EVERYMAN,
I WILL GO WITH THEE,
AND BE THY GUIDE,
IN THY MOST NEED
TO GO BY THY SIDE

EVERYMAN'S LIBRARY

ERNEST HEMINGWAY

THE
COLLECTED
STORIES

EDITED AND INTRODUCED
BY JAMES FENTON

EVERYMAN'S LIBRARY

187

First included in Everyman's Library, 1995
Stories reprinted from *The First Forty-Nine Stories* © Hemingway Foreign
Rights Trust, 1939. By kind permission of
Jonathan Cape Ltd.
Previously uncollected stories copyright © 1995 by Mary, John, Patrick
and Gregory Hemingway.
Drafts and Fragments from *The Nick Adams Stories* copyright © 1972 by
The Ernest Hemingway Foundation.
Stories first published in the Finca Vigía edition of *The Complete Short
Stories* copyright © 1987 by The Ernest Hemingway Foundation.
'Judgment of Manitou', 'A Matter of Colour', 'Sepi Jingan' copyright
© 1971 by The Ernest Hemingway Foundation.
'The Mercenaries', 'Crossroads – An Anthology', 'Portrait of an Idealist
in Love', 'The Ash Heel's Tendon', 'The Current' copyright © 1985 by
Mary, John, Patrick and Gregory Hemingway.
This collection © Everyman's Library, 1995
Introduction © James Fenton, 1995
Bibliography and Chronology © Everyman's Library, 1995
Typography by Peter B. Willberg

ISBN 978-1-85715-187-9

A CIP catalogue record for this book is available from the
British Library

Published by Everyman's Library,
50 Albemarle Street, London W1S 4BD

Distributed by Penguin Random House UK
20 Vauxhall Bridge Road, London SW1V 2SA

Printed and bound in Germany by GGP Media GmbH, Pössneck

ERNEST HEMINGWAY

CONTENTS

PART ONE: STORIES COLLECTED IN HEMINGWAY'S LIFETIME

From *Three Stories and Ten Poems* (1923)

in our time (1924)

In Our Time (1925 and 1930)

Men Without Women (1927)

Winner Take Nothing (1933)

CONTENTS

Stories from *The Fifth Column and the First Forty-Nine Stories* (1938)

PART TWO: STORIES AND FRAGMENTS FROM POSTHUMOUS COLLECTIONS

Uncollected Stories published in Hemingway's Lifetime

Drafts and Fragments first published in *The Nick Adams Stories* (1972)

ERNEST HEMINGWAY

INTRODUCTION

Hemingway's greatest achievement was his style, the simplicity and economy of which was so influential that it is almost impossible to imagine modern fiction without it. The style was forged first of all in reportage and in the short stories, and many people, myself among them, believe that the short stories represent the very best of his work. But when we turn to existing editions in order to see how Hemingway began, and how his writing developed, we find a situation very far from clear. The collections do not tell us quite what we are looking for.

The purpose of this edition then, is to give the most complete and comprehensibly organized collection of Hemingway's short fiction to date, and to correct some of the anomalies that have crept into other editions. Hemingway published four individual collections of stories during his lifetime. They are the tiny experimental prose volume, *in our time* (1924), the much expanded *In Our Time* (1925, with an extra story added in 1930), *Men Without Women* (1927) and *Winner Take Nothing* (1933). The arrangement of each of these volumes was, it seems to me, a matter of artistic choice, and I have reproduced each of them in its most complete form.

The anomalies begin in 1938 when Hemingway put together an omnibus, *The Fifth Column and the First Forty-Nine Stories*. There were excellent publishing reasons for the arrangement of this book, which placed the recent topical play, *The Fifth Column*, and the latest stories at the front of the collection, to draw attention to its novelty. But publishing reasons are not necessarily the same as artistic reasons, and the novelty of that arrangement has long since vanished.

What's left is a confusion. A modern volume called *The Snows of Kilimanjaro*, for instance, turns out to be the 1936 story of that name bound up with the early material from *In Our Time*. A current edition of *Winner Take Nothing* turns out to contain a much later story, 'The Short Happy Life of Francis Macomber', which really belongs, both chronologically and artistically, with 'The Snows of Kilimanjaro'.

A volume called *The Nick Adams Stories* (1972), with a preface by Philip Young, put together published and unpublished work featuring the hero of that name, arranging the material as if – seen as a whole – it might form a fragmentary biography of the character. The editor distinguished typographically between the published and the unpublished material. But the presentation is open to very serious objection. The first story, 'Three Shots', appears as a preface to the famous 'Indian Camp'. But 'Three Shots' is rejected material. Hemingway is famous for his ability to pare down a story, to exclude material in order to charge what was left with an added significance. To interweave the abandoned with the eventually published material is to undermine the very aesthetic the author hoped to promote. 'Three Shots' is very interesting, but 'Indian Camp' should be kept in isolation from it.

In 1985, Peter Griffin published a study of Hemingway's early years, *Along With Youth*, which was billed as containing five new short stories. These were five works from the immature pre-Paris period, placed in the setting of a biography, and not therefore recommended to the general reader on grounds of literary merit. But still, there they were – additions to the corpus.

The Finca Vigía edition of *The Complete Short Stories of Ernest Hemingway* followed in 1987, but did not use all of the Nick Adams material, and did not include what Peter Griffin had printed. Much was added to the basic canon of *The First Forty-Nine*, but not all of what was added has commanded assent as being short story material. It is true that 'One Trip Across' and 'Tradesman's Return' were originally published as short stories. But they so swiftly came to constitute the first and second parts of *To Have and Have Not* that those original versions are much better seen as a disclosure of work in progress. (Hemingway himself, his letters show, declassified them as short stories.) Anyone who wants to read these two yarns can find them in the novel in the form Hemingway settled on (which is not so dramatically different from the original).

For the rest of the Finca Vigía material, it all comes with

various caveats, to which I shall return later. The main point is that the material in the second part of the present edition differs from that in the first in being, in some sense, unauthorized. There are some remarkable stories, which happened never to have been collected, but there are also works which Hemingway printed in magazine form but did not want reprinted. There are fragments of abandoned novels. And there are items which, though written in story form, seem like family anecdotes.

There is more material in the Hemingway archives – fragments, stories of various kinds – which remains unpublished, but it seems to me to belong to a different kind of scholarly edition. In the present case, I decided to confine my choice of material to what has already appeared in print, and to bring together in one volume what is scattered over several. I don't say that this is a satisfactory procedure, but I think it less unsatisfactory than any other I can think of, short of the eventual complete, minute, scholarly re-examination of the whole corpus.

For the general reader, it is enough perhaps to know that the stories published between 1923 and 1938 form the classic body of work. After that, by and large, Hemingway was doing other things. I would hesitate to say that he declined as a short story writer. *The Old Man and the Sea* (1951) is really a long short story. *A Moveable Feast* (written around 1959) is a non-fiction work cast as a series of stories, left unfinished at the time of Hemingway's death in 1961. But the reader will see from the publication dates given with the list of contents that the majority of the good work belongs to two great bursts of creative energy, one in the Twenties, the other in the Thirties.

*

Hemingway's first book, a miscellany called *Three Stories and Ten Poems*, contains a tale which was lost sight of for a while, since later publishers thought it obscene. Gertrude Stein, according to *A Moveable Feast*, disliked it too. 'It's good,' she said. 'That's not the question at all. But it is *inaccrochable*. That means it is like a picture that a painter paints and then he cannot hang it when he has a show and nobody will buy it because they cannot hang it either.'

The story in question, 'Up in Michigan', was referred to by Hemingway as the first he wrote, in Paris in 1921. By this he means the first of his published oeuvre. Earlier stories, written in America, have been published. 'Up in Michigan' and 'My Old Man' are unusual in that they survived the suitcase of mature work to date which his wife Hadley lost in 1922. This famous event – the suitcase was stolen at the Gare de Lyon – sent the young Hemingway back almost to square one as a writer. 'Up in Michigan' survived because it had been set aside after Gertrude Stein's objections. 'My Old Man', a work criticized as being too heavily indebted to a story by Sherwood Anderson, survived because it was out on offer to a magazine. The other story in Hemingway's first book was 'Out of Season', but it and 'My Old Man' I have left in their proper place, in the first full volume of stories.

Hemingway was not at the forefront of experimental, modernist writing in its most evolved sense. Indeed it might be said that his achievement was rather that he continued and kept alive the tradition of Kipling, that he dignified the traditional and popular form of adventure story and yarn-spinning. But he did this from within the context of modernism.

Stein gave him advice. Joyce was appreciative of his work. Pound was behind the publication of his second small book, *in our time* (1924) which appeared in a series devoted to an 'inquest' into the current state of English prose. This I have reprinted in the form in which it first appeared. The shortness of these short stories, their closeness to anecdote or reportage, their sense of themselves as found objects, must have seemed daring and refreshing at the time. Hemingway was seeing how much he could achieve with how little, and it was this economy of means for which his prose became famous.

The title of the collection is an abbreviation of a sentence from the *Book of Common Prayer*, 'Give peace in our time, O Lord.' The arrangement of the sketches is paratactical, that is to say that they are placed side by side, rather than coaxed into forming an argument. Nevertheless, there are patterns intended, as Hemingway wrote to Pound, with whom he had discussed the work at length:

The bulls start, then reappear and then finish. The war starts clear and noble just like it did, Mons etc., then gets close and blurred and finished with the feller who goes home and gets clap. The refugees leave Thrace, due to the Greek ministers who are shot. The whole thing closes with the talk with the King of Greece ... The radicals start noble in the young Magyar story and get bitched. America appears in the cops shooting the guys who robbed the cigar store. It has form all right. The king closes it in swell shape. Oh that king.

The next stage was to take the paratactical method further, to alternate between short story and prose miniature, in order to build up further the picture of 'our time'. This is the achievement of the 1925 volume (to which Hemingway added 'On the Quai at Smyrna' in a 1930 edition).

D. H. Lawrence, who reviewed the expanded *In Our Time*, was enthusiastic:

It is a short book: and it does not pretend to be about one man. But it is. It is as much as we need to know about a man's life ... these few sketches are enough to create the man and all his history: we need know no more.

What Lawrence sees in Hemingway is the character of the lone trapper or cowboy, with a state of mind he defines thus:

It is a state of *conscious*, accepted indifference to everything except freedom from work and the moment's interest ... Nothing matters. Everything happens. One wants to keep oneself loose. Avoid one thing only: getting connected up. Don't get connected up. If you get held by anything, break. Don't be held. Break it, and get away.

So what Lawrence admired was negativity honestly expressed: Hemingway 'doesn't love anybody, and it nauseates him to pretend that he does. He doesn't even *want* to love anybody.'

This is to mistake the book for the man. Hemingway did care, things did matter to him and he was very far from indifferent to the world. But the man who wrote *In Our Time* had been through a large number of new and shaking experiences in a very short time, particularly during 1917-19. And he was slow to unpack the experiences he had acquired.

Depending on whether you believe Hemingway or his perhaps most astute biographer, Kenneth S. Lynn, he had either been rejected by the army on grounds of poor eyesight or had failed to sign up as a soldier, but had applied instead and had been accepted as an ambulance driver by the Red Cross. He had gone to Europe for the first time. He had seen war for the first time. He had been wounded. He had recovered. He had fallen in love with his nurse. He had tried to get back to his friends at the front, but had proved to be too ill to take the strain. He had embarked on a friendship with a man whose interest had turned out (according to another biographer) to be dismayingly homosexual. He had returned to America to hear himself described as a cripple. He had been a local hero. Finally the nurse he loved had jilted him. All this in little more than a year.

The first of these great events seems to me one of the most important. If Hemingway was lying when he said that he had been rejected by the army, then clearly his not signing up was a matter of shame to him. If he was telling the truth, I suspect that the rejection would have been bitterly felt.

Not everyone feels such things so intensely. Many are simply relieved not to have to fight. But the real test for someone of Hemingway's cast of mind is: to serve in war as a soldier under military discipline. Hemingway in later life did many things that approximated to this. He carried arms in Spain, but he was a journalist. During the Second World War, he engaged in quixotic reconnaissance activities in Cuba, supposedly chasing submarines on a yacht equipped with a machine-gun. During the German retreat in France, he was apparently involved in mopping-up operations with a group of French irregulars (see the story 'Black Ass at the Crossroads'). But he was never a soldier under a soldier's discipline, and he knew this meant that his courage had not been put to the ultimate test.

So he sought out the company of courageous men – soldiers, bullfighters, hunters – and sought to associate himself with their deeds. But he was not only interested in courage. Cowardice too was a great theme for him, as were defeat and the decline of powers. The unsettled question was a continual source of material for his stories.

Hemingway also wrote as a rejected and as a wounded man. 'A Very Short Story' is an account of the rejection. 'Soldier's Home' is a fictional version of the author's own predicament after the war – nagging mother, adoring sister, a history of 'weakness' among the menfolk in the family. Krebs is in a state of mind which makes him incapable of love or work or any purposeful activity. The best he can do is watch his kid sister play baseball.

The fact that Hemingway had indeed been traumatized we may conclude from a much later Nick Adams story, 'A Way You'll Never Be' (1933), in which Nick does what Hemingway did in real life. He returns to the front but finds that he gets the horrors and that his sanity begins to slip. Hemingway waited a long time before using this material – a fact which suggests that the memory indeed held its horror for him, and there is plenty throughout the fiction to suggest that, as the horror played itself out, a part of its meaning for Hemingway was that it had destroyed, he feared, his ability to love, or to go on loving a woman to the point, for instance, of having a child.

The placing of 'Indian Camp' at the beginning, and 'Big Two-Hearted River' at the end of the collection suggests perhaps a design: in the former story the boy Nick is rudely introduced to the nature of birth and death, although he ends the story 'quite sure that he would never die'. In the latter, it was suggested by Philip Young that if we imagine Nick as having returned from the war, then 'its submerged tensions – the impression that Nick is exorcizing some nameless anxiety – become perfectly understandable'.

And a parallel suggests itself between this story and the actual case of many Vietnam war veterans, who came back, found city or home life impossible and took to the woods, made their own camps or cabins, kept themselves aloof. Some did this because they had become violent men, who felt themselves to be a danger to society. One supposes that for others the overt act in which they were engaged – the practising of survival skills – had a symbolic meaning. They went to the woods in order to survive there.

The idea that war is the unmentioned subject of 'Big Two-Hearted River' is made plausible by a passage in *A Moveable Feast*:

When I stopped writing I did not want to leave the river where I could see the trout in the pool, its surface pushing and swelling smooth against the resistance of the log-driven piles of the bridge. The story was about coming back from the war but there was no mention of the war in it.

This technique of cutting out any reference to the real subject-matter of a story so that the reader must do the work of inferring it – this is quintessential Hemingway. 'Three Shots', for instance, is not an independent short story but only the rejected opening to 'Indian Camp'. If you take the rejected material alongside the published story, it becomes plain that the subject is cowardice: the child accused of cowardice by his uncle has, by the end of the story, faced up to the violence of birth and death rather better than his uncle has.

But the bold excision Hemingway made has removed the structure of that plot, and therefore the implication of a comeuppance for the uncle, and has left the story more ambiguous, more a thing to be savoured for its own sake. And in the case of 'Big Two-Hearted River' another bold cut removed all the material that Philip Young later reprinted as 'On Writing'. Once again, if you put back the rejected material, which originally formed the latter part of the story, you begin to see that the original conscious aim was to describe an ambitious young man striking out into the unknown, his purpose being to become a great writer.

But then Hemingway took a second look and (quite rightly) thought that the passage on writing was tripe. This excision is utterly radical. It changes everything, in a way that the cut in 'Indian Camp' does not. Nobody could infer from the story as published that it ever had anything to do with an ambition to rival Pound and Joyce. It appears too, if the passage in *A Moveable Feast* is indeed about 'Big Two-Hearted River', that Hemingway forgot what the story was originally about, and came only to remember what he eventually *decided* it was about – 'coming back from the war'.

INTRODUCTION

A Moveable Feast is a thrilling book for any aspiring writer, and good to read alongside these stories, since it tells us about the circumstances in which they were written, and the spirit behind them. But it should not be thought one hundred per cent reliable. Rather what he gives us is a clue to his thinking:

> it was a very simple story called 'Out of Season' and I had omitted the real end of it which was that the old man hanged himself. This was omitted on my new theory that you could omit anything as long as you knew that you omitted and the omitted part would strengthen the story and make people feel something more than they understood.

When one reads this, and then goes back to 'Out of Season', it almost seems as if Hemingway has misremembered the title of the story he was talking about, so little of the omitted death remains in the story as published. But it is true that editing, cropping, omission are the keys to the style of these stories.

In Our Time sets out Hemingway's stall. The virtues are all there. So too are some of the incipient vices. Those who enjoy satirizing Hemingway will find all the tricks they are looking for in 'Big Two-Hearted River'.

Hemingway writes well when his temperament is equable, badly when we feel that the story has been composed out of some unacknowledged malice. 'Mr. and Mrs. Elliot', for instance, feels unpleasant and sneering. Sure enough, it turns out to have been based on an actual couple and their supposed sexual mismatch. Its publication was a gross act of cruelty on Hemingway's part, the original Mrs Elliot having died in childbirth a month before Hemingway wrote the story, about which he was utterly impenitent. And this virulence seems all the more striking when we look for what the offence might have been, and find only that the original Mr Elliot had been rich and educated at both Harvard and Yale, and that the Hemingways had enjoyed their hospitality.

But see, when Hemingway writes equably, what an incomparably superior story 'Cat in the Rain' is, which deals, although this is not said, with another woman who wants a child. The joke, in 'Mr. and Mrs. Elliot' is supposed to be that Mrs Elliott ends up sleeping with her girlfriend. But see another later story, 'The Sea Change', which Hemingway strongly hinted was based on a situation he knew intimately, and which shows a girl taking leave of absence from her boyfriend in order to have an affair with a woman.

The same animus, the same sneering tone, would have wrecked everything. Instead, the writing is perfectly equable and the effects so lightly sketched that, although we believe that it is a great humiliation for the boyfriend to be left *for a woman*, that humiliation has yet to sink in. We are not at all sure what the future holds for him, or quite what the significance is of that final moment when the abandoned husband takes his place at the bar with the other men. Among the drafts there is one ending which implies that he does so angrily, with an insult to the men, and another (he asks the barman 'What can you recommend to a recent convert?') which seems to suggest that he has taken to heart what his girlfriend has said, and that he is about to plunge into the world of homosexuality. Hemingway seems to have decided to leave the whole matter in the balance. The boyfriend knows that he is a changed man. That's all, for the moment.

The tact of this decision reminds us that, while Hemingway is often remembered, and indeed revered, for a kind of machismo, in his best writing he is far more sophisticated about human nature than the machismo ethic would allow. *Men Without Women* is very largely a collection of stories about men without women, or men losing women. It contains one classic story about homoeroticism – 'A Simple Enquiry' – and others that ring the changes on the male perspective.

There is absolutely no getting away from the fact that Hemingway writes best about men, and white men at that. The blacks and Indians in his stories are always important figures in the landscape, but they do not have a fully rounded point of view. The index entry for heroines in Jeffrey Meyers's biography lists them under the following categories: bitter, castrating, predatory, pregnant, selfish, sleeping, submissive and victims. Women are supremely important beings *in a man's life*, and some of them have a point of view. But we do not turn to Hemingway for his insights into womanhood.

*

The last story Hemingway collected in his lifetime was 'Old Man at the Bridge', a slight work, cabled from the Spanish Civil War, and of interest as belonging to the propaganda of that period. It was followed by 'The Denunciation', 'The Butterfly and the Tank' and 'Night Before Battle' of which it is worth noting that Hemingway vigorously opposed their reprinting. 'The Denunciation' is a particularly uneasy work. Paul Smith remarks that 'there is a deep sense of shame at the heart of this fiction', and I agree. The debate over questions such as denunciation was virulently conducted during the Spanish Civil War, in which Hemingway attacked John Dos Passos for taking too close an interest in the fate of his translator, who had been executed secretly. The article he wrote at the time, 'Treachery in Aragon', taken with 'The Denunciation' show the worst side of Hemingway the fellow traveller. The absolute opposite point of view, in which the hatred of the Spanish soldiers for the military police on the battlefield is angrily depicted, gives us the best of the Spanish stories, 'Under the Ridge'. 'Landscape with Figures', unpublished by Hemingway (another exercise in the vindictive mode), and the Cuban epilogue 'Nobody Ever Dies' complete this group, which were once to have been the basis of a collection, before their author became distracted by his Spanish novel.

'The Good Lion' and 'The Faithful Bull' are mere curiosities. 'A Man of the World' and 'Get a Seeing-Eyed Dog' were originally published as 'Two Tales of Darkness' and are the last short stories Hemingway published in magazine form.

About the Nick Adams material in the next section, I have already said that 'Three Shots' is the rejected opening of 'Indian Camp', and 'On Writing' is the rejected conclusion to 'Big Two-Hearted River'. 'Night Before Landing' is the beginning of an abandoned novel, *Along With Youth*.

'Summer People', as printed in *The Nick Adams Stories*, contains a notorious misreading of the manuscript. Having made love to Kate, Nick says 'You've got to get dressed, slut.' In fact, Kate's nicknames are Butstein and Stut. Nick is not in the habit of fucking a girl and calling her a whore. The transcribers also omitted a whole page of manuscript, clearly inadvertently (just as they absent-mindedly dropped the last word of 'Three Shots', which is 'absent-mindedly') from this final scene. The 'rich slobs' in their cars out from Charlevoix, who hog the road and fail to dip their headlights, are 'rich Jews' in the original. The love-making scene was clearly cut in the manuscript, but restored by the editors and I have indicated where the excision comes. It is worth pointing out that Hemingway was unclear, during the composition of this piece, whether it was about a man called Allen Wemedge, or a man called Nick Adams who had the nickname Wemedge.

'The Last Good Country' is an unfinished novel, which the editors bowdlerized. I have returned to the original text, because the effect of those bowdlerizations has been to obscure Nick's sexual history, which is precocious, but only partly to obscure the incestuous fantasies of the sister. Much better to see the whole problem laid out plainly. It was a novel going nowhere, and no doubt it made the editors uneasy with its theme of incest. But it hardly seems fair to the material to put more sex into 'Summer People' while cutting it out of the longer work.

The material first printed in the Complete Short Stories includes two sections of a novel, 'A Train Trip' and 'The Porter' and material from an early version of *Islands in the Stream*, 'The Strange Country'. I have dropped 'An African Story', which is filleted from various chapters of *The Garden of Eden*, itself a posthumous novel. It is a story being written by the novel's hero, of which we get glimpses. To present it as a whole short story, without the intervening passage, seems somewhat bold. 'Landscape with Figures' must have been written before early 1939, and is clearly a genuine short story, as I believe is 'Black Ass at the Crossroads'. The very painful Cuban pieces, 'I Guess Everything Reminds You of Something' and 'Great News from the Mainland', are described variously as finished short stories and family anecdotes. It is worth remembering that Hemingway's fiction began in anecdote (*in our time*), and that the short story 'Che Ti Dice La Patria?' started its published life as a piece of straight reportage. There is in the archive what appears to be an anecdote from experience, about a death from influenza in an Italian hospital during the First World War, but it is written in the third person, as if in preparation for its life as a short story.

There is, in other words, a high degree of overlap. Anecdotes become stories, stories become novels, novels run out of steam, and find their place here only under the rubric 'short fiction', and because thematically they relate to the classic canon of finished work. Part One represents that canon, and I do not think that Part Two traduces it, as long as people pay attention to the labelling, and do not expect an equivalence between collected, rejected, unfinished and abandoned work.

James Fenton

I should like to thank the staff of the Hemingway Archive at the J.F.K. Library in Boston for their courtesy, and George Packer for dropping everything in order to retranscribe 'The Last Good Country.'

SELECT BIBLIOGRAPHY

———

BIBLIOGRAPHIES

HANNEMAN, AUDRE, *Ernest Hemingway: A Comprehensive Bibliography*, Princeton University Press, Princeton, NJ, 1967. *Supplement*, 1975.
SAMUELS, LEE, *A Hemingway Check List*, Scribner, New York, 1951.

AUTOBIOGRAPHY, LETTERS, JOURNALISM

BAKER, CARLOS (ed.), *Ernest Hemingway: Selected Letters, 1917–1961*, Granada, London and New York, 1981.
HEMINGWAY, ERNEST, *A Moveable Feast*, Scribner, New York, 1964.
WHITE, WILLIAM (ed.), *Ernest Hemingway, By-Line: Selected Articles and Dispatches of Four Decades*, Scribner, New York, 1967.

BIOGRAPHIES

BAKER, CARLOS, *Ernest Hemingway: A Life Story*, Scribner, New York, and Collins, London, 1969.
BRUCCOLI, MATTHEW, *Scott and Ernest*, Random House, New York, 1978.
CALLAGHAN, MORLEY, *That Summer in Paris*, Coward-McCann, New York, 1963.
FENTON, CHARLES, *The Apprenticeship of Ernest Hemingway*, Mentor, New York, and Vision Press, London, 1954.
FORD, HUGH, *Published in Paris*, Garnstone, London, 1975.
HEMINGWAY, GREGORY, *Papa*, Houghton Mifflin, Boston, 1976.
HEMINGWAY, LEICESTER, *My Brother, Ernest Hemingway*, Fawcett, New York, 1962.
HEMINGWAY, MARY, *How It Was*, Ballantine, New York, 1976.
HOTCHNER, A. E., *Papa Hemingway*, Bantam, New York, 1966.
LYNN, KENNETH, S., *Hemingway*, Simon and Schuster, London and New York, 1987.
MEYERS, JEFFREY, *Hemingway: A Biography*, Harper and Row, New York and London, 1985.
MILLER, MADELAINE HEMINGWAY, *Ernie*, Crown, New York, 1966.
ROSS, LILLIAN, *Portrait of Hemingway*, Simon and Schuster, New York, 1961.
STEIN, GERTRUDE, *The Autobiography of Alice B. Toklas*, Harcourt Brace, New York, 1933.
WICKES, GEORGE, *Americans in Paris*, Doubleday, Garden City, 1969.

CRITICISM

BAKER, CARLOS, *Hemingway: The Writer as Artist*, Princeton University Press, Princeton NJ, 1972 (4th revised edition).

BAKER, CARLOS (ed.), *Hemingway and His Critics: An International Anthology*, Hill and Wang, New York, 1961.

BENSON, JACKSON J., *Hemingway: The Writer's Art of Self-Defense*, University of Minnesota Press, Minnesota, 1969.

BRADBURY, MALCOLM, *The Modern American Novel*, Oxford University Press, London, 1990/New York, Viking, 1993 (revised edition).

BURGESS, ANTHONY, *Ernest Hemingway*, Thames and Hudson, London, 1978.

COWLEY, MALCOLM, *A Second Flowering: Works and Days of the Lost Generation*, Viking, New York, 1973.

GELLEN, JAY (ed.), A Farewell to Arms: *Twentieth Century Interpretations*, Prentice Hall, Englewood Cliffs, NJ, 1970.

HOFFMAN, FREDERICK, J., *The Mortal No: Death and the Modern Imagination*, Princeton University Press, Princeton, NJ, 1964.

KLEIN, HOLGER (ed.), *The First World War in Fiction*, Macmillan, London, 1976.

LEE, A. ROBERT (ed.), *Ernest Hemingway: New Critical Essays*, Vision, London, 1983.

MCCAFFERY, J. K. M. (ed.), *Ernest Hemingway: The Man and His Work*, World, Cleveland, 1950.

MEYERS, JEFFREY (ed.), *Hemingway: The Critical Heritage*, Routledge, London, 1982.

REYNOLDS, MICHAEL, *Hemingway's First War: The Making of* A Farewell to Arms, Princeton University Press, Princeton, NJ, 1976.

SMITH, PAUL, *A Reader's Guide to the Short Stories of Ernest Hemingway*, Macmillan, Boston, 1989.

WATTS, EMILY STIPES, *Ernest Hemingway and the Arts*, University of Illinois Press, Urbana and London, 1971.

WEEKS, ROBERT P. (ed.), *Hemingway: A Collection of Critical Essays*, Prentice Hall, Englewood Cliffs, NJ, 1962.

WILSON, EDMUND, *The Wound and the Bow: Seven Studies in Literature*, Methuen, London, 1961.

CHRONOLOGY

DATE	AUTHOR'S LIFE	LITERARY CONTEXT
1899	Ernest Hemingway born 21 July to Clarence Hemingway and Grace Hemingway (neé Hall) at Oak Park near Chicago.	
1900		Conrad: *Lord Jim*. Dreiser: *Sister Carrie*. Freud: *The Interpretation of Dreams*.
1901		Mann: *Buddenbrooks*.
1902	His father gives him his first fishing rod.	Conrad: *Youth*.
1903		Henry James: *The Ambassadors*. London: *Call of the Wild*.
1904		Conrad: *Nostromo*.
1905		Wharton: *The House of Mirth*.
1907		Adams: *The Education of Henry Adams*. William James: *Pragmatism*.
1909	His father gives him his first shotgun. He is allowed to shoot three shells a day during the holidays which are spent hunting and fishing with his father.	Stein: *Three Lives*.
1912		Mann: *Death in Venice*.
1913	Enters Oak Park High School, and is an outstanding student. He goes in for a variety of sports including football and boxing. Although he studies hard, he runs away from home and school twice.	Lawrence: *Sons and Lovers*. Wharton: *The Custom of the Country*. Proust: *Swann's Way*.
1914		Joyce: *Dubliners*. Burroughs: *Tarzan of the Apes*.
1916	Edits the school magazine, *The Trapeze*.	Joyce: *A Portrait of the Artist as a Young Man*.
1917	Graduates from Oak Park High School and joins the *Kansas City Star* as a junior reporter.	T. S. Eliot: 'The Love Song of J. Alfred Prufrock'.

Planck's quantum theory. First Zeppelin flight.

Assassination of President McKinley; succeeded by Theodore Roosevelt. First award of Nobel Prizes.

Wright brothers' first successful powered flight. Alaskan frontier question between US and Canada settled by arbitration.

Einstein's theory of relativity.
Cubist exhibition in Paris.

Woodrow Wilson elected President. Sinking of the *Titanic*. New Mexico admitted to statehood in the US.
Armory Show of Post-Impressionist paintings open in New York.

Britain declares war on Germany, 4 August. President Wilson proclaims US neutrality. Panama Canal opens.

US declares war on Germany, 6 April. Bolshevik Revolution in Russia.

DATE	AUTHOR'S LIFE	LITERARY CONTEXT
1918	Joins the Red Cross as an ambulance driver. He is sent to Italy and is wounded on the Piave front while performing an act of rescue. He is decorated for bravery under fire by both the Italian and US governments. In hospital in Milan he falls in love with a nurse, Agnes von Kurowsky.	Joyce: *Exiles*. Strachey: *Eminent Victorians*.
1919	Returns to Oak Park as a war hero. Suffers from terrible nightmares and insomnia. Spends most of his time reading and drinking until the summer when he starts writing seriously but without commercial success.	Anderson: *Winesburg, Ohio*. Dos Passos: *One Man's Initiation – 1917*.
1920	Joins the *Toronto Star*.	Fitzgerald: *This Side of Paradise*. Lewis: *Main Street*. Pound: *Hugh Selwyn Mauberly*. Eliot: *The Sacred Wood*.
1921	Marries Hadley Richardson and goes with her to Paris as correspondent of the *Toronto Star*.	Dos Passos: *Three Soldiers*. Lawrence: *Women in Love*. Pirandello: *Six Characters in Search of an Author*.
1922	Meets Gertrude Stein and Ezra Pound. Travels all over Europe as a roving correspondent. Covers the war between Turkey and Greece. Interviews Mussolini. Sees his first bullfight.	Joyce: *Ulysses*. Eliot: *The Waste Land*. Lewis: *Babbitt*. Spengler: *The Decline of the West*. Hašek: *The Good Soldier Švejk*.
1923	His first son, John, is born. Gertrude Stein and Alice B. Toklas are godmothers. *Three Stories and Ten Poems*.	Stevens: *Harmonium*. Lawrence: *Studies in Classic American Literature*.
1924	Publishes *In Our Time*. Assists Ford Madox Ford on *Transatlantic Review*. Becomes a bullfight 'groupie'. Begins *The Sun Also Rises*, writing 'to the point of exhaustion'.	Forster: *A Passage to India*. Ford: *Parade's End* (to 1928). Mann: *The Magic Mountain*.

CHRONOLOGY

DATE	AUTHOR'S LIFE	LITERARY CONTEXT
1925	*In Our Time* meets with critical approval in the US.	Fitzgerald: *The Great Gatsby.* Woolf: *Mrs Dalloway.* Eliot: *Poems 1905–1925.* Dreiser: *An American Tragedy.* Stein: *The Making of Americans.* Dos Passos: *Manhattan Transfer.* Anderson: *Dark Laughter.* Bulgakov: *The White Guard.* Kafka: *The Trial.*
1926	Publishes *The Torrents of Spring* and *The Sun Also Rises*. Has an affair with Pauline Pfeiffer, an American reporter.	Fitzgerald: *All the Sad Young Men.* Faulkner: *Soldier's Pay.* Lawrence: *The Plumed Serpent.* Kafka: *The Castle.*
1927	*Men Without Women*, a volume of stories, confirms Hemingway's importance. He divorces Hadley and marries Pauline. Becomes a practising Catholic.	Woolf: *To the Lighthouse.* Cather: *Death Comes for the Archbishop.* Wilder: *The Bridge of San Luis Rey.*
1928	Returns to the US and sets up home at Key West, Florida. His second son, Patrick, is born. *The Sun Also Rises* begins to bring in a lot of money and Hemingway spends much time hunting and fishing. Begins writing *A Farewell to Arms*. His father, incurably ill, commits suicide. Hemingway helps found, and becomes a contributor to, *Esquire*.	Lawrence: *Lady Chatterley's Lover.* O'Neill: *Strange Interlude.* Bulgakov: *The Master and Margarita* (to 1940).
1929	Publishes *A Farewell to Arms*.	Faulkner: *Sartoris* and *The Sound and the Fury.* Wolfe: *Look Homeward Angel.* Remarque: *All Quiet on the Western Front.* Graves: *Goodbye to All That.*
1930	Visits Spain and works on *Death in the Afternoon*. *A Farewell to Arms*, adapted by Lawrence Stallings, is staged in New York without much success.	Dos Passos: *The 42nd Parallel.* Faulkner: *As I Lay Dying.* Hammett: *The Maltese Falcon.* Crane: *The Bridge.* Freud: *Civilization and its Discontents.* Musil: *The Man without Qualities* (to 1932).

CHRONOLOGY

DATE	AUTHOR'S LIFE	LITERARY CONTEXT
1931	Finishes *Death in the Afternoon*.	Wilson: *Axel's Castle*. Remarque: *The Road Back*.
1932	Publishes *Death in the Afternoon*. Hemingway is taken to task by writers on the Left for avoiding major political and economic issues in his work. His third son, Gregory, is born.	Faulkner: *Light in August*. Caldwell: *Tobacco Road*. Céline: *Journey to the End of the Night*.
1933	Visits Africa. Publishes *Winner Take Nothing*.	West: *Miss Lonelyhearts*.
1934	Buys a big boat for deep sea fishing. Catches a record fish which he presents to the Miami Deep Sea Fishing Club where it can be found to this day.	Fitzgerald: *Tender is the Night*. Miller: *Tropic of Cancer*. Farrell: *The Young Manhood of Studs Lonigan*. Williams: *Collected Poems 1921–1931*. Waugh: *A Handful of Dust*.
1935	Publishes *Green Hills of Africa*. Helps found International Game Fish Association. Shoots himself in the foot while trying to kill a huge shark.	Odets: *Waiting for Lefty*. Wolfe: *Of Time and the River*.
1936	Sends a donation of $40,000 to the Republicans in Spain. Meets Martha Gellhorn, an American journalist.	Eliot: *Collected Poems*. Dos Passos: *The Big Money*. Faulkner: *Absalom, Absalom!* Céline: *Death on the Instalment Plan*.
1937	Publishes *To Have and Have Not* in part as a reply to his Leftist critics. Goes to Spain as a war correspondent. Apart from reporting on the war there, he spends a lot of time locating food and funds for the combatants, especially the wounded. Returns to the US to raise money for the Republican cause and works on the film *The Spanish Earth* which has its première at the White House.	Stevens: *The Man with the Blue Guitar*. Steinbeck: *Of Mice and Men*.
1938	Finishes his pro-Republican play, *The Fifth Column*, which is a commercial failure. Begins an affair with Martha Gellhorn in Madrid. Returns to Key West and Pauline but is 'taciturn and	Beckett: *Murphy*. Sartre: *Nausea*. Cummings: *Collected Poems*. Waugh: *Scoop*.

CHRONOLOGY

DATE	AUTHOR'S LIFE	LITERARY CONTEXT
1938 *cont*	withdrawn'. Returns to Spain and then to Cuba where he settles and begins *For Whom the Bell Tolls*.	
1939		Joyce: *Finnegans Wake*. Miller: *Tropic of Capricorn*. Steinbeck: *The Grapes of Wrath*.
1940	Marries Martha Gellhorn two weeks after divorcing Pauline. *For Whom the Bell Tolls* is published and is immensely popular.	Wright: *Native Son*. Greene: *The Power and the Glory*. Chandler: *Farewell my Lovely*.
1941	The Hemingways go to the Far East to report on the Sino–Japanese War. Returning to Cuba, Hemingway fits out his boat in order to chase German submarines.	Fitzgerald: *The Last Tycoon*. Welty: *A Curtain of Green*. Wilson: *The Wound and the Bow*.
1942		Paul: *A Narrow Street*. Camus: *The Stranger*.
1944	Goes to Europe as a war correspondent. While in London he is involved in a car crash and is reported as dead by the world press. Enters Paris with his own partisan unit. Awarded the Bronze Star. Meets Mary Welsh, an American journalist. During his stay in Paris, Hemingway also meets Picasso, Sartre and Simone de Beauvoir.	Eliot: *Four Quartets*. Sartre: *Huis Clos*. Camus: *Caligula*. Anouilh: *Antigone*.
1945	Divorces Martha and returns to Havana.	Orwell: *Animal Farm*. Thurber: *The Thurber Carnival*. Waugh: *Brideshead Revisited*. Borges: *Fictions*.
1946	Marries Mary Welsh.	Wilson: *Memoirs of Hecate County*. John Hersey: *Hiroshima*.
1947	Remains in Havana writing and attending boxing matches and cockfights.	Williams: *A Streetcar Named Desire*. Mackenzie: *Whisky Galore*. Sartre: *The Roads to Freedom* (to 1950). Camus: *The Plague*.

CHRONOLOGY

HISTORICAL EVENTS

Germany invades Poland; Britain and France declare war on Germany. First commercial transatlantic flights. Barcelona captured by Nationalists under Franco; surrender of Madrid to Nationalists; end of Spanish Civil War. Vivien Leigh and Clark Gable star in *Gone with the Wind*.
The Battle of Britain. Britain leases naval and military bases to US. Paris occupied by Germany. Trotsky assassinated in Mexico. Disney: *Fantasia*. Development of Penicillin. Extraction of plutonium from uranium.

Hitler invades Russia. Japanese attack US fleet at Pearl Harbor; meeting of Churchill and Roosevelt; US enters the war, 11 December. US introduce 'lease-lend' system of aid to Britain. Orson Welles: *Citizen Kane*. Irving Berlin: *White Christmas*. Beginnings of 'bebop'.

Rommel defeated at El Alamein. Build-up of American air force in Free China. World's first nuclear reactor constructed at Chicago University.
Allied landings in Normandy; German retreat; liberation of Paris. Roosevelt elected for fourth term in US.

US and Russian forces join at River Elbe; suicide of Hitler. Yalta Conference: last meeting of Roosevelt, Churchill and Stalin. First atomic explosion (experimental) at Alamogordo, New Mexico, 16 July. Atomic bombs dropped on Hiroshima (6 August) and Nagasaki (9 August) with tremendous loss of life. San Francisco Conference: formation of United Nations; Falangist Spain refused admission. Attlee government in UK. Truman succeeds Roosevelt in US.
Churchill's 'Iron Curtain' speech at Fulton, US. UNESCO established, 4 November. US navy atomic tests at Bikini and Eniwetok Atolls.

First report of flying saucers in US. Formation of General Agreement on Tariffs and Trade (GATT). Marshall Plan instituted: US aid for European postwar recovery. Pilotless US plane crosses Atlantic. Christian Dior's 'New Look'.

ERNEST HEMINGWAY

DATE	AUTHOR'S LIFE	LITERARY CONTEXT
1948	Visits Italy with Mary.	Mailer: *The Naked and the Dead.* Irwin Shaw: *The Young Lions.* Leavis: *The Great Tradition.*
1949		de Beauvoir: *The Second Sex.* Greene: *The Third Man.* Orwell: *Nineteen Eighty-four.* Miller: *Death of a Salesman.*
1950	Publishes *Across the River and Into the Trees* which has a poor reception.	Eliot: *The Cocktail Party.*
1951		Jones: *From Here to Eternity.* Salinger: *The Catcher in the Rye.* Yourcenar: *Memoirs of Hadrian.*
1952	Publishes *The Old Man and the Sea* which restores his reputation.	Steinbeck: *East of Eden.* Waugh: *Men at Arms.* Beckett: *Waiting for Godot.*
1953	Hemingway is awarded the Pulitzer Prize. Returns to Spain and then to Africa. He is reported dead when his plane crashes while on safari.	Faulkner: *Requiem for a Nun.* Williams: *Camino Real.*
1954	Awarded the Nobel Prize. He is unable – or unwilling – to attend the ceremony. He also receives the Annual Prize of the American Academy of Arts and Letters.	Amis: *Lucky Jim.*
1955		Williams: *Cat on a Hot Tin Roof.* Miller: *A View from the Bridge.* Nabokov: *Lolita.* Lampedusa: *The Leopard.* Waugh: *Officers and Gentlemen.*
1956		Osborne: *Look Back in Anger.*
1957	Suffering from ill health, Hemingway returns to the US.	Céline: *Castle to Castle.*
1958		Capote: *Breakfast at Tiffany's.* Kerouac: *On the Road.* Pasternak: *Doctor Zhivago.*

CHRONOLOGY

DATE	AUTHOR'S LIFE	LITERARY CONTEXT
1959	Spends a happy year in Spain.	Burroughs: *The Naked Lunch*.
1960	Works on a lengthy study of bullfighting called *The Dangerous Summer*. Compiles a volume of reminiscences entitled *A Moveable Feast*. Ill, he attends a clinic in Minnesota.	
1961	After severe loss of weight and electroshock treatments for depression, Hemingway commits suicide on 2 July. This was his third attempt that year.	Heller: *Catch 22*. Williams: *Night of the Iguana*. Waugh: *Unconditional Surrender*.

CHRONOLOGY

in our time

by

ernest hemingway

A GIRL IN CHICAGO: Tell us about
the French women, Hank. What are
they like?
BILL SMITH: How old are the French
women, Hank?

paris:

printed at the three mountains press *and for sale
at* shakespeare & company, *in the rue de l'odéon;
london: william jackson, tod's court, cursitor street, chancery lane.*

1924

Title page of first edition. Courtesy of Princeton
University Library

THREE STORIES

Up in Michigan

Out of Season

My Old Man

& TEN POEMS

Mitraigliatrice

Oklahoma

Oily Weather

Roosevelt

Captives

Champs d'Honneur

Riparto d'Assalto

Montparnasse

Along With Youth

Chapter Heading

ERNEST HEMINGWAY

Title page of first edition. Courtesy of Princeton
University Library

PART ONE

STORIES COLLECTED IN HEMINGWAY'S LIFETIME

From   THREE STORIES
AND TEN POEMS

UP IN MICHIGAN

Jim Gilmore came to Hortons Bay from Canada. He bought the blacksmith shop from old man Horton. Jim was short and dark with big mustaches and big hands. He was a good horseshoer and did not look much like a blacksmith even with his leather apron on. He lived upstairs above the blacksmith shop and took his meals at A. J. Smith's.

Liz Coates worked for Smith's. Mrs. Smith, who was a very large clean woman, said Liz Coates was the neatest girl she'd ever seen. Liz had good legs and always wore clean gingham aprons and Jim noticed that her hair was always neat behind. He liked her face because it was so jolly but he never thought about her.

Liz liked Jim very much. She liked it the way he walked over from the shop and often went to the kitchen door to watch for him to start down the road. She liked it about his mustache. She liked it about how white his teeth were when he smiled. She liked it very much that he didn't look like a blacksmith. She liked it how much A. J. Smith and Mrs. Smith liked Jim. One day she found that she liked it the way the hair was black on his arms and how white they were above the tanned line when he washed up in the washbasin outside the house. Liking that made her feel funny.

Hortons Bay, the town, was only five houses on the main road between Boyne City and Charlevoix. There was the general store and postoffice with a high false front and maybe a wagon hitched out in front, Smith's house, Stroud's house, Fox's house, Horton's house and Van Hoosen's house. The houses were in a big grove of elm trees and the road was very sandy. There was farming country and timber each way up the road. Up the road a ways was the Methodist church and down the road the other direction was the township school. The blacksmith shop was painted red and faced the school.

A steep sandy road ran down the hill to the bay through the timber. From Smith's back door you could look out across the woods that ran down to the lake and across the bay. It was very beautiful in the spring and summer, the bay blue and bright and usually whitecaps on the lake out beyond the point from the breeze blowing from Charlevoix and Lake Michigan. From Smith's back door Liz could see ore barges way out in the lake going toward Boyne City. When she looked at them they didn't seem to be moving at all but if she went in and dried some more dishes and then came out again they would be out of sight beyond the point.

All the time now Liz was thinking about Jim Gilmore. He didn't seem to notice her much. He talked about the shop to A. J. Smith and about the Republican Party and about James G. Blaine. In the evenings he read the Toledo Blade and the Grand Rapids paper by the lamp in the front room or went out spearing fish in the bay with a jacklight with A. J. Smith. In the fall he and Smith and Charley Wyman took a wagon and tent, grub, axes, their rifles and two dogs and went on a trip to the pine plains beyond Vanderbilt deer hunting. Liz and Mrs. Smith were cooking for four days for them before they started. Liz wanted to make something special for Jim to take but she didn't finally because she was afraid to ask Mrs. Smith for the eggs and flour and afraid if she bought them Mrs. Smith would catch her cooking. It would have been all right with Mrs. Smith but Liz was afraid.

All the time Jim was gone on the deer hunting trip Liz thought about him. It was awful while he was gone. She couldn't sleep well from thinking about him but she discovered it was fun to think about him too. If she let herself go it was better. The night before they were to come back she didn't sleep at all, that is she didn't think she slept because it was all mixed up in a dream about not sleeping and really not sleeping. When she saw the wagon coming down the road she felt weak and sick sort of inside. She couldn't wait till she saw Jim and it seemed as though everything would be all right when he came. The wagon stopped outside under the big elm and Mrs. Smith and Liz went out. All the men had beards and there were three deer in the back of the wagon, their thin legs sticking stiff over the edge of the wagon box. Mrs. Smith kissed Alonzo and he hugged her. Jim said 'Hello Liz.' and grinned. Liz hadn't known just what would happen when Jim got back but she was sure it would be something. Nothing had happened. The men were just home that was all. Jim pulled the burlap sacks off the deer and Liz looked at them. One was a big buck. It was stiff and hard to lift out of the wagon.

'Did you shoot it Jim?' Liz asked.

'Yeah. Aint it a beauty?' Jim got it onto his back to carry to the smokehouse.

That night Charley Wyman stayed to supper at Smith's. It was too late to get back to Charlevoix. The men washed up and waited in the front room for supper.

'Aint there something left in that crock Jimmy?' A. J. Smith asked and Jim went out to the wagon in the barn and fetched in the jug of whiskey the men had taken hunting with them. It was a four gallon jug and there was quite a little slopped back and forth in the bottom. Jim took a long pull on his way back to the house. It was hard to lift such a big jug up to drink out of it. Some of the whiskey ran down on his shirt front. The two men smiled when Jim came in with the jug. A. J. Smith sent for glasses and Liz brought them. A. J. poured out three big shots.

'Well here's looking at you A. J.' said Charley Wyman.

'That damn big buck Jimmy.' said A. J.

'Here's all the ones we missed A. J.' said Jim and downed his liquor.

'Tastes good to a man.'

'Nothing like it this time of year for what ails you.'

'How about another boys?'

'Here's how A. J.'

'Down the creek boys.'

'Here's to next year.'

Jim began to feel great. He loved the taste and the feel of whiskey. He was glad to be back to a comfortable bed and warm food and the shop. He had another drink. The men came in to supper feeling hilarious but acting very respectable. Liz sat at the table after she put on the food and ate with the family. It was a good dinner. The men ate seriously. After supper they went into the front room again and Liz cleaned off with Mrs. Smith. Then Mrs. Smith went up stairs and pretty soon Smith came out and went up stairs too. Jim and Charley were still in the front room. Liz was sitting in the kitchen next to the stove pretending to read a book and thinking about Jim. She didn't want to go to bed yet because she knew Jim would be coming out and she wanted to see him as he went out so she could take the way he looked up to bed with her.

She was thinking about him hard and then Jim came out. His eyes were shining and his hair was a little rumpled. Liz looked down at her book. Jim came over back of her chair and stood there and she could feel him breathing and then he put his arms around her. Her breasts felt plump and firm and the nipples were erect under his hands. Liz was terribly frightened, no one had ever touched her, but she thought, 'He's come to me finally. He's really come.'

She held herself stiff because she was so frightened and did not know anything else to do and then Jim held her tight against the chair and kissed her. It was such a sharp, aching, hurting feeling that she thought she couldn't stand it. She felt Jim right through the back of the chair and she couldn't stand it and then something clicked inside of her and the feeling was warmer and softer. Jim held her tight hard against the chair and she wanted it now and Jim whispered, 'Come on for a walk.'

Liz took her coat off the peg on the kitchen wall and they went out the door. Jim had his arm around her and every little way they stopped and pressed against each other and Jim kissed her. There was no moon and they walked ankle deep in the sandy road through the trees down to the dock and the warehouse on the bay. The water was lapping in the piles and the point was dark across the bay. It was cold but Liz was hot all over from being with Jim. They sat down in the shelter of the warehouse and Jim pulled Liz close to him. She was frightened. One of Jim's hands went inside her dress and stroked over her breast and the other hand was in her lap. She was very frightened and didn't know how he was going to go about things but she snuggled close to him. Then the hand that felt so big in her lap went away and was on her leg and started to move up it.

'Don't Jim,' Liz said. Jim slid the hand further up.

'You musn't Jim. You musn't.' Neither Jim nor Jim's big hand paid any attention to her.

The boards were hard. Jim had her dress up and was trying to do something to her. She was frightened but she wanted it. She had to have it but it frightened her.

'You musn't do it Jim. You musn't.'

'I got to. I'm going to. You know we got to.'

'No we haven't Jim. We aint got to. Oh it isn't right. Oh it's so big and it hurts so. You can't. Oh Jim. Jim. Oh.'

The hemlock planks of the dock were hard and splintery and cold and Jim was heavy on her and he had hurt her. Liz pushed him, she was so uncomfortable and cramped. Jim was asleep. He wouldn't move. She worked out from under him and sat up and straightened her skirt and coat and tried to do something with her hair. Jim was sleeping with his mouth a little open. Liz leaned over and kissed him on the cheek. He was still asleep. She lifted his head a little and shook it. He rolled his head over and swallowed. Liz started to cry. She walked over to the edge of the dock and looked down to the water. There was a mist coming up from the bay. She was cold and miserable and everything felt gone. She walked back to where Jim was lying and shook him once more to make sure. She was crying.

'Jim' she said, 'Jim. Please Jim.'

Jim stirred and curled a little tighter. Liz took off her coat and leaned over and covered him with it. She tucked it around him neatly and carefully. Then she walked across the dock and up the steep sandy road to go to bed. A cold mist was coming up through the woods from the bay.

in our time

to
robert mᶜalmon and william bird
publishers of the city of paris
and to

captain eric edward dorman–smith, m.c.,
of his majesty's fifth fusiliers
this book
is respectfully dedicated

chapter 1

EVERYBODY was drunk. The whole battery was drunk going along the road in the dark. We were going to the Champagne. The lieutenant kept riding his horse out into the fields and saying to him, 'I'm drunk, I tell you, mon vieux. Oh, I am so soused.' We went along the road all night in the dark and the adjutant kept riding up alongside my kitchen and saying, 'You must put it out. It is dangerous. It will be observed.' We were fifty kilometers from the front but the adjutant worried about the fire in my kitchen. It was funny going along that road. That was when I was a kitchen corporal.

chapter 2

THE first matador got the horn through his sword hand and the crowd hooted him out. The second matador slipped and the bull caught him through the belly and he hung on to the horn with one hand and held the other tight against the place, and the bull rammed him wham against the wall and the horn came out, and he lay in the sand, and then got up like crazy drunk and tried to slug the men carrying him away and yelled for his sword but he fainted. The kid came out and had to kill five bulls because you can't have more than three matadors, and the last bull he was so tired he couldn't get the sword in. He couldn't hardly lift his arm. He tried five times and the crowd was quiet because it was a good bull and it looked like him or the bull and then he finally made it. He sat down in the sand and puked and they held a cape over him while the crowd hollered and threw things down into the bull ring.

chapter 3

MINARETS stuck up in the rain out of Adrianople across the mud flats. The carts were jammed for thirty miles along the Karagatch road. Water buffalo and cattle were hauling carts through the mud. No end and no beginning. Just carts loaded with everything they owned. The old men and women, soaked through, walked along keeping the cattle moving. The Maritza was running yellow almost up to the bridge. Carts were jammed solid on the bridge with camels bobbing along through them. Greek cavalry herded along the procession. Women and kids were in the carts crouched with mattresses, mirrors, sewing machines, bundles. There was a woman having a kid with a young girl holding a blanket over her and crying. Scared sick looking at it. It rained all through the evacuation.

chapter 4

WE were in a garden at Mons. Young Buckley came in with his patrol from across the river. The first German I saw climbed up over the garden wall. We waited till he got one leg over and then potted him. He had so much equipment on and looked awfully surprised and fell down into the garden. Then three more came over further down the wall. We shot them. They all came just like that.

chapter 5

IT was a frightfully hot day. We'd jammed an absolutely perfect barricade across the bridge. It was simply priceless. A big old wrought iron grating from the front of a house. Too heavy to lift and you could shoot through it and they would have to climb over it. It was absolutely topping. They tried to get over it, and we potted them from forty yards. They rushed it, and officers came out alone and worked on it. It was an absolutely perfect obstacle. Their officers were very fine. We were frightfully put out when we heard the flank had gone, and we had to fall back.

chapter 6

THEY shot the six cabinet ministers at half-past six in the morning against the wall of a hospital. There were pools of water in the courtyard. There were wet dead leaves on the paving of the courtyard. It rained hard. All the shutters of the hospital were nailed shut. One of the ministers was sick with typhoid. Two soldiers carried him downstairs and out into the rain. They tried to hold him up against the wall but he sat down in a puddle of water. The other five stood very quietly against the wall. Finally the officer told the soldiers it was no good trying to make him stand up. When they fired the first volley he was sitting down in the water with his head on his knees.

chapter 7

NICK sat against the wall of the church where they had dragged him to be clear of machine gun fire in the street. Both legs stuck out awkwardly. He had been hit in the spine. His face was sweaty and dirty. The sun shone on his face. The day was very hot. Rinaldi, big backed, his equipment sprawling, lay face downward against the wall. Nick looked straight ahead brilliantly. The pink wall of the house opposite had fallen out from the roof, and an iron bedstead hung twisted toward the street. Two Austrian dead lay in the rubble in the shade of the house. Up the street were other dead. Things were getting forward in the town. It was going well. Stretcher bearers would be along any time now. Nick turned his head carefully and looked down at Rinaldi. 'Senta Rinaldi. Senta. You and me we've made a separate peace.' Rinaldi lay still in the sun breathing with difficulty. 'Not patriots.' Nick turned his head carefully away smiling sweatily. Rinaldi was a disappointing audience.

chapter 8

WHILE the bombardment was knocking the trench to pieces at Fossalta, he lay very flat and sweated and prayed oh jesus christ get me out of here. Dear jesus please get me out. Christ please please please christ. If you'll only keep me from getting killed I'll do anything you say. I believe in you and I'll tell everyone in the world that you are the only thing that matters. Please please dear jesus. The shelling moved further up the line. We went to work on the trench and in the morning the sun came up and the day was hot and muggy and cheerful and quiet. The next night back at Mestre he did not tell the girl he went upstairs with at the Villa Rossa about Jesus. And he never told anybody.

chapter 9

AT two o'clock in the morning two Hungarians got into a cigar store at Fifteenth Street and Grand Avenue. Drevitts and Boyle drove up from the Fifteenth Street police station in a Ford. The Hungarians were backing their wagon out of an alley. Boyle shot one off the seat of the wagon and one out of the wagon box. Drevetts got frightened when he found they were both dead. Hell Jimmy, he said, you oughtn't to have done it. There's liable to be a hell of a lot of trouble.

– They're crooks ain't they? said Boyle. They're wops ain't they? Who the hell is going to make any trouble?

– That's all right maybe this time, said Drevitts, but how did you know they were wops when you bumped them?

– Wops, said Boyle, I can tell wops a mile off.

chapter 10

ONE hot evening in Milan they carried him up onto the roof and he could look out over the top of the town. There were chimney swifts in the sky. After a while it got dark and the searchlights came out. The others went down and took the bottles with them. He and Ag could hear them below on the balcony. Ag sat on the bed. She was cool and fresh in the hot night.

Ag stayed on night duty for three months. They were glad to let her. When they operated on him she prepared him for the operating table, and they had a joke about friend or enema. He went under the anæsthetic holding tight on to himself so that he would not blab about anything during the silly, talky time. After he got on crutches he used to take the temperature so Ag would not have to get up from the bed. There were only a few patients, and they all knew about it. They all liked Ag. As he walked back along the halls he thought of Ag in his bed.

Before he went back to the front they went into the Duomo and prayed. It was dim and quiet, and there were other people praying. They wanted to get married, but there was not enough time for the banns, and neither of them had birth certificates. They felt as though they were married, but they wanted everyone to know about it, and to make it so they could not lose it.

Ag wrote him many letters that he never got until after the armistice. Fifteen came in a bunch and he sorted them by the dates and read them all straight through. They were about the hospital, and how much she loved him and how it was impossible to get along without him and how terrible it was missing him at night.

After the armistice they agreed he should go home to get a job so they might be married. Ag would not come home until he had a good job and could come to New York to meet her. It was understood he would not drink, and he did not want to see his friends or anyone in the States. Only to get a job and be married. On the train from Padova to Milan they quarrelled about her not being willing to come home at once. When they had to say good-bye in the station at Padova they kissed good-bye, but were not finished with the quarrel. He felt sick about saying good-bye like that.

He went to America on a boat from Genoa. Ag went back to Torre di Mosta to open a hospital. It was lonely and rainy there, and there was a battalion of *arditi* quartered in the town. Living in the muddy, rainy town in the winter the major of the battalion made love to Ag, and she had never known Italians before, and finally wrote a letter to the States that theirs had been only a boy and girl affair. She was sorry, and she knew he would probably not be able to understand, but might some day forgive her, and be grateful to her, and she expected, absolutely unexpectedly, to be married in the spring. She loved him as always, but she realized now it was only a boy and girl love. She hoped he would have a great career, and believed in him absolutely. She knew it was for the best.

The Major did not marry her in the spring, or any other time. Ag never got an answer to her letter to Chicago about it. A short time after he contracted gonorrhea from a sales girl from The Fair riding in a taxicab through Lincoln Park.

chapter 11

In 1919 he was travelling on the railroads in Italy carrying a square of oilcloth from the headquarters of the party written in indelible pencil and saying here was a comrade who had suffered very much under the whites in Budapest and requesting comrades to aid him in any way. He used this instead of a ticket. He was very shy and quite young and the train men passed him on from one crew to another. He had no money, and they fed him behind the counter in railway eating houses.

He was delighted with Italy. It was a beautiful country he said. The people were all kind. He had been in many towns, walked much and seen many pictures. Giotto, Masaccio, and Piero della Francesca he bought reproductions of and carried them wrapped in a copy of *Avanti*. Mantegna he did not like.

He reported at Bologna, and I took him with me up into the Romagna where it was necessary I go to see a man. We had a good trip together. It was early September and the country was pleasant. He was a Magyar, a very nice boy and very shy. Horthy's men had done some bad things to him. He talked about it a little. In spite of Italy, he believed altogether in the world revolution.

– But how is the movement going in Italy? he asked.

– Very badly, I said.

– But it will go better, he said. You have everything here. It is the one country that everyone is sure of. It will be the starting point of everything.

At Bologna he said good-bye to us to go on the train to Milano and then to Aosta to walk over the pass into Switzerland. I spoke to him about the Mantegnas in Milano. No, he said, very shyly, he did not like Mantegna. I wrote out for him where to eat in Milano and the addresses of comrades. He thanked me very much, but his mind was already looking forward to walking over the pass. He was very eager to walk over the pass while the weather held good. The last I heard of him the Swiss had him in jail near Sion.

chapter 12

THEY whack whacked the white horse on the legs
and he knee-ed himself up. The picador twisted the
stirrups straight and pulled and hauled up into the
saddle. The horse's entrails hung down in a blue
bunch and swung backward and forward as he began
to canter, the *monos* whacking him on the back of his
legs with the rods. He cantered jerkily along the barrera. He stopped stiff and one of the *monos* held his
bridle and walked him forward. The picador kicked
in his spurs, leaned forward and shook his lance at the
bull. Blood pumped regularly from between the
horse's front legs. He was nervously wobbly. The bull
could not make up his mind to charge.

chapter 13

THE crowd shouted all the time and threw pieces of bread down into the ring, then cushions and leather wine bottles, keeping up whistling and yelling. Finally the bull was too tired from so much bad sticking and folded his knees and lay down and one of the *cuadrilla* leaned out over his neck and killed him with the *puntillo*. The crowd came over the barrera and around the torero and two men grabbed him and held him and some one cut off his pigtail and was waving it and a kid grabbed it and ran away with it. Afterwards I saw him at the café. He was very short with a brown face and quite drunk and he said after all it has happened before like that. I am not really a good bull fighter.

chapter 14

IF it happened right down close in front of you, you could see Villalta snarl at the bull and curse him, and when the bull charged he swung back firmly like an oak when the wind hits it, his legs tight together, the muleta trailing and the sword following the curve behind. Then he cursed the bull, flopped the muleta at him, and swung back from the charge his feet firm, the muleta curving and each swing the crowd roaring.

When he started to kill it was all in the same rush. The bull looking at him straight in front, hating. He drew out the sword from the folds of the muleta and sighted with the same movement and called to the bull, Toro! Toro! and the bull charged and Villalta charged and just for a moment they became one. Villalta became one with the bull and then it was over. Villalta standing straight and the red hilt of the sword sticking out dully between the bull's shoulders. Villalta, his hand up at the crowd and the bull roaring blood, looking straight at Villalta and his legs caving.

chapter 15

I heard the drums coming down the street and then the fifes and the pipes and then they came around the corner, all dancing. The street full of them. Maera saw him and then I saw him. When they stopped the music for the crouch he hunched down in the street with them all and when they started it again he jumped up and went dancing down the street with them. He was drunk all right.

You go down after him, said Maera, he hates me.

So I went down and caught up with them and grabbed him while he was crouched down waiting for the music to break loose and said, Come on Luis. For Christ sake you've got bulls this afternoon. He didn't listen to me, he was listening so hard for the music to start.

I said, Don't be a damn fool Luis. Come on back to the hotel.

Then the music started up again and he jumped up and twisted away from me and started dancing. I grabbed his arm and he pulled loose and said, Oh leave me alone. You're not my father.

I went back to the hotel and Maera was on the balcony looking out to see if I'd be bringing him back. He went inside when he saw me and came downstairs disgusted.

Well, I said, after all he's just an ignorant Mexican savage.

Yes, Maera said, and who will kill his bulls after he gets a *cogida?*

We, I suppose, I said.

Yes, we, said Maera. We kills the savages' bulls, and the drunkards' bulls, and the *riau-riau* dancers' bulls. Yes. We kill them. We kill them all right. Yes. Yes. Yes.

chapter 16

MAERA lay still, his head on his arms, his face in the sand. He felt warm and sticky from the bleeding. Each time he felt the horn coming. Sometimes the bull only bumped him with his head. Once the horn went all the way through him and he felt it go into the sand. Someone had the bull by the tail. They were swearing at him and flopping the cape in his face. Then the bull was gone. Some men picked Maera up and started to run with him toward the barriers through the gate out the passage way around under the grand stand to the infirmary. They laid Maera down on a cot and one of the men went out for the doctor. The others stood around. The doctor came running from the corral where he had been sewing up picador horses. He had to stop and wash his hands. There was a great shouting going on in the grandstand overhead. Maera wanted to say something and found he could not talk. Maera felt everything getting larger and larger and larger and then smaller and smaller. Then it got larger and larger and larger and then smaller and smaller. Then everything commenced to run faster and faster as when they speed up a cinematograph film. Then he was dead.

chapter 17

THEY hanged Sam Cardinella at six o'clock in the morning in the corridor of the county jail. The corridor was high and narrow with tiers of cells on either side. All the cells were occupied. The men had been brought in for the hanging. Five men sentenced to be hanged were in the five top cells. Three of the men to be hanged were negroes. They were very frightened. One of the white men sat on his cot with his head in his hands. The other lay flat on his cot with a blanket wrapped around his head.

They came out onto the gallows through a door in the wall. There were six or seven of them including two priests. They were carrying Sam Cardinella. He had been like that since about four o'clock in the morning.

While they were strapping his legs together two guards held him up and the two priests were whispering to him. 'Be a man, my son,' said one priest. When they came toward him with the cap to go over his head Sam Cardinella lost control of his sphincter muscle. The guards who had been holding him up dropped him. They were both disgusted. 'How about a chair, Will?' asked one of the guards. 'Better get one,' said a man in a derby hat.

When they all stepped back on the scaffolding back of the drop, which was very heavy, built of oak and steel and swung on ball bearings, Sam Cardinella was left sitting there strapped tight, the younger of the two priests kneeling beside the chair. The priest skipped back onto the scaffolding just before the drop fell.

chapter 18

THE king was working in the garden. He seemed very glad to see me. We walked through the garden. This is the queen, he said. She was clipping a rose bush. Oh how do you do, she said. We sat down at a table under a big tree and the king ordered whiskey and soda. We have good whiskey anyway, he said. The revolutionary committee, he told me, would not allow him to go outside the palace grounds. Plastiras is a very good man I believe, he said, but frightfully difficult. I think he did right though shooting those chaps. If Kerensky had shot a few men things might have been altogether different. Of course the great thing in this sort of an affair is not to be shot oneself!

It was very jolly. We talked for a long time. Like all Greeks he wanted to go to America.

IN OUR TIME

to   HADLEY RICHARDSON HEMINGWAY

A girl in Chicago: – *Tell us about the French women,
Hank. What are they like?*
Bill Smith: – *How old are the French women, Hank?*

ON THE QUAI AT SMYRNA

The strange thing was, he said, how they screamed every night at midnight. I do not know why they screamed at that time. We were in the harbor and they were all on the pier and at midnight they started screaming. We used to turn the searchlight on them to quiet them. That always did the trick. We'd run the searchlight up and down over them two or three times and they stopped it. One time I was senior officer on the pier and a Turkish officer came up to me in a frightful rage because one of our sailors had been most insulting to him. So I told him the fellow would be sent on ship and be most severely punished. I asked him to point him out. So he pointed out a gunner's mate, most inoffensive chap. Said he'd been most frightfully and repeatedly insulting; talking to me through an interpreter. I couldn't imagine how the gunner's mate knew enough Turkish to be insulting. I called him over and said, 'And just in case you should have spoken to any Turkish officers.'

'I haven't spoken to any of them, sir.'

'I'm quite sure of it,' I said, 'but you'd best go on board ship and not come ashore again for the rest of the day.'

Then I told the Turk the man was being sent on board ship and would be most severely dealt with. Oh most rigorously. He felt topping about it. Great friends we were.

The worst, he said, were the women with dead babies. You couldn't get the women to give up their dead babies. They'd have babies dead for six days. Wouldn't give them up. Nothing you could do about it. Had to take them away finally. Then there was an old lady, most extraordinary case. I told it to a doctor and he said I was lying. We were clearing them off the pier, had to clear off the dead ones, and this old woman was lying on a sort of litter. They said, 'Will you have a look at her, sir?' So I had a look at her and just then she died and went absolutely stiff. Her legs drew up and she drew up from the waist and went quite rigid. Exactly as though she had been dead over night. She was quite dead and absolutely rigid. I told a medical chap about it and he told me it was impossible.

They were all out there on the pier and it wasn't at all like an earthquake or that sort of thing because they never knew about the Turk. They never knew what the old Turk would do. You remember when they ordered us not to come in to take off any more? I had the wind up when we came in that morning. He had any amount of batteries and could have blown us clean out of the water. We were going to come in, run close along the pier, let go the front and rear anchors and then shell the Turkish quarter of the town. They would have blown us out of water but we would have blown the town simply to hell. They just fired a few blank charges at us as we came in. Kemal came down and sacked the Turkish commander. For exceeding his authority or some such thing. He got a bit above himself. It would have been the hell of a mess.

You remember the harbor. There were plenty of nice things floating around in it. That was the only time in my life I got so I dreamed about things. You didn't mind the women who were having babies as you did those with the dead ones. They had them all right. Surprising how few of them died. You just covered them over with something and let them go to it. They'd always pick out the darkest place in the hold to have them. None of them minded anything once they got off the pier.

The Greeks were nice chaps too. When they evacuated they had all their baggage animals they couldn't take off with them so they just broke their forelegs and dumped them into the shallow water. All those mules with their forelegs broken pushed over into the shallow water. It was all a pleasant business. My word yes a most pleasant business.

CHAPTER I

Everybody was drunk. The whole battery was drunk going along the road in the dark. We were going to the Champagne. The lieutenant kept riding his horse out into the fields and saying to him, 'I'm drunk, I tell you, mon vieux. *Oh, I am so soused.' We went along the road all night in the dark and the adjutant kept riding up alongside my kitchen and saying, 'You must put it out. It is dangerous. It will be observed.' We were fifty kilometers from the front but the adjutant worried about the fire in my kitchen. It was funny going along that road. That was when I was a kitchen corporal.*

INDIAN CAMP

At the lake shore there was another rowboat drawn up. The two Indians stood waiting.

Nick and his father got in the stern of the boat and the Indians shoved it off and one of them got in to row. Uncle George sat in the stern of the camp rowboat. The young Indian shoved the camp boat off and got in to row Uncle George.

The two boats started off in the dark. Nick heard the oarlocks of the other boat quite a way ahead of them in the mist. The Indians rowed with quick choppy strokes. Nick lay back with his father's arm around him. It was cold on the water. The Indian who was rowing them was working very hard, but the other boat moved further ahead in the mist all the time.

'Where are we going, Dad?' Nick asked.

'Over to the Indian camp. There is an Indian lady very sick.'

'Oh,' said Nick.

Across the bay they found the other boat beached. Uncle George was smoking a cigar in the dark. The young Indian pulled the boat way up on the beach. Uncle George gave both the Indians cigars.

They walked up from the beach through a meadow that was soaking wet with dew, following the young Indian who carried a lantern. Then they went into the woods and followed a trail that led to the logging road that ran back into the hills. It was much lighter on the logging road as the timber was cut away on both sides. The young Indian stopped and blew out his lantern and they all walked on along the road.

They came around a bend and a dog came out barking. Ahead were the lights of the shanties where the Indian bark-peelers lived. More dogs rushed out at them. The two Indians sent them back to the shanties. In the shanty nearest the road there was a light in the window. An old woman stood in the doorway holding a lamp.

Inside on a wooden bunk lay a young Indian woman. She had been trying to have her baby for two days. All the old women in the camp had been helping her. The men had moved off up the road to sit in the dark and smoke out of range of the noise she made. She screamed just as Nick and the two Indians followed his father and Uncle George into the shanty. She lay in

the lower bunk, very big under a quilt. Her head was turned to one side. In the upper bunk was her husband. He had cut his foot very badly with an ax three days before. He was smoking a pipe. The room smelled very bad.

Nick's father ordered some water to be put on the stove, and while it was heating he spoke to Nick.

'This lady is going to have a baby, Nick,' he said.

'I know,' said Nick.

'You don't know,' said his father. 'Listen to me. What she is going through is called being in labor. The baby wants to be born and she wants it to be born. All her muscles are trying to get the baby born. That is what is happening when she screams.'

'I see,' Nick said.

Just then the woman cried out.

'Oh, Daddy, can't you give her something to make her stop screaming?' asked Nick.

'No. I haven't any anæsthetic,' his father said. 'But her screams are not important. I don't hear them because they are not important.'

The husband in the upper bunk rolled over against the wall.

The woman in the kitchen motioned to the doctor that the water was hot. Nick's father went into the kitchen and poured about half of the water out of the big kettle into a basin. Into the water left in the kettle he put several things he unwrapped from a handkerchief.

'Those must boil,' he said, and began to scrub his hands in the basin of hot water with a cake of soap he had brought from the camp. Nick watched his father's hands scrubbing each other with the soap. While his father washed his hands very carefully and thoroughly, he talked.

'You see, Nick, babies are supposed to be born head first but sometimes they're not. When they're not they make a lot of trouble for everybody. Maybe I'll have to operate on this lady. We'll know in a little while.'

When he was satisfied with his hands he went in and went to work.

'Pull back that quilt, will you, George?' he said. 'I'd rather not touch it.'

Later when he started to operate Uncle George and three Indian men held the woman still. She bit Uncle George on the arm and Uncle George said, 'Damn squaw bitch!' and the young Indian who had rowed Uncle George over laughed at him. Nick held the basin for his father. It all took a long time. His father picked the baby up and slapped it to make it breathe and handed it to the old woman.

'See, it's a boy, Nick,' he said. 'How do you like being an interne?'

Nick said, 'All right.' He was looking away so as not to see what his father was doing.

'There. That gets it,' said his father and put something into the basin.

Nick didn't look at it.

'Now,' his father said, 'there's some stitches to put in. You can watch this or not, Nick, just as you like. I'm going to sew up the incision I made.'

Nick did not watch. His curiosity had been gone for a long time.

His father finished and stood up. Uncle George and the three Indian men stood up. Nick put the basin out in the kitchen.

Uncle George looked at his arm. The young Indian smiled reminiscently.

'I'll put some peroxide on that, George,' the doctor said. He bent over the Indian woman. She was quiet now and her eyes were closed. She looked very pale. She did not know what had become of the baby or anything.

'I'll be back in the morning,' the doctor said, standing up. 'The nurse should be here from St. Ignace by noon and she'll bring everything we need.'

He was feeling exalted and talkative as football players are in the dressing room after a game.

'That's one for the medical journal, George,' he said. 'Doing a Cæsarian with a jack-knife and sewing it up with nine-foot, tapered gut leaders.'

Uncle George was standing against the wall, looking at his arm.

'Oh, you're a great man, all right,' he said.

'Ought to have a look at the proud father. They're usually the worst sufferers in these little affairs,' the doctor said. 'I must say he took it all pretty quietly.'

He pulled back the blanket from the Indian's head. His hand came away wet. He mounted on the edge of the lower bunk with the lamp in one hand and looked in. The Indian lay with his face toward the wall. His throat had been cut from ear to ear. The blood had flowed down into a pool where his body sagged the bunk. His head rested on his left arm. The open razor lay, edge up, in the blankets.

'Take Nick out of the shanty, George,' the doctor said.

There was no need of that. Nick, standing in the door of the kitchen, had a good view of the upper bunk when his father, the lamp in one hand, tipped the Indian's head back.

It was just beginning to be daylight when they walked along the logging road back toward the lake.

'I'm terribly sorry I brought you along, Nickie,' said his father, all his post-operative exhilaration gone. 'It was an awful mess to put you through.'

'Do ladies always have such a hard time having babies?' Nick asked.

'No, that was very, very exceptional.'

'Why did he kill himself, Daddy?'

'I don't know, Nick. He couldn't stand things, I guess.'

'Do many men kill themselves, Daddy?'

'Not very many, Nick.'

'Do many women?'

'Hardly ever.'

'Don't they ever?'

'Oh, yes. They do sometimes.'

'Daddy?'

'Yes.'

'Where did Uncle George go?'

'He'll turn up all right.'

'Is dying hard, Daddy?'

'No, I think it's pretty easy, Nick. It all depends.'

They were seated in the boat, Nick in the stern, his father rowing. The sun was coming up over the hills. A bass jumped, making a circle in the water. Nick trailed his hand in the water. It felt warm in the sharp chill of the morning.

In the early morning on the lake sitting in the stern of the boat with his father rowing, he felt quite sure that he would never die.

CHAPTER II

Minarets stuck up in the rain out of Adrianople across the mud flats. The carts were jammed for thirty miles along the Karagatch road. Water buffalo and cattle were hauling carts through the mud. No end and no beginning. Just carts loaded with everything they owned. The old men and women, soaked through, walked along keeping the cattle moving. The Maritza was running yellow almost up to the bridge. Carts were jammed solid on the bridge with camels bobbing along through them. Greek cavalry herded along the procession. Women and kids were in the carts crouched with mattresses, mirrors, sewing machines, bundles. There was a woman having a kid with a young girl holding a blanket over her and crying. Scared sick looking at it. It rained all through the evacuation.

THE DOCTOR AND THE
DOCTOR'S WIFE

Dick Boulton came from the Indian camp to cut up logs for Nick's father. He brought his son Eddy and another Indian named Billy Tabeshaw with him. They came in through the back gate out of the woods, Eddy carrying the long cross-cut saw. It flopped over his shoulder and made a musical sound as he walked. Billy Tabeshaw carried two big cant-hooks. Dick had three axes under his arm.

He turned and shut the gate. The others went on ahead of him down to the lake shore where the logs were buried in the sand.

The logs had been lost from the big log booms that were towed down the lake to the mill by the steamer *Magic*. They had drifted up onto the beach and if nothing were done about them sooner or later the crew of the *Magic* would come along the shore in a rowboat, spot the logs, drive an iron spike with a ring on it into the end of each one and then tow them out into the lake to make a new boom. But the lumbermen might never come for them because a few logs were not worth the price of a crew to gather them. If no one came for them they would be left to waterlog and rot on the beach.

Nick's father always assumed that this was what would happen, and hired the Indians to come down from the camp and cut the logs up with the cross-cut saw and split them with a wedge to make cord wood and chunks for the open fireplace. Dick Boulton walked around past the cottage down to the lake. There were four big beech logs lying almost buried in the sand. Eddy hung the saw up by one of its handles in the crotch of a tree. Dick put the three axes down on the little dock. Dick was a half-breed and many of the farmers around the lake believed he was really a white man. He was very lazy but a great worker once he was started. He took a plug of tobacco out of his pocket, bit off a chew and spoke in Ojibway to Eddy and Billy Tabeshaw.

They sunk the ends of their cant-hooks into one of the logs and swung against it to loosen it in the sand. They swung their weight against the shafts of the cant-hooks. The log moved in the sand. Dick Boulton turned to Nick's father.

'Well, Doc,' he said, 'that's a nice lot of timber you've stolen.'

'Don't talk that way, Dick,' the doctor said. 'It's driftwood.'

Eddy and Billy Tabeshaw had rocked the log out of the wet sand and rolled it toward the water.

'Put it right in,' Dick Boulton shouted.

'What are you doing that for?' asked the doctor.

'Wash it off. Clean off the sand on account of the saw. I want to see who it belongs to,' Dick said.

The log was just awash in the lake. Eddy and Billy Tabeshaw leaned on their cant-hooks sweating in the sun. Dick kneeled down in the sand and looked at the mark of the scaler's hammer in the wood at the end of the log.

'It belongs to White and McNally,' he said, standing up and brushing off his trousers' knees.

The doctor was very uncomfortable.

'You'd better not saw it up then, Dick,' he said, shortly.

'Don't get huffy, Doc,' said Dick. 'Don't get huffy. I don't care who you steal from. It's none of my business.'

'If you think the logs are stolen, leave them alone and take your tools back to the camp,' the doctor said. His face was red.

'Don't go off at half cock, Doc,' Dick said. He spat tobacco juice on the log. It slid off, thinning in the water. 'You know they're stolen as well as I do. It don't make any difference to me.'

'All right. If you think the logs are stolen, take your stuff and get out.'

'Now, Doc –'

'Take your stuff and get out.'

'Listen, Doc.'

'If you call me Doc once again, I'll knock your eye teeth down your throat.'

'Oh, no, you won't, Doc.'

Dick Boulton looked at the doctor. Dick was a big man. He knew how big a man he was. He liked to get into fights. He was happy. Eddy and Billy Tabeshaw leaned on their cant-hooks and looked at the doctor. The doctor chewed the beard on his lower lip and looked at Dick Boulton. Then he turned away and walked up the hill to the cottage. They could see from his back how angry he was. They all watched him walk up the hill and go inside the cottage.

Dick said something in Ojibway. Eddy laughed but Billy Tabeshaw looked very serious. He did not understand English but he had sweat all the time the row was going on. He was fat with only a few hairs of mustache like a Chinaman. He picked up the two cant-hooks. Dick picked up the axes and Eddy took the saw down from the tree. They started off and walked up past the cottage and out the back gate into the woods. Dick left the gate open. Billy Tabeshaw went back and fastened it. They were gone through the woods.

In the cottage the doctor, sitting on the bed in his room, saw a pile of medical journals on the floor by the bureau. They were still in their wrappers unopened. It irritated him.

'Aren't you going back to work, dear?' asked the doctor's wife from the room where she was lying with the blinds drawn.

'No!'

'Was anything the matter?'

'I had a row with Dick Boulton.'

'Oh,' said his wife. 'I hope you didn't lose your temper, Henry.'

'No,' said the doctor.

'Remember, that he who ruleth his spirit is greater than he that taketh a city,' said his wife. She was a Christian Scientist. Her Bible, her copy of *Science and Health* and her *Quarterly* were on a table beside her bed in the darkened room.

Her husband did not answer. He was sitting on his bed now, cleaning a shotgun. He pushed the magazine full of the heavy yellow shells and pumped them out again. They were scattered on the bed.

'Henry,' his wife called. Then paused a moment. 'Henry!'

'Yes,' the doctor said.

'You didn't say anything to Boulton to anger him, did you?'

'No,' said the doctor.

'What was the trouble about, dear?'

'Nothing much.'

'Tell me, Henry. Please don't try and keep anything from me. What was the trouble about?'

'Well, Dick owes me a lot of money for pulling his squaw through pneumonia and I guess he wanted a row so he wouldn't have to take it out in work.'

His wife was silent. The doctor wiped his gun carefully with a rag. He pushed the shells back in against the spring of the magazine. He sat with the gun on his knees. He was very fond of it. Then he heard his wife's voice from the darkened room.

'Dear, I don't think, I really don't think that any one would really do a thing like that.'

'No?' the doctor said.

'No. I can't really believe that any one would do a thing of that sort intentionally.'

The doctor stood up and put the shotgun in the corner behind the dresser.

'Are you going out, dear?' his wife said.

'I think I'll go for a walk,' the doctor said.

'If you see Nick, dear, will you tell him his mother wants to see him?' his wife said.

The doctor went out on the porch. The screen door slammed behind him. He heard his wife catch her breath when the door slammed.

'Sorry,' he said, outside her window with the blinds drawn.

'It's all right, dear,' she said.

He walked in the heat out the gate and along the path into the hemlock woods. It was cool in the woods even on such a hot day. He found Nick sitting with his back against a tree, reading.

'Your mother wants you to come and see her,' the doctor said.

'I want to go with you,' Nick said.

His father looked down at him.

'All right. Come on, then,' his father said. 'Give me the book, I'll put it in my pocket.'

'I know where there's black squirrels, Daddy,' Nick said.

'All right,' said his father. 'Let's go there.'

CHAPTER III

We were in a garden at Mons. Young Buckley came in with his patrol from across the river. The first German I saw climbed up over the garden wall. We waited till he got one leg over and then potted him. He had so much equipment on and looked awfully surprised and fell down into the garden. Then three more came over further down the wall. We shot them. They all came just like that.

THE END OF SOMETHING

In the old days Hortons Bay was a lumbering town. No one who lived in it was out of sound of the big saws in the mill by the lake. Then one year there were no more logs to make lumber. The lumber schooners came into the bay and were loaded with the cut of the mill that stood stacked in the yard. All the piles of lumber were carried away. The big mill building had all its machinery that was removable taken out and hoisted on board one of the schooners by the men who had worked in the mill. The schooner moved out of the bay toward the open lake carrying the two great saws, the travelling carriage that hurled the logs against the revolving, circular saws and all the rollers, wheels, belts and iron piled on a hull-deep load of lumber. Its open hold covered with canvas and lashed tight, the sails of the schooner filled and it moved out into the open lake, carrying with it everything that had made the mill a mill and Hortons Bay a town.

The one-story bunk houses, the eating-house, the company store, the mill offices, and the big mill itself stood deserted in the acres of sawdust that covered the swampy meadow by the shore of the bay.

Ten years later there was nothing of the mill left except the broken white limestone of its foundations showing through the swampy second growth as Nick and Marjorie rowed along the shore. They were trolling along the edge of the channel-bank where the bottom dropped off suddenly from sandy shallows to twelve feet of dark water. They were trolling on their way to the point to set night lines for rainbow trout.

'There's our old ruin, Nick,' Marjorie said.

Nick, rowing, looked at the white stone in the green trees.

'There it is,' he said.

'Can you remember when it was a mill?' Marjorie asked.

'I can just remember,' Nick said.

'It seems more like a castle,' Marjorie said.

Nick said nothing. They rowed on out of sight of the mill, following the shore line. Then Nick cut across the bay.

'They aren't striking,' he said.

'No,' Marjorie said. She was intent on the rod all the time they trolled, even when she talked. She loved to fish. She loved to fish with Nick.

Close beside the boat a big trout broke the surface of the water. Nick pulled hard on one oar so the boat would turn and the bait spinning far behind would pass where the trout was feeding. As the trout's back came up out of the water the minnows jumped wildly. They sprinkled the surface like a handful of shot thrown into the water. Another trout broke water, feeding on the other side of the boat.

'They're feeding,' Marjorie said.

'But they won't strike,' Nick said.

He rowed the boat around to troll past both the feeding fish, then headed it for the point. Marjorie did not reel in until the boat touched the shore.

They pulled the boat up the beach and Nick lifted out a pail of live perch. The perch swam in the water in the pail. Nick caught three of them with his hands and cut their heads off and skinned them while Marjorie chased with her hands in the bucket, finally caught a perch, cut its head off and skinned it. Nick looked at her fish.

'You don't want to take the ventral fin out,' he said. 'It'll be all right for bait but it's better with the ventral fin in.'

He hooked each of the skinned perch through the tail. There were two hooks attached to a leader on each rod. Then Marjorie rowed the boat out over the channel-bank, holding the line in her teeth, and looking toward Nick, who stood on the shore holding the rod and letting the line run out from the reel.

'That's about right,' he called.

'Should I let it drop?' Marjorie called back, holding the line in her hand.

'Sure. Let it go.' Marjorie dropped the line overboard and watched the baits go down through the water.

She came in with the boat and ran the second line out the same way. Each time Nick set a heavy slab of driftwood across the butt of the rod to hold it solid and propped it up at an angle with a small slab. He reeled in the slack line so the line ran taut out to where the bait rested on the sandy floor of the channel and set the click on the reel. When a trout, feeding on the bottom, took the bait it would run with it, taking line out of the reel in a rush and making the reel sing with the click on.

Marjorie rowed up the point a little way so she would not disturb the line. She pulled hard on the oars and the boat went way up the beach. Little waves came in with it. Marjorie stepped out of the boat and Nick pulled the boat high up the beach.

'What's the matter, Nick?' Marjorie asked.

'I don't know,' Nick said, getting wood for a fire.

They made a fire with driftwood. Marjorie went to the boat and brought a blanket. The evening breeze blew the smoke toward the point, so Marjorie spread the blanket out between the fire and the lake.

Marjorie sat on the blanket with her back to the fire and waited for Nick. He came over and sat down beside her on the blanket. In back of them was the close second-growth timber of the point and in front was the bay with the mouth of Hortons Creek. It was not quite dark. The fire-light went as far as the water. They could both see the two steel rods at an angle over the dark water. The fire glinted on the reels.

Marjorie unpacked the basket of supper.

'I don't feel like eating,' said Nick.

'Come on and eat, Nick.'

'All right.'

They ate without talking, and watched the two rods and the fire-light in the water.

'There's going to be a moon tonight,' said Nick. He looked across the bay to the hills that were beginning to sharpen against the sky. Beyond the hills he knew the moon was coming up.

'I know it,' Marjorie said happily.

'You know everything,' Nick said.

'Oh, Nick, please cut it out! Please, please don't be that way!'

'I can't help it,' Nick said. 'You do. You know everything. That's the trouble. You know you do.'

Marjorie did not say anything.

'I've taught you everything. You know you do. What don't you know, anyway?'

'Oh, shut up,' Marjorie said. 'There comes the moon.'

They sat on the blanket without touching each other and watched the moon rise.

'You don't have to talk silly,' Marjorie said. 'What's really the matter?'

'I don't know.'

'Of course you know.'

'No I don't.'

'Go on and say it.'

Nick looked on at the moon, coming up over the hills.

'It isn't fun any more.'

He was afraid to look at Marjorie. Then he looked at her. She sat there with her back toward him. He looked at her back. 'It isn't fun any more. Not any of it.'

She didn't say anything. He went on. 'I feel as though everything was gone to hell inside of me. I don't know, Marge. I don't know what to say.'

He looked on at her back.

'Isn't love any fun?' Marjorie said.

'No,' Nick said. Marjorie stood up. Nick sat there his head in his hands.

'I'm going to take the boat,' Marjorie called to him. 'You can walk back around the point.'

'All right,' Nick said. 'I'll push the boat off for you.'

'You don't need to,' she said. She was afloat in the boat on the water with the moonlight on it. Nick went back and lay down with his face in the blanket by the fire. He could hear Marjorie rowing on the water.

He lay there for a long time. He lay there while he heard Bill come into the clearing walking around through the woods. He felt Bill coming up to the fire. Bill didn't touch him, either.

'Did she go all right?' Bill said.

'Yes,' Nick said, lying, his face on the blanket.

'Have a scene?'

'No, there wasn't any scene.'

'How do you feel?'

'Oh, go away, Bill! Go away for a while.'

Bill selected a sandwich from the lunch basket and walked over to have a look at the rods.

CHAPTER IV

It was a frightfully hot day. We'd jammed an absolutely perfect barricade across the bridge. It was simply priceless. A big old wrought-iron grating from the front of a house. Too heavy to lift and you could shoot through it and they would have to climb over it. It was absolutely topping. They tried to get over it, and we potted them from forty yards. They rushed it, and officers came out alone and worked on it. It was an absolutely perfect obstacle. Their officers were very fine. We were frightfully put out when we heard the flank had gone, and we had to fall back.

THE THREE-DAY BLOW

The rain stopped as Nick turned into the road that went up through the orchard. The fruit had been picked and the fall wind blew through the bare trees. Nick stopped and picked up a Wagner apple from beside the road, shiny in the brown grass from the rain. He put the apple in the pocket of his Mackinaw coat.

The road came out of the orchard on to the top of the hill. There was the cottage, the porch bare, smoke coming from the chimney. In back was the garage, the chicken coop and the second-growth timber like a hedge against the woods behind. The big trees swayed far over in the wind as he watched. It was the first of the autumn storms.

As Nick crossed the open field above the orchard the door of the cottage opened and Bill came out. He stood on the porch looking out.

'Well, Wemedge,' he said.

'Hey, Bill,' Nick said, coming up the steps.

They stood together, looking out across the country, down over the orchard, beyond the road, across the lower fields and the woods of the point to the lake. The wind was blowing straight down the lake. They could see the surf along Ten Mile point.

'She's blowing,' Nick said.

'She'll blow like that for three days,' Bill said.

'Is your dad in?' Nick said.

'No. He's out with the gun. Come on in.'

Nick went inside the cottage. There was a big fire in the fireplace. The wind made it roar. Bill shut the door.

'Have a drink?' he said.

He went out to the kitchen and came back with two glasses and a pitcher of water. Nick reached the whiskey bottle from the shelf above the fireplace.

'All right?' he said.

'Good,' said Bill.

They sat in front of the fire and drank the Irish whiskey and water.

'It's got a swell, smoky taste,' Nick said, and looked at the fire through the glass.

'That's the peat,' Bill said.

'You can't get peat into liquor,' Nick said.

'That doesn't make any difference,' Bill said.

'You ever seen any peat?' Nick asked.

'No,' said Bill.

'Neither have I,' Nick said.

His shoes, stretched out on the hearth, began to steam in front of the fire.

'Better take your shoes off,' Bill said.

'I haven't got any socks on.'

'Take them off and dry them and I'll get you some,' Bill said. He went upstairs into the loft and Nick heard him walking about overhead. Upstairs was open under the roof and was where Bill and his father and he, Nick, sometimes slept. In back was a dressing room. They moved the cots back out of the rain and covered them with rubber blankets.

Bill came down with a pair of heavy wool socks.

'It's getting too late to go around without socks,' he said.

'I hate to start them again,' Nick said. He pulled the socks on and slumped back in the chair, putting his feet up on the screen in front of the fire.

'You'll dent in the screen,' Bill said. Nick swung his feet over to the side of the fireplace.

'Got anything to read?' he asked.

'Only the paper.'

'What did the Cards do?'

'Dropped a double header to the Giants.'

'That ought to cinch it for them.'

'It's a gift,' Bill said. 'As long as McGraw can buy every good ball player in the league there's nothing to it.'

'He can't buy them all,' Nick said.

'He buys all the ones he wants,' Bill said. 'Or he makes them discontented so they have to trade them to him.'

'Like Heinie Zim,' Nick agreed.

'That bonehead will do him a lot of good.'

Bill stood up.

'He can hit,' Nick offered. The heat from the fire was baking his legs.

'He's a sweet fielder, too,' Bill said. 'But he loses ball games.'

'Maybe that's what McGraw wants him for,' Nick suggested.

'Maybe,' Bill agreed.

'There's always more to it than we know about,' Nick said.

'Of course. But we've got pretty good dope for being so far away.'

'Like how much better you can pick them if you don't see the horses.'

'That's it.'

Bill reached down the whiskey bottle. His big hand went all the way around it. He poured the whiskey into the glass Nick held out.

'How much water?'

'Just the same.'

He sat down on the floor beside Nick's chair.

'It's good when the fall storms come, isn't it?' Nick said.

'It's swell.'

'It's the best time of year,' Nick said.

'Wouldn't it be hell to be in town?' Bill said.

'I'd like to see the World Series,' Nick said.

'Well, they're always in New York or Philadelphia now,' Bill said. 'That doesn't do us any good.'

'I wonder if the Cards will ever win a pennant?'

'Not in our lifetime,' Bill said.

'Gee, they'd go crazy,' Nick said.

'Do you remember when they got going that once before they had the train wreck?'

'Boy!' Nick said, remembering.

Bill reached over to the table under the window for the book that lay there, face down, where he had put it when he went to the door. He held his glass in one hand and the book in the other, leaning back against Nick's chair.

'What are you reading?'

'*Richard Feverel*.'

'I couldn't get into it.'

'It's all right,' Bill said. 'It ain't a bad book, Wemedge.'

'What else have you got I haven't read?' Nick asked.

'Did you read the *Forest Lovers*?'

'Yup. That's the one where they go to bed every night with the naked sword between them.'

'That's a good book, Wemedge.'

'It's a swell book. What I couldn't ever understand was what good the sword would do. It would have to stay edge up all the time because if it went over flat you could roll right over it and it wouldn't make any trouble.'

'It's a symbol,' Bill said.

'Sure,' said Nick, 'but it isn't practical.'

'Did you ever read *Fortitude*?'

'It's fine,' Nick said. 'That's a real book. That's where his old man is after him all the time. Have you got any more by Walpole?'

'*The Dark Forest*,' Bill said. 'It's about Russia.'

'What does he know about Russia?' Nick asked.

'I don't know. You can't ever tell about those guys. Maybe he was there when he was a boy. He's got a lot of dope on it.'

'I'd like to meet him,' Nick said.

'I'd like to meet Chesterton,' Bill said.

'I wish he was here now,' Nick said. 'We'd take him fishing to the 'Voix tomorrow.'

'I wonder if he'd like to go fishing,' Bill said.

'Sure,' said Nick. 'He must be about the best guy there is. Do you remember the *Flying Inn*?'

> ' "If an angel out of heaven
>   Gives you something else to drink,
>   Thank him for his kind intentions;
>   Go and pour them down the sink." '

'That's right,' said Nick. 'I guess he's a better guy than Walpole.'

'Oh, he's a better guy, all right,' Bill said.

'But Walpole's a better writer.'

'I don't know,' Nick said. 'Chesterton's a classic.'

'Walpole's a classic, too,' Bill insisted.

'I wish we had them both here,' Nick said. 'We'd take them both fishing to the 'Voix tomorrow.'

'Let's get drunk,' Bill said.

'All right,' Nick agreed.

'My old man won't care,' Bill said.

'Are you sure?' said Nick.

'I know it,' Bill said.

'I'm a little drunk now,' Nick said.

'You aren't drunk,' Bill said.

He got up from the floor and reached for the whiskey bottle. Nick held out his glass. His eyes fixed on it while Bill poured.

Bill poured the glass half full of whiskey.

'Put in your own water,' he said. 'There's just one more shot.'

'Got any more?' Nick asked.

'There's plenty more but dad only likes me to drink what's open.'

'Sure,' said Nick.

'He says opening bottles is what makes drunkards,' Bill explained.

'That's right,' said Nick. He was impressed. He had never thought of that before. He had always thought it was solitary drinking that made drunkards.

'How is your dad?' he asked respectfully.

'He's all right,' Bill said. 'He gets a little wild sometimes.'

'He's a swell guy,' Nick said. He poured water into his glass out of the pitcher. It mixed slowly with the whiskey. There was more whiskey than water.

'You bet your life he is,' Bill said.

'My old man's all right,' Nick said.

'You're damn right he is,' said Bill.

'He claims he's never taken a drink in his life,' Nick said, as though announcing a scientific fact.

'Well, he's a doctor. My old man's a painter. That's different.'

'He's missed a lot,' Nick said sadly.

'You can't tell,' Bill said. 'Everything's got its compensations.'

'He says he's missed a lot himself,' Nick confessed.

'Well, dad's had a tough time,' Bill said.

'It all evens up,' Nick said.

They sat looking into the fire and thinking of this profound truth.

'I'll get a chunk from the back porch,' Nick said. He had noticed while looking into the fire that the fire was dying down. Also he wished to show he could hold his liquor and be practical. Even if his father had never touched a drop Bill was not going to get him drunk before he himself was drunk.

'Bring one of the big beech chunks,' Bill said. He was also being consciously practical.

Nick came in with the log through the kitchen and in passing knocked a pan off the kitchen table. He laid the log down and picked up the pan. It had contained dried apricots, soaking in water. He carefully picked up all the apricots off the floor, some of them had gone under the stove, and put them back in the pan. He dipped some more water onto them from the pail by the table. He felt quite proud of himself. He had been thoroughly practical.

He came in carrying the log and Bill got up from the chair and helped him put it on the fire.

'That's a swell log,' Nick said.

'I'd been saving it for the bad weather,' Bill said. 'A log like that will burn all night.'

'There'll be coals left to start the fire in the morning,' Nick said.

'That's right,' Bill agreed. They were conducting the conversation on a high plane.

'Let's have another drink,' Nick said.

'I think there's another bottle open in the locker,' Bill said.

He kneeled down in the corner in front of the locker and brought out a square-faced bottle.

'It's Scotch,' he said.

'I'll get some more water,' Nick said. He went out into the kitchen again. He filled the pitcher with the dipper dipping cold spring water from the pail. On his way back to the living room he passed a mirror in the dining room and looked in it. His face looked strange. He smiled at the face in the mirror and it grinned back at him. He winked at it and went on. It was not his face but it didn't make any difference.

Bill had poured out the drinks.

'That's an awfully big shot,' Nick said.

'Not for us, Wemedge,' Bill said.

'What'll we drink to?' Nick asked, holding up the glass.

'Let's drink to fishing,' Bill said.

'All right,' Nick said. 'Gentlemen, I give you fishing.'

'All fishing,' Bill said. 'Everywhere.'

'Fishing,' Nick said. 'That's what we drink to.'

'It's better than baseball,' Bill said.

'There isn't any comparison,' said Nick. 'How did we ever get talking about baseball?'

'It was a mistake,' Bill said. 'Baseball is a game for louts.'

They drank all that was in their glasses.

'Now let's drink to Chesterton.'

'And Walpole,' Nick interposed.

Nick poured out the liquor. Bill poured in the water. They looked at each other. They felt very fine.

'Gentlemen,' Bill said, 'I give you Chesterton and Walpole.'

'Exactly, gentlemen,' Nick said.

They drank. Bill filled up the glasses. They sat down in the big chairs in front of the fire.

'You were very wise, Wemedge,' Bill said.

'What do you mean?' asked Nick.

'To bust off that Marge business,' Bill said.

'I guess so,' said Nick.

'It was the only thing to do. If you hadn't, by now you'd be back home working trying to get enough money to get married.'

Nick said nothing.

'Once a man's married he's absolutely bitched,' Bill went on. 'He hasn't got anything more. Nothing. Not a damn thing. He's done for. You've seen the guys that get married.'

Nick said nothing.

'You can tell them,' Bill said. 'They get this sort of fat married look. They're done for.'

'Sure,' said Nick.

'It was probably bad busting it off,' Bill said. 'But you always fall for somebody else and then it's all right. Fall for them but don't let them ruin you.'

'Yes,' said Nick.

'If you'd have married her you would have had to marry the whole family. Remember her mother and that guy she married.'

Nick nodded.

'Imagine having them around the house all the time and going to Sunday dinners at their house, and having them over to dinner and her telling Marge all the time what to do and how to act.'

Nick sat quiet.

'You came out of it damned well,' Bill said. 'Now she can marry somebody of her own sort and settle down and be happy. You can't mix oil and water and you can't mix that sort of thing any more than if I'd marry Ida that works for Strattons. She'd probably like it, too.'

Nick said nothing. The liquor had all died out of him and left him alone. Bill wasn't there. He wasn't sitting in front of the fire or going fishing tomorrow with Bill and his dad or anything. He wasn't drunk. It was all gone. All he knew was that he had once had Marjorie and that he had lost her. She was gone and he had sent her away. That was all that mattered. He might never see her again. Probably he never would. It was all gone, finished.

'Let's have another drink,' Nick said.

Bill poured it out. Nick splashed in a little water.

'If you'd gone on that way we wouldn't be here now,' Bill said.

That was true. His original plan had been to go down home

and get a job. Then he had planned to stay in Charlevoix all winter so he could be near Marge. Now he did not know what he was going to do.

'Probably we wouldn't even be going fishing tomorrow,' Bill said. 'You had the right dope, all right.'

'I couldn't help it,' Nick said.

'I know. That's the way it works out,' Bill said.

'All of a sudden everything was over,' Nick said. 'I don't know why it was. I couldn't help it. Just like when the three-day blows come now and rip all the leaves off the trees.'

'Well, it's over. That's the point,' Bill said.

'It was my fault,' Nick said.

'It doesn't make any difference whose fault it was,' Bill said.

'No, I suppose not,' Nick said.

The big thing was that Marjorie was gone and that probably he would never see her again. He had talked to her about how they would go to Italy together and the fun they would have. Places they would be together. It was all gone now.

'So long as it's over that's all that matters,' Bill said. 'I tell you, Wemedge, I was worried while it was going on. You played it right. I understand her mother is sore as hell. She told a lot of people you were engaged.'

'We weren't engaged,' Nick said.

'It was all around that you were.'

'I can't help it,' Nick said. 'We weren't.'

'Weren't you going to get married?' Bill asked.

'Yes. But we weren't engaged,' Nick said.

'What's the difference?' Bill asked judicially.

'I don't know. There's a difference.'

'I don't see it,' said Bill.

'All right,' said Nick. 'Let's get drunk.'

'All right,' Bill said. 'Let's get really drunk.'

'Let's get drunk and then go swimming,' Nick said.

He drank off his glass.

'I'm sorry as hell about her but what could I do?' he said. 'You know what her mother was like!'

'She was terrible,' Bill said.

'All of a sudden it was over,' Nick said. 'I oughtn't to talk about it.'

'You aren't,' Bill said. 'I talked about it and now I'm through. We won't ever speak about it again. You don't want to think about it. You might get back into it again.'

Nick had not thought about that. It had seemed so absolute. That was a thought. That made him feel better.

'Sure,' he said. 'There's always that danger.'

He felt happy now. There was not anything that was irrevocable. He might go into town Saturday night. Today was Thursday.

'There's always a chance,' he said.

'You'll have to watch yourself,' Bill said.

'I'll watch myself,' he said.

He felt happy. Nothing was finished. Nothing was ever lost. He would go into town on Saturday. He felt lighter, as he had felt before Bill started to talk about it. There was always a way out.

'Let's take the guns and go down to the point and look for your dad,' Nick said.

'All right.'

Bill took down the two shotguns from the rack on the wall. He opened a box of shells. Nick put on his Mackinaw coat and his shoes. His shoes were stiff from the drying. He was still quite drunk but his head was clear.

'How do you feel?' Nick asked.

'Swell. I've just got a good edge on.' Bill was buttoning up his sweater.

'There's no use getting drunk.'

'No. We ought to get outdoors.'

They stepped out the door. The wind was blowing a gale.

'The birds will lie right down in the grass with this,' Nick said.

They struck down toward the orchard.

'I saw a woodcock this morning,' Bill said.

'Maybe we'll jump him,' Nick said.

'You can't shoot in this wind,' Bill said.

Outside now the Marge business was no longer so tragic. It was not even very important. The wind blew everything like that away.

'It's coming right off the big lake,' Nick said.

Against the wind they heard the thud of a shotgun.

'That's dad,' Bill said. 'He's down in the swamp.'

'Let's cut down that way,' Nick said.

'Let's cut across the lower meadow and see if we jump anything,' Bill said.

'All right,' Nick said.

None of it was important now. The wind blew it out of his head. Still he could always go into town Saturday night. It was a good thing to have in reserve.

CHAPTER V

They shot the six cabinet ministers at half-past six in the morning against the wall of a hospital. There were pools of water in the courtyard. There were wet dead leaves on the paving of the courtyard. It rained hard. All the shutters of the hospital were nailed shut. One of the ministers was sick with typhoid. Two soldiers carried him downstairs and out into the rain. They tried to hold him up against the wall but he sat down in a puddle of water. The other five stood very quietly against the wall. Finally the officer told the soldiers it was no good trying to make him stand up. When they fired the first volley he was sitting down in the water with his head on his knees.

THE BATTLER

Nick stood up. He was all right. He looked up the track at the lights of the caboose going out of sight around the curve. There was water on both sides of the track, then tamarack swamp.

He felt of his knee. The pants were torn and the skin was barked. His hands were scraped and there were sand and cinders driven up under his nails. He went over to the edge of the track down the little slope to the water and washed his hands. He washed them carefully in the cold water, getting the dirt out from the nails. He squatted down and bathed his knee.

That lousy crut of a brakeman. He would get him some day. He would know him again. That was a fine way to act.

'Come here, kid,' he said. 'I got something for you.'

He had fallen for it. What a lousy kid thing to have done. They would never suck him in that way again.

'Come here, kid, I got something for you.' Then *wham* and he lit on his hands and knees beside the track.

Nick rubbed his eye. There was a big bump coming up. He would have a black eye, all right. It ached already. That son of a crutting brakeman.

He touched the bump over his eye with his fingers. Oh, well, it was only a black eye. That was all he had gotten out of it. Cheap at the price. He wished he could see it. Could not see it looking into the water, though. It was dark and he was a long way off from anywhere. He wiped his hands on his trousers and stood up, then climbed the embankment to the rails.

He started up the track. It was well ballasted and made easy walking, sand and gravel packed between the ties, solid walking. The smooth roadbed like a causeway went on ahead through the swamp. Nick walked along. He must get to somewhere.

Nick had swung on to the freight train when it slowed down for the yards outside of Walton Junction. The train, with Nick on it, had passed through Kalkaska as it started to get dark. Now he must be nearly to Mancelona. Three or four miles of swamp. He stepped along the track, walking so he kept on the ballast between the ties, the swamp ghostly in the rising mist. His eye ached and he was hungry. He kept on hiking, putting the miles of track back of him. The swamp was all the same on both sides of the track.

Ahead there was a bridge. Nick crossed it, his boots ringing hollow on the iron. Down below the water showed black between the slits of ties. Nick kicked a loose spike and it dropped into the water. Beyond the bridge were hills. It was high and dark on both sides of the track. Up the track Nick saw a fire.

He came up the track toward the fire carefully. It was off to one side of the track, below the railway embankment. He had only seen the light from it. The track came out through a cut and where the fire was burning the country opened out and fell away into woods. Nick dropped carefully down the embankment and cut into the woods to come up to the fire through the trees. It was a beechwood forest and the fallen beechnut burrs were under his shoes as he walked between the trees. The fire was bright now, just at the edge of the trees. There was a man sitting by it. Nick waited behind the tree and watched. The man looked to be alone. He was sitting there with his head in his hands looking at the fire. Nick stepped out and walked into the firelight.

The man sat there looking into the fire. When Nick stopped quite close to him he did not move.

'Hello!' Nick said.

The man looked up.

'Where did you get the shiner?' he said.

'A brakeman busted me.'

'Off the through freight?'

'Yes.'

'I saw the bastard,' the man said. 'He went through here 'bout an hour and a half ago. He was walking along the top of the cars slapping his arms and singing.'

'The bastard!'

'It must have made him feel good to bust you,' the man said seriously.

'I'll bust him.'

'Get him with a rock sometime when he's going through,' the man advised.

'I'll get him.'

'You're a tough one, aren't you?'

'No,' Nick answered.

'All you kids are tough.'

'You got to be tough,' Nick said.

'That's what I said.'

The man looked at Nick and smiled. In the firelight Nick saw that his face was misshapen. His nose was sunken, his eyes were slits, he had queer-shaped lips. Nick did not perceive all this at once, he only saw the man's face was queerly formed and mutilated. It was like putty in color. Dead looking in the firelight.

'Don't you like my pan?' the man asked.

Nick was embarrassed.

'Sure,' he said.

'Look here!' the man took off his cap.

He had only one ear. It was thickened and tight against the side of his head. Where the other ear should have been there was a stump.

'Ever see one like that?'

'No,' said Nick. It made him a little sick.

'I could take it,' the man said. 'Don't you think I could take it, kid?'

'You bet!'

'They all bust their hands on me,' the little man said. 'They couldn't hurt me.'

He looked at Nick. 'Sit down,' he said. 'Want to eat?'

'Don't bother,' Nick said. 'I'm going on to the town.'

'Listen!' the man said. 'Call me Ad.'

'Sure!'

'Listen,' the little man said. 'I'm not quite right.'

'What's the matter?'

'I'm crazy.'

He put on his cap. Nick felt like laughing.

'You're all right,' he said.

'No, I'm not. I'm crazy. Listen, you ever been crazy?'

'No,' Nick said. 'How does it get you?'

'I don't know,' Ad said. 'When you got it you don't know about it. You know me, don't you?'

'No.'

'I'm Ad Francis.'

'Honest to God?'

'Don't you believe it?'

'Yes.'

Nick knew it must be true.

'You know how I beat them?'

'No,' Nick said.

'My heart's slow. It only beats forty a minute. Feel it.'

Nick hesitated.

'Come on,' the man took hold of his hand. 'Take hold of my wrist. Put your fingers there.'

The little man's wrist was thick and the muscles bulged above the bone. Nick felt the slow pumping under his fingers.

'Got a watch?'

'No.'

'Neither have I,' Ad said. 'It ain't any good if you haven't got a watch.'

Nick dropped his wrist.

'Listen,' Ad Francis said. 'Take ahold again. You count and I'll count up to sixty.'

Feeling the slow hard throb under his fingers Nick started to count. He heard the little man counting slowly, one, two, three, four, five, and on – aloud.

'Sixty,' Ad finished. 'That's a minute. What did you make it?'

'Forty,' Nick said.

'That's right,' Ad said happily. 'She never speeds up.'

A man dropped down the railroad embankment and came across the clearing to the fire.

'Hello, Bugs!' Ad said.

'Hello!' Bugs answered. It was a negro's voice. Nick knew from the way he walked that he was a negro. He stood with his back to them, bending over the fire. He straightened up.

'This is my pal Bugs,' Ad said. 'He's crazy, too.'

'Glad to meet you,' Bugs said. 'Where you say you're from?'

'Chicago,' Nick said.

'That's a fine town,' the negro said. 'I didn't catch your name.'

'Adams. Nick Adams.'

'He says he's never been crazy, Bugs,' Ad said.

'He's got a lot coming to him,' the negro said. He was un-wrapping a package by the fire.

'When are we going to eat, Bugs?' the prizefighter asked.

'Right away.'

'Are you hungry, Nick?'

'Hungry as hell.'

'Hear that, Bugs?'

'I hear most of what goes on.'

'That ain't what I asked you.'

'Yes. I heard what the gentleman said.'

Into a skillet he was laying slices of ham. As the skillet grew hot the grease sputtered and Bugs, crouching on long nig-ger legs over the fire, turned the ham and broke eggs into the skillet, tipping it from side to side to baste the eggs with the hot fat.

'Will you cut some bread out of that bag, Mister Adams?' Bugs turned from the fire.

'Sure.'

Nick reached in the bag and brought out a loaf of bread. He cut six slices. Ad watched him and leaned forward.

'Let me take your knife, Nick,' he said.

'No, you don't,' the negro said. 'Hang onto your knife, Mister Adams.'

The prizefighter sat back.

'Will you bring me the bread, Mister Adams?' Bugs asked. Nick brought it over.

'Do you like to dip your bread in the ham fat?' the negro asked.

'You bet!'

'Perhaps we'd better wait until later. It's better at the finish of the meal. Here.'

The negro picked up a slice of ham and laid it on one of the pieces of bread, then slid an egg on top of it.

'Just close that sandwich, will you, please, and give it to Mister Francis.'

Ad took the sandwich and started eating.

'Watch out how that egg runs,' the negro warned. 'This is for you, Mister Adams. The remainder for myself.'

Nick bit into the sandwich. The negro was sitting opposite him beside Ad. The hot fried ham and eggs tasted wonderful.

'Mister Adams is right hungry,' the negro said. The little man whom Nick knew by name as a former champion fighter was silent. He had said nothing since the negro had spoken about the knife.

'May I offer you a slice of bread dipped right in the hot ham fat?' Bugs said.

'Thanks a lot.'

The little white man looked at Nick.

'Will you have some, Mister Adolph Francis?' Bugs offered from the skillet.

Ad did not answer. He was looking at Nick.

'Mister Francis?' came the nigger's soft voice.

Ad did not answer. He was looking at Nick.

'I spoke to you, Mister Francis,' the nigger said softly.

Ad kept on looking at Nick. He had his cap down over his eyes. Nick felt nervous.

'How the hell do you get that way?' came out from under the cap sharply at Nick.

'Who the hell do you think you are? You're a snotty bastard. You come in here where nobody asks you and eat a man's food and when he asks to borrow a knife you get snotty.'

He glared at Nick, his face was white and his eyes almost out of sight under the cap.

'You're a hot sketch. Who the hell asked you to butt in here?'

'Nobody.'

'You're damn right nobody did. Nobody asked you to stay either. You come in here and act snotty about my face and smoke my cigars and drink my liquor and then talk snotty. Where the hell do you think you get off?'

Nick said nothing. Ad stood up.

'I'll tell you, you yellow-livered Chicago bastard. You're going to get your can knocked off. Do you get that?'

Nick stepped back. The little man came toward him slowly, stepping flat-footed forward, his left foot stepping forward, his right dragging up to it.

'Hit me,' he moved his head. 'Try and hit me.'

'I don't want to hit you.'

'You won't get out of it that way. You're going to take a beating, see? Come on and lead at me.'

'Cut it out,' Nick said.

'All right, then, you bastard.'

The little man looked down at Nick's feet. As he looked down the negro, who had followed behind him as he moved away from the fire, set himself and tapped him across the base of the skull. He fell forward and Bugs dropped the cloth-wrapped blackjack on the grass. The little man lay there, his face in the grass. The negro picked him up, his head hanging, and carried him to the fire. His face looked bad, the eyes open. Bugs laid him down gently.

'Will you bring me the water in the bucket, Mister Adams,' he said. 'I'm afraid I hit him just a little hard.'

The negro splashed water with his hand on the man's face and pulled his ears gently. The eyes closed.

Bugs stood up.

'He's all right,' he said. 'There's nothing to worry about. I'm sorry, Mister Adams.'

'It's all right.' Nick was looking down at the little man. He saw the blackjack on the grass and picked it up. It had a flexible handle and was limber in his hand. It was made of worn black leather with a handkerchief wrapped around the heavy end.

'That's a whalebone handle,' the negro smiled. 'They don't make them any more. I didn't know how well you could take care of yourself and, anyway, I didn't want you to hurt him or mark him up no more than he is.'

The negro smiled again.

'You hurt him yourself.'

'I know how to do it. He won't remember nothing of it. I have to do it to change him when he gets that way.'

Nick was still looking down at the little man, lying, his eyes closed in the firelight. Bugs put some wood on the fire.

'Don't you worry about him none, Mister Adams. I seen him like this plenty of times before.'

'What made him crazy?' Nick asked.

'Oh, a lot of things,' the negro answered from the fire. 'Would you like a cup of this coffee, Mister Adams?'

He handed Nick the cup and smoothed the coat he had placed under the unconscious man's head.

'He took too many beatings, for one thing,' the negro sipped the coffee. 'But that just made him sort of simple. Then his sister was his manager and they was always being written up in the papers all about brothers and sisters and how she loved her brother and how he loved his sister, and then they got married in New York and that made a lot of unpleasantness.'

'I remember about it.'

'Sure. Of course they wasn't brother and sister no more than a rabbit, but there was a lot of people didn't like it either way and they commenced to have disagreements, and one day she just went off and never come back.'

He drank the coffee and wiped his lips with the pink palm of his hand.

'He just went crazy. Will you have some more coffee, Mister Adams?'

'Thanks.'

'I seen her a couple of times,' the negro went on. 'She was an awful good-looking woman. Looked enough like him to be twins. He wouldn't be bad-looking without his face all busted.'

He stopped. The story seemed to be over.

'I met him in jail,' the negro said. 'He was busting people all the time after she went away and they put him in jail. I was in for cuttin' a man.'

He smiled, and went on soft-voiced:

'Right away I liked him and when I got out I looked him up. He likes to think I'm crazy and I don't mind. I like to be with him and I like seeing the country and I don't have to commit no larceny to do it. I like living like a gentleman.'

'What do you all do?' Nick asked.

'Oh, nothing. Just move around. He's got money.'

'He must have made a lot of money.'

'Sure. He spent all his money, though. Or they took it away from him. She sends him money.'

He poked up the fire.

'She's a mighty fine woman,' he said. 'She looks enough like him to be his own twin.'

The negro looked over at the little man, lying breathing heavily. His blond hair was down over his forehead. His mutilated face looked childish in repose.

'I can wake him up any time now, Mister Adams. If you don't mind I wish you'd sort of pull out. I don't like to not be hospitable, but it might disturb him back again to see you. I hate to have to thump him and it's the only thing to do when he gets started. I have to sort of keep him away from people. You don't mind, do you, Mister Adams? No, don't thank me, Mister Adams. I'd have warned you about him but he seemed to have taken such a liking to you and I thought things were going to be all right. You'll hit a town about two miles up the track. Mancelona they call it. Good-bye. I wish we could ask you to stay the night but it's just out of the question. Would you like to take some of that ham and some bread with you? No? You better take a sandwich,' all this in a low, smooth, polite nigger voice.

'Good. Well, good-bye, Mister Adams. Good-bye and good luck!'

Nick walked away from the fire across the clearing to the railway tracks. Out of the range of the fire he listened. The low soft voice of the negro was talking. Nick could not hear the words. Then he heard the little man say, 'I got an awful headache, Bugs.'

'You'll feel better, Mister Francis,' the negro's voice soothed. 'Just you drink a cup of this hot coffee.'

Nick climbed the embankment and started up the track. He found he had a ham sandwich in his hand and put it in his pocket. Looking back from the mounting grade before the track curved into the hills he could see the firelight in the clearing.

CHAPTER VI

Nick sat against the wall of the church where they had dragged him to be clear of machine-gun fire in the street. Both legs stuck out awkwardly. He had been hit in the spine. His face was sweaty and dirty. The sun shone on his face. The day was very hot. Rinaldi, big backed, his equipment sprawling, lay face downward against the wall. Nick looked straight ahead brilliantly. The pink wall of the house opposite had fallen out from the roof, and an iron bedstead hung twisted toward the street. Two Austrian dead lay in the rubble in the shade of the house. Up the street were other dead. Things were getting forward in the town. It was going well. Stretcher bearers would be along any time now. Nick turned his head carefully and looked at Rinaldi. 'Senta Rinaldi. Senta. You and me we've made a separate peace.' Rinaldi lay still in the sun breathing with difficulty. 'Not patriots.' Nick turned his head carefully away smiling sweatily. Rinaldi was a disappointing audience.

A VERY SHORT STORY

One hot evening in Padua they carried him up onto the roof and he could look out over the top of the town. There were chimney swifts in the sky. After a while it got dark and the searchlights came out. The others went down and took the bottles with them. He and Luz could hear them below on the balcony. Luz sat on the bed. She was cool and fresh in the hot night.

Luz stayed on night duty for three months. They were glad to let her. When they operated on him she prepared him for the operating table; and they had a joke about friend or enema. He went under the anæsthetic holding tight on to himself so he would not blab about anything during the silly, talky time. After he got on crutches he used to take the temperatures so Luz would not have to get up from the bed. There were only a few patients, and they all knew about it. They all liked Luz. As he walked back along the halls he thought of Luz in his bed.

Before he went back to the front they went into the Duomo and prayed. It was dim and quiet, and there were other people praying. They wanted to get married, but there was not enough time for the banns, and neither of them had birth certificates. They felt as though they were married, but they wanted every one to know about it, and to make it so they could not lose it.

Luz wrote him many letters that he never got until after the armistice. Fifteen came in a bunch to the front and he sorted them by the dates and read them all straight through. They were all about the hospital, and how much she loved him and how it was impossible to get along without him and how terrible it was missing him at night.

After the armistice they agreed he should go home to get a job so they might be married. Luz would not come home until he had a good job and could come to New York to meet her. It was understood he would not drink, and he did not want to see his friends or any one in the States. Only to get a job and be married. On the train from Padua to Milan they quarrelled about her not being willing to come home at once. When they had to say good-bye, in the station at Milan, they kissed good-bye, but were not finished with the quarrel. He felt sick about saying good-bye like that.

He went to America on a boat from Genoa. Luz went back to

Pordenone to open a hospital. It was lonely and rainy there, and there was a battalion of *arditi* quartered in the town. Living in the muddy, rainy town in the winter, the major of the battalion made love to Luz, and she had never known Italians before, and finally wrote to the States that theirs had been only a boy and girl affair. She was sorry, and she knew he would probably not be able to understand, but might some day forgive her, and be grateful to her, and she expected, absolutely unexpectedly, to be married in the spring. She loved him as always, but she realized now it was only a boy and girl love. She hoped he would have a great career, and believed in him absolutely. She knew it was for the best.

The major did not marry her in the spring, or any other time. Luz never got an answer to the letter to Chicago about it. A short time after he contracted gonorrhea from a sales girl in a loop department store while riding in a taxicab through Lincoln Park.

CHAPTER VII

While the bombardment was knocking the trench to pieces at Fossalta, he lay very flat and sweated and prayed oh jesus christ get me out of here. Dear jesus please get me out. Christ please please please christ. If you'll only keep me from getting killed I'll do anything you say. I believe in you and I'll tell every one in the world that you are the only one that matters. Please please dear jesus. The shelling moved further up the line. We went to work on the trench and in the morning the sun came up and the day was hot and muggy and cheerful and quiet. The next night back at Mestre he did not tell the girl he went upstairs with at the Villa Rossa about Jesus. And he never told anybody.

SOLDIER'S HOME

Krebs went to the war from a Methodist college in Kansas. There is a picture which shows him among his fraternity brothers, all of them wearing exactly the same height and style collar. He enlisted in the Marines in 1917 and did not return to the United States until the second division returned from the Rhine in the summer of 1919.

There is a picture which shows him on the Rhine with two German girls and another corporal. Krebs and the corporal look too big for their uniforms. The German girls are not beautiful. The Rhine does not show in the picture.

By the time Krebs returned to his home town in Oklahoma the greeting of heroes was over. He came back much too late. The men from the town who had been drafted had all been welcomed elaborately on their return. There had been a great deal of hysteria. Now the reaction had set in. People seemed to think it was rather ridiculous for Krebs to be getting back so late, years after the war was over.

At first Krebs, who had been at Belleau Wood, Soissons, the Champagne, St. Mihiel and in the Argonne did not want to talk about the war at all. Later he felt the need to talk but no one wanted to hear about it. His town had heard too many atrocity stories to be thrilled by actualities. Krebs found that to be listened to at all he had to lie, and after he had done this twice he, too, had a reaction against the war and against talking about it. A distaste for everything that had happened to him in the war set in because of the lies he had told. All of the times that had been able to make him feel cool and clear inside himself when he thought of them; the times so long back when he had done the one thing, the only thing for a man to do, easily and naturally, when he might have done something else, now lost their cool, valuable quality and then were lost themselves.

His lies were quite unimportant lies and consisted in attributing to himself things other men had seen, done or heard of, and stating as facts certain apocryphal incidents familiar to all soldiers. Even his lies were not sensational at the pool room. His acquaintances, who had heard detailed accounts of German women found chained to machine guns in the Argonne forest and who could not comprehend, or were barred by their patriotism from interest in, any German machine gunners who were not chained, were not thrilled by his stories.

Krebs acquired the nausea in regard to experience that is the result of untruth or exaggeration, and when he occasionally met another man who had really been a soldier and they talked a few minutes in the dressing room at a dance he fell into the easy pose of the old soldier among other soldiers: that he had been badly, sickeningly frightened all the time. In this way he lost everything.

During this time, it was late summer, he was sleeping late in bed, getting up to walk down town to the library to get a book, eating lunch at home, reading on the front porch until he became bored and then walking down through the town to spend the hottest hours of the day in the cool dark of the pool room. He loved to play pool.

In the evening he practised on his clarinet, strolled down town, read and went to bed. He was still a hero to his two young sisters. His mother would have given him breakfast in bed if he had wanted it. She often came in when he was in bed and asked him to tell her about the war, but her attention always wandered. His father was non-committal.

Before Krebs went away to the war he had never been allowed to drive the family motor car. His father was in the real estate business and always wanted the car to be at his command when he required it to take clients out into the country to show them a piece of farm property. The car always stood outside the First National Bank building where his father had an office on the second floor. Now, after the war, it was still the same car.

Nothing was changed in the town except that the young girls had grown up. But they lived in such a complicated world of already defined alliances and shifting feuds that Krebs did not feel the energy or the courage to break into it. He liked to look at them, though. There were so many good-looking young girls. Most of them had their hair cut short. When he went away only little girls wore their hair like that or girls that were fast. They all wore sweaters and shirt waists with round Dutch collars. It was a pattern. He liked to look at them from the front porch as they walked on the other side of the street. He liked to watch them walking under the shade of the trees. He liked the round Dutch collars above their sweaters. He liked their silk stockings and flat shoes. He liked their bobbed hair and the way they walked.

When he was in town their appeal to him was not very strong. He did not like them when he saw them in the Greek's ice cream parlor. He did not want them themselves really. They were too complicated. There was something else. Vaguely he wanted a girl but he did not want to have to work to get her. He would have liked to have a girl but he did not want to have to spend a long time getting her. He did not want to get into the intrigue and the politics. He did not want to have to do any courting. He did not want to tell any more lies. It wasn't worth it.

He did not want any consequences. He did not want any consequences ever again. He wanted to live along without consequences. Besides he did not really need a girl. The army had taught him that. It was all right to pose as though you had to have a girl. Nearly everybody did that. But it wasn't true. You did not need a girl. That was the funny thing. First a fellow boasted how girls mean nothing to him, that he never thought of them, that they could not touch him. Then a fellow boasted that he could not get along without girls, that he had to have them all the time, that he could not go to sleep without them.

That was all a lie. It was all a lie both ways. You did not need a girl unless you thought about them. He learned that in the army. Then sooner or later you always got one. When you were really ripe for a girl you always got one. You did not have to think about it. Sooner or later it would come. He had learned that in the army.

Now he would have liked a girl if she had come to him and not wanted to talk. But here at home it was all too complicated. He knew he could never get through it all again. It was not worth the trouble. That was the thing about French girls and German girls. There was not all this talking. You couldn't talk much and you did not need to talk. It was simple and you were friends. He thought about France and then he began to think about Germany. On the whole he had liked Germany better. He did not want to leave Germany. He did not want to come home. Still, he had come home. He sat on the front porch.

He liked the girls that were walking along the other side of the street. He liked the look of them much better than the French girls or the German girls. But the world they were in was not the world he was in. He would like to have one of them. But it was not worth it. They were such a nice pattern. He liked the pattern. It was exciting. But he would not go through all the talking. He did not want one badly enough. He liked to look at them all, though. It was not worth it. Not now when things were getting good again.

He sat there on the porch reading a book on the war. It was a history and he was reading about all the engagements he had been in. It was the most interesting reading he had ever done. He wished there were more maps. He looked forward with a good feeling to reading all the really good histories when they would come out with good detail maps. Now he was really learning about the war. He had been a good soldier. That made a difference.

One morning after he had been home about a month his mother came into his bedroom and sat on the bed. She smoothed her apron.

'I had a talk with your father last night, Harold,' she said, 'and he is willing for you to take the car out in the evenings.'

'Yeah?' said Krebs, who was not fully awake. 'Take the car out? Yeah?'

'Yes. Your father has felt for some time that you should be able to take the car out in the evenings whenever you wished but we only talked it over last night.'

'I'll bet you made him,' Krebs said.

'No. It was your father's suggestion that we talk the matter over.'

'Yeah. I'll bet you made him,' Krebs sat up in bed.

'Will you come down to breakfast, Harold?' his mother said.

'As soon as I get my clothes on,' Krebs said.

His mother went out of the room and he could hear her frying something downstairs while he washed, shaved and dressed to go down into the dining-room for breakfast. While he was eating breakfast his sister brought in the mail.

'Well, Hare,' she said. 'You old sleepy-head. What do you ever get up for?'

Krebs looked at her. He liked her. She was his best sister.

'Have you got the paper?' he asked.

She handed him *The Kansas City Star* and he shucked off its brown wrapper and opened it to the sporting page. He folded *The Star* open and propped it against the water pitcher with his cereal dish to steady it, so he could read while he ate.

'Harold,' his mother stood in the kitchen doorway, 'Harold, please don't muss up the paper. Your father can't read his *Star* if it's been mussed.'

'I won't muss it,' Krebs said.

His sister sat down at the table and watched him while he read.

'We're playing indoor over at school this afternoon,' she said. 'I'm going to pitch.'

'Good,' said Krebs. 'How's the old wing?'

'I can pitch better than lots of the boys. I tell them all you taught me. The other girls aren't much good.'

'Yeah?' said Krebs.

'I tell them all you're my beau. Aren't you my beau, Hare?'

'You bet.'

'Couldn't your brother really be your beau just because he's your brother?'

'I don't know.'

'Sure you know. Couldn't you be my beau, Hare, if I was old enough and if you wanted to?'

'Sure. You're my girl now.'

'Am I really your girl?'

'Sure.'

'Do you love me?'

'Uh, huh.'

'Will you love me always?'

'Sure.'

'Will you come over and watch me play indoor?'

'Maybe.'

'Aw, Hare, you don't love me. If you loved me, you'd want to come over and watch me play indoor.'

Krebs's mother came into the dining-room from the kitchen. She carried a plate with two fried eggs and some crisp bacon on it and a plate of buckwheat cakes.

'You run along, Helen,' she said. 'I want to talk to Harold.'

She put the eggs and bacon down in front of him and brought in a jug of maple syrup for the buckwheat cakes. Then she sat down across the table from Krebs.

'I wish you'd put down the paper a minute, Harold,' she said.

Krebs took down the paper and folded it.

'Have you decided what you are going to do yet, Harold?' his mother said, taking off her glasses.

'No,' said Krebs.

'Don't you think it's about time?' His mother did not say this in a mean way. She seemed worried.

'I hadn't thought about it,' Krebs said.

'God has some work for every one to do,' his mother said. 'There can be no idle hands in His Kingdom.'

'I'm not in His Kingdom,' Krebs said.

'We are all of us in His Kingdom.'

Krebs felt embarrassed and resentful as always.

'I've worried about you so much, Harold,' his mother went on. 'I know the temptations you must have been exposed to. I know how weak men are. I know what your own dear grandfather, my own father, told us about the Civil War and I have prayed for you. I pray for you all day long, Harold.'

Krebs looked at the bacon fat hardening on his plate.

'Your father is worried, too,' his mother went on. 'He thinks you have lost your ambition, that you haven't got a definite aim in life. Charley Simmons, who is just your age, has a good job and is going to be married. The boys are all settling down; they're all determined to get somewhere; you can see that boys like Charley Simmons are on their way to being really a credit to the community.'

Krebs said nothing.

'Don't look that way, Harold,' his mother said. 'You know we love you and I want to tell you for your own good how matters stand. Your father does not want to hamper your freedom. He thinks you should be allowed to drive the car. If you want to take some of the nice girls out riding with you, we are only too pleased. We want you to enjoy yourself. But you are going to have to settle down to work, Harold. Your father doesn't care what you start in at. All work is honorable as he says. But you've got to make a start at something. He asked me to speak to you this morning and then you can stop in and see him at his office.'

'Is that all?' Krebs said.

'Yes. Don't you love your mother, dear boy?'

'No,' Krebs said.

His mother looked at him across the table. Her eyes were shiny. She started crying.

'I don't love anybody,' Krebs said.

It wasn't any good. He couldn't tell her, he couldn't make her see it. It was silly to have said it. He had only hurt her. He went over and took hold of her arm. She was crying with her head in her hands.

'I didn't mean it,' he said. 'I was just angry at something. I didn't mean I didn't love you.'

His mother went on crying. Krebs put his arm on her shoulder.

'Can't you believe me, mother?'

His mother shook her head.

'Please, please, mother. Please believe me.'

'All right,' his mother said chokily. She looked up at him. 'I believe you, Harold.'

Krebs kissed her hair. She put her face up to him.

'I'm your mother,' she said. 'I held you next to my heart when you were a tiny baby.'

Krebs felt sick and vaguely nauseated.

'I know, Mummy,' he said. 'I'll try and be a good boy for you.'

'Would you kneel and pray with me, Harold?' his mother asked.

They knelt down beside the dining-room table and Krebs's mother prayed.

'Now, you pray, Harold,' she said.

'I can't,' Krebs said.

'Try, Harold.'

'I can't.'

'Do you want me to pray for you?'

'Yes.'

So his mother prayed for him and then they stood up and Krebs kissed his mother and went out of the house. He had tried so to keep his life from being complicated. Still, none of it had touched him. He had felt sorry for his mother and she had made him lie. He would go to Kansas City and get a job and she would feel all right about it. There would be one more scene maybe before he got away. He would not go down to his father's office. He would miss that one. He wanted his life to go smoothly. It had just gotten going that way. Well, that was all over now, anyway. He would go over to the schoolyard and watch Helen play indoor baseball.

CHAPTER VIII

At two o'clock in the morning two Hungarians got into a cigar store at Fifteenth Street and Grand Avenue. Drevitts and Boyle drove up from the Fifteenth Street police station in a Ford. The Hungarians were backing their wagon out of an alley. Boyle shot one off the seat of the wagon and one out of the wagon box. Drevitts got frightened when he found they were both dead. Hell Jimmy, he said, you oughtn't to have done it. There's liable to be a hell of a lot of trouble.

— They're crooks, ain't they? said Boyle. They're wops, ain't they? Who the hell is going to make any trouble?

— That's all right maybe this time, said Drevitts, but how did you know they were wops when you bumped them?

— Wops, said Boyle, I can tell wops a mile off.

THE REVOLUTIONIST

In 1919 he was travelling on the railroads in Italy, carrying a square of oilcloth from the headquarters of the party written in indelible pencil and saying here was a comrade who had suffered very much under the Whites in Budapest and requesting comrades to aid him in any way. He used this instead of a ticket. He was very shy and quite young and the train men passed him on from one crew to another. He had no money, and they fed him behind the counter in railway eating houses.

He was delighted with Italy. It was a beautiful country, he said. The people were all kind. He had been in many towns, walked much, and seen many pictures. Giotto, Masaccio, and Piero della Francesca he bought reproductions of and carried them wrapped in a copy of *Avanti*. Mantegna he did not like.

He reported at Bologna, and I took him with me up into the Romagna where it was necessary I go to see a man. We had a good trip together. It was early September and the country was pleasant. He was a Magyar, a very nice boy and very shy. Horthy's men had done some bad things to him. He talked about it a little. In spite of Hungary, he believed altogether in the world revolution.

'But how is the movement going in Italy?' he asked.

'Very badly,' I said.

'But it will go better,' he said. 'You have everything here. It is the one country that every one is sure of. It will be the starting point of everything.'

I did not say anything.

At Bologna he said good-bye to us to go on the train to Milano and then to Aosta to walk over the pass into Switzerland. I spoke to him about the Mantegnas in Milano. 'No,' he said, very shyly, he did not like Mantegna. I wrote out for him where to eat in Milano and the addresses of comrades. He thanked me very much, but his mind was already looking forward to walking over the pass. He was very eager to walk over the pass while the weather held good. He loved the mountains in the autumn. The last I heard of him the Swiss had him in jail near Sion.

CHAPTER IX

The first matador got the horn through his sword hand and the crowd hooted him. The second matador slipped and the bull caught him through the belly and he hung on to the horn with one hand and held the other tight against the place, and the bull rammed him wham against the wall and the horn came out, and he lay in the sand, and then got up like crazy drunk and tried to slug the men carrying him away and yelled for his sword but he fainted. The kid came out and had to kill five bulls because you can't have more than three matadors, and the last bull he was so tired he couldn't get the sword in. He couldn't hardly lift his arm. He tried five times and the crowd was quiet because it was a good bull and it looked like him or the bull and then he finally made it. He sat down in the sand and puked and they held a cape over him while the crowd hollered and threw things down into the bull ring.

MR. AND MRS. ELLIOT

Mr. and Mrs. Elliot tried very hard to have a baby. They tried as often as Mrs. Elliot could stand it. They tried in Boston after they were married and they tried coming over on the boat. They did not try very often on the boat because Mrs. Elliot was quite sick. She was sick and when she was sick she was sick as Southern women are sick. That is women from the Southern part of the United States. Like all Southern women Mrs. Elliot disintegrated very quickly under sea sickness, travelling at night, and getting up too early in the morning. Many of the people on the boat took her for Elliot's mother. Other people who knew they were married believed she was going to have a baby. In reality she was forty years old. Her years had been precipitated suddenly when she started travelling.

She had seemed much younger, in fact she had seemed not to have any age at all, when Elliot had married her after several weeks of making love to her after knowing her for a long time in her tea shop before he had kissed her one evening.

Hubert Elliot was taking postgraduate work in law at Harvard when he was married. He was a poet with an income of nearly ten thousand dollars a year. He wrote very long poems very rapidly. He was twenty-five years old and had never gone to bed with a woman until he married Mrs. Elliot. He wanted to keep himself pure so that he could bring to his wife the same purity of mind and body that he expected of her. He called it to himself living straight. He had been in love with various girls before he kissed Mrs. Elliot and always told them sooner or later that he had led a clean life. Nearly all the girls lost interest in him. He was shocked and really horrified at the way girls would become engaged to and marry men whom they must know had dragged themselves through the gutter. He once tried to warn a girl he knew against a man of whom he had almost proof that he had been a rotter at college and a very unpleasant incident had resulted.

Mrs. Elliot's name was Cornelia. She had taught him to call her Calutina, which was her family nickname in the South. His mother cried when he brought Cornelia home after their marriage but brightened very much when she learned they were going to live abroad.

Cornelia had said, 'You dear sweet boy,' and held him closer than ever when he had told her how he had kept himself clean for her. Cornelia was pure too. 'Kiss me again like that,' she said.

Hubert explained to her that he had learned that way of kissing from hearing a fellow tell a story once. He was delighted with his experiment and they developed it as far as possible. Sometimes when they had been kissing together a long time, Cornelia would ask him to tell her again that he had kept himself really straight for her. The declaration always set her off again.

At first Hubert had no idea of marrying Cornelia. He had never thought of her that way. She had been such a good friend of his, and then one day in the little back room of the shop they had been dancing to the gramophone while her girl friend was in the front of the shop and she had looked up into his eyes and he had kissed her. He could never remember just when it was decided that they were to be married. But they were married.

They spent the night of the day they were married in a Boston hotel. They were both disappointed but finally Cornelia went to sleep. Hubert could not sleep and several times went out and walked up and down the corridor of the hotel in his new Jaeger bathrobe that he had bought for his wedding trip. As he walked he saw all the pairs of shoes, small shoes and big shoes, outside the doors of the hotel rooms. This set his heart to pounding and he hurried back to his own room but Cornelia was asleep. He did not like to waken her and soon everything was quite all right and he slept peacefully.

The next day they called on his mother and the next day they sailed for Europe. It was possible to try to have a baby but Cornelia could not attempt it very often although they wanted a baby more than anything else in the world. They landed at Cherbourg and came to Paris. They tried to have a baby in Paris. Then they decided to go to Dijon where there was summer school and where a number of people who crossed on the boat with them had gone. They found there was nothing to do in Dijon. Hubert, however, was writing a great number of poems and Cornelia typed them for him. They were all very long poems. He was very severe about mistakes and would make her re-do an entire page if there was one mistake. She cried a good deal and they tried several times to have a baby before they left Dijon.

They came to Paris and most of their friends from the boat came back too. They were tired of Dijon and anyway would now be able to say that after leaving Harvard or Columbia or

Wabash they had studied at the University of Dijon down in the Côte d'Or. Many of them would have preferred to go to Languedoc, Montpellier or Perpignan if there are universities there. But all those places are too far away. Dijon is only four and a half hours from Paris and there is a diner on the train.

So they all sat around the Café du Dôme, avoiding the Rotonde across the street because it is always so full of foreigners, for a few days and then the Elliots rented a château in Touraine through an advertisement in the New York *Herald*. Elliot had a number of friends by now all of whom admired his poetry and Mrs. Elliot had prevailed upon him to send over to Boston for her girl friend who had been in the tea shop. Mrs. Elliot became much brighter after her girl friend came and they had many good cries together. The girl friend was several years older than Cornelia and called her Honey. She too came from a very old Southern family.

The three of them, with several of Elliot's friends who called him Hubie, went down to the château in Touraine. They found Touraine to be a very flat hot country very much like Kansas. Elliot had nearly enough poems for a book now. He was going to bring it out in Boston and had already sent his check to, and made a contract with, a publisher.

In a short time the friends began to drift back to Paris. Touraine had not turned out the way it looked when it started. Soon all the friends had gone off with a rich young and unmarried poet to a seaside resort near Trouville. There they were all very happy.

Elliot kept on at the château in Touraine because he had taken it for all summer. He and Mrs. Elliot tried very hard to have a baby in the big hot bedroom on the big, hard bed. Mrs. Elliot was learning the touch system on the typewriter, but she found that while it increased the speed it made more mistakes. The girl friend was now typing practically all of the manuscripts. She was very neat and efficient and seemed to enjoy it.

Elliot had taken to drinking white wine and lived apart in his own room. He wrote a great deal of poetry during the night and in the morning looked very exhausted. Mrs. Elliot and the girl friend now slept together in the big mediæval bed. They had many a good cry together. In the evening they all sat at dinner together in the garden under a plane tree and the hot evening wind blew and Elliot drank white wine and Mrs. Elliot and the girl friend made conversation and they were all quite happy.

CHAPTER X

They whack-whacked the white horse on the legs and he kneed himself up. The picador twisted the stirrups straight and pulled and hauled up into the saddle. The horse's entrails hung down in a blue bunch and swung backward and forward as he began to canter, the monos *whacking him on the back of his legs with the rods. He cantered jerkily along the* barrera. *He stopped stiff and one of the* monos *held his bridle and walked him forward. The picador kicked in his spurs, leaned forward and shook his lance at the bull. Blood pumped regularly from between the horse's front legs. He was nervously wobbly. The bull could not make up his mind to charge.*

CAT IN THE RAIN

There were only two Americans stopping at the hotel. They did not know any of the people they passed on the stairs on their way to and from their room. Their room was on the second floor facing the sea. It also faced the public garden and the war monument. There were big palms and green benches in the public garden. In the good weather there was always an artist with his easel. Artists liked the way the palms grew and the bright colors of the hotels facing the gardens and the sea. Italians came from a long way off to look up at the war monument. It was made of bronze and glistened in the rain. It was raining. The rain dripped from the palm trees. Water stood in pools on the gravel paths. The sea broke in a long line in the rain and slipped back down the beach to come up and break again in a long line in the rain. The motor cars were gone from the square by the war monument. Across the square in the doorway of the café a waiter stood looking out at the empty square.

The American wife stood at the window looking out. Outside right under their window a cat was crouched under one of the dripping green tables. The cat was trying to make herself so compact that she would not be dripped on.

'I'm going down and get that kitty,' the American wife said.

'I'll do it,' her husband offered from the bed.

'No, I'll get it. The poor kitty out trying to keep dry under a table.'

The husband went on reading, lying propped up with the two pillows at the foot of the bed.

'Don't get wet,' he said.

The wife went downstairs and the hotel owner stood up and bowed to her as she passed the office. His desk was at the far end of the office. He was an old man and very tall.

'*Il piove*,' the wife said. She liked the hotel-keeper.

'*Sì, sì, Signora, brutto tempo*. It's very bad weather.'

He stood behind his desk in the far end of the dim room. The wife liked him. She liked the deadly serious way he received any complaints. She liked his dignity. She liked the way he wanted to serve her. She liked the way he felt about being a hotel-keeper. She liked his old, heavy face and big hands.

Liking him she opened the door and looked out. It was raining harder. A man in a rubber cape was crossing the empty square to the café. The cat would be around to the right. Perhaps she could go along under the eaves. As she stood in the doorway an umbrella opened behind her. It was the maid who looked after their room.

'You must not get wet,' she smiled, speaking Italian. Of course, the hotel-keeper had sent her.

With the maid holding the umbrella over her, she walked along the gravel path until she was under their window. The table was there, washed bright green in the rain, but the cat was gone. She was suddenly disappointed. The maid looked up at her.

'*Ha perduto qualche cosa, Signora?*'

'There was a cat,' said the American girl.

'A cat?'

'*Sì, il gatto.*'

'A cat?' the maid laughed. 'A cat in the rain?'

'Yes,' she said, 'under the table.' Then, 'Oh, I wanted it so much. I wanted a kitty.'

When she talked English the maid's face tightened.

'Come, Signora,' she said. 'We must get back inside. You will be wet.'

'I suppose so,' said the American girl.

They went back along the gravel path and passed in the door. The maid stayed outside to close the umbrella. As the American girl passed the office, the padrone bowed from his desk. Something felt very small and tight inside the girl. The padrone made her feel very small and at the same time really important. She had a momentary feeling of being of supreme importance. She went on up the stairs. She opened the door of the room. George was on the bed, reading.

'Did you get the cat?' he asked, putting the book down.

'It was gone.'

'Wonder where it went to,' he said, resting his eyes from reading.

She sat down on the bed.

'I wanted it so much,' she said. 'I don't know why I wanted it so much. I wanted that poor kitty. It isn't any fun to be a poor kitty out in the rain.'

George was reading again.

She went over and sat in front of the mirror of the dressing table looking at herself with the hand glass. She studied her profile, first one side and then the other. Then she studied the back of her head and her neck.

'Don't you think it would be a good idea if I let my hair grow out?' she asked, looking at her profile again.

George looked up and saw the back of her neck, clipped close like a boy's.

'I like it the way it is.'

'I get so tired of it,' she said. 'I get so tired of looking like a boy.'

George shifted his position in the bed. He hadn't looked away from her since she started to speak.

'You look pretty darn nice,' he said.

She laid the mirror down on the dresser and went over to the window and looked out. It was getting dark.

'I want to pull my hair back tight and smooth and make a big knot at the back that I can feel,' she said. 'I want to have a kitty to sit on my lap and purr when I stroke her.'

'Yeah?' George said from the bed.

'And I want to eat at a table with my own silver and I want candles. And I want it to be spring and I want to brush my hair out in front of a mirror and I want a kitty and I want some new clothes.'

'Oh, shut up and get something to read,' George said. He was reading again.

His wife was looking out of the window. It was quite dark now and still raining in the palm trees.

'Anyway, I want a cat,' she said, 'I want a cat. I want a cat now. If I can't have long hair or any fun, I can have a cat.'

George was not listening. He was reading his book. His wife looked out of the window where the light had come on in the square.

Someone knocked at the door.

'*Avanti*,' George said. He looked up from his book.

In the doorway stood the maid. She held a big tortoise-shell cat pressed tight against her and swung down against her body.

'Excuse me,' she said, 'the padrone asked me to bring this for the Signora.'

CHAPTER XI

The crowd shouted all the time and threw pieces of bread down into the ring, then cushions and leather wine bottles, keeping up whistling and yelling. Finally the bull was too tired from so much bad sticking and folded his knees and lay down and one of the cuadrilla *leaned out over his neck and killed him with the* puntillo. *The crowd came over the* barrera *and around the torero and two men grabbed him and held him and some one cut off his pigtail and was waving it and a kid grabbed it and ran away with it. Afterwards I saw him at the café. He was very short with a brown face and quite drunk and he said after all it has happened before like that. I am not really a good bull fighter.*

OUT OF SEASON

On the four lire Peduzzi had earned by spading the hotel garden he got quite drunk. He saw the young gentleman coming down the path and spoke to him mysteriously. The young gentleman said he had not eaten but would be ready to go as soon as lunch was finished. Forty minutes or an hour.

At the cantina near the bridge they trusted him for three more grappas because he was so confident and mysterious about his job for the afternoon. It was a windy day with the sun coming out from behind clouds and then going under in sprinkles of rain. A wonderful day for trout fishing.

The young gentleman came out of the hotel and asked him about the rods. Should his wife come behind with the rods? 'Yes,' said Peduzzi, 'let her follow us.' The young gentleman went back into the hotel and spoke to his wife. He and Peduzzi started down the road. The young gentleman had a musette over his shoulder. Peduzzi saw the wife, who looked as young as the young gentleman, and was wearing mountain boots and a blue beret, start out to follow them down the road, carrying the fishing rods, unjointed, one in each hand. Peduzzi didn't like her to be way back there. 'Signorina,' he called, winking at the young gentleman, 'come up here and walk with us. Signora, come up here. Let us all walk together.' Peduzzi wanted them all three to walk down the street of Cortina together.

The wife stayed behind, following rather sullenly. 'Signorina,' Peduzzi called tenderly, 'come up here with us.' The young gentleman looked back and shouted something. The wife stopped lagging behind and walked up.

Everyone they met walking through the main street of the town Peduzzi greeted elaborately. *Buon dì*, Arturo! Tipping his hat. The bank clerk stared at him from the door of the Fascist café. Groups of three and four people standing in front of the shops stared at the three. The workmen in their stone-powdered jackets working on the foundations of the new hotel looked up as they passed. Nobody spoke or gave any sign to them except the town beggar, lean and old, with a spittle-thickened beard, who lifted his hat as they passed.

Peduzzi stopped in front of a store with the window full of bottles and brought his empty grappa bottle from an inside pocket of his old military coat. 'A little to drink, some marsala for the Signora, something, something to drink.' He gestured with the bottle. It was a wonderful day. 'Marsala, you like marsala, Signorina? A little marsala?'

The wife stood sullenly. 'You'll have to play up to this,' she said. 'I can't understand a word he says. He's drunk, isn't he?'

The young gentleman appeared not to hear Peduzzi. He was thinking, what in hell makes him say marsala? That's what Max Beerbohm drinks.

'*Geld*,' Peduzzi said finally, taking hold of the young gentleman's sleeve. '*Lire*.' He smiled, reluctant to press the subject but needing to bring the young gentleman into action.

The young gentleman took out his pocketbook and gave him a ten-lira note. Peduzzi went up the steps to the door of the Specialty of Domestic and Foreign Wines shop. It was locked.

'It is closed until two,' someone passing in the street said scornfully. Peduzzi came down the steps. He felt hurt. 'Never mind,' he said, 'we can get it at the Concordia.'

They walked down the road to the Concordia three abreast. On the porch of the Concordia, where the rusty bobsleds were stacked, the young gentleman said, '*Was wollen Sie?*' Peduzzi handed him the ten-lira note folded over and over. 'Nothing,' he said, 'anything.' He was embarrassed. 'Marsala, maybe. I don't know. Marsala?'

The door of the Concordia shut on the young gentleman and the wife. 'Three marsalas,' said the young gentleman to the girl behind the pastry counter. 'Two, you mean?' she asked. 'No,' he said, 'one for a *vecchio*.' 'Oh,' she said, 'a *vecchio*,' and laughed, getting down the bottle. She poured out the three muddy looking drinks into three glasses. The wife was sitting at a table under the line of newspapers on sticks. The young gentleman put one of the marsalas in front of her. 'You might as well drink it,' he said, 'maybe it'll make you feel better.' She sat and looked at the glass. The young gentleman went outside the door with a glass for Peduzzi but could not see him.

'I don't know where he is,' he said, coming back into the pastry room carrying the glass.

'He wanted a quart of it,' said the wife.

'How much is a quarter litre?' the young gentleman asked the girl.

'Of the *bianco*? One lira.'

'No, of the marsala. Put these two in, too,' he said, giving her his own glass and the one poured for Peduzzi. She filled the quarter litre wine measure with a funnel. 'A bottle to carry it,' said the young gentleman.

She went to hunt for a bottle. It all amused her.

'I'm sorry you feel so rotten, Tiny,' he said. 'I'm sorry I talked the way I did at lunch. We were both getting at the same thing from different angles.'

'It doesn't make any difference,' she said. 'None of it makes any difference.'

'Are you too cold?' he asked. 'I wish you'd worn another sweater.'

'I've got on three sweaters.'

The girl came in with a very slim brown bottle and poured the marsala into it. The young gentleman paid five lire more. They went out the door. The girl was amused. Peduzzi was walking up and down at the other end out of the wind and holding the rods.

'Come on,' he said, 'I will carry the rods. What difference does it make if anybody sees them? No one will trouble us. No one will make any trouble for me in Cortina. I know them at the *municipio*. I have been a soldier. Everybody in this town likes me. I sell frogs. What if it is forbidden to fish? Not a thing. Nothing. No trouble. Big trout, I tell you. Lots of them.'

They were walking down the hill toward the river. The town was in back of them. The sun had gone under and it was sprinkling rain. 'There,' said Peduzzi, pointing to a girl in the doorway of a house they passed. 'My daughter.'

'His doctor,' the wife said, 'has he got to show us his doctor?'

'He said his daughter,' said the young gentleman.

The girl went into the house as Peduzzi pointed.

They walked down the hill across the fields and then turned to follow the river bank. Peduzzi talked rapidly with much winking and knowingness. As they walked three abreast the wife caught his breath across the wind. Once he nudged her in the ribs. Part of the time he talked in d'Ampezzo dialect and sometimes in Tyroler German dialect. He could not make out which the young gentleman and his wife understood the best so he was being bilingual. But as the young gentleman said, '*Ja, Ja*,' Peduzzi decided to talk altogether in Tyroler. The young gentleman and the wife understood nothing.

'Everybody in the town saw us going through with these rods. We're probably being followed by the game police now. I wish we weren't in on this damn thing. This damned old fool is so drunk, too.'

'Of course you haven't got the guts to just go back,' said the wife. 'Of course you have to go on.'

'Why don't you go back? Go on back, Tiny.'

'I'm going to stay with you. If you go to jail we might as well both go.'

They turned sharp down the bank and Peduzzi stood, his coat blowing in the wind, gesturing at the river. It was brown and muddy. Off on the right there was a dump heap.

'Say it to me in Italian,' said the young gentleman.

'*Un' mezz'ora. Piu d'un' mezz'ora.*'

'He says it's at least a half hour more. Go on back, Tiny. You're cold in this wind anyway. It's a rotten day and we aren't going to have any fun, anyway.'

'All right,' she said, and climbed up the grassy bank.

Peduzzi was down at the river and did not notice her till she was almost out of sight over the crest. 'Frau!' he shouted. 'Frau! Fräulein! You're not going.'

She went on over the crest of the hill.

'She's gone!' said Peduzzi. It shocked him.

He took off the rubber bands that held the rod segments together and commenced to joint up one of the rods.

'But you said it was half an hour further.'

'Oh, yes. It is good half an hour down. It is good here, too.'

'Really?'

'Of course. It is good here and good there, too.'

The young gentleman sat down on the bank and jointed up a rod, put on the reel and threaded the line through the guides. He felt uncomfortable and afraid that any minute a gamekeeper or a posse of citizens would come over the bank from the town. He could see the houses of the town and the campanile over the edge of the hill. He opened his leader box. Peduzzi leaned over and dug his flat, hard thumb and forefinger in and tangled the moistened leaders.

'Have you some lead?'

'No.'

'You must have some lead.' Peduzzi was excited. 'You must have *piombo. Piombo.* A little *piombo.* Just here. Just above the hook or your bait will float on the water. You must have it. Just a little *piombo.*'

'Have you got some?'

'No.' He looked through his pockets desperately. Sifting through the cloth dirt in the linings of his inside military pockets. 'I haven't any. We must have *piombo*.'

'We can't fish then,' said the young gentleman, and unjointed the rod, reeling the line back through the guides. 'We'll get some *piombo* and fish tomorrow.'

'But listen, *caro*, you must have *piombo*. The line will lie flat on the water.' Peduzzi's day was going to pieces before his eyes. 'You must have *piombo*. A little is enough. Your stuff is all clean and new but you have no lead. I would have brought some. You said you had everything.'

The young gentleman looked at the stream discolored by the melting snow. 'I know,' he said, 'we'll get some *piombo* and fish tomorrow.'

'At what hour in the morning? Tell me that.'

'At seven.'

The sun came out. It was warm and pleasant. The young gentleman felt relieved. He was no longer breaking the law. Sitting on the bank he took the bottle of marsala out of his pocket and passed it to Peduzzi. Peduzzi passed it back. The young gentleman took a drink of it and passed it to Peduzzi again. Peduzzi passed it back again. 'Drink,' he said, 'drink. It's your marsala.' After another short drink the young gentleman handed the bottle over. Peduzzi had been watching it closely. He took the bottle very hurriedly and tipped it up. The gray hairs in the folds of his neck oscillated as he drank, his eyes fixed on the end of the narrow brown bottle. He drank it all. The sun shone while he drank. It was wonderful. This was a great day, after all. A wonderful day.

'*Senta, caro!* In the morning at seven.' He had called the young gentleman *caro* several times and nothing had happened. It was good marsala. His eyes glistened. Days like this stretched out ahead. It would begin at seven in the morning.

They started to walk up the hill toward the town. The young gentleman went on ahead. He was quite a way up the hill. Peduzzi called to him.

'Listen, *caro*, can you let me take five lire for a favor?'

'For today?' asked the young gentleman frowning.

'No, not today. Give it to me today for tomorrow. I will provide everything for tomorrow. *Pane, salami, formaggio*, good stuff for all of us. You and I and the Signora. Bait for fishing, minnows, not worms only. Perhaps I can get some marsala. All for five lire. Five lire for a favor.'

The young gentleman looked through his pocketbook and took out a two-lira note and two ones.

'Thank you, *caro*. Thank you,' said Peduzzi, in the tone of one member of the Carleton Club accepting the *Morning Post* from another. This was living. He was through with the hotel garden, breaking up frozen manure with a dung fork. Life was opening out.

'Until seven o'clock then, *caro*,' he said, slapping the young gentleman on the back. 'Promptly at seven.'

'I may not be going,' said the young gentleman putting his purse back in his pocket.

'What,' said Peduzzi, 'I will have minnows, Signor. Salami, everything. You and I and the Signora. The three of us.'

'I may not be going,' said the young gentleman, 'very probably not. I will leave word with the padrone at the hotel office.'

CHAPTER XII

If it happened right down close in front of you, you could see Villalta snarl at the bull and curse him, and when the bull charged he swung back firmly like an oak when the wind hits it, his legs tight together, the muleta trailing and the sword following the curve behind. Then he cursed the bull, flopped the muleta at him, and swung back from the charge his feet firm, the muleta curving and at each swing the crowd roaring.

When he started to kill it was all in the same rush. The bull looking at him straight in front, hating. He drew out the sword from the folds of the muleta and sighted with the same movement and called to the bull, Toro! Toro! and the bull charged and Villalta charged and just for a moment they became one. Villalta became one with the bull and then it was over. Villalta standing straight and the red hilt of the sword sticking out dully between the bull's shoulders. Villalta, his hand up at the crowd and the bull roaring blood, looking straight at Villalta and his legs caving.

CROSS-COUNTRY SNOW

The funicular car bucked once more and then stopped. It could not go farther, the snow drifted solidly across the track. The gale scouring the exposed surface of the mountain had swept the snow surface into a wind-board crust. Nick, waxing his skis in the baggage car, pushed his boots into the toe irons and shut the clamp tight. He jumped from the car sideways onto the hard wind-board, made a jump turn and crouching and trailing his sticks slipped in a rush down the slope.

On the white below George dipped and rose and dipped out of sight. The rush and the sudden swoop as he dropped down a steep undulation in the mountain side plucked Nick's mind out and left him only the wonderful flying, dropping sensation in his body. He rose to a slight up-run and then the snow seemed to drop out from under him as he went down, down, faster and faster in a rush down the last, long steep slope. Crouching so he was almost sitting back on his skis, trying to keep the center of gravity low, the snow driving like a sandstorm, he knew the pace was too much. But he held it. He would not let go and spill. Then a patch of soft snow, left in a hollow by the wind, spilled him and he went over and over in a clashing of skis, feeling like a shot rabbit, then stuck, his legs crossed, his skis sticking straight up and his nose and ears jammed full of snow.

George stood a little farther down the slope, knocking the snow from his wind jacket with big slaps.

'You took a beauty, Nick,' he called to Nick. 'That's lousy soft snow. It bagged me the same way.'

'What's it like over the khud?' Nick kicked his skis around as he lay on his back and stood up.

'You've got to keep to your left. It's a good fast drop with a Christy at the bottom on account of a fence.'

'Wait a sec and we'll take it together.'

'No, you come on and go first. I like to see you take the khuds.'

Nick Adams came up past George, big back and blond head still faintly snowy, then his skis started slipping at the edge and he swooped down, hissing in the crystalline powder snow and seeming to float up and drop down as he went up and down the billowing khuds. He held to his left and at the end, as he rushed toward the fence, keeping his knees locked tight together and turning his body like tightening a screw brought his skis sharply around to the right in a smother of snow and slowed into a loss of speed parallel to the hillside and the wire fence.

He looked up the hill. George was coming down in telemark position, kneeling; one leg forward and bent, the other trailing; his sticks hanging like some insect's thin legs, kicking up puffs of snow as they touched the surface and finally the whole kneeling, trailing figure coming around in a beautiful right curve, crouching, the legs shot forward and back, the body leaning out against the swing, the sticks accenting the curve like points of light, all in a wild cloud of snow.

'I was afraid to Christy,' George said, 'the snow was too deep. You made a beauty.'

'I can't telemark with my leg,' Nick said.

Nick held down the top strand of the wire fence with his ski and George slid over. Nick followed him down to the road. They thrust bent-kneed along the road into a pine forest. The road became polished ice, stained orange and a tobacco yellow from the teams hauling logs. The skiers kept to the stretch of snow along the side. The road dipped sharply to a stream and then ran straight up-hill. Through the woods they could see a long, low-eaved, weather-beaten building. Through the trees it was a faded yellow. Closer the window frames were painted green. The paint was peeling. Nick knocked his clamps loose with one of his ski sticks and kicked off the skis.

'We might as well carry them up here,' he said.

He climbed the steep road with the skis on his shoulder, kicking his heel nails into the icy footing. He heard George breathing and kicking in his heels just behind him. They stacked the skis against the side of the inn and slapped the snow off each other's trousers, stamped their boots clean, and went in.

Inside it was quite dark. A big porcelain stove shone in the corner of the room. There was a low ceiling. Smooth benches back of dark, wine-stained tables were along each side of the rooms. Two Swiss sat over their pipes and two decies of cloudy new wine next to the stove. The boys took off their jackets and sat against the wall on the other side of the stove. A voice in the next room stopped singing and a girl in a blue apron came in through the door to see what they wanted to drink.

'A bottle of Sion,' Nick said. 'Is that all right, Gidge?'

'Sure,' said George. 'You know more about wine than I do. I like any of it.'

The girl went out.

'There's nothing really can touch skiing, is there?' Nick said. 'The way it feels when you first drop off on a long run.'

'Huh,' said George. 'It's too swell to talk about.'

The girl brought the wine in and they had trouble with the cork. Nick finally opened it. The girl went out and they heard her singing in German in the next room.

'Those specks of cork in it don't matter,' said Nick.

'I wonder if she's got any cake.'

'Let's find out.'

The girl came in and Nick noticed that her apron covered swellingly her pregnancy. I wonder why I didn't see that when she first came in, he thought.

'What were you singing?' he asked her.

'Opera, German opera.' She did not care to discuss the subject. 'We have some apple strudel if you want it.'

'She isn't so cordial, is she?' said George.

'Oh, well. She doesn't know us and she thought we were going to kid her about her singing, maybe. She's from up where they speak German probably and she's touchy about being here and then she's got that baby coming without being married and she's touchy.'

'How do you know she isn't married?'

'No ring. Hell, no girls get married around here till they're knocked up.'

The door came open and a gang of woodcutters from up the road came in, stamping their boots and steaming in the room. The waitress brought in three litres of new wine for the gang and they sat at the two tables, smoking and quiet, with their hats off, leaning back against the wall or forward on the table. Outside the horses on the wood sledges made an occasional sharp jangle of bells as they tossed their heads.

George and Nick were happy. They were fond of each other. They knew they had the run back home ahead of them.

'When have you got to go back to school?' Nick asked.

'Tonight,' George answered. 'I've got to get the ten-forty from Montreux.'

'I wish you could stick over and we could do the Dent du Lys tomorrow.'

'I got to get educated,' George said. 'Gee, Nick, don't you

wish we could just bum together? Take our skis and go on the train to where there was good running and then go on and put up at pubs and go right across the Oberland and up the Valais and all through the Engadine and just take repair kit and extra sweaters and pyjamas in our rucksacks and not give a damn about school or anything.'

'Yes, and go through the *Schwarzwald* that way. Gee, the swell places.'

'That's where you went fishing last summer, isn't it?'

'Yes.'

They ate the strudel and drank the rest of the wine.

George leaned back against the wall and shut his eyes.

'Wine always makes me feel this way,' he said.

'Feel bad?' Nick asked.

'No. I feel good, but funny.'

'I know,' Nick said.

'Sure,' said George.

'Should we have another bottle?' Nick asked.

'Not for me,' George said.

They sat there, Nick leaning his elbows on the table, George slumped back against the wall.

'Is Helen going to have a baby?' George said, coming down to the table from the wall.

'Yes.'

'When?'

'Late next summer.'

'Are you glad?'

'Yes. Now.'

'Will you go back to the States?'

'I guess so.'

'Do you want to?'

'No.'

'Does Helen?'

'No.'

George sat silent. He looked at the empty bottle and the empty glasses.

'It's hell, isn't it?' he said.

'No. Not exactly,' Nick said.

'Why not?'

'I don't know,' Nick said.

'Will you ever go skiing together in the States?' George said.

'I don't know,' said Nick.

'The mountains aren't much,' George said.

'No,' said Nick. 'They're too rocky. There's too much timber and they're too far away.'

'Yes,' said George, 'that's the way it is in California.'

'Yes,' Nick said, 'that's the way it is everywhere I've ever been.'

'Yes,' said George, 'that's the way it is.'

The Swiss got up and paid and went out.

'I wish we were Swiss,' George said.

'They've all got goiter,' said Nick.

'I don't believe it,' George said.

'Neither do I,' said Nick.

They laughed.

'Maybe we'll never go skiing again, Nick,' George said.

'We've got to,' said Nick. 'It isn't worth while if you can't.'

'We'll go, all right,' George said.

'We've got to,' Nick agreed.

'I wish we could make a promise about it,' George said.

Nick stood up. He buckled his wind jacket tight. He leaned over George and picked up the two ski poles from against the wall. He stuck one of the ski poles into the floor.

'There isn't any good in promising,' he said.

They opened the door and went out. It was very cold. The snow had crusted hard. The road ran up the hill into the pine trees.

They took down their skis from where they leaned against the wall in the inn. Nick put on his gloves. George was already started up the road, his skis on his shoulder. Now they would have the run home together.

CHAPTER XIII

I heard the drums coming down the street and then the fifes and the pipes and then they came around the corner, all dancing. The street was full of them. Maera saw him and then I saw him. When they stopped the music for the crouch he hunched down in the street with them all and when they started it again he jumped up and went dancing down the street with them. He was drunk all right.

You go down after him, said Maera, he hates me.

So I went down and caught up with them and grabbed him while he was crouched down waiting for the music to break loose and said, Come on Luis. For Christ's sake you've got bulls this afternoon. He didn't listen to me, he was listening so hard for the music to start.

I said, Don't be a damn fool Luis. Come on back to the hotel.

Then the music started up again and he jumped up and twisted away from me and started dancing. I grabbed his arm and he pulled loose and said, Oh leave me alone. You're not my father.

I went back to the hotel and Maera was on the balcony looking out to see if I'd be bringing him back. He went inside when he saw me and came downstairs disgusted.

Well, I said, after all he's just an ignorant Mexican savage.

Yes, Maera said, and who will kill his bulls after he gets a cogida*?*

We, I suppose, I said.

Yes, we, said Maera. We kills the savages' bulls, and the drunkards' bulls, and the riau-riau *dancers' bulls. Yes. We kill them. We kill them all right. Yes. Yes. Yes.*

MY OLD MAN

I guess looking at it, now, my old man was cut out for a fat guy, one of those regular little roly fat guys you see around, but he sure never got that way, except a little toward the last, and then it wasn't his fault, he was riding over the jumps only and he could afford to carry plenty of weight then. I remember the way he'd pull on a rubber shirt over a couple of jerseys and a big sweat shirt over that, and get me to run with him in the forenoon in the hot sun. He'd have, maybe, taken a trial trip with one of Razzo's skins early in the morning after just getting in from Torino at four o'clock in the morning and beating it out to the stables in a cab and then with the dew all over everything and the sun just starting to get going, I'd help him pull off his boots and he'd get into a pair of sneakers and all these sweaters and we'd start out.

'Come on, kid,' he'd say, stepping up and down on his toes in front of the jock's dressing room, 'let's get moving.'

Then we'd start off jogging around the infield once, maybe, with him ahead, running nice, and then turn out the gate and along one of those roads with all the trees along both sides of them that run out from San Siro. I'd go ahead of him when we hit the road and I could run pretty good and I'd look around again and he'd begun to sweat. Sweating heavy and he'd just be dogging it along with his eyes on my back, but when he'd catch me looking at him he'd grin and say, 'Sweating plenty?' When my old man grinned, nobody could help but grin too. We'd keep right on running out toward the mountains and then my old man would yell, 'Hey, Joe!' and I'd look back and he'd be sitting under a tree with a towel he'd had around his waist wrapped around his neck.

I'd come back and sit down beside him and he'd pull a rope out of his pocket and start skipping rope out in the sun with the sweat pouring off his face and him skipping rope out in the white dust with the rope going cloppetty, cloppetty, clop, clop, clop, and the sun hotter, and him working harder up and down a patch of the road. Say, it was a treat to see my old man skip rope, too. He could whirr it fast or lop it slow and fancy. Say, you ought to have seen wops look at us sometimes, when they'd come by, going into town walking along with big white steers hauling the cart. They sure looked as though they thought the old man was nuts. He'd start the rope whirring till they'd stop dead still and watch him, then give the steers a cluck and a poke with the goad and get going again.

When I'd sit watching him working out in the hot sun I sure felt fond of him. He sure was fun and he done his work so hard and he'd finish up with a regular whirring that'd drive the sweat out on his face like water and then sling the rope at the tree and come over and sit down with me and lean back against the tree with the towel and a sweater wrapped around his neck.

'Sure is hell keeping it down, Joe,' he'd say and lean back and shut his eyes and breathe long and deep, 'it ain't like when you're a kid.' Then he'd get up and before he started to cool we'd jog along back to the stables. That's the way it was keeping down to weight. He was worried all the time. Most jocks can just about ride off all they want to. A jock loses about a kilo every time he rides, but my old man was sort of dried out and he couldn't keep down his kilos without all that running.

I remember once at San Siro, Regoli, a little wop, that was riding for Buzoni, came out across the paddock going to the bar for something cool; and flicking his boots with his whip, after he'd just weighed in and my old man had just weighed in too, and came out with the saddle under his arm looking red-faced and tired and too big for his silks and he stood there looking at young Regoli standing up to the outdoors bar, cool and kid-looking, and I said, 'What's the matter, Dad?' cause I thought maybe Regoli had bumped him or something and he just looked at Regoli and said, 'Oh, to hell with it,' and went on to the dressing room.

Well, it would have been all right, maybe, if we'd stayed in Milan and ridden at Milan and Torino, 'cause if there ever were any easy courses, it's those two. 'Pianola, Joe,' my old man said when he dismounted in the winning stall after what the wops thought was a hell of a steeplechase. I asked him once. 'This course rides itself. It's the pace you're going at, that makes riding the jumps dangerous, Joe. We ain't going any pace here, and they ain't really bad jumps either. But it's the pace always – not the jumps – that makes the trouble.'

San Siro was the swellest course I'd ever seen but the old man said it was a dog's life. Going back and forth between Mirafiore and San Siro and riding just about every day in the week with a train ride every other night.

I was nuts about the horses, too. There's something about it, when they come out and go up the track to the post. Sort of dancy and tight looking with the jock keeping a tight hold on them and maybe easing off a little and letting them run a little going up. Then once they were at the barrier it got me worse than anything. Especially at San Siro with that big green infield and the mountains way off and the fat wop starter with his big whip and the jocks fiddling them around and then the barrier snapping up and that bell going off and them all getting off in a bunch and then commencing to string out. You know the way a bunch of skins gets off. If you're up in the stand with a pair of glasses all you see is them plunging off and then that bell goes off and it seems like it rings for a thousand years and then they come sweeping round the turn. There wasn't ever anything like it for me.

But my old man said one day, in the dressing room, when he was getting into his street clothes, 'None of these things are horses, Joe. They'd kill that bunch of skates for their hides and hoofs up at Paris.' That was the day he'd won the Premio Commercio with Lantorna shooting her out of the field the last hundred meters like pulling a cork out of a bottle.

It was right after the Premio Commercio that we pulled out and left Italy. My old man and Holbrook and a fat wop in a straw hat that kept wiping his face with a handkerchief were having an argument at a table in the Galleria. They were all talking French and the two of them was after my old man about something. Finally he didn't say anything any more but just sat there and looked at Holbrook, and the two of them kept after him, first one talking and then the other, and the fat wop always butting in on Holbrook.

'You go out and buy me a *Sportsman*, will you, Joe?' my old man said, and handed me a couple of soldi without looking away from Holbrook.

So I went out of the Galleria and walked over to in front of the Scala and bought a paper, and came back and stood a little way away because I didn't want to butt in and my old man was sitting back in his chair looking down at his coffee and fooling with a spoon and Holbrook and the big wop were standing and the big wop was wiping his face and shaking his head. And I came up and my old man acted just as though the two of them weren't standing there and said, 'Want an ice, Joe?' Holbrook looked down at my old man and said slow and careful, 'You son of a bitch,' and he and the fat wop went out through the tables.

My old man sat there and sort of smiled at me, but his face was white and he looked sick as hell and I was scared and felt sick inside because I knew something had happened and I didn't see how anybody could call my old man a son of a bitch, and get away with it. My old man opened up the *Sportsman* and studied the handicaps for a while and then he said, 'You got to take a lot of things in this world, Joe.' And three days later we left Milan for good on the Turin train for Paris, after an auction sale out in front of Turner's stables of everything we couldn't get into a trunk and a suitcase.

We got into Paris early in the morning in a long, dirty station the old man told me was the Gare de Lyon. Paris was an awful big town after Milan. Seems like in Milan everybody is going somewhere and all the trams run somewhere and there ain't any sort of a mix-up, but Paris is all balled up and they never do straighten it out. I got to like it, though, part of it, anyway, and say, it's got the best race courses in the world. Seems as though that were the thing that keeps it all going and about the only thing you can figure on is that every day the buses will be going out to whatever track they're running at, going right out through everything to the track. I never really got to know Paris well, because I just came in about once or twice a week with the old man from Maisons and he always sat at the Café de la Paix on the Opéra side with the rest of the gang from Maisons and I guess that's one of the busiest parts of the town. But, say, it is funny that a big town like Paris wouldn't have a Galleria, isn't it?

Well, we went out to live at Maisons-Lafitte, where just about everybody lives except the gang at Chantilly, with a Mrs. Meyers that runs a boarding house. Maisons is about the swellest place to live I've ever seen in all my life. The town ain't so much, but there's a lake and a swell forest that we used to go off bumming in all day, a couple of us kids, and my old man made me a sling shot and we got a lot of things with it but the best one was a magpie. Young Dick Atkinson shot a rabbit with it one day and we put it under a tree and were all sitting around and Dick had some cigarettes and all of a sudden the rabbit jumped up and beat it into the brush and we chased it but we couldn't find it. Gee, we had fun at Maisons. Mrs. Meyers used to give me lunch in the morning and I'd be gone all day. I learned to talk French quick. It's an easy language.

As soon as we got to Maisons, my old man wrote to Milan for his license and he was pretty worried till it came. He used to sit

around the Café de Paris in Maisons with the gang, there were
lots of guys he'd known when he rode up at Paris, before the
war, lived at Maisons, and there's a lot of time to sit around
because the work around a racing stable, for the jocks, that is, is
all cleaned up by nine o'clock in the morning. They take the
first bunch of skins out to gallop them at 5:30 in the morning
and they work the second lot at 8 o'clock. That means getting
up early all right and going to bed early, too. If a jock's riding
for somebody too, he can't go boozing around because the
trainer always has an eye on him if he's a kid and if he ain't a
kid he's always got an eye on himself. So mostly if a jock ain't
working he sits around the Café de Paris with the gang and
they can all sit around about two or three hours in front of some
drink like a vermouth and seltz and they talk and tell stories
and shoot pool and it's sort of like a club or the Galleria in
Milan. Only it ain't really like the Galleria because there everybody is going by all the time and there's everybody around at the
tables.

Well, my old man got his license all right. They sent it
through to him without a word and he rode a couple of times.
Amiens, up country and that sort of thing, but he didn't seem to
get any engagement. Everybody liked him and whenever I'd
come into the Café in the forenoon I'd find somebody drinking
with him because my old man wasn't tight like most of these
jockeys that have got the first dollar they made riding at the
World's Fair in St. Louis in nineteen ought four. That's what my
old man would say when he'd kid George Burns. But it seemed
like everybody steered clear of giving my old man any mounts.

We went out to wherever they were running every day with
the car from Maisons and that was the most fun of all. I was glad
when the horses came back from Deauville and the summer.
Even though it meant no more bumming in the woods, 'cause
then we'd ride to Enghien or Tremblay or St. Cloud and watch
them from the trainers' and jockeys' stand. I sure learned about
racing from going out with that gang and the fun of it was going
every day.

I remember once out at St. Cloud. It was a big two hundred
thousand franc race with seven entries and Kzar a big favourite.
I went around to the paddock to see the horses with my old man
and you never saw such horses. This Kzar is a great big yellow
horse that looks like just nothing but run. I never saw such a
horse. He was being led around the paddocks with his head

down and when he went by me I felt all hollow inside he was so beautiful. There never was such a wonderful, lean, running built horse. And he went around the paddock putting his feet just so and quiet and careful and moving easy like he knew just what he had to do and not jerking and standing up on his legs and getting wild eyed like you see these selling platers with a shot of dope in them. The crowd was so thick I couldn't see him again except just his legs going by and some yellow and my old man started out through the crowd and I followed him over to the jocks' dressing room back in the trees and there was a big crowd around there, too, but the man at the door in a derby nodded to my old man and we got in and everybody was sitting around and getting dressed and pulling shirts over their heads and pulling boots on and it all smelled hot and sweaty and linimenty and outside was the crowd looking in.

The old man went over and sat down beside George Gardner that was getting into his pants and said, 'What's the dope, George?' just in an ordinary tone of voice 'cause there ain't any use him feeling around because George either can tell him or he can't tell him.

'He won't win,' George says very low, leaning over and buttoning the bottoms of his breeches.

'Who will?' my old man says, leaning over close so nobody can hear.

'Kircubbin,' George says, 'and if he does, save me a couple of tickets.'

My old man says something in a regular voice to George and George says, 'Don't ever bet on anything I tell you,' kidding like, and we beat it out and through all the crowd that was looking in, over to the 100 franc mutuel machine. But I knew something big was up because George is Kzar's jockey. On the way he gets one of the yellow odds-sheets with the starting prices on and Kzar is only paying 5 for 10, Cefisidote is next at 3 to 1 and fifth down the list this Kircubbin at 8 to 1. My old man bets five thousand on Kircubbin to win and puts on a thousand to place and we went around back of the grandstand to go up the stairs and get a place to watch the race.

We were jammed in tight and first a man in a long coat with a gray tall hat and a whip folded up in his hand came out and then one after another the horses, with the jocks up and a stable boy holding the bridle on each side and walking along, followed the old guy. That big yellow horse Kzar came first. He didn't

look so big when you first looked at him until you saw the
length of his legs and the whole way he's built and the way he
moves. Gosh, I never saw such a horse. George Gardner was
riding him and they moved along slow, back of the old guy in
the gray tall hat that walked along like he was a ring master in a
circus. Back of Kzar, moving along smooth and yellow in the
sun, was a good-looking black with a nice head with Tommy
Archibald riding him; and after the black was a string of five
more horses all moving along slow in a procession past the
grand-stand and the *pesage*. My old man said the black was Kircubbin and I took a good look at him and he was a nice-looking
horse, all right, but nothing like Kzar.

Everybody cheered Kzar when he went by and he sure was
one swell-looking horse. The procession of them went around
on the other side past the *pelouse* and then back up to the near
end of the course and the circus master had the stable boys turn
them loose one after another so they could gallop by the stands
on their way up to the post and let everybody have a good look
at them. They weren't at the post hardly any time at all when
the gong started and you could see them way off across the infield all in a bunch starting on the first swing like a lot of little
toy horses. I was watching them through the glasses and Kzar
was running well back, with one of the bays making the pace.
They swept down and around and came pounding past and Kzar
was way back when they passed us and this Kircubbin horse in
front and going smooth. Gee, it's awful when they go by you
and then you have to watch them go farther away and get smaller and smaller and then all bunched up on the turns and then
come around towards into the stretch and you feel like swearing
and god-damming worse and worse. Finally they made the last
turn and came into the straightaway with this Kircubbin horse
way out in front. Everybody was looking funny and saying
'Kzar' in sort of a sick way and them pounding nearer down the
stretch, and then something came out of the pack right into my
glasses like a horse-headed yellow streak and everybody began to
yell 'Kzar' as though they were crazy. Kzar came on faster than
I'd ever seen anything in my life and pulled up on Kircubbin that
was going fast as any black horse could go with the jock flogging
hell out of him with the gad and they were right dead neck and
neck for a second but Kzar seemed going about twice as fast with
those great jumps and that head out – but it was while they were
neck and neck that they passed the winning post and when the

numbers went up in the slots the first one was 2 and that meant that Kircubbin had won.

I felt all trembly and funny inside, and then we were all jammed in with the people going downstairs to stand in front of the board where they'd post what Kircubbin paid. Honest, watching the race I'd forgot how much my old man had bet on Kircubbin. I'd wanted Kzar to win so damned bad. But now it was all over it was swell to know we had the winner.

'Wasn't it a swell race, Dad?' I said to him.

He looked at me sort of funny with his derby on the back of his head. 'George Gardner's a swell jockey, all right,' he said. 'It sure took a great jock to keep that Kzar horse from winning.'

Of course I knew it was funny all the time. But my old man saying that right out like that sure took the kick all out of it for me and I didn't get the real kick back again ever, even when they posted the numbers upon the board and the bell rang to pay off and we saw that Kircubbin paid 67.50 for 10. All round people were saying, 'Poor Kzar! Poor Kzar!' And I thought, I wish I were a jockey and could have rode him instead of that son of a bitch. And that was funny, thinking of George Gardner as a son of a bitch because I'd always liked him and besides he'd given us the winner, but I guess that's what he is, all right.

My old man had a big lot of money after that race and he took to coming into Paris oftener. If they raced at Tremblay he'd have them drop him in town on their way back to Maisons and he and I'd sit out in front of the Café de la Paix and watch the people go by. It's funny sitting there. There's streams of people going by and all sorts of guys come up and want to sell you things, and I loved to sit there with my old man. That was when we'd have the most fun. Guys would come by selling funny rabbits that jumped if you squeezed a bulb and they'd come up to us and my old man would kid with them. He could talk French just like English and all those kind of guys knew him 'cause you can always tell a jockey – and then we always sat at the same table and they got used to seeing us there. There were guys selling matrimonial papers and girls selling rubber eggs that when you squeezed them a rooster came out of them and one old wormy-looking guy that went by with post-cards of Paris, showing them to everybody, and, of course, nobody ever bought any, and then he would come back and show the under side of the pack and they would all be smutty post-cards and lots of people would dig down and buy them.

Gee, I remember the funny people that used to go by. Girls around supper time looking for somebody to take them out to eat and they'd speak to my old man and he'd make some joke at them in French and they'd pat me on the head and go on. Once there was an American woman sitting with her kid daughter at the next table to us and they were both eating ices and I kept looking at the girl and she was awfully good looking and I smiled at her and she smiled at me but that was all that ever came of it because I looked for her mother and her every day and I made up ways that I was going to speak to her and I wondered if I got to know her if her mother would let me take her out to Auteuil or Tremblay but I never saw either of them again. Anyway, I guess it wouldn't have been any good, anyway, because looking back on it I remember the way I thought out would be best to speak to her was to say, 'Pardon me, but perhaps I can give you a winner at Enghien today?' and, after all, maybe she would have thought I was a tout instead of really trying to give her a winner.

We'd sit at the Café de la Paix, my old man and me, and we had a big drag with the waiter because my old man drank whiskey and it cost five francs, and that meant a good tip when the saucers were counted up. My old man was drinking more than I'd ever seen him, but he wasn't riding at all now and besides he said that whiskey kept his weight down. But I noticed he was putting it on, all right, just the same. He'd busted away from his old gang out at Maisons and seemed to like just sitting around on the boulevard with me. But he was dropping money every day at the track. He'd feel sort of doleful after the last race, if he'd lost on the day, until we'd get to our table and he'd have his first whiskey and then he'd be fine.

He'd be reading the *Paris-Sport* and he'd look over at me and say, 'Where's your girl, Joe?' to kid me on account I had told him about the girl that day at the next table. And I'd get red, but I liked being kidded about her. It gave me a good feeling. 'Keep your eye peeled for her, Joe,' he'd say, 'she'll be back.'

He'd ask me questions about things and some of the things I'd say he'd laugh. And then he'd get started talking about things. About riding down in Egypt, or at St. Moritz on the ice before my mother died, and about during the war when they had regular races down in the south of France without any purses, or betting or crowd or anything just to keep the breed up. Regular races with the jocks riding hell out of the horses. Gee, I could listen to my old man talk by the hour, especially when he'd had a couple or so of drinks. He'd tell me about when he was a boy in Kentucky and going coon hunting, and the old days in the States before everything went on the bum there. And he'd say, 'Joe, when we've got a decent stake, you're going back there to the States and go to school.'

'What've I got to go back there to go to school for when everything's on the bum there?' I'd ask him.

'That's different,' he'd say and get the waiter over and pay the pile of saucers and we'd get a taxi to the Gare St. Lazare and get on the train out to Maisons.

One day at Auteuil, after a selling steeplechase, my old man bought in the winner for 30,000 francs. He had to bid a little to get him but the stable let the horse go finally and my old man had his permit and his colors in a week. Gee, I felt proud when my old man was an owner. He fixed it up for stable space with Charles Drake and cut out coming in to Paris, and started his running and sweating out again, and him and I were the whole stable gang. Our horse's name was Gilford, he was Irish bred and a nice, sweet jumper. My old man figured that training him and riding him, himself, he was a good investment. I was proud of everything and I thought Gilford was as good a horse as Kzar. He was a good, solid jumper, a bay, with plenty of speed on the flat, if you asked him for it, and he was a nice-looking horse, too.

Gee, I was fond of him. The first time he started with my old man up, he finished third in a 2500 meter hurdle race and when my old man got off him, all sweating and happy in the place stall, and went in to weigh, I felt as proud of him as though it was the first race he'd ever placed in. You see, when a guy ain't been riding for a long time, you can't make yourself really believe that he has ever rode. The whole thing was different now, 'cause down in Milan, even big races never seemed to make any difference to my old man, if he won he wasn't ever excited or anything, and now it was so I couldn't hardly sleep the night before a race and I knew my old man was excited, too, even if he didn't show it. Riding for yourself makes an awful difference.

Second time Gilford and my old man started, was a rainy Sunday at Auteuil, in the Prix du Marat, a 4500 meter steeplechase. As soon as he'd gone out I beat it up in the stand with the new glasses my old man had bought for me to watch them. They started way over at the far end of the course and there was some trouble at the barrier. Something with goggle blinders on was making a great fuss and rearing around and busted the barrier

once, but I could see my old man in our black jacket, with a
white cross and a black cap, sitting up on Gilford, and patting
him with his hand. Then they were off in a jump and out of sight
behind the trees and the gong going for dear life and the pari-
mutuel wickets rattling down. Gosh, I was so excited, I was
afraid to look at them, but I fixed the glasses on the place where
they would come out back of the trees and then out they came
with the old black jacket going third and they all sailing over the
jump like birds. Then they went out of sight again and then they
came pounding out and down the hill and all going nice and
sweet and easy and taking the fence smooth in a bunch, and
moving away from us all solid. Looked as though you could
walk across on their backs they were all so bunched and going
so smooth. Then they bellied over the big double Bullfinch and
something came down. I couldn't see who it was, but in a
minute the horse was up and galloping free and the field, all
bunched still, sweeping around the long left turn into the
straightaway. They jumped the stone wall and came jammed
down the stretch toward the big water-jump right in front of the
stands. I saw them coming and hollered at my old man as he
went by, and he was leading by about a length and riding way
out, and light as a monkey, and they were racing for the water-
jump. They took off over the big hedge of the water-jump in a
pack and then there was a crash, and two horses pulled sideways
out off it, and kept on going, and three others were piled up. I
couldn't see my old man anywhere. One horse kneed himself up
and the jock had hold of the bridle and mounted and went
slamming on after the place money. The other horse was up and
away by himself, jerking his head and galloping with the bridle
rein hanging and the jock staggered over to one side of the track
against the fence. Then Gilford rolled over to one side off my
old man and got up and started to run on three legs with his front
off hoof dangling and there was my old man laying there on the
grass flat out with his face up and blood all over the side of his
head. I ran down the stand and bumped into a jam of people and
got to the rail and a cop grabbed me and held me and two big
stretcher-bearers were going out after my old man and around
on the other side of the course I saw three horses, strung way
out, coming out of the trees and taking the jump.

My old man was dead when they brought him in and while a
doctor was listening to his heart with a thing plugged in his ears,
I heard a shot up the track that meant they'd killed Gilford. I lay

down beside my old man, when they carried the stretcher into the hospital room, and hung onto the stretcher and cried and cried, and he looked so white and gone and so awfully dead, and I couldn't help feeling that if my old man was dead maybe they didn't need to have shot Gilford. His hoof might have got well. I don't know. I loved my old man so much.

Then a couple of guys came in and one of them patted me on the back and then went over and looked at my old man and then pulled a sheet off the cot and spread it over him; and the other was telephoning in French for them to send the ambulance to take him out to Maisons. And I couldn't stop crying, crying and choking, sort of, and George Gardner came in and sat down beside me on the floor and put his arm around me and says, 'Come on, Joe, old boy. Get up and we'll go out and wait for the ambulance.'

George and I went out to the gate and I was trying to stop bawling and George wiped off my face with his handkerchief and we were standing back a little ways while the crowd was going out of the gate and a couple of guys stopped near us while we were waiting for the crowd to get through the gate and one of them was counting a bunch of mutuel tickets and he said, 'Well, Butler got his, all right.'

The other guy said, 'I don't give a good goddam if he did, the crook. He had it coming to him on the stuff he's pulled.'

'I'll say he had,' said the other guy, and tore the bunch of tickets in two.

And George Gardner looked at me to see if I'd heard and I had all right and he said, 'Don't you listen to what those bums said, Joe. Your old man was one swell guy.'

But I don't know. Seems like when they get started they don't leave a guy nothing.

CHAPTER XIV

Maera lay still, his head on his arms, his face in the sand. He felt warm and sticky from the bleeding. Each time he felt the horn coming. Sometimes the bull only bumped him with his head. Once the horn went all the way through him and he felt it go into the sand. Some one had the bull by the tail. They were swearing at him and flopping the cape in his face. Then the bull was gone. Some men picked Maera up and started to run with him toward the barriers through the gate out the passageway around under the grandstand to the infirmary. They laid Maera down on a cot and one of the men went out for the doctor. The others stood around. The doctor came running from the corral where he had been sewing up picador horses. He had to stop and wash his hands. There was a great shouting going on in the grandstand overhead. Maera felt everything getting larger and larger and then smaller and smaller. Then it got larger and larger and larger and then smaller and smaller. Then everything commenced to run faster and faster as when they speed up a cinematograph film. Then he was dead.

BIG TWO-HEARTED RIVER
PART I

The train went on up the track out of sight, around one of the hills of burnt timber. Nick sat down on the bundle of canvas and bedding the baggage man had pitched out of the door of the baggage car. There was no town, nothing but the rails and the burned-over country. The thirteen saloons that had lined the one street of Seney had not left a trace. The foundations of the Mansion House hotel stuck up above the ground. The stone was chipped and split by the fire. It was all that was left of the town of Seney. Even the surface had been burned off the ground.

Nick looked at the burned-over stretch of hillside, where he had expected to find the scattered houses of the town and then walked down the railroad track to the bridge over the river. The river was there. It swirled against the log spiles of the bridge. Nick looked down into the clear, brown water, colored from the pebbly bottom, and watched the trout keeping themselves steady in the current with wavering fins. As he watched them they changed their positions by quick angles, only to hold steady in the fast water again. Nick watched them a long time.

He watched them holding themselves with their noses into the current, many trout in deep, fast moving water, slightly distorted as he watched far down through the glassy convex surface of the pool, its surface pushing and swelling smooth against the resistance of the log-driven piles of the bridge. At the bottom of the pool were the big trout. Nick did not see them at first. Then he saw them at the bottom of the pool, big trout looking to hold themselves on the gravel bottom in a varying mist of gravel and sand, raised in spurts by the current.

Nick looked down into the pool from the bridge. It was a hot day. A kingfisher flew up the stream. It was a long time since Nick had looked into a stream and seen trout. They were very satisfactory. As the shadow of the kingfisher moved up the stream, a big trout shot upstream in a long angle, only his shadow marking the angle, then lost his shadow as he came through the surface of the water, caught the sun, and then, as he went back into the stream under the surface, his shadow seemed to float down the stream with the current, unresisting, to his post under the bridge where he tightened facing up into the current.

Nick's heart tightened as the trout moved. He felt all the old feeling.

He turned and looked down the stream. It stretched away, pebbly-bottomed with shallows and big boulders and a deep pool as it curved away around the foot of a bluff.

Nick walked back up the ties to where his pack lay in the cinders beside the railway track. He was happy. He adjusted the pack harness around the bundle, pulling straps tight, slung the pack on his back, got his arms through the shoulder straps and took some of the pull off his shoulders by leaning his forehead against the wide band of the tump-line. Still, it was too heavy. It was much too heavy. He had his leather rod-case in his hand and leaning forward to keep the weight of the pack high on his shoulders he walked along the road that paralleled the railway track, leaving the burned town behind in the heat, and then turned off around a hill with a high, fire-scarred hill on either side onto a road that went back into the country. He walked along the road feeling the ache from the pull of the heavy pack. The road climbed steadily. It was hard work walking uphill. His muscles ached and the day was hot, but Nick felt happy. He felt he had left everything behind, the need for thinking, the need to write, other needs. It was all back of him.

From the time he had gotten down off the train and the baggage man had thrown his pack out of the open car door things had been different. Seney was burned, the country was burned over and changed, but it did not matter. It could not all be burned. He knew that. He hiked along the road, sweating in the sun, climbing to cross the range of hills that separated the railway from the pine plains.

The road ran on, dipping occasionally, but always climbing. Nick went on up. Finally the road after going parallel to the burnt hillside reached the top. Nick leaned back against a stump and slipped out of the pack harness. Ahead of him, as far as he could see, was the pine plain. The burned country stopped off at the left with the range of hills. On ahead islands of dark pine trees rose out of the plain. Far off to the left was the line of the river. Nick followed it with his eye and caught glints of the water in the sun.

There was nothing but the pine plain ahead of him, until the far blue hills that marked the Lake Superior height of land. He could hardly see them, faint and far away in the heat-light over the plain. If he looked too steadily they were gone. But if he only half-looked they were there, the far-off hills of the height of land.

Nick sat down against the charred stump and smoked a cigarette. His pack balanced on the top of the stump, harness holding ready, a hollow molded in it from his back. Nick sat smoking, looking out over the country. He did not need to get his map out. He knew where he was from the position of the river.

As he smoked, his legs stretched out in front of him, he noticed a grasshopper walk along the ground and up onto his woolen sock. The grasshopper was black. As he had walked along the road, climbing, he had started many grasshoppers from the dust. They were all black. They were not the big grasshoppers with yellow and black or red and black wings whirring out from their black wing sheathing as they fly up. These were just ordinary hoppers, but all a sooty black in color. Nick had wondered about them as he walked, without really thinking about them. Now, as he watched the black hopper that was nibbling at the wool of his sock with its fourway lip, he realized that they had all turned black from living in the burned-over land. He realized that the fire must have come the year before, but the grasshoppers were all black now. He wondered how long they would stay that way.

Carefully he reached his hand down and took hold of the hopper by the wings. He turned him up, all his legs walking in the air, and looked at his jointed belly. Yes, it was black too, iridescent where the back and head were dusty.

'Go on, hopper,' Nick said, speaking out loud for the first time. 'Fly away somewhere.'

He tossed the grasshopper up into the air and watched him sail away to a charcoal stump across the road.

Nick stood up. He leaned his back against the weight of his pack where it rested upright on the stump and got his arms through the shoulder straps. He stood with the pack on his back on the brow of the hill looking out across the country toward the distant river and then struck down the hillside away from the road. Underfoot the ground was good walking. Two hundred yards down the hillside the fire line stopped. Then it was sweet fern, growing ankle high, to walk through, and clumps of jackpines; a long undulating country with frequent rises and descents, sandy underfoot and the country alive again.

Nick kept his direction by the sun. He knew where he wanted

to strike the river and he kept on through the pine plain, mounting small rises to see other rises ahead of him and sometimes from the top of a rise a great solid island of pines off to his right or his left. He broke off some sprigs of the heathery sweet fern, and put them under his pack straps. The chafing crushed it and he smelled it as he walked.

He was tired and very hot, walking across the uneven, shadeless pine plain. At any time he knew he could strike the river by turning off to his left. It could not be more than a mile away. But he kept on toward the north to hit the river as far upstream as he could go in one day's walking.

For some time as he walked Nick had been in sight of one of the big islands of pine standing out above the rolling high ground he was crossing. He dipped down and then as he came slowly up to the crest of the bridge he turned and made toward the pine trees.

There was no underbrush in the island of pine trees. The trunks of the trees went straight up or slanted toward each other. The trunks were straight and brown without branches. The branches were high above. Some interlocked to make a solid shadow on the brown forest floor. Around the grove of trees was a bare space. It was brown and soft underfoot as Nick walked on it. This was the over-lapping of the pine needle floor, extending out beyond the width of the high branches. The trees had grown tall and the branches moved high, leaving in the sun this bare space they had once covered with shadow. Sharp at the edge of this extension of the forest floor commenced the sweet fern.

Nick slipped off his pack and lay down in the shade. He lay on his back and looked up into the pine trees. His neck and back and the small of his back rested as he stretched. The earth felt good against his back. He looked up at the sky, through the branches, and then shut his eyes. He opened them and looked up again. There was a wind high up in the branches. He shut his eyes again and went to sleep.

Nick woke stiff and cramped. The sun was nearly down. His pack was heavy and the straps painful as he lifted it on. He leaned over with the pack on and picked up the leather rod-case and started out from the pine trees across the sweet fern swale, toward the river. He knew it could not be more than a mile.

He came down a hillside covered with stumps into a meadow. At the edge of the meadow flowed the river. Nick was glad to get to the river. He walked upstream through the meadow. His trousers were soaked with the dew as he walked. After the hot day, the dew had come quickly and heavily. The river made no sound. It was too fast and smooth. At the edge of the meadow, before he mounted to a piece of high ground to make camp, Nick looked down the river at the trout rising. They were rising to insects come from the swamp on the other side of the stream when the sun went down. The trout jumped out of water to take them. While Nick walked through the little stretch of meadow alongside the stream, trout had jumped high out of water. Now as he looked down the river, the insects must be settling on the surface, for the trout were feeding steadily all down the stream. As far down the long stretch as he could see, the trout were rising, making circles all down the surface of the water, as though it were starting to rain.

The ground rose, wooded and sandy, to overlook the meadow, the stretch of river and the swamp. Nick dropped his pack and rod-case and looked for a level piece of ground. He was very hungry and he wanted to make his camp before he cooked. Between two jack pines, the ground was quite level. He took the ax out of the pack and chopped out two projecting roots. That leveled a piece of ground large enough to sleep on. He smoothed out the sandy soil with his hand and pulled all the sweet fern bushes by their roots. His hands smelled good from the sweet fern. He smoothed the uprooted earth. He did not want anything making lumps under the blankets. When he had the ground smooth, he spread his three blankets. One he folded double, next to the ground. The other two he spread on top.

With the ax he slit off a bright slab of pine from one of the stumps and split it into pegs for the tent. He wanted them long and solid to hold in the ground. With the tent unpacked and spread on the ground, the pack, leaning against a jackpine, looked much smaller. Nick tied the rope that served the tent for a ridge-pole to the trunk of one of the pine trees and pulled the tent up off the ground with the other end of the rope and tied it to the other pine. The tent hung on the rope like a canvas blanket on a clothesline. Nick poked a pole he had cut up under the back peak of the canvas and then made it a tent by pegging out the sides. He pegged the sides out taut and drove the pegs deep, hitting them down into the ground with the flat of the ax until the rope loops were buried and the canvas was drum tight.

Across the open mouth of the tent Nick fixed cheesecloth to keep out mosquitoes. He crawled inside under the mosquito bar with various things from the pack to put at the head of the bed under the slant of the canvas. Inside the tent the light came through the brown canvas. It smelled pleasantly of canvas. Already there was something mysterious and homelike. Nick was happy as he crawled inside the tent. He had not been unhappy all day. This was different though. Now things were done. There had been this to do. Now it was done. It had been a hard trip. He was very tired. That was done. He had made his camp. He was settled. Nothing could touch him. It was a good place to camp. He was there, in the good place. He was in his home where he had made it. Now he was hungry.

He came out, crawling under the cheesecloth. It was quite dark outside. It was lighter in the tent.

Nick went over to the pack and found, with his fingers, a long nail in a paper sack of nails, in the bottom of the pack. He drove it into the pine tree, holding it close and hitting it gently with the flat of the ax. He hung the pack up on the nail. All his supplies were in the pack. They were off the ground and sheltered now.

Nick was hungry. He did not believe he had ever been hungrier. He opened and emptied a can of pork and beans and a can of spaghetti into the frying pan.

'I've got a right to eat this kind of stuff, if I'm willing to carry it,' Nick said. His voice sounded strange in the darkening woods. He did not speak again.

He started a fire with some chunks of pine he got with the ax from a stump. Over the fire he stuck a wire grill, pushing the four legs down into the ground with his boot. Nick put the frying pan on the grill over the flames. He was hungrier. The beans and spaghetti warmed. Nick stirred them and mixed them together. They began to bubble, making little bubbles that rose with difficulty to the surface. There was a good smell. Nick got out a bottle of tomato catchup and cut four slices of bread. The little bubbles were coming faster now. Nick sat down beside the fire and lifted the frying pan off. He poured about half the contents out into the tin plate. It spread slowly on the plate. Nick knew it was too hot. He poured on some tomato catchup. He knew the beans and spaghetti were still too hot. He looked at the fire, then at the tent, he was not going to spoil it all by burning his tongue. For years he had never enjoyed fried bananas because he had never been able to wait for them to cool. His tongue was very sensitive. He was very hungry. Across the river in the swamp, in the almost dark, he saw a mist rising. He looked at the tent once more. All right. He took a full spoonful from the plate.

'Chrise,' Nick said, 'Geezus Chrise,' he said happily.

He ate the whole plateful before he remembered the bread. Nick finished the second plateful with the bread, mopping the plate shiny. He had not eaten since a cup of coffee and a ham sandwich in the station restaurant at St. Ignace. It had been a very fine experience. He had been that hungry before, but had not been able to satisfy it. He could have made camp hours before if he had wanted to. There were plenty of good places to camp on the river. But this was good.

Nick tucked two big chips of pine under the grill. The fire flared up. He had forgotten to get water for the coffee. Out of the pack he got a folding canvas bucket and walked down the hill, across the edge of the meadow, to the stream. The other bank was in the white mist. The grass was wet and cold as he knelt on the bank and dipped the canvas bucket into the stream. It bellied and pulled hard in the current. The water was ice cold. Nick rinsed the bucket and carried it full up to the camp. Up away from the stream it was not so cold.

Nick drove another big nail and hung up the bucket full of water. He dipped the coffee pot half full, put some more chips under the grill onto the fire and put the pot on. He could not remember which way he made coffee. He could remember an argument about it with Hopkins, but not which side he had taken. He decided to bring it to a boil. He remembered now that was Hopkins's way. He had once argued about everything with Hopkins. While he waited for the coffee to boil, he opened a small can of apricots. He liked to open cans. He emptied the can of apricots out into a tin cup. While he watched the coffee on the fire, he drank the juice syrup of the apricots, carefully at first to keep from spilling, then meditatively, sucking the apricots down. They were better than fresh apricots.

The coffee boiled as he watched. The lid came up and coffee and grounds ran down the side of the pot. Nick took it off the grill. It was a triumph for Hopkins. He put sugar in the empty apricot cup and poured some of the coffee out to cool. It was too hot to pour and he used his hat to hold the handle of the coffee pot. He would not let it steep in the pot at all. Not the first cup. It should be straight Hopkins all the way. Hop deserved that. He was a very serious coffee drinker. He was the most serious man Nick had ever known. Not heavy, serious. That was a long time ago. Hopkins spoke without moving his lips. He had played polo. He made millions of dollars in Texas. He had borrowed carfare to go to Chicago, when the wire came that his first big well had come in. He could have wired for money. That would have been too slow. They called Hop's girl the Blonde Venus. Hop did not mind because she was not his real girl. Hopkins said very confidently that none of them would make fun of his real girl. He was right. Hopkins went away when the telegram came. That was on the Black River. It took eight days for the telegram to reach him. Hopkins gave away his .22 caliber Colt automatic pistol to Nick. He gave his camera to Bill. It was to remember him always by. They were all going fishing again next summer. The Hop Head was rich. He would get a yacht and they would all cruise along the north shore of Lake Superior. He was excited but serious. They said good-bye and all felt bad. It broke up the trip. They never saw Hopkins again. That was a long time ago on the Black River.

Nick drank the coffee, the coffee according to Hopkins. The coffee was bitter. Nick laughed. It made a good ending to the story. His mind was starting to work. He knew he could choke it because he was tired enough. He spilled the coffee out of the pot and shook the grounds loose into the fire. He lit a cigarette and went inside the tent. He took off his shoes and trousers, sitting on the blankets, rolled the shoes up inside the trousers for a pillow and got in between the blankets.

Out through the front of the tent he watched the glow of the fire, when the night wind blew on it. It was a quiet night. The swamp was perfectly quiet. Nick stretched under the blanket comfortably. A mosquito hummed close to his ear. Nick sat up and lit a match. The mosquito was on the canvas, over his head. Nick moved the match quickly up to it. The mosquito made a satisfactory hiss in the flame. The match went out. Nick lay down again under the blanket. He turned on his side and shut his eyes. He was sleepy. He felt sleep coming. He curled up under the blanket and went to sleep.

CHAPTER XV

They hanged Sam Cardinella at six o'clock in the morning in the corridor of the county jail. The corridor was high and narrow with tiers of cells on either side. All the cells were occupied. The men had been brought in for the hanging. Five men sentenced to be hanged were in the five top cells. Three of the men to be hanged were negroes. They were very frightened. One of the white men sat on his cot with his head in his hands. The other lay flat on his cot with a blanket wrapped around his head.

They came out onto the gallows through a door in the wall. There were seven of them including two priests. They were carrying Sam Cardinella. He had been like that since about four o'clock in the morning.

While they were strapping his legs together two guards held him up and the two priests were whispering to him. 'Be a man, my son,' said one priest. When they came toward him with the cap to go over his head Sam Cardinella lost control of his sphincter muscle. The guards who had been holding him up both dropped him. They were both disgusted. 'How about a chair, Will?' asked one of the guards. 'Better get one,' said a man in a derby hat.

When they all stepped back on the scaffolding back of the drop, which was very heavy, built of oak and steel and swung on ball bearings, Sam Cardinella was left sitting there strapped tight, the younger of the two priests kneeling beside the chair. The priest skipped back onto the scaffolding just before the drop fell.

BIG TWO-HEARTED RIVER
PART II

In the morning the sun was up and the tent was starting to get hot. Nick crawled out under the mosquito netting stretched across the mouth of the tent, to look at the morning. The grass was wet on his hands as he came out. He held his trousers and his shoes in his hands. The sun was just up over the hill. There was the meadow, the river and the swamp. There were birch trees in the green of the swamp on the other side of the river.

The river was clear and smoothly fast in the early morning. Down about two hundred yards were three logs all the way across the stream. They made the water smooth and deep above them. As Nick watched, a mink crossed the river on the logs and went into the swamp. Nick was excited. He was excited by the early morning and the river. He was really too hurried to eat breakfast, but he knew he must. He built a little fire and put on the coffee pot.

While the water was heating in the pot he took an empty bottle and went down over the edge of the high ground to the meadow. The meadow was wet with dew and Nick wanted to catch grasshoppers for bait before the sun dried the grass. He found plenty of good grasshoppers. They were at the base of the grass stems. Sometimes they clung to a grass stem. They were cold and wet with the dew, and could not jump until the sun warmed them. Nick picked them up, taking only the medium-sized brown ones, and put them into the bottle. He turned over a log and just under the shelter of the edge were several hundred hoppers. It was a grasshopper lodging house. Nick put about fifty of the medium browns into the bottle. While he was picking up the hoppers the others warmed in the sun and commenced to hop away. They flew when they hopped. At first they made one flight and stayed stiff when they landed, as though they were dead.

Nick knew that by the time he was through with breakfast they would be as lively as ever. Without dew in the grass it would take him all day to catch a bottle full of good grasshoppers and he would have to crush many of them, slamming at them with his hat. He washed his hands at the stream. He was excited to be near it. Then he walked up to the tent. The hoppers were already jumping stiffly in the grass. In the bottle, warmed by the sun, they were jumping in a mass. Nick put in a pine stick as a cork. It plugged the mouth of the bottle enough, so the hoppers could not get out and left plenty of air passage.

He had rolled the log back and knew he could get grasshoppers there every morning.

Nick laid the bottle full of jumping grasshoppers against a pine trunk. Rapidly he mixed some buckwheat flour with water and stirred it smooth, one cup of flour, one cup of water. He put a handful of coffee in the pot and dipped a lump of grease out of a can and slid it sputtering across the hot skillet. On the smoking skillet he poured smoothly the buckwheat batter. It spread like lava, the grease spitting sharply. Around the edges the buckwheat cake began to firm, then brown, then crisp. The surface was bubbling slowly to porousness. Nick pushed under the browned under surface with a fresh pine chip. He shook the skillet sideways and the cake was loose on the surface. I won't try and flop it, he thought. He slid the chip of clean wood all the way under the cake, and flopped it over onto its face. It sputtered in the pan.

When it was cooked Nick regreased the skillet. He used all the batter. It made another big flapjack and one smaller one.

Nick ate a big flapjack and a smaller one, covered with apple butter. He put apple butter on the third cake, folded it over twice, wrapped it in oiled paper and put it in his shirt pocket. He put the apple butter jar back in the pack and cut bread for two sandwiches.

In the pack he found a big onion. He sliced it in two and peeled the silky outer skin. Then he cut one half into slices and made onion sandwiches. He wrapped them in oiled paper and buttoned them in the other pocket of his khaki shirt. He turned the skillet upside down on the grill, drank the coffee, sweetened and yellow brown with the condensed milk in it, and tidied up the camp. It was a good camp.

Nick took his fly rod out of the leather rod-case, jointed it, and shoved the rod-case back into the tent. He put on the reel and threaded the line through the guides. He had to hold it from hand to hand, as he threaded it, or it would slip back through its own weight. It was a heavy, double tapered fly line. Nick had paid eight dollars for it a long time ago. It was made heavy to lift back in the air and come forward flat and heavy and straight to make it possible to cast a fly which has no weight. Nick opened the aluminum leader box. The leaders were coiled between the damp flannel pads. Nick had wet the pads at the water cooler on the train up to St. Ignace. In the damp pads the gut leaders had softened and Nick unrolled one and tied it by a loop at the end to the heavy fly line. He fastened a hook on the end of the leader. It was a small hook; very thin and springy.

Nick took it from his hook book, sitting with the rod across his lap. He tested the knot and the spring of the rod by pulling the line taut. It was a good feeling. He was careful not to let the hook bite into his finger.

He started down to the stream, holding his rod, the bottle of grasshoppers hung from his neck by a thong tied in half hitches around the neck of the bottle. His landing net hung by a hook from his belt. Over his shoulder was a long flour sack tied at each corner into an ear. The cord went over his shoulder. The sack flapped against his legs.

Nick felt awkward and professionally happy with all his equipment hanging from him. The grasshopper bottle swung against his chest. In his shirt the breast pockets bulged against him with the lunch and his fly book.

He stepped into the stream. It was a shock. His trousers clung tight to his legs. His shoes felt the gravel. The water was a rising cold shock.

Rushing, the current sucked against his legs. Where he stepped in, the water was over his knees. He waded with the current. The gravel slid under his shoes. He looked down at the swirl of water below each leg and tipped up the bottle to get a grasshopper.

The first grasshopper gave a jump in the neck of the bottle and went out into the water. He was sucked under in the whirl by Nick's right leg and came to the surface a little way down stream. He floated rapidly, kicking. In a quick circle, breaking the smooth surface of the water, he disappeared. A trout had taken him.

Another hopper poked his face out of the bottle. His antennæ wavered. He was getting his front legs out of the bottle to jump. Nick took him by the head and held him while he threaded the slim hook under his chin, down through his thorax and into the last segments of his abdomen. The grasshopper took hold of the hook with his front feet, spitting tobacco juice on it. Nick dropped him into the water.

Holding the rod in his right hand he let out line against the

pull of the grasshopper in the current. He stripped off line from
the reel with his left hand and let it run free. He could see the
hopper in the little waves of the current. It went out of sight.

There was a tug on the line. Nick pulled against the taut line.
It was his first strike. Holding the now living rod across the current, he brought in the line with his left hand. The rod bent in
jerks, the trout pumping against the current. Nick knew it was
a small one. He lifted the rod straight up in the air. It bowed
with the pull.

He saw the trout in the water jerking with his head and body
against the shifting tangent of the line in the stream.

Nick took the line in his left hand and pulled the trout,
thumping tiredly against the current, to the surface. His back
was mottled the clear, water-over-gravel color, his side flashing
in the sun. The rod under his right arm, Nick stooped, dipping
his right hand into the current. He held the trout, never still,
with his moist right hand, while he unhooked the barb from his
mouth, then dropped him back into the stream.

He hung unsteadily in the current, then settled to the bottom
beside a stone. Nick reached down his hand to touch him, his
arm to the elbow under water. The trout was steady in the moving stream, resting on the gravel, beside a stone. As Nick's
fingers touched him, touched his smooth, cool, underwater feeling he was gone, gone in a shadow across the bottom of the
stream.

He's all right, Nick thought. He was only tired.

He had wet his hand before he touched the trout, so he would
not disturb the delicate mucus that covered him. If a trout was
touched with a dry hand, a white fungus attacked the unprotected spot. Years before when he had fished crowded streams,
with fly fishermen ahead of him and behind him, Nick had again
and again come on dead trout, furry with white fungus, drifted
against a rock, or floating belly up in some pool. Nick did not
like to fish with other men on the river. Unless they were of
your party, they spoiled it.

He wallowed down the stream, above his knees in the current,
through the fifty yards of shallow water above the pile of logs
that crossed the stream. He did not rebait his hook and held it in
his hand as he waded. He was certain he could catch small trout
in the shallows, but he did not want them. There would be no
big trout in the shallows this time of day.

Now the water deepened up his thighs sharply and coldly.

Ahead was the smooth dammed-back flood of water above the logs. The water was smooth and dark; on the left, the lower edge of the meadow; on the right the swamp.

Nick leaned back against the current and took a hopper from the bottle. He threaded the hopper on the hook and spat on him for good luck. Then he pulled several yards of line from the reel and tossed the hopper out ahead onto the fast, dark water. It floated down towards the logs, then the weight of the line pulled the bait under the surface. Nick held the rod in his right hand, letting the line run out through his fingers.

There was a long tug. Nick struck and the rod came alive and dangerous, bent double, the line tightening, coming out of water, tightening, all in a heavy, dangerous, steady pull. Nick felt the moment when the leader would break if the strain increased and let the line go.

The reel ratcheted into a mechanical shriek as the line went out in a rush. Too fast. Nick could not check it, the line rushing out, the reel note rising as the line ran out.

With the core of the reel showing, his heart feeling stopped with the excitement, leaning back against the current that mounted icily his thighs, Nick thumbed the reel hard with his left hand. It was awkward getting his thumb inside the fly reel frame.

As he put on pressure the line tightened into sudden hardness and beyond the logs a huge trout went high out of water. As he jumped, Nick lowered the tip of the rod. But he felt, as he dropped the tip to ease the strain, the moment when the strain was too great; the hardness too tight. Of course, the leader had broken. There was no mistaking the feeling when all spring left the line and it became dry and hard. Then it went slack.

His mouth dry, his heart down, Nick reeled in. He had never seen so big a trout. There was a heaviness, a power not to be held, and then the bulk of him, as he jumped. He looked as broad as a salmon.

Nick's hand was shaky. He reeled in slowly. The thrill had been too much. He felt, vaguely, a little sick, as though it would be better to sit down.

The leader had broken where the hook was tied to it. Nick took it in his hand. He thought of the trout somewhere on the bottom, holding himself steady over the gravel, far down below the light, under the logs, with the hook in his jaw. Nick knew the trout's teeth would cut through the snell of the hook. The hook would imbed itself in his jaw. He'd bet the trout was angry. Anything that size would be angry. That was a trout. He had been solidly hooked. Solid as a rock. He felt like a rock, too, before he started off. By God, he was a big one. By God, he was the biggest one I ever heard of.

Nick climbed out onto the meadow and stood, water running down his trousers and out of his shoes, his shoes squelchy. He went over and sat on the logs. He did not want to rush his sensations any.

He wriggled his toes in the water, in his shoes, and got out a cigarette from his breast pocket. He lit it and tossed the match into the fast water below the logs. A tiny trout rose at the match, as it swung around in the fast current. Nick laughed. He would finish the cigarette.

He sat on the logs, smoking, drying in the sun, the sun warm on his back, the river shallow ahead entering the woods, curving into the woods, shallows, light glittering, big water-smooth rocks, cedars along the bank and white birches, the logs warm in the sun, smooth to sit on, without bark, gray to the touch; slowly the feeling of disappointment left him. It went away slowly, the feeling of disappointment that came sharply after the thrill that made his shoulders ache. It was all right now. His rod lying out on the logs, Nick tied a new hook on the leader, pulling the gut tight until it grimped into itself in a hard knot.

He baited up, then picked up the rod and walked to the far end of the logs to get into the water, where it was not too deep. Under and beyond the logs was a deep pool. Nick walked around the shallow shelf near the swamp shore until he came out on the shallow bed of the stream.

On the left, where the meadow ended and the woods began, a great elm tree was uprooted. Gone over in a storm, it lay back into the woods, its roots clotted with dirt, grass growing in them, rising a solid bank beside the stream. The river cut to the edge of the uprooted tree. From where Nick stood he could see deep channels, like ruts, cut in the shallow bed of the stream by the flow of the current. Pebbly where he stood and pebbly and full of boulders beyond; where it curved near the tree roots, the bed of the stream was marly and between the ruts of deep water green weed fronds swung in the current.

Nick swung the rod back over his shoulder and forward, and the line, curving forward, laid the grasshopper down on one of the deep channels in the weeds. A trout struck and Nick hooked him.

Holding the rod far out toward the uprooted tree and sloshing backward in the current, Nick worked the trout, plunging, the rod bending alive, out of the danger of the weeds into the open river. Holding the rod, pumping alive against the current, Nick brought the trout in. He rushed, but always came, the spring of the rod yielding to the rushes, sometimes jerking under water, but always bringing him in. Nick eased downstream with the rushes. The rod above his head he led the trout over the net, then lifted.

The trout hung heavy in the net, mottled trout back and silver sides in the meshes. Nick unhooked him; heavy sides, good to hold, big undershot jaw, and slipped him, heaving and big sliding, into the long sack that hung from his shoulders in the water.

Nick spread the mouth of the sack against the current and it filled, heavy with water. He held it up, the bottom in the stream, and the water poured out through the sides. Inside at the bottom was the big trout, alive in the water.

Nick moved downstream. The sack out ahead of him sunk heavy in the water, pulling from his shoulders.

It was getting hot, the sun hot on the back of his neck.

Nick had one good trout. He did not care about getting many trout. Now the stream was shallow and wide. There were trees along both banks. The trees of the left bank made short shadows on the current in the forenoon sun. Nick knew there were trout in each shadow. In the afternoon, after the sun had crossed toward the hills, the trout would be in the cool shadows on the other side of the stream.

The very biggest ones would lie up close to the bank. You could always pick them up there on the Black. When the sun was down they all moved out into the current. Just when the sun made the water blinding in the glare before it went down, you were liable to strike a big trout anywhere in the current. It was almost impossible to fish then, the surface of the water was blinding as a mirror in the sun. Of course, you could fish upstream, but in a stream like the Black, or this, you had to wallow against the current and in a deep place, the water piled up on you. It was no fun to fish upstream with this much current.

Nick moved along through the shallow stretch watching the banks for deep holes. A beech tree grew close beside the river, so that the branches hung down into the water. The stream went back in under the leaves. There were always trout in a place like that.

Nick did not care about fishing that hole. He was sure he would get hooked in the branches.

It looked deep though. He dropped the grasshopper so the current took it under water, back in under the overhanging branch. The line pulled hard and Nick struck. The trout threshed heavily, half out of water in the leaves and branches. The line was caught. Nick pulled hard and the trout was off. He reeled in and holding the hook in his hand, walked down the stream.

Ahead, close to the left bank, was a big log. Nick saw it was hollow; pointing up river the current entered it smoothly, only a little ripple spread each side of the log. The water was deepening. The top of the hollow log was gray and dry. It was partly in the shadow.

Nick took the cork out of the grasshopper bottle and a hopper clung to it. He picked him off, hooked him and tossed him out. He held the rod far out so that the hopper on the water moved into the current flowing into the hollow log. Nick lowered the rod and the hopper floated in. There was a heavy strike. Nick swung the rod against the pull. It felt as though he were hooked into the log itself, except for the live feeling.

He tried to force the fish out into the current. It came, heavily.

The line went slack and Nick thought the trout was gone. Then he saw him, very near, in the current, shaking his head, trying to get the hook out. His mouth was clamped shut. He was fighting the hook in the clear flowing current.

Looping in the line with his left hand, Nick swung the rod to make the line taut and tried to lead the trout toward the net, but he was gone, out of sight, the line pumping. Nick fought him against the current, letting him thump in the water against the spring of the rod. He shifted the rod to his left hand, worked the trout upstream, holding his weight, fighting on the rod, and then let him down into the net. He lifted him clear of the water, a heavy half circle in the net, the net dripping, unhooked him and slid him into the sack.

He spread the mouth of the sack and looked down in at the two big trout alive in the water.

Through the deepening water, Nick waded over to the hollow log. He took the sack off, over his head, the trout flopping as it came out of water, and hung it so the trout were deep in the

water. Then he pulled himself up on the log and sat, the water
from his trousers and boots running down into the stream. He
laid his rod down, moved along to the shady end of the log and
took the sandwiches out of his pocket. He dipped the sandwiches in the cold water. The current carried away the crumbs.
He ate the sandwiches and dipped his hat full of water to drink,
the water running out through his hat just ahead of his drinking.

It was cool in the shade, sitting on the log. He took a cigarette
out and struck a match to light it. The match sunk into the gray
wood, making a tiny furrow. Nick leaned over the side of the
log, found a hard place and lit the match. He sat smoking and
watching the river.

Ahead the river narrowed and went into a swamp. The river
became smooth and deep and the swamp looked solid with cedar
trees, their trunks close together, their branches solid. It would
not be possible to walk through a swamp like that. The branches
grew so low. You would have to keep almost level with the
ground to move at all. You could not crash through the
branches. That must be why the animals that lived in swamps
were built the way they were, Nick thought.

He wished he had brought something to read. He felt like
reading. He did not feel like going on into the swamp. He
looked down the river. A big cedar slanted all the way across the
stream. Beyond that the river went into the swamp.

Nick did not want to go in there now. He felt a reaction
against deep wading with the water deepening up under his
armpits, to hook big trout in places impossible to land them. In
the swamp the banks were bare, the big cedars came together
overhead, the sun did not come through, except in patches; in
the fast deep water, in the half light, the fishing would be tragic.
In the swamp fishing was a tragic adventure. Nick did not want
it. He did not want to go down the stream any further today.

He took out his knife, opened it and stuck it in the log. Then
he pulled up the sack, reached into it and brought out one of the
trout. Holding him near the tail, hard to hold, alive, in his hand,
he whacked him against the log. The trout quivered, rigid. Nick
laid him on the log in the shade and broke the neck of the other
fish the same way. He laid them side by side on the log. They
were fine trout.

Nick cleaned them, slitting them from the vent to the tip of
the jaw. All the insides and the gills and tongue came out in one
piece. They were both males; long gray-white strips of milt,

smooth and clean. All the insides clean and compact, coming out all together. Nick tossed the offal ashore for the minks to find.

He washed the trout in the stream. When he held them back up in the water they looked like live fish. Their color was not gone yet. He washed his hands and dried them on the log. Then he laid the trout on the sack spread out on the log, rolled them up in it, tied the bundle and put it in the landing net. His knife was still standing, blade stuck in the log. He cleaned it on the wood and put it in his pocket.

Nick stood up on the log, holding his rod, the landing net hanging heavy, then stepped into the water and splashed ashore. He climbed the bank and cut up into the woods, toward the high ground. He was going back to camp. He looked back. The river just showed through the trees. There were plenty of days coming when he could fish the swamp.

L'ENVOI

The king was working in the garden. He seemed very glad to see me.
We walked through the garden. This is the queen, he said. She was
clipping a rose bush. Oh how do you do, she said. We sat down at a
table under a big tree and the king ordered whiskey and soda. We have
good whiskey anyway, he said. The revolutionary committee, he told
me, would not allow him to go outside the palace grounds. Plastiras is a
very good man I believe, he said, but frightfully difficult. I think he did
right though shooting those chaps. If Kerensky had shot a few men
things might have been altogether different. Of course the great thing in
this sort of an affair is not to be shot oneself!

It was very jolly. We talked for a long time. Like all Greeks he
wanted to go to America.

MEN WITHOUT WOMEN

to EVAN SHIPMAN

THE UNDEFEATED

Manuel Garcia climbed the stairs to Don Miguel Retana's office. He set down his suitcase and knocked on the door. There was no answer. Manuel, standing in the hallway, felt there was someone in the room. He felt it through the door.

'Retana,' he said, listening.

There was no answer.

He's there, all right, Manuel thought.

'Retana,' he said and banged the door.

'Who's there?' said someone in the office.

'Me, Manolo,' Manuel said.

'What do you want?' asked the voice.

'I want to work,' Manuel said.

Something in the door clicked several times and it swung open. Manuel went in, carrying his suitcase.

A little man sat behind a desk at the far side of the room. Over his head was a bull's head, stuffed by a Madrid taxidermist; on the walls were framed photographs and bull-fight posters.

The little man sat looking at Manuel.

'I thought they'd killed you,' he said.

Manuel knocked with his knuckles on the desk. The little man sat looking at him across the desk.

'How many corridas you had this year?' Retana asked.

'One,' he answered.

'Just that one?' the little man asked.

'That's all.'

'I read about it in the papers,' Retana said. He leaned back in the chair and looked at Manuel.

Manuel looked up at the stuffed bull. He had seen it often before. He felt a certain family interest in it. It had killed his brother, the promising one, about nine years ago. Manuel remembered the day. There was a brass plate on the oak shield the bull's head was mounted on. Manuel could not read it, but he imagined it was in memory of his brother. Well, he had been a good kid.

The plate said: 'The Bull "Mariposa" of the Duke of Veragua, which accepted 9 varas for 7 caballos, and caused the death of Antonio Garcia, Novillero, April 27, 1909.'

Retana saw him looking at the stuffed bull's head.

'The lot the Duke sent me for Sunday will make a scandal,' he said. 'They're all bad in the legs. What do they say about them at the Café?'

'I don't know,' Manuel said. 'I just got in.'

'Yes,' Retana said. 'You still have your bag.'

He looked at Manuel, leaning back behind the big desk.

'Sit down,' he said. 'Take off your cap.'

Manuel sat down; his cap off, his face was changed. He looked pale, and his *coleta* pinned forward on his head, so that it would not show under the cap, gave him a strange look.

'You don't look well,' Retana said.

'I just got out of the hospital,' Manuel said.

'I heard they'd cut your leg off,' Retana said.

'No,' said Manuel. 'It got all right.'

Retana leaned forward across the desk and pushed a wooden box of cigarettes toward Manuel.

'Have a cigarette,' he said.

'Thanks.'

Manuel lit it.

'Smoke?' he said, offering the match to Retana.

'No,' Retana waved his hand, 'I never smoke.'

Retana watched him smoking.

'Why don't you get a job and go to work?' he said.

'I don't want to work,' Manuel said. 'I am a bullfighter.'

'There aren't any bullfighters any more,' Retana said.

'I'm a bullfighter,' Manuel said.

'Yes, while you're in there,' Retana said.

Manuel laughed.

Retana sat, saying nothing and looking at Manuel.

'I'll put you in a nocturnal if you want,' Retana offered.

'When?' Manuel asked.

'Tomorrow night.'

'I don't like to substitute for anybody,' Manuel said. That was the way they all got killed. That was the way Salvador got killed. He tapped with his knuckles on the table.

'It's all I've got,' Retana said.

'Why don't you put me on next week?' Manuel suggested.

'You wouldn't draw,' Retana said. 'All they want is Litri and Rubito and La Torre. Those kids are good.'

'They'd come to see me get it,' Manuel said, hopefully.

'No, they wouldn't. They don't know who you are any more.'

'I've got a lot of stuff,' Manuel said.

'I'm offering to put you on tomorrow night,' Retana said. 'You can work with young Hernandez and kill two *novillos* after the Charlots.'

'Whose *novillos*?' Manuel asked.

'I don't know. Whatever stuff they've got in the corrals. What the veterinaries won't pass in the daytime.'

'I don't like to substitute,' Manuel said.

'You can take it or leave it,' Retana said. He leaned forward over the papers. He was no longer interested. The appeal that Manuel had made to him for a moment when he thought of the old days was gone. He would like to get him to substitute for Larita because he could get him cheaply. He could get others cheaply too. He would like to help him though. Still he had given him the chance. It was up to him.

'How much do I get?' Manuel asked. He was still playing with the idea of refusing. But he knew he could not refuse.

'Two hundred and fifty pesetas,' Retana said. He had thought of five hundred, but when he opened his mouth it said two hundred and fifty.

'You pay Villalta seven thousand,' Manuel said.

'You're not Villalta,' Retana said.

'I know it,' Manuel said.

'He draws it, Manolo,' Retana said in explanation.

'Sure,' said Manuel. He stood up. 'Give me three hundred, Retana.'

'All right,' Retana agreed. He reached in the drawer for a paper.

'Can I have fifty now?' Manuel asked.

'Sure,' said Retana. He took a fifty-peseta note out of his pocket-book and laid it, spread out flat, on the table.

Manuel picked it up and put it in his pocket.

'What about a *cuadrilla*?' he asked.

'There's the boys that always work for me nights,' Retana said. 'They're all right.'

'How about picadors?' Manuel asked.

'They're not much,' Retana admitted.

'I've got to have one good pic,' Manuel said.

'Get him then,' Retana said. 'Go and get him.'

'Not out of this,' Manuel said. 'I'm not paying for any *cuadrilla* out of sixty duros.'

Retana said nothing but looked at Manuel across the big desk.

'You know I've got to have one good pic,' Manuel said.

Retana said nothing but looked at Manuel from a long way off.

'It isn't right,' Manuel said.

Retana was still considering him, leaning back in his chair, considering him from a long way away.

'There're the regular pics,' he offered.

'I know,' Manuel said. 'I know your regular pics.'

Retana did not smile. Manuel knew it was over.

'All I want is an even break,' Manuel said reasonably. 'When I go out there I want to be able to call my shots on the bull. It only takes one good picador.'

He was talking to a man who was no longer listening.

'If you want something extra,' Retana said, 'go and get it. There will be a regular *cuadrilla* out there. Bring as many of your own pics as you want. The *charlotada* is over by 10.30.'

'All right,' Manuel said. 'If that's the way you feel about it.'

'That's the way,' Retana said.

'I'll see you tomorrow night,' Manuel said.

'I'll be out there,' Retana said.

Manuel picked up his suitcase and went out.

'Shut the door,' Retana called.

Manuel looked back. Retana was sitting forward looking at some papers. Manuel pulled the door tight until it clicked.

He went down the stairs and out of the door into the hot brightness of the street. It was very hot in the street and the light on the white buildings was sudden and hard on his eyes. He walked down the shady side of the steep street toward the Puerta del Sol. The shade felt solid and cool as running water. The heat came suddenly as he crossed the intersecting streets. Manuel saw no one he knew in all the people he passed.

Just before the Puerta del Sol he turned into a café.

It was quiet in the café. There were a few men sitting at tables against the wall. At one table four men played cards. Most of the men sat against the wall smoking, empty coffee-cups and liqueur-glasses before them on the tables. Manuel went through the long room to a small room in back. A man sat at a table in the corner asleep. Manuel sat down at one of the tables.

A waiter came in and stood beside Manuel's table.

'Have you seen Zurito?' Manuel asked him.

'He was in before lunch,' the waiter answered. 'He won't be back before five o'clock.'

'Bring me some coffee and milk and a shot of the ordinary,' Manuel said.

The waiter came back into the room carrying a tray with a big coffee-glass and a liqueur-glass on it. In his left hand he held a bottle of brandy. He swung these down to the table and a boy who had followed him poured coffee and milk into the glass from two shiny, spouted pots with long handles.

Manuel took off his cap and the waiter noticed his pigtail pinned forward on his head. He winked at the coffee-boy as he poured out the brandy into the little glass beside Manuel's coffee. The coffee-boy looked at Manuel's pale face curiously.

'You fighting here?' asked the waiter, corking up the bottle.

'Yes,' Manuel said. 'Tomorrow.'

The waiter stood there, holding the bottle on one hip.

'You in the Charlie Chaplins?' he asked.

The coffee-boy looked away, embarrassed.

'No. In the ordinary.'

'I thought they were going to have Chaves and Hernandez,' the waiter said.

'No. Me and another.'

'Who? Chaves or Hernandez?'

'Hernandez, I think.'

'What's the matter with Chaves?'

'He got hurt.'

'Where did you hear that?'

'Retana.'

'Hey, Looie,' the waiter called to the next room, 'Chaves got *cogida*.'

Manuel had taken the wrapper off the lumps of sugar and dropped them into his coffee. He stirred it and drank it down, sweet, hot, and warming in his empty stomach. He drank off the brandy.

'Give me another shot of that,' he said to the waiter.

The waiter uncorked the bottle and poured the glass full, slopping another drink into the saucer. Another waiter had come up in front of the table. The coffee-boy was gone.

'Is Chaves hurt bad?' the second waiter asked Manuel.

'I don't know,' Manuel said, 'Retana didn't say.'

'A hell of a lot he cares,' the tall waiter said. Manuel had not seen him before. He must have just come up.

'If you stand in with Retana in this town, you're a made man,' the tall waiter said. 'If you aren't in with him, you might just as well go out and shoot yourself.'

'You said it,' the other waiter who had come in said. 'You said it then.'

'You're right I said it,' said the tall waiter. 'I know what I'm talking about when I talk about that bird.'

'Look what he's done for Villalta,' the first waiter said.

'And that ain't all,' the tall waiter said. 'Look what he's done for Marcial Lalanda. Look what he's done for Nacional.'

'You said it, kid,' agreed the short waiter.

Manuel looked at them, standing talking in front of his table. He had drunk his second brandy. They had forgotten about him. They were not interested in him.

'Look at that bunch of camels,' the tall waiter went on. 'Did you ever see this Nacional II?'

'I seen him last Sunday, didn't I?' the original waiter said.

'He's a giraffe,' the short waiter said.

'What did I tell you?' the tall waiter said. 'Those are Retana's boys.'

'Say, give me another shot of that,' Manuel said. He had poured the brandy the waiter had slopped over in the saucer into his glass and drank it while they were talking.

The original waiter poured his glass full mechanically, and the three of them went out of the room talking.

In the far corner the man was still asleep, snoring slightly on the intaking breath, his head back against the wall.

Manuel drank his brandy. He felt sleepy himself. It was too hot to go out into the town. Besides there was nothing to do. He wanted to see Zurito. He would go to sleep while he waited. He kicked his suitcase under the table to be sure it was there. Perhaps it would be better to put it back under the seat, against the wall. He leaned down and shoved it under. Then he leaned forward on the table and went to sleep.

When he woke there was someone sitting across the table from him. It was a big man with a heavy brown face like an Indian. He had been sitting there some time. He had waved the waiter away and sat reading the paper and occasionally looking down at Manuel, asleep, his head on the table. He read the paper laboriously, forming the words with his lips as he read. When it tired him he looked at Manuel. He sat heavily in the chair, his black Cordoba hat tipped forward.

Manuel sat up and looked at him.

'Hello, Zurito,' he said.

'Hello, kid,' the big man said.

'I've been asleep.' Manuel rubbed his forehead with the back of his fist.

'I thought maybe you were.'

'How's everything?'

'Good. How is everything with you?'

'Not so good.'

They were both silent. Zurito, the picador, looked at Manuel's white face. Manuel looked down at the picador's enormous hands folding the paper to put away in his pocket.

'I got a favor to ask you, Manos,' Manuel said.

Manosduros was Zurito's nickname. He never heard it without thinking of his huge hands. He put them forward on the table self-consciously.

'Let's have a drink,' he said.

'Sure,' said Manuel.

The waiter came and went and came again. He went out of the room looking back at the two men at the table.

'What's the matter, Manolo?' Zurito set down his glass.

'Would you pic two bulls for me tomorrow night?' Manuel asked, looking up at Zurito across the table.

'No,' said Zurito. 'I'm not pic-ing.'

Manuel looked down at his glass. He had expected that answer; now he had it. Well, he had it.

'I'm sorry, Manolo, but I'm not pic-ing.' Zurito looked at his hands.

'That's all right,' Manuel said.

'I'm too old,' Zurito said.

'I just asked you,' Manuel said.

'Is it the nocturnal tomorrow?'

'That's it. I figured if I had just one good pic, I could get away with it.'

'How much are you getting?'

'Three hundred pesetas.'

'I get more than that for pic-ing.'

'I know,' said Manuel. 'I didn't have any right to ask you.'

'What do you keep on doing it for?' Zurito asked. 'Why don't you cut off your *coleta*, Manolo?'

'I don't know,' Manuel said.

'You're pretty near as old as I am,' Zurito said.

'I don't know,' Manuel said. 'I got to do it. If I can fix it so that I get an even break, that's all I want. I got to stick with it, Manos.'

'No, you don't.'

'Yes, I do. I've tried keeping away from it.'

'I know how you feel. But it isn't right. You ought to get out and stay out.'

'I can't do it. Besides, I've been going good lately.'

Zurito looked at his face.

'You've been in the hospital.'

'But I was going great when I got hurt.'

Zurito said nothing. He tipped the cognac out of his saucer into his glass.

'The papers said they never saw a better *faena*,' Manuel said.

Zurito looked at him.

'You know when I get going I'm good,' Manuel said.

'You're too old,' the picador said.

'No,' said Manuel. 'You're ten years older than I am.'

'With me it's different.'

'I'm not too old,' Manuel said.

They sat silent, Manuel watching the picador's face.

'I was going great till I got hurt,' Manuel offered.

'You ought to have seen me, Manos,' Manuel said, reproachfully.

'I don't want to see you,' Zurito said. 'It makes me nervous.'

'You haven't seen me lately.'

'I've seen you plenty.'

Zurito looked at Manuel, avoiding his eyes.

'You ought to quit it, Manolo.'

'I can't,' Manuel said. 'I'm going good now, I tell you.'

Zurito leaned forward, his hands on the table.

'Listen. I'll pic for you and if you don't go big tomorrow night, you'll quit. See? Will you do that?'

'Sure.'

Zurito leaned back, relieved.

'You got to quit,' he said. 'No monkey business. You got to cut the *coleta*.'

'I won't have to quit,' Manuel said. 'You watch me. I've got the stuff.'

Zurito stood up. He felt tired from arguing.

'You got to quit,' he said. 'I'll cut your *coleta* myself.'

'No, you won't,' Manuel said. 'You won't have a chance.'

Zurito called the waiter.

'Come on,' said Zurito. 'Come on up to the house.'

Manuel reached under the seat for his suitcase. He was happy. He knew Zurito would pic for him. He was the best picador living. It was all simple now.

'Come on up to the house and we'll eat,' Zurito said.

Manuel stood in the *patio de caballos* waiting for the Charlie Chaplins to be over. Zurito stood beside him. Where they stood it was dark. The high door that led into the bull-ring was shut. Above them they heard a shout, then another shout of laughter. Then there was silence. Manuel liked the smell of the stables about the *patio de caballos*. It smelt good in the dark. There was another roar from the arena and then applause, prolonged applause, going on and on.

'You ever seen these fellows?' Zurito asked, big and looming beside Manuel in the dark.

'No,' Manuel said.

'They're pretty funny,' Zurito said. He smiled to himself in the dark.

The high, double, tight-fitting door into the bull-ring swung open and Manuel saw the ring in the hard light of the arc-lights, the plaza, dark all the way around, rising high; around the edge of the ring were running and bowing two men dressed like tramps, followed by a third in the uniform of a hotel bell-boy who stooped and picked up the hats and canes thrown down onto the sand and tossed them back up into the darkness.

The electric light went on in the patio.

'I'll climb onto one of those ponies while you collect the kids,' Zurito said.

Behind them came the jingle of the mules, coming out to go into the arena and be hitched onto the dead bull.

The members of the *cuadrilla*, who had been watching the burlesque from the runway between the *barrera* and the seats, came walking back and stood in a group talking, under the electric light in the patio. A good-looking lad in a silver-and-orange suit came up to Manuel and smiled.

'I'm Hernandez,' he said and put out his hand.

Manuel shook it.

'They're regular elephants we've got tonight,' the boy said cheerfully.

'They're big ones with horns,' Manuel agreed.

'You drew the worst lot,' the boy said.

'That's all right,' Manuel said. 'The bigger they are, the more meat for the poor.'

'Where did you get that one?' Hernandez grinned.

'That's an old one,' Manuel said. 'You line up your *cuadrilla*, so I can see what I've got.'

'You've got some good kids,' Hernandez said. He was very cheerful. He had been on twice before in nocturnals and was beginning to get a following in Madrid. He was happy the fight would start in a few minutes.

'Where are the pics?' Manuel asked.

'They're back in the corrals fighting about who gets the beautiful horses,' Hernandez grinned.

The mules came through the gate in a rush, the whips snapping, bells jangling and the young bull ploughing a furrow of sand.

They formed up for the *paseo* as soon as the bull had gone through.

Manuel and Hernandez stood in front. The youths of the *cuadrillas* were behind, their heavy capes furled over their arms. In back, the four picadors, mounted, holding their steel-tipped push-poles erect in the half-dark of the corral.

'It's a wonder Retana wouldn't give us enough light to see the horses by,' one picador said.

'He knows we'll be happier if we don't get too good a look at these skins,' another pic answered.

'This thing I'm on barely keeps me off the ground,' the first picador said.

'Well, they're horses.'

'Sure, they're horses.'

They talked, sitting their gaunt horses in the dark.

Zurito said nothing. He had the only steady horse of the lot. He had tried him, wheeling him in the corrals and he responded to the bit and the spurs. He had taken the bandage off his right eye and cut the strings where they had tied his ears tight shut at the base. He was a good, solid horse, solid on his legs. That was all he needed. He intended to ride him all through the *corrida*. He had already, since he had mounted, sitting in the half-dark in the big, quilted saddle, waiting for the *paseo*, pic-ed through the whole *corrida* in his mind. The other picadors went on talking on both sides of him. He did not hear them.

The two matadors stood together in front of their three *peones*, their capes furled over their left arms in the same fashion. Manuel was thinking about the three lads in back of him. They were all three Madrileños, like Hernandez, boys about nineteen. One of them, a gypsy, serious, aloof, and dark-faced, he liked the look of. He turned.

'What's your name, kid?' he asked the gypsy.

'Fuentes,' the gypsy said.

'That's a good name,' Manuel said.

The gypsy smiled, showing his teeth.

'You take the bull and give him a little run when he comes out,' Manuel said.

'All right,' the gypsy said. His face was serious. He began to think about just what he would do.

'Here she goes,' Manuel said to Hernandez.

'All right. We'll go.'

Heads up, swinging with the music, their right arms swinging free, they stepped out, crossing the sanded arena under the arc-lights, the *cuadrillas* opening out behind, the picadors riding after, behind came the bull-ring servants and the jingling mules. The crowd applauded Hernandez as they marched across the arena. Arrogant, swinging, they looked straight ahead as they marched.

They bowed before the president, and the procession broke up into its component parts. The bull-fighters went over to the *barrera* and changed their heavy mantles for the light fighting capes. The mules went out. The picadors galloped jerkily around the ring, and two rode out the gate they had come in by. The servants swept the sand smooth.

Manuel drank a glass of water poured for him by one of Retana's deputies, who was acting as his manager and sword-handler. Hernandez came over from speaking with his own manager.

'You got a good hand, kid,' Manuel complimented him.

'They like me,' Hernandez said happily.

'How did the *paseo* go?' Manuel asked Retana's man.

'Like a wedding,' said the handler. 'Fine. You came out like Joselito and Belmonte.'

Zurito rode by, a bulky equestrian statue. He wheeled his horse and faced him toward the *toril* on the far side of the ring where the bull would come out. It was strange under the arc-light. He pic-ed in the hot afternoon sun for big money. He didn't like this arc-light business. He wished they would get started.

Manuel went up to him.

'Pic him, Manos,' he said. 'Cut him down to size for me.'

'I'll pic him, kid,' Zurito spat on the sand. 'I'll make him jump out of the ring.'

'Lean on him, Manos,' Manuel said.

'I'll lean on him,' Zurito said. 'What's holding it up?'

'He's coming now,' Manuel said.

Zurito sat there, his feet in the box-stirrups, his great legs in the buckskin-covered armor gripping the horse, the reins in his left hand, the long pic held in his right hand, his broad hat well down over his eyes to shade them from the lights, watching the distant door of the *toril*. His horse's ears quivered. Zurito patted him with his left hand.

The red door of the *toril* swung back and for a moment Zurito looked into the empty passageway far across the arena. Then the bull came out in a rush, skidding on his four legs as he came out under the lights, then charging in a gallop, moving softly in a fast gallop, silent except as he woofed through wide nostrils as he charged, glad to be free after the dark pen.

In the first row of seats, slightly bored, leaning forward to write on the cement wall in front of his knees, the substitute bull-fight critic of *El Heraldo* scribbled: 'Campagnero, Negro, 42, came out at 90 miles an hour with plenty of gas –'

Manuel, leaning against the *barrera*, watching the bull, waved his hand and the gypsy ran out, trailing his cape. The bull, in full gallop, pivoted and charged the cape, his head down, his tail rising. The gypsy moved in a zigzag, and as he passed, the bull caught sight of him and abandoned the cape to charge the man. The gyp sprinted and vaulted the red fence of the *barrera* as the bull struck it with his horns. He tossed into it twice with his horns, banging into the wood blindly.

The critic of *El Heraldo* lit a cigarette and tossed the match at the bull, then wrote in his note-book, 'large and with enough horns to satisfy the cash customers, Campagnero showed a tendency to cut into the terrain of the bull-fighters.'

Manuel stepped out on the hard sand as the bull banged into the fence. Out of the corner of his eye he saw Zurito sitting the white horse close to the *barrera*, about a quarter of the way around the ring to the left. Manuel held the cape close in front of him, a fold in each hand, and shouted at the bull. 'Huh! Huh!' The bull turned, seemed to brace against the fence as he charged in a scramble, driving into the cape as Manuel side-stepped, pivoted on his heels with the charge of the bull, and swung the cape just ahead of the horns. At the end of the swing he was facing the bull again and held the cape in the same position close in front of his body, and pivoted again as the bull recharged. Each time, as he swung, the crowd shouted.

Four times he swung with the bull, lifting the cape so it billowed full, and each time bringing the bull around to charge again. Then, at the end of the fifth swing, he held the cape against his hip and pivoted, so the cape swung out like a ballet dancer's skirt and wound the bull around himself like a belt, to step clear, leaving the bull facing Zurito on the white horse, come up and planted firm, the horse facing the bull, its ears forward, its lips nervous, Zurito, his hat over his eyes, leaning forward, the long pole sticking out before and behind in a sharp angle under his right arm, held half-way down, the triangular iron point facing the bull.

El Heraldo's second-string critic, drawing on his cigarette, his eyes on the bull, wrote: 'The veteran Manolo designed a series of acceptable *verónicas*, ending in a very Belmontistic *recorte* that earned applause from the regulars, and we entered the *tercio* of the cavalry.'

Zurito sat his horse, measuring the distance between the bull and the end of the pic. As he looked, the bull gathered himself together and charged, his eyes on the horse's chest. As he lowered his head to hook, Zurito sunk the point of the pic in the swelling hump of muscle above the bull's shoulder, leaned all his weight on the shaft, and with his left hand pulled the white horse into the air, front hoofs pawing, and swung him to the right as he pushed the bull under and through so the horns passed safely under the horse's belly and the horse came down, quivering, the bull's tail brushing his chest as he charged the cape Hernandez offered him.

Hernandez ran sideways, taking the bull out and away with the cape, toward the other picador. He fixed him with a swing of the cape, squarely facing the horse and rider, and stepped back. As the bull saw the horse he charged. The picador's lance slid along his back, and as the shock of the charge lifted the horse, the picador was already half-way out of the saddle, lifting his right leg clear as he missed with the lance and falling to the left side to keep the horse between him and the bull. The horse, lifted and gored, crashed over with the bull driving into him, the picador gave a shove with his boots against the horse and lay clear, waiting to be lifted and hauled away and put on his feet.

Manuel let the bull drive into the fallen horse; he was in no hurry, the picador was safe; besides, it did a picador like that good to worry. He'd stay on longer next time. Lousy pics! He looked across the sand at Zurito a little way out from the *barrera*, his horse rigid, waiting.

'Huh!' he called to the bull, '*Tomar!*' holding the cape in both hands so it would catch his eye. The bull detached himself from the horse and charged the cape, and Manuel, running sideways and holding the cape spread wide, stopped, swung on his heels, and brought the bull sharply around facing Zurito.

'Campagnero accepted a pair of *varas* for the death of one *rosinante*, with Hernandez and Manolo at the *quites*,' *El Heraldo*'s critic wrote. 'He pressed on the iron and clearly showed he was no horse-lover. The veteran Zurito resurrected some of his old stuff with the pike-pole, notably the *suerte* –'

'*Olé! Olé!*' the man sitting beside him shouted. The shout was lost in the roar of the crowd, and he slapped the critic on the back. The critic looked up to see Zurito, directly below him, leaning far out over his horse, the length of the pic rising in a sharp angle under his armpit, holding the pic almost by the point, bearing down with all his weight, holding the bull off, the bull pushing and driving to get at the horse, and Zurito, far out, on top of him, holding him, holding him, and slowly pivoting the horse against the pressure, so that at last he was clear. Zurito felt the moment when the horse was clear and the bull could come past, and relaxed the absolute steel lock of his resistance, and the triangular steel point of the pic ripped in the bull's hump of shoulder muscle as he tore loose to find Hernandez's cape before his muzzle. He charged blindly into the cape and the boy took him out into the open arena.

Zurito sat patting his horse and looking at the bull charging the cape that Hernandez swung for him out under the bright light while the crowd shouted.

'You see that one?' he said to Manuel.

'It was a wonder,' Manuel said.

'I got him that time,' Zurito said. 'Look at him now.'

At the conclusion of a closely turned pass of the cape the bull slid to his knees. He was up at once, but far out across the sand Manuel and Zurito saw the shine of the pumping flow of blood, smooth against the black of the bull's shoulder.

'I got him that time,' Zurito said.

'He's a good bull,' Manuel said.

'If they gave me another shot at him, I'd kill him,' Zurito said.

'They'll change the thirds on us,' Manuel said.

'Look at him now,' Zurito said.

'I got to go over there,' Manuel said, and started on a run for the other side of the ring, where the *monos* were leading a horse

out by the bridle toward the bull, whacking him on the legs with
rods and all, in a procession, trying to get him toward the bull,
who stood, dropping his head, pawing, unable to make up his
mind to charge.

Zurito, sitting his horse, walking him toward the scene, not
missing any detail, scowled.

Finally the bull charged, the horse leaders ran for the *barrera*,
the picador hit too far back, and the bull got under the horse,
lifted him, threw him onto his back.

Zurito watched. The *monos*, in their red shirts, running out to
drag the picador clear. The picador, now on his feet, swearing
and flopping his arms. Manuel and Hernandez standing ready
with their capes. And the bull, the great, black bull, with a horse
on his back, hooves dangling, the bridle caught in the horns.
Black bull with a horse on his back, staggering short-legged,
then arching his neck and lifting, thrusting, charging to slide the
horse off, horse sliding down. Then the bull into a lunging
charge at the cape Manuel spread for him.

The bull was slower now, Manuel felt. He was bleeding badly.
There was a sheen of blood all down his flank.

Manuel offered him the cape again. There he came, eyes
open, ugly, watching the cape. Manuel stepped to the side and
raised his arms, tightening the cape ahead of the bull for the
verónica.

Now he was facing the bull. Yes, his head was going down a
little. He was carrying it lower. That was Zurito.

Manuel flopped the cape; there he comes; he side-stepped and
swung in another *verónica*. He's shooting awfully accurately, he
thought. He's had enough fight, so he's watching now. He's
hunting now. Got his eye on me. But I always give him the cape.

He shook the cape at the bull; there he comes; he side-
stepped. Awful close that time. I don't want to work that close
to him.

The edge of the cape was wet with blood where it had swept
along the bull's back as he went by.

All right, here's the last one.

Manuel, facing the bull, having turned with him each charge,
offered the cape with his two hands. The bull looked at him.
Eyes watching, horns straight forward, the bull looked at
him, watching.

'Huh!' Manuel said, '*Toro!*' and leaning back, swung the cape
forward. Here he comes. He side-stepped, swung the cape in

back of him, and pivoted, so the bull followed a swirl of cape and then was left with nothing, fixed by the pass, dominated by the cape. Manuel swung the cape under his muzzle with one hand, to show the bull was fixed, and walked away.

There was no applause.

Manuel walked across the sand toward the *barrera*, while Zurito rode out of the ring. The trumpet had blown to change the act to the planting of the *banderillas* while Manuel had been working with the bull. He had not consciously noticed it. The *monos* were spreading canvas over the two dead horses and sprinkling sawdust around them.

Manuel came up to the *barrera* for a drink of water. Retana's man handed him the heavy porous jug.

Fuentes, the tall gypsy, was standing holding a pair of *banderillas*, holding them together, slim, red sticks, fish-hook points out. He looked at Manuel.

'Go on out there,' Manuel said.

The gypsy trotted out. Manuel set down the jug and watched. He wiped his face with his handkerchief.

The critic of *El Heraldo* reached for the bottle of warm champagne that stood between his feet, took a drink, and finished his paragraph.

'– the aged Manolo rated no applause for a vulgar series of lances with the cape and we entered the third of the palings.'

Alone in the center of the ring the bull stood, still fixed. Fuentes, tall, flat-backed, walking toward him arrogantly, his arms spread out, the two slim, red sticks, one in each hand, held by the fingers, points straight forward. Fuentes walked forward. Back of him and to one side was a peon with a cape. The bull looked at him and was no longer fixed.

His eyes watched Fuentes, now standing still. Now he leaned back, calling to him. Fuentes twitched the two *banderillas* and the light on the steel points caught the bull's eye.

His tail went up and he charged.

He came straight, his eyes on the man. Fuentes stood still, leaning back, the *banderillas* pointing forward. As the bull lowered his head to hook, Fuentes leaned backward, his arms came together and rose, his two hands touching, the *banderillas* two descending red lines, and leaning forward drove the points into the bull's shoulder, leaning far in over the bull's horns and pivoting on the two upright sticks, his legs tight together, his body curving to one side to let the bull pass.

'*Olé!*' from the crowd.

The bull was hooking wildly, jumping like a trout, all four feet off the ground. The red shaft of the *banderillas* tossed as he jumped.

Manuel, standing at the *barrera*, noticed that he hooked always to the right.

'Tell him to drop the next pair on the right,' he said to the kid who started to run out to Fuentes with the new *banderillas*.

A heavy hand fell on his shoulder. It was Zurito.

'How do you feel, kid?' he asked.

Manuel was watching the bull.

Zurito leaned forward on the *barrera*, leaning the weight of his body on his arms. Manuel turned to him.

'You're going good,' Zurito said.

Manuel shook his head. He had nothing to do now until the next third. The gypsy was very good with the *banderillas*. The bull would come to him in the next third in good shape. He was a good bull. It had all been easy up to now. The final stuff with the sword was all he worried over. He did not really worry. He did not even think about it. But standing there he had a heavy sense of apprehension. He looked out at the bull, planning his *faena*, his work with the red cloth that was to reduce the bull, to make him manageable.

The gypsy was walking out toward the bull again, walking heel-and-toe, insultingly, like a ballroom dancer, the red shafts of the *banderillas* twitching with his walk. The bull watched him, not fixed now, hunting him, but waiting to get close enough so he could be sure of getting him, getting the horns into him.

As Fuentes walked forward the bull charged. Fuentes ran across the quarter of a circle as the bull charged and, as he passed running backward, stopped, swung forward, rose on his toes, arms straight out, and sunk the *banderillas* straight down into the tight of the big shoulder muscles as the bull missed him.

The crowd were wild about it.

'That kid won't stay in this night stuff long,' Retana's man said to Zurito.

'He's good,' Zurito said.

'Watch him now.'

They watched.

Fuentes was standing with his back against the *barrera*. Two of the *cuadrilla* were back of him, with their capes ready to flop over the fence to distract the bull.

The bull, with his tongue out, his barrel heaving, was watching the gypsy. He thought he had him now. Back against the red planks. Only a short charge away. The bull watched him.

The gypsy bent back, drew back his arms, the *banderillas* pointing at the bull. He called to the bull, stamped one foot. The bull was suspicious. He wanted the man. No more barbs in the shoulder.

Fuentes walked a little closer to the bull. Bent back. Called again. Somebody in the crowd shouted a warning.

'He's too damn close,' Zurito said.

'Watch him,' Retana's man said.

Leaning back, inciting the bull with the *banderillas*, Fuentes jumped, both feet off the ground. As he jumped the bull's tail rose and he charged. Fuentes came down on his toes, arms straight out, whole body arching forward, and drove the shafts straight down as he swung his body clear of the right horn.

The bull crashed into the *barrera* where the flopping capes had attracted his eye as he lost the man.

The gypsy came running along the *barrera* toward Manuel, taking the applause of the crowd. His vest was ripped where he had not quite cleared the point of the horn. He was happy about it, showing it to the spectators. He made the tour of the ring. Zurito saw him go by, smiling, pointing at his vest. He smiled.

Somebody else was planting the last pair of *banderillas*. Nobody was paying any attention.

Retana's man tucked a baton inside the red cloth of a *muleta*, folded the cloth over it, and handed it over the *barrera* to Manuel. He reached in the leather sword-case, took out a sword, and holding it by its leather scabbard, reached it over the fence to Manuel. Manuel pulled the blade out by the red hilt and the scabbard fell limp.

He looked at Zurito. The big man saw he was sweating.

'Now you get him, kid,' Zurito said.

Manuel nodded.

'He's in good shape,' Zurito said.

'Just like you want him,' Retana's man assured him.

Manuel nodded.

The trumpeter, up under the roof, blew for the final act, and Manuel walked across the arena toward where, up in the dark boxes, the president must be.

In the front row of seats the substitute bull-fight critic of *El Heraldo* took a long drink of the warm champagne. He had decided it was not worth while to write a running story and would write up the *corrida* back in the office. What the hell was it anyway? Only a nocturnal. If he missed anything he would get it out of the morning papers. He took another drink of the champagne. He had a date at Maxim's at twelve. Who were these bull-fighters anyway? Kids and bums. A bunch of bums. He put his pad of paper in his pocket and looked over toward Manuel, standing very much alone in the ring, gesturing with his hat in a salute toward a box he could not see high up in the dark plaza. Out in the ring the bull stood quiet, looking at nothing.

'I dedicate this bull to you, Mr. President, and to the public of Madrid, the most intelligent and generous of the world,' was what Manuel was saying. It was a formula. He said it all. It was a little long for nocturnal use.

He bowed at the dark, straightened, tossed his hat over his shoulder, and, carrying the *muleta* in his left hand and the sword in his right, walked out toward the bull.

Manuel walked toward the bull. The bull looked at him; his eyes were quick. Manuel noticed the way the *banderillas* hung down on his left shoulder and the steady sheen of blood from Zurito's pic-ing. He noticed the way the bull's feet were. As he walked forward, holding the *muleta* in his left hand and the sword in his right, he watched the bull's feet. The bull could not charge without gathering his feet together. Now he stood square on them, dully.

Manuel walked toward him, watching his feet. This was all right. He could do this. He must work to get the bull's head down, so he could go in past the horns and kill him. He did not think about the sword, not about killing the bull. He thought about one thing at a time. The coming things oppressed him, though. Walking forward, watching the bull's feet, he saw successively his eyes, his wet muzzle, and the wide, forward-pointing spread of his horns. The bull had light circles about his eyes. His eyes watched Manuel. He felt he was going to get this little one with the white face.

Standing still now and spreading the red cloth of the *muleta* with the sword, pricking the point into the cloth so that the sword, now held in his left hand, spread the red flannel like the jib of a boat, Manuel noticed the points of the bull's horns. One of them was splintered from banging against the *barrera*. The other was sharp as a porcupine quill. Manuel noticed while spreading the *muleta* that the white base of the horn was stained red. While he noticed these things he did not lose sight of the bull's feet. The bull watched Manuel steadily.

He's on the defensive now, Manuel thought. He's reserving himself. I've got to bring him out of that and get his head down. Always get his head down. Zurito had his head down once, but he's come back. He'll bleed when I start him going and that will bring it down.

Holding the *muleta*, with the sword in his left hand widening it in front of him, he called to the bull.

The bull looked at him.

He leaned back insultingly and shook the wide-spread flannel.

The bull saw the *muleta*. It was a bright scarlet under the arc-light. The bull's legs tightened.

Here he comes. Whoosh! Manuel turned as the bull came and raised the *muleta* so that it passed over the bull's horns and swept down his broad back from head to tail. The bull had gone clean up in the air with the charge. Manuel had not moved.

At the end of the pass the bull turned like a cat coming around a corner and faced Manuel.

He was on the offensive again. His heaviness was gone. Manuel noted the fresh blood shining down the black shoulder and dripping down the bull's leg. He drew the sword out of the *muleta* and held it in his right hand. The *muleta* held low down in his left hand, leaning toward the left, he called to the bull. The bull's legs tightened, his eyes on the *muleta*. Here he comes, Manuel thought. Yuh!

He swung with the charge, sweeping the *muleta* ahead of the bull, his feet firm, the sword following the curve, a point of light under the arcs.

The bull recharged as the *pase natural* finished and Manuel raised the *muleta* for a *pase de pecho*. Firmly planted, the bull came by his chest under the raised *muleta*. Manuel leaned his head back to avoid the clattering *banderillo* shafts. The hot, black bull body touched his chest as it passed.

Too damn close, Manuel thought. Zurito, leaning on the *barrera*, spoke rapidly to the gypsy, who trotted out toward Manuel with a cape. Zurito pulled his hat down low and looked out across the arena at Manuel.

Manuel was facing the bull again, the *muleta* held low and to the left. The bull's head was down as he watched the *muleta*.

'If it was Belmonte doing that stuff, they'd go crazy,' Retana's man said.

Zurito said nothing. He was watching Manuel out in the center of the arena.

'Where did the boss dig this fellow up?' Retana's man asked.

'Out of the hospital,' Zurito said.

'That's where he's going damn quick,' Retana's man said. Zurito turned on him.

'Knock on that,' he said, pointing to the *barrera*.

'I was just kidding, man,' Retana's man said.

'Knock on the wood.'

Retana's man leaned forward and knocked three times on the *barrera*.

'Watch the *faena*,' Zurito said.

Out in the center of the ring, under the lights, Manuel was kneeling, facing the bull, and as he raised the *muleta* in both hands the bull charged, tail up.

Manuel swung his body clear and, as the bull recharged, brought around the *muleta* in a half-circle that pulled the bull to his knees.

'Why, that one's a great bull-fighter,' Retana's man said.

'No, he's not,' said Zurito.

Manuel stood up and, the *muleta* in his left hand, the sword in his right, acknowledged the applause from the dark plaza.

The bull had humped himself up from his knees and stood waiting, his head hung low.

Zurito spoke to two of the other lads of the *cuadrilla* and they ran out to stand back of Manuel with their capes. There were four men back of him now. Hernandez had followed him since he first came out with the *muleta*. Fuentes stood watching, his cape held against his body, tall, in repose, watching lazy-eyed. Now the two came up. Hernandez motioned them to stand one at each side. Manuel stood alone, facing the bull.

Manuel waved back the men with the capes. Stepping back cautiously, they saw his face was white and sweating.

Didn't they know enough to keep back? Did they want to catch the bull's eye with the capes after he was fixed and ready? He had enough to worry about without that kind of thing.

The bull was standing, his four feet square, looking at the *muleta*. Manuel furled the *muleta* in his left hand. The bull's eyes watched it. His body was heavy on his feet. He carried his head low, but not too low.

Manuel lifted the *muleta* at him. The bull did not move. Only his eyes watched.

He's all lead, Manuel thought. He's all square. He's framed right. He'll take it.

He thought in bull-fight terms. Sometimes he had a thought and the particular piece of slang would not come into his mind and he could not realize the thought. His instincts and his knowledge worked automatically, and his brain worked slowly and in words. He knew all about bulls. He did not have to think about them. He just did the right thing. His eyes noted things and his body performed the necessary measures without thought. If he thought about it, he would be gone.

Now, facing the bull, he was conscious of many things at the same time. There were the horns, the one splintered, the other smoothly sharp, the need to profile himself toward the left horn, lance himself short and straight, lower the *muleta* so the bull would follow it, and, going in over the horns, put the sword all the way into a little spot about as big as a five-peseta piece straight in back of the neck, between the sharp pitch of the bull's shoulders. He must do all this and must then come out from between the horns. He was conscious he must do all this, but his only thought was in words: '*Corto y derecho.*'

'*Corto y derecho,*' he thought, furling the *muleta*. Short and straight. *Corto y derecho*, he drew the sword out of the *muleta*, profiled on the splintered left horn, dropped the *muleta* across his body, so his right hand with the sword on the level with his eye made the sign of the cross, and, rising on his toes, sighted along the dipping blade of the sword at the spot high up between the bull's shoulders.

Corto y derecho he launched himself on the bull.

There was a shock, and he felt himself go up in the air. He pushed on the sword as he went up and over, and it flew out of his hand. He hit the ground and the bull was on him. Manuel, lying on the ground, kicked at the bull's muzzle with his slippered feet. Kicking, kicking, the bull after him, missing him in his excitement, bumping him with his head, driving the horns into the sand. Kicking like a man keeping a ball in the air, Manuel kept the bull from getting a clean thrust at him.

Manuel felt the wind on his back from the capes flopping at the bull, and then the bull was gone, gone over him in a rush. Dark, as his belly went over. Not even stepped on.

Manuel stood up and picked up the *muleta*. Fuentes handed

him the sword. It was bent where it had struck the shoulder-blade. Manuel straightened it on his knee and ran toward the bull, standing now beside one of the dead horses. As he ran, his jacket flopped where it had been ripped under his armpit.

'Get him out of there,' Manuel shouted to the gypsy. The bull had smelled the blood of the dead horse and ripped into the canvas-cover with his horns. He charged Fuentes's cape, with the canvas hanging from his splintered horn, and the crowd laughed. Out in the ring, he tossed his head to rid himself of the canvas. Hernandez, running up from behind him, grabbed the end of the canvas and neatly lifted it off the horn.

The bull followed it in a half-charge and stopped still. He was on the defensive again. Manuel was walking toward him with the sword and *muleta*. Manuel swung the *muleta* before him. The bull would not charge.

Manuel profiled toward the bull, sighting along the dipping blade of the sword. The bull was motionless, seemingly dead on his feet, incapable of another charge.

Manuel rose to his toes, sighting along the steel, and charged.

Again there was the shock and he felt himself being borne back in a rush, to strike hard on the sand. There was no chance of kicking this time. The bull was on top of him. Manuel lay as though dead, his head on his arms, and the bull bumped him. Bumped his back, bumped his face in the sand. He felt the horn go into the sand between his folded arms. The bull hit him in the small of the back. His face drove into the sand. The horn drove through one of his sleeves and the bull ripped it off. Manuel was tossed clear and the bull followed the capes.

Manuel got up, found the sword and *muleta*, tried the point of the sword with his thumb, and then ran toward the *barrera* for a new sword.

Retana's man handed him the sword over the edge of the *barrera*.

'Wipe off your face,' he said.

Manuel, running again toward the bull, wiped his bloody face with his handkerchief. He had not seen Zurito. Where was Zurito?

The *cuadrilla* had stepped away from the bull and waited with their capes. The bull stood, heavy and dull again after the action.

Manuel walked toward him with the *muleta*. He stopped and shook it. The bull did not respond. He passed it right and left, left and right before the bull's muzzle. The bull's eyes watched it and turned with the swing, but he would not charge. He was waiting for Manuel.

Manuel was worried. There was nothing to do but go in. *Corto y derecho*. He profiled close to the bull, crossed the *muleta* in front of his body and charged. As he pushed in the sword, he jerked his body to the left to clear the horn. The bull passed him and the sword shot up in the air, twinkling under the arc-lights, to fall red-hilted on the sand.

Manuel ran over and picked it up. It was bent and he straightened it over his knee.

As he came running toward the bull, fixed again now, he passed Hernandez standing with his cape.

'He's all bone,' the boy said encouragingly.

Manuel nodded, wiping his face. He put the bloody handkerchief in his pocket.

There was the bull. He was close to the *barrera* now. Damn him. Maybe he was all bone. Maybe there was not any place for the sword to go in. The hell there wasn't! He'd show them.

He tried a pass with the *muleta* and the bull did not move. Manuel chopped the *muleta* back and forth in front of the bull. Nothing doing.

He furled the *muleta*, drew the sword out, profiled and drove in on the bull. He felt the sword buckle as he shoved it in, leaning his weight on it, and then it shot high in the air, end-over-ending into the crowd. Manuel had jerked clear as the sword jumped.

The first cushions thrown down out of the dark missed him. Then one hit him in the face, his bloody face looking toward the crowd. They were coming down fast. Spotting the sand. Somebody threw an empty champagne-bottle from close range. It hit Manuel on the foot. He stood there watching the dark, where the things were coming from. Then something whished through the air and struck by him. Manuel leaned over and picked it up. It was his sword. He straightened it over his knee and gestured with it to the crowd.

'Thank you,' he said. 'Thank you.'

Oh, the dirty bastards! Dirty bastards! Oh, the lousy, dirty bastards! He kicked into a cushion as he ran.

There was the bull. The same as ever. All right, you dirty, lousy bastard!

Manuel passed the *muleta* in front of the bull's black muzzle. Nothing doing.

You won't! All right. He stepped close and jammed the sharp peak of the *muleta* into the bull's damp muzzle.

The bull was on him as he jumped back and as he tripped on a cushion he felt the horn go into him, into his side. He grabbed the horn with his two hands and rode backward, holding tight onto the place. The bull tossed him and he was clear. He lay still. It was all right. The bull was gone.

He got up coughing and feeling broken and gone. The dirty bastards!

'Give me the sword,' he shouted. 'Give me the stuff.'

Fuentes came up with the *muleta* and the sword.

Hernandez put his arm around him.

'Go on to the infirmary, man,' he said. 'Don't be a damn fool.'

'Get away from me,' Manuel said. 'Get to hell away from me.'

He twisted free. Hernandez shrugged his shoulders. Manuel ran toward the bull.

There was the bull standing, heavy, firmly planted.

All right, you bastard! Manuel drew the sword out of the *muleta*, sighted with the same movement, and flung himself onto the bull. He felt the sword go in all the way. Right up to the guard. Four fingers and his thumb into the bull. The blood was hot on his knuckles, and he was on top of the bull.

The bull lurched with him as he lay on, and seemed to sink; then he was standing clear. He looked at the bull going down slowly over on his side, then suddenly four feet in the air.

Then he gestured at the crowd, his hand warm from the bull blood.

All right, you bastards! He wanted to say something, but he started to cough. It was hot and choking. He looked down for the *muleta*. He must go over and salute the president. President hell! He was sitting down looking at something. It was the bull. His four feet up. Thick tongue out. Things crawling around on his belly and under his legs. Crawling where the hair was thin. Dead bull. To hell with the bull! To hell with them all! He started to get to his feet and commenced to cough. He sat down again, coughing. Somebody came and pushed him up.

They carried him across the ring to the infirmary, running with him across the sand, standing blocked at the gate as the mules came in, then around under the dark passageway, men grunting as they took him up the stairway, and then laid him down.

The doctor and two men in white were waiting for him. They laid him out on the table. They were cutting away his shirt. Manuel felt tired. His whole chest felt scalding inside. He started to cough and they held something to his mouth. Everybody was very busy.

There was an electric light in his eyes. He shut his eyes.

He heard someone coming very heavily up the stairs. Then he did not hear it. Then he heard a noise far off. That was the crowd. Well, somebody would have to kill his other bull. They had cut away all his shirt. The doctor smiled at him. There was Retana.

'Hello, Retana!' Manuel said. He could not hear his voice.

Retana smiled at him and said something. Manuel could not hear it.

Zurito stood beside the table, bending over where the doctor was working. He was in his picador clothes, without his hat.

Zurito said something to him. Manuel could not hear it.

Zurito was speaking to Retana. One of the men in white smiled and handed Retana a pair of scissors. Retana gave them to Zurito. Zurito said something to Manuel. He could not hear it.

To hell with this operating-table. He'd been on plenty of operating-tables before. He was not going to die. There would be a priest if he was going to die.

Zurito was saying something to him. Holding up the scissors.

That was it. They were going to cut off his *coleta*. They were going to cut off his pigtail.

Manuel sat up on the operating-table. The doctor stepped back, angry. Someone grabbed him and held him.

'You couldn't do a thing like that, Manos,' he said.

He heard suddenly, clearly, Zurito's voice.

'That's all right,' Zurito said. 'I won't do it. I was joking.'

'I was going good,' Manuel said. 'I didn't have any luck. That was all.'

Manuel lay back. They had put something over his face. It was all familiar. He inhaled deeply. He felt very tired. He was very, very tired. They took the thing away from his face.

'I was going good,' Manuel said weakly. 'I was going great.'

Retana looked at Zurito and started for the door.

'I'll stay here with him,' Zurito said.

Retana shrugged his shoulders.

Manuel opened his eyes and looked at Zurito.

'Wasn't I going good, Manos?' he asked, for confirmation.

'Sure,' said Zurito. 'You were going great.'

The doctor's assistant put the cone over Manuel's face and he inhaled deeply. Zurito stood awkwardly, watching.

IN ANOTHER COUNTRY

In the fall the war was always there, but we did not go to it any more. It was cold in the fall in Milan and the dark came very early. Then the electric lights came on, and it was pleasant along the streets looking in the windows. There was much game hanging outside the shops, and the snow powdered in the fur of the foxes and the wind blew their tails. The deer hung stiff and heavy and empty, and small birds blew in the wind and the wind turned their feathers. It was a cold fall and the wind came down from the mountains.

We were all at the hospital every afternoon, and there were different ways of walking across the town through the dusk to the hospital. Two of the ways were alongside canals, but they were long. Always, though, you crossed a bridge across a canal to enter the hospital. There was a choice of three bridges. On one of them a woman sold roasted chestnuts. It was warm, standing in front of her charcoal fire, and the chestnuts were warm afterward in your pocket. The hospital was very old and very beautiful, and you entered through a gate and walked across a courtyard and out a gate on the other side. There were usually funerals starting from the courtyard. Beyond the old hospital were the new brick pavilions, and there we met every afternoon and were all very polite and interested in what was the matter, and sat in the machines that were to make so much difference.

The doctor came up to the machine where I was sitting and said: 'What did you like best to do before the war? Did you practice a sport?'

I said: 'Yes, football.'

'Good,' he said. 'You will be able to play football again better than ever.'

My knee did not bend and the leg dropped straight from the knee to the ankle without a calf, and the machine was to bend the knee and make it move as in riding a tricycle. But it did not bend yet, and instead the machine lurched when it came to the bending part. The doctor said: 'That will all pass. You are a fortunate young man. You will play football again like a champion.'

In the next machine was a major who had a little hand like a baby's. He winked at me when the doctor examined his hand, which was between two leather straps that bounced up and down and flapped the stiff fingers, and said: 'And will I too play football, captain-doctor?' He had been a very great fencer, and before the war the greatest fencer in Italy.

The doctor went to his office in a back room and brought a photograph which showed a hand that had been withered almost as small as the major's, before it had taken a machine course, and after was a little larger. The major held the photograph with his good hand and looked at it very carefully. 'A wound?' he asked.

'An industrial accident,' the doctor said.

'Very interesting, very interesting,' the major said, and handed it back to the doctor.

'You have confidence?'

'No,' said the major.

There were three boys who came each day who were about the same age I was. They were all three from Milan, and one of them was to be a lawyer, and one was to be a painter, and one had intended to be a soldier, and after we were finished with the machines, sometimes we walked back together to the Café Cova, which was next door to the Scala. We walked the short way through the communist quarter because we were four together. The people hated us because we were officers, and from a wine-shop some one would call out, '*A basso gli ufficiali!*' as we passed. Another boy who walked with us sometimes and made us five wore a black silk handkerchief across his face because he had no nose then and his face was to be rebuilt. He had gone out to the front from the military academy and been wounded within an hour after he had gone into the front line for the first time. They rebuilt his face, but he came from a very old family and they could never get the nose exactly right. He went to South America and worked in a bank. But this was a long time ago, and then we did not any of us know how it was going to be afterward. We only knew then that there was always the war, but that we were not going to it any more.

We all had the same medals, except the boy with the black silk bandage across his face, and he had not been at the front long enough to get any medals. The tall boy with a very pale face who was to be a lawyer had been a lieutenant of *Arditi* and had three medals of the sort we each had only one of. He had lived a very long time with death and was a little detached. We were all a little detached, and there was nothing that held us together except that we met every afternoon at the hospital. Although, as we walked to the Cova through the tough part of town, walking in the dark, with light and singing coming out of the wine-shops, and sometimes having to walk into the street when the men and women would crowd together on the sidewalk so that we would have had to jostle them to get by, we felt held together by there being something that had happened that they, the people who disliked us, did not understand.

We ourselves all understood the Cova, where it was rich and warm and not too brightly lighted, and noisy and smoky at certain hours, and there were always girls at the tables and the illustrated papers on a rack on the wall. The girls at the Cova were very patriotic, and I found that the most patriotic people in Italy were the café girls – and I believe they are still patriotic.

The boys at first were very polite about my medals and asked me what I had done to get them. I showed them the papers, which were written in very beautiful language and full of *fratellanza* and *abnegazione*, but which really said, with the adjectives removed, that I had been given the medals because I was an American. After that their manner changed a little toward me, although I was their friend against outsiders. I was a friend, but I was never really one of them after they had read the citations, because it had been different with them and they had done very different things to get their medals. I had been wounded, it was true; but we all knew that being wounded, after all, was really an accident. I was never ashamed of the ribbons, though, and sometimes, after the cocktail hour, I would imagine myself having done all the things they had done to get their medals; but walking home at night through the empty streets with the cold wind and all the shops closed, trying to keep near the street lights, I knew that I would never have done such things, and I was very much afraid to die, and often lay in bed at night by myself, afraid to die and wondering how I would be when I went back to the front again.

The three with the medals were like hunting-hawks; and I was not a hawk, although I might seem a hawk to those who had never hunted; they, the three, knew better and so we drifted apart. But I stayed good friends with the boy who had been wounded his first day at the front, because he would never know now how he would have turned out; so he could never be accepted either, and I liked him because I thought perhaps he would not have turned out to be a hawk either.

The major, who had been the great fencer, did not believe in

bravery, and spent much time while we sat in the machines cor-
recting my grammar. He had complimented me on how I spoke
Italian, and we talked together very easily. One day I had said
that Italian seemed such an easy language to me that I could not
take a great interest in it; everything was so easy to say. 'Ah, yes,'
the major said. 'Why, then, do you not take up the use of grammar?' So we took up the use of grammar, and soon Italian was
such a difficult language that I was afraid to talk to him until I
had the grammar straight in my mind.

The major came very regularly to the hospital. I do not think
he ever missed a day, although I am sure he did not believe in
the machines. There was a time when none of us believed in the
machines, and one day the major said it was all nonsense. The
machines were new then and it was we who were to prove
them. It was an idiotic idea, he said, 'a theory, like another.' I
had not learned my grammar, and he said I was a stupid impossible disgrace, and he was a fool to have bothered with me.
He was a small man and he sat straight up in his chair with his
right hand thrust into the machine and looked straight ahead at
the wall while the straps thumped up and down with his fingers
in them.

'What will you do when the war is over if it is over?' he asked
me. 'Speak grammatically!'

'I will go to the States.'

'Are you married?'

'No, but I hope to be.'

'The more of a fool you are,' he said. He seemed very angry.
'A man must not marry.'

'Why, Signor Maggiore?'

'Don't call me "Signor Maggiore." '

'Why must not a man marry?'

'He cannot marry. He cannot marry,' he said angrily. 'If he is
to lose everything, he should not place himself in a position to
lose that. He should not place himself in a position to lose. He
should find things he cannot lose.'

He spoke very angrily and bitterly, and looked straight ahead
while he talked.

'But why should he necessarily lose it?'

'He'll lose it,' the major said. He was looking at the wall.
Then he looked down at the machine and jerked his little hand
out from between the straps and slapped it hard against his thigh.
'He'll lose it,' he almost shouted. 'Don't argue with me!' Then

he called to the attendant who ran the machines. 'Come and turn this damned thing off.'

He went back into the other room for the light treatment and the massage. Then I heard him ask the doctor if he might use his telephone and he shut the door. When he came back into the room, I was sitting in another machine. He was wearing his cape and had his cap on, and he came directly toward my machine and put his arm on my shoulder.

'I am so sorry,' he said, and patted me on the shoulder with his good hand. 'I would not be rude. My wife has just died. You must forgive me.'

'Oh –' I said, feeling sick for him. 'I am *so* sorry.'

He stood there biting his lower lip. 'It is very difficult,' he said. 'I cannot resign myself.'

He looked straight past me and out through the window. Then he began to cry. 'I am utterly unable to resign myself,' he said and choked. And then crying, his head up looking at nothing, carrying himself straight and soldierly, with tears on both his cheeks and biting his lips, he walked past the machines and out the door.

The doctor told me that the major's wife, who was very young and whom he had not married until he was definitely invalided out of the war, had died of pneumonia. She had been sick only a few days. No one expected her to die. The major did not come to the hospital for three days. Then he came at the usual hour, wearing a black band on the sleeve of his uniform. When he came back, there were large framed photographs around the wall, of all sorts of wounds before and after they had been cured by the machines. In front of the machine the major used were three photographs of hands like his that were completely restored. I do not know where the doctor got them. I always understood we were the first to use the machines. The photographs did not make much difference to the major because he only looked out of the window.

HILLS LIKE WHITE ELEPHANTS

The hills across the valley of the Ebro were long and white. On this side there was no shade and no trees and the station was between two lines of rails in the sun. Close against the side of the station there was the warm shadow of the building and a curtain, made of strings of bamboo beads, hung across the open door into the bar, to keep out flies. The American and the girl with him sat at a table in the shade, outside the building. It was very hot and the express from Barcelona would come in forty minutes. It stopped at this junction for two minutes and went on to Madrid.

'What should we drink?' the girl asked. She had taken off her hat and put it on the table.

'It's pretty hot,' the man said.

'Let's drink beer.'

'*Dos cervezas,*' the man said into the curtain.

'Big ones?' a woman asked from the doorway.

'Yes. Two big ones.'

The woman brought two glasses of beer and two felt pads. She put the felt pads and the beer glasses on the table and looked at the man and the girl. The girl was looking off at the line of hills. They were white in the sun and the country was brown and dry.

'They look like white elephants,' she said.

'I've never seen one,' the man drank his beer.

'No, you wouldn't have.'

'I might have,' the man said. 'Just because you say I wouldn't have doesn't prove anything.'

The girl looked at the bead curtain. 'They've painted something on it,' she said. 'What does it say?'

'Anis del Toro. It's a drink.'

'Could we try it?'

The man called 'Listen' through the curtain. The woman came out from the bar.

'Four reales.'

'We want two Anis del Toro.'

'With water?'

'Do you want it with water?'

'I don't know,' the girl said. 'Is it good with water?'

'It's all right.'

'You want them with water?' asked the woman.

'Yes, with water.'

'It tastes like licorice,' the girl said and put the glass down.

'That's the way with everything.'

'Yes,' said the girl. 'Everything tastes of licorice. Especially all the things you've waited so long for, like absinthe.'

'Oh, cut it out.'

'You started it,' the girl said. 'I was being amused. I was having a fine time.'

'Well, let's try and have a fine time.'

'All right. I was trying. I said the mountains looked like white elephants. Wasn't that bright?'

'That was bright.'

'I wanted to try this new drink: That's all we do, isn't it – look at things and try new drinks?'

'I guess so.'

The girl looked across at the hills.

'They're lovely hills,' she said. 'They don't really look like white elephants. I just meant the coloring of their skin through the trees.'

'Should we have another drink?'

'All right.'

The warm wind blew the bead curtain against the table.

'The beer's nice and cool,' the man said.

'It's lovely,' the girl said.

'It's really an awfully simple operation, Jig,' the man said. 'It's not really an operation at all.'

The girl looked at the ground the table legs rested on.

'I know you wouldn't mind it, Jig. It's really not anything. It's just to let the air in.'

The girl did not say anything.

'I'll go with you and I'll stay with you all the time. They just let the air in and then it's all perfectly natural.'

'Then what will we do afterward?'

'We'll be fine afterward. Just like we were before.'

'What makes you think so?'

'That's the only thing that bothers us. It's the only thing that's made us unhappy.'

The girl looked at the bead curtain, put her hand out and took hold of two of the strings of beads.

'And you think then we'll be all right and be happy.'

'I know we will. You don't have to be afraid. I've known lots of people that have done it.'

'So have I,' said the girl. 'And afterward they were all so happy.'

'Well,' the man said, 'if you don't want to you don't have to. I wouldn't have you do it if you didn't want to. But I know it's perfectly simple.'

'And you really want to?'

'I think it's the best thing to do. But I don't want you to do it if you don't really want to.'

'And if I do it you'll be happy and things will be like they were and you'll love me?'

'I love you now. You know I love you.'

'I know. But if I do it, then it will be nice again if I say things are like white elephants, and you'll like it?'

'I'll love it. I love it now but I just can't think about it. You know how I get when I worry.'

'If I do it you won't ever worry?'

'I won't worry about that because it's perfectly simple.'

'Then I'll do it. Because I don't care about me.'

'What do you mean?'

'I don't care about me.'

'Well, I care about you.'

'Oh, yes. But I don't care about me. And I'll do it and then everything will be fine.'

'I don't want you to do it if you feel that way.'

The girl stood up and walked to the end of the station. Across, on the other side, were fields of grain and trees along the banks of the Ebro. Far away, beyond the river, were mountains. The shadow of a cloud moved across the field of grain and she saw the river through the trees.

'And we could have all this,' she said. 'And we could have everything and every day we make it more impossible.'

'What did you say?'

'I said we could have everything.'

'We can have everything.'

'No, we can't.'

'We can have the whole world.'

'No, we can't.'

'We can go everywhere.'

'No, we can't. It isn't ours any more.'

'It's ours.'

'No, it isn't. And once they take it away, you never get it back.'

'But they haven't taken it away.'

'We'll wait and see.'

'Come on back in the shade,' he said. 'You mustn't feel that way.'

'I don't feel any way,' the girl said. 'I just know things.'

'I don't want you to do anything that you don't want to do –'

'Nor that isn't good for me,' she said. 'I know. Could we have another beer?'

'All right. But you've got to realize –'

'I realize,' the girl said. 'Can't we maybe stop talking?'

They sat down at the table and the girl looked across at the hills on the dry side of the valley and the man looked at her and at the table.

'You've got to realize,' he said, 'that I don't want you to do it if you don't want to. I'm perfectly willing to go through with it if it means anything to you.'

'Doesn't it mean anything to you? We could get along.'

'Of course it does. But I don't want anybody but you. I don't want any one else. And I know it's perfectly simple.'

'Yes, you know it's perfectly simple.'

'It's all right for you to say that, but I do know it.'

'Would you do something for me now?'

'I'd do anything for you.'

'Would you please please please please please please please stop talking?'

He did not say anything but looked at the bags against the wall of the station. There were labels on them from all the hotels where they had spent nights.

'But I don't want you to,' he said, 'I don't care anything about it.'

'I'll scream,' the girl said.

The woman came out through the curtains with two glasses of beer and put them down on the damp felt pads. 'The train comes in five minutes,' she said.

'What did she say?' asked the girl.

'That the train is coming in five minutes.'

The girl smiled brightly at the woman, to thank her.

'I'd better take the bags over to the other side of the station,' the man said. She smiled at him.

'All right. Then come back and we'll finish the beer.'

He picked up the two heavy bags and carried them around the station to the other tracks. He looked up the tracks but could not see the train. Coming back, he walked through the bar-room, where people waiting for the train were drinking. He drank an Anis at the bar and looked at the people. They were all waiting reasonably for the train. He went out through the bead curtain. She was sitting at the table and smiled at him.

'Do you feel better?' he asked.

'I feel fine,' she said. 'There's nothing wrong with me. I feel fine.'

THE KILLERS

The door of Henry's lunch-room opened and two men came in.
They sat down at the counter.

'What's yours?' George asked them.

'I don't know,' one of the men said. 'What do you want to
eat, Al?'

'I don't know,' said Al. 'I don't know what I want to eat.'

Outside it was getting dark. The street-light came on outside
the window. The two men at the counter read the menu. From
the other end of the counter Nick Adams watched them. He had
been talking to George when they came in.

'I'll have a roast pork tenderloin with apple sauce and mashed
potatoes,' the first man said.

'It isn't ready yet.'

'What the hell do you put it on the card for?'

'That's the dinner,' George explained. 'You can get that at six
o'clock.'

George looked at the clock on the wall behind the counter.

'It's five o'clock.'

'The clock says twenty minutes past five,' the second man said.

'It's twenty minutes fast.'

'Oh, to hell with the clock,' the first man said. 'What have
you got to eat?'

'I can give you any kind of sandwiches,' George said. 'You can
have ham and eggs, bacon and eggs, liver and bacon, or a steak.'

'Give me chicken croquettes with green peas and cream sauce
and mashed potatoes.'

'That's the dinner.'

'Everything we want's the dinner, eh? That's the way you
work it.'

'I can give you ham and eggs, bacon and eggs, liver –'

'I'll take ham and eggs,' the man called Al said. He wore a
derby hat and a black overcoat buttoned across the chest. His
face was small and white and he had tight lips. He wore a silk
muffler and gloves.

'Give me bacon and eggs,' said the other man. He was about
the same size as Al. Their faces were different, but they were
dressed like twins. Both wore overcoats too tight for them. They
sat leaning forward, their elbows on the counter.

'Got anything to drink?' Al asked.

'Silver beer, bevo, ginger-ale,' George said.

'I mean you got anything to *drink*?'

'Just those I said.'

'This is a hot town,' said the other. 'What do they call it?'

'Summit.'

'Ever hear of it?' Al asked his friend.

'No,' said the friend.

'What do you do here nights?' Al asked.

'They eat the dinner,' his friend said. 'They all come here and eat the big dinner.'

'That's right,' George said.

'So you think that's right?' Al asked George.

'Sure.'

'You're a pretty bright boy, aren't you?'

'Sure,' said George.

'Well, you're not,' said the other little man. 'Is he, Al?'

'He's dumb,' said Al. He turned to Nick. 'What's your name?'

'Adams.'

'Another bright boy,' Al said. 'Ain't he a bright boy, Max?'

'The town's full of bright boys,' Max said.

George put the two platters, one of ham and eggs, the other of bacon and eggs, on the counter. He set down two side-dishes of fried potatoes and closed the wicket into the kitchen.

'Which is yours?' he asked Al.

'Don't you remember?'

'Ham and eggs.'

'Just a bright boy,' Max said. He leaned forward and took the ham and eggs. Both men ate with their gloves on. George watched them eat.

'What are *you* looking it?' Max looked at George.

'Nothing.'

'The hell you were. You were looking at me.'

'Maybe the boy meant it for a joke, Max,' Al said.

George laughed.

'*You* don't have to laugh,' Max said to him. '*You* don't have to laugh at all, see?'

'All right,' said George.

'So he thinks it's all right.' Max turned to Al. 'He thinks it's all right. That's a good one.'

'Oh, he's a thinker,' Al said. They went on eating.

'What's the bright boy's name down the counter?' Al asked Max.

'Hey, bright boy,' Max said to Nick. 'You go around on the other side of the counter with your boy friend.'

'What's the idea?' Nick asked.

'There isn't any idea.'

'You better go around, bright boy,' Al said. Nick went around behind the counter.

'What's the idea?' George asked.

'None of your damn business,' Al said. 'Who's out in the kitchen?'

'The nigger.'

'What do you mean the nigger?'

'The nigger that cooks.'

'Tell him to come in.'

'What's the idea?'

'Tell him to come in.'

'Where do you think you are?'

'We know damn well where we are,' the man called Max said. 'Do we look silly?'

'You talk silly,' Al said to him. 'What the hell do you argue with this kid for? Listen,' he said to George, 'tell the nigger to come out here.'

'What are you going to do to him?'

'Nothing. Use your head, bright boy. What would we do to a nigger?'

George opened the slit that opened back into the kitchen. 'Sam,' he called. 'Come in here a minute.'

The door to the kitchen opened and the nigger came in. 'What was it?' he asked. The two men at the counter took a look at him.

'All right, nigger. You stand right there,' Al said.

Sam, the nigger, standing in his apron, looked at the two men sitting at the counter. 'Yes, sir,' he said. Al got down from his stool.

'I'm going back to the kitchen with the nigger and bright boy,' he said. 'Go on back to the kitchen, nigger. You go with him, bright boy.' The little man walked after Nick and Sam, the cook, back into the kitchen. The door shut after them. The man called Max sat at the counter opposite George. He didn't look at George but looked in the mirror that ran along back of the counter. Henry's had been made over from a saloon into a lunch-counter.

'Well, bright boy,' Max said, looking into the mirror, 'why don't you say something?'

'What's it all about?'

'Hey, Al,' Max called, 'bright boy wants to know what it's all about.'

'Why don't you tell him?' Al's voice came from the kitchen.

'What do you think it's all about?'

'I don't know.'

'What do you think?'

Max looked into the mirror all the time he was talking.

'I wouldn't say.'

'Hey, Al, bright boy says he wouldn't say what he thinks it's all about.'

'I can hear you, all right,' Al said from the kitchen. He had propped open the slit that dishes passed through into the kitchen with a catsup bottle. 'Listen, bright boy,' he said from the kitchen to George. 'Stand a little further along the bar. You move a little to the left, Max.' He was like a photographer arranging for a group picture.

'Talk to me, bright boy,' Max said. 'What do you think's going to happen?'

George did not say anything.

'I'll tell you,' Max said. 'We're going to kill a Swede. Do you know a big Swede named Ole Andreson?'

'Yes.'

'He comes here to eat every night, don't he?'

'Sometimes he comes here.'

'He comes here at six o'clock, don't he?'

'If he comes.'

'We know all that, bright boy,' Max said. 'Talk about something else. Ever go to the movies?'

'Once in a while.'

'You ought to go to the movies more. The movies are fine for a bright boy like you.'

'What are you going to kill Ole Andreson for? What did he ever do to you?'

'He never had a chance to do anything to us. He never even seen us.'

'And he's only going to see us once,' Al said from the kitchen.

'What are you going to kill him for, then?' George asked.

'We're killing him for a friend. Just to oblige a friend, bright boy.'

'Shut up,' said Al from the kitchen. 'You talk too goddam much.'

'Well, I got to keep bright boy amused. Don't I, bright boy?'

'You talk too damn much,' Al said. 'The nigger and my bright boy are amused by themselves. I got them tied up like a couple of girl friends in the convent.'

'I suppose you were in a convent?'

'You never know.'

'You were in a kosher convent. That's where you were.'

George looked up at the clock.

'If anybody comes in you tell them the cook is off, and if they keep after it, you tell them you'll go back and cook yourself. Do you get that, bright boy?'

'All right,' George said. 'What you going to do with us afterward?'

'That'll depend,' Max said. 'That's one of those things you never know at the time.'

George looked up at the clock. It was a quarter past six. The door from the street opened. A street-car motorman came in.

'Hello, George,' he said. 'Can I get supper?'

'Sam's gone out,' George said. 'He'll be back in about half an hour.'

'I'd better go up the street,' the motorman said. George looked at the clock. It was twenty minutes past six.

'That was nice, bright boy,' Max said. 'You're a regular little gentleman.'

'He knew I'd blow his head off,' Al said from the kitchen.

'No,' said Max. 'It ain't that. Bright boy is nice. He's a nice boy. I like him.'

At six-fifty-five George said: 'He's not coming.'

Two other people had been in the lunch-room. Once George had gone out to the kitchen and made a ham-and-egg sandwich 'to go' that a man wanted to take with him. Inside the kitchen he saw Al, his derby hat tipped back, sitting on a stool beside the wicket with the muzzle of a sawed-off shotgun resting on the ledge. Nick and the cook were back to back in the corner, a towel tied in each of their mouths. George had cooked the sandwich, wrapped it up in oiled paper, put it in a bag, brought it in, and the man had paid for it and gone out.

'Bright boy can do everything,' Max said. 'He can cook and everything. You'd make some girl a nice wife, bright boy.'

'Yes?' George said. 'Your friend, Ole Andreson, isn't going to come.'

'We'll give him ten minutes,' Max said.

Max watched the mirror and the clock. The hands of the clock marked seven o'clock, and then five minutes past seven.

'Come on, Al,' said Max. 'We better go. He's not coming.'

'Better give him five minutes,' Al said from the kitchen.

In the five minutes a man came in, and George explained that the cook was sick.

'Why the hell don't you get another cook?' the man asked. 'Aren't you running a lunch-counter?' He went out.

'Come on, Al,' Max said.

'What about the two bright boys and the nigger?'

'They're all right.'

'You think so?'

'Sure. We're through with it.'

'I don't like it,' said Al. 'It's sloppy. You talk too much.'

'Oh, what the hell,' said Max. 'We got to keep amused, haven't we?'

'You talk too much, all the same,' Al said. He came out from the kitchen. The cutoff barrels of the shotgun made a slight bulge under the waist of his too tight-fitting overcoat. He straightened his coat with his gloved hands.

'So long, bright boy,' he said to George. 'You got a lot of luck.'

'That's the truth,' Max said. 'You ought to play the races, bright boy.'

The two of them went out the door. George watched them, through the window, pass under the arc-light and cross the street. In their tight over-coats and derby hats they looked like a vaudeville team. George went back through the swinging-door into the kitchen and untied Nick and the cook.

'I don't want any more of that,' said Sam, the cook. 'I don't want any more of that.'

Nick stood up. He had never had a towel in his mouth before.

'Say,' he said. 'What the hell?' He was trying to swagger it off.

'They were going to kill Ole Andreson,' George said. 'They were going to shoot him when he came in to eat.'

'Ole Andreson?'

'Sure.'

The cook felt the corners of his mouth with his thumbs.

'They all gone?' he asked.

'Yeah,' said George. 'They're gone now.'

'I don't like it,' said the cook. 'I don't like any of it at all.'

'Listen,' George said to Nick. 'You better go see Ole Andreson.'

'All right.'

'You better not have anything to do with it at all,' Sam, the cook, said. 'You better stay way out of it.'

'Don't go if you don't want to,' George said.

'Mixing up in this ain't going to get you anywhere,' the cook said. 'You stay out of it.'

'I'll go see him,' Nick said to George. 'Where does he live?'

The cook turned away.

'Little boys always know what they want to do,' he said.

'He lives up at Hirsch's rooming-house,' George said to Nick.

'I'll go up there.'

Outside the arc-light shone through the bare branches of a tree. Nick walked up the street beside the car-tracks and turned at the next arc-light down a side-street. Three houses up the street was Hirsch's rooming-house. Nick walked up the two steps and pushed the bell. A woman came to the door.

'Is Ole Andreson here?'

'Do you want to see him?'

'Yes, if he's in.'

Nick followed the woman up a flight of stairs and back to the end of a corridor. She knocked on the door.

'Who is it?'

'It's somebody to see you, Mr. Andreson,' the woman said.

'It's Nick Adams.'

'Come in.'

Nick opened the door and went into the room. Ole Andreson was lying on the bed with all his clothes on. He had been a heavyweight prizefighter and he was too long for the bed. He lay with his head on two pillows. He did not look at Nick.

'What was it?' he asked.

'I was up at Henry's,' Nick said, 'and two fellows came in and tied up me and the cook, and they said they were going to kill you.'

It sounded silly when he said it. Ole Andreson said nothing.

'They put us out in the kitchen,' Nick went on. 'They were going to shoot you when you came in to supper.'

Ole Andreson looked at the wall and did not say anything.

'George thought I better come and tell you about it.'

'There isn't anything I can do about it,' Ole Andreson said.

'I'll tell you what they were like.'

'I don't want to know what they were like,' Ole Andreson said. He looked at the wall. 'Thanks for coming to tell me about it.'

'That's all right.'

Nick looked at the big man lying on the bed.

'Don't you want me to go and see the police?'

'No,' Ole Andreson said. 'That wouldn't do any good.'

'Isn't there something I could do?'

'No. There ain't anything to do.'

'Maybe it was just a bluff.'

'No. It ain't just a bluff.'

Ole Andreson rolled over toward the wall.

'The only thing is,' he said, talking toward the wall, 'I just can't make up my mind to go out. I been in here all day.'

'Couldn't you get out of town?'

'No,' Ole Andreson said. 'I'm through with all that running around.'

He looked at the wall.

'There ain't anything to do now.'

'Couldn't you fix it up some way?'

'No. I got in wrong.' He talked in the same flat voice. 'There ain't anything to do. After a while I'll make up my mind to go out.'

'I better go back and see George,' Nick said.

'So long,' said Ole Andreson. He did not look toward Nick. 'Thanks for coming around.'

Nick went out. As he shut the door he saw Ole Andreson with all his clothes on, lying on the bed looking at the wall.

'He's been in his room all day,' the landlady said down-stairs. 'I guess he don't feel well. I said to him: "Mr. Andreson, you ought to go out and take a walk on a nice fall day like this," but he didn't feel like it.'

'He doesn't want to go out.'

'I'm sorry he don't feel well,' the woman said. 'He's an aw-fully nice man. He was in the ring, you know.'

'I know it.'

'You'd never know it except from the way his face is,' the woman said. They stood talking just inside the street door. 'He's just as gentle.'

'Well, good-night, Mrs. Hirsch,' Nick said.

'I'm not Mrs. Hirsch,' the woman said. 'She owns the place. I just look after it for her. I'm Mrs. Bell.'

'Well, good-night, Mrs. Bell,' Nick said.

'Good-night,' the woman said.

Nick walked up the dark street to the corner under the arc-light, and then along the car-tracks to Henry's eating-house. George was inside, back of the counter.

'Did you see Ole?'

'Yes,' said Nick. 'He's in his room and he won't go out.'

The cook opened the door from the kitchen when he heard Nick's voice.

'I don't even listen to it,' he said and shut the door.

'Did you tell him about it?' George asked.

'Sure. I told him but he knows what it's all about.'

'What's he going to do?'

'Nothing.'

'They'll kill him.'

'I guess they will.'

'He must have got mixed up in something in Chicago.'

'I guess so,' said Nick.

'It's a hell of a thing.'

'It's an awful thing,' Nick said.

They did not say anything. George reached down for a towel and wiped the counter.

'I wonder what he did?' Nick said.

'Double-crossed somebody. That's what they kill them for.'

'I'm going to get out of this town,' Nick said.

'Yes,' said George. 'That's a good thing to do.'

'I can't stand to think about him waiting in the room and knowing he's going to get it. It's too damned awful.'

'Well,' said George, 'you better not think about it.'

CHE TI DICE LA PATRIA?

The road of the pass was hard and smooth and not yet dusty in the early morning. Below were the hills with oak and chestnut trees, and far away below was the sea. On the other side were snowy mountains.

We came down from the pass through wooded country. There were bags of charcoal piled beside the road, and through the trees we saw charcoal-burners' huts. It was Sunday and the road, rising and falling, but always dropping away from the altitude of the pass, went through the scrub woods and through villages.

Outside the villages there were fields with vines. The fields were brown and the vines coarse and thick. The houses were white, and in the streets the men, in their Sunday clothes, were playing bowls. Against the walls of some of the houses there were pear trees, their branches candelabraed against the white walls. The pear trees had been sprayed, and the walls of the houses were stained a metallic blue-green by the spray vapor. There were small clearings around the villages where the vines grew, and then the woods.

In a village, twenty kilometers above Spezia, there was a crowd in the square, and a young man carrying a suitcase came up to the car and asked us to take him in to Spezia.

'There are only two places, and they are occupied,' I said. We had an old Ford coupé.

'I will ride on the outside.'

'You will be uncomfortable.'

'That makes nothing. I must go to Spezia.'

'Should we take him?' I asked Guy.

'He seems to be going anyway,' Guy said. The young man handed in a parcel through the window.

'Look after this,' he said. Two men tied his suitcase on the back of the car, above our suitcases. He shook hands with every one, explained that to a Fascist and a man as used to travelling as himself there was no discomfort, and climbed up on the running-board on the left-hand side of the car, holding on inside, his right arm through the open window.

'You can start,' he said. The crowd waved. He waved with his free hand.

'What did he say?' Guy asked me.

'That we could start.'

'Isn't he nice?' Guy said.

The road followed a river. Across the river were mountains. The sun was taking the frost out of the grass. It was bright and cold and the air came through the open wind-shield.

'How do you think he likes it out there?' Guy was looking up the road. His view out of his side of the car was blocked by our guest. The young man projected from the side of the car like the figurehead of a ship. He had turned his coat collar up and pulled his hat down and his nose looked cold in the wind.

'Maybe he'll get enough of it,' Guy said. 'That's the side our bum tire's on.'

'Oh, he'd leave us if we blew out,' I said. 'He wouldn't get his travelling-clothes dirty.'

'Well, I don't mind him,' Guy said – 'except the way he leans out on the turns.'

The woods were gone; the road had left the river to climb; the radiator was boiling; the young man looked annoyedly and suspiciously at the steam and rusty water; the engine was grinding, with both Guy's feet on the first-speed pedal, up and up, back and forth and up, and, finally, out level. The grinding stopped, and in the new quiet there was a great churning bubbling in the radiator. We were at the top of the last range above Spezia and the sea. The road descended with short, barely rounded turns. Our guest hung out on the turns and nearly pulled the top-heavy car over.

'You can't tell him not to,' I said to Guy. 'It's his sense of self-preservation.'

'The great Italian sense.'

'The greatest Italian sense.'

We came down around curves, through deep dust, the dust powdering the olive trees. Spezia spread below along the sea. The road flattened outside the town. Our guest put his head in the window.

'I want to stop.'

'Stop it,' I said to Guy.

We slowed up, at the side of the road. The young man got down, went to the back of the car and untied the suitcase.

'I stop here, so you won't get into trouble carrying passengers,' he said. 'My package.'

I handed him the package. He reached in his pocket.

'How much do I owe you?'

'Nothing.'

'Why not?'

'I don't know,' I said.

'Then thanks,' the young man said, not 'thank you,' or 'thank you very much,' or 'thank you a thousand times,' all of which you formerly said in Italy to a man when he handed you a time-table or explained about a direction. The young man uttered the lowest form of the word 'thanks' and looked after us suspiciously as Guy started the car. I waved my hand at him. He was too dignified to reply. We went on into Spezia.

'That's a young man that will go a long way in Italy,' I said to Guy.

'Well,' said Guy, 'he went twenty kilometers with us.'

A MEAL IN SPEZIA

We came into Spezia looking for a place to eat. The street was wide and the houses high and yellow. We followed the tram-track into the center of town. On the walls of the houses were stencilled eye-bugging portraits of Mussolini, with hand-painted '*vivas*,' the double V in black paint with drippings of paint down the wall. Side-streets went down to the harbor. It was bright and the people were all out for Sunday. The stone paving had been sprinkled and there were damp stretches in the dust. We went close to the curb to avoid a tram.

'Let's eat somewhere simple,' Guy said.

We stopped opposite two restaurant signs. We were standing across the street and I was buying the papers. The two restaurants were side by side. A woman standing in the doorway of one smiled at us and we crossed the street and went in.

It was dark inside and at the back of the room three girls were sitting at a table with an old woman. Across from us, at another table, sat a sailor. He sat there neither eating nor drinking. Fur-ther back, a young man in a blue suit was writing at a table. His hair was pomaded and shining and he was very smartly dressed and clean-cut looking.

The light came through the doorway, and through the win-dow where vegetables, fruit, steaks, and chops were arranged in a show-case. A girl came and took our order and another girl stood in the doorway. We noticed that she wore nothing under her house dress. The girl who took our order put her arm around Guy's neck while we were looking at the menu. There were three girls in all, and they all took turns going and standing in the doorway. The old woman at the table in the back of the room spoke to them and they sat down again with her.

There was no doorway leading from the room except into the kitchen. A curtain hung over it. The girl who had taken our order came in from the kitchen with spaghetti. She put it on the table and brought a bottle of red wine and sat down at the table.

'Well,' I said to Guy, 'you wanted to eat some place simple.'

'This isn't simple. This is complicated.'

'What do you say?' asked the girl. 'Are you Germans?'

'South Germans,' I said. 'The South Germans are a gentle, lovable people.'

'Don't understand,' she said.

'What's the mechanics of this place?' Guy asked. 'Do I have to let her put her arm around my neck?'

'Certainly,' I said. 'Mussolini has abolished the brothels. This is a restaurant.'

The girl wore a one-piece dress. She leaned forward against the table and put her hands on her breasts and smiled. She smiled better on one side than on the other and turned the good side toward us. The charm of the good side had been enhanced by some event which had smoothed the other side of her nose in, as warm wax can be smoothed. Her nose, however, did not look like warm wax. It was very cold and firmed, only smoothed in. 'You like me?' she asked Guy.

'He adores you,' I said. 'But he doesn't speak Italian.'

'*Ich spreche Deutsch*,' she said, and stroked Guy's hair.

'Speak to the lady in your native tongue, Guy.'

'Where do you come from?' asked the lady.

'Potsdam.'

'And you will stay here now for a little while?'

'In this so dear Spezia?' I asked.

'Tell her we have to go,' said Guy. 'Tell her we are very ill, and have no money.'

'My friend is a misogynist,' I said, 'an old German misogynist.'

'Tell him I love him.'

I told him.

'Will you shut your mouth and get us out of here?' Guy said. The lady had placed another arm around his neck. 'Tell him he is mine,' she said. I told him.

'Will you get us out of here?'

'You are quarrelling,' the lady said. 'You do not love one another.'

'We are Germans,' I said proudly, 'old South Germans.'

'Tell him he is a beautiful boy,' the lady said. Guy is thirty-eight and takes some pride in the fact that he is taken for a travelling salesman in France. 'You are a beautiful boy,' I said.

'Who says so?' Guy asked, 'you or her?'

'She does. I'm just your interpreter. Isn't that what you got me in on this trip for?'

'I'm glad it's her,' said Guy. 'I didn't want to have to leave you here too.'

'I don't know. Spezia's a lovely place.'

'Spezia,' the lady said. 'You are talking about Spezia.'

'Lovely place,' I said.

'It is my country,' she said. 'Spezia is my home and Italy is my country.'

'She says that Italy is her country.'

'Tell her it looks like her country,' Guy said.

'What have you for dessert?' I asked.

'Fruit,' she said. 'We have bananas.'

'Bananas are all right,' Guy said. 'They've got skins on.'

'Oh, he takes bananas,' the lady said. She embraced Guy.

'What does she say?' he asked, keeping his face out of the way.

'She is pleased because you take bananas.'

'Tell her I don't take bananas.'

'The Signor does not take bananas.'

'Ah,' said the lady, crestfallen, 'he doesn't take bananas.'

'Tell her I take a cold bath every morning,' Guy said.

'The Signor takes a cold bath every morning.'

'No understand,' the lady said.

Across from us, the property sailor had not moved. No one in the place paid any attention to him.

'We want the bill,' I said.

'Oh, no. You must stay.'

'Listen,' the clean-cut young man said from the table where he was writing, 'let them go. These two are worth nothing.'

The lady took my hand. 'You won't stay? You won't ask him to stay?'

'We have to go,' I said. 'We have to get to Pisa, or if possible, Firenze, tonight. We can amuse ourselves in those cities at the end of the day. It is now the day. In the day we must cover distance.'

'To stay a little while is nice.'

'To travel is necessary during the light of day.'

'Listen,' the clean-cut young man said. 'Don't bother to talk with these two. I tell you they are worth nothing and I know.'

'Bring us the bill,' I said. She brought the bill from the old woman and went back and sat at the table. Another girl came in from the kitchen. She walked the length of the room and stood in the doorway.

'Don't bother with these two,' the clean-cut young man said in a wearied voice. 'Come and eat. They are worth nothing.'

We paid the bill and stood up. All the girls, the old woman, and the clean-cut young man sat down at table together. The property sailor sat with his head in his hands. No one had spoken to him all the time we were at lunch. The girl brought us our change that the old woman counted out for her and went back to her place at the table. We left a tip on the table and went out. When we were seated in the car ready to start, the girl came out and stood in the door. We started and I waved to her. She did not wave, but stood there looking after us.

AFTER THE RAIN

It was raining hard when we passed through the suburbs of Genoa and, even going very slowly behind the tram-cars and the motor trucks, liquid mud splashed on to the sidewalks, so that people stepped into doorways as they saw us coming. In San Pier d'Arena, the industrial suburb outside of Genoa, there is a wide street with two car-tracks and we drove down the center to avoid sending the mud on to the men going home from work. On our left was the Mediterranean. There was a big sea running and waves broke and the wind blew the spray against the car. A river-bed that, when we had passed, going into Italy, had been wide, stony and dry, was running brown, and up to the banks. The brown water discolored the sea and as the waves thinned and cleared in breaking, the light came through the yellow water and the crests, detached by the wind, blew across the road.

A big car passed us, going fast, and a sheet of muddy water rose up and over our wind-shield and radiator. The automatic wind-shield cleaner moved back and forth, spreading the film over the glass. We stopped and ate lunch at Sestri. There was no heat in the restaurant and we kept our hats and coats on. We could see the car outside, through the window. It was covered with mud and was stopped beside some boats that had been pulled up beyond the waves. In the restaurant you could see your breath.

The *pasta asciutta* was good; the wine tasted of alum, and we poured water in it. Afterward the waiter brought beefsteak and fried potatoes. A man and a woman sat at the far end of the restaurant. He was middle-aged and she was young and wore black. All during the meal she would blow out her breath in the cold damp air. The man would look at it and shake his head. They ate without talking and the man held her hand under the table. She was good-looking and they seemed very sad. They had a travelling-bag with them.

We had the papers and I read the account of the Shanghai fighting aloud to Guy. After the meal, he left with the waiter in search for a place which did not exist in the restaurant, and I cleaned off the wind-shield, the lights and the license plates with a rag. Guy came back and we backed the car out and started. The waiter had taken him across the road and into an old house. The people in the house were suspicious and the waiter had remained with Guy to see nothing was stolen.

'Although I don't know how, me not being a plumber, they expected me to steal anything,' Guy said.

As we came up on a headland beyond the town, the wind struck the car and nearly tipped it over.

'It's good it blows us away from the sea,' Guy said.

'Well,' I said, 'they drowned Shelley somewhere along here.'

'That was down by Viareggio,' Guy said. 'Do you remember what we came to this country for?'

'Yes,' I said, 'but we didn't get it.'

'We'll be out of it tonight.'

'If we can get past Ventimiglia.'

'We'll see. I don't like to drive this coast at night.' It was early afternoon and the sun was out. Below, the sea was blue with whitecaps running toward Savona. Back, beyond the cape, the brown and blue water joined. Out ahead of us, a tramp steamer was going up the coast.

'Can you still see Genoa?' Guy asked.

'Oh, yes.'

'That next big cape ought to put it out of sight.'

'We'll see it a long time yet. I can still see Portofino Cape behind it.'

Finally we could not see Genoa. I looked back as we came out and there was only the sea, and below, in the bay, a line of beach with fishing-boats and above, on the side of the hill, a town and then capes far down the coast.

'It's gone now,' I said to Guy.

'Oh, it's been gone a long time now.'

'But we couldn't be sure till we got way out.'

There was a sign with a picture of an S-turn and *Svolta Pericolosa*. The road curved around the headland and the wind blew through the crack in the wind-shield. Below the cape was a flat stretch beside the sea. The wind had dried the mud and the wheels were beginning to lift dust. On the flat road we passed a Fascist riding a bicycle, a heavy revolver in a holster on his back. He held the middle of the road on his bicycle and we turned out for him. He looked up at us as we passed. Ahead there was a railway crossing, and as we came toward it the gates went down.

As we waited, the Fascist came up on his bicycle. The train went by and Guy started the engine.

'Wait,' the bicycle man shouted from behind the car. 'Your number's dirty.'

I got out with a rag. The number had been cleaned at lunch.

'You can read it,' I said.

'You think so?'

'Read it.'

'I cannot read it. It is dirty.'

I wiped it off with the rag.

'How's that?'

'Twenty-five lire.'

'What?' I said. 'You could have read it. It's only dirty from the state of the roads.'

'You don't like Italian roads?'

'They are dirty.'

'Fifty lire.' He spat in the road. 'Your car is dirty and you are dirty too.'

'Good. And give me a receipt with your name.'

He took out a receipt book, made in duplicate, and perforated, so one side could be given to the customer, and the other side filled in and kept as a stub. There was no carbon to record what the customer's ticket said.

'Give me fifty lire.'

He wrote in indelible pencil, tore out the slip and handed it to me. I read it.

'This is for twenty-five lire.'

'A mistake,' he said, and changed the twenty-five to fifty.

'And now the other side. Make it fifty in the part you keep.'

He smiled a beautiful Italian smile and wrote something on the receipt stub, holding it so I could not see.

'Go on,' he said, 'before your number gets dirty again.'

We drove for two hours after it was dark and slept in Mentone that night. It seemed very cheerful and clean and sane and lovely. We had driven from Ventimiglia to Pisa and Florence, across the Romagna to Rimini, back through Forli, Imola, Bologna, Parma, Piacenza and Genoa, to Ventimiglia again. The whole trip had taken only ten days. Naturally, in such a short trip, we had no opportunity to see how things were with the country or the people.

FIFTY GRAND

'How are you going yourself, Jack?' I asked him.

'You seen this Walcott?' he says.

'Just in the gym.'

'Well,' Jack says, 'I'm going to need a lot of luck with that boy.'

'He can't hit you, Jack,' Soldier said.

'I wish to hell he couldn't.'

'He couldn't hit you with a handful of bird-shot.'

'Bird-shot'd be all right,' Jack says. 'I wouldn't mind bird-shot any.'

'He looks easy to hit,' I said.

'Sure,' Jack says, 'he ain't going to last long. He ain't going to last like you and me, Jerry. But right now he's got everything.'

'You'll left-hand him to death.'

'Maybe,' Jack says. 'Sure. I got a chance to.'

'Handle him like you handled Kid Lewis.'

'Kid Lewis,' Jack said. 'That kike!'

The three of us, Jack Brennan, Soldier Bartlett, and I were in Hanley's. There were a couple of broads sitting at the next table to us. They had been drinking.

'What do you mean, kike?' one of the broads says. 'What do you mean, kike, you big Irish bum?'

'Sure,' Jack says. 'That's it.'

'Kikes,' this broad goes on. 'They're always talking about kikes, these big Irishmen. What do you mean, kikes?'

'Come on. Let's get out of here.'

'Kikes,' this broad goes on. 'Whoever saw you ever buy a drink? Your wife sews your pockets up every morning. These Irishmen and their kikes! Ted Lewis could lick you too.'

'Sure,' Jack says. 'And you give away a lot of things free too, don't you?'

We went out. That was Jack. He could say what he wanted to when he wanted to say it.

Jack started training out at Danny Hogan's health farm over in Jersey. It was nice out there but Jack didn't like it much. He didn't like being away from his wife and the kids, and he was sore and grouchy most of the time. He liked me and we got along fine together; and he liked Hogan, but after a while Sol-

dier Bartlett commenced to get on his nerves. A kidder gets to
be an awful thing around a camp if his stuff goes sort of sour.
Soldier was always kidding Jack, just sort of kidding him all the
time. It wasn't very funny and it wasn't very good, and it began
to get to Jack. It was sort of stuff like this. Jack would finish up
with the weights and the bag and pull on the gloves.

'You want to work?' he'd say to Soldier.

'Sure. How you want me to work?' Soldier would ask. 'Want
me to treat you rough like Walcott? Want me to knock you
down a few times?'

'That's it,' Jack would say. He didn't like it any, though.

One morning we were all out on the road. We'd been out
quite a way and now we were coming back. We'd go along fast
for three minutes and then walk a minute, and then go fast for
three minutes again. Jack wasn't ever what you would call a
sprinter. He'd move around fast enough in the ring if he had to,
but he wasn't any too fast on the road. All the time we were
walking Soldier was kidding him. We came up the hill to the
farm-house.

'Well,' says Jack, 'you better go back to town, Soldier.'

'What do you mean?'

'You better go back to town and stay there.'

'What's the matter?'

'I'm sick of hearing you talk.'

'Yes?' says Soldier.

'Yes,' says Jack.

'You'll be a damn sight sicker when Walcott gets through
with you.'

'Sure,' says Jack, 'maybe I will. But I know I'm sick of you.'

So Soldier went off on the train to town that same morning.
I went down with him to the train. He was good and sore.

'I was just kidding him,' he said. We were waiting on the
platform. 'He can't pull that stuff with me, Jerry.'

'He's nervous and crabby,' I said. 'He's a good fellow, Soldier.'

'The hell he is. The hell he's ever been a good fellow.'

'Well,' I said, 'so long, Soldier.'

The train had come in. He climbed up with his bag.

'So long, Jerry,' he says. 'You be in town before the fight?'

'I don't think so.'

'See you then.'

He went in and the conductor swung up and the train went
out. I rode back to the farm in the cart. Jack was on the porch

writing a letter to his wife. The mail had come and I got the papers and went over on the other side of the porch and sat down to read. Hogan came out the door and walked over to me.

'Did he have a jam with Soldier?'

'Not a jam,' I said. 'He just told him to go back to town.'

'I could see it coming,' Hogan said. 'He never liked Soldier much.'

'No. He don't like many people.'

'He's a pretty cold one,' Hogan said.

'Well, he's always been fine to me.'

'Me too,' Hogan said. 'I got no kick on him. He's a cold one, though.'

Hogan went in through the screen door and I sat there on the porch and read the papers. It was just starting to get fall weather and it's nice country there in Jersey, up in the hills, and after I read the paper through I sat there and looked out at the country and the road down below against the woods with cars going along it, lifting the dust up. It was fine weather and pretty nice-looking country. Hogan came to the door and I said, 'Say, Hogan, haven't you got anything to shoot out here?'

'No,' Hogan said. 'Only sparrows.'

'Seen the paper?' I said to Hogan.

'What's in it?'

'Sande booted three of them in yesterday.'

'I got that on the telephone last night.'

'You follow them pretty close, Hogan?' I asked.

'Oh, I keep in touch with them,' Hogan said.

'How about Jack?' I says. 'Does he still play them?'

'Him?' said Hogan. 'Can you see him doing it?'

Just then Jack came around the corner with the letter in his hand. He's wearing a sweater and an old pair of pants and boxing shoes.

'Got a stamp, Hogan?' he asks.

'Give me the letter,' Hogan said. 'I'll mail it for you.'

'Say, Jack,' I said, 'didn't you used to play the ponies?'

'Sure.'

'I knew you did. I knew I used to see you out at Sheepshead.'

'What did you lay off them for?' Hogan asked.

'Lost money.'

Jack sat down on the porch by me. He leaned back against a post. He shut his eyes in the sun.

'Want a chair?' Hogan asked.

'No,' said Jack. 'This is fine.'

'It's a nice day,' I said. 'It's pretty nice out in the country.'

'I'd a damn sight rather be in town with the wife.'

'Well, you only got another week.'

'Yes,' Jack says. 'That's so.'

We sat there on the porch. Hogan was inside at the office.

'What do you think about the shape I'm in?' Jack asked me.

'Well, you can't tell,' I said. 'You got a week to get around into form.'

'Don't stall me.'

'Well,' I said, 'you're not right.'

'I'm not sleeping,' Jack said.

'You'll be all right in a couple of days.'

'No,' says Jack, 'I got the insomnia.'

'What's on your mind?'

'I miss the wife.'

'Have her come out.'

'No. I'm too old for that.'

'We'll take a long walk before you turn in and get you good and tired.'

'Tired!' Jack says. 'I'm tired all the time.'

He was that way all week. He wouldn't sleep at night and he'd get up in the morning feeling that way, you know, when you can't shut your hands. 'He's stale as poorhouse cake,' Hogan said. 'He's nothing.'

'I never seen Walcott,' I said.

'He'll kill him,' said Hogan. 'He'll tear him in two.'

'Well,' I said, 'everybody's got to get it sometime.'

'Not like this, though,' Hogan said. 'They'll think he never trained. It gives the farm a black eye.'

'You hear what the reporters said about him?'

'Didn't I! They said he was awful. They said they oughtn't to let him fight.'

'Well,' I said, 'they're always wrong, ain't they?'

'Yes,' said Hogan. 'But this time they're right.'

'What the hell do they know about whether a man's right or not?'

'Well,' said Hogan, 'they're not such fools.'

'All they did was pick Willard at Toledo. This Lardner, he's so wise now, ask him about when he picked Willard at Toledo.'

'Aw, he wasn't out,' Hogan said. 'He only writes the big fights.'

'I don't care who they are,' I said. 'What the hell do they know? They can write maybe, but what the hell do they know?'

'You don't think Jack's in any shape, do you?' Hogan asked.

'No. He's through. All he needs is to have Corbett pick him to win for it to be all over.'

'Well, Corbett'll pick him,' Hogan says.

'Sure. He'll pick him.'

That night Jack didn't sleep any either. The next morning was the last day before the fight. After breakfast we were out on the porch again.

'What do you think about, Jack, when you can't sleep?' I said.

'Oh, I worry,' Jack says. 'I worry about property I got up in the Bronx, I worry about property I got in Florida. I worry about the kids. I worry about the wife. Sometimes I think about fights. I think about that kike Ted Lewis and I get sore. I got some stocks and I worry about them. What the hell don't I think about?'

'Well,' I said, 'tomorrow night it'll all be over.'

'Sure,' said Jack. 'That always helps a lot, don't it? That just fixes everything all up, I suppose. Sure.'

He was sore all day. We didn't do any work. Jack just moved around a little to loosen up. He shadow-boxed a few rounds. He didn't even look good doing that. He skipped the rope a little while. He couldn't sweat.

'He'd be better not to do any work at all,' Hogan said. We were standing watching him skip rope. 'Don't he ever sweat at all any more?'

'He can't sweat.'

'Do you suppose he's got the con? He never had any trouble making weight did he?'

'No, he hasn't got any con. He just hasn't got anything inside any more.'

'He ought to sweat,' said Hogan.

Jack came over, skipping the rope. He was skipping up and down in front of us, forward and back, crossing his arms every third time.

'Well,' he says. 'What are you buzzards talking about?'

'I don't think you ought to work any more,' Hogan says. 'You'll be stale.'

'Wouldn't that be awful?' Jack says and skips away down the floor, slapping the rope hard.

That afternoon John Collins showed up out at the farm. Jack

was up in his room. John came out in a car from town. He had a couple of friends with him. The car stopped and they all got out.

'Where's Jack?' John asked me.

'Up in his room, lying down.'

'Lying down?'

'Yes,' I said.

'How is he?'

I looked at the two fellows that were with John.

'They're friends of his,' John said.

'He's pretty bad,' I said.

'What's the matter with him?'

'He don't sleep.'

'Hell,' said John. 'That Irishman could never sleep.'

'He isn't right,' I said.

'Hell,' John said. 'He's never right. I've had him for ten years and he's never been right yet.'

The fellows who were with him laughed.

'I want you to shake hands with Mr. Morgan and Mr. Steinfelt,' John said. 'This is Mr. Doyle. He's been training Jack.'

'Glad to meet you,' I said.

'Let's go up and see the boy,' the fellow called Morgan said.

'Let's have a look at him,' Steinfelt said.

We all went upstairs.

'Where's Hogan?' John asked.

'He's out in the barn with a couple of his customers,' I said.

'He got many people out here now?' John asked.

'Just two.'

'Pretty quiet, ain't it?' Morgan said.

'Yes,' I said. 'It's pretty quiet.'

We were outside Jack's room. John knocked on the door. There wasn't any answer.

'Maybe he's asleep,' I said.

'What the hell's he sleeping in the daytime for?'

John turned the handle and we all went in. Jack was lying asleep on the bed. He was face down and his face was in the pillow. Both his arms were around the pillow.

'Hey, Jack!' John said to him.

Jack's head moved a little on the pillow. 'Jack!' John says, leaning over him. Jack just dug a little deeper in the pillow. John touched him on the shoulder. Jack sat up and looked at us. He hadn't shaved and he was wearing an old sweater.

'Christ! Why can't you let me sleep?' he says to John.

'Don't be sore,' John says. 'I didn't mean to wake you up.'

'Oh no,' Jack says. 'Of course not.'

'You know Morgan and Steinfelt,' John said.

'Glad to see you,' Jack says.

'How do you feel, Jack?' Morgan asks him.

'Fine,' Jack says. 'How the hell would I feel?'

'You look fine,' Steinfelt says.

'Yes, don't I,' says Jack. 'Say,' he says to John. 'You're my manager. You get a big enough cut. Why the hell don't you come out here when the reporters was out! You want Jerry and me to talk to them?'

'I had Lew fighting in Philadelphia,' John said.

'What the hell's that to me?' Jack says. 'You're my manager. You get a big enough cut, don't you? You aren't making me any money in Philadelphia, are you? Why the hell aren't you out here when I ought to have you?'

'Hogan was here.'

'Hogan,' Jack says. 'Hogan's as dumb as I am.'

'Soldier Bahtlett was out here wukking with you for a while, wasn't he?' Steinfelt said to change the subject.

'Yes, he was out here,' Jack says. 'He was out here all right.'

'Say, Jerry,' John said to me. 'Would you go and find Hogan and tell him we want to see him in about half an hour?'

'Sure,' I said.

'Why the hell can't he stick around?' Jack says. 'Stick around, Jerry.'

Morgan and Steinfelt looked at each other.

'Quiet down, Jack,' John said to him.

'I better go find Hogan,' I said.

'All right, if you want to go,' Jack says. 'None of these guys are going to send you away, though.'

'I'll go find Hogan,' I said.

Hogan was out in the gym in the barn. He had a couple of his health-farm patients with the gloves on. They neither one wanted to hit the other, for fear the other would come back and hit him.

'That'll do,' Hogan said when he saw me come in. 'You can stop the slaughter. You gentlemen take a shower and Bruce will rub you down.'

They climbed out through the ropes and Hogan came over to me.

'John Collins is out with a couple of friends to see Jack,' I said.
'I saw them come up in the car.'

'Who are the two fellows with John?'

'They're what you call wise boys,' Hogan said. 'Don't you know them two?'

'No,' I said.

'That's Happy Steinfelt and Lew Morgan. They got a pool-room.'

'I been away a long time,' I said.

'Sure,' said Hogan. 'That Happy Steinfelt's a big operator.'

'I've heard his name,' I said.

'He's a pretty smooth boy,' Hogan said. 'They're a couple of sharpshooters.'

'Well,' I said. 'They want to see us in half an hour.'

'You mean they don't want to see us until a half an hour?'

'That's it.'

'Come on in the office,' Hogan said. 'To hell with those sharpshooters.'

After about thirty minutes or so Hogan and I went upstairs. We knocked on Jack's door. They were talking inside the room.

'Wait a minute,' somebody said.

'To hell with that stuff,' Hogan said. 'When you want to see me I'm down in the office.'

We heard the door unlock. Steinfelt opened it.

'Come on in, Hogan,' he says. 'We're all going to have a drink.'

'Well,' says Hogan. 'That's something.'

We went in. Jack was sitting on the bed. John and Morgan were sitting on a couple of chairs. Steinfelt was standing up.

'You're a pretty mysterious lot of boys,' Hogan said.

'Hello, Danny,' John says.

'Hello, Danny,' Morgan says and shakes hands.

Jack doesn't say anything. He just sits there on the bed. He ain't with the others. He's all by himself. He was wearing an old blue jersey and pants and had on boxing shoes. He needed a shave. Steinfelt and Morgan were dressers. John was quite a dresser too. Jack sat there looking Irish and tough.

Steinfelt brought out a bottle and Hogan brought in some glasses and everybody had a drink. Jack and I took one and the rest of them went on and had two or three each.

'Better save some for your ride back,' Hogan said.

'Don't you worry. We got plenty,' Morgan said.

Jack hadn't drunk anything since the one drink. He was standing up and looking at them. Morgan was sitting on the bed where Jack had sat.

'Have a drink, Jack,' John said and handed him the glass and the bottle.

'No,' Jack said, 'I never liked to go to these wakes.'

They all laughed. Jack didn't laugh.

They were all feeling pretty good when they left. Jack stood on the porch when they got into the car. They waved to him.

'So long,' Jack said.

We had supper. Jack didn't say anything all during the meal except, 'Will you pass me this?' or 'Will you pass me that?' The two health-farm patients ate at the same table with us. They were pretty nice fellows. After we finished eating we went out on the porch. It was dark early.

'Like to take a walk, Jerry?' Jack asked.

'Sure,' I said.

We put on our coats and started out. It was quite a way down to the main road and then we walked along the main road about a mile and a half. Cars kept going by and we would pull out to the side until they were past. Jack didn't say anything. After we had stepped out into the bushes to let a big car go by Jack said, 'To hell with this walking. Come on back to Hogan's.'

We went along a side road that cut up over the hill and cut across the fields back to Hogan's. We could see the lights of the house up on the hill. We came around to the front of the house and there standing in the doorway was Hogan.

'Have a good walk?' Hogan asked.

'Oh, fine,' Jack said. 'Listen, Hogan. Have you got any liquor?'

'Sure,' says Hogan. 'What's the idea?'

'Send it up to the room,' Jack says. 'I'm going to sleep to-night.'

'You're the doctor,' Hogan says.

'Come on up to the room, Jerry,' Jack says.

Upstairs Jack sat on the bed with his head in his hands.

'Ain't it a life?' Jack says.

Hogan brought in a quart of liquor and two glasses.

'Want some ginger ale?'

'What do you think I want to do, get sick?'

'I just asked you,' said Hogan.

'Have a drink?' said Jack.

'No, thanks,' said Hogan. He went out.

'How about you, Jerry?'

'I'll have one with you,' I said.

Jack poured out a couple of drinks. 'Now,' he said, 'I want to take it slow and easy.'

'Put some water in it,' I said.

'Yes,' Jack said. 'I guess that's better.'

We had a couple of drinks without saying anything. Jack started to pour me another.

'No,' I said, 'that's all I want.'

'All right,' Jack said. He poured himself out another big shot and put water in it. He was lighting up a little.

'That was a fine bunch out here this afternoon,' he said. 'They don't take any chances, those two.'

Then a little later, 'Well,' he says, 'they're right. What the hell's the good in taking chances?'

'Don't you want another, Jerry?' he said. 'Come on, drink along with me.'

'I don't need it, Jack,' I said. 'I feel all right.'

'Just have one more,' Jack said. It was softening him up.

'All right,' I said.

Jack poured one for me and another big one for himself.

'You know,' he said, 'I like liquor pretty well. If I hadn't been boxing I would have drunk quite a lot.'

'Sure,' I said.

'You know,' he said, 'I missed a lot, boxing.'

'You made plenty of money.'

'Sure, that's what I'm after. You know I miss a lot, Jerry.'

'How do you mean?'

'Well,' he says, 'like about the wife. And being away from home so much. It don't do my girls any good. "Who's your old man?" some of those society kids'll say to them. "My old man's Jack Brennan." That don't do them any good.'

'Hell,' I said, 'all that makes a difference is if they got dough.'

'Well,' says Jack, 'I got the dough for them all right.'

He poured out another drink. The bottle was about empty.

'Put some water in it,' I said. Jack poured in some water.

'You know,' he says, 'you ain't got any idea how I miss the wife.'

'Sure.'

'You ain't got any idea. You can't have an idea what it's like.'

'It ought to be better out in the country than in town.'

'With me now,' Jack said, 'it don't make any difference where I am. You can't have an idea what it's like.'

'Have another drink.'

'Am I getting soused? Do I talk funny?'

'You're coming on all right.'

'You can't have an idea what it's like. They ain't anybody can have an idea what it's like.'

'Except the wife,' I said.

'She knows,' Jack said. 'She knows all right. She knows. You bet she knows.'

'Put some water in that,' I said.

'Jerry,' says Jack, 'you can't have an idea what it gets to be like.'

He was good and drunk. He was looking at me steady. His eyes were sort of too steady.

'You'll sleep all right,' I said.

'Listen Jerry,' Jack says. 'You want to make some money? Get some money down on Walcott.'

'Yes?'

'Listen, Jerry,' Jack put down the glass. 'I'm not drunk now, see? You know what I'm betting on him? Fifty grand.'

'That's a lot of dough.'

'Fifty grand,' Jack says, 'at two to one. I'll get twenty-five thousand bucks. Get some money on him, Jerry.'

'It sounds good,' I said.

'How can I beat him?' Jack says. 'It ain't crooked. How can I beat him? Why not make money on it?'

'Put some water in that,' I said.

'I'm through after this fight,' Jack says. 'I'm through with it. I got to take a beating. Why shouldn't I make money on it?'

'Sure.'

'I ain't slept for a week,' Jack says. 'All night I lay awake and worry my can off. I can't sleep, Jerry. You ain't got an idea what it's like when you can't sleep.'

'Sure.'

'I can't sleep. That's all. I just can't sleep. What's the use of taking care of yourself all these years when you can't sleep?'

'It's bad.'

'You ain't got an idea what it's like, Jerry, when you can't sleep.'

'Put some water in that,' I said.

Well, about eleven o'clock Jack passes out and I put him to

bed. Finally he's so he can't keep from sleeping. I helped him get his clothes off and got him into bed.

'You'll sleep all right, Jack,' I said.

'Sure,' Jack says, 'I'll sleep now.'

'Good night, Jack,' I said.

'Good night, Jerry,' Jack says. 'You're the only friend I got.'

'Oh, hell,' I said.

'You're the only friend I got,' Jack says, 'the only friend I got.'

'Go to sleep,' I said.

'I'll sleep,' Jack says.

Downstairs Hogan was sitting at the desk in the office reading the papers. He looked up. 'Well, you get your boy friend to sleep?' he asks.

'He's off.'

'It's better for him than not sleeping,' Hogan said.

'Sure.'

'You'd have a hell of a time explaining that to these sport writers though,' Hogan said.

'Well, I'm going to bed myself,' I said.

'Good night,' said Hogan.

In the morning I came downstairs about eight o'clock and got some breakfast. Hogan had his two customers out in the barn doing exercises. I went out and watched them.

'One! Two! Three! Four!' Hogan was counting for them. 'Hello, Jerry,' he said. 'Is Jack up yet?'

'No. He's still sleeping.'

I went back to my room and packed up to go in to town. About nine-thirty I heard Jack getting up in the next room. When I heard him go downstairs I went down after him. Jack was sitting at the breakfast table. Hogan had come in and was standing beside the table.

'How do you feel, Jack?' I asked him.

'Not so bad.'

'Sleep well?' Hogan asked.

'I slept all right,' Jack said. 'I got a thick tongue but I ain't got a head.'

'Good,' said Hogan. 'That was good liquor.'

'Put it on the bill,' Jack says.

'What time you want to go into town?' Hogan asked.

'Before lunch,' Jack says. 'The eleven o'clock train.'

'Sit down, Jerry,' Jack said. Hogan went out.

I sat down at the table. Jack was eating a grapefruit. When

he'd find a seed he'd spit it out in the spoon and dump it on the plate.

'I guess I was pretty stewed last night,' he started.

'You drank some liquor.'

'I guess I said a lot of fool things.'

'You weren't bad.'

'Where's Hogan?' he asked. He was through with the grape-fruit.

'He's out in front in the office.'

'What did I say about betting on the fight?' Jack asked. He was holding the spoon and sort of poking at the grapefruit with it.

The girl came in with some ham and eggs and took away the grapefruit.

'Bring me another glass of milk,' Jack said to her. She went out.

'You said you had fifty grand on Walcott,' I said.

'That's right,' Jack said.

'That's a lot of money.'

'I don't feel too good about it,' Jack said.

'Something might happen.'

'No,' Jack said. 'He wants the title bad. They'll be shooting with him all right.'

'You can't ever tell.'

'No. He wants the title. It's worth a lot of money to him.'

'Fifty grand is a lot of money,' I said.

'It's business,' said Jack. 'I can't win. You know I can't win anyway.'

'As long as you're in there you got a chance.'

'No,' Jack says. 'I'm all through. It's just business.'

'How do you feel?'

'Pretty good,' Jack said. 'The sleep was what I needed.'

'You might go good.'

'I'll give them a good show,' Jack said.

After breakfast Jack called up his wife on the long-distance. He was inside the booth telephoning.

'That's the first time he's called her up since he's out here,' Hogan said.

'He writes her every day.'

'Sure,' Hogan says, 'a letter only costs two cents.'

Hogan said good-by to us and Bruce, the nigger rubber, drove us down to the train in the cart.

'Good-by, Mr. Brennan,' Bruce said at the train, 'I sure hope you knock his can off.'

'So long,' Jack said. He gave Bruce two dollars. Bruce had worked on him a lot. He looked kind of disappointed. Jack saw me looking at Bruce holding the two dollars.

'It's all in the bill,' he said. 'Hogan charged me for the rubbing.'

On the train going into town Jack didn't talk. He sat in the corner of the seat with his ticket in his hat-band and looked out of the window. Once he turned and spoke to me.

'I told the wife I'd take a room at the Shelby tonight,' he said. 'It's just around the corner from the Garden. I can go up to the house tomorrow morning.'

'That's a good idea,' I said. 'Your wife ever see you fight, Jack?'

'No,' Jack says. 'She never seen me fight.'

I thought he must be figuring on taking an awful beating if he doesn't want to go home afterward. In town we took a taxi up to the Shelby. A boy came out and took our bags and we went in to the desk.

'How much are the rooms?' Jack asked.

'We only have double rooms,' the clerk says. 'I can give you a nice double room for ten dollars.'

'That's too steep.'

'I can give you a double room for seven dollars.'

'With a bath?'

'Certainly.'

'You might as well bunk with me, Jerry,' Jack says.

'Oh,' I said, 'I'll sleep down at my brother-in-law's.'

'I don't mean for you to pay it,' Jack says. 'I just want to get my money's worth.'

'Will you register, please?' the clerk says. He looked at the names. 'Number 238, Mr. Brennan.'

We went up in the elevator. It was a nice big room with two beds and a door opening into a bath-room.

'This is pretty good,' Jack says.

The boy who brought us up pulled up the curtains and brought in our bags. Jack didn't make any move, so I gave the boy a quarter. We washed up and Jack said we better go out and get something to eat.

We ate a lunch at Jimmy Hanley's place. Quite a lot of the boys were there. When we were about half through eating, John came in and sat down with us. Jack didn't talk much.

'How are you on the weight, Jack?' John asked him. Jack was putting away a pretty good lunch.

'I could make it with my clothes on,' Jack said. He never had to worry about taking off weight. He was a natural welterweight and he'd never gotten fat. He'd lost weight out at Hogan's.

'Well, that's one thing you never had to worry about,' John said.

'That's one thing,' Jack says.

We went around to the Garden to weigh in after lunch. The match was made at a hundred forty-seven pounds at three o'clock. Jack stepped on the scales with a towel around him. The bar didn't move. Walcott had just weighed and was standing with a lot of people around him.

'Let's see what you weigh, Jack,' Freedman, Walcott's manager, said.

'All right, weigh *him* then,' Jack jerked his head toward Walcott.

'Drop the towel,' Freedman said.

'What do you make it?' Jack asked the fellows who were weighing.

'One hundred and forty-three pounds,' the fat man who was weighing said.

'You're down fine, Jack,' Freedman says.

'Weigh *him*,' Jack says.

Walcott came over. He was a blond with wide shoulders and arms like a heavyweight. He didn't have much legs. Jack stood about half a head taller than he did.

'Hello, Jack,' he said. His face was plenty marked up.

'Hello,' said Jack. 'How you feel?'

'Good,' Walcott says. He dropped the towel from around his waist and stood on the scales. He had the widest shoulders and back you ever saw.

'One hundred and forty-six pounds and twelve ounces.'

Walcott stepped off and grinned at Jack.

'Well,' John says to him, 'Jack's spotting you about four pounds.'

'More than that when I come in, kid,' Walcott says. 'I'm going to go and eat now.'

We went back and Jack got dressed. 'He's a pretty tough-looking boy,' Jack says to me.

'He looks as though he'd been hit plenty of times.'

'Oh, yes,' Jack says. 'He ain't hard to hit.'

'Where are you going?' John asked when Jack was dressed.

'Back to the hotel,' Jack says. 'You looked after everything?'

'Yes,' John says. 'It's all looked after.'

'I'm going to lie down a while,' Jack says.

'I'll come around for you about a quarter to seven and we'll go and eat.'

'All right.'

Up at the hotel Jack took off his shoes and his coat and lay down for a while. I wrote a letter. I looked over a couple of times and Jack wasn't sleeping. He was lying perfectly still but every once in a while his eyes would open. Finally he sits up.

'Want to play some cribbage, Jerry?' he says.

'Sure,' I said.

He went over to his suitcase and got out the cards and the cribbage board. We played cribbage and he won three dollars off me. John knocked at the door and came in.

'Want to play some cribbage, John?' Jack asked him.

John put his hat down on the table. It was all wet. His coat was wet too.

'Is it raining?' Jack asks.

'It's pouring,' John says. 'The taxi I had got tied up in the traffic and I got out and walked.'

'Come on, play some cribbage,' Jack says.

'You ought to go and eat.'

'No,' says Jack. 'I don't want to eat yet.'

So they played cribbage for about half an hour and Jack won a dollar and a half off him.

'Well, I suppose we got to go eat,' Jack says. He went to the window and looked out.

'Is it still raining?'

'Yes.'

'Let's eat in the hotel,' John says.

'All right,' Jack says, 'I'll play you once more to see who pays for the meal.'

After a little while Jack gets up and says, 'You buy the meal, John,' and we went downstairs and ate in the big dining-room.

After we ate we went upstairs and Jack played cribbage with John again and won two dollars and a half off him. Jack was feeling pretty good. John had a bag with him with all his stuff in it. Jack took off his shirt and collar and put on a jersey and a sweater, so he wouldn't catch cold when he came out, and put his ring clothes and his bathrobe in a bag.

'You all ready?' John asks him. 'I'll call up and have them get a taxi.'

Pretty soon the telephone rang and they said the taxi was waiting.

We rode down in the elevator and went out through the lobby, and got in a taxi and rode around to the Garden. It was raining hard but there was a lot of people outside on the streets. The Garden was sold out. As we came in on our way to the dressing-room I saw how full it was. It looked like half a mile down to the ring. It was all dark. Just the lights over the ring.

'It's a good thing, with this rain, they didn't try and pull this fight in the ball park,' John said.

'They got a good crowd,' Jack says.

'This is a fight that would draw a lot more than the Garden could hold.'

'You can't tell about the weather,' Jack says.

John came to the door of the dressing-room and poked his head in. Jack was sitting there with his bathrobe on, he had his arms folded and was looking at the floor. John had a couple of handlers with him. They looked over his shoulder. Jack looked up.

'Is he in?' he asked.

'He's just gone down,' John said.

We started down. Walcott was just getting into the ring. The crowd gave him a big hand. He climbed through between the ropes and put his two fists together and smiled, and shook them at the crowd, first at one side of the ring, then at the other, and then sat down. Jack got a good hand coming down through the crowd. Jack is Irish and the Irish always get a pretty good hand. An Irishman don't draw in New York like a Jew or an Italian but they always get a good hand. Jack climbed up and bent down to go through the ropes and Walcott came over from his corner and pushed the rope down for Jack to go through. The crowd thought that was wonderful. Walcott put his hand on Jack's shoulder and they stood there just for a second.

'So you're going to be one of these popular champions,' Jack says to him. 'Take your goddam hand off my shoulder.'

'Be yourself,' Walcott says.

This is all great for the crowd. How gentlemanly the boys are before the fight. How they wish each other luck.

Solly Freedman came over to our corner while Jack is bandaging his hands and John is over in Walcott's corner. Jack puts his thumb through the slit in the bandage and then wrapped his hand nice and smooth. I taped it around the wrist and twice across the knuckles.

'Hey,' Freedman says. 'Where do you get all that tape?'

'Feel of it,' Jack says. 'It's soft, ain't it? Don't be a hick.'

Freedman stands there all the time while Jack bandages the other hand, and one of the boys that's going to handle him brings the gloves and I pull them on and work them around.

'Say, Freedman,' Jack asks, 'what nationality is this Walcott?'

'I don't know,' Solly says. 'He's some sort of a Dane.'

'He's a Bohemian,' the lad who brought the gloves said.

The referee called them out to the center of the ring and Jack walks out. Walcott comes out smiling. They met and the referee put his arm on each of their shoulders.

'Hello, popularity,' Jack says to Walcott.

'Be yourself.'

'What do you call yourself "Walcott" for?' Jack says. 'Didn't you know he was a nigger?'

'Listen –' says the referee, and he gives them the same old line. Once Walcott interrupts him. He grabs Jack's arm and says, 'Can I hit when he's got me like this?'

'Keep your hands off me,' Jack says. 'There ain't no moving-pictures of this.'

They went back to their corners. I lifted the bathrobe off Jack and he leaned on the ropes and flexed his knees a couple of times and scuffed his shoes in the rosin. The gong rang and Jack turned quick and went out. Walcott came toward him and they touched gloves and as soon as Walcott dropped his hands Jack jumped his left into his face twice. There wasn't anybody ever boxed better than Jack. Walcott was after him, going forward all the time with his chin on his chest. He's a hooker and he carries his hands pretty low. All he knows is to get in there and sock. But every time he gets in there close, Jack has the left hand in his face. It's just as though it's automatic. Jack just raises the left hand up and it's in Walcott's face. Three or four times Jack brings the right over but Walcott gets it on the shoulder or high up on the head. He's just like all these hookers. The only thing he's afraid of is another one of the same kind. He's covered everywhere you can hurt him. He don't care about a left hand in his face.

After about four rounds Jack has him bleeding bad and his face all cut up, but every time Walcott's got in close he's socked so hard he's got two big red patches on both sides just below Jack's ribs. Every time he gets in close, Jack ties him up, then gets one hand loose and uppercuts him, but when Walcott gets his hands loose he socks Jack in the body so they can hear it outside in the street. He's a socker.

It goes along like that for three rounds more. They don't talk any. They're working all the time. We worked over Jack plenty too, in between the rounds. He don't look good at all but he never does much work in the ring. He don't move around much and that left hand is just automatic. It's just like it was connected with Walcott's face and Jack just had to wish it in every time. Jack is always calm in close and he doesn't waste any juice. He knows everything about working in close too and he's getting away with a lot of stuff. While they were in our corner I watched him tie Walcott up, get his right hand loose, turn it and come up with an uppercut that got Walcott's nose with the heel of the glove. Walcott was bleeding bad and leaned his nose on Jack's shoulder so as to give Jack some of it too, and Jack sort of lifted his shoulder sharp and caught him against the nose, and then brought down the right hand and did the same thing again.

Walcott was sore as hell. By the time they'd gone five rounds he hated Jack's guts. Jack wasn't sore; that is, he wasn't any sorer than he always was. He certainly did used to make the fellows he fought hate boxing. That was why he hated Kid Lewis so. He never got the Kid's goat. Kid Lewis always had about three new dirty things Jack couldn't do. Jack was as safe as a church all the time he was in there, as long as he was strong. He certainly was treating Walcott rough. The funny thing was it looked as though Jack was an open classic boxer. That was because he had all that stuff too.

After the seventh round Jack says, 'My left's getting heavy.'

From then he started to take a beating. It didn't show at first. But instead of him running the fight it was Walcott was running it, instead of being safe all the time now he was in trouble. He couldn't keep him out with the left hand now. It looked as though it was the same as ever, only now instead of Walcott's punches just missing him they were just hitting him. He took an awful beating in the body.

'What's the round?' Jack asked.

'The eleventh.'

'I can't stay,' Jack says. 'My legs are going bad.'

Walcott had been just hitting him for a long time. It was like a baseball catcher pulls the ball and takes some of the shock off. From now on Walcott commenced to land solid. He certainly was a socking-machine. Jack was just trying to block everything now. It didn't show what an awful beating he was taking. In between the rounds I worked on his legs. The muscles would flutter under my hands all the time I was rubbing them. He was sick as hell.

'How's it go?' he asked John, turning around, his face all swollen.

'It's his fight.'

'I think I can last,' Jack says. 'I don't want this bohunk to stop me.'

It was going just the way he thought it would. He knew he couldn't beat Walcott. He wasn't strong any more. He was all right though. His money was all right and now he wanted to finish it off right to please himself. He didn't want to be knocked out.

The gong rang and we pushed him out. He went out slow. Walcott came right out after him. Jack put the left in his face and Walcott took it, came in under it and started working on Jack's body. Jack tried to tie him up and it was just like trying to hold on to a buzz-saw. Jack broke away from it and missed with the right. Walcott clipped him with a left hook and Jack went down. He went down on his hands and knees and looked at us. The referee started counting. Jack was watching us and shaking his head. At eight John motioned to him. You couldn't hear on account of the crowd. Jack got up. The referee had been holding Walcott back with one arm while he counted.

When Jack was on his feet Walcott started toward him.

'Watch yourself, Jimmy,' I heard Solly Freedman yell to him.

Walcott came up to Jack looking at him. Jack stuck the left hand at him. Walcott just shook his head. He backed Jack up against the ropes, measured him and then hooked the left very light to the side of Jack's head and socked the right into the body as hard as he could sock, just as low as he could get it. He must have hit him five inches below the belt. I thought the eyes would come out of Jack's head. They stuck way out. His mouth come open.

The referee grabbed Walcott. Jack stepped forward. If he went down there went fifty thousand bucks. He walked as though all his insides were going to fall out.

'It wasn't low,' he said. 'It was a accident.'

The crowd were yelling so you couldn't hear anything.

'I'm all right,' Jack says. They were right in front of us. The referee looks at John and then he shakes his head.

'Come on, you polak son-of-a-bitch,' Jack says to Walcott.

John was hanging onto the ropes. He had the towel ready to chuck in. Jack was standing just a little way out from the ropes. He took a step forward. I saw the sweat come out on his face like somebody had squeezed it and a big drop went down his nose.

'Come on and fight,' Jack says to Walcott.

The referee looked at John and waved Walcott on.

'Go in there, you slob,' he says.

Walcott went in. He didn't know what to do either. He never thought Jack could have stood it. Jack put the left in his face. There was such a hell of a lot of yelling going on. They were right in front of us. Walcott hit him twice. Jack's face was the worst thing I ever saw – the look on it! He was holding himself and all his body together and it all showed on his face. All the time he was thinking and holding his body in where it was busted.

Then he started to sock. His face looked awful all the time. He started to sock with his hands low down by his side, swinging at Walcott. Walcott covered up and Jack was swinging wild at Walcott's head. Then he swung the left and it hit Walcott in the groin and the right hit Walcott right bang where he'd hit Jack. Way low below the belt. Walcott went down and grabbed himself there and rolled and twisted around.

The referee grabbed Jack and pushed him toward his corner. John jumps into the ring. There was all this yelling going on. The referee was talking with the judges and then the announcer got into the ring with the megaphone and says, 'Walcott on a foul.'

The referee is talking to John and he says, 'What could I do? Jack wouldn't take the foul. Then when he's groggy he fouls him.'

'He'd lost it anyway,' John says.

Jack's sitting on the chair. I've got his gloves off and he's holding himself in down there with both hands. When he's got something supporting it his face doesn't look so bad.

'Go over and say you're sorry,' John says into his ear. 'It'll look good.'

Jack stands up and the sweat comes out all over his face. I put the bathrobe around him and he holds himself in with one hand under the bathrobe and goes across the ring. They've picked Walcott up and they're working on him. There're a lot of people in Walcott's corner. Nobody speaks to Jack. He leans over Walcott.

'I'm sorry,' Jack says. 'I didn't mean to foul you.'

Walcott doesn't say anything. He looks too damned sick.

'Well, you're the champion now,' Jack says to him. 'I hope you get a hell of a lot of fun out of it.'

'Leave the kid alone,' Solly Freedman says.

'Hello, Solly,' Jack says. 'I'm sorry I fouled your boy.'

Freedman just looks at him.

Jack went to his corner walking that funny jerky way and we got him down through the ropes and through the reporters' tables and out down the aisle. A lot of people want to slap Jack on the back. He goes out through all that mob in his bathrobe to the dressing-room. It's a popular win for Walcott. That's the way the money was bet in the Garden.

Once we got inside the dressing-room Jack lay down and shut his eyes.

'We want to get to the hotel and get a doctor,' John says.

'I'm all busted inside,' Jack says.

'I'm sorry as hell, Jack,' John says.

'It's all right,' Jack says.

He lies there with his eyes shut.

'They certainly tried a nice double-cross,' John said.

'Your friends Morgan and Steinfelt,' Jack said. 'You got nice friends.'

He lies there, his eyes are open now. His face has still got that awful drawn look.

'It's funny how fast you can think when it means that much money,' Jack says.

'You're some boy, Jack,' John says.

'No,' Jack says. 'It was nothing.'

A SIMPLE ENQUIRY

Outside, the snow was higher than the window. The sunlight came in through the window and shone on a map on the pine-board wall of the hut. The sun was high and the light came in over the top of the snow. A trench had been cut along the open side of the hut, and each clear day the sun, shining on the wall, reflected heat against the snow and widened the trench. It was late March. The major sat at a table against the wall. His adjutant sat at another table.

Around the major's eyes were two white circles where his snow-glasses had protected his face from the sun on the snow. The rest of his face had been burned and then tanned and then burned through the tan. His nose was swollen and there were edges of loose skin where blisters had been. While he worked at the papers he put the fingers of his left hand into a saucer of oil and then spread the oil over his face, touching it very gently with the tips of his fingers. He was very careful to drain his fingers on the edge of the saucer so there was only a film of oil on them, and after he had stroked his forehead and his cheeks, he stroked his nose very delicately between his fingers. When he had finished he stood up, took the saucer of oil and went into the small room of the hut where he slept. 'I'm going to take a little sleep,' he said to the adjutant. In that army an adjutant is not a commissioned officer. 'You will finish up.'

'Yes, *signor maggiore*,' the adjutant answered. He leaned back in his chair and yawned. He took a paper-covered book out of the pocket of his coat and opened it; then laid it down on the table and lit his pipe. He leaned forward on the table to read and puffed at his pipe. Then he closed the book and put it back in his pocket. He had too much paper-work to get through. He could not enjoy reading until it was done. Outside, the sun went behind a mountain and there was no more light on the wall of the hut. A soldier came in and put some pine branches, chopped into irregular lengths, into the stove. 'Be soft, Pinin,' the adjutant said to him. 'The major is sleeping.'

Pinin was the major's orderly. He was a dark-faced boy, and he fixed the stove, putting the pine wood in carefully, shut the door, and went into the back of the hut again. The adjutant went on with his papers.

'Tonani,' the major called.

'*Signor maggiore?*'

'Send Pinin in to me.'

'Pinin!' the adjutant called. Pinin came into the room. 'The major wants you,' the adjutant said.

Pinin walked across the main room of the hut toward the major's door. He knocked on the half-opened door. '*Signor maggiore?*'

'Come in,' the adjutant heard the major say, 'and shut the door.'

Inside the room the major lay on his bunk. Pinin stood beside the bunk. The major lay with his head on the rucksack that he had stuffed with spare clothing to make a pillow. His long, burned, oiled face looked at Pinin. His hands lay on the blankets.

'You are nineteen?' he asked.

'Yes, *signor maggiore.*'

'You have ever been in love?'

'How do you mean, *signor maggiore?*'

'In love – with a girl?'

'I have been with girls.'

'I did not ask that. I asked if you had been in love – with a girl.'

'Yes, *signor maggiore.*'

'You are in love with this girl now? You don't write her. I read all your letters.'

'I am in love with her,' Pinin said, 'but I do not write her.'

'You are sure of this?'

'I am sure.'

'Tonani,' the major said in the same tone of voice, 'can you hear me talking?'

There was no answer from the next room.

'He can not hear,' the major said. 'And you are quite sure that you love a girl?'

'I am sure.'

'And,' the major looked at him quickly, 'that you are not corrupt?'

'I don't know what you mean, corrupt.'

'All right,' the major said. 'You needn't be superior.'

Pinin looked at the floor. The major looked at his brown face, down and up him, and at his hands. Then he went on, not smiling, 'And you don't really want –' the major paused. Pinin looked at the floor. 'That your great desire isn't really –' Pinin looked at the floor. The major leaned his head back on the rucksack and smiled. He was really relieved: life in the army was too complicated. 'You're a good boy,' he said. 'You're a good boy, Pinin. But don't be superior and be careful some one else doesn't come along and take you.'

Pinin stood still beside the bunk.

'Don't be afraid,' the major said. His hands were folded on the blankets. 'I won't touch you. You can go back to your platoon if you like. But you had better stay on as my servant. You've less chance of being killed.'

'Do you want anything of me, *signor maggiore*?'

'No,' the major said. 'Go on and get on with whatever you were doing. Leave the door open when you go out.'

Pinin went out, leaving the door open. The adjutant looked up at him as he walked awkwardly across the room and out the door. Pinin was flushed and moved differently than he had moved when he brought in the wood for the fire. The adjutant looked after him and smiled. Pinin came in with more wood for the stove. The major, lying on his bunk, looking at his cloth-covered helmet and his snow-glasses that hung from a nail on the wall, heard him walk across the floor. The little devil, he thought, I wonder if he lied to me.

TEN INDIANS

After one Fourth of July, Nick, driving home late from town in the big wagon with Joe Garner and his family, passed nine drunken Indians along the road. He remembered there were nine because Joe Garner, driving along in the dusk, pulled up the horses, jumped down into the road and dragged an Indian out of the wheel rut. The Indian had been asleep, face down in the sand. Joe dragged him into bushes and got back up on the wagon-box.

'That makes nine of them,' Joe said, 'just between here and the edge of town.'

'Them Indians,' said Mrs. Garner.

Nick was on the back seat with the two Garner boys. He was looking out from the back seat to see the Indian where Joe had dragged him alongside of the road.

'Was it Billy Tabeshaw?' Carl asked.

'No.'

'His pants looked mighty like Billy.'

'All Indians wear the same kind of pants.'

'I didn't see him at all,' Frank said. 'Pa was down into the road and back up again before I seen a thing. I thought he was killing a snake.'

'Plenty of Indians'll kill snakes tonight, I guess,' Joe Garner said.

'Them Indians,' said Mrs. Garner.

They drove along. The road turned off from the main highway and went up into the hills. It was hard pulling for the horses and the boys got down and walked. The road was sandy. Nick looked back from the top of the hill by the schoolhouse. He saw the lights of Petoskey and, off across Little Traverse Bay, the lights of Harbour Springs. They climbed back in the wagon again.

'They ought to put some gravel on that stretch,' Joe Garner said. The wagon went along the road through the woods. Joe and Mrs. Garner sat close together on the front seat. Nick sat between the two boys. The road came out into a clearing.

'Right here was where Pa ran over the skunk.'

'It was further on.'

'It don't make no difference where it was,' Joe said without turning his head. 'One place is just as good as another to run over a skunk.'

'I saw two skunks last night,' Nick said.

'Where?'

'Down by the lake. They were looking for dead fish along the beach.'

'They were coons probably,' Carl said.

'They were skunks. I guess I know skunks.'

'You ought to,' Carl said. 'You got an Indian girl.'

'Stop talking that way, Carl,' said Mrs. Garner.

'Well, they smell about the same.'

Joe Garner laughed.

'You stop laughing, Joe,' Mrs. Garner said. 'I won't have Carl talk that way.'

'Have you got an Indian girl, Nickie?' Joe asked.

'No.'

'He has too, Pa,' Frank said. 'Prudence Mitchell's his girl.'

'She's not.'

'He goes to see her every day.'

'I don't.' Nick, sitting between the two boys in the dark, felt hollow and happy inside himself to be teased about Prudence Mitchell. 'She ain't my girl,' he said.

'Listen to him,' said Carl. 'I see them together every day.'

'Carl can't get a girl,' his mother said, 'not even a squaw.'

Carl was quiet.

'Carl ain't no good with girls,' Frank said.

'You shut up.'

'You're all right, Carl,' Joe Garner said. 'Girls never got a man anywhere. Look at your pa.'

'Yes, that's what you would say,' Mrs. Garner moved close to Joe as the wagon jolted. 'Well, you had plenty of girls in your time.'

'I'll bet Pa wouldn't ever have had a squaw for a girl.'

'Don't you think it,' Joe said. 'You better watch out to keep Prudie, Nick.'

His wife whispered to him and Joe laughed.

'What you laughing at?' asked Frank.

'Don't you say it, Garner,' his wife warned. Joe laughed again.

'Nickie can have Prudence,' Joe Garner said. 'I got a good girl.'

'That's the way to talk,' Mrs. Garner said.

The horses were pulling heavily in the sand. Joe reached out in the dark with the whip.

'Come on, pull into it. You'll have to pull harder than this tomorrow.'

They trotted down the long hill, the wagon jolting. At the farmhouse everybody got down. Mrs. Garner unlocked the door, went inside, and came out with a lamp in her hand. Carl and Nick unloaded the things from the back of the wagon. Frank sat on the front seat to drive to the barn and put up the horses. Nick went up the steps and opened the kitchen door. Mrs. Garner was building a fire in the stove. She turned from pouring kerosene on the wood.

'Good-by, Mrs. Garner,' Nick said. 'Thanks for taking me.'

'Oh shucks, Nickie.'

'I had a wonderful time.'

'We like to have you. Won't you stay and eat some supper?'

'I better go. I think Dad probably waited for me.'

'Well, get along then. Send Carl up to the house, will you?'

'All right.'

'Good-night, Nickie.'

'Good-night, Mrs. Garner.'

Nick went out the farmyard and down to the barn. Joe and Frank were milking.

'Good-night,' Nick said. 'I had a swell time.'

'Good-night, Nick,' Joe Garner called. 'Aren't you going to stay and eat?'

'No, I can't. Will you tell Carl his mother wants him?'

'All right. Good-night, Nickie.'

Nick walked barefoot along the path through the meadow below the barn. The path was smooth and the dew was cool on his bare feet. He climbed a fence at the end of the meadow, went down through a ravine, his feet wet in the swamp mud, and then climbed up through the dry beech woods until he saw the lights of the cottage. He climbed over the fence and walked around to the front porch. Through the window he saw his father sitting by the table, reading in the light from the big lamp. Nick opened the door and went in.

'Well, Nickie,' his father said, 'was it a good day?'

'I had a swell time, Dad. It was a swell Fourth of July.'

'Are you hungry?'

'You bet.'

'What did you do with your shoes?'

'I left them in the wagon at Garner's.'

'Come on out to the kitchen.'

Nick's father went ahead with the lamp. He stopped and lifted the lid of the ice-box. Nick went on into the kitchen. His father brought in a piece of cold chicken on a plate and a pitcher of milk and put them on the table before Nick. He put down the lamp.

'There's some pie too,' he said. 'Will that hold you?'

'It's grand.'

His father sat down in a chair beside the oil-cloth-covered table. He made a big shadow on the kitchen wall.

'Who won the ball game?'

'Petoskey. Five to three.'

His father sat watching him eat and filled his glass from the milk-pitcher. Nick drank and wiped his mouth on his napkin. His father reached over to the shelf for the pie. He cut Nick a big piece. It was huckleberry pie.

'What did you do, Dad?'

'I went out fishing in the morning.'

'What did you get?'

'Only perch.'

His father sat watching Nick eat the pie.

'What did you do this afternoon?' Nick asked.

'I went for a walk up by the Indian camp.'

'Did you see anybody?'

'The Indians were all in town getting drunk.'

'Didn't you see anybody at all?'

'I saw your friend, Prudie.'

'Where was she?'

'She was in the woods with Frank Washburn. I ran onto them. They were having quite a time.'

His father was not looking at him.

'What were they doing?'

'I didn't stay to find out.'

'Tell me what they were doing.'

'I don't know,' his father said. 'I just heard them threshing around.'

'How did you know it was them?'

'I saw them.'

'I thought you said you didn't see them.'

'Oh, yes, I saw them.'

'Who was it with her?' Nick asked.

'Frank Washburn.'

'Were they – were they –'

'Were they what?'

'Were they happy?'

'I guess so.'

His father got up from the table and went out the kitchen screen door. When he came back Nick was looking at his plate. He had been crying.

'Have some more?' His father picked up the knife to cut the pie.

'No,' said Nick.

'You better have another piece.'

'No, I don't want any.'

His father cleared off the table.

'Where were they in the woods?' Nick asked.

'Up back of the camp.' Nick looked at his plate. His father said, 'You better go to bed, Nick.'

'All right.'

Nick went into his room, undressed, and got into bed. He heard his father moving around in the living room. Nick lay in the bed with his face in the pillow.

'My heart's broken,' he thought. 'If I feel this way my heart must be broken.'

After a while he heard his father blow out the lamp and go into his own room. He heard a wind come up in the trees outside and felt it come in cool through the screen. He lay for a long time with his face in the pillow, and after a while he forgot to think about Prudence and finally he went to sleep. When he awoke in the night he heard the wind in the hemlock trees outside the cottage and the waves of the lake coming in on the shore, and he went back to sleep. In the morning there was a big wind blowing and the waves were running high up on the beach and he was awake a long time before he remembered that his heart was broken.

A CANARY FOR ONE

The train passed very quickly a long, red stone house with a garden and four thick palm-trees with tables under them in the shade. On the other side was the sea. Then there was a cutting through red stone and clay, and the sea was only occasionally and far below against rocks.

'I bought him in Palermo,' the American lady said. 'We only had an hour ashore and it was Sunday morning. The man wanted to be paid in dollars and I gave him a dollar and a half. He really sings very beautifully.'

It was very hot in the train and it was very hot in the *lit salon* compartment. There was no breeze came through the open window. The American lady pulled the window-blind down and there was no more sea, even occasionally. On the other side there was glass, then the corridor, then an open window, and outside the window were dusty trees and an oiled road and flat fields of grapes, with gray-stone hills behind them.

There was smoke from many tall chimneys – coming into Marseilles, and the train slowed down and followed one track through many others into the station. The train stayed twenty-five minutes in the station at Marseilles and the American lady bought a copy of *The Daily Mail* and a half-bottle of Evian water. She walked a little way along the station platform, but she stayed near the steps of the car because at Cannes, where it stopped for twelve minutes, the train had left with no signal of departure and she had gotten on only just in time. The American lady was a little deaf and she was afraid that perhaps signals of departure were given and that she did not hear them.

The train left the station in Marseilles and there was not only the switchyards and the factory smoke but, looking back, the town of Marseilles and the harbor with stone hills behind it and the last of the sun on the water. As it was getting dark the train passed a farmhouse burning in a field. Motor-cars were stopped along the road and bedding and things from inside the farm-house were spread in the field. Many people were watching the house burn. After it was dark the train was in Avignon. People got on and off. At the news-stand Frenchmen, returning to Paris, bought that day's French papers. On the station platform were negro soldiers. They wore brown uniforms and were tall

and their faces shone, close under the electric light. Their faces
were very black and they were too tall to stare. The train left
Avignon station with the negroes standing there. A short white
sergeant was with them.

Inside the *lit salon* compartment the porter had pulled down
the three beds from inside the wall and prepared them for sleeping. In the night the American lady lay without sleeping because
the train was a *rapide* and went very fast and she was afraid of the
speed in the night. The American lady's bed was the one next to
the window. The canary from Palermo, a cloth spread over his
cage, was out of the draft in the corridor that went into the
compartment wash-room. There was a blue light outside
the compartment, and all night the train went very fast and the
American lady lay awake and waited for a wreck.

In the morning the train was near Paris, and after the American lady had come out from the wash-room, looking very
wholesome and middle-aged and American in spite of not having slept, and had taken the cloth off the birdcage and hung the
cage in the sun, she went back to the restaurant-car for breakfast.
When she came back to the *lit salon* compartment again, the beds
had been pushed back into the wall and made into seats, the
canary was shaking his feathers in the sunlight that came through
the open window, and the train was much nearer Paris.

'He loves the sun,' the American lady said. 'He'll sing now in
a little while.'

The canary shook his feathers and pecked into them. 'I've
always loved birds,' the American lady said. 'I'm taking him
home to my little girl. There – he's singing now.'

The canary chirped and the feathers on his throat stood out,
then he dropped his bill and pecked into his feathers again. The
train crossed a river and passed through a very carefully tended
forest. The train passed through many outside of Paris towns.
There were tram-cars in the towns and big advertisements for
the Belle Jardinière and Dubonnet and Pernod on the walls toward the train. All that the train passed through looked as
though it were before breakfast. For several minutes I had not
listened to the American lady, who was talking to my wife.

'Is your husband American too?' asked the lady.

'Yes,' said my wife. 'We're both Americans.'

'I thought you were English.'

'Oh, no.'

'Perhaps that was because I wore braces,' I said. I had started to say suspenders and changed it to braces in the mouth, to keep my English character. The American lady did not hear. She was really quite deaf; she read lips, and I had not looked toward her. I had looked out of the window. She went on talking to my wife.

'I'm so glad you're Americans. American men make the best husbands,' the American lady was saying. 'That was why we left the Continent, you know. My daughter fell in love with a man in Vevey.' She stopped. 'They were simply madly in love.' She stopped again. 'I took her away, of course.'

'Did she get over it?' asked my wife.

'I don't think so,' said the American lady. 'She wouldn't eat anything and she wouldn't sleep at all. I've tried so very hard, but she doesn't seem to take an interest in anything. She doesn't care about things. I couldn't have her marrying a foreigner.' She paused. 'Some one, a very good friend, told me once, "No foreigner can make an American girl a good husband." '

'No,' said my wife, 'I suppose not.'

The American lady admired my wife's travelling-coat, and it turned out that the American lady had bought her own clothes for twenty years now from the same *maison de couture* in the Rue Saint Honoré. They had her measurements, and a *vendeuse* who knew her and her tastes picked the dresses out for her and they were sent to America. They came to the post-office near where she lived up-town in New York, and the duty was never exorbitant because they opened the dresses there in the post-office to appraise them and they were always very simple-looking and with no gold lace nor ornaments that would make the dresses look expensive. Before the present *vendeuse*, named Thérèse, there had been another *vendeuse*, named Amélie. Altogether there had only been these two in the twenty years. It had always been the same couturier. Prices, however, had gone up. The exchange, though, equalized that. They had her daughter's measurements now too. She was grown up and there was not much chance of their changing now.

The train was now coming into Paris. The fortifications were levelled but grass had not grown. There were many cars standing on tracks – brown wooden restaurant-cars and brown wooden sleeping-cars that would go to Italy at five o'clock that night, if that train still left at five; the cars were marked Paris-Rome, and cars, with seats on the roofs, that went back and forth to the suburbs with, at certain hours, people in all the seats and on the roofs, if that were the way it were still done, and passing were the white walls and many windows of houses. Nothing had eaten any breakfast.

'Americans make the best husbands,' the American lady said to my wife. I was getting down the bags. 'American men are the only men in the world to marry.'

'How long ago did you leave Vevey?' asked my wife.

'Two years ago this fall. It's her, you know, that I'm taking the canary to.'

'Was the man your daughter was in love with a Swiss?'

'Yes,' said the American lady. 'He was from a very good family in Vevey. He was going to be an engineer. They met there in Vevey. They used to go on long walks together.'

'I know Vevey,' said my wife. 'We were there on our honeymoon.'

'Were you really? That must have been lovely. I had no idea, of course, that she'd fall in love with him.'

'It was a very lovely place,' said my wife.

'Yes,' said the American lady. 'Isn't it lovely? Where did you stop there?'

'We stayed at the Trois Couronnes,' said my wife.

'It's such a fine old hotel,' said the American lady.

'Yes,' said my wife. 'We had a very fine room and in the fall the country was lovely.'

'Were you there in the fall?'

'Yes,' said my wife.

We were passing three cars that had been in a wreck. They were splintered open and the roofs sagged in.

'Look,' I said. 'There's been a wreck.'

The American lady looked and saw the last car. 'I was afraid of just that all night,' she said. 'I have terrific presentiments about things sometimes. I'll never travel on a *rapide* again at night. There must be other comfortable trains that don't go so fast.'

Then the train was in the dark of the Gare de Lyon, and then stopped and porters came up to the windows. I handed bags through the windows, and we were out on the dim longness of the platform, and the American lady put herself in charge of one of three men from Cook's who said: 'Just a moment, madame, and I'll look for your name.'

The porter brought a truck and piled on the baggage, and my wife said good-by and I said good-by to the American lady, whose name had been found by the man from Cook's on a

typewritten page in a sheaf of typewritten pages which he replaced in his pocket.

We followed the porter with the truck down the long cement
platform beside the train. At the end was a gate and a man took
the tickets.

We were returning to Paris to set up separate residences.

AN ALPINE IDYLL

It was hot coming down into the valley even in the early morning. The sun melted the snow from the skis we were carrying and dried the wood. It was spring in the valley but the sun was very hot. We came along the road into Galtur carrying our skis and rucksacks. As we passed the churchyard a burial was just over. I said, '*Grüss Gott*,' to the priest as he walked past us coming out of the churchyard. The priest bowed.

'It's funny a priest never speaks to you,' John said.

'You'd think they'd like to say "*Grüss Gott*." '

'They never answer,' John said.

We stopped in the road and watched the sexton shovelling in the new earth. A peasant with a black beard and high leather boots stood beside the grave. The sexton stopped shovelling and straightened his back. The peasant in the high boots took the spade from the sexton and went on filling in the grave – spreading the earth evenly as a man spreading manure in a garden. In the bright May morning the grave-filling looked unreal. I could not imagine any one being dead.

'Imagine being buried on a day like this,' I said to John.

'I wouldn't like it.'

'Well,' I said, 'we don't have to do it.'

We went on up the road past the houses of the town to the inn. We had been skiing in the Silvretta for a month, and it was good to be down in the valley. In the Silvretta the skiing had been all right, but it was spring skiing, the snow was good only in the early morning and again in the evening. The rest of the time it was spoiled by the sun. We were both tired of the sun. You could not get away from the sun. The only shadows were made by rocks or by the hut that was built under the protection of a rock beside a glacier, and in the shade the sweat froze in your underclothing. You could not sit outside the hut without dark glasses. It was pleasant to be burned black but the sun had been very tiring. You could not rest in it. I was glad to be down away from snow. It was too late in the spring to be up in the Silvretta. I was a little tired of skiing. We had stayed too long. I could taste the snow water we had been drinking melted off the tin roof of the hut. The taste was a part of the way I felt about skiing. I was glad there were other things beside skiing, and I was glad to be down, away from the unnatural high mountain spring, into this May morning in the valley.

The innkeeper sat on the porch of the inn, his chair tipped back against the wall. Beside him sat the cook.

'*Ski-heil!*' said the innkeeper.

'*Heil!*' we said and leaned the skis against the wall and took off our packs.

'How was it up above?' asked the innkeeper.

'*Schön*. A little too much sun.'

'Yes. There's too much sun this time of year.'

The cook sat on in his chair. The innkeeper went in with us and unlocked his office and brought out our mail. There was a bundle of letters and some papers.

'Let's get some beer,' John said.

'Good. We'll drink it inside.'

The proprietor brought two bottles and we drank them while we read the letters.

'We better have some more beer,' John said. A girl brought it this time. She smiled as she opened the bottles.

'Many letters,' she said.

'Yes. Many.'

'*Prosit*,' she said and went out, taking the empty bottles.

'I'd forgotten what beer tasted like.'

'I hadn't,' John said. 'Up in the hut I used to think about it a lot.'

'Well,' I said, 'we've got it now.'

'You oughtn't to ever do anything too long.'

'No. We were up there too long.'

'Too damn long,' John said. 'It's no good doing a thing too long.'

The sun came through the open window and shone through the beer bottles on the table. The bottles were half full. There was a little froth on the beer in the bottles, not much because it was very cold. It collared up when you poured it into the tall glasses. I looked out of the open window at the white road. The trees beside the road were dusty. Beyond was a green field and a stream. There were trees along the stream and a mill with a water wheel. Through the open side of the mill I saw a long log and a saw in it rising and falling. No one seemed to be tending it. There were four crows walking in the green field. One crow sat in a tree watching. Outside on the porch the cook got off his chair and passed into the hall that led back into the kitchen.

Inside, the sunlight shone through the empty glasses on the table. John was leaning forward with his head on his arms.

Through the window I saw two men come up the front steps. They came into the drinking room. One was the bearded peasant in the high boots. The other was the sexton. They sat down at the table under the window. The girl came in and stood by their table. The peasant did not seem to see her. He sat with his hands on the table. He wore his old army clothes. There were patches on the elbows.

'What will it be?' asked the sexton. The peasant did not pay any attention.

'What will you drink?'

'Schnapps,' the peasant said.

'And a quarter litre of red wine,' the sexton told the girl.

The girl brought the drinks and the peasant drank the schnapps. He looked out of the window. The sexton watched him. John had his head forward on the table. He was asleep.

The innkeeper came in and went over to the table. He spoke in dialect and the sexton answered him. The peasant looked out of the window. The innkeeper went out of the room. The peasant stood up. He took a folded ten-thousand kronen note out of a leather pocketbook and unfolded it. The girl came up.

'*Alles?*' she asked.

'*Alles,*' he said.

'Let me buy the wine,' the sexton said.

'*Alles,*' the peasant repeated to the girl. She put her hand in the pocket of her apron, brought it out full of coins and counted out the change. The peasant went out the door. As soon as he was gone the innkeeper came into the room again and spoke to the sexton. He sat down at the table. They talked in dialect. The sexton was amused. The innkeeper was disgusted. The sexton stood up from the table. He was a little man with a mustache. He leaned out of the window and looked up the road.

'There he goes in,' he said.

'In the Löwen?'

'*Ja.*'

They talked again and then the innkeeper came over to our table. The innkeeper was a tall man and old. He looked at John asleep.

'He's pretty tired.'

'Yes, we were up early.'

'Will you want to eat soon?'

'Any time,' I said. 'What is there to eat?'

'Anything you want. The girl will bring the eating-card.'

The girl brought the menu. John woke up. The menu was written in ink on a card and the card slipped into a wooden paddle.

'There's the *Speisekarte*,' I said to John. He looked at it. He was still sleepy.

'Won't you have a drink with us?' I asked the innkeeper. He sat down. 'Those peasants are beasts,' said the innkeeper.

'We saw that one at a funeral coming into town.'

'That was his wife.'

'Oh.'

'He's a beast. All these peasants are beasts.'

'How do you mean?'

'You wouldn't believe it. You wouldn't believe what just happened about that one.'

'Tell me.'

'You wouldn't believe it.' The innkeeper spoke to the sexton. 'Franz, come over here.' The sexton came, bringing his little bottle of wine and his glass.

'The gentlemen are just come down from the Wiesbadenerhütte,' the innkeeper said. We shook hands.

'What will you drink?' I asked.

'Nothing,' Franz shook his finger.

'Another quarter litre?'

'All right.'

'Do you understand dialect?' the innkeeper asked.

'No.'

'What's it all about?' John asked.

'He's going to tell us about the peasant we saw filling the grave, coming into town.'

'I can't understand it, anyway,' John said. 'It goes too fast for me.'

'That peasant,' the innkeeper said, 'today he brought his wife in to be buried. She died last November.'

'December,' said the sexton.

'That makes nothing. She died last December then, and he notified the commune.'

'December eighteenth,' said the sexton.

'Anyway, he couldn't bring her over to be buried until the snow was gone.'

'He lives on the other side of the Paznaun,' said the sexton. 'But he belongs to this parish.'

'He couldn't bring her out at all?' I asked.

'No. He can only come, from where he lives, on skis until the snow melts. So today he brought her in to be buried and the priest, when he looked at her face, didn't want to bury her. You go on and tell it,' he said to the sexton. 'Speak German, not dialect.'

'It was very funny with the priest,' said the sexton. 'In the report to the commune she died of heart trouble. We knew she had heart trouble here. She used to faint in church sometimes. She did not come for a long time. She wasn't strong to climb. When the priest uncovered her face he asked Olz, "Did your wife suffer much?" "No," said Olz. "When I came in the house she was dead across the bed."

'The priest looked at her again. He didn't like it.

' "How did her face get that way?"

' "I don't know," Olz said.

' "You'd better find out," the priest said, and put the blanket back. Olz didn't say anything. The priest looked at him. Olz looked back at the priest. "You want to know?"

' "I must know," the priest said.'

'This is where it's good,' the innkeeper said. 'Listen to this. Go on Franz.'

' "Well," said Olz, "when she died I made the report to the commune and I put her in the shed across the top of the big wood. When I started to use the big wood she was stiff and I put her up against the wall. Her mouth was open and when I came into the shed at night to cut up the big wood, I hung the lantern from it."

' "Why did you do that?" asked the priest.

' "I don't know," said Olz.

' "Did you do that many times?"

' "Every time I went to work in the shed at night."

' "It was very wrong," said the priest. "Did you love your wife?"

' "*Ja*, I loved her," Olz said. "I loved her fine." '

'Did you understand it all?' asked the innkeeper. 'You understand it all about his wife?'

'I heard it.'

'How about eating?' John asked.

'You order,' I said. 'Do you think it's true?' I asked the innkeeper.

'Sure it's true,' he said. 'These peasants are beasts.'

'Where did he go now?'

'He's gone to drink at my colleague's, the Löwen.'

'He didn't want to drink with me,' said the sexton.

'He didn't want to drink with me, after *he* knew about his wife,' said the innkeeper.

'Say,' said John. 'How about eating?'

'All right,' I said.

A PURSUIT RACE

William Campbell had been in a pursuit race with a burlesque show ever since Pittsburgh. In a pursuit race, in bicycle racing, riders start at equal intervals to ride after one another. They ride very fast because the race is usually limited to a short distance and if they slow their riding another rider who maintains his pace will make up the space that separated them equally at the start. As soon as a rider is caught and passed he is out of the race and must get down from his bicycle and leave the track. If none of the riders are caught the winner of the race is the one who has gained the most distance. In most pursuit races, if there are only two riders, one of the riders is caught inside of six miles. The burlesque show caught William Campbell at Kansas City.

William Campbell had hoped to hold a slight lead over the burlesque show until they reached the Pacific coast. As long as he preceded the burlesque show as advance man he was being paid. When the burlesque show caught up with him he was in bed. He was in bed when the manager of the burlesque troupe came into his room and after the manager had gone out he decided that he might as well stay in bed. It was very cold in Kansas City and he was in no hurry to go out. He did not like Kansas City. He reached under the bed for a bottle and drank. It made his stomach feel better. Mr. Turner, the manager of the burlesque show, had refused a drink.

William Campbell's interview with Mr. Turner had been a little strange. Mr. Turner had knocked on the door. Campbell had said: 'Come in!' When Mr. Turner came into the room he saw clothing on a chair, an open suitcase, the bottle on a chair beside the bed, and some one lying in the bed completely covered by the bed-clothes.

'Mister Campbell,' Mr. Turner said.

'You can't fire me,' William Campbell said from underneath the covers. It was warm and white and close under the covers. 'You can't fire me because I've got down off my bicycle.'

'You're drunk,' Mr. Turner said.

'Oh, yes,' William Campbell said, speaking directly against the sheet and feeling the texture with his lips.

'You're a fool,' Mr. Turner said. He turned off the electric light. The electric light had been burning all night. It was now ten o'clock in the morning. 'You're a drunken fool. When did you get into this town?'

'I got into this town last night,' William Campbell said, speaking against the sheet. He found he liked to talk through a sheet. 'Did you ever talk through a sheet?'

'Don't try to be funny. You aren't funny.'

'I'm not being funny. I'm just talking through a sheet.'

'You're talking through a sheet all right.'

'You can go now, Mr. Turner,' Campbell said. 'I don't work for you any more.'

'You know that anyway.'

'I know a lot,' William Campbell said. He pulled down the sheet and looked at Mr. Turner. 'I know enough so I don't mind looking at you at all. Do you want to hear what I know?'

'No.'

'Good,' said William Campbell. 'Because really I don't know anything at all. I was just talking.' He pulled the sheet up over his face again. 'I love it under a sheet,' he said. Mr. Turner stood beside the bed. He was a middle-aged man with a large stomach and a bald head and he had many things to do. 'You ought to stop off here, Billy, and take a cure,' he said. 'I'll fix it up if you want to do it.'

'I don't want to take a cure,' William Campbell said. 'I don't want to take a cure at all. I am perfectly happy. All my life I have been perfectly happy.'

'How long have you been this way?'

'What a question!' William Campbell breathed in and out through the sheet.

'How long have you been stewed, Billy?'

'Haven't I done my work?'

'Sure. I just asked you how long you've been stewed, Billy.'

'I don't know. But I've got my wolf back,' he touched the sheet with his tongue. 'I've had him for a week.'

'The hell you have.'

'Oh, yes. My dear wolf. Every time I take a drink he goes outside the room. He can't stand alcohol. The poor little fellow.' He moved his tongue round and round on the sheet. 'He's a lovely wolf. He's just like he always was.' William Campbell shut his eyes and took a deep breath.

'You got to take a cure, Billy,' Mr. Turner said. 'You won't mind the Keeley. It isn't bad.'

'The Keeley,' William Campbell said. 'It isn't far from London.' He shut his eyes and opened them, moving the eyelashes against the sheet. 'I just love sheets,' he said. He looked at Mr. Turner.

'Listen, you think I'm drunk.'

'You *are* drunk.'

'No, I'm not.'

'You're drunk and you've had D.T.'s.'

'No.' William Campbell held the sheet around his head. 'Dear sheet,' he said. He breathed against it gently. 'Pretty sheet. You love me, don't you, sheet? It's all in the price of the room. Just like in Japan. No,' he said. 'Listen Billy, dear Sliding Billy, I have a surprise for you. I'm not drunk. I'm hopped to the eyes.'

'No,' said Mr. Turner.

'Take a look.' William Campbell pulled up the right sleeve of his pyjama jacket under the sheet, then shoved the right forearm out. 'Look at that.' On the forearm, from just above the wrist to the elbow, were small blue circles around tiny dark blue punctures. The circles almost touched one another. 'That's the new development,' William Campbell said. 'I drink a little now once in a while, just to drive the wolf out of the room.'

'They got a cure for that,' 'Sliding Billy' Turner said.

'No,' William Campbell said. 'They haven't got a cure for anything.'

'You can't just quit like that, Billy,' Turner said. He sat on the bed.

'Be careful of my sheet,' William Campbell said.

'You can't just quit at your age and take to pumping yourself full of that stuff just because you got in a jam.'

'There's a law against it. If that's what you mean.'

'No, I mean you got to fight it out.'

Billy Campbell caressed the sheet with his lips and his tongue. 'Dear sheet,' he said. 'I can kiss this sheet and see right through it at the same time.'

'Cut it out about the sheet. You can't just take to that stuff, Billy.'

William Campbell shut his eyes. He was beginning to feel a slight nausea. He knew that this nausea would increase steadily, without there ever being the relief of sickness, until something were done against it. It was at this point that he suggested that Mr. Turner have a drink. Mr. Turner declined. William Campbell took a drink from the bottle. It was a temporary measure. Mr. Turner watched him. Mr. Turner had been in this room much longer than he should have been, he had many things to do; although living in daily association with people who used drugs, he had a horror of drugs, and he was very fond of William Campbell; he did not wish to leave him. He was very sorry for him and he felt a cure might help. He knew there were good cures in Kansas City. But he had to go. He stood up.

'Listen, Billy,' William Campbell said, 'I want to tell you something. You're called "Sliding Billy." That's because you can slide. I'm called just Billy. That's because I never could slide at all. I can't slide, Billy. I can't slide. It just catches. Every time I try it, it catches.' He shut his eyes. 'I can't slide, Billy. It's awful when you can't slide.'

'Yes,' said 'Sliding Billy' Turner.

'Yes, what?' William Campbell looked at him.

'You were saying.'

'No,' said William Campbell. 'I wasn't saying. It must have been a mistake.'

'You were saying about sliding.'

'No. It couldn't have been about sliding. But listen, Billy, and I'll tell you a secret. Stick to sheets, Billy. Keep away from women and horses and, and –' he stopped '– eagles, Billy. If you love horses you'll get horse-shit, and if you love eagles you'll get eagle-shit.' He stopped and put his head under the sheet.

'I got to go,' said 'Sliding Billy' Turner.

'If you love women you'll get a dose,' William Campbell said. 'If you love horses –'

'Yes, you said that.'

'Said what?'

'About horses and eagles.'

'Oh, yes. And if you love sheets.' He breathed on the sheet and stroked his nose against it. 'I don't know about sheets,' he said. 'I just started to love this sheet.'

'I have to go,' Mr. Turner said. 'I got a lot to do.'

'That's all right,' William Campbell said. 'Everybody's got to go.'

'I better go.'

'All right, you go.'

'Are you all right, Billy?'

'I was never so happy in my life.'

'And you're all right?'

'I'm fine. You go along. I'll just lie here for a little while. Around noon I'll get up.'

But when Mr. Turner came up to William Campbell's room at noon William Campbell was sleeping and as Mr. Turner was a man who knew what things in life were very valuable he did not wake him.

TODAY IS FRIDAY

Three Roman soldiers are in a drinking-place at eleven o'clock at night. There are barrels around the wall. Behind the wooden counter is a Hebrew wine-seller. The three Roman soldiers are a little cock-eyed.

  1st Roman Soldier – You tried the red?

  2d Soldier – No, I ain't tried it.

  1st Soldier – You better try it.

  2d Soldier – All right, George, we'll have a round of the red.

  Hebrew Wine-seller – Here you are, gentlemen. You'll like that. [*He sets down an earthenware pitcher that he has filled from one of the casks.*] That's a nice little wine.

  1st Soldier – Have a drink of it yourself. [*He turns to the third Roman soldier who is leaning on a barrel.*] What's the matter with you?

  3d Roman Soldier – I got a gut-ache.

  2d Soldier – You've been drinking water.

  1st Soldier – Try some of the red.

  3d Soldier – I can't drink the damn stuff. It makes my gut sour.

  1st Soldier – You been out here too long.

  3d Soldier – Hell, don't I know it?

  1st Soldier – Say, George, can't you give this gentleman something to fix up his stomach?

  Hebrew Wine-seller – I got it right here.

  [*The third Roman soldier tastes the cup that the wine-seller has mixed for him.*]

  3d Soldier – Hey, what you put in that, camel chips?

  Wine-seller – You drink that right down, Lootenant. That'll fix you up right.

  3d Soldier – Well, I couldn't feel any worse.

  1st Soldier – Take a chance on it. George fixed me up fine the other day.

  Wine-seller – You were in bad shape, Lootenant. I know what fixes up a bad stomach.

  [*The third Roman soldier drinks the cup down.*]

  3d Roman Soldier – Jesus Christ. [*He makes a face.*]

  2d Soldier – That false alarm!

  1st Soldier – Oh, I don't know. He was pretty good in there today.

  2d Soldier – Why didn't he come down off the cross?

1st Soldier – He didn't want to come down off the cross. That's not his play.

2d Soldier – Show me a guy that doesn't want to come down off the cross.

1st Soldier – Aw, hell, you don't know anything about it. Ask George there. Did he want to come down off the cross, George?

Wine-seller – I'll tell you, gentlemen, I wasn't out there. It's a thing I haven't taken any interest in.

2d Soldier – Listen, I seen a lot of them – here and plenty of other places. Any time you show me one that doesn't want to get down off the cross when the time comes – when the time comes, I mean – I'll climb right up with him.

1st Soldier – I thought he was pretty good in there today.

3d Soldier – He was all right.

2d Roman Soldier – You guys don't know what I'm talking about. I'm not saying whether he was good or not. What I mean is, when the time comes. When they first start nailing him, there isn't none of them wouldn't stop it if they could.

1st Soldier – Didn't you follow it, George?

Wine-seller – No, I didn't take any interest in it, Lootenant.

1st Soldier – I was surprised how he acted.

3d Soldier – The part I don't like is the nailing them on. You know, that must get to you pretty bad.

2d Soldier – It isn't that that's so bad, as when they first lift 'em up. [*He makes a lifting gesture with his two palms together.*] When the weight starts to pull on 'em. That's when it gets 'em.

3d Roman Soldier – It take some of them pretty bad.

1st Soldier – Ain't I seen 'em? I seen plenty of them. I tell you, he was pretty good in there today.

[*The second Roman soldier smiles at the Hebrew wine-seller.*]

2d Soldier – You're a regular Christer, big boy.

1st Soldier – Sure, go on and kid him. But listen while I tell you something. He was pretty good in there today.

2d Soldier – What about some more wine?

[*The wine-seller looks up expectantly. The third Roman soldier is sitting with his head down. He does not look well.*]

3d Soldier – I don't want any more.

2d Soldier – Just for two, George.

[*The wine-seller puts out a pitcher of wine, a size smaller than the last one. He leans forward on the wooden counter.*]

1st Roman Soldier – You see his girl?

2d Soldier – Wasn't I standing right by her?

1st Soldier – She's a nice-looker.

2d Soldier – I knew her before he did. [*He winks at the wine-seller.*]

1st Soldier – I used to see her around the town.

2d Soldier – She used to have a lot of stuff. He never brought *her* no good luck.

1st Soldier – Oh, he ain't lucky. But he looked pretty good to me in there today.

2d Soldier – What become of his gang?

1st Soldier – Oh, they faded out. Just the women stuck by him.

2d Roman Soldier – They were a pretty yellow crowd. When they seen him go up there they didn't want any of it.

1st Soldier – The women stuck all right.

2d Soldier – Sure, they stuck all right.

1st Roman Soldier – You see me slip the old spear into him?

2d Roman Soldier – You'll get into trouble doing that some day.

1st Soldier – It was the least I could do for him. I'll tell you he looked pretty good to me in there today.

Hebrew wine-seller – Gentlemen, you know I got to close.

1st Roman Soldier – We'll have one more round.

2d Roman Soldier – What's the use? This stuff don't get you anywhere. Come on, let's go.

1st Soldier – Just another round.

3d Roman Soldier – [*Getting up from the barrel.*] No, come on. Let's go. I feel like hell tonight.

1st Soldier – Just one more.

2d Soldier – No, come on. We're going to go. Good-night, George. Put it on the bill.

Wine-seller – Good-night, gentlemen. [*He looks a little worried.*] You couldn't let me have a little something on account, Lootenant?

2d Roman Soldier – What the hell, George! Wednesday's pay-day.

Wine-seller – It's all right, Lootenant. Good-night, gentlemen.
  [*The three Roman soldiers go out the door into the street.*]
  [*Outside in the street.*]

2d Roman Soldier – George is a kike just like all the rest of them.

1st Roman Soldier – Oh, George is a nice fella.

2d Soldier – Everybody's a nice fella to you tonight.

3d Roman Soldier – Come on, let's go up to the barracks. I feel like hell tonight.

2d Soldier – You been out here too long.

3d Roman Soldier – No, it ain't just that. I feel like hell.

2d Soldier – You been out here too long. That's all.

CURTAIN

BANAL STORY

So he ate an orange, slowly spitting out the seeds. Outside, the snow was turning to rain. Inside, the electric stove seemed to give no heat and rising from his writing-table, he sat down upon the stove. How good it felt! Here, at last, was life.

He reached for another orange. Far away in Paris, Mascart had knocked Danny Frush cuckoo in the second round. Far off in Mesopotamia, twenty-one feet of snow had fallen. Across the world in distant Australia, the English cricketers were sharpening up their wickets. *There* was Romance.

Patrons of the arts and letters have discovered *The Forum*, he read. It is the guide, philosopher, and friend of the thinking minority. Prize short-stories – will their authors write our best-sellers of tomorrow?

You will enjoy these warm, homespun, American tales, bits of real life on the open ranch, in crowded tenement or comfortable home, and all with a healthy undercurrent of humor.

I must read them, he thought.

He read on. Our children's children – what of them? Who of them? New means must be discovered to find room for us under the sun. Shall this be done by war or can it be done by peaceful methods?

Or will we all have to move to Canada?

Our deepest convictions – will Science upset them? Our civilization – is it inferior to older orders of things?

And meanwhile, in the far-off dripping jungles of Yucatan, sounded the chopping of the axes of the gum-choppers.

Do we want big men – or do we want them cultured? Take Joyce. Take President Coolidge. What star must our college students aim at? There is Jack Britton. There is Doctor Henry Van Dyke. Can we reconcile the two? Take the case of Young Stribling.

And what of our daughters who must make their own Soundings? Nancy Hawthorne is obliged to make her own Soundings in the sea of life. Bravely and sensibly she faces the problems which come to every girl of eighteen.

It was a splendid booklet.

Are you a girl of eighteen? Take the case of Joan of Arc. Take the case of Bernard Shaw. Take the case of Betsy Ross.

Think of these things in 1925 – Was there a risqué page in Puritan history? Were there two sides to Pocahontas? Did she have a fourth dimension?

Are modern paintings – and poetry – Art? Yes and No. Take Picasso.

Have tramps codes of conduct? Send your mind adventuring.

There is Romance everywhere. *Forum* writers talk to the point, are possessed of humor and wit. But they do not try to be smart and are never long-winded.

Live the full life of the mind, exhilarated by new ideas, intoxicated by the Romance of the unusual. He laid down the booklet.

And meanwhile, stretched flat on a bed in a darkened room in his house in Triana, Manuel Garcia Maera lay with a tube in each lung, drowning with the pneumonia. All the papers in Andalucia devoted special supplements to his death, which had been expected for some days. Men and boys bought full-length colored pictures of him to remember him by, and lost the picture they had of him in their memories by looking at the lithographs. Bull-fighters were very relieved he was dead, because he did always in the bull-ring the things they could only do sometimes. They all marched in the rain behind his coffin and there were one hundred and forty-seven bull-fighters followed him out to the cemetery, where they buried him in the tomb next to Joselito. After the funeral every one sat in the cafés out of the rain, and many colored pictures of Maera were sold to men who rolled them up and put them away in their pockets.

NOW I LAY ME

That night we lay on the floor in the room and I listened to the silk-worms eating. The silk-worms fed in racks of mulberry leaves and all night you could hear them eating and a dropping sound in the leaves. I myself did not want to sleep because I had been living for a long time with the knowledge that if I ever shut my eyes in the dark and let myself go, my soul would go out of my body. I had been that way for a long time, ever since I had been blown up at night and felt it go out of me and go off and then come back. I tried never to think about it, but it had started to go since, in the nights, just at the moment of going off to sleep, and I could only stop it by a very great effort. So while now I am fairly sure that it would not really have gone out, yet then, that summer, I was unwilling to make the experiment.

I had different ways of occupying myself while I lay awake. I would think of a trout stream I had fished along when I was a boy and fish its whole length very carefully in my mind; fishing very carefully under all the logs, all the turns of the bank, the deep holes and the clear shallow stretches, sometimes catching trout and sometimes losing them. I would stop fishing at noon to eat my lunch; sometimes on a log over the stream; sometimes on a high bank under a tree, and I always ate my lunch very slowly and watched the stream below me while I ate. Often I ran out of bait because I would take only ten worms with me in a tobacco tin when I started. When I had used them all I had to find more worms, and sometimes it was very difficult digging in the bank of the stream where the cedar trees kept out the sun and there was no grass but only the bare moist earth and often I could find no worms. Always though I found some kind of bait, but one time in the swamp I could find no bait at all and had to cut up one of the trout I had caught and use him for bait.

Sometimes I found insects in the swamp meadows, in the grass or under ferns, and used them. There were beetles and in-sects with legs like grass stems, and grubs in old rotten logs; white grubs with brown pinching heads that would not stay on the hook and emptied into nothing in the cold water, and wood ticks under logs where sometimes I found angle-worms that slipped into the ground as soon as the log was raised. Once I used a salamander from under an old log. The salamander was very small and neat and agile and a lovely color. He had tiny feet that tried to hold on to the hook, and after that one time I never used a salamander, although I found them very often. Nor did I use crickets, because of the way they acted about the hook.

Sometimes the stream ran through an open meadow, and in the dry grass I would catch grasshoppers and use them for bait and sometimes I would catch grasshoppers and toss them into the stream and watch them float along swimming on the stream and circling on the surface as the current took them and then disappear as a trout rose. Sometimes I would fish four or five different streams in the night; starting as near as I could get to their source and fishing them down stream. When I had finished too quickly and the time did not go, I would fish the stream over again, starting where it emptied into the lake and fishing back up stream, trying for all the trout I had missed coming down. Some nights too I made up streams, and some of them were very exciting, and it was like being awake and dreaming. Some of those streams I still remember and think that I have fished in them, and they are confused with streams I really know. I gave them all names and went to them on the train and sometimes walked for miles to get to them.

But some nights I could not fish, and on those nights I was cold-awake and said my prayers over and over and tried to pray for all the people I had ever known. That took up a great amount of time, for if you try to remember all the people you have ever known, going back to the earliest thing you remember – which was, with me, the attic of the house where I was born and my mother and father's wedding-cake in a tin box hanging from one of the rafters, and, in the attic, jars of snakes and other specimens that my father had collected as a boy and preserved in alcohol, the alcohol sunken in the jars so the backs of some of the snakes and specimens were exposed and had turned white – if you thought back that far, you remembered a great many people. If you prayed for all of them, saying a Hail Mary and an Our Father for each one, it took a long time and finally it would be light, and then you could go to sleep, if you were in a place where you could sleep in the daylight.

On those nights I tried to remember everything that had ever happened to me, starting with just before I went to the war and remembering back from one thing to another. I found I could only remember back to that attic in my grandfather's house.

Then I would start there and remember this way again, until I reached the war.

I remember, after my grandfather died we moved away from that house and to a new house designed and built by my mother. Many things that were not to be moved were burned in the back-yard and I remember those jars from the attic being thrown in the fire, and how they popped in the heat and the fire flamed up from the alcohol. I remember the snakes burning in the fire in the back-yard. But there were no people in that, only things. I could not remember who burned the things even, and I would go on until I came to people and then stop and pray for them.

About the new house I remember how my mother was always cleaning things out and making a good clearance. One time when my father was away on a hunting trip she made a good thorough cleaning out in the basement and burned everything that should not have been there. When my father came home and got down from his buggy and hitched the horse, the fire was still burning in the road beside the house. I went out to meet him. He handed me his shotgun and looked at the fire. 'What's this?' he asked.

'I've been cleaning out the basement, dear,' my mother said from the porch. She was standing there smiling, to meet him. My father looked at the fire and kicked at something. Then he leaned over and picked something out of the ashes. 'Get a rake, Nick,' he said to me. I went to the basement and brought a rake and my father raked very carefully in the ashes. He raked out stone axes and stone skinning knives and tools for making arrow-heads and pieces of pottery and many arrow-heads. They had all been blackened and chipped by the fire. My father raked them all out very carefully and spread them on the grass by the road. His shotgun in its leather case and his game-bags were on the grass where he had left them when he stepped down from the buggy.

'Take the gun and the bags in the house, Nick, and bring me a paper,' he said. My mother had gone inside the house. I took the shotgun, which was heavy to carry and banged against my legs, and the two game-bags and started toward the house. 'Take them one at a time,' my father said. 'Don't try and carry too much at once.' I put down the game-bags and took in the shot-gun and brought out a newspaper from the pile in my father's office. My father spread all the blackened, chipped stone imple-ments on the paper and then wrapped them up. 'The best arrow-heads went all to pieces,' he said. He walked into the house with the paper package and I stayed outside on the grass with the two game-bags. After a while I took them in. In remembering that, there were only two people, so I would pray for them both.

Some nights, though, I could not remember my prayers even. I could only get as far as 'On earth as it is in heaven' and then have to start all over and be absolutely unable to get past that. Then I would have to recognize that I could not remember and give up saying my prayers that night and try something else. So on some nights I would try to remember all the animals in the world by name and then the birds and then fishes and then countries and cities and then kinds of food and the names of all the streets I could remember in Chicago, and when I could not remember anything at all any more I would just listen. And I do not remember a night on which you could not hear things. If I could have a light I was not afraid to sleep, because I knew my soul would only go out of me if it were dark. So, of course, many nights I was where I could have a light and then I slept because I was nearly always tired and often very sleepy. And I am sure many times too that I slept without knowing it – but I never slept knowing it, and on this night I listened to the silk-worms. You can hear silk-worms eating very clearly in the night and I lay with my eyes open and listened to them.

There was only one other person in the room and he was awake too. I listened to him being awake, for a long time. He could not lie as quietly as I could because, perhaps, he had not had as much practice being awake. We were lying on blankets spread over straw and when he moved the straw was noisy, but the silk-worms were not frightened by any noise we made and ate on steadily. There were the noises of night seven kilometers behind the lines outside but they were different from the small noises inside the room in the dark. The other man in the room tried lying quietly. Then he moved again. I moved too, so he would know I was awake. He had lived ten years in Chicago. They had taken him for a soldier in nineteen fourteen when he had come back to visit his family, and they had given him me for an orderly because he spoke English. I heard him listening, so I moved again in the blankets.

'Can't you sleep, Signor Tenente?' he asked.

'No.'

'I can't sleep, either.'

'What's the matter?'

'I don't know. I can't sleep.'

'You feel all right?'

'Sure. I feel good. I just can't sleep.'

'You want to talk a while?' I asked.

'Sure. What can you talk about in this damn place.'

'This place is pretty good,' I said.

'Sure,' he said. 'It's all right.'

'Tell me about out in Chicago,' I said.

'Oh,' he said, 'I told you all that once.'

'Tell me about how you got married.'

'I told you that.'

'Was the letter you got Monday – from her?'

'Sure. She writes me all the time. She's making good money with the place.'

'You'll have a nice place when you go back.'

'Sure. She runs it fine. She's making a lot of money.'

'Don't you think we'll wake them up, talking?' I asked.

'No. They can't hear. Anyway, they sleep like pigs. I'm different,' he said. 'I'm nervous.'

'Talk quiet,' I said. 'Want a smoke?'

We smoked skilfully in the dark.

'You don't smoke much, Signor Tenente.'

'No. I've just about cut it out.'

'Well,' he said, 'it don't do you any good and I suppose you get so you don't miss it. Did you ever hear a blind man won't smoke because he can't see the smoke come out?'

'I don't believe it.'

'I think it's all bull, myself,' he said. 'I just heard it somewhere. You know how you hear things.'

We were both quiet and I listened to the silk-worms.

'You hear those damn silk-worms?' he asked. 'You can hear them chew.'

'It's funny,' I said.

'Say, Signor Tenente, is there something really the matter that you can't sleep? I never see you sleep. You haven't slept nights ever since I been with you.'

'I don't know, John,' I said. 'I got in pretty bad shape along early last spring and at night it bothers me.'

'Just like I am,' he said. 'I shouldn't have ever got in this war. I'm too nervous.'

'Maybe it will get better.'

'Say, Signor Tenente, what did you get in this war for, anyway?'

'I don't know, John. I wanted to, then.'

'Wanted to,' he said. 'That's a hell of a reason.'

'We oughtn't to talk out loud,' I said.

'They sleep just like pigs,' he said. 'They can't understand the English language, anyway. They don't know a damn thing. What are you going to do when it's over and we go back to the States?'

'I'll get a job on a paper.'

'In Chicago?'

'Maybe.'

'Do you ever read what this fellow Brisbane writes? My wife cuts it out for me and sends it to me.'

'Sure.'

'Did you ever meet him?'

'No, but I've seen him.'

'I'd like to meet that fellow. He's a fine writer. My wife don't read English but she takes the paper just like when I was home and she cuts out the editorials and the sport page and sends them to me.'

'How are your kids?'

'They're fine. One of the girls is in the fourth grade now. You know, Signor Tenente, if I didn't have the kids I wouldn't be your orderly now. They'd have made me stay in the line all the time.'

'I'm glad you've got them.'

'So am I. They're fine kids but I want a boy. Three girls and no boy. That's a hell of a note.'

'Why don't you try and go to sleep?'

'No, I can't sleep now. I'm wide awake now, Signor Tenente. Say, I'm worried about you not sleeping though.'

'It'll be all right, John.'

'Imagine a young fellow like you not to sleep.'

'I'll get all right. It just takes a while.'

'You got to get all right. A man can't get along that don't sleep. Do you worry about anything? You got anything on your mind?'

'No, John, I don't think so.'

'You ought to get married, Signor Tenente. Then you wouldn't worry.'

'I don't know.'

'You ought to get married. Why don't you pick out some nice Italian girl with plenty of money? You could get any one you want. You're young and you got good decorations and you look nice. You been wounded a couple of times.'

'I can't talk the language well enough.'

'You talk it fine. To hell with talking the language. You don't have to talk to them. Marry them.'

'I'll think about it.'

'You know some girls, don't you?'

'Sure.'

'Well, you marry the one with the most money. Over here, the way they're brought up, they'll all make you a good wife.'

'I'll think about it.'

'Don't think about it, Signor Tenente. Do it.'

'All right.'

'A man ought to be married. You'll never regret it. Every man ought to be married.'

'All right,' I said. 'Let's try and sleep a while.'

'All right, Signor Tenente. I'll try it again. But you remember what I said.'

'I'll remember it,' I said. 'Now let's sleep a while, John.'

'All right,' he said. 'I hope you sleep, Signor Tenente.'

I heard him roll in his blankets on the straw and then he was very quiet and I listened to him breathing regularly. Then he started to snore. I listened to him snore for a long time and then I stopped listening to him snore and listened to the silk-worms eating. They ate steadily, making a dropping in the leaves. I had a new thing to think about and I lay in the dark with my eyes open and thought of all the girls I had ever known and what kind of wives they would make. It was a very interesting thing to think about and for a while it killed off trout-fishing and interfered with my prayers. Finally, though, I went back to trout-fishing, because I found that I could remember all the streams and there was always something new about them, while the girls, after I had thought about them a few times, blurred and I could not call them into my mind and finally they all blurred and all became rather the same and I gave up thinking about them almost altogether. But I kept on with my prayers and I prayed very often for John in the nights and his class was removed from active service before the October offensive. I was glad he was not there, because he would have been a great worry to me. He came to the hospital in Milan to see me several months after and was very disappointed that I had not yet married, and I know he would feel very badly if he knew that, so far, I have never married. He was going back to America and he was very certain about marriage and knew it would fix up everything.

WINNER TAKE NOTHING

"Unlike all other forms of lutte or
combat the conditions are that the
winner shall take nothing; neither
his ease, nor his pleasure, nor any
notions of glory; nor, if he win far
enough, shall there be any reward
within himself."

to ADA and ARCHIBALD MacLEISH

AFTER THE STORM

It wasn't about anything, something about making punch, and then we started fighting and I slipped and he had me down kneeling on my chest and choking me with both hands like he was trying to kill me and all the time I was trying to get the knife out of my pocket to cut him loose. Everybody was too drunk to pull him off me. He was choking me and hammering my head on the floor and I got the knife out and opened it up; and I cut the muscle right across his arm and he let go of me. He couldn't have held on if he wanted to. Then he rolled and hung onto that arm and started to cry and I said:

'What the hell you want to choke me for?'

I'd have killed him. I couldn't swallow for a week. He hurt my throat bad.

Well, I went out of there and there were plenty of them with him and some came out after me and I made a turn and was down by the docks and I met a fellow and he said somebody killed a man up the street. I said 'Who killed him?' and he said 'I don't know who killed him but he's dead all right,' and it was dark and there was water standing in the street and no lights and windows broke and boats all up in the town and trees blown down and everything all blown and I got a skiff and went out and found my boat where I had her inside of Mango Key and she was all right only she was full of water. So I bailed her out and pumped her out and there was a moon but plenty of clouds and still plenty rough and I took it down along; and when it was daylight I was off Eastern Harbor.

Brother, that was some storm. I was the first boat out and you never saw water like that was. It was just as white as a lye barrel and coming from Eastern Harbor to Sou'west Key you couldn't recognize the shore. There was a big channel blown right out through the middle of the beach. Trees and all blown out and a channel cut through and all the water white as chalk and everything on it; branches and whole trees and dead birds, and all floating. Inside the keys were all the pelicans in the world and all kinds of birds flying. They must have gone inside there when they knew it was coming.

I lay at Sou'west Key a day and nobody came after me. I was the first boat out and I seen a spar floating and I knew there must be a wreck and I started out to look for her. I found her. She was a three-masted schooner and I could just see the stumps of her spars out of water. She was in too deep water and I didn't get anything off of her. So I went on looking for something else. I had the start on all of them and I knew I ought to get whatever there was. I went on down over the sand-bars from where I left that three-masted schooner and I didn't find anything and I went on a long way. I was way out toward the quicksands and I didn't find anything so I went on. Then when I was in sight of the Rebecca light I saw all kinds of birds making over something and I headed over for them to see what it was and there was a cloud of birds all right.

I could see something looked like a spar up out of the water and when I got over close the birds all went up in the air and stayed all around me. The water was clear out there and there was a spar of some kind sticking out just above the water and when I come up close to it I saw it was all dark under water like a long shadow and I came right over it and there under water was a liner; just lying there all under water as big as the whole world. I drifted over her in the boat. She lay on her side and the stern was deep down. The port holes were all shut tight and I could see the glass shine in the water and the whole of her; the biggest boat I ever saw in my life laying there and I went along the whole length of her and then I went over and anchored and I had the skiff on the deck forward and I shoved it down into the water and sculled over with the birds all around me.

I had a water glass like we use sponging and my hand shook so I could hardly hold it. All the port holes were shut that you could see going along over her but way down below near the bottom something must have been open because there were pieces of things floating out all the time. You couldn't tell what they were. Just pieces. That's what the birds were after. You never saw so many birds. They were all around me; crazy yelling.

I could see everything sharp and clear. I could see her rounded over and she looked a mile long under the water. She was lying on a clear white bank of sand and the spar was a sort of foremast or some sort of tackle that slanted out of water the way she was laying on her side. Her bow wasn't very far under. I could stand on the letters of her name on her bow and my head was just out of water. But the nearest port hole was twelve feet down. I could just reach it with the grains pole and I tried to break it with that but I couldn't. The glass was too stout. So I sculled back to the boat and got a wrench and lashed it to the end of the grains pole and I couldn't break it. There I was looking down through the glass at that liner with everything in her and I was the first one to her and I couldn't get into her. She must have had five million dollars worth in her.

It made me shaky to think how much she must have in her. Inside the port hole that was closest I could see something but I couldn't make it out through the water glass. I couldn't do any good with the grains pole and I took off my clothes and stood and took a couple of deep breaths and dove over off the stern with the wrench in my hand and swam down. I could hold on for a second to the edge of the port hole and I could see in and there was a woman inside with her hair floating all out. I could see her floating plain and I hit the glass twice with the wrench hard and I heard the noise clink in my ears but it wouldn't break and I had to come up.

I hung onto the dinghy and got my breath and then I climbed in and took a couple of breaths and dove again. I swam down and took hold of the edge of the port hole with my fingers and held it and hit the glass as hard as I could with the wrench. I could see the woman floated in the water through the glass. Her hair was tied once close to her head and it floated all out in the water. I could see the rings on one of her hands. She was right up close to the port hole and I hit the glass twice and I didn't even crack it. When I came up I thought I wouldn't make it to the top before I'd have to breathe.

I went down once more and I cracked the glass, only cracked it, and when I came up my nose was bleeding and I stood on the bow of the liner with my bare feet on the letters of her name and my head just out and rested there and then I swam over to the skiff and pulled up into it and sat there waiting for my head to stop aching and looking down into the water glass, but I bled so I had to wash out the water glass. Then I lay back in the skiff and held my hand under my nose to stop it and I lay there with my head back looking up and there was a million birds above and all around.

When I quit bleeding I took another look through the glass and then I sculled over to the boat to try and find something heavier than the wrench but I couldn't find a thing; not even a sponge hook. I went back and the water was clearer all the time and you could see everything that floated out over that white bank of sand. I looked for sharks but there weren't any. You could have seen a shark a long way away. The water was so clear and the sand white. There was a grapple for an anchor on the skiff and I cut it off and went overboard and down with it. It carried me right down and past the port hole and I grabbed and couldn't hold anything and went on down and down, sliding along the curved side of her. I had to let go of the grapple. I heard it bump once and it seemed like a year before I came up through to the top of the water. The skiff was floated away with the tide and I swam over to her with my nose bleeding in the water while I swam and I was plenty glad there weren't sharks; but I was tired.

My head felt cracked open and I lay in the skiff and rested and then I sculled back. It was getting along in the afternoon. I went down once more with the wrench and it didn't do any good. That wrench was too light. It wasn't any good diving unless you had a big hammer or something heavy enough to do good. Then I lashed the wrench to the grains pole again and I watched through the water glass and pounded on the glass and hammered until the wrench came off and I saw it in the glass, clear and sharp, go sliding down along her and then off and down to the quicksand and go in. Then I couldn't do a thing. The wrench was gone and I'd lost the grapple so I sculled back to the boat. I was too tired to get the skiff aboard and the sun was pretty low. The birds were all pulling out and leaving her and I headed for Sou'west Key towing the skiff and the birds going on ahead of me and behind me. I was plenty tired.

That night it came on to blow and it blew for a week. You couldn't get out to her. They come out from town and told me the fellow I'd had to cut was all right except for his arm and I went back to town and they put me under five hundred dollar bond. It came out all right because some of them, friends of mine, swore he was after me with an ax, but by the time we got back out to her the Greeks had blown her open and cleaned her out. They got the safe out with dynamite. Nobody ever knows how much they got. She carried gold and they got it all. They stripped her clean. I found her and I never got a nickel out of her.

It was a hell of a thing all right. They say she was just outside of Havana harbor when the hurricane hit and she couldn't get in or the owners wouldn't let the captain chance coming in; they say he wanted to try; so she had to go with it and in the dark they were running with it trying to go through the gulf between

Rebecca and Tortugas when she struck on the quicksands. Maybe her rudder was carried away. Maybe they weren't even steering. But anyway they couldn't have known they were quicksands and when she struck the captain must have ordered them to open up the ballast tanks so she'd lay solid. But it was quicksand she'd hit and when they opened the tank she went in stern first and then over on her beam ends. There were four hundred and fifty passengers and the crew on board of her and they must all have been aboard of her when I found her. They must have opened the tanks as soon as she struck and the minute she settled on it the quicksands took her down. Then her boilers must have burst and that must have been what made those pieces that came out. It was funny there weren't any sharks though. There wasn't a fish. I could have seen them on that clear white sand.

Plenty of fish now though; jewfish, the biggest kind. The biggest part of her's under the sand now but they live inside of her; the biggest kind of jewfish. Some weigh three to four hundred pounds. Sometime we'll go out and get some. You can see the Rebecca light from where she is. They've got a buoy on her now. She's right at the end of the quicksand right at the edge of the gulf. She only missed going through by about a hundred yards. In the dark in the storm they just missed it; raining the way it was they couldn't have seen the Rebecca. Then they're not used to that sort of thing. The captain of a liner isn't used to scudding that way. They have a course and they tell me they set some sort of a compass and it steers itself. They probably didn't know where they were when they ran with that blow but they come close to making it. Maybe they'd lost the rudder though. Anyway there wasn't another thing for them to hit till they'd get to Mexico once they were in that gulf. Must have been something though when they struck in that rain and wind and he told them to open her tanks. Nobody could have been on deck in that blow and rain. Everybody must have been below. They couldn't have lived on deck. There must have been some scenes inside all right because you know she settled fast. I saw that wrench go into the sand. The captain couldn't have known it was quicksand when she struck unless he knew these waters. He just knew it wasn't rock. He must have seen it all up in the bridge. He must have known what it was about when she settled. I wonder how fast she made it. I wonder if the mate was there with him. Do you think they stayed inside the bridge or do you think they took it outside? They never found any bodies. Not a one. Nobody floating. They float a long way with life belts too. They must have took it inside. Well, the Greeks got it all. Everything. They must have come fast all right. They picked her clean. First there was the birds, then me, then the Greeks, and even the birds got more out of her than I did.

A CLEAN, WELL-LIGHTED PLACE

It was late and every one had left the café except an old man who sat in the shadow the leaves of the tree made against the electric light. In the day time the street was dusty, but at night the dew settled the dust and the old man liked to sit late because he was deaf and now at night it was quiet and he felt the difference. The two waiters inside the café knew that the old man was a little drunk, and while he was a good client they knew that if he became too drunk he would leave without paying, so they kept watch on him.

'Last week he tried to commit suicide,' one waiter said.

'Why?'

'He was in despair.'

'What about?'

'Nothing.'

'How do you know it was nothing?'

'He has plenty of money.'

They sat together at a table that was close against the wall near the door of the café and looked at the terrace where the tables were all empty except where the old man sat in the shadow of the leaves of the tree that moved slightly in the wind. A girl and a soldier went by in the street. The street light shone on the brass number on his collar. The girl wore no head covering and hurried beside him.

'The guard will pick him up,' one waiter said.

'What does it matter if he gets what he's after?'

'He had better get off the street now. The guard will get him. They went by five minutes ago.'

The old man sitting in the shadow rapped on his saucer with his glass. The younger waiter went over to him.

'What do you want?'

The old man looked at him. 'Another brandy,' he said.

'You'll be drunk,' the waiter said. The old man looked at him. The waiter went away.

'He'll stay all night,' he said to his colleague. 'I'm sleepy now. I never get into bed before three o'clock. He should have killed himself last week.'

The waiter took the brandy bottle and another saucer from the counter inside the café and marched out to the old man's table. He put down the saucer and poured the glass full of brandy.

'You should have killed yourself last week,' he said to the deaf man. The old man motioned with his finger. 'A little more,' he said. The waiter poured on into the glass so that the brandy slopped over and ran down the stem into the top saucer of the pile. 'Thank you,' the old man said. The waiter took the bottle back inside the café. He sat down at the table with his colleague again.

'He's drunk now,' he said.

'He's drunk every night.'

'What did he want to kill himself for?'

'How should I know.'

'How did he do it?'

'He hung himself with a rope.'

'Who cut him down?'

'His niece.'

'Why did they do it?'

'Fear for his soul.'

'How much money has he got?'

'He's got plenty.'

'He must be eighty years old.'

'Anyway I should say he was eighty.'

'I wish he would go home. I never get to bed before three o'clock. What kind of hour is that to go to bed?'

'He stays up because he likes it.'

'He's lonely. I'm not lonely. I have a wife waiting in bed for me.'

'He had a wife once too.'

'A wife would be no good to him now.'

'You can't tell. He might be better with a wife.'

'His niece looks after him. You said she cut him down.'

'I know.'

'I wouldn't want to be that old. An old man is a nasty thing.'

'Not always. This old man is clean. He drinks without spilling. Even now, drunk. Look at him.'

'I don't want to look at him. I wish he would go home. He has no regard for those who must work.'

The old man looked from his glass across the square, then over at the waiters.

'Another brandy,' he said, pointing to his glass. The waiter who was in a hurry came over.

'Finished,' he said, speaking with that omission of syntax stupid people employ when talking to drunken people or foreigners. 'No more tonight. Close now.'

'Another,' said the old man.

'No. Finished.' The waiter wiped the edge of the table with a towel and shook his head.

The old man stood up, slowly counted the saucers, took a leather coin purse from his pocket and paid for the drinks, leaving half a peseta tip.

The waiter watched him go down the street, a very old man walking unsteadily but with dignity.

'Why didn't you let him stay and drink?' the unhurried waiter asked. They were putting up the shutters. 'It is not half-past two.'

'I want to go home to bed.'

'What is an hour?'

'More to me than to him.'

'An hour is the same.'

'You talk like an old man yourself. He can buy a bottle and drink at home.'

'It's not the same.'

'No, it is not,' agreed the waiter with a wife. He did not wish to be unjust. He was only in a hurry.

'And you? You have no fear of going home before your usual hour?'

'Are you trying to insult me?'

'No, *hombre*, only to make a joke.'

'No,' the waiter who was in a hurry said, rising from pulling down the metal shutters. 'I have confidence. I am all confidence.'

'You have youth, confidence, and a job,' the older waiter said. 'You have everything.'

'And what do you lack?'

'Everything but work.'

'You have everything I have.'

'No. I have never had confidence and I am not young.'

'Come on. Stop talking nonsense and lock up.'

'I am of those who like to stay late at the café,' the older waiter said. 'With all those who do not want to go to bed. With all those who need a light for the night.'

'I want to go home and into bed.'

'We are of two different kinds,' the older waiter said. He was now dressed to go home. 'It is not only a question of youth and confidence although those things are very beautiful. Each night I am reluctant to close up because there may be some one who needs the café.'

'*Hombre*, there are *bodegas* open all night long.'

'You do not understand. This is a clean and pleasant café. It is well lighted. The light is very good and also, now, there are shadows of the leaves.'

'Good night,' said the younger waiter.

'Good night,' the other said. Turning off the electric light he continued the conversation with himself. It is the light of course but it is necessary that the place be clean and pleasant. You do not want music. Certainly you do not want music. Nor can you stand before a bar with dignity although that is all that is provided for these hours. What did he fear? It was not fear or dread. It was a nothing that he knew too well. It was all a nothing and a man was nothing too. It was only that and light was all it needed and a certain cleanness and order. Some lived in it and never felt it but he knew it all was *nada y pues nada y nada y pues nada*. Our *nada* who art in *nada, nada* be thy name thy kingdom *nada* thy will be *nada* in *nada* as it is in *nada*. Give us this *nada* our daily *nada* and *nada* us our *nada* as we *nada* our *nadas* and *nada* us not into *nada* but deliver us from *nada*; *pues nada*. Hail nothing full of nothing, nothing is with thee. He smiled and stood before a bar with a shining steam pressure coffee machine.

'What's yours?' asked the barman.

'*Nada*.'

'*Otro loco más*,' said the barman and turned away.

'A little cup,' said the waiter.

The barman poured it for him.

'The light is very bright and pleasant but the bar is unpolished,' the waiter said.

The barman looked at him but did not answer. It was too late at night for conversation.

'You want another *copita?*' the barman asked.

'No, thank you,' said the waiter and went out. He disliked bars and *bodegas*. A clean, well-lighted café was a very different thing. Now, without thinking further, he would go home to his room. He would lie in the bed and finally, with daylight, he would go to sleep. After all, he said to himself, it is probably only insomnia. Many must have it.

THE LIGHT OF THE WORLD

When he saw us come in the door the bartender looked up and then reached over and put the glass covers on the two free-lunch bowls.

'Give me a beer,' I said. He drew it, cut the top off with the spatula and then held the glass in his hand. I put the nickel on the wood and he slid the beer toward me.

'What's yours?' he said to Tom.

'Beer.'

He drew that beer and cut it off and when he saw the money he pushed the beer across to Tom.

'What's the matter?' Tom asked.

The bartender didn't answer him. He just looked over our heads and said, 'What's yours?' to a man who'd come in.

'Rye,' the man said. The bartender put out the bottle and glass and a glass of water.

Tom reached over and took the glass off the free-lunch bowl. It was a bowl of pickled pig's feet and there was a wooden thing that worked like a scissors, with two wooden forks at the end to pick them up with.

'No,' said the bartender and put the glass cover back on the bowl. Tom held the wooden scissors fork in his hand. 'Put it back,' said the bartender.

'You know where,' said Tom.

The bartender reached a hand forward under the bar, watching us both. I put fifty cents on the wood and he straightened up.

'What was yours?' he said.

'Beer,' I said, and before he drew the beer he uncovered both the bowls.

'Your goddam pig's feet stink,' Tom said, and spit what he had in his mouth on the floor. The bartender didn't say anything. The man who had drunk the rye paid and went out without looking back.

'You stink yourself,' the bartender said. 'All you punks stink.'

'He says we're punks,' Tommy said to me.

'Listen,' I said. 'Let's get out.'

'You punks clear the hell out of here,' the bartender said.

'I said we were going out,' I said. 'It wasn't your idea.'

'We'll be back,' Tommy said.

'No you won't,' the bartender told him.

'Tell him how wrong he is,' Tom turned to me.

'Come on,' I said.

Outside it was good and dark.

'What the hell kind of place is this?' Tommy said.

'I don't know,' I said. 'Let's go down to the station.'

We'd come in that town at one end and we were going out the other. It smelled of hides and tan bark and the big piles of sawdust. It was getting dark as we came in, and now that it was dark it was cold and the puddles of water in the road were freezing at the edges.

Down at the station there were five whores waiting for the train to come in, and six white men and four Indians. It was crowded and hot from the stove and full of stale smoke. As we came in nobody was talking and the ticket window was down.

'Shut the door, can't you?' somebody said.

I looked to see who said it. It was one of the white men. He wore stagged trousers and lumbermen's rubbers and a mackinaw shirt like the others, but he had no cap and his face was white and his hands were white and thin.

'Aren't you going to shut it?'

'Sure,' I said, and shut it.

'Thank you,' he said. One of the other men snickered.

'Ever interfere with a cook?' he said to me.

'No.'

'You can interfere with this one,' he looked at the cook. 'He likes it.'

The cook looked away from him holding his lips tight together.

'He puts lemon juice on his hands,' the man said. 'He wouldn't get them in dishwater for anything. Look how white they are.'

One of the whores laughed out loud. She was the biggest whore I ever saw in my life and the biggest woman. And she had on one of those silk dresses that change colors. There were two other whores that were nearly as big but the big one must have weighed three hundred and fifty pounds. You couldn't believe she was real when you looked at her. All three had those changeable silk dresses. They sat side by side on the bench. They were huge. The other two were just ordinary looking whores, peroxide blondes.

'Look at his hands,' the man said and nodded his head at the cook. The whore laughed again and shook all over.

The cook turned and said to her quickly, 'You big disgusting mountain of flesh.'

She just keep on laughing and shaking.

'Oh, my Christ,' she said. She had a nice voice. 'Oh, my sweet Christ.'

The two other whores, the big ones, acted very quiet and placid as though they didn't have much sense, but they were big, nearly as big as the biggest one. They'd have both gone well over two hundred and fifty pounds. The other two were dignified.

Of the men, besides the cook and the one who talked, there were two other lumberjacks, one that listened, interested but bashful, and the other that seemed getting ready to say something, and two Swedes. Two Indians were sitting down at the end of the bench and one standing up against the wall.

The man who was getting ready to say something spoke to me very low, 'Must be like getting on top of a hay mow.'

I laughed and said it to Tommy.

'I swear to Christ I've never been anywhere like this,' he said. 'Look at the three of them.' Then the cook spoke up.

'How old are you boys?'

'I'm ninety-six and he's sixty-nine,' Tommy said.

'Ho! Ho! Ho!' the big whore shook with laughing. She had a really pretty voice. The other whores didn't smile.

'Oh, can't you be decent?' the cook said. 'I asked just to be friendly.'

'We're seventeen and nineteen,' I said.

'What's the matter with you?' Tommy turned to me.

'That's all right.'

'You can call me Alice,' the big whore said and then she began to shake again.

'Is that your name?' Tommy asked.

'Sure,' she said. 'Alice. Isn't it?' she turned to the man who sat by the cook.

'Alice. That's right.'

'That's the sort of name you'd have,' the cook said.

'It's my real name,' Alice said.

'What's the other girls' names?' Tom asked.

'Hazel and Ethel,' Alice said. Hazel and Ethel smiled. They weren't very bright.

'What's your name?' I said to one of the blondes.

'Frances,' she said.

'Frances what?'

'Frances Wilson. What's it to you?'

'What's yours?' I asked the other one.

'Oh, don't be fresh,' she said.

'He just wants us all to be friends,' the man who talked said. 'Don't you want to be friends?'

'No,' the peroxide one said. 'Not with you.'

'She's just a spitfire,' the man said. 'A regular little spitfire.'

The one blonde looked at the other and shook her head.

'Goddamned mossbacks,' she said.

Alice commenced to laugh again and to shake all over.

'There's nothing funny,' the cook said. 'You all laugh but there's nothing funny. You two young lads; where are you bound for?'

'Where are you going yourself?' Tom asked him.

'I want to go to Cadillac,' the cook said. 'Have you ever been there? My sister lives there.'

'He's a sister himself,' the man in the stagged trousers said.

'Can't you stop that sort of thing?' the cook asked. 'Can't we speak decently?'

'Cadillac is where Steve Ketchel came from and where Ad Wolgast is from,' the shy man said.

'Steve Ketchel,' one of the blondes said in a high voice as though the name had pulled a trigger in her. 'His own father shot and killed him. Yes, by Christ, his own father. There aren't any more men like Steve Ketchel.'

'Wasn't his name Stanley Ketchel?' asked the cook.

'Oh, shut up,' said the blonde. 'What do you know about Steve? Stanley. He was no Stanley. Steve Ketchel was the finest and most beautiful man that ever lived. I never saw a man as clean and as white and as beautiful as Steve Ketchel. There never was a man like that. He moved just like a tiger and he was the finest, free-est spender that ever lived.'

'Did you know him?' one of the men asked.

'Did I know him? Did I know him? Did I love him? You ask me that? I knew him like you know nobody in the world and I loved him like you love God. He was the greatest, finest, whitest, most beautiful man that ever lived, Steve Ketchel, and his own father shot him down like a dog.'

'Were you out on the coast with him?'

'No. I knew him before that. He was the only man I ever loved.'

Every one was very respectful to the peroxide blonde, who said all this in a high stagey way, but Alice was beginning to shake again. I felt it sitting by her.

'You should have married him,' the cook said.

'I wouldn't hurt his career,' the peroxide blonde said. 'I wouldn't be a drawback to him. A wife wasn't what he needed. Oh, my God, what a man he was.'

'That was a fine way to look at it,' the cook said. 'Didn't Jack Johnson knock him out though?'

'It was a trick,' Peroxide said. 'That big dinge took him by surprise. He'd just knocked Jack Johnson down, the big black bastard. That nigger beat him by a fluke.'

The ticket window went up and the three Indians went over to it.

'Steve knocked him down,' Peroxide said. 'He turned to smile at me.'

'I thought you said you weren't on the coast,' some one said.

'I went out just for that fight. Steve turned to smile at me and that black son of a bitch from hell jumped up and hit him by surprise. Steve could lick a hundred like that black bastard.'

'He was a great fighter,' the lumberjack said.

'I hope to God he was,' Peroxide said. 'I hope to God they don't have fighters like that now. He was like a god, he was. So white and clean and beautiful and smooth and fast and like a tiger or like lightning.'

'I saw him in the moving pictures of the fight,' Tom said. We were all very moved. Alice was shaking all over and I looked and saw she was crying. The Indians had gone outside on the platform.

'He was more than any husband could ever be,' Peroxide said. 'We were married in the eyes of God and I belong to him right now and always will and all of me is his. I don't care about my body. They can take my body. My soul belongs to Steve Ketchel. By God, he was a man.'

Everybody felt terribly. It was sad and embarrassing. Then Alice, who was still shaking, spoke. 'You're a dirty liar,' she said in that low voice. 'You never laid Steve Ketchel in your life and you know it.'

'How can you say that?' Peroxide said proudly.

'I say it because it's true,' Alice said. 'I'm the only one here that ever knew Steve Ketchel and I come from Mancelona and I knew him there and it's true and you know it's true and God can strike me dead if it isn't true.'

'He can strike me too,' Peroxide said.

'This is true, true, true, and you know it. Not just made up and I know exactly what he said to me.'

'What did he say?' Peroxide asked, complacently.

Alice was crying so she could hardly speak from shaking so. 'He said "You're a lovely piece, Alice." That's exactly what he said.'

'It's a lie,' Peroxide said.

'It's true,' Alice said. 'That's truly what he said.'

'It's a lie,' Peroxide said proudly.

'No, it's true, true, true, to Jesus and Mary true.'

'Steve couldn't have said that. It wasn't the way he talked,' Peroxide said happily.

'It's true,' said Alice in her nice voice. 'And it doesn't make any difference to me whether you believe it or not.' She wasn't crying any more and she was calm.

'It would be impossible for Steve to have said that,' Peroxide declared.

'He said it,' Alice said and smiled. 'And I remember when he said it and I *was* a lovely piece then exactly as he said, and right now I'm a better piece than you, you dried up old hot-water bottle.'

'You can't insult me,' said Peroxide. 'You big mountain of pus. I have my memories.'

'No,' Alice said in that sweet lovely voice, 'you haven't got any real memories except having your tubes out and when you started C. and M. Everything else you just read in the papers. I'm clean and you know it and men like me, even though I'm big, and you know it, and I never lie and you know it.'

'Leave me with my memories,' Peroxide said. 'With my true, wonderful memories.'

Alice looked at her and then at us and her face lost that hurt look and she smiled and she had about the prettiest face I ever saw. She had a pretty face and a nice smooth skin and a lovely voice and she was nice all right and really friendly. But my God she was big. She was as big as three women. Tom saw me looking at her and he said, 'Come on. Let's go.'

'Good-bye,' said Alice. She certainly had a nice voice.
'Good-bye,' I said.
'Which way are you boys going?' asked the cook.
'The other way from you,' Tom told him.

GOD REST YOU MERRY, GENTLEMEN

In those days the distances were all very different, the dirt blew off the hills that now have been cut down, and Kansas City was very like Constantinople. You may not believe this. No one believes this; but it is true. On this afternoon it was snowing and inside an automobile dealer's show window, lighted against the early dark, there was a racing motor car finished entirely in silver with Dans Argent lettered on the hood. This I believed to mean the silver dance or the silver dancer, and, slightly puzzled which it meant but happy in the sight of the car and pleased by my knowledge of a foreign language, I went along the street in the snow. I was walking from the Woolf Brothers' saloon where, on Christmas and Thanksgiving Day, a free turkey dinner was served, toward the city hospital which was on a high hill that overlooked the smoke, the buildings and the streets of the town. In the reception room of the hospital were the two ambulance surgeons Doc Fischer and Doctor Wilcox, sitting, the one before a desk, the other in a chair against the wall.

Doc Fischer was thin, sand-blond, with a thin mouth, amused eyes and gambler's hands. Doctor Wilcox was short, dark and carried an indexed book, *The Young Doctor's Friend and Guide*, which, being consulted on any given subject, told symptoms and treatment. It was also cross-indexed so that being consulted on symptoms it gave diagnoses. Doc Fischer had suggested that any future editions should be further cross-indexed so that if consulted as to the treatments being given, it would reveal ailments and symptoms. 'As an aid to memory,' he said.

Doctor Wilcox was sensitive about this book but could not get along without it. It was bound in limp leather and fitted his coat pocket and he had bought it at the advice of one of his professors who had said, 'Wilcox, you have no business being a physician and I have done everything in my power to prevent you from being certified as one. Since you are now a member of this learned profession I advise you, in the name of humanity, to obtain a copy of *The Young Doctor's Friend and Guide*, and use it, Doctor Wilcox. Learn to use it.'

Doctor Wilcox had said nothing but he had bought the leather-bound guide that same day.

'Well, Horace,' Doc Fischer said as I came in the receiving room which smelt of cigarettes, iodoform, carbolic and an over-heated radiator.

'Gentlemen,' I said.

'What news along the rialto?' Doc Fischer asked. He affected a certain extravagance of speech which seemed to me to be of the utmost elegance.

'The free turkey at Woolf's,' I answered.

'You partook?'

'Copiously.'

'Many of the confrères present?'

'All of them. The whole staff.'

'Much Yuletide cheer?'

'Not much.'

'Doctor Wilcox here has partaken slightly,' Doc Fischer said. Doctor Wilcox looked up at him, then at me.

'Want a drink?' he asked.

'No, thanks,' I said.

'That's all right,' Doctor Wilcox said.

'Horace,' Doc Fischer said, 'you don't mind me calling you Horace, do you?'

'No.'

'Good old Horace. We've had an extremely interesting case.'

'I'll say,' said Doctor Wilcox.

'You know the lad who was in here yesterday?'

'Which one?'

'The lad who sought eunuch-hood.'

'Yes.' I had been there when he came in. He was a boy about sixteen. He came in with no hat on and was very excited and frightened but determined. He was curly haired and well built and his lips were prominent.

'What's the matter with you, son?' Doctor Wilcox asked him.

'I want to be castrated,' the boy said.

'Why?' Doc Fischer asked.

'I've prayed and I've done everything and nothing helps.'

'Helps what?'

'That awful lust.'

'What awful lust?'

'The way I get. The way I can't stop getting. I pray all night about it.'

'Just what happens?' Doc Fischer asked.

The boy told him. 'Listen, boy,' Doc Fischer said. 'There's

nothing wrong with you. That's the way you're supposed to be. There's nothing wrong with that.'

'It is wrong,' said the boy. 'It's a sin against purity. It's a sin against our Lord and Saviour.'

'No,' said Doc Fischer. 'It's a natural thing. It's the way you are supposed to be and later on you will think you are very fortunate.'

'Oh, you don't understand,' the boy said.

'Listen,' Doc Fischer said and he told the boy certain things.

'No. I won't listen. You can't make me listen.'

'Please listen,' Doc Fischer said.

'You're just a goddamned fool,' Doctor Wilcox said to the boy.

'Then you won't do it?' the boy asked.

'Do what?'

'Castrate me.'

'Listen,' Doc Fischer said. 'No one will castrate you. There is nothing wrong with your body. You have a fine body and you must not think about that. If you are religious remember that what you complain of is no sinful state but the means of consummating a sacrament.'

'I can't stop it happening,' the boy said. 'I pray all night and I pray in the daytime. It is a sin, a constant sin against purity.'

'Oh, go and –' Doctor Wilcox said.

'When you talk like that I don't hear you,' the boy said with dignity to Doctor Wilcox. 'Won't you please do it?' he asked Doc Fischer.

'No,' said Doc Fischer. 'I've told you, boy.'

'Get him out of here,' Doctor Wilcox said.

'I'll get out,' the boy said. 'Don't touch me. I'll get out.'

That was about five o'clock on the day before.

'So what happened?' I asked.

'So at one o'clock this morning,' Doc Fischer said, 'we receive the youth self-mutilated with a razor.'

'Castrated?'

'No,' said Doc Fischer. 'He didn't know what castrate meant.'

'He may die,' Doctor Wilcox said.

'Why?'

'Loss of blood.'

'The good physician here, Doctor Wilcox, my colleague, was on call and he was unable to find this emergency listed in his book.'

'The hell with you talking that way,' Doctor Wilcox said.

'I only mean it in the friendliest way, Doctor,' Doc Fischer said, looking at his hands, at his hands that had, with his willingness to oblige and his lack of respect for Federal statutes, made him his trouble. 'Horace here will bear me out that I only speak of it in the very friendliest way. It was an amputation the young man performed, Horace.'

'Well, I wish you wouldn't ride me about it,' Doctor Wilcox said. 'There isn't any need to ride me.'

'Ride you, Doctor, on the day, the very anniversary, of our Saviour's birth?'

'*Our* Saviour? Ain't you a Jew?' Doctor Wilcox said.

'So I am. So I am. It always is slipping my mind. I've never given it its proper importance. So good of you to remind me. *Your* Saviour. That's right. *Your* Saviour, undoubtedly *your* Saviour – and the ride for Palm Sunday.'

'You're too damned smart,' Doctor Wilcox said.

'An excellent diagnosis, Doctor. I was always too damned smart. Too damned smart on the coast certainly. Avoid it, Horace. You haven't much tendency but sometimes I see a gleam. But what a diagnosis – and without the book.'

'The hell with you,' Doctor Wilcox said.

'All in good time, Doctor,' Doc Fischer said. 'All in good time. If there is such a place I shall certainly visit it. I have even had a very small look into it. No more than a peek, really. I looked away almost at once. And do you know what the young man said, Horace, when the good Doctor here brought him in? He said, "Oh, I asked you to do it. I asked you so many times to do it." '

'On Christmas Day, too,' Doctor Wilcox said.

'The significance of the particular day is not important,' Doc Fischer said.

'Maybe not to you,' said Doctor Wilcox.

'You hear him, Horace?' Doc Fischer said. 'You hear him? Having discovered my vulnerable point, my achilles tendon so to speak, the doctor pursues his advantage.'

'You're too damned smart,' Doctor Wilcox said.

THE SEA CHANGE

'All right,' said the man. 'What about it?'

'No,' said the girl, 'I can't.'

'You mean you won't.'

'I can't,' said the girl. 'That's all that I mean.'

'You mean that you won't.'

'All right,' said the girl. 'You have it your own way.'

'I don't have it my own way. I wish to God I did.'

'You did for a long time,' the girl said.

It was early, and there was no one in the café except the bar-man and these two who sat together at a table in the corner. It was the end of the summer and they were both tanned, so that they looked out of place in Paris. The girl wore a tweed suit, her skin was a smooth golden brown, her blonde hair was cut short and grew beautifully away from her forehead. The man looked at her.

'I'll kill her,' he said.

'Please don't,' the girl said. She had very fine hands and the man looked at them. They were slim and brown and very beau-tiful.

'I will. I swear to God I will.'

'It won't make you happy.'

'Couldn't you have gotten into something else? Couldn't you have gotten into some other jam?'

'It seems not,' the girl said. 'What are you going to do about it?'

'I told you.'

'No; I mean really.'

'I don't know,' he said. She looked at him and put out her hand. 'Poor old Phil,' she said. He looked at her hands, but he did not touch her hand with his.

'No, thanks,' he said.

'It doesn't do any good to say I'm sorry?'

'No.'

'Nor to tell you how it is?'

'I'd rather not hear.'

'I love you very much.'

'Yes, this proves it.'

'I'm sorry,' she said, 'if you don't understand.'

'I understand. That's the trouble. I understand.'

'You do,' she said. 'That makes it worse, of course.'

'Sure,' he said, looking at her. 'I'll understand all the time. All day and all night. Especially all night. I'll understand. You don't have to worry about that.'

'I'm sorry,' she said.

'If it was a man –'

'Don't say that. It wouldn't be a man. You know that. Don't you trust me?'

'That's funny,' he said. 'Trust you. That's really funny.'

'I'm sorry,' she said. 'That's all I seem to say. But when we do understand each other there's no use to pretend we don't.'

'No,' he said. 'I suppose not.'

'I'll come back if you want me.'

'No. I don't want you.'

Then they did not say anything for a while.

'You don't believe I love you, do you?' the girl asked.

'Let's not talk rot,' the man said.

'Don't you really believe I love you?'

'Why don't you prove it?'

'You didn't use to be that way. You never asked me to prove anything. That isn't polite.'

'You're a funny girl.'

'You're not. You're a fine man and it breaks my heart to go off and leave you –'

'You have to, of course.'

'Yes,' she said. 'I have to and you know it.'

He did not say anything and she looked at him and put her hand out again. The barman was at the far end of the bar. His face was white and so was his jacket. He knew these two and thought them a handsome young couple. He had seen many handsome young couples break up and new couples form that were never so handsome long. He was not thinking about this, but about a horse. In half an hour he could send across the street to find if the horse had won.

'Couldn't you just be good to me and let me go?' the girl asked.

'What do you think I'm going to do?'

Two people came in the door and went up to the bar.

'Yes, sir,' the barman took the orders.

'You can't forgive me? When you know about it?' the girl asked.

'No.'

'You don't think things we've had and done should make any difference in understanding?'

' "Vice is a monster of such fearful mien," ' the young man said bitterly, 'that to be something or other needs but to be seen. Then we something, something, then embrace.' He could not remember the words. 'I can't quote,' he said.

'Let's not say vice,' she said. 'That's not very polite.'

'Perversion,' he said.

'James,' one of the clients addressed the barman, 'you're looking very well.'

'You're looking very well yourself,' the barman said.

'Old James,' the other client said. 'You're fatter, James.'

'It's terrible,' the barman said, 'the way I put it on.'

'Don't neglect to insert the brandy, James,' the first client said.

'No, sir,' said the barman. 'Trust me.'

The two at the bar looked over at the two at the table, then looked back at the barman again. Towards the barman was the comfortable direction.

'I'd like it better if you didn't use words like that,' the girl said. 'There's no necessity to use a word like that.'

'What do you want me to call it?'

'You don't have to call it. You don't have to put any name to it.'

'That's the name for it.'

'No,' she said. 'We're made up of all sorts of things. You've known that. You've used it well enough.'

'You don't have to say that again.'

'Because that explains it to you.'

'All right,' he said. 'All right.'

'You mean all wrong. I know. It's all wrong. But I'll come back. I told you I'd come back. I'll come back right away.'

'No, you won't.'

'I'll come back.'

'No, you won't. Not to me.'

'You'll see.'

'Yes,' he said. 'That's the hell of it. You probably will.'

'Of course I will.'

'Go on, then.'

'Really?' She could not believe him, but her voice was happy.

'Go on,' his voice sounded strange to him. He was looking at her, at the way her mouth went and the curve of her cheek bones, at her eyes and at the way her hair grew on her forehead and at the edge of her ear and at her neck.

'Not really. Oh, you're too sweet,' she said. 'You're too good to me.'

'And when you come back tell me all about it.' His voice sounded very strange. He did not recognize it. She looked at him quickly. He was settled into something.

'You want me to go?' she asked seriously.

'Yes,' he said seriously. 'Right away.' His voice was not the same, and his mouth was very dry. 'Now,' he said.

She stood up and went out quickly. She did not look back at him. He watched her go. He was not the same-looking man as he had been before he had told her to go. He got up from the table, picked up the two checks and went over to the bar with them.

'I'm a different man, James,' he said to the barman. 'You see in me quite a different man.'

'Yes, sir?' said James.

'Vice,' said the brown young man, 'is a very strange thing, James.' He looked out the door. He saw her going down the street. As he looked in the glass, he saw he was really quite a different-looking man. The other two at the bar moved down to make room for him.

'You're right there, sir,' James said.

The other two moved down a little more, so that he would be quite comfortable. The young man saw himself in the mirror behind the bar. 'I said I was a different man, James,' he said. Looking into the mirror he saw that this was quite true.

'You look very well, sir,' James said. 'You must have had a very good summer.'

A WAY YOU'LL NEVER BE

The attack had gone across the field, been held up by machine-gun fire from the sunken road and from the group of farm houses, encountered no resistance in the town, and reached the bank of the river. Coming along the road on a bicycle, getting off to push the machine when the surface of the road became too broken, Nicholas Adams saw what had happened by the position of the dead.

They lay alone or in clumps in the high grass of the field and along the road, their pockets out, and over them were flies and around each body or group of bodies were the scattered papers.

In the grass and the grain, beside the road, and in some places scattered over the road, there was much material: a field kitchen, it must have come over when things were going well; many of the calf-skin-covered haversacks, stick bombs, helmets, rifles, sometimes one butt-up, the bayonet stuck in the dirt, they had dug quite a little at the last; stick bombs, helmets, rifles, entrenching tools, ammunition boxes, star-shell pistols, their shells scattered about, medical kits, gas masks, empty gas-mask cans, a squat, tripodded machine gun in a nest of empty shells, full belts protruding from the boxes, the water-cooling can empty and on its side, the breech block gone, the crew in odd positions, and around them, in the grass, more of the typical papers.

There were mass prayer books, group postcards showing the machine-gun unit standing in ranked and ruddy cheerfulness as in a football picture for a college annual; now they were humped and swollen in the grass; propaganda postcards showing a soldier in Austrian uniform bending a woman backward over a bed; the figures were impressionistically drawn; very attractively depicted and had nothing in common with actual rape in which the woman's skirts are pulled over her head to smother her, one comrade sometimes sitting upon the head. There were many of these inciting cards which had evidently been issued just before the offensive. Now they were scattered with the smutty post-cards, photographic; the small photographs of village girls by village photographers, the occasional pictures of children, and the letters, letters, letters. There was always much paper about the dead and the débris of this attack was no exception.

These were new dead and no one had bothered with anything

but their pockets. Our own dead, or what he thought of, still, as our own dead, were surprisingly few, Nick noticed. Their coats had been opened too and their pockets were out, and they showed, by their positions, the manner and the skill of the attack. The hot weather had swollen them all alike regardless of nationality.

The town had evidently been defended, at the last, from the line of the sunken road and there had been few or no Austrians to fall back into it. There were only three bodies in the street and they looked to have been killed running. The houses of the town were broken by the shelling and the street had much rubble of plaster and mortar and there were broken beams, broken tiles, and many holes, some of them yellow-edged from the mustard gas. There were many pieces of shell, and shrapnel balls were scattered in the rubble. There was no one in the town at all.

Nick Adams had seen no one since he had left Fornaci, although, riding along the road through the over-foliaged country, he had seen guns hidden under screens of mulberry leaves to the left of the road, noticing them by the heat-waves in the air above the leaves where the sun hit the metal. Now he went on through the town, surprised to find it deserted, and came out on the low road beneath the bank of the river. Leaving the town there was a bare open space where the road slanted down and he could see the placid reach of the river and the low curve of the opposite bank and the whitened, sun-baked mud where the Austrians had dug. It was all very lush and over-green since he had seen it last and becoming historical had made no change in this, the lower river.

The battalion was along the bank to the left. There was a series of holes in the top of the bank with a few men in them. Nick noticed where the machine guns were posted and the signal rockets in their racks. The men in the holes in the side of the bank were sleeping. No one challenged. He went on and as he came around a turn in the mud bank a young second lieutenant with a stubble of beard and red-rimmed, very blood-shot eyes pointed a pistol at him.

'Who are you?'

Nick told him.

'How do I know this?'

Nick showed him the tessera with photograph and identification and the seal of the third army. He took hold of it.

'I will keep this.'

'You will not,' Nick said. 'Give me back the card and put your gun away. There. In the holster.'

'How am I to know who you are?'

'The tessera tells you.'

'And if the tessera is false? Give me that card.'

'Don't be a fool,' Nick said cheerfully. 'Take me to your company commander.'

'I should send you to battalion headquarters.'

'All right,' said Nick. 'Listen, do you know the Captain Paravicini? The tall one with the small mustache who was an architect and speaks English?'

'You know him?'

'A little.'

'What company does he command?'

'The second.'

'He is commanding the battalion.'

'Good,' said Nick. He was relieved to know that Para was all right. 'Let us go to the battalion.'

As Nick had left the edge of the town three shrapnel had burst high and to the right over one of the wrecked houses and since then there had been no shelling. But the face of this officer looked like the face of a man during a bombardment. There was the same tightness and the voice did not sound natural. His pistol made Nick nervous.

'Put it away,' he said. 'There's the whole river between them and you.'

'If I thought you were a spy I would shoot you now,' the second lieutenant said.

'Come on,' said Nick. 'Let us go to the battalion.' This officer made him very nervous.

The Captain Paravicini, acting major, thinner and more English-looking than ever, rose when Nick saluted from behind the table in the dugout that was battalion headquarters.

'Hello,' he said. 'I didn't know you. What are you doing in that uniform?'

'They've put me in it.'

'I am very glad to see you, Nicolo.'

'Right. You look well. How was the show?'

'We made a very fine attack. Truly. A very fine attack. I will show you. Look.'

He showed on the map how the attack had gone.

'I came from Fornaci,' Nick said. 'I could see how it had been. It was very good.'

'It was extraordinary. Altogether extraordinary. Are you attached to the regiment?'

'No. I am supposed to move around and let them see the uniform.'

'How odd.'

'If they see one American uniform that is supposed to make them believe others are coming.'

'But how will they know it is an American uniform?'

'You will tell them.'

'Oh. Yes, I see. I will send a corporal with you to show you about and you will make a tour of the lines.'

'Like a bloody politician,' Nick said.

'You would be much more distinguished in civilian clothes. They are what is really distinguished.'

'With a homburg hat,' said Nick.

'Or with a very furry fedora.'

'I'm supposed to have my pockets full of cigarettes and postal cards and such things,' Nick said. 'I should have a musette full of chocolate. These I should distribute with a kind word and a pat on the back. But there weren't any cigarettes and postcards and no chocolate. So they said to circulate around anyway.'

'I'm sure your appearance will be very heartening to the troops.'

'I wish you wouldn't,' Nick said. 'I feel badly enough about it as it is. In principle, I would have brought you a bottle of brandy.'

'In principle,' Para said and smiled, for the first time, showing yellowed teeth. 'Such a beautiful expression. Would you like some grappa?'

'No, thank you,' Nick said.

'It hasn't any ether in it.'

'I can taste that still,' Nick remembered suddenly and completely.

'You know I never knew you were drunk until you started talking coming back in the camions.'

'I was stinking in every attack,' Nick said.

'I can't do it,' Para said. 'I took it in the first show, the very first show, and it only made me very upset and then frightfully thirsty.'

'You don't need it.'

'You're much braver in an attack than I am.'

'No,' Nick said. 'I know how I am and I prefer to get stinking. I'm not ashamed of it.'

'I've never seen you drunk.'

'No?' said Nick. 'Never? Not when we rode from Mestre to Portogrande that night and I wanted to go to sleep and used the bicycle for a blanket and pulled it up under my chin?'

'That wasn't in the lines.'

'Let's not talk about how I am,' Nick said. 'It's a subject I know too much about to want to think about it any more.'

'You might as well stay here a while,' Paravicini said. 'You can take a nap if you like. They didn't do much to this in the bombardment. It's too hot to go out yet.'

'I suppose there is no hurry.'

'How are you really?'

'I'm fine. I'm perfectly all right.'

'No. I mean really.'

'I'm all right. I can't sleep without a light of some sort. That's all I have now.'

'I said it should have been trepanned. I'm no doctor but I know that.'

'Well, they thought it was better to have it absorb, and that's what I got. What's the matter? I don't seem crazy to you, do I?'

'You seem in top-hole shape.'

'It's a hell of a nuisance once they've had you certified as nutty,' Nick said. 'No one ever has any confidence in you again.'

'I would take a nap, Nicolo,' Paravicini said. 'This isn't battalion headquarters as we used to know it. We're just waiting to be pulled out. You oughtn't to go out in the heat now – it's silly. Use that bunk.'

'I might just lie down,' Nick said.

Nick lay on the bunk. He was very disappointed that he felt this way and more disappointed, even, that it was so obvious to Captain Paravicini. This was not as large a dugout as the one where that platoon of the class of 1899, just out at the front, got hysterics during the bombardment before the attack, and Para had had him walk them two at a time outside to show them nothing would happen, he wearing his own chin strap tight across his mouth to keep his lips quiet. Knowing they could not hold it when they took it. Knowing it was all a bloody balls – if he can't stop crying, break his nose to give him something else to think about. I'd shoot one but it's too late

now. They'd all be worse. Break his nose. They've put it back
to five-twenty. We've only got four minutes more. Break
that other silly bugger's nose and kick his silly ass out of here.
Do you think they'll go over? If they don't, shoot two and try
to scoop the others out some way. Keep behind them, sergeant.
It's no use to walk ahead and find there's nothing coming behind you. Bail them out as you go. What a bloody balls. All
right. That's right. Then, looking at the watch, in that quiet
tone, that valuable quiet tone, 'Savoia.' Making it cold, no time
to get it, he couldn't find his own after the cave-in, one
whole end had caved in; it was that started them; making it
cold up that slope the only time he hadn't done it stinking. And
after they came back the *teleferica* house burned, it seemed, and
some of the wounded got down four days later and some did
not get down, but we went up and we went back and we came
down – we always came down. And there was Gaby Delys,
oddly enough, with feathers on; you called me baby doll a year
ago tadada you said that I was rather nice to know tadada with
feathers on, with feathers off, the great Gaby, and my name's
Harry Pilcer, too, we used to step out of the far side of the
taxis when it got steep going up the hill and he could see that
hill every night when he dreamed with Sacré Cœur, blown
white, like a soap bubble. Sometimes his girl was there and
sometimes she was with some one else and he could not understand that, but those were the nights the river ran so much wider
and stiller than it should and outside of Fossalta there was
a low house painted yellow with willows all around it and a low
stable and there was a canal, and he had been there a thousand times and never seen it, but there it was every night as
plain as the hill, only it frightened him. That house meant more
than anything and every night he had it. That was what he
needed but it frightened him especially when the boat lay there
quietly in the willows on the canal, but the banks weren't like
this river. It was all lower, as it was at Portogrande, where they
had seen them come wallowing across the flooded ground holding the rifles high until they fell with them in the water. Who
ordered that one? If it didn't get so damned mixed up he could
follow it all right. That was why he noticed everything in such
detail to keep it all straight so he would know just where he was,
but suddenly it confused without reason as now, he lying in a
bunk at battalion headquarters, with Para commanding a battalion and he in a bloody American uniform. He sat up and looked

around; they all watching him. Para was gone out. He lay down again.

The Paris part came earlier and he was not frightened of it except when she had gone off with some one else and the fear that they might take the same driver twice. That was what frightened about that. Never about the front. He never dreamed about the front now any more but what frightened him so that he could not get rid of it was that long yellow house and the different width of the river. Now he was back here at the river, he had gone through that same town, and there was no house. Nor was the river that way. Then where did he go each night and what was the peril, and why would he wake, soaking wet, more frightened than he had ever been in a bombardment, because of a house and a long stable and a canal?

He sat up; swung his legs carefully down; they stiffened any time they were out straight for long; returned the stares of the adjutant, the signallers and the two runners by the door and put on his cloth-covered trench helmet.

'I regret the absence of the chocolate, the postal cards and cigarettes,' he said. 'I am, however, wearing the uniform.'

'The major is coming back at once,' the adjutant said. In that army an adjutant is not a commissioned officer.

'The uniform is not very correct,' Nick told them. 'But it gives you the idea. There will be several millions of Americans here shortly.'

'Do you think they will send Americans down here?' asked the adjutant.

'Oh, absolutely. Americans twice as large as myself, healthy, with clean hearts, sleep at night, never been wounded, never been blown up, never had their heads caved in, never been scared, don't drink, faithful to the girls they left behind them, many of them never had crabs, wonderful chaps. You'll see.'

'Are you an Italian?' asked the adjutant.

'No, American. Look at the uniform. Spagnolini made it but it's not quite correct.'

'A North or South American?'

'North,' said Nick. He felt it coming on now. He would quiet down.

'But you speak Italian.'

'Why not? Do you mind if I speak Italian? Haven't I a right to speak Italian?'

'You have Italian medals.'

'Just the ribbons and the papers. The medals come later. Or you give them to people to keep and the people go away; or they are lost with your baggage. You can purchase others in Milan. It is the papers that are of importance. You must not feel badly about them. You will have some yourself if you stay at the front long enough.'

'I am a veteran of the Eritrea campaign,' said the adjutant stiffly. 'I fought in Tripoli.'

'It's quite something to have met you,' Nick put out his hand. 'Those must have been trying days. I noticed the ribbons. Were you, by any chance, on the Carso?'

'I have just been called up for this war. My class was too old.'

'At one time I was under the age limit,' Nick said. 'But now I am reformed out of the war.'

'But why are you here now?'

'I am demonstrating the American uniform,' Nick said. 'Don't you think it is very significant? It is a little tight in the collar but soon you will see untold millions wearing this uniform swarming like locusts. The grasshopper, you know, what we call the grasshopper in America, is really a locust. The true grasshopper is small and green and comparatively feeble. You must not, however, make a confusion with the seven-year locust or cicada which emits a peculiar sustained sound which at the moment I cannot recall. I try to recall it but I cannot. I can almost hear it and then it is quite gone. You will pardon me if I break off our conversation?'

'See if you can find the major,' the adjutant said to one of the two runners. 'I can see you have been wounded,' he said to Nick.

'In various places,' Nick said. 'If you are interested in scars I can show you some very interesting ones but I would rather talk about grasshoppers. What we call grasshoppers that is; and what are, really, locusts. These insects at one time played a very important part in my life. It might interest you and you can look at the uniform while I am talking.'

The adjutant made a motion with his hand to the second runner who went out.

'Fix your eyes on the uniform. Spagnolini made it, you know. You might as well look, too,' Nick said to the signallers. 'I really have no rank. We're under the American consul. It's perfectly all right for you to look. You can stare, if you like. I will tell you about the American locust. We always preferred one that we

called the medium-brown. They last the best in the water and
fish prefer them. The larger ones that fly making a noise somewhat similar to that produced by a rattlesnake rattling his rattlers,
a very dry sound, have vivid colored wings, some are bright red,
others yellow barred with black, but their wings go to pieces in
the water and they make a very blowsy bait, while the medium-
brown is a plump, compact, succulent hopper that I can recommend as far as one may well recommend something you
gentlemen will probably never encounter. But I must insist that
you will never gather a sufficient supply of these insects for a
day's fishing by pursuing them with your hands or trying to hit
them with a bat. That is sheer nonsense and a useless waste of
time. I repeat, gentlemen, that you will get nowhere at it. The
correct procedure, and one which should be taught all young
officers at every small-arms course if I had anything to say about
it, and who knows but what I will have, is the employment of a
seine or net made of common mosquito netting. Two officers
holding this length of netting at alternate ends, or let us say one
at each end, stoop, hold the bottom extremity of the net in one
hand and the top extremity in the other and run into the wind.
The hoppers, flying with the wind, fly against the length of netting and are imprisoned in its folds. It is no trick at all to catch a
very great quantity indeed, and no officer, in my opinion, should
be without a length of mosquito netting suitable for the impro-
visation of one of these grasshopper seines. I hope I have made
myself clear, gentlemen. Are there any questions? If there is anything in the course you do not understand please ask questions.
Speak up. None? Then I would like to close on this note. In the
words of that great soldier and gentleman, Sir Henry Wilson:
Gentlemen, either you must govern or you must be governed.
Let me repeat it. Gentlemen, there is one thing I would like to
have you remember. One thing I would like you to take with
you as you leave this room. Gentlemen, either you must govern
– or you must be governed. That is all, gentlemen. Good-day.'

He removed his cloth-covered helmet, put it on again and,
stooping, went out the low entrance of the dugout. Para, accompanied by the two runners, was coming down the line of the
sunken road. It was very hot in the sun and Nick removed the
helmet.

'There ought to be a system for wetting these things,' he said.
'I shall wet this one in the river.' He started up the bank.

'Nicolo,' Paravicini called. 'Nicolo. Where are you going?'

'I don't really have to go.' Nick came down the slope, holding the helmet in his hands. 'They're a damned nuisance wet or dry. Do you wear yours all the time?'

'All the time,' said Para. 'It's making me bald. Come inside.'

Inside Para told him to sit down.

'You know they're absolutely no damned good,' Nick said. 'I remember when they were a comfort when we first had them, but I've seen them full of brains too many times.'

'Nicolo,' Para said. 'I think you should go back. I think it would be better if you didn't come up to the line until you had those supplies. There's nothing here for you to do. If you move around, even with something worth giving away, the men will group and that invites shelling. I won't have it.'

'I know it's silly,' Nick said. 'It wasn't my idea. I heard the brigade was here so I thought I would see you or some one else I knew. I could have gone to Zenzon or to San Dona. I'd like to go to San Dona to see the bridge again.'

'I won't have you circulating around to no purpose,' Captain Paravicini said.

'All right,' said Nick. He felt it coming on again.

'You understand?'

'Of course,' said Nick. He was trying to hold it in.

'Anything of that sort should be done at night.'

'Naturally,' said Nick. He knew he could not stop it now.

'You see, I am commanding the battalion,' Para said.

'And why shouldn't you be?' Nick said. Here it came. 'You can read and write, can't you?'

'Yes,' said Para gently.

'The trouble is you have a damned small battalion to command. As soon as it gets to strength again they'll give you back your company. Why don't they bury the dead? I've seen them now. I don't care about seeing them again. They can bury them any time as far as I'm concerned and it would be much better for you. You'll all get bloody sick.'

'Where did you leave your bicycle?'

'Inside the last house.'

'Do you think it will be all right?'

'Don't worry,' Nick said. 'I'll go in a little while.'

'Lie down a little while, Nicolo.'

'All right.'

He shut his eyes, and in place of the man with the beard who looked at him over the sights of the rifle, quite calmly before squeezing off, the white flash and clublike impact, on his knees, hot-sweet choking, coughing it onto the rock while they went past him, he saw a long, yellow house with a low stable and the river much wider than it was and stiller. 'Christ,' he said, 'I might as well go.'

He stood up.

'I'm going, Para,' he said. 'I'll ride back now in the afternoon. If any supplies have come I'll bring them down tonight. If not I'll come at night when I have something to bring.'

'It is still hot to ride,' Captain Paravicini said.

'You don't need to worry,' Nick said. 'I'm all right now for quite a while. I had one then but it was easy. They're getting much better. I can tell when I'm going to have one because I talk so much.'

'I'll send a runner with you.'

'I'd rather you didn't. I know the way.'

'You'll be back soon?'

'Absolutely.'

'Let me send –'

'No,' said Nick. 'As a mark of confidence.'

'Well, *ciao* then.'

'*Ciao*,' said Nick. He started back along the sunken road toward where he had left the bicycle. In the afternoon the road would be shady once he had passed the canal. Beyond that there were trees on both sides that had not been shelled at all. It was on that stretch that, marching, they had once passed the Terza Savoia cavalry regiment riding in the snow with their lances. The horses' breath made plumes in the cold air. No, that was somewhere else. Where was that?

'I'd better get to that damned bicycle,' Nick said to himself. 'I don't want to lose the way to Fornaci.'

THE MOTHER OF A QUEEN

When his father died he was only a kid and his manager buried him perpetually. That is, so he would have the plot permanently. But when his mother died his manager thought they might not always be so hot on each other. They were sweethearts; sure he's a queen, didn't you know that, of course he is. So he just buried her for five years.

Well, when he came back to Mexico from Spain he got the first notice. It said it was the first notice that the five years were up and would he make arrangements for the continuing of his mother's grave. It was only twenty dollars for perpetual. I had the cash box then and I said let me attend to it, Paco. But he said no, he would look after it. He'd look after it right away. It was his mother and he wanted to do it himself.

Then in a week he got the second notice. I read it to him and I said I thought he had looked after it.

No, he said, he hadn't.

'Let me do it,' I said. 'It's right here in the cash box.'

No, he said. Nobody could tell him what to do. He'd do it himself when he got around to it. 'What's the sense in spending money sooner than necessary?'

'All right,' I said, 'but see you look after it.' At this time he had a contract for six fights at four thousand pesos a fight besides his benefit fight. He made over fifteen thousand dollars there in the capital alone. He was just tight, that's all.

The third notice came in another week and I read it to him. It said that if he did not make the payment by the following Saturday his mother's grave would be opened and her remains dumped on the common boneheap. He said he would go attend to it that afternoon when he went to town.

'Why not have me do it?' I asked him.

'Keep out of my business,' he said. 'It's my business and I'm going to do it.'

'All right, if that's the way you feel about it,' I said. 'Do your own business.'

He got the money out of the cash box, although then he always carried a hundred or more pesos with him all the time, and he said he would look after it. He went out with the money and so of course I thought he had attended to it.

A week later the notice came that they had no response to the final warning and so his mother's body had been dumped on the boneheap; on the public boneheap.

'Jesus Christ,' I said to him, 'you said you'd pay that and you took money out of the cash box to do it and now what's happened to your mother? My God, think of it! The public boneheap and your own mother. Why didn't you let me look after it? I would have sent it when the first notice came.'

'It's none of your business. It's *my* mother.'

'It's none of *my* business, yes, but it was *your* business. What kind of blood is it in a man that will let that be done to his mother? You don't deserve to have a mother.'

'It is my mother,' he said. 'Now she is so much dearer to me. Now I don't have to think of her buried in one place and be sad. Now she is all about me in the air, like the birds and the flowers. Now she will always be with me.'

'Jesus Christ,' I said, 'what kind of blood have you anyway? I don't want you to even speak to me.'

'She is all around me,' he said. 'Now I will never be sad.'

At that time he was spending all kinds of money around women trying to make himself seem a man and fool people, but it didn't have any effect on people that knew anything about him. He owed me over six hundred pesos and he wouldn't pay me. 'Why do you want it now?' he'd say. 'Don't you trust me? Aren't we friends?'

'It isn't friends or trusting you. It's that I paid the accounts out of my own money while you were away and now I need the money back and you have it to pay me.'

'I haven't got it.'

'You have it,' I said. 'It's in the cash box now and you can pay me.'

'I need that money for something,' he said. 'You don't know all the needs I have for money.'

'I stayed here all the time you were in Spain and you authorized me to pay these things as they came up, all these things of the house, and you didn't send any money while you were gone and I paid over six hundred pesos in my own money and now I need it and you can pay me.'

'I'll pay you soon,' he said. 'Right now I need the money badly.'

'For what?'

'For my own business.'

'Why don't you pay me some on account?'

'I can't,' he said. 'I need that money too badly. But I will pay you.'

He had only fought twice in Spain, they couldn't stand him there, they saw through him quick enough, and he had seven new fighting suits made and this is the kind of thing he was: he had them packed so badly that four of them were ruined by sea water on the trip back and he couldn't even wear them.

'My God,' I said to him, 'you go to Spain. You stay there the whole season and only fight two times. You spend all the money you took with you on suits and then have them spoiled by salt water so you can't wear them. That is the kind of season you have and then you talk to me about running your own business. Why don't you pay me the money you owe me so I can leave?'

'I want you here,' he said, 'and I will pay you. But now I need the money.'

'You need it too badly to pay for your own mother's grave to keep your mother buried. Don't you?' I said.

'I am happy about what has happened to my mother,' he said. 'You cannot understand.'

'Thank Christ I can't,' I said. 'You pay me what you owe me or I will take it out of the cash box.'

'I will keep the cash box myself,' he said.

'No, you won't,' I said.

That very afternoon he came to me with a punk, some fellow from his own town who was broke, and said, 'Here is a *paisano* who needs money to go home because his mother is very sick.' This fellow was just a punk, you understand, a nobody he'd never seen before, but from his home town, and he wanted to be the big, generous matador with a fellow townsman.

'Give him fifty pesos from the cash box,' he told me.

'You just told me you had no money to pay me,' I said. 'And now you want to give fifty pesos to this punk.'

'He is a fellow townsman,' he said, 'and he is in distress.'

'You bitch,' I said. I gave him the key of the cash box. 'Get it yourself. I'm going to town.'

'Don't be angry,' he said. 'I'm going to pay you.'

I got the car out to go to town. It was his car but he knew I drove it better than he did. Everything he did I could do better. He knew it. He couldn't even read and write. I was going to see somebody and see what I could do about making him pay me.

He came out and said, 'I'm coming with you and I'm going to pay you. We are good friends. There is no need to quarrel.'

We drove into the city and I was driving. Just before we came into the town he pulled out twenty pesos.

'Here's the money,' he said.

'You motherless bitch,' I said to him and told him what he could do with the money. 'You give fifty pesos to that punk and then offer me twenty when you owe me six hundred. I wouldn't take a nickel from you. You know what you can do with it.'

I got out of the car without a peso in my pocket and I didn't know where I was going to sleep that night. Later I went out with a friend and got my things from his place. I never spoke to him again until this year. I met him walking with three friends in the evening on the way to the Callao cinema in the Gran Via in Madrid. He put his hand out to me.

'Hello Roger, old friend,' he said to me. 'How are you? People say you are talking against me. That you say all sorts of unjust things about me.'

'All I say is you never had a mother,' I said to him. That's the worst thing you can say to insult a man in Spanish.

'That's true,' he said. 'My poor mother died when I was so young it seems as though I never had a mother. It's very sad.'

There's a queen for you. You can't touch them. Nothing, nothing can touch them. They spend money on themselves or for vanity, but they never pay. Try to get one to pay. I told him what I thought of him right there on the Gran Via, in front of three friends, but he speaks to me now when I meet him as though we were friends. What kind of blood is it that makes a man like that?

ONE READER WRITES

She sat at the table in her bedroom with a newspaper folded open before her and only stopping to look out of the window at the snow which was falling and melting on the roof as it fell. She wrote this letter, writing it steadily with no necessity to cross out or rewrite anything.

Roanoke, Virginia
February 6, 1933

Dear Doctor —

May I write you for some very important advice – I have a decision to make and don't know just whom to trust most I dare not ask my parents – and so I come to you – and only because I need not see you, can I confide in you even. Now here is the situation – I married a man in U. S. service in 1929 and that same year he was sent to China, Shanghai – he staid three years – and came home – he was discharged from the service some few months ago – and went to his mother's home in Helena, Arkansas. He wrote for me to come home – I went, and found he is taking a course of injections and I naturally ask, and found he is being treated for I don't know how to spell the word but it sound like this 'sifilus' – Do you know what I mean – now tell me will it ever be safe for me to live with him again – I did not come in close contact with him at any time since his return from China. He assures me he will be OK after this doctor finishes with him – Do you think it right – I often heard my Father say one could well wish themselves dead if once they became a victim of that malady – I believe my Father but want to believe my Husband most – Please, please tell me what to do – I have a daughter born while her Father was in China –

Thanking you and trusting wholly in your advice I am

and signed her name.

Maybe he can tell me what's right to do, she said to herself. Maybe he can tell me. In the picture in the paper he looks like he'd know. He looks smart, all right. Every day he tells somebody what to do. He ought to know. I want to do whatever is right. It's such a long time though. It's a long time. And it's been a long time. My Christ, it's been a long time. He had to go wherever they sent him, I know, but I don't know what he had to get it for. Oh, I wish to Christ he wouldn't have got it. I don't care what he did to get it. But I wish to Christ he hadn't ever got it. It does seem like he didn't have to have got it. I don't know what to do. I wish to Christ he hadn't got any kind of malady. I don't know why he had to get a malady.

HOMAGE TO SWITZERLAND

PART I

PORTRAIT OF MR. WHEELER IN MONTREUX

Inside the station café it was warm and light. The wood of the tables shone from wiping and there were baskets of pretzels in glazed paper sacks. The chairs were carved, but the seats were worn and comfortable. There was a carved wooden clock on the wall and a bar at the far end of the room. Outside the window it was snowing.

Two of the station porters sat drinking new wine at the table under the clock. Another porter came in and said the Simplon-Orient Express was an hour late at Saint-Maurice. He went out. The waitress came over to Mr. Wheeler's table.

'The Express is an hour late, sir,' she said. 'Can I bring you some coffee?'

'If you think it won't keep me awake.'

'Please?' asked the waitress.

'Bring me some,' said Mr. Wheeler.

'Thank you.'

She brought the coffee from the kitchen and Mr. Wheeler looked out the window at the snow falling in the light from the station platform.

'Do you speak other languages besides English?' he asked the waitress.

'Oh, yes, sir. I speak German and French and the dialects.'

'Would you like a drink of something?'

'Oh, no, sir. It is not permitted to drink in the café with the clients.'

'You won't take a cigar?'

'Oh, no, sir. I don't smoke, sir.'

'That is all right,' said Mr. Wheeler. He looked out of the window again, drank the coffee, and lit a cigarette.

'Fräulein,' he called. The waitress came over.

'What would you like, sir?'

'You,' he said.

'You must not joke me like that.'

'I'm not joking.'

'Then you must not say it.'

'I haven't time to argue,' Mr. Wheeler said. 'The train comes in forty minutes. If you'll go upstairs with me I'll give you a hundred francs.'

'You should not say such things, sir. I will ask the porter to speak with you.'

'I don't want a porter,' Mr. Wheeler said. 'Nor a policeman nor one of those boys that sell cigarettes. I want you.'

'If you talk like that you must go out. You cannot stay here and talk like that.'

'Why don't you go away, then? If you go away I can't talk to you.'

The waitress went away. Mr. Wheeler watched to see if she spoke to the porters. She did not.

'Mademoiselle!' he called. The waitress came over. 'Bring me a bottle of Sion, please.'

'Yes, sir.'

Mr. Wheeler watched her go out, then come in with the wine and bring it to his table. He looked toward the clock.

'I'll give you two hundred francs,' he said.

'Please do not say such things.'

'Two hundred francs is a great deal of money.'

'You will not say such things!' the waitress said. She was losing her English. Mr. Wheeler looked at her interestedly.

'Two hundred francs.'

'You are hateful.'

'Why don't you go away then? I can't talk to you if you're not here.'

The waitress left the table and went over to the bar. Mr. Wheeler drank the wine and smiled to himself for some time.

'Mademoiselle,' he called. The waitress pretended not to hear him. 'Mademoiselle,' he called again. The waitress came over.

'You wish something?'

'Very much. I'll give you three hundred francs.'

'You are hateful.'

'Three hundred francs Swiss.'

She went away and Mr. Wheeler looked after her. A porter opened the door. He was the one who had Mr. Wheeler's bags in his charge.

'The train is coming, sir,' he said in French. Mr. Wheeler stood up.

'Mademoiselle,' he called. The waitress came toward the table. 'How much is the wine?'

'Seven francs.'

Mr. Wheeler counted out eight francs and left them on the table. He put on his coat and followed the porter onto the platform where the snow was falling.

'*Au revoir*, Mademoiselle,' he said. The waitress watched him go. He's ugly, she thought, ugly and hateful. Three hundred francs for a thing that is nothing to do. How many times have I done that for nothing. And no place to go here. If he had sense he would know there was no place. No time and no place to go. Three hundred francs to do that. What people those Americans.

Standing on the cement platform beside his bags, looking down the rails toward the headlight of the train coming through the snow, Mr. Wheeler was thinking that it was very inexpensive sport. He had only spent, actually, aside from the dinner, seven francs for a bottle of wine and a franc for the tip. Seventy-five centimes would have been better. He would have felt better now if the tip had been seventy-five centimes. One franc Swiss is five francs French. Mr. Wheeler was headed for Paris. He was very careful about money and did not care for women. He had been in that station before and he knew there was no upstairs to go to. Mr. Wheeler never took chances.

PART II

MR. JOHNSON TALKS ABOUT IT AT VEVEY

Inside the station café it was warm and light; the tables were shiny from wiping and on some there were red and white striped table cloths; and there were blue and white striped table cloths on the others and on all of them baskets with pretzels in glazed paper sacks. The chairs were carved but the wood seats were worn and comfortable. There was a clock on the wall, a zinc bar at the far end of the room, and outside the window it was snowing. Two of the station porters sat drinking new wine at the table under the clock.

Another porter came in and said the Simplon-Orient Express was an hour late at Saint-Maurice. The waitress came over to Mr. Johnson's table.

'The Express is an hour late, sir,' she said. 'Can I bring you some coffee?'

'If it's not too much trouble.'

'Please?' asked the waitress.

'I'll take some.'

'Thank you.'

She brought the coffee from the kitchen and Mr. Johnson looked out the window at the snow falling in the light from the station platform.

'Do you speak other languages besides English?' he asked the waitress.

'Oh, yes, I speak German and French and the dialects.'

'Would you like a drink of something?'

'Oh, no, sir. It is not permitted to drink in the café with the clients.'

'Have a cigar?'

'Oh, no, sir,' she laughed. 'I don't smoke, sir.'

'Neither do I,' said Johnson. 'It's a dirty habit.'

The waitress went away and Johnson lit a cigarette and drank the coffee. The clock on the wall marked a quarter to ten. His watch was a little fast. The train was due at ten-thirty – an hour late meant eleven-thirty. Johnson called to the waitress.

'Signorina!'

'What would you like, sir?'

'You wouldn't like to play with me?' Johnson asked. The waitress blushed.

'No, sir.'

'I don't mean anything violent. You wouldn't like to make up a party and see the night life of Vevey? Bring a girl friend if you like.'

'I must work,' the waitress said. 'I have my duty here.'

'I know,' said Johnson. 'But couldn't you get a substitute? They used to do that in the Civil War.'

'Oh, no, sir. I must be here myself in the person.'

'Where did you learn your English?'

'At the Berlitz school, sir.'

'Tell me about it,' Johnson said. 'Were the Berlitz undergraduates a wild lot? What about all this necking and petting? Were there many smoothies? Did you ever run into Scott Fitzgerald?'

'Please?'

'I mean were your college days the happiest days of your life? What sort of team did Berlitz have last fall?'

'You are joking, sir?'

'Only feebly,' said Johnson. 'You're an awfully good girl. And you don't want to play with me?'

'Oh, no, sir,' said the waitress. 'Would you like me to bring you something?'

'Yes,' said Johnson. 'Would you bring me the wine list?'

'Yes, sir.'

Johnson walked over with the wine list to the table where the three porters sat. They looked up at him. They were old men.

'*Wollen Sie trinken?*' he asked. One of them nodded and smiled.

'*Oui, monsieur.*'

'You speak French?'

'*Oui, monsieur.*'

'What shall we drink? *Connais-vous des champagnes?*'

'*Non, monsieur.*'

'*Faut les connaître,*' said Johnson. 'Fräulein,' he called the waitress. 'We will drink champagne.'

'Which champagne would you prefer, sir?'

'The best,' said Johnson. '*Laquelle est le best?*' he asked the porters.

'*Le meilleur?*' asked the porter who had spoken first.

'By all means.'

The porter took out a pair of gold-rimmed glasses from his coat pocket and looked over the list. He ran his finger down the four typewritten names and prices.

'Sportsman,' he said. 'Sportsman is the best.'

'You agree, gentlemen?' Johnson asked the other porters. The one porter nodded. The other said in French, 'I don't know them personally but I've often heard speak of Sportsman. It's good.'

'A bottle of Sportsman,' Johnson said to the waitress. He looked at the price on the wine card: eleven francs Swiss. 'Make it two Sportsmen. Do you mind if I sit here with you?' he asked the porter who had suggested Sportsman.

'Sit down. Put yourself here, please.' The porter smiled at him. He was folding his spectacles and putting them away in their case. 'Is it the gentleman's birthday?'

'No,' said Johnson. 'It's not a fête. My wife has decided to divorce me.'

'So,' said the porter. 'I hope not.' The other porter shook his head. The third porter seemed a little deaf.

'It is doubtless a common experience,' said Johnson, 'like the first visit to the dentist or the first time a girl is unwell, but I have been upset.'

'It is understandable,' said the oldest porter. 'I understand it.'

'None of you gentlemen is divorced?' Johnson asked. He had stopped clowning with the language and was speaking good French now and had been for some time.

'No,' said the porter who had ordered Sportsman. 'They don't divorce much here. There are gentlemen who are divorced but not many.'

'With us,' said Johnson, 'it's different. Practically every one is divorced.'

'That's true,' the porter confirmed. 'I've read it in the paper.'

'I myself am somewhat in retard,' Johnson went on. 'This is the first time I have been divorced. I am thirty-five.'

'*Mais vous êtes encore jeune,*' said the porter. He explained to the two others. '*Monsieur n'a que trente-cinq ans.*' The other porters nodded. 'He's very young,' said one.

'And it is really the first time you've been divorced?' asked the porter.

'Absolutely,' said Johnson. 'Please open the wine, mademoiselle.'

'And is it very expensive?'

'Ten thousand francs.'

'Swiss money?'

'No, French money.'

'Oh, yes. Two thousand francs Swiss. All the same it's not cheap.'

'No.'

'And why does one do it?'

'One is asked to.'

'But why do they ask that?'

'To marry someone else.'

'But it's idiotic.'

'I agree with you,' said Johnson. The waitress filled the four glasses. They all raised them.

'*Prosit,*' said Johnson.

'*A votre santé, monsieur,*' said the porter. The other two porters said '*Salut.*' The champagne tasted like sweet pink cider.

'Is it a system always to respond in a different language in Switzerland?' Johnson asked.

'No,' said the porter. 'French is more cultivated. Besides, this is La Suisse romande.'

'But you speak German?'

'Yes. Where I come from they speak German.'

'I see,' said Johnson, 'and you say you have never been divorced?'

'No. It would be too expensive. Besides I have never married.'

'Ah,' said Johnson. 'And these other gentlemen?'

'They are married.'

'You like being married?' Johnson asked one of the porters.

'What?'

'You like the married state?'

'*Oui. C'est normale.*'

'Exactly,' said Johnson. '*Et vous, monsieur?*'

'*Ça va*,' said the other porter.

'*Pour moi*,' said Johnson, '*ça ne va pas*.'

'Monsieur is going to divorce,' the first porter explained.

'Oh,' said the second porter.

'Ah ha,' the third porter said.

'Well,' said Johnson, 'the subject seems to be exhausted. You're not interested in my troubles,' he addressed the first porter.

'But, yes,' said the porter.

'Well, let's talk about something else.'

'As you wish.'

'What can we talk about?'

'You do the sport?'

'No,' said Johnson. 'My wife does, though.'

'What do you do for amusement?'

'I am a writer.'

'Does that make much money?'

'No. But later on when you get known it does.'

'It is interesting.'

'No,' said Johnson, 'it is not interesting. I am sorry gentlemen, but I have to leave you. Will you please drink the other bottle?'

'But the train does not come for three-quarters of an hour.'

'I know,' said Johnson. The waitress came and he paid for the wine and his dinner.

'You're going out, sir?' she asked.

'Yes,' said Johnson, 'just for a little walk. I'll leave my bags here.'

He put on his muffler, his coat, and his hat. Outside the snow was falling heavily. He looked back through the window at the three porters sitting at the table. The waitress was filling their glasses from the last wine of the opened bottle. She took the unopened bottle back to the bar. That makes them three francs something apiece, Johnson thought. He turned and walked down the platform. Inside the café he had thought that talking about it would blunt it; but it had not blunted it; it had only made him feel nasty.

PART III

THE SON OF A FELLOW MEMBER AT TERRITET

In the station café at Territet it was a little too warm; the lights were bright and the tables shiny from polishing. There were baskets with pretzels in glazed paper sacks on the tables and cardboard pads for beer glasses in order that the moist glasses would not make rings on the wood. The chairs were carved but the wooden seats were worn and quite comfortable. There was a clock on the wall, a bar at the far end of the room, and outside the window it was snowing. There was an old man drinking coffee at a table under the clock and reading the evening paper. A porter came in and said the Simplon-Orient Express was an hour late at Saint-Maurice. The waitress came over to Mr. Harris's table. Mr. Harris had just finished dinner.

'The Express is an hour late, sir. Can I bring you some coffee?'

'If you like.'

'Please?' asked the waitress.

'All right,' said Mr. Harris.

'Thank you, sir,' said the waitress.

She brought the coffee from the kitchen and Mr. Harris put sugar in it, crunched the lumps with his spoon, and looked out the window at the snow falling in the light from the station platform.

'Do you speak other languages besides English?' he asked the waitress.

'Oh, yes, sir. I speak German and French and the dialects.'

'Which do you like best?'

'They are all very much the same, sir. I can't say I like one better than another.'

'Would you like a drink of something or a coffee?'

'Oh, no, sir, it is not permitted to drink in the café with the clients.'

'You wouldn't take a cigar?'

'Oh, no, sir,' she laughed. 'I don't smoke, sir.'

'Neither do I,' said Harris, 'I don't agree with David Belasco.'

'Please?'

'Belasco. David Belasco. You can always tell him because he has his collar on backwards. But I don't agree with him. Then, too, he's dead now.'

'Will you excuse me, sir?' asked the waitress.

'Absolutely,' said Harris. He sat forward in the chair and looked out of the window. Across the room the old man had folded his paper. He looked at Mr. Harris and then picked up his coffee cup and saucer and walked to Harris's table.

'I beg your pardon if I intrude,' he said in English, 'but it has just occurred to me that you might be a member of the National Geographic Society.'

'Please sit down,' Harris said. The gentleman sat down.

'Won't you have another coffee or a liqueur?'

'Thank you,' said the gentleman.

'Won't you have a kirsch with me?'

'Perhaps. But you must have it with me.'

'No, I insist.' Harris called the waitress. The old gentleman took out from an inside pocket of his coat a leather pocket-book. He took off a wide rubber band and drew out several papers, selected one, and handed it to Harris.

'That is my certificate of membership,' he said. 'Do you know Frederick J. Roussel in America?'

'I'm afraid I don't.'

'I believe he is very prominent.'

'Where does he come from? Do you know what part of the States?'

'From Washington, of course. Isn't that the headquarters of the Society?'

'I believe it is.'

'You believe it is. Aren't you sure?'

'I've been away a long time,' Harris said.

'You're not a member, then?'

'No. But my father is. He's been a member for a great many years.'

'Then he would know Frederick J. Roussel. He is one of the officers of the society. You will observe that it is by Mr. Roussel that I was nominated for membership.'

'I'm awfully glad.'

'I am sorry you are not a member. But you could obtain nomination through your father?'

'I think so,' said Harris. 'I must when I go back.'

'I would advise you to,' said the gentleman. 'You see the magazine, of course?'

'Absolutely.'

'Have you seen the number with the colored plates of the North American fauna?'

'Yes. I have it in Paris.'

'And the number containing the panorama of the volcanoes of Alaska?'

'That was a wonder.'

'I enjoyed very much, too, the wild animal photographs of George Shiras three.'

'They were damned fine.'

'I beg your pardon?'

'They were excellent. That fellow Shiras – '

'You call him that fellow?'

'We're old friends,' said Harris.

'I see. You know George Shiras three. He must be very interesting.'

'He is. He's about the most interesting man I know.'

'And do you know George Shiras two? Is he interesting too?'

'Oh, he's not so interesting.'

'I should imagine he would be very interesting.'

'You know, a funny thing. He's not so interesting. I've often wondered why.'

'H'm,' said the gentleman. 'I should have thought any one in that family would be interesting.'

'Do you remember the panorama of the Sahara Desert?' Harris asked.

'The Sahara Desert? That was nearly fifteen years ago.'

'That's right. That was one of my father's favorites.'

'He doesn't prefer the newer numbers?'

'He probably does. But he was very fond of the Sahara panorama.'

'It was excellent. But to me its artistic value far exceeded its scientific interest.'

'I don't know,' said Harris. 'The wind blowing all that sand and that Arab with his camel kneeling toward Mecca.'

'As I recall, the Arab was standing holding the camel.'

'You're quite right,' said Harris. 'I was thinking of Colonel Lawrence's book.'

'Lawrence's book deals with Arabia, I believe.'

'Absolutely,' said Harris. 'It was the Arab reminded me of it.'

'He must be a very interesting young man.'

'I believe he is.'

'Do you know what he is doing now?'

'He's in the Royal Air Force.'

'And why does he do that?'

'He likes it.'

'Do you know if he belongs to the National Geographic Society?'

'I wonder if he does.'

'He would make a very good member. He is the sort of person they want as a member. I would be very happy to nominate him if you think they would like to have him.'

'I think they would.'

'I have nominated a scientist from Vevey and a colleague of mine from Lausanne and they were both elected. I believe they would be very pleased if I nominated Colonel Lawrence.'

'It's a splendid idea,' said Harris. 'Do you come here to the café often?'

'I come here for coffee after dinner.'

'Are you in the University?'

'I am not active any longer.'

'I'm just waiting for the train,' said Harris. 'I'm going up to Paris and sail from Havre for the States.'

'I have never been to America. But I would like to go very much. Perhaps I shall attend a meeting of the society some time. I would be very happy to meet your father.'

'I'm sure he would have liked to meet you but he died last year. Shot himself, oddly enough.'

'I am very truly sorry. I am sure his loss was a blow to science as well as to his family.'

'Science took it awfully well.'

'This is my card,' Harris said. 'His initials were E. J. instead of E. D. I know he would have liked to know you.'

'It would have been a great pleasure.' The gentleman took out a card from the pocketbook and gave it to Harris. It read:

> DR. SIGISMUND WYER, PH.D.
> Member of the National Geographic
> Society, Washington, D. C., U. S. A.

'I will keep it very carefully,' Harris said.

A DAY'S WAIT

He came into the room to shut the windows while we were still in bed and I saw he looked ill. He was shivering, his face was white, and he walked slowly as though it ached to move.

'What's the matter, Schatz?'

'I've got a headache.'

'You better go back to bed.'

'No. I'm all right.'

'You go to bed. I'll see you when I'm dressed.'

But when I came downstairs he was dressed, sitting by the fire, looking a very sick and miserable boy of nine years. When I put my hand on his forehead I knew he had a fever.

'You go up to bed,' I said, 'you're sick.'

'I'm all right,' he said.

When the doctor came he took the boy's temperature.

'What is it?' I asked him.

'One hundred and two.'

Downstairs, the doctor left three different medicines in different colored capsules with instructions for giving them. One was to bring down the fever, another a purgative, the third to overcome an acid condition. The germs of influenza can only exist in an acid condition, he explained. He seemed to know all about influenza and said there was nothing to worry about if the fever did not go above one hundred and four degrees. This was a light epidemic of flu and there was no danger if you avoided pneumonia.

Back in the room I wrote the boy's temperature down and made a note of the time to give the various capsules.

'Do you want me to read to you?'

'All right. If you want to,' said the boy. His face was very white and there were dark areas under his eyes. He lay still in the bed and seemed very detached from what was going on.

I read aloud from Howard Pyle's *Book of Pirates*; but I could see he was not following what I was reading.

'How do you feel, Schatz?' I asked him.

'Just the same, so far,' he said.

I sat at the foot of the bed and read to myself while I waited for it to be time to give another capsule. It would have been natural for him to go to sleep, but when I looked up he was looking at the foot of the bed, looking very strangely.

'Why don't you try to go to sleep? I'll wake you up for the medicine.'

'I'd rather stay awake.'

After a while he said to me, 'You don't have to stay in here with me, Papa, if it bothers you.'

'It doesn't bother me.'

'No, I mean you don't have to stay if it's going to bother you.'

I thought perhaps he was a little lightheaded and after giving him the prescribed capsules at eleven o'clock I went out for a while.

It was a bright, cold day, the ground covered with a sleet that had frozen so that it seemed as if all the bare trees, the bushes, the cut brush and all the grass and the bare ground had been varnished with ice. I took the young Irish setter for a little walk up the road and along a frozen creek, but it was difficult to stand or walk on the glassy surface and the red dog slipped and slithered and I fell twice, hard, once dropping my gun and having it slide away over the ice.

We flushed a covey of quail under a high clay bank with overhanging brush and I killed two as they went out of sight over the top of the bank. Some of the covey lit in trees, but most of them scattered into brush piles and it was necessary to jump on the ice-coated mounds of brush several times before they would flush. Coming out while you were poised unsteadily on the icy, springy brush they made difficult shooting and I killed two, missed five, and started back pleased to have found a covey close to the house and happy there were so many left to find on another day.

At the house they said the boy had refused to let any one come into the room.

'You can't come in,' he said. 'You mustn't get what I have.'

I went up to him and found him in exactly the position I had left him, white-faced, but with the tops of his cheeks flushed by the fever, staring still, as he had stared, at the foot of the bed.

I took his temperature.

'What is it?'

'Something like a hundred,' I said. It was one hundred and two and four tenths.

'It was a hundred and two,' he said.

'Who said so?'

'The doctor.'

'Your temperature is all right,' I said. 'It's nothing to worry about.'

'I don't worry,' he said, 'but I can't keep from thinking.'

'Don't think,' I said. 'Just take it easy.'

'I'm taking it easy,' he said and looked straight ahead. He was evidently holding tight onto himself about something.

'Take this with water.'

'Do you think it will do any good?'

'Of course it will.'

I sat down and opened the *Pirate* book and commenced to read, but I could see he was not following, so I stopped.

'About what time do you think I'm going to die?' he asked.

'What?'

'About how long will it be before I die?'

'You aren't going to die. What's the matter with you?'

'Oh, yes, I am. I heard him say a hundred and two.'

'People don't die with a fever of one hundred and two. That's a silly way to talk.'

'I know they do. At school in France the boys told me you can't live with forty-four degrees. I've got a hundred and two.'

He had been waiting to die all day, ever since nine o'clock in the morning.

'You poor Schatz,' I said. 'Poor old Schatz. It's like miles and kilometers. You aren't going to die. That's a different thermometer. On that thermometer thirty-seven is normal. On this kind it's ninety-eight.'

'Are you sure?'

'Absolutely,' I said. 'It's like miles and kilometers. You know, like how many kilometers we make when we do seventy miles in the car?'

'Oh,' he said.

But his gaze at the foot of the bed relaxed slowly. The hold over himself relaxed too, finally, and the next day it was very slack and he cried very easily at little things that were of no importance.

A NATURAL HISTORY
OF THE DEAD

It has always seemed to me that the war has been omitted as a field for the observations of the naturalist. We have charming and sound accounts of the flora and fauna of Patagonia by the late W. H. Hudson, the Reverend Gilbert White has written most interestingly of the Hoopoe on its occasional and not at all common visits to Selborne, and Bishop Stanley has given us a valuable, although popular, *Familiar History of Birds*. Can we not hope to furnish the reader with a few rational and interesting facts about the dead? I hope so.

When that persevering traveller, Mungo Park, was at one period of his course fainting in the vast wilderness of an African desert, naked and alone, considering his days as numbered and nothing appearing to remain for him to do but to lie down and die, a small moss-flower of extraordinary beauty caught his eye. 'Though the whole plant,' says he, 'was no larger than one of my fingers, I could not contemplate the delicate conformation of its roots, leaves and capsules without admiration. Can that Being who planted, watered and brought to perfection, in this obscure part of the world, a thing which appears of so small importance, look with unconcern upon the situation and suffering of creatures formed after his own image? Surely not. Reflections like these would not allow me to despair; I started up and, disregarding both hunger and fatigue, travelled forward, assured that relief was at hand; and I was not disappointed.'

With a disposition to wonder and adore in like manner, as Bishop Stanley says, can any branch of Natural History be studied without increasing that faith, love and hope which we also, every one of us, need in our journey through the wilderness of life? Let us therefore see what inspiration we may derive from the dead.

In war the dead are usually the male of the human species although this does not hold true with animals, and I have frequently seen dead mares among the horses. An interesting aspect of war, too, is that it is only there that the naturalist has an opportunity to observe the dead of mules. In twenty years of observation in civil life I had never seen a dead mule and had begun to entertain doubts as to whether these animals were really mortal. On rare occasions I had seen what I took to be dead mules, but on close approach these always proved to be living creatures who seemed to be dead through their quality of complete repose. But in war these animals succumb in much the same manner as the more common and less hardy horse.

Most of those mules that I saw dead were along mountain roads or lying at the foot of steep declivities whence they had been pushed to rid the road of their encumbrance. They seemed a fitting enough sight in the mountains where one was accustomed to their presence and looked less incongruous there than they did later, at Smyrna, where the Greeks broke the legs of all their baggage animals and pushed them off the quay into the shallow water to drown. The numbers of broken-legged mules and horses drowning in the shallow water called for a Goya to depict them. Although, speaking literally, one can hardly say that they called for a Goya since there has only been one Goya, long dead, and it is extremely doubtful if these animals, were they able to call, would call for pictorial representation of their plight but, more likely, would, if they were articulate, call for some one to alleviate their condition.

Regarding the sex of the dead it is a fact that one becomes so accustomed to the sight of all the dead being men that the sight of a dead woman is quite shocking. I first saw inversion of the usual sex of the dead after the explosion of a munition factory which had been situated in the countryside near Milan, Italy. We drove to the scene of the disaster in trucks along poplar-shaded roads, bordered with ditches containing much minute animal life, which I could not clearly observe because of the great clouds of dust raised by the trucks. Arriving where the munition plant had been, some of us were put to patrolling about those large stocks of munitions which for some reason had not exploded, while others were put at extinguishing a fire which had gotten into the grass of an adjacent field; which task being concluded, we were ordered to search the immediate vicinity and surrounding fields for bodies. We found and carried to an improvised mortuary a good number of these and, I must admit, frankly, the shock it was to find that these dead were women rather than men. In those days women had not yet commenced to wear their hair cut short, as they did later for several years in Europe and America, and the most disturbing thing, perhaps because it was the most unaccustomed, was the presence and, even more disturbing, the occasional absence of this long hair. I remember that after we had searched quite thoroughly for the complete dead we collected fragments. Many of these were detached from a heavy, barbed-wire fence which had surrounded the position of the factory and from the still existent portions of which we picked many of these detached bits which illustrated only too well the tremendous energy of high explosive. Many fragments we found a considerable distance away in the fields, they being carried farther by their own weight.

On our return to Milan I recall one or two of us discussing the occurrence and agreeing that the quality of unreality and the fact that there were no wounded did much to rob the disaster of a horror which might have been much greater. Also the fact that it had been so immediate and that the dead were in consequence still as little unpleasant as possible to carry and deal with made it quite removed from the usual battlefield experience. The pleasant, though dusty, ride through the beautiful Lombard countryside also was a compensation for the unpleasantness of the duty and on our return, while we exchanged impressions, we all agreed that it was indeed fortunate that the fire which broke out just before we arrived had been brought under control as rapidly as it had and before it had attained any of the seemingly huge stocks of unexploded munitions. We agreed too that the picking up of the fragments had been an extraordinary business; it being amazing that the human body should be blown into pieces which exploded along no anatomical lines, but rather divided as capriciously as the fragmentation in the burst of a high explosive shell.

A naturalist, to obtain accuracy of observation, may confine himself in his observations to one limited period and I will take first that following the Austrian offensive of June, 1918, in Italy as one in which the dead were present in their greatest numbers, a withdrawal having been forced and an advance later made to recover the ground lost so that the positions after the battle were the same as before except for the presence of the dead. Until the dead are buried they change somewhat in appearance each day. The color change in Caucasian races is from white to yellow, to yellow-green, to black. If left long enough in the heat the flesh comes to resemble coal-tar, especially where it has been broken or torn, and it has quite a visible tarlike iridescence. The dead grow larger each day until sometimes they become quite too big for their uniforms, filling these until they seem blown tight enough to burst. The individual members may increase in girth

to an unbelievable extent and faces fill as taut and globular as
balloons. The surprising thing, next to their progressive cor-
pulence, is the amount of paper that is scattered about the dead.
Their ultimate position, before there is any question of burial,
depends on the location of the pockets in the uniform. In the
Austrian army these pockets were in the back of the breeches
and the dead, after a short time, all consequently lay on their
faces, the two hip pockets pulled out and, scattered around them
in the grass, all those papers their pockets had contained. The
heat, the flies, the indicative positions of the bodies in the grass,
and the amount of paper scattered are the impressions one re-
tains. The smell of a battlefield in hot weather one cannot recall.
You can remember that there was such a smell, but nothing ever
happens to you to bring it back. It is unlike the smell of a regiment, which may come to you suddenly while riding in the
street car and you will look across and see the man who has
brought it to you. But the other thing is gone as completely as
when you have been in love; you remember things that happened, but the sensation cannot be recalled.

One wonders what that persevering traveller, Mungo Park,
would have seen on a battlefield in hot weather to restore his
confidence. There were always poppies in the wheat in the end
of June and in July, and the mulberry trees were in full leaf and
one could see the heat waves rise from the barrels of the guns
where the sun struck them through the screens of leaves; the
earth was turned a bright yellow at the edge of holes where
mustard gas shells had been and the average broken house is finer
to see than one that has been shelled, but few travellers would
take a good full breath of that early summer air and have any
such thoughts as Mungo Park about those formed in His own
image.

The first thing that you found about the dead was that, hit
badly enough, they died like animals. Some quickly from a little
wound you would not think would kill a rabbit. They died from
little wounds as rabbits die sometimes from three or four small
grains of shot that hardly seem to break the skin. Others would
die like cats; a skull broken in and iron in the brain, they lie alive
two days like cats that crawl into the coal bin with a bullet in the
brain and will not die until you cut their heads off. Maybe cats
do not die then, they say they have nine lives, I do not know,
but most men die like animals, not men. I'd never seen a natural
death, so called, and so I blamed it on the war and like the per-

severing traveller, Mungo Park, knew that there was something else; that always absent something else, and then I saw one.

The only natural death I've ever seen, outside of loss of blood, which isn't bad, was death from Spanish influenza. In this you drown in mucus, choking, and how you know the patient's dead is: at the end he turns to be a little child again, though with his manly force, and fills the sheets as full as any diaper with one vast, final, yellow cataract that flows and dribbles on after he's gone. So now I want to see the death of any self-called Humanist* because a persevering traveller like Mungo Park or me lives on and maybe yet will live to see the actual death of members of this literary sect and watch the noble exits that they make. In my musings as a naturalist it has occurred to me that while decorum is an excellent thing some must be indecorous if the race is to be carried on since the position prescribed for procreation is indecorous, highly indecorous, and it occurred to me that perhaps that is what these people are, or were: the children of decorous cohabitation. But regardless of how they started I hope to see the finish of a few, and speculate how worms will try that long preserved sterility; with their quaint pamphlets gone to bust and into foot-notes all their lust.

While it is, perhaps, legitimate to deal with these self-designated citizens in a natural history of the dead, even though the designation may mean nothing by the time this work is published, yet it is unfair to the other dead, who were not dead in their youth of choice, who owned no magazines, many of whom had doubtless never even read a review, that one has seen in the hot weather with a half-pint of maggots working where their mouths have been. It was not always hot weather for the dead, much of the time it was the rain that washed them clean when they lay in it and made the earth soft when they were buried in it and sometimes then kept on until the earth was mud and washed them out and you had to bury them again. Or in the winter in the mountains you had to put them in the snow and when the snow melted in the spring some one else had to bury them. They had beautiful burying grounds in the mountains, war in the mountains is the most beautiful of all war, and in one

*The reader's indulgence is requested for this mention of an extinct phenomenon. The reference, like all references to fashions, dates the story but it is retained because of its mild historical interest and because its omission would spoil the rhythm.

of them, at a place called Pocol, they buried a general who was
shot through the head by a sniper. This is where those writers
are mistaken who write books called *Generals Die in Bed*, because
this general died in a trench dug in snow, high in the mountains,
wearing an Alpine hat with an eagle feather in it and a hole in
front you couldn't put your little finger in and a hole in back you
could put your fist in, if it were a small fist and you wanted to
put it there, and much blood in the snow. He was a damned fine
general, and so was General von Behr who commanded the Ba-
varian Alpenkorps troops at the battle of Caporetto and was
killed in his staff car by the Italian rearguard as he drove into
Udine ahead of his troops, and the titles of all such books should
be *Generals Usually Die in Bed*, if we are to have any sort of
accuracy in such things.

In the mountains too, sometimes, the snow fell on the dead
outside the dressing station on the side that was protected by the
mountain from any shelling. They carried them into a cave that
had been dug into the mountainside before the earth froze. It
was in this cave that a man whose head was broken as a flower-
pot may be broken, although it was all held together by mem-
branes and a skillfully applied bandage now soaked and hardened, with the structure of his brain disturbed by a piece of
broken steel in it, lay a day, a night, and a day. The stretcher-
bearers asked the doctor to go in and have a look at him. They
saw him each time they made a trip and even when they did not
look at him they heard him breathing. The doctor's eyes were
red and the lids swollen, almost shut from tear gas. He looked at
the man twice; once in daylight, once with a flashlight. That too
would have made a good etching for Goya, the visit with the
flashlight, I mean. After looking at him the second time the doctor believed the stretcher-bearers when they said the soldier was
still alive.

'What do you want me to do about it?' he asked.

There was nothing they wanted done. But after a while they
asked permission to carry him out and lay him with the badly
wounded.

'No. No. No!' said the doctor, who was busy. 'What's the
matter? Are you afraid of him?'

'We don't like to hear him in there with the dead.'

'Don't listen to him. If you take him out of there you will
have to carry him right back in.'

'We wouldn't mind that, Captain Doctor.'

'No,' said the doctor. 'No. Didn't you hear me say no?'

'Why don't you give him an overdose of morphine?' asked an artillery officer who was waiting to have a wound in his arm dressed.

'Do you think that is the only use I have for morphine? Would you like me to have to operate without morphine? You have a pistol, go out and shoot him yourself.'

'He's been shot already,' said the officer. 'If some of you doctors were shot you'd be different.'

'Thank you very much,' said the doctor waving a forceps in the air. 'Thank you a thousand times. What about these eyes?' He pointed the forceps at them. 'How would you like these?'

'Tear gas. We call it lucky if it's tear gas.'

'Because you leave the line,' said the doctor. 'Because you come running here with your tear gas to be evacuated. You rub onions in your eyes.'

'You are beside yourself. I do not notice your insults. You are crazy.'

The stretcher-bearers came in.

'Captain Doctor,' one of them said.

'Get out of here!' said the doctor.

They went out.

'I will shoot the poor fellow,' the artillery officer said. 'I am a humane man. I will not let him suffer.'

'Shoot him then,' said the doctor. 'Shoot him. Assume the responsibility. I will make a report. Wounded shot by lieutenant of artillery in first curing post. Shoot him. Go ahead shoot him.'

'You are not a human being.'

'My business is to care for the wounded, not to kill them. That is for gentlemen of the artillery.'

'Why don't you care for him then?'

'I have done so. I have done all that can be done.'

'Why don't you send him down on the cable railway?'

'Who are you to ask me questions? Are you my superior officer? Are you in command of this dressing post? Do me the courtesy to answer.'

The lieutenant of artillery said nothing. The others in the room were all soldiers and there were no other officers present.

'Answer me,' said the doctor holding a needle up in his forceps. 'Give me a response.'

'F — yourself,' said the artillery officer.

'So,' said the doctor. 'So, you said that. All right. All right. We shall see.'

The lieutenant of artillery stood up and walked toward him.

'F — yourself,' he said. 'F — yourself. F — your mother. F — your sister. . . .'

The doctor tossed the saucer full of iodine in his face. As he came toward him, blinded, the lieutenant fumbled for his pistol. The doctor skipped quickly behind him, tripped him and, as he fell to the floor, kicked him several times and picked up the pistol in his rubber gloves. The lieutenant sat on the floor holding his good hand to his eyes.

'I'll kill you!' he said. 'I'll kill you as soon as I can see.'

'I am the boss,' said the doctor. 'All is forgiven since you know I am the boss. You cannot kill me because I have your pistol. Sergeant! Adjutant! Adjutant!'

'The adjutant is at the cable railway,' said the sergeant.

'Wipe out this officer's eyes with alcohol and water. He has got iodine in them. Bring me the basin to wash my hands. I will take this officer next.'

'You won't touch me.'

'Hold him tight. He is a little delirious.'

One of the stretcher-bearers came in.

'Captain Doctor.'

'What do you want?'

'The man in the dead-house –'

'Get out of here.'

'Is dead, Captain Doctor. I thought you would be glad to know.'

'See, my poor lieutenant? We dispute about nothing. In time of war we dispute about nothing.'

'F — you,' said the lieutenant of artillery. He still could not see. 'You've blinded me.'

'It is nothing,' said the doctor. 'Your eyes will be all right. It is nothing. A dispute about nothing.'

'Ayee! Ayee! Ayee!' suddenly screamed the lieutenant. 'You have blinded me! You have blinded me!'

'Hold him tight,' said the doctor. 'He is in much pain. Hold him very tight.'

WINE OF WYOMING

It was a hot afternoon in Wyoming; the mountains were a long way away and you could see snow on their tops, but they made no shadow, and in the valley the grain-fields were yellow, the road was dusty with cars passing, and all the small wooden houses at the edge of town were baking in the sun. There was a tree made shade over Fontan's back porch and I sat there at a table and Madame Fontan brought up cold beer from the cellar. A motor-car turned off the main road and came up the side road, and stopped beside the house. Two men got out and came in through the gate. I put the bottles under the table. Madame Fontan stood up.

'Where's Sam?' one of the men asked at the screen door.

'He ain't here. He's at the mines.'

'You got some beer?'

'No. Ain't got any beer. That's a last bottle. All gone.'

'What's he drinking?'

'That's a last bottle. All gone.'

'Go on, give us some beer. You know me.'

'Ain't got any beer. That's a last bottle. All gone.'

'Come on, let's go some place where we can get some real beer,' one of them said, and they went out to the car. One of them walked unsteadily. The motor-car jerked in starting, whirled on the road, and went on and away.

'Put the beer on the table,' Madame Fontan said. 'What's the matter, yes, all right. What's the matter? Don't drink off the floor.'

'I didn't know who they were,' I said.

'They're drunk,' she said. 'That's what makes the trouble. Then they go somewhere else and say they got it here. Maybe they don't even remember.' She spoke French, but it was only French occasionally, and there were many English words and some English constructions.

'Where's Fontan?'

'Il fait de la vendange. Oh, my God, il est crazy pour le vin.'

'But you like the beer?'

'Oui, j'aime la bière, mais Fontan, il est crazy pour le vin.'

She was a plump old woman with a lovely ruddy complexion and white hair. She was very clean and the house was very clean and neat. She came from Lens.

'Where did you eat?'

'At the hotel.'

'Mangez ici. Il ne faut pas manger à l'hôtel ou au restaurant. Mangez ici!'

'I don't want to make you trouble. And besides they eat all right at the hotel.'

'I never eat at the hotel. Maybe they eat all right there. Only once in my life I ate at a restaurant in America. You know what they gave me? They gave me pork that was raw!'

'Really?'

'I don't lie to you. It was pork that wasn't cooked! Et mon fils il est marié avec une américaine, et tout le temps il a mangé les *beans* en *can*.'

'How long has he been married?'

'Oh, my God, I don't know. His wife weighs two hundred twenty-five pounds. She don't work. She don't cook. She gives him beans en can.'

'What does she do?'

'All the time she reads. Rien que des books. Tout le temps elle stay in the bed and read books. Already she can't have another baby. She's too fat. There ain't any room.'

'What's the matter with her?'

'She reads books all the time. He's a good boy. He works hard. He worked in the mines; now he works on a ranch. He never worked on a ranch before, and the man that owns the ranch said to Fontan that he never saw anybody work better on that ranch than that boy. Then he comes home and she feeds him nothing.'

'Why doesn't he get a divorce?'

'He ain't got no money to get a divorce. Besides, il est *crazy* pour elle.'

'Is she beautiful?'

'He thinks *so*. When he brought her home I thought I would die. He's such a good boy and works hard all the time and never run around or make any trouble. Then he goes away to work in the oil-fields and brings home this Indienne that weighs right then one hundred eighty-five pounds.'

'Elle est Indienne?'

'She's Indian all right. My God, yes. All the time she says son-ofabitsh goddam. She don't work.'

'Where is she now?'

'Au show.'

'Where's that?'

'*Au show. Moving* pictures. All she does is read and go to the show.'

'Have you got any more beer?'

'My God, yes. Sure. You come and eat with us tonight.'

'All right. What should I bring?'

'Don't bring anything. Nothing at all. Maybe Fontan will have some of the wine.'

That night I had dinner at Fontan's. We ate in the dining-room and there was a clean tablecloth. We tried the new wine. It was very light and clear and good, and still tasted of the grapes. At the table there were Fontan and Madame and the little boy, André.

'What did you do today?' Fontan asked. He was an old man with small mine-tired body, a drooping gray mustache, and bright eyes, and was from the Centre near Saint-Etienne.

'I worked on my book.'

'Were your books all right?' asked Madame.

'He means he writes a book like a writer. Un roman,' Fontan explained.

'Pa, can I go to the show?' André asked.

'Sure,' said Fontan. André turned to me.

'How old do you think I am? Do you think I look fourteen years old?' He was a thin little boy, but his face looked sixteen.

'Yes. You look fourteen.'

'When I go to the show I crouch down like this and try to look small.' His voice was very high and breaking. 'If I give them a quarter they keep it all but if I give them only fifteen cents they let me in all right.'

'I only give you fifteen cents, then,' said Fontan.

'No. Give me the whole quarter. I'll get it changed on the way.'

'Il faut revenir tout de suite après le show,' Madame Fontan said.

'I come right back.' André went out the door. The night was cooling outside. He left the door open and a cool breeze came in.

'Mangez!' said Madame Fontan. 'You haven't eaten anything.' I had eaten two helpings of chicken and French fried potatoes, three ears of sweet corn, some sliced cucumbers, and two help-ings of salad.

'Perhaps he wants some kek,' Fontan said.

'I should have gotten some kek for him,' Madame Fontan said. 'Mangez du fromage. Mangez du crimcheez. Vous n'avez rien mangé. I ought have gotten kek. Americans always eat kek.'

'Mais j'ai rudement bien mangé.'

'Mangez! Vous n'avez rien mangé. Eat it all. We don't save anything. Eat it all up.'

'Eat some more salad,' Fontan said.

'I'll get some more beer,' Madame Fontan said. 'If you work all day in a book-factory you get hungry.'

'Elle ne comprend pas que vous êtes écrivain,' Fontan said. He was a delicate old man who used the slang and knew the popular songs of his period of military service in the end of the 1890's. 'He writes the books himself,' he explained to Madame.

'You write the books yourself?' Madame asked.

'Sometimes.'

'Oh!' she said. 'Oh! You write them yourself. Oh! Well, you get hungry if you do that too. Mangez! Je vais chercher de la bière.'

We heard her walking on the stairs to the cellar. Fontan smiled at me. He was very tolerant of people who had not his experience and worldly knowledge.

When André came home from the show we were still sitting in the kitchen and were talking about hunting.

'Labor *day* we all went to Clear Creek,' Madame said. 'Oh, my God, you ought to have been there all right. We all went in the truck. Tout le monde est allé dans le truck. Nous sommes partis le dimanche. C'est le truck de Charley.'

'On a mangé, on a bu du vin, de la bière, et il y avait aussi un français qui a apporté de l'absinthe,' Fontan said. 'Un français de la Californie!'

'My God, nous avons chanté. There's a farmer comes to see what's the matter, and we give him something to drink, and he stayed with us awhile. There was some Italians come too, and they want to stay with us too. We sung a song about the Italians and they don't understand it. They didn't know we didn't want them, but we didn't have nothing to do with them, and after a while they went away.'

'How many fish did you catch?'

'Très peu. We went to fish a little while, but then we came back to sing again. Nous avons chanté, vous savez.'

'In the night,' said Madame, 'toutes les femmes ont dormi dans le truck. Les hommes à côté du feu. In the night I hear

Fontan come to get some more wine, and I tell him, Fontan, my God, leave some for tomorrow. Tomorrow they won' have anything to drink, and then they'll be sorry.'

'Mais nous avons tout bu,' Fontan said. 'Et le lendemain il ne reste rien.'

'What did you do?'

'Nous avons pêché sérieusement.'

'Good trout, all right, too. My God, yes. All the same; half-pound one ounce.'

'How big?'

'Half-pound one ounce. Just right to eat. All the same size; half-pound one ounce.'

'How do you like America?' Fontan asked me.

'It's my country, you see. So I like it, because it's my country. Mais on ne mange pas très bien. D'antan, oui. Mais maintenant, no.'

'No,' said Madame. 'On ne mange pas bien.' She shook her head. 'Et aussi, il y a trop de Polack. Quand j'étais petite ma mère m'a dit, "vous mangez comme les Polacks." Je n'ai jamais compris ce que c'est qu'un Polack. Mais maintenant en Amérique je comprends. Il y a trop de Polack. Et, my God, ils sont sales, les Polacks.'

'It is fine for hunting and fishing,' I said.

'Oui. Ça, c'est le meilleur. La chasse et la pêche,' Fontan said. 'Qu'est-ce que vous avez comme fusil?'

'A twelve-gauge pump.'

'Il est bon, le pump,' Fontan nodded his head.

'Je veux aller à la chasse moi-même,' André said in his high, little boy's voice.

'Tu ne peux pas,' Fontan said. He turned to me.

'Ils sont des sauvages, les boys, vous savez. Ils sont des sauvages. Ils veulent shooter les uns les autres.'

'Je veux aller tout seul,' André said, very shrill and excited.

'You can't go,' Madame Fontan said. 'You are too young.'

'Je veux aller tout seul,' André said shrilly. 'Je veux shooter les rats d'eau.'

'What are rats d'eau?' I asked.

'You don't know them? Sure you know them. What they call the muskrats.'

André had brought the twenty-two-calibre rifle out from the cupboard and was holding it in his hands under the light.

'Ils sont des sauvages,' Fontan explained. 'Ils veulent shooter les uns les autres.'

'Je veux aller tout seul,' André shrilled. He looked desperately along the barrel of the gun. 'Je veux shooter les rats d'eau. Je connais beaucoup de rats d'eau.'

'Give me the gun,' Fontan said. He explained again to me. 'They're savages. They would shoot one another.'

André held tight on to the gun.

'On peut looker. On ne fait pas de mal. On peut looker.'

'Il est crazy pour le shooting,' Madame Fontan said. 'Mais il est trop jeune.'

André put the twenty-two-calibre rifle back in the cupboard.

'When I'm bigger I'll shoot the muskrats and the jack-rabbits too,' he said in English. 'One time I went out with Papa and he shot a jack-rabbit just a little bit and I shot it and hit it.'

'C'est vrai,' Fontan nodded. 'Il a tué un jack.'

'But he hit it first,' André said. 'I want to go all by myself and shoot all by myself. Next year I can do it.' He went over in a corner and sat down to read a book. I had picked it up when we came into the kitchen to sit after supper. It was a library book – *Frank on a Gunboat*.

'Il aime les books,' Madame Fontan said. 'But it's better than to run around at night with the other boys and steal things.'

'Books are all right,' Fontan said. 'Monsieur il fait les books.'

'Yes, that's so, all right. But too many books are bad,' Madame Fontan said. 'Ici, c'est une maladie, les books. C'est comme les churches. Ici il y a trop de churches. En France il y a seulement les catholiques et les protestants – et très peu de protestants. Mais ici rien que de churches. Quand j'étais venu ici je disais, oh, my God, what are all the churches?'

'C'est vrai,' Fontan said. 'Il y a trop de churches.'

'The other day,' Madame Fontan said, 'there was a little French girl here with her mother, the cousin of Fontan, and she said to me, "En Amérique il ne faut pas être catholique. It's not good to be catholique. The Americans don't like you to be ca-tholique. It's like the dry law." I said to her, "What you going to be? Heh? It's better to be catholique if you're catholique." But she said, "No, it isn't any good to be catholique in Ameri-ca." But I think it's better to be catholique if you are. Ce n'est pas bon de changer sa religion. My God, no.'

'You go to the mass here?'

'No. I don't go in America, only sometimes in a long while. Mais je reste catholique. It's no good to change the religion.'

'On dit que Schmidt est catholique,' Fontan said.

'On dit, mais on ne sait jamais,' Madame Fontan said. 'I don't think Schmidt is catholique. There's not many catholique in America.'

'We are catholique,' I said.

'Sure, but you live in France,' Madame Fontan said. 'Je ne crois pas que Schmidt est catholique. Did he ever live in France?'

'Les Polacks sont catholiques,' Fontan said.

'That's true,' Madame Fontan said. 'They go to church, then they fight with knives all the way home and kill each other all day Sunday. But they're not real catholiques. They're Polack catholiques.'

'All catholiques are the same,' Fontan said. 'One catholique is like another.'

'I don't believe Schmidt is catholique,' Madame Fontan said. 'That's awful funny if he's catholique. Moi, je ne crois pas.'

'Il est catholique,' I said.

'Schmidt is catholique,' Madame Fontan mused. 'I wouldn't have believed it. My God, il est catholique.'

'Marie va chercher de la bière,' Fontan said. 'Monsieur a soif – moi aussi.'

'Yes, all right,' Madame Fontan said from the next room. She went downstairs and we heard the stairs creaking. André sat reading in the corner. Fontan and I sat at the table, and he poured the beer from the last bottle into our two glasses, leaving a little in the bottom.

'C'est un bon pays pour la chasse,' Fontan said. 'J'aime beaucoup shooter les canards.'

'Mais il y a très bonne chasse aussi en France,' I said.

'C'est vrai,' Fontan said. 'Nous avons beaucoup de gibier làbas.'

Madame Fontan came up the stairs with the beer bottles in her hands. 'Il est catholique,' she said 'My God, Schmidt est catholique.'

'You think he'll be the President?' Fontan asked.

'No,' I said.

The next afternoon I drove out to Fontan's, through the shade of the town, then along the dusty road, turning up the side road and leaving the car beside the fence. It was another hot day.

Madame Fontan came to the back door. She looked like Mrs. Santa Claus, clean and rosy-faced and white-haired, and waddling when she walked.

'My God, hello,' she said. 'It's hot, my God.' She went back into the house to get some beer. I sat on the back porch and looked through the screen and the leaves of the tree at the heat and, away off, the mountains. There were furrowed brown mountains, and above them three peaks and a glacier with snow that you could see through the trees. The snow looked very white and pure and unreal. Madame Fontan came out and put down the bottles on the table.

'What you see out there?'

'The snow.'

'C'est jolie, la neige.'

'Have a glass, too.'

'All right.'

She sat down on a chair beside me. 'Schmidt,' she said. 'If he's the President, you think we get the wine and beer all right?'

'Sure,' I said. 'Trust Schmidt.'

'Already we paid seven hundred fifty-five dollars in fines when they arrested Fontan. Twice the police arrested us and once the government. All the money we made all the time Fontan worked in the mines and I did washing. We paid it all. They put Fontan in jail. Il n'a jamais fait de mal à personne.'

'He's a good man,' I said. 'It's a crime.'

'We don't charge too much money. The wine one dollar a litre. The beer ten cents a bottle. We never sell the beer before it's good. Lots of places they sell the beer right away when they make it, and then it gives everybody a headache. What's the matter with that? They put Fontan in jail and they take seven hundred fifty-five dollars.'

'It's wicked,' I said. 'Where is Fontan?'

'He stays with the wine. He has to watch it now to catch it just right,' she smiled. She did not think about the money any more. 'Vous savez, il est crazy pour le vin. Last night he brought a little bit home with him, what you drank, and a little bit of the new. The last new. It ain't ready yet, but he drank a little bit, and this morning he put a little bit in his coffee. Dans son café, vous savez! Il est crazy pour le vin! Il est comme ça. Son pays est comme ça. Where I live in the north they don't drink any wine. Everybody drinks beer. By where we lived there was a big brewery right near us. When I was a little girl I didn't like the smell of the hops in the carts. Nor in the fields. Je n'aime pas les houblons. No, my God, not a bit. The man that owns the brewery said to me and my sister to go to the brewery and drink the beer, and then we'd like the hops. That's true. Then we liked them all right. He had them give us the beer. We liked them all right then. But Fontan, il est crazy pour le vin. One time he killed a jack-rabbit and he wanted me to cook it with a sauce with wine, make a black sauce with wine and butter and mushrooms and onion and everything in it, for the jack. My God, I make the sauce all right, and he eat it all and said, "La sauce est meilleure que le jack." Dans son pays c'est comme ça. Il y a beaucoup de gibier et de vin. Moi, j'aime les pommes de terre, le saucisson, et la bière. C'est bon, la bière. C'est très bon pour la santé.'

'It's good,' I said. 'It and wine too.'

'You're like Fontan. But there was a thing here that I never saw. I don't think you've ever seen it either. There were Americans came here and they put whiskey in the beer.'

'No,' I said.

'Oui. My God, yes, that's true. Et aussi une femme qui a vomis sur la table!'

'Comment?'

'C'est vrai. Elle a vomis sur la table. Et après elle a vomis dans ses shoes. And afterward they come back and say they want to come again and have another party the next Saturday, and I say no, my God, no! When they came I locked the door.'

'They're bad when they're drunk.'

'In the winter-time when the boys go to the dance they come in the cars and wait outside and say to Fontan, "Hey, Sam, sell us a bottle wine," or they buy the beer, and then they take the moonshine out of their pockets in a bottle and pour it in the beer and drink it. My God, that's the first time I ever saw that in my life. They put whiskey in the beer. My God, I don't understand *that!*'

'They want to get sick, so they'll know they're drunk.'

'One time a fellow comes here came to me and said he wanted me to cook them a big supper and they drink one two bottles of wine, and their girls come too, and then they go to the dance. All right, I said. So I made a big supper, and when they come already they drank a lot. Then they put whiskey in the wine. My God, yes. I said to Fontan, "On va être malade!" "Oui," il dit. Then these girls were sick, nice girls too, all-right girls. They were sick right at the table. Fontan tried to take them by the arm and show them where they could be sick all right in the cabinet, but the fellows said no, they were all right right there at the table.'

Fontan had come in. 'When they come again I locked the door. "No," I said. "Not for hundred fifty dollars." My God, no.'

'There is a word for such people when they do like that, in French,' Fontan said. He stood looking very old and tired from the heat.

'What?'

'Cochon,' he said delicately, hesitating to use such a strong word. 'They were like the cochon. C'est un mot très fort,' he apologized, 'mais vomir sur la table –' he shook his head sadly.

'Cochons,' I said. 'That's what they are – cochons. Salauds.'

The grossness of the words was distasteful to Fontan. He was glad to speak of something else.

'Il y a des gens très gentils, très sensibles, qui viennent aussi,' he said. 'There are officers from the fort. Very nice men. Good fellas. Everybody that was ever in France they want to come and drink wine. They like wine all right.'

'There was one man,' Madame Fontan said, 'and his wife never lets him get out. So he tells her he's tired, and goes to bed, and when she goes to the show he comes straight down here, sometimes in his pyjamas just with a coat over them. "Maria, some beer," he says, "for God's sake." He sits in his pyjamas and drinks the beer, and then he goes up to the fort and gets back in bed before his wife comes home from the show.'

'C'est un original,' Fontan said, 'mais vraiment gentil. He's a nice fella.'

'My God, yes, nice fella all right,' Madame Fontan said. 'He's always in bed when his wife gets back from the show.'

'I have to go away tomorrow,' I said. 'To the Crow Reservation. We go there for the opening of the prairie-chicken season.'

'Yes? You come back here before you go away. You come back here all right?'

'Absolutely.'

'Then the wine will be done,' Fontan said. 'We'll drink a bottle together.'

'Three bottles,' Madame Fontan said.

'I'll be back,' I said.

'We count on you,' Fontan said.

'Good night,' I said.

★ ★ ★

We got in early in the afternoon from the shooting-trip. We had been up that morning since five o'clock. The day before we had had good shooting, but that morning we had not seen a prairie-chicken. Riding in the open car, we were very hot and we stopped to eat our lunch out of the sun, under a tree beside the road. The sun was high and the patch of shade was very small. We ate sandwiches and crackers with sandwich filling on them, and were thirsty and tired, and glad when we finally were out and on the main road back to town. We came up behind a prairie-dog town and stopped the car to shoot at the prairie-dogs with the pistol. We shot two, but then stopped, because the bullets that missed glanced off the rocks and the dirt, and sung off across the fields, and beyond the fields there were some trees along a watercourse, with a house, and we did not want to get in trouble from stray bullets going toward the house. So we drove on, and finally were on the road coming down-hill toward the outlying houses of the town. Across the plain we could see the mountains. They were blue that day, and the snow on the high mountains shone like glass. The summer was ending, but the new snow had not yet come to stay on the high mountains; there was only the old sun-melted snow and the ice, and from a long way away it shone very brightly.

We wanted something cool and some shade. We were sunburned and our lips blistered from the sun and alkali dust. We turned up the side road to Fontan's, stopped the car outside the house, and went in. It was cool inside the dining-room. Madame Fontan was alone.

'Only two bottles beer,' she said. 'It's all gone. The new is no good yet.'

I gave her some birds. 'That's good,' she said. 'All right. Thanks. That's good.' She went out to put the birds away where it was cooler. When we finished the beer I stood up. 'We have to go,' I said.

'You come back tonight all right? Fontan he's going to have the wine.'

'We'll come back before we go away.'

'You go away?'

'Yes. We have to leave in the morning.'

'That's too bad you go away. You come tonight. Fontan will have the wine. We'll make a fête before you go.'

'We'll come before we go.'

But that afternoon there were telegrams to send, the car to be gone over – a tire had been cut by a stone and needed vulcanizing – and, without the car, I walked into the town, doing things that had to be done before we could go. When it was suppertime I was too tired to go out. We did not want a foreign language. All we wanted was to go early to bed.

As I lay in bed before I went to sleep, with all the things of the summer piled around ready to be packed, the windows open and the air coming in cool from the mountains, I thought it was a shame not to have gone to Fontan's – but in a little while I was asleep. The next day we were busy all morning packing and ending the summer. We had lunch and were ready to start by two o'clock.

'We must go and say good-by to the Fontans,' I said.

'Yes, we must.'

'I'm afraid they expected us last night.'

'I suppose we could have gone.'

'I wish we'd gone.'

We said good-by to the man at the desk at the hotel, and to Larry and our other friends in the town, and then drove out to Fontan's. Both Monsieur and Madame were there. They were glad to see us. Fontan looked old and tired.

'We thought you would come last night,' Madame Fontan said. 'Fontan had three bottles of wine. When you did not come he drank it all up.'

'We can only stay a minute,' I said. 'We just came to say good-by. We wanted to come last night. We intended to come, but we were too tired after the trip.'

'Go get some wine,' Fontan said.

'There is no wine. You drank it all up.'

Fontan looked very upset.

'I'll go get some,' he said. 'I'll just be gone a few minutes. I drank it up last night. We had it for you.'

'I knew you were tired. "My God," I said, "they're too tired all right to come," ' Madame Fontan said. 'Go get some wine, Fontan.'

'I'll take you in the car,' I said.

'All right,' Fontan said. 'That way we'll go faster.'

We drove down the road in the motor-car and turned up a side road about a mile away.

'You'll like that wine,' Fontan said. 'It's come out well. You can drink it for supper tonight.'

We stopped in front of a frame house. Fontan knocked on the door. There was no answer. We went around to the back. The back door was locked too. There were empty tin cans around the back door. We looked in the window. There was nobody inside. The kitchen was dirty and sloppy, but all the doors and windows were tight shut.

'That son of a bitch. Where is she gone out?' Fontan said. He was desperate.

'I know where I can get a key,' he said. 'You stay here.' I watched him go down to the next house down the road, knock on the door, talk to the woman who came out, and finally come back. He had a key. We tried it on the front door and the back, but it wouldn't work.

'That son of a bitch,' Fontan said. 'She's gone away somewhere.'

Looking through the window I could see where the wine was stored. Close to the window you could smell the inside of the house. It smelled sweet and sickish like an Indian house. Suddenly Fontan took a loose board and commenced digging at the earth beside the back door.

'I can get in,' he said. 'Son of a bitch, I can get in.'

There was a man in the back yard of the next house doing something to one of the front wheels of an old Ford.

'You better not,' I said. 'That man will see you. He's watching.'

Fontan straightened up. 'We'll try the key once more,' he said. We tried the key and it did not work. It turned half-way in either direction.

'We can't get in,' I said. 'We better go back.'

'I'll dig up the back,' Fontan offered.

'No, I wouldn't let you take the chance.'

'I'll do it.'

'No,' I said. 'That man would see. Then they would seize it.'

We went out to the car and drove back to Fontan's, stopping on the way to leave the key. Fontan did not say anything but swear in English. He was incoherent and crushed. We went in the house.

'That son of a bitch!' he said. 'We couldn't get the wine. My own wine that I made.'

All the happiness went from Madame Fontan's face. Fontan sat down in a corner with his head in his hands.

'We must go,' I said. 'It doesn't make any difference about the wine. You drink to us when we're gone.'

'Where did that crazy go?' Madame Fontan asked.

'I don't know,' Fontan said. 'I don't know where she go. Now you go away without any wine.'

'That's all right,' I said.

'That's no good,' Madame Fontan said. She shook her head.

'We have to go,' I said. 'Good-by and good luck. Thank you for the fine times.'

Fontan shook his head. He was disgraced. Madame Fontan looked sad.

'Don't feel bad about the wine,' I said.

'He wanted you to drink his wine,' Madame Fontan said. 'You can come back next year?'

'No. Maybe the year after.'

'You see?' Fontan said to her.

'Good-by,' I said. 'Don't think about the wine. Drink some for us when we're gone.' Fontan shook his head. He did not smile. He knew when he was ruined.

'That son of a bitch,' Fontan said to himself.

'Last night he had three bottles,' Madame Fontan said to comfort him. He shook his head.

'Good-by,' he said.

Madame Fontan had tears in her eyes.

'Good-by,' she said. She felt badly for Fontan.

'Good-by,' we said. We all felt very badly. They stood in the doorway and we got in, and I started the motor. We waved. They stood together sadly on the porch. Fontan looked very old, and Madame Fontan looked sad. She waved to us and Fontan went in the house. We turned up the road.

'They felt so badly. Fontan felt terribly.'

'We ought to have gone last night.'

'Yes, we ought to have.'

We were through the town and out on the smooth road beyond, with the stubble of grain-fields on each side and the mountains off to the right. It looked like Spain, but it was Wyoming.

'I hope they have a lot of good luck.'

'They won't,' I said, 'and Schmidt won't be President either.'

The cement road stopped. The road was gravelled now and we left the plain and started up between two foot-hills; the road in a curve and commencing to climb. The soil of the hills was red, the sage grew in gray clumps, and as the road rose we could see across the hills and away across the plain of the valley to the mountains. They were farther away now and they looked more like Spain than ever. The road curved and climbed again, and ahead there were some grouse dusting in the road. They flew as we came toward them, their wings beating fast, then sailing in long slants, and lit on the hillside below.

'They are so big and lovely. They're bigger than European partridges.'

'It's a fine country for la chasse, Fontan says.'

'And when the chasse is gone?'

'They'll be dead then.'

'The boy won't.'

'There's nothing to prove he won't be,' I said.

'We ought to have gone last night.'

'Oh, yes,' I said. 'We ought to have gone.'

THE GAMBLER, THE NUN, AND THE RADIO

They brought them in around midnight and then, all night long, every one along the corridor heard the Russian.

'Where is he shot?' Mr. Frazer asked the night nurse.

'In the thigh, I think.'

'What about the other one?'

'Oh, he's going to die, I'm afraid.'

'Where is he shot?'

'Twice in the abdomen. They only found one of the bullets.'

They were both beet workers, a Mexican and a Russian, and they were sitting drinking coffee in an all-night restaurant when some one came in the door and started shooting at the Mexican. The Russian crawled under a table and was hit, finally, by a stray shot fired at the Mexican as he lay on the floor with two bullets in his abdomen. That was what the paper said.

The Mexican told the police he had no idea who shot him. He believed it to be an accident.

'An accident that he fired eight shots at you and hit you twice, there?'

'*Sí, señor*,' said the Mexican, who was named Cayetano Ruiz.

'An accident that he hit me at all, the *cabrón*,' he said to the interpreter.

'What does he say?' asked the detective sergeant, looking across the bed at the interpreter.

'He says it was an accident.'

'Tell him to tell the truth, that he is going to die,' the detective said.

'Na,' said Cayetano. 'But tell him that I feel very sick and would prefer not to talk so much.'

'He says that he is telling the truth,' the interpreter said. Then, speaking confidently, to the detective, 'He don't know who shot him. They shot him in the back.'

'Yes,' said the detective. 'I understand that, but why did the bullets all go in the front?'

'Maybe he is spinning around,' said the interpreter.

'Listen,' said the detective, shaking his finger almost at Cayetano's nose, which projected, waxen yellow, from his dead-man's face in which his eyes were alive as a hawk's. 'I don't give a damn who shot you, but I've got to clear this thing up. Don't you want the man who shot you to be punished? Tell him that,' he said to the interpreter.

'He says to tell who shot you.'

'*Mandarlo al carajo*,' said Cayetano, who was very tired.

'He says he never saw the fellow at all,' the interpreter said. 'I tell you straight they shot him in the back.'

'Ask him who shot the Russian.'

'Poor Russian,' said Cayetano. 'He was on the floor with his head enveloped in his arms. He started to give cries when they shoot him and he is giving cries ever since. Poor Russian.'

'He says some fellow that he doesn't know. Maybe the same fellow that shot him.'

'Listen,' the detective said. 'This isn't Chicago. You're not a gangster. You don't have to act like a moving picture. It's all right to tell who shot you. Anybody would tell who shot them. That's all right to do. Suppose you don't tell who he is and he shoots somebody else. Suppose he shoots a woman or a child. You can't let him get away with that. You tell him,' he said to Mr. Frazer. 'I don't trust that damn interpreter.'

'I am very reliable,' the interpreter said. Cayetano looked at Mr. Frazer.

'Listen, amigo,' said Mr. Frazer. 'The policeman says that we are not in Chicago but in Hailey, Montana. You are not a bandit and this has nothing to do with the cinema.'

'I believe him,' said Cayetano softly. '*Ya lo creo*.'

'One can, with honor, denounce one's assailant. Every one does it here, he says. He says what happens if after shooting you, this man shoots a woman or a child?'

'I am not married,' Cayetano said.

'He says any woman, any child.'

'The man is not crazy,' Cayetano said.

'He says you should denounce him,' Mr. Frazer finished.

'Thank you,' Cayetano said. 'You are of the great translators. I speak English, but badly. I understand it all right. How did you break your leg?'

'A fall off a horse.'

'What bad luck. I am very sorry. Does it hurt much?'

'Not now. At first, yes.'

'Listen, amigo,' Cayetano began, 'I am very weak. You will pardon me. Also I have much pain; enough pain. It is very possible that I die. Please get this policeman out of here because

I am very tired.' He made as though to roll to one side; then held himself still.

'I told him everything exactly as you said and he said to tell you, truly, that he doesn't know who shot him and that he is very weak and wishes you would question him later on,' Mr. Frazer said.

'He'll probably be dead later on.'

'That's quite possible.'

'That's why I want to question him now.'

'Somebody shot him in the back, I tell you,' the interpreter said.

'Oh, for Chrisake,' the detective sergeant said, and put his notebook in his pocket.

Outside in the corridor the detective sergeant stood with the interpreter beside Mr. Frazer's wheeled chair.

'I suppose you think somebody shot him in the back too?'

'Yes,' Frazer said. 'Somebody shot him in the back. What's it to you?'

'Don't get sore,' the sergeant said. 'I wish I could talk spick.'

'Why don't you learn?'

'You don't have to get sore. I don't get any fun out of asking that spick questions. If I could talk spick it would be different.'

'You don't need to talk Spanish,' the interpreter said. 'I am a very reliable interpreter.'

'Oh, for Chrisake,' the sergeant said. 'Well, so long. I'll come up and see you.'

'Thanks. I'm always in.'

'I guess you are all right. That was bad luck all right. Plenty bad luck.'

'It's coming along good now since he spliced the bone.'

'Yes, but it's a long time. A long, long time.'

'Don't let anybody shoot you in the back.'

'That's right,' he said. 'That's right. Well, I'm glad you're not sore.'

'So long,' said Mr. Frazer.

Mr. Frazer did not see Cayetano again for a long time, but each morning Sister Cecilia brought news of him. He was so uncomplaining she said and he was very bad now. He had peritonitis and they thought he could not live. Poor Cayetano, she said. He had such beautiful hands and such a fine face and he never complains. The odor, now, was really terrific. He would point toward his nose with one finger and smile and shake his head, she said. He felt badly about the odor. It embarrassed him, Sister Cecilia said. Oh, he was such a fine patient. He always smiled. He wouldn't go to confession to Father but he promised to say his prayers, and not a Mexican had been to see him since he had been brought in. The Russian was going out at the end of the week. I could never feel anything about the Russian, Sister Cecilia said. Poor fellow, he suffered too. It was a greased bullet and dirty and the wound infected, but he made so much noise and then I always like the bad ones. That Cayetano, he's a bad one. Oh, he must really be a bad one, a thoroughly bad one, he's so fine and delicately made and he's never done any work with his hands. He's not a beet worker. I know he's not a beet worker. His hands are as smooth and not a callous on them. I know he's a bad one of some sort. I'm going down and pray for him now. Poor Cayetano, he's having a dreadful time and he doesn't make a sound. What did they have to shoot him for? Oh, that poor Cayetano! I'm going right down and pray for him.

She went right down and prayed for him.

In that hospital a radio did not work very well until it was dusk. They said it was because there was so much ore in the ground or something about the mountains, but anyway it did not work well at all until it began to get dark outside; but all night it worked beautifully and when one station stopped you could go farther west and pick up another. The last one that you could get was Seattle, Washington, and due to the difference in time, when they signed off at four o'clock in the morning it was five o'clock in the morning in the hospital; and at six o'clock you could get the morning revellers in Minneapolis. That was on account of the difference in time, too, and Mr. Frazer used to like to think of the morning revellers arriving at the studio and picture how they would look getting off a street-car before daylight in the morning carrying their instruments. Maybe that was wrong and they kept their instruments at the place they revelled, but he always pictured them with their instruments. He had never been in Minneapolis and believed he probably would never go there, but he knew what it looked like that early in the morning.

Out of the window of the hospital you could see a field with tumbleweed coming out of the snow, and a bare clay butte. One morning the doctor wanted to show Mr. Frazer two pheasants that were out there in the snow, and pulling the bed toward the window, the reading light fell off the iron bedstead and hit Mr. Frazer on the head. This does not sound so funny now but it was very funny then. Every one was looking out the window, and the doctor, who was a most excellent doctor, was pointing at the pheasants and pulling the bed toward the window, and then, just as in a comic section, Mr. Frazer was knocked out by the leaded base of the lamp hitting the top of his head. It seemed the antithesis of healing or whatever people were in the hospital for, and every one thought it was very funny, as a joke on Mr. Frazer and on the doctor. Everything is much simpler in a hospital, including the jokes.

From the other window, if the bed was turned, you could see the town, with a little smoke above it, and the Dawson mountains looking like real mountains with the winter snow on them. Those were the two views since the wheeled chair had proved to be premature. It is really best to be in bed if you are in a hospital; since two views, with time to observe them, from a room the temperature of which you control, are much better than any number of views seen for a few minutes from hot, empty rooms that are waiting for some one else, or just abandoned, which you are wheeled in and out of. If you stay long enough in a room the view, whatever it is, acquires a great value and becomes very important and you would not change it, not even by a different angle. Just as, with the radio, there are certain things that you become fond of, and you welcome them and resent the new things. The best tunes they had that winter were 'Sing Something Simple,' 'Singsong Girl,' and 'Little White Lies.' No other tunes were as satisfactory, Mr. Frazer felt. 'Betty Co-ed' was a good tune too, but the parody of the words which came unavoidably into Mr. Frazer's mind, grew so steadily and increasingly obscene that there being no one to appreciate it, he finally abandoned it and let the song go back to football.

About nine o'clock in the morning they would start using the X-ray machine, and then the radio, which, by then, was only getting Hailey, became useless. Many people in Hailey who owned radios protested about the hospital's X-ray machine which ruined their morning reception, but there was never any action taken, although many felt it was a shame the hospital could not use their machine at a time when people were not using their radios.

About the time when it became necessary to turn off the radio Sister Cecilia came in.

'How's Cayetano, Sister Cecilia?' Mr. Frazer asked.

'Oh, he's very bad.'

'Is he out of his head?'

'No, but I'm afraid he's going to die.'

'How are you?'

'I'm very worried about him, and do you know that absolutely no one has come to see him? He could die just like a dog for all those Mexicans care. They're really dreadful.'

'Do you want to come up and hear the game this afternoon?'

'Oh, no,' she said. 'I'd be too excited. I'll be in the chapel praying.'

'We ought to be able to hear it pretty well,' Mr. Frazer said. 'They're playing out on the coast and the difference in time will bring it late enough so we can get it all right.'

'Oh, no. I couldn't do it. The world series nearly finished me. When the Athletics were at bat I was praying right out loud: "Oh, Lord, direct their batting eyes! Oh, Lord, may he hit one! Oh, Lord, may he hit safely!" Then when they filled the bases in the third game, you remember, it was too much for me. "Oh, Lord, may he hit it out of the lot! Oh, Lord, may he drive it clean over the fence!" Then you know when the Cardinals would come to bat it was simply dreadful. "Oh, Lord, may they not see it! Oh, Lord, don't let them even catch a glimpse of it! Oh, Lord, may they fan!" And this game is even worse. It's Notre Dame. Our Lady. No, I'll be in the chapel. For Our Lady. They're playing for Our Lady. I wish you'd write something sometime for Our Lady. You could do it. You know you could do it, Mr. Frazer.'

'I don't know anything about her that I could write. It's mostly been written already,' Mr. Frazer said. 'You wouldn't like the way I write. She wouldn't care for it either.'

'You'll write about her sometime,' Sister said. 'I know you will. You must write about Our Lady.'

'You'd better come up and hear the game.'

'It would be too much for me. No, I'll be in the chapel doing what I can.'

That afternoon they had been playing about five minutes when a probationer came into the room and said, 'Sister Cecilia wants to know how the game is going?'

'Tell her they have a touchdown already.'

In a little while the probationer came into the room again.

'Tell her they're playing them off their feet,' Mr. Frazer said.

A little later he rang the bell for the nurse who was on floor duty. 'Would you mind going down to the chapel or sending word down to Sister Cecilia that Notre Dame has them fourteen to nothing at the end of the first quarter and that it's all right. She can stop praying.'

In a few minutes Sister Cecilia came into the room. She was very excited. 'What does fourteen to nothing mean? I don't know anything about this game. That's a nice safe lead in baseball. But I don't know anything about football. It may not mean a thing. I'm going right back down to the chapel and pray until it's finished.'

'They have them beaten,' Frazer said. 'I promise you. Stay and listen with me.'

'No. No. No. No. No. No. No,' she said. 'I'm going right down to the chapel to pray.'

Mr. Frazer sent down word whenever Notre Dame scored, and finally, when it had been dark a long time, the final result.

'How's Sister Cecilia?'

'They're all at chapel,' she said.

The next morning Sister Cecilia came in. She was very pleased and confident.

'I knew they couldn't beat Our Lady,' she said. 'They couldn't. Cayetano's better too. He's much better. He's going to have visitors. He can't see them yet, but they are going to come and that will make him feel better and know he's not forgotten by his own people. I went down and saw that O'Brien boy at Police Headquarters and told him that he's got to send some Mexicans up to see poor Cayetano. He's going to send some this afternoon. Then that poor man will feel better. It's wicked the way no one has come to see him.'

That afternoon about five o'clock three Mexicans came into the room.

'Can one?' asked the biggest one, who had very thick lips and was quite fat.

'Why not?' Mr. Frazer answered. 'Sit down, gentlemen. Will you take something?'

'Many thanks,' said the big one.

'Thanks,' said the darkest and smallest one.

'Thanks, no,' said the thin one. 'It mounts to my head.' He tapped his head.

The nurse brought some glasses. 'Please give them the bottle,' Frazer said. 'It is from Red Lodge,' he explained.

'That of Red Lodge is the best,' said the big one. 'Much better than that of Big Timber.'

'Clearly,' said the smallest one, 'and costs more too.'

'In Red Lodge it is of all prices,' said the big one.

'How many tubes has the radio?' asked the one who did not drink.

'Seven.'

'Very beautiful,' he said. 'What does it cost?'

'I don't know,' Mr. Frazer said. 'It is rented.'

'You gentlemen are friends of Cayetano?'

'No,' said the big one. 'We are friends of he who wounded him.'

'We were sent here by the police,' the smallest one said.

'We have a little place,' the big one said. 'He and I,' indicating the one who did not drink. 'He has a little place too,' indicating the small, dark one. 'The police tell us we have to come – so we come.'

'I am very happy you have come.'

'Equally,' said the big one.

'Will you have another little cup?'

'Why not?' said the big one.

'With your permission,' said the smallest one.

'Not me,' said the thin one. 'It mounts to my head.'

'It is very good,' said the smallest one.

'Why not try some,' Mr. Frazer asked the thin one. 'Let a little mount to your head.'

'Afterwards comes the headache,' said the thin one.

'Could you not send friends of Cayetano to see him?' Frazer asked.

'He has no friends.'

'Every man has friends.'

'This one, no.'

'What does he do?'

'He is a card-player.'

'Is he good?'

'I believe it.'

'From me,' said the smallest one, 'he won one hundred and eighty dollars. Now there is no longer one hundred and eighty dollars in the world.'

'From me,' said the thin one, 'he won two hundred and eleven dollars. Fix yourself on that figure.'

'I never played with him,' said the fat one.

'He must be very rich,' Mr. Frazer suggested.

'He is poorer than we,' said the little Mexican. 'He has no more than the shirt on his back.'

'And that shirt is of little value now,' Mr. Frazer said. 'Perforated as it is.'

'Clearly.'

'The one who wounded him was a card-player?'

'No, a beet worker. He has had to leave town.'

'Fix yourself on this,' said the smallest one. 'He was the best guitar player ever in this town. The finest.'

'What a shame.'

'I believe it,' said the biggest one. 'How he could touch the guitar.'

'There are no good guitar players left?'

'Not the shadow of a guitar player.'

'There is an accordion player who is worth something,' the thin man said.

'There are a few who touch various instruments,' the big one said. 'You like music?'

'How would I not?'

'We will come one night with music? You think the sister would allow it? She seems very amiable.'

'I am sure she would permit it when Cayetano is able to hear it.'

'Is she a little crazy?' asked the thin one.

'Who?'

'That sister.'

'No,' Mr. Frazer said. 'She is a fine woman of great intelligence and sympathy.'

'I distrust all priests, monks, and sisters,' said the thin one.

'He had bad experiences when a boy,' the smallest one said.

'I was acolyte,' the thin one said proudly. 'Now I believe in nothing. Neither do I go to mass.'

'Why? Does it mount to your head?'

'No,' said the thin one. 'It is alcohol that mounts to my head. Religion is the opium of the poor.'

'I thought marijuana was the opium of the poor,' Frazer said.

'Did you ever smoke opium?' the big one asked.

'No.'

'Nor I,' he said. 'It seems it is very bad. One commences and cannot stop. It is a vice.'

'Like religion,' said the thin one.

'This one,' said the smallest Mexican, 'is very strong against religion.'

'It is necessary to be very strong against something,' Mr. Frazer said politely.

'I respect those who have faith even though they are ignorant,' the thin one said.

'Good,' said Mr. Frazer.

'What can we bring you?' asked the big Mexican. 'Do you lack for anything?'

'I would be glad to buy some beer if there is good beer.'

'We will bring beer.'

'Another *copita* before you go?'

'It is very good.'

'We are robbing you.'

'I can't take it. It goes to my head. Then I have a bad headache and sick at the stomach.'

'Good-by, gentlemen.'

'Good-by and thanks.'

They went out and there was supper and then the radio, turned to be as quiet as possible and still be heard, and the stations finally signing off in this order: Denver, Salt Lake City, Los Angeles, and Seattle. Mr. Frazer received no picture of Denver from the radio. He could see Denver from the *Denver Post*, and correct the picture from *The Rocky Mountain News*. Nor did he ever have any feel of Salt Lake City or Los Angeles from what he heard from those places. All he felt about Salt Lake City was that it was clean, but dull, and there were too many ballrooms mentioned in too many big hotels for him to see Los Angeles. He could not feel it for the ballrooms. But Seattle he came to know very well, the taxicab company with the big white cabs (each cab equipped with radio itself) he rode in every night out to the roadhouse on the Canadian side where he followed the course of parties by the musical selections they phoned for. He lived in Seattle from two o'clock on, each night, hearing the pieces that all the different people asked for, and it was as real as Minneapolis, where the revellers left their beds each morning to make that trip down to the studio. Mr. Frazer grew very fond of Seattle, Washington.

The Mexicans came and brought beer but it was not good beer. Mr. Frazer saw them but he did not feel like talking, and when they went he knew they would not come again. His nerves had become tricky and he disliked seeing people while he was in this condition. His nerves went bad at the end of five weeks, and while he was pleased they lasted that long yet he resented being forced to make the same experiment when he already knew the answer. Mr. Frazer had been through this all before. The only thing which was new to him was the radio. He played it all night long, turned so low he could barely hear it, and he was learning to listen to it without thinking.

Sister Cecilia came into the room about ten o'clock in the morning on that day and brought the mail. She was very handsome, and Mr. Frazer liked to see her and to hear her talk, but the mail, supposedly coming from a different world, was more important. However, there was nothing in the mail of any interest.

'You look *so* much better,' she said. 'You'll be leaving us soon.'

'Yes,' Mr. Frazer said. 'You look very happy this morning.'

'Oh, I am. This morning I feel as though I might be a saint.'

Mr. Frazer was a little taken aback at this.

'Yes,' Sister Cecilia went on. 'That's what I want to be. A saint. Ever since I was a little girl I've wanted to be a saint. When I was a girl I thought if I renounced the world and went into the convent I would be a saint. That was what I wanted to be and that was what I thought I had to do to be one. I expected I would be a saint. I was absolutely sure I would be one. For just a moment I thought I was one. I was so happy and it seemed so simple and easy. When I awoke in the morning I expected I would be a saint, but I wasn't. I've never become one. I want so to be one. All I want is to be a saint. That is all I've ever wanted. And this morning I feel as though I might be one. Oh, I hope I will get to be one.'

'You'll be one. Everybody gets what they want. That's what they always tell me.'

'I don't know now. When I was a girl it seemed so simple. I knew I would be a saint. Only I believed it took time when I found it did not happen suddenly. Now it seems almost impossible.'

'I'd say you had a good chance.'

'Do you really think so? No, I don't want just to be encouraged. Don't just encourage me. I want to be a saint. I want so to be a saint.'

'Of course you'll be a saint,' Mr. Frazer said.

'No, probably I won't be. But, oh, if I could only be a saint! I'd be perfectly happy.'

'You're three to one to be a saint.'

'No, don't encourage me. But, oh, if I could only be a saint! If I could only be a saint!'

'How's your friend Cayetano?'

'He's going to get well but he's paralyzed. One of the bullets hit the big nerve that goes down through his thigh and that leg is paralyzed. They only found it out when he got well enough so that he could move.'

'Maybe the nerve will regenerate.'

'I'm praying that it will,' Sister Cecilia said. 'You ought to see him.'

'I don't feel like seeing anybody.'

'You know you'd like to see him. They could wheel him in here.'

'All right.'

They wheeled him in, thin, his skin transparent, his hair black and needing to be cut, his eyes very laughing, his teeth bad when he smiled.

'*Hola, amigo! Qué tal?*'

'As you see,' said Mr. Frazer. 'And thou?'

'Alive and with the leg paralyzed.'

'Bad,' Mr. Frazer said. 'But the nerve can regenerate and be as good as new.'

'So they tell me.'

'What about the pain?'

'Not now. For a while I was crazy with it in the belly. I thought the pain alone would kill me.'

Sister Cecilia was observing them happily.

'She tells me you never made a sound,' Mr. Frazer said.

'So many people in the ward,' the Mexican said deprecatingly. 'What class of pain do you have?'

'Big enough. Clearly not as bad as yours. When the nurse goes out I cry an hour, two hours. It rests me. My nerves are bad now.'

'You have the radio. If I had a private room and a radio I would be crying and yelling all night long.'

'I doubt it.'

'*Hombre, sí.* It's very healthy. But you cannot do it with so many people.'

'At least,' Mr. Frazer said, 'the hands are still good. They tell me you make your living with the hands.'

'And the head,' he said, tapping his forehead. 'But the head isn't worth as much.'

'Three of your countrymen were here.'

'Sent by the police to see me.'

'They brought some beer.'

'It probably was bad.'

'It was bad.'

'Tonight, sent by the police, they come to serenade me.' He laughed, then tapped his stomach. 'I cannot laugh yet. As musicians they are fatal.'

'And the one who shot you?'

'Another fool. I won thirty-eight dollars from him at cards. That is not to kill about.'

'The three told me you win much money.'

'And am poorer than the birds.'

'How?'

'I am a poor idealist. I am the victim of illusions.' He laughed, then grinned and tapped his stomach. 'I am a professional gambler but I like to gamble. To really gamble. Little gambling is all crooked. For real gambling you need luck. I have no luck.'

'Never?'

'Never. I am completely without luck. Look, this *cabrón* who shoots me just now. Can he shoot? No. The first shot he fires into nothing. The second is intercepted by a poor Russian. That would seem to be luck. What happens? He shoots me twice in the belly. He is a lucky man. I have no luck. He could not hit a horse if he were holding the stirrup. All luck.'

'I thought he shot you first and the Russian after.'

'No, the Russian first, me after. The paper was mistaken.'

'Why didn't you shoot him?'

'I never carry a gun. With my luck, if I carried a gun I would be hanged ten times a year. I am a cheap card player, only that.' He stopped, then continued. 'When I make a sum of money I gamble and when I gamble I lose. I have passed at dice for three thousand dollars and crapped out for the six. With good dice. More than once.'

'Why continue?'

'If I live long enough the luck will change. I have bad luck now for fifteen years. If I ever get any good luck I will be rich.'

He grinned. 'I am a good gambler, really I would enjoy being rich.'

'Do you have bad luck with all games?'

'With everything and with women.' He smiled again, showing his bad teeth.

'Truly?'

'Truly.'

'And what is there to do?'

'Continue, slowly, and wait for luck to change.'

'But with women?'

'No gambler has luck with women. He is too concentrated. He works nights. When he should be with the woman. No man who works nights can hold a woman if the woman is worth anything.'

'You are a philosopher.'

'No, hombre. A gambler of the small towns. One small town, then another, another, then a big town, then start over again.'

'Then shot in the belly.'

'The first time,' he said. 'That has only happened once.'

'I tire you talking?' Mr. Frazer suggested.

'No,' he said. 'I must tire you.'

'And the leg?'

'I have no great use for the leg. I am all right with the leg or not. I will be able to circulate.'

'I wish you luck, truly, and with all my heart,' Mr. Frazer said.

'Equally,' he said. 'And that the pain stops.'

'It will not last, certainly. It is passing. It is of no importance.'

'That it passes quickly.'

'Equally.'

That night the Mexicans played the accordion and other instruments in the ward and it was cheerful and the noise of the inhalations and exhalations of the accordion, and of the bells, the traps, and the drum came down the corridor. In that ward there was a rodeo rider who had come out of the chutes on Midnight on a hot dusty afternoon with the big crowd watching, and now, with a broken back, was going to learn to work in leather and to cane chairs when he got well enough to leave the hospital. There was a carpenter who had fallen with a scaffolding and broken both ankles and both wrists. He had lit like a cat but without a cat's resiliency. They could fix him up so that he could work again but it would take a long time. There was a boy from

a farm, about sixteen years old, with a broken leg that had been
badly set and was to be rebroken. There was Cayetano Ruiz, a
small-town gambler with a paralyzed leg. Down the corridor
Mr. Frazer could hear them all laughing and merry with the
music made by the Mexicans who had been sent by the police.
The Mexicans were having a good time. They came in, very
excited, to see Mr. Frazer and wanted to know if there was anything he wanted them to play, and they came twice more to play
at night of their own accord.

The last time they played Mr. Frazer lay in his room with the
door open and listened to the noisy, bad music and could not
keep from thinking. When they wanted to know what he
wished played, he asked for the Cucaracha, which has the sinister lightness and deftness of so many of the tunes men have gone
to die to. They played noisily and with emotion. The tune was
better than most of such tunes, to Mr. Frazer's mind, but the
effect was all the same.

In spite of this introduction of emotion, Mr. Frazer went on
thinking. Usually he avoided thinking all he could, except when
he was writing, but now he was thinking about those who were
playing and what the little one had said.

Religion is the opium of the people. He believed that, that
dyspeptic little joint-keeper. Yes, and music is the opium of the
people. Old mount-to-the-head hadn't thought of that. And
now economics is the opium of the people; along with patriotism the opium of the people in Italy and Germany. What about
sexual intercourse; was that an opium of the people? Of some of
the people. Of some of the best of the people. But drink was a
sovereign opium of the people, oh, an excellent opium. Although some prefer the radio, another opium of the people, a
cheap one he had just been using. Along with these went gambling, an opium of the people if there ever was one, one of the
oldest. Ambition was another, an opium of the people, along
with a belief in any new form of government. What you wanted
was the minimum of government, always less government. Liberty, what we believed in, now the name of a MacFadden publication. We believed in that although they had not found a new
name for it yet. But what was the real one? What was the real,
the actual, opium of the people? He knew it very well. It was
gone just a little way around the corner in that well-lighted part
of his mind that was there after two or more drinks in the evening; that he knew was there (it was not really there of course).

What was it? He knew very well. What was it? Of course; bread was the opium of the people. Would he remember that and would it make sense in the daylight? Bread is the opium of the people.

'Listen,' Mr. Frazer said to the nurse when she came. 'Get that little thin Mexican in here, will you, please?'

'How do you like it?' the Mexican said at the door.

'Very much.'

'It is a historic tune,' the Mexican said. 'It is the tune of the real revolution.'

'Listen,' said Mr. Frazer. 'Why should the people be operated on without an anæsthetic?'

'I do not understand.'

'Why are not all the opiums of the people good? What do you want to do with the people?'

'They should be rescued from ignorance.'

'Don't talk nonsense. Education is an opium of the people. You ought to know that. You've had a little.'

'You do not believe in education?'

'No,' said Mr. Frazer. 'In knowledge, yes.'

'I do not follow you.'

'Many times I do not follow myself with pleasure.'

'You want to hear the Cucaracha another time?' asked the Mexican worriedly.

'Yes,' said Mr. Frazer. 'Play the Cucaracha another time. It's better than the radio.'

Revolution, Mr. Frazer thought, is no opium. Revolution is a catharsis; an ecstasy which can only be prolonged by tyranny. The opiums are for before and for after. He was thinking well, a little too well.

They would go now in a little while, he thought, and they would take the Cucaracha with them. Then he would have a little spot of the giant killer and play the radio, you could play the radio so that you could hardly hear it.

FATHERS AND SONS

There had been a sign to detour in the center of the main street of this town, but cars had obviously gone through, so, believing it was some repair which had been completed, Nicholas Adams drove on through the town along the empty, brick-paved street, stopped by traffic lights that flashed on and off on this traffic-less Sunday, and would be gone next year when the payments on the system were not met; on under the heavy trees of the small town that are a part of your heart if it is your town and you have walked under them, but that are only too heavy, that shut out the sun and that dampen the houses for a stranger; out past the last house and onto the highway that rose and fell straight away ahead with banks of red dirt sliced cleanly away and the second-growth timber on both sides. It was not his country but it was the middle of fall and all of this country was good to drive through and to see. The cotton was picked and in the clearings there were patches of corn, some cut with streaks of red sorghum, and, driving easily, his son asleep on the seat by his side, the day's run made, knowing the town he would reach for the night, Nick noticed which corn fields had soy beans or peas in them, how the thickets and the cut-over land lay, where the cabins and houses were in relation to the fields and the thickets; hunting the country in his mind as he went by; sizing up each clearing as to feed and cover and figuring where you would find a covey and which way they would fly.

In shooting quail you must not get between them and their habitual cover, once the dogs have found them, or when they flush they will come pouring at you, some rising steep, some skimming by your ears, whirring into a size you have never seen them in the air as they pass, the only way being to turn and take them over your shoulder as they go, before they set their wings and angle down into the thicket. Hunting this country for quail as his father had taught him, Nicholas Adams started thinking about his father. When he first thought about him it was always the eyes. The big frame, the quick movements, the wide shoulders, the hooked, hawk nose, the beard that covered the weak chin, you never thought about – it was always the eyes. They were protected in his head by the formation of the brows; set deep as though a special protection had been devised for some very valuable instrument. They saw much farther and much quicker than the human eye sees and they were the great gift his father had. His father saw as a big-horn ram or as an eagle sees, literally.

He would be standing with his father on one shore of the lake, his own eyes were very good then, and his father would say, 'They've run up the flag.' Nick could not see the flag or the flag pole. 'There,' his father would say, 'it's your sister Dorothy. She's got the flag up and she's walking out onto the dock.'

Nick would look across the lake and he could see the long wooded shore-line, the higher timber behind, the point that guarded the bay, the clear hills of the farm and the white of their cottage in the trees but he could not see any flag pole, or any dock, only the white of the beach and the curve of the shore.

'Can you see the sheep on the hillside toward the point?'

'Yes.'

They were a whitish patch on the gray-green of the hill.

'I can count them,' his father said.

Like all men with a faculty that surpasses human requirements, his father was very nervous. Then, too, he was sentimental, and, like most sentimental people, he was both cruel and abused. Also, he had much bad luck, and it was not all of it his own. He had died in a trap that he had helped only a little to set, and they had all betrayed him in their various ways before he died. All sentimental people are betrayed so many times. Nick could not write about him yet, although he would, later, but the quail country made him remember him as he was when Nick was a boy and he was very grateful to him for two things: fishing and shooting. His father was as sound on those two things as he was unsound on sex, for instance, and Nick was glad that it had been that way; for some one has to give you your first gun or the opportunity to get it and use it, and you have to live where there is game or fish if you are to learn about them, and now, at thirty-eight, he loved to fish and to shoot exactly as much as when he first had gone with his father. It was a passion that had never slackened and he was very grateful to his father for bringing him to know it.

While for the other, that his father was not sound about, all the equipment you will ever have is provided and each man learns all there is for him to know about it without advice; and it makes no difference where you live. He remembered very clearly the only two pieces of information his father had given

him about that. Once when they were out shooting together
Nick shot a red squirrel out of a hemlock tree. The squirrel fell,
wounded, and when Nick picked him up bit the boy clean
through the ball of the thumb.

'The dirty little bugger,' Nick said and smacked the squirrel's
head against the tree. 'Look how he bit me.'

His father looked and said, 'Suck it out clean and put some
iodine on when you get home.'

'The little bugger,' Nick said.

'Do you know what a bugger is?' his father asked him.

'We call anything a bugger,' Nick said.

'A bugger is a man who has intercourse with animals.'

'Why?' Nick said.

'I don't know,' his father said. 'But it is a heinous crime.'

Nick's imagination was both stirred and horrified by this and
he thought of various animals but none seemed attractive or
practical and that was the sum total of direct sexual knowledge
bequeathed him by his father except on one other subject. One
morning he read in the paper that Enrico Caruso had been arrested for mashing.

'What is mashing?'

'It is one of the most heinous of crimes,' his father answered.
Nick's imagination pictured the great tenor doing something
strange, bizarre, and heinous with a potato masher to a beautiful
lady who looked like the pictures of Anna Held on the inside of
cigar boxes. He resolved, with considerable horror, that when
he was old enough he would try mashing at least once.

His father had summed up the whole matter by stating that
masturbation produced blindness, insanity, and death, while a
man who went with prostitutes would contract hideous venereal
diseases and that the thing to do was to keep your hands off of
people. On the other hand his father had the finest pair of eyes
he had ever seen and Nick had loved him very much and for a
long time. Now, knowing how it had all been, even remembering the earliest times before things had gone badly was not good
remembering. If he wrote it he could get rid of it. He had gotten
rid of many things by writing them. But it was still too early for
that. There were still too many people. So he decided to think
of something else. There was nothing to do about his father and
he had thought it all through many times. The handsome job the
undertaker had done on his father's face had not blurred in his
mind and all the rest of it was quite clear, including the respon-

sibilities. He had complimented the undertaker. The undertaker had been both proud and smugly pleased. But it was not the undertaker that had given him that last face. The undertaker had only made certain dashingly executed repairs of doubtful artistic merit. The face had been making itself and being made for a long time. It had modelled fast in the last three years. It was a good story but there were still too many people alive for him to write it.

Nick's own education in those earlier matters had been acquired in the hemlock woods behind the Indian camp. This was reached by a trail which ran from the cottage through the woods to the farm and then by a road which wound through the slashings to the camp. Now if he could still feel all of that trail with bare feet. First there was the pine-needle loam through the hemlock woods behind the cottage where the fallen logs crumbled into wood dust and long splintered pieces of wood hung like javelins in the tree that had been struck by lightning. You crossed the creek on a log and if you stepped off there was the black muck of the swamp. You climbed a fence out of the woods and the trail was hard in the sun across the field with cropped grass and sheep sorrel and mullen growing and to the left the quaky bog of the creek bottom where the killdeer plover fed. The spring house was in that creek. Below the barn there was fresh warm manure and the other older manure that was caked dry on top. Then there was another fence and the hard, hot trail from the barn to the house and the hot sandy road that ran down to the woods, crossing the creek, on a bridge this time, where the cat-tails grew that you soaked in kerosene to make jacklights with for spearing fish at night.

Then the main road went off to the left, skirting the woods and climbing the hill, while you went into the woods on the wide clay and shale road, cool under the trees, and broadened for them to skid out the hemlock bark the Indians cut. The hemlock bark was piled in long rows of stacks, roofed over with more bark, like houses, and the peeled logs lay huge and yellow where the trees had been felled. They left the logs in the woods to rot, they did not even clear away or burn the tops. It was only the bark they wanted for the tannery at Boyne City; hauling it across the lake on the ice in winter, and each year there was less forest and more open, hot, shadeless, weed-grown slashing.

But there was still much forest then, virgin forest where the trees grew high before there were any branches and you walked on the brown, clean, springy-needled ground with no undergrowth and it was cool on the hottest days and they three lay against the trunk of a hemlock wider than two beds are long, with the breeze high in the tops and the cool light that came in patches, and Billy said:

'You want Trudy again?'

'You want to?'

'Un Huh.'

'Come on.'

'No, here.'

'But Billy –'

'I no mind Billy. He my brother.'

Then afterwards they sat, the three of them, listening for a black squirrel that was in the top branches where they could not see him. They were waiting for him to bark again because when he barked he would jerk his tail and Nick would shoot where he saw any movement. His father gave him only three cartridges a day to hunt with and he had a single-barrel twenty-gauge shotgun with a very long barrel.

'Son of a bitch never move,' Billy said.

'You shoot, Nickie. Scare him. We see him jump. Shoot him again,' Trudy said. It was a long speech for her.

'I've only got two shells,' Nick said.

'Son of a bitch,' said Billy.

They sat against the tree and were quiet. Nick was feeling hollow and happy.

'Eddie says he going to come some night sleep in bed with you sister Dorothy.'

'What?'

'He said.'

Trudy nodded.

'That's all he want do,' she said. Eddie was their older half-brother. He was seventeen.

'If Eddie Gilby ever comes at night and even speaks to Dorothy you know what I'd do to him? I'd kill him like this.' Nick cocked the gun and hardly taking aim pulled the trigger, blowing a hole as big as your hand in the head or belly of that half-breed bastard Eddie Gilby. 'Like that. I'd kill him like that.'

'He better not come then,' Trudy said. She put her hand in Nick's pocket.

'He better watch out plenty,' said Billy.

'He's big bluff,' Trudy was exploring with her hand in Nick's pocket. 'But don't you kill him. You get plenty trouble.'

'I'd kill him like that,' Nick said. Eddie Gilby lay on the ground with all his chest shot away. Nick put his foot on him proudly.

'I'd scalp him,' he said happily.

'No,' said Trudy. 'That's dirty.'

'I'd scalp him and send it to his mother.'

'His mother dead,' Trudy said. 'Don't you kill him, Nickie. Don't you kill him for me.'

'After I scalped him I'd throw him to the dogs.'

Billy was very depressed. 'He better watch out,' he said gloomily.

'They'd tear him to pieces,' Nick said, pleased with the picture. Then, having scalped that half-breed renegade and standing, watching the dogs tear him, his face unchanging, he fell backward against the tree, held tight around the neck, Trudy holding, choking him, and crying, 'No kill him! No kill him! No kill him! No. No. No. Nickie. Nickie. Nickie!'

'What's the matter with you?'

'No kill him.'

'I got to kill him.'

'He just a big bluff.'

'All right,' Nickie said. 'I won't kill him unless he comes around the house. Let go of me.'

'That's good,' Trudy said. 'You want to do anything now? I feel good now.'

'If Billy goes away.' Nick had killed Eddie Gilby, then pardoned him his life, and he was a man now.

'You go, Billy. You hang around all the time. Go on.'

'Son a bitch,' Billy said. 'I get tired this. What we come? Hunt or what?'

'You can take the gun. There's one shell.'

'All right. I get a big black one all right.'

'I'll holler,' Nick said.

Then, later, it was a long time after and Billy was still away.

'You think we make a baby?' Trudy folded her brown legs together happily and rubbed against him. Something inside Nick had gone a long way away.

'I don't think so,' he said.

'Make plenty baby what the hell.'

They heard Billy shoot.

'I wonder if he got one.'

'Don't care,' said Trudy.

Billy came through the trees. He had the gun over his shoulder and he held a black squirrel by the front paws.

'Look,' he said. 'Bigger than a cat. You all through?'

'Where'd you get him?'

'Over there. Saw him jump first.'

'Got to go home,' Nick said.

'No,' said Trudy.

'I got to get there for supper.'

'All right.'

'Want to hunt tomorrow?'

'All right.'

'You can have the squirrel.'

'All right.'

'Come out after supper?'

'No.'

'How you feel?'

'Good.'

'All right.'

'Give me kiss on the face,' said Trudy.

Now, as he rode along the highway in the car and it was getting dark, Nick was all through thinking about his father. The end of the day never made him think of him. The end of the day had always belonged to Nick alone and he never felt right unless he was alone at it. His father came back to him in the fall of the year, or in the early spring when there had been jacksnipe on the prairie, or when he saw shocks of corn, or when he saw a lake, or if he ever saw a horse and buggy, or when he saw, or heard, wild geese, or in a duck blind; remembering the time an eagle dropped through the whirling snow to strike a canvas-covered decoy, rising, his wings beating, the talons caught in the canvas. His father was with him, suddenly, in deserted orchards and in new-plowed fields, in thickets, on small hills, or when going through dead grass, whenever splitting wood or hauling water, by grist mills, cider mills and dams and always with open fires. The towns he lived in were not towns his father knew. After he was fifteen he had shared nothing with him.

His father had frost in his beard in cold weather and in hot weather he sweated very much. He liked to work in the sun on the farm because he did not have to and he loved manual work, which Nick did not. Nick loved his father but hated the smell of him and once when he had to wear a suit of his father's underwear that had gotten too small for his father it made him feel sick and he took it off and put it under two stones in the creek and said that he had lost it. He had told his father how it was when his father had made him put it on but his father had said it was freshly washed. It had been, too. When Nick had asked him to smell of it his father sniffed at it indignantly and said that it was clean and fresh. When Nick came home from fishing without it and said he lost it he was whipped for lying.

Afterwards he had sat inside the woodshed with the door open, his shotgun loaded and cocked, looking across at his father sitting on the screen porch reading the paper, and thought, 'I can blow him to hell. I can kill him.' Finally he felt his anger go out of him and he felt a little sick about it being the gun that his father had given him. Then he had gone to the Indian camp, walking there in the dark, to get rid of the smell. There was only one person in his family that he liked the smell of; one sister. All the others he avoided all contact with. That sense blunted when he started to smoke. It was a good thing. It was good for a bird dog but it did not help a man.

'What was it like, Papa, when you were a little boy and used to hunt with the Indians?'

'I don't know,' Nick was startled. He had not even noticed the boy was awake. He looked at him sitting beside him on the seat. He had felt quite alone but this boy had been with him. He wondered for how long. 'We used to go all day to hunt black squirrels,' he said. 'My father only gave me three shells a day because he said that would teach me to hunt and it wasn't good for a boy to go banging around. I went with a boy named Billy Gilby and his sister Trudy. We used to go out nearly every day all one summer.'

'Those are funny names for Indians.'

'Yes, aren't they,' Nick said.

'But tell me what they were like.'

'They were Ojibways,' Nick said. 'And they were very nice.'

'But what were they like to be with?'

'It's hard to say,' Nick Adams said. Could you say she did first what no one has ever done better and mention plump brown legs, flat belly, hard little breasts, well holding arms, quick searching tongue, the flat eyes, the good taste of mouth, then uncomfortably, tightly, sweetly, moistly, lovely, tightly, achingly, fully, finally, unendingly, never-endingly, never-to-endingly, suddenly ended, the great bird flown like an owl in the twilight, only it was daylight in the woods and hemlock needles stuck against your belly. So that when you go in a place where Indians have lived you smell them gone and all the empty pain killer bottles and the flies that buzz do not kill the sweetgrass smell, the smoke smell and that other like a fresh cased marten skin. Nor any jokes about them nor old squaws take that away. Nor the sick sweet smell they get to have. Nor what they did finally. It wasn't how they ended. They all ended the same. Long time ago good. Now no good.

And about the other. When you have shot one bird flying you have shot all birds flying. They are all different and they fly in different ways but the sensation is the same and the last one is as good as the first. He could thank his father for that.

'You might not like them,' Nick said to the boy. 'But I think you would.'

'And my grandfather lived with them too when he was a boy, didn't he?'

'Yes. When I asked him what they were like he said that he had many friends among them.'

'Will I ever live with them?'

'I don't know,' Nick said. 'That's up to you.'

'How old will I be when I get a shotgun and can hunt by myself?'

'Twelve years old if I see you are careful.'

'I wish I was twelve now.'

'You will be, soon enough.'

'What was my grandfather like? I can't remember him except that he gave me an air rifle and an American flag when I came over from France that time. What was he like?'

'He's hard to describe. He was a great hunter and fisherman and he had wonderful eyes.'

'Was he greater than you?'

'He was a much better shot and his father was a great wing shot too.'

'I'll bet he wasn't better than you.'

'Oh, yes he was. He shot very quickly and beautifully. I'd rather see him shoot than any man I ever knew. He was always very disappointed in the way I shot.'

'Why do we never go to pray at the tomb of my grandfather?'

'We live in a different part of the country. It's a long way from here.'

'In France that wouldn't make any difference. In France we'd go. I think I ought to go to pray at the tomb of my grandfather.'

'Sometime we'll go.'

'I hope we won't live somewhere so that I can never go to pray at your tomb when you are dead.'

'We'll have to arrange it.'

'Don't you think we might all be buried at a convenient place? We could all be buried in France. That would be fine.'

'I don't want to be buried in France,' Nick said.

'Well, then, we'll have to get some convenient place in America. Couldn't we all be buried out at the ranch?'

'That's an idea.'

'Then I could stop and pray at the tomb of my grandfather on the way to the ranch.'

'You're awfully practical.'

'Well, I don't feel good never to have even visited the tomb of my grandfather.'

'We'll have to go,' Nick said. 'I can see we'll have to go.'

From THE FIFTH COLUMN
AND THE FIRST
FORTY-NINE STORIES

THE CAPITAL OF THE WORLD

Madrid is full of boys named Paco, which is the diminutive of the name Francisco, and there is a Madrid joke about a father who came to Madrid and inserted an advertisement in the personal columns of *El Liberal* which said: PACO MEET ME AT HOTEL MONTANA NOON TUESDAY ALL IS FORGIVEN PAPA and how a squadron of Guardia Civil had to be called out to disperse the eight hundred young men who answered the advertisement. But this Paco, who waited on table at the Pension Luarca, had no father to forgive him, nor anything for the father to forgive. He had two older sisters who were chambermaids at the Luarca, who had gotten their place through coming from the same small village as a former Luarca chambermaid who had proven hardworking and honest and hence given her village and its products a good name; and these sisters had paid his way on the auto-bus to Madrid and gotten him his job as an apprentice waiter. He came from a village in a part of Extramadura where conditions were incredibly primitive, food scarce, and comforts unknown and he had worked hard ever since he could remember.

He was a well built boy with very black, rather curly hair, good teeth and a skin that his sisters envied, and he had a ready and unpuzzled smile. He was fast on his feet and did his work well and he loved his sisters, who seemed beautiful and sophisticated; he loved Madrid, which was still an unbelievable place, and he loved his work which, done under bright lights, with clean linen, the wearing of evening clothes, and abundant food in the kitchen, seemed romantically beautiful.

There were from eight to a dozen other people who lived at the Luarca and ate in the dining room but for Paco, the youngest of the three waiters who served at table, the only ones who really existed were the bullfighters.

Second-rate matadors lived at that pension because the address in the Calle San Jerónimo was good, the food was excellent and the room and board was cheap. It is necessary for a bullfighter to give the appearance, if not of prosperity, at least of respectability, since decorum and dignity rank above courage as the virtues most highly prized in Spain, and bullfighters stayed at the Luarca until their last pesetas were gone. There is no record of any bullfighter having left the Luarca for a better or more expensive hotel; second-rate bullfighters never became first rate; but the descent from the Luarca was swift since any one could stay there who was making anything at all and a bill was never presented to a guest unasked until the woman who ran the place knew that the case was hopeless.

At this time there were three full matadors living at the Luarca as well as two very good picadors, and one excellent *banderillero*. The Luarca was luxury for the picadors and the *banderilleros* who, with their families in Seville, required lodging in Madrid during the Spring season; but they were well paid and in the fixed employ of fighters who were heavily contracted during the coming season and the three of these subalterns would probably make much more apiece than any of the three matadors. Of the three matadors one was ill and trying to conceal it; one had passed his short vogue as a novelty; and the third was a coward.

The coward had at one time, until he had received a peculiarly atrocious horn wound in the lower abdomen at the start of his first season as a full matador, been exceptionally brave and remarkably skillful and he still had many of the hearty mannerisms of his days of success. He was jovial to excess and laughed constantly with and without provocation. He had, when successful, been very addicted to practical jokes but he had given them up now. They took an assurance that he did not feel. This matador had an intelligent, very open face and he carried himself with much style.

The matador who was ill was careful never to show it and was meticulous about eating a little of all the dishes that were presented at the table. He had a great many handkerchiefs which he laundered himself in his room and, lately, he had been selling his fighting suits. He had sold one, cheaply, before Christmas and another in the first week of April. They had been very expensive suits, had always been well kept and he had one more. Before he had become ill he had been a very promising, even a sensational, fighter and, while he himself could not read, he had clippings which said that in his debut in Madrid he had been better than Belmonte. He ate alone at a small table and looked up very little.

The matador who had once been a novelty was very short and brown and very dignified. He also ate alone at a separate table and he smiled very rarely and never laughed. He came from Valladolid, where the people are extremely serious, and he was a capable matador; but his style had become old-fashioned before he had ever succeeded in endearing himself to the public through his virtues, which were courage and a calm capability, and his name on a poster would draw no one to a bull ring. His novelty had been that he was so short that he could barely see over the bull's withers, but there were other short fighters, and he had never succeeded in imposing himself on the public's fancy.

Of the picadors one was a thin, hawk-faced, gray-haired man, lightly built but with legs and arms like iron, who always wore cattlemen's boots under his trousers, drank too much every evening and gazed amorously at any woman in the pension. The other was huge, dark, brown-faced, good-looking, with black hair like an Indian and enormous hands. Both were great picadors although the first was reputed to have lost much of his ability through drink and dissipation, and the second was said to be too headstrong and quarrelsome to stay with any matador more than a single season.

The *banderillero* was middle-aged, gray, cat-quick in spite of his years and, sitting at the table he looked a moderately prosperous business man. His legs were still good for this season, and when they should go he was intelligent and experienced enough to keep regularly employed for a long time. The difference would be that when his speed of foot would be gone he would always be frightened where now he was assured and calm in the ring and out of it.

On this evening every one had left the dining room except the hawk-faced picador who drank too much, the birthmarked-faced auctioneer of watches at the fairs and festivals of Spain, who also drank too much, and two priests from Galicia who were sitting at a corner table and drinking if not too much certainly enough. At that time wine was included in the price of the room and board at the Luarca and the waiters had just brought fresh bottles of Valdepeñas to the tables of the auctioneer, then to the picador and, finally, to the two priests.

The three waiters stood at the end of the room. It was the rule of the house that they should all remain on duty until the diners whose tables they were responsible for should all have left, but the one who served the table of the two priests had an appointment to go to an Anarcho-Syndicalist meeting and Paco had agreed to take over his table for him.

Upstairs the matador who was ill was lying face down on his bed alone. The matador who was no longer a novelty was sitting looking out of his window preparatory to walking out to the café. The matador who was a coward had the older sister of Paco in his room with him and was trying to get her to do something which she was laughingly refusing to do. This matador was saying 'Come on, little savage.'

'No,' said the sister. 'Why should I?'

'For a favor.'

'You've eaten and now you want me for dessert.'

'Just once. What harm can it do?'

'Leave me alone. Leave me alone, I tell you.'

'It is a very little thing to do.'

'Leave me alone, I tell you.'

Down in the dining room the tallest of the waiters, who was overdue at the meeting, said 'Look at those black pigs drink.'

'That's no way to speak,' said the second waiter. 'They are decent clients. They do not drink too much.'

'For me it is a good way to speak,' said the tall one. 'There are the two curses of Spain, the bulls and the priests.'

'Certainly not the individual bull and the individual priest,' said the second waiter.

'Yes,' said the tall waiter. 'Only through the individual can you attack the class. It is necessary to kill the individual bull and the individual priest. All of them. Then there are no more.'

'Save it for the meeting,' said the other waiter.

'Look at the barbarity of Madrid,' said the tall waiter. 'It is now half-past eleven o'clock and these are still guzzling.'

'They only started to eat at ten,' said the other waiter. 'As you know there are many dishes. That wine is cheap and these have paid for it. It is not a strong wine.'

'How can there be solidarity of workers with fools like you?' asked the tall waiter.

'Look,' said the second waiter who was a man of fifty. 'I have worked all my life. In all that remains of my life I must work. I have no complaints against work. To work is normal.'

'Yes, but the lack of work kills.'

'I have always worked,' said the older waiter. 'Go on to the meeting. There is no necessity to stay.'

'You are a good comrade,' said the tall waiter. 'But you lack all ideology.'

'*Mejor si me falta eso que el otro*,' said the older waiter (meaning it is better to lack that than work). 'Go on to the *mitin*.'

Paco had said nothing. He did not yet understand politics but it always gave him a thrill to hear the tall waiter speak of the necessity for killing the priests and the Guardia Civil. The tall waiter represented to him revolution and revolution also was romantic. He himself would like to be a good Catholic, a revolutionary, and have a steady job like this, while, at the same time, being a bullfighter.

'Go on to the meeting, Ignacio,' he said. 'I will respond for your work.'

'The two of us,' said the older waiter.

'There isn't enough for one,' said Paco. 'Go on to the meeting.'

'*Pues, me voy*,' said the tall waiter. 'And thanks.'

In the meantime, upstairs, the sister of Paco had gotten out of the embrace of the matador as skilfully as a wrestler breaking a hold and said, now angry, 'These are the hungry people. A failed bullfighter. With your ton-load of fear. If you have so much of that, use it in the ring.'

'That is the way a whore talks.'

'A whore is also a woman, but I am not a whore.'

'You'll be one.'

'Not through you.'

'Leave me,' said the matador who, now, repulsed and refused, felt the nakedness of his cowardice returning.

'Leave you? What hasn't left you?' said the sister. 'Don't you want me to make up the bed? I'm paid to do that.'

'Leave me,' said the matador, his broad good-looking face wrinkled into a contortion that was like crying. 'You whore. You dirty little whore.'

'Matador,' she said, shutting the door. 'My matador.'

Inside the room the matador sat on the bed. His face still had the contortion which, in the ring, he made into a constant smile which frightened those people in the first rows of seats who knew what they were watching. 'And this,' he was saying aloud. 'And this. And this.'

He could remember when he had been good and it had only been three years before. He could remember the weight of the heavy gold-brocaded fighting jacket on his shoulders on that hot afternoon in May when his voice had still been the same in the ring as in the café, and how he sighted along the point-dipping blade at the place in the top of the shoulders where it was dusty in the short-haired black hump of muscle above the wide, wood-knocking, splintered-tipped horns that lowered as he went in to kill, and how the sword pushed in as easy as into a mound of stiff butter with the palm of his hand pushing the pommel, his left arm crossed low, his left shoulder forward, his weight on his left leg, and then his weight wasn't on his leg. His weight was on his lower belly and as the bull raised his head the horn was out of sight in him and he swung over on it twice before they pulled him off it. So now when he went into kill, and it was seldom, he could not look at the horns and what did any whore know about what he went through before be fought? And what had they been through that laughed at him? They were all whores and they knew what they could do with it.

Down in the dining room the picador sat looking at the priests. If there were women in the room he stared at them. If there were no women he would stare with enjoyment at a for-eigner, *un inglés*, but lacking women or strangers, he now stared with enjoyment and insolence at the two priests. While he stared the birth-marked auctioneer rose and folding his napkin went out, leaving over half the wine in the last bottle he had ordered. If his accounts had been paid up at the Luarca he would have finished the bottle.

The two priests did not stare back at the picador. One of them was saying, 'It is ten days since I have been here waiting to see him and all day I sit in the ante-chamber and he will not receive me.'

'What is there to do?'

'Nothing. What can one do? One cannot go against author-ity.'

'I have been here for two weeks and nothing. I wait and they will not see me.'

'We are from the abandoned country. When the money runs out we can return.'

'To the abandoned country. What does Madrid care about Galicia? We are a poor province.'

'One understands the action of our brother Basilio.'

'Still I have no real confidence in the integrity of Basilio Al-varez.'

'Madrid is where one learns to understand. Madrid kills Spain.'

'If they would simply see one and refuse.'

'No. You must be broken and worn out by waiting.'

'Well, we shall see. I can wait as well as another.'

At this moment the picador got to his feet, walked over to the priests' table and stood, gray-headed and hawk-faced, staring at them and smiling.

'A *torero*,' said one priest to the other.

'And a good one,' said the picador and walked out of the dining room, gray-jacketed, trim-waisted, bow-legged, in tight breeches over his high-heeled cattlemen's boots that clicked on the floor as he swaggered quite steadily, smiling to himself. He lived in a small, tight, professional world of personal efficiency, nightly alcoholic triumph, and insolence. Now he lit a cigar and tilting his hat at an angle in the hallway went out to the café.

The priests left immediately after the picador, hurriedly conscious of being the last people in the dining room, and there was no one in the room now but Paco and the middle-aged waiter. They cleared the tables and carried the bottles into the kitchen.

In the kitchen was the boy who washed the dishes. He was three years older than Paco and was very cynical and bitter.

'Take this,' the middle-aged waiter said, and poured out a glass of the Valdepeñas and handed it to him.

'Why not?' the boy took the glass.

'*Tu*, Paco?' the older waiter asked.

'Thank you,' said Paco. The three of them drank.

'I will be going,' said the middle-aged waiter.

'Good night,' they told him.

He went out and they were alone. Paco took a napkin one of the priests had used and standing straight, his heels planted, lowered the napkin and with head following the movement, swung his arms in the motion of a slow sweeping *verónica*. He turned, and advancing his right foot slightly, made the second pass, gained a little terrain on the imaginary bull and made a third pass, slow, perfectly timed and suave, then gathered the napkin to his waist and swung his hips away from the bull in a *media-verónica*.

The dishwasher, whose name was Enrique, watched him critically and sneeringly.

'How is the bull?' he said.

'Very brave,' said Paco. 'Look.'

Standing slim and straight he made four more perfect passes, smooth, elegant and graceful.

'And the bull?' asked Enrique standing against the sink, holding his wine glass and wearing his apron.

'Still has lots of gas,' said Paco.

'You make me sick,' said Enrique.

'Why?'

'Look.'

Enrique removed his apron and citing the imaginary bull he sculptured four perfect, languid gypsy *verónicas* and ended up with a *rebolera* that made the apron swing in a stiff arc past the bull's nose as he walked away from him.

'Look at that,' he said. 'And I wash dishes.'

'Why?'

'Fear,' said Enrique. '*Miedo*. The same fear you would have in a ring with a bull.'

'No,' said Paco. 'I wouldn't be afraid.'

'*Leche!*' said Enrique. 'Every one is afraid. But a *torero* can control his fear so that he can work the bull. I went in an amateur fight and I was so afraid I couldn't keep from running. Every one thought it was very funny. So would you be afraid. If it wasn't for fear every bootblack in Spain would be a bullfighter. You, a country boy, would be frightened worse than I was.'

'No,' said Paco.

He had done it too many times in his imagination. Too many times he had seen the horns, seen the bull's wet muzzle, the ear twitching, then the head go down and the charge, the hoofs thudding and the hot bull pass him as he swung the cape, to recharge as he swung the cape again, then again, and again, and again, to end winding the bull around him in his great *mediaverónica*, and walk swingingly away, with bull hairs caught in the gold ornaments of his jacket from the close passes; the bull standing hypnotized and the crowd applauding. No, he would not be afraid. Others, yes. Not he. He knew he would not be afraid. Even if he ever was afraid he knew that he could do it anyway. He had confidence. 'I wouldn't be afraid,' he said.

Enrique said, '*Leche*,' again.

Then he said, 'If we should try it?'

'How?'

'Look,' said Enrique. 'You think of the bull but you do not think of the horns. The bull has such force that the horns rip like a knife, they stab like a bayonet, and they kill like a club. Look,' he opened a table drawer and took out two meat knives. 'I will bind these to the legs of a chair. Then I will play bull for you with the chair held before my head. The knives are the horns. If you make those passes then they mean something.'

'Lend me your apron,' said Paco. 'We'll do it in the dining room.'

'No,' said Enrique, suddenly not bitter. 'Don't do it, Paco.'

'Yes,' said Paco. 'I'm not afraid.'

'You will be when you see the knives come.'

'We'll see,' said Paco. 'Give me the apron.'

At this time, while Enrique was binding the two heavy-bladed razor-sharp meat knives fast to the legs of the chair with two soiled napkins holding the haft of each knife, wrapping them tight and then knotting them, the two chambermaids, Paco's sisters, were on their way to the cinema to see Greta Garbo in *Anna Christie*. Of the two priests, one was sitting in his underwear reading his breviary and the other was wearing a nightshirt and saying the rosary. All the bullfighters except the one who was ill had made their evening appearance at the Café Fornos, where the big, dark-haired picador was playing billiards, the short, serious matador was sitting at a crowded table before a coffee and milk, along with the middle-aged *banderillero* and other serious workmen.

The drinking, gray-headed picador was sitting with a glass of *cazalas* brandy before him staring with pleasure at a table where the matador whose courage was gone sat with another matador who had renounced the sword to become a *banderillero* again, and two very houseworn-looking prostitutes.

The auctioneer stood on the street corner talking with friends. The tall waiter was at the Anarcho-Syndicalist meeting waiting for an opportunity to speak. The middle-aged waiter was seated on the terrace of the Café Alvarez drinking a small beer. The woman who owned the Luarca was already asleep in her bed, where she lay on her back with the bolster between her legs; big, fat, honest, clean, easy-going, very religious and never having ceased to miss or pray daily for her husband, dead, now, twenty years. In his room, alone, the matador who was ill lay face down on his bed with his mouth against a handkerchief.

Now, in the deserted dining room, Enrique tied the last knot in the napkins that bound the knives to the chair legs and lifted the chair. He pointed the legs with the knives on them forward and held the chair over his head with the two knives pointing straight ahead, one on each side of his head.

'It's heavy,' he said. 'Look, Paco. It is very dangerous. Don't do it.' He was sweating.

Paco stood facing him, holding the apron spread, holding a fold of it bunched in each hand, thumbs up, first finger down, spread to catch the eye of the bull.

'Charge straight,' he said. 'Turn like a bull. Charge as many times as you want.'

'How will you know when to cut the pass?' asked Enrique. 'It's better to do three and then a *media*.'

'All right,' said Paco. 'But come straight. Huh, *torito*! Come on, little bull!'

Running with head down Enrique came toward him and Paco swung the apron just ahead of the knife blade as it passed close in front of his belly and as it went by it was, to him, the real horn, white-tipped, black, smooth, and as Enrique passed him and turned to rush again it was the hot, blood-flanked mass of the bull that thudded by, then turned like a cat and came again as he swung the cape slowly. Then the bull turned and came again and, as he watched the onrushing point, he stepped his left foot two inches too far forward and the knife did not pass, but had slipped in as easily as into a wineskin and there was a hot scalding rush above and around the sudden inner rigidity of steel and Enrique shouting, 'Ay! Ay! Let me get it out! Let me get it out!' and Paco slipped forward on the chair, the apron cape still held, Enrique pulling on the chair as the knife turned in him, in him, Paco.

The knife was out now and he sat on the floor in the widening warm pool.

'Put the napkin over it. Hold it!' said Enrique. 'Hold it tight. I will run for the doctor. You must hold in the hemorrhage.'

'There should be a rubber cup,' said Paco. He had seen that used in the ring.

'I came straight,' said Enrique, crying. 'All I wanted was to show the danger.'

'Don't worry,' said Paco, his voice sounding far away. 'But bring the doctor.'

In the ring they lifted you and carried you, running with you, to the operating room. If the femoral artery emptied itself before you reached there they called the priest.

'Advise one of the priests,' said Paco, holding the napkin tight against his lower abdomen. He could not believe that this had happened to him.

But Enrique was running down the Calle San Jerónimo to the all-night first-aid station and Paco was alone, first sitting up, then huddled over, then slumped on the floor, until it was over, feeling his life go out of him as dirty water empties from a bathtub when the plug is drawn. He was frightened and he felt faint and he tried to say an act of contrition and he remembered how it started but before he had said, as fast as he could, 'Oh, my God, I am heartily sorry for having offended Thee who art worthy of all my love and I firmly resolve . . .,' he felt too faint and he was lying face down on the floor and it was over very quickly. A severed femoral artery empties itself faster than you can believe.

As the doctor from the first-aid station came up the stairs accompanied by a policeman who held on to Enrique by the arm, the two sisters of Paco were still in the moving-picture palace of the Gran Via, where they were intensely disappointed in the Garbo film, which showed the great star in miserable low surroundings when they had been accustomed to see her surrounded by great luxury and brilliance. The audience disliked the film thoroughly and were protesting by whistling and stamping their feet. All the other people from the hotel were doing almost what they had been doing when the accident happened, except that the two priests had finished their devotions and were preparing for sleep, and the gray-haired picador had moved his drink over to the table with the two houseworn prostitutes. A little later he went out of the café with one of them. It was the one for whom the matador who had lost his nerve had been buying drinks.

The boy Paco had never known about any of this nor about what all these people would be doing on the next day and on other days to come. He had no idea how they really lived nor how they ended. He did not even realize they ended. He died, as the Spanish phrase has it, full of illusions. He had not had time in his life to lose any of them, nor even, at the end, to complete an act of contrition. He had not even had time to be disappointed in the Garbo picture which disappointed all Madrid for a week.

Kilimanjaro is a snow-covered mountain 19,710 feet high, and is said to be the highest mountain in Africa. Its western summit is called the Masai 'Ngàje Ngài,' the House of God. Close to the western summit there is the dried and frozen carcass of a leopard. No one has explained what the leopard was seeking at that altitude.

THE SNOWS OF KILIMANJARO

'The marvellous thing is that it's painless,' he said. 'That's how you know when it starts.'

'Is it really?'

'Absolutely. I'm awfully sorry about the odor though. That must bother you.'

'Don't! Please don't.'

'Look at them,' he said. 'Now is it sight or is it scent that brings them like that?'

The cot the man lay on was in the wide shade of a mimosa tree and as he looked out past the shade onto the glare of the plain there were three of the big birds squatted obscenely, while in the sky a dozen more sailed, making quick-moving shadows as they passed.

'They've been there since the day the truck broke down,' he said. 'Today's the first time any have lit on the ground. I watched the way they sailed very carefully at first in case I ever wanted to use them in a story. That's funny now.'

'I wish you wouldn't,' she said.

'I'm only talking,' he said. 'It's much easier if I talk. But I don't want to bother you.'

'You know it doesn't bother me,' she said. 'It's that I've gotten so very nervous not being able to do anything. I think we might make it as easy as we can until the plane comes.'

'Or until the plane doesn't come.'

'Please tell me what I can do. There must be something I can do.'

'You can take the leg off and that might stop it, though I doubt it. Or you can shoot me. You're a good shot now. I taught you to shoot, didn't I?'

'Please don't talk that way. Couldn't I read to you?'

'Read what?'

'Anything in the book bag that we haven't read.'

'I can't listen to it,' he said. 'Talking is the easiest. We quarrel and that makes the time pass.'

'I don't quarrel. I never want to quarrel. Let's not quarrel any more. No matter how nervous we get. Maybe they will be back with another truck today. Maybe the plane will come.'

'I don't want to move,' the man said. 'There is no sense in moving now except to make it easier for you.'

'That's cowardly.'

'Can't you let a man die as comfortably as he can without calling him names? What's the use of slanging me?'

'You're not going to die.'

'Don't be silly. I'm dying now. Ask those bastards.' He looked over to where the huge, filthy birds sat, their naked heads sunk in the hunched feathers. A fourth planed down, to run quick-legged and then waddle slowly toward the others.

'They are around every camp. You never notice them. You can't die if you don't give up.'

'Where did you read that? You're such a bloody fool.'

'You might think about some one else.'

'For Christ's sake,' he said, 'that's been my trade.'

He lay then and was quiet for a while and looked across the heat shimmer of the plain to the edge of the bush. There were a few Tommies that showed minute and white against the yellow and, far off, he saw a herd of zebra, white against the green of the bush. This was a pleasant camp under big trees against a hill, with good water, and close by, a nearly dry water hole where sand grouse flighted in the mornings.

'Wouldn't you like me to read?' she asked. She was sitting on a canvas chair beside his cot. 'There's a breeze coming up.'

'No thanks.'

'Maybe the truck will come.'

'I don't give a damn about the truck.'

'I do.'

'You give a damn about so many things that I don't.'

'Not so many, Harry.'

'What about a drink?'

'It's supposed to be bad for you. It said in Black's to avoid all alcohol. You shouldn't drink.'

'Molo!' he shouted.

'Yes Bwana.'

'Bring whiskey-soda.'

'Yes Bwana.'

'You shouldn't,' she said. 'That's what I mean by giving up. It says it's bad for you. I know it's bad for you.'

'No,' he said. 'It's good for me.'

So now it was all over, he thought. So now he would never have a chance to finish it. So this was the way it ended, in a bickering over a drink. Since the gangrene started in his right leg he had no pain and with the pain the horror had gone and all he felt now was a great tiredness and anger that this was the end of it. For this, that now was coming, he had very little curiosity. For years it had obsessed him; but now it meant nothing in itself. It was strange how easy being tired enough made it.

Now he would never write the things that he had saved to write until he knew enough to write them well. Well, he would not have to fail at trying to write them either. Maybe you could never write them, and that was why you put them off and de-layed the starting. Well he would never know, now.

'I wish we'd never come,' the woman said. She was looking at him, holding the glass and biting her lip. 'You never would have gotten anything like this in Paris. You always said you loved Paris. We could have stayed in Paris or gone anywhere. I'd have gone anywhere. I said I'd go anywhere you wanted. If you wanted to shoot we could have gone shooting in Hungary and been comfortable.'

'Your bloody money,' he said.

'That's not fair,' she said. 'It was always yours as much as mine. I left everything and I went wherever you wanted to go and I've done what you wanted to do. But I wish we'd never come here.'

'You said you loved it.'

'I did when you were all right. But now I hate it. I don't see why that had to happen to your leg. What have we done to have that happen to us?'

'I suppose what I did was to forget to put iodine on it when I first scratched it. Then I didn't pay any attention to it because I never infect. Then, later, when it got bad, it was probably using that weak carbolic solution when the other antiseptics ran out that paralyzed the minute blood vessels and started the gan-grene.' He looked at her, 'What else?'

'I don't mean that.'

'If we would have hired a good mechanic instead of a half-baked Kikuyu driver, he would have checked the oil and never burned out that bearing in the truck.'

'I don't mean that.'

'If you hadn't left your own people, your goddamned Old Westbury, Saratoga, Palm Beach people to take me on –'

'Why, I loved you. That's not fair. I love you now. I'll always love you. Don't you love me?'

'No,' said the man. 'I don't think so. I never have.'

'Harry, what are you saying? You're out of your head.'

'No. I haven't any head to go out of.'

'Don't drink that,' she said. 'Darling, please don't drink that. We have to do everything we can.'

'You do it,' he said. 'I'm tired.'

* * *

Now in his mind he saw a railway station at Karagatch and he was standing with his pack and that was the headlight of the Simplon-Orient cutting the dark now and he was leaving Thrace then after the retreat. That was one of the things he had saved to write, with, in the morning at breakfast, looking out the window and seeing snow on the mountains in Bulgaria and Nansen's Secretary asking the old man if it were snow and the old man looking at it and saying, No, that's not snow. It's too early for snow. And the Secretary repeating to the other girls, No, you see. It's not snow and them all saying, It's not snow we were mistaken. But it was the snow all right and he sent them on into it when he evolved exchange of populations. And it was snow they tramped along in until they died that winter.

It was snow too that fell all Christmas week that year up in the Gauertal, that year they lived in the woodcutter's house with the big square porcelain stove that filled half the room, and they slept on mattresses filled with beech leaves, the time the deserter came with his feet bloody in the snow. He said the police were right behind him and they gave him woolen socks and held the gendarmes talking until the tracks had drifted over.

In Schrunz, on Christmas day, the snow was so bright it hurt your eyes when you looked out from the Weinstube and saw every one coming home from church. That was where they walked up the sleigh-smoothed urine-yellowed road along the river with the steep pine hills, skis heavy on the shoulder, and where they ran that great run down the glacier above the Madlener-haus, the snow as smooth to see as cake frosting and as light as powder and he remembered the noiseless rush the speed made as you dropped down like a bird.

They were snow-bound a week in the Madlener-haus that time in the blizzard playing cards in the smoke by the lantern light and the stakes were higher all the time as Herr Lent lost more. Finally he lost it all. Everything, the Skischule money and all the season's profit and then his capital. He could see him with his long nose, picking up the cards and then opening, 'Sans Voir.' There was always gambling then. When there was no snow you gambled and when there was too much you gambled. He thought of all the time in his life he had spent gambling.

But he had never written a line of that, nor of that cold, bright Christmas day with the mountains showing across the plain that Barker had flown across the lines to bomb the Austrian officers' leave train, machine-gunning them as they scattered and ran. He remembered Barker afterwards coming into the mess and starting to tell about it. And how quiet it got and then somebody saying, 'You bloody murderous bastard.'

Those were the same Austrians they killed then that he skied with later. No not the same. Hans, that he skied with all that year, had been in the Kaiser-Jägers and when they went hunting hares together up the little valley above the saw-mill they had talked of the fighting on Pasubio and of the attack on Perticara and Asalone and he had never written a word of that. Nor of Monte Corona, nor the Sette Communi, nor of Arsiero.

How many winters had he lived in the Vorarlberg and the Arlberg? It was four and then he remembered the man who had the fox to sell when they had walked into Bludenz, that time to buy presents, and the cherry-pit taste of good kirsch, the fast-slipping rush of running powder-snow on crust, singing 'Hi! Ho! said Rolly!' as you ran down the last stretch to the steep drop, taking it straight, then running the orchard in three turns and out across the ditch and onto the icy road behind the inn. Knocking your bindings loose, kicking the skis free and leaning them up against the wooden wall of the inn, the lamplight coming from the window, where inside, in the smoky, new-wine smelling warmth, they were playing the accordion.

'Where did we stay in Paris?' he asked the woman who was sitting by him in a canvas chair, now, in Africa.

'At the Crillon. You know that.'

'Why do I know that?'

'That's where we always stayed.'

'No. Not always.'

'There and at the Pavillion Henri-Quatre in St. Germain. You said you loved it there.'

'Love is a dunghill,' said Harry. 'And I'm the cock that gets on it to crow.'

'If you have to go away,' she said, 'is it absolutely necessary to kill off everything you leave behind? I mean do you have to take away everything? Do you have to kill your horse, and your wife and burn your saddle and your armour?'

'Yes,' he said. 'Your damned money was my armour. My Swift and my Armour.'

'Don't.'

'All right. I'll stop that. I don't want to hurt you.'

'It's a little bit late now.'

'All right then. I'll go on hurting you. It's more amusing. The only thing I ever really liked to do with you I can't do now.'

'No, that's not true. You liked to do many things and everything you wanted to do I did.'

'Oh, for Christ sake stop bragging, will you?'

He looked at her and saw her crying.

'Listen,' he said. 'Do you think that it is fun to do this? I don't know why I'm doing it. It's trying to kill to keep yourself alive, I imagine. I was all right when we started talking. I didn't mean to start this, and now I'm crazy as a coot and being as cruel to you as I can be. Don't pay any attention, darling, to what I say. I love you, really. You know I love you. I've never loved any one else the way I love you.'

He slipped into the familiar lie he made his bread and butter by.

'You're sweet to me.'

'You bitch,' he said. 'You rich bitch. That's poetry. I'm full of poetry now. Rot and poetry. Rotten poetry.'

'Stop it. Harry, why do you have to turn into a devil now?'

'I don't like to leave anything,' the man said. 'I don't like to leave things behind.'

★ ★ ★

It was evening now and he had been asleep. The sun was gone behind the hill and there was a shadow all across the plain and the small animals were feeding close to camp; quick dropping heads and switching tails, he watched them keeping well out away from the bush now. The birds no longer waited on the ground. They were all perched heavily in a tree. There were many more of them. His personal boy was sitting by the bed.

'Memsahib's gone to shoot,' the boy said. 'Does Bwana want?'

'Nothing.'

She had gone to kill a piece of meat and, knowing how he liked to watch the game, she had gone well away so she would not disturb this little pocket of the plain that he could see. She was always thoughtful, he thought. On anything she knew about, or had read, or that she had ever heard.

It was not her fault that when he went to her he was already over. How could a woman know that you meant nothing that you said; that you spoke only from habit and to be comfortable? After he no longer meant what he said, his lies were more successful with women than when he had told them the truth.

It was not so much that he lied as that there was no truth to tell. He had had his life and it was over and then he went on living it again with different people and more money, with the best of the same places, and some new ones.

You kept from thinking and it was all marvellous. You were equipped with good insides so that you did not go to pieces that way, the way most of them had, and you made an attitude that you cared nothing for the work you used to do, now that you could no longer do it. But, in yourself, you said that you would write about these people; about the very rich; that you were really not of them but a spy in their country; that you would leave it and write of it and for once it would be written by some one who knew what he was writing of. But he would never do it, because each day of not writing, of comfort, of being that which he despised, dulled his ability and softened his will to work so that, finally, he did no work at all. The people he knew now were all much more comfortable when he did not work. Africa was where he had been happiest in the good time of his life, so he had come out here to start again. They had made this safari with the minimum of comfort. There was no hardship; but there was no luxury and he had thought that he could get back into training that way. That in some way he could work the fat off his soul the way a fighter went into the mountains to work and train in order to burn it out of his body.

She had liked it. She said she loved it. She loved anything that was exciting, that involved a change of scene, where there were new people and where things were pleasant. And he had felt the illusion of returning strength of will to work. Now if this was how it ended, and he knew it was, he must not turn like some snake biting itself because its back was broken. It wasn't this woman's fault. If it had not been she it would have been another. If he lived by a lie he should try to die by it. He heard a shot beyond the hill.

She shot very well this good, this rich bitch, this kindly caretaker and destroyer of his talent. Nonsense. He had destroyed his talent himself. Why should he blame this woman because she kept him well? He had destroyed his talent by not using it, by betrayals of himself and what he believed in, by drinking so much that he blunted the edge of his perceptions, by laziness, by sloth, and by snobbery, by pride and by prejudice, by hook and by crook. What was this? A catalogue of old books? What was his talent anyway? It was a talent all right but instead of using it, he had traded on it. It was never what he had done, but always what he could do. And he had chosen to make his living with something else instead of a pen or a pencil. It was strange, too, wasn't it, that when he fell in love with another woman, that woman should always have more money than the last one? But when he no longer was in love, when he was only lying, as to this woman, now, who had the most money of all, who had all the money there was, who had had a husband and children, who had taken lovers and been dissatisfied with them, and who loved him dearly as a writer, as a man, as a companion and as a proud possession; it was strange that when he did not love her at all and was lying, that he should be able to give her more for her money than when he had really loved.

We must all be cut out for what we do, he thought. However you make your living is where your talent lies. He had sold vitality, in one form or another, all his life and when your affections are not too involved you give much better value for the money. He had found that out but he would never write that, now, either. No, he would not write that, although it was well worth writing.

Now she came in sight, walking across the open toward the camp. She was wearing jodhpurs and carrying her rifle. The two boys had a Tommie slung and they were coming along behind her. She was still a good-looking woman, he thought, and she had a pleasant body. She had a great talent and appreciation for the bed, she was not pretty, but he liked her face, she read enormously, liked to ride and shoot and, certainly, she drank too much. Her husband had died when she was still a comparatively young woman and for a while she had devoted herself to her two just-grown children, who did not need her and were embarrassed at having her about, to her stable of horses, to books, and to bottles. She liked to read in the evening before dinner and she drank Scotch and soda while she read. By dinner she was fairly drunk and after a bottle of wine at dinner she was usually drunk enough to sleep.

That was before the lovers. After she had the lovers she did not drink so much because she did not have to be drunk to sleep. But the lovers bored her. She had been married to a man who had never bored her and these people bored her very much.

Then one of her two children was killed in a plane crash and after that was over she did not want the lovers, and drink being no anæsthetic she had to make another life. Suddenly, she had been acutely frightened of being alone. But she wanted some one that she respected with her.

It had begun very simply. She liked what he wrote and she had always envied the life he led. She thought he did exactly what he wanted to. The steps by which she had acquired him and the way in which she had finally fallen in love with him were all part of a regular progression in which she had built herself a new life and he had traded away what remained of his old life.

He had traded it for security, for comfort too, there was no denying that, and for what else? He did not know. She would have bought him anything he wanted. He knew that. She was a damned nice woman too. He would as soon be in bed with her as any one; rather with her, because she was richer, because she was very pleasant and appreciative and because she never made scenes. And now this life that she had built again was coming to a term because he had not used iodine two weeks ago when a thorn had scratched his knee as they moved forward trying to photograph a herd of waterbuck standing, their heads up, peering while their nostrils searched the air, their ears spread wide to hear the first noise that would send them rushing into the bush. They had bolted, too, before he got the picture.

Here she came now.

He turned his head on the cot to look toward her. 'Hello,' he said.

'I shot a Tommy ram,' she told him. 'He'll make you good broth and I'll have them mash some potatoes with the Klim. How do you feel?'

'Much better.'

'Isn't that lovely? You know I thought perhaps you would. You were sleeping when I left.'

'I had a good sleep. Did you walk far?'

'No. Just around behind the hill. I made quite a good shot on the Tommy.'

'You shoot marvellously, you know.'

'I love it. I've loved Africa. Really. If *you're* all right it's the most fun that I've ever had. You don't know the fun it's been to shoot with you. I've loved the country.'

'I love it too.'

'Darling, you don't know how marvellous it is to see you feeling better. I couldn't stand it when you felt that way. You won't talk to me like that again, will you? Promise me?'

'No,' he said. 'I don't remember what I said.'

'You don't have to destroy me. Do you? I'm only a middle-aged woman who loves you and wants to do what you want to do. I've been destroyed two or three times already. You wouldn't want to destroy me again, would you?'

'I'd like to destroy you a few times in bed,' he said.

'Yes. That's the good destruction. That's the way we're made to be destroyed. The plane will be here tomorrow.'

'How do you know?'

'I'm sure. It's bound to come. The boys have the wood all ready and the grass to make the smudge. I went down and looked at it again today. There's plenty of room to land and we have the smudges ready at both ends.'

'What makes you think it will come tomorrow?'

'I'm sure it will. It's overdue now. Then, in town, they will fix up your leg and then we will have some good destruction. Not that dreadful talking kind.'

'Should we have a drink? The sun is down.'

'Do you think you should?'

'I'm having one.'

'We'll have one together. Molo, *letti dui* whiskey-soda!' she called.

'You'd better put on your mosquito boots,' he told her.

'I'll wait till I bathe . . .'

While it grew dark they drank and just before it was dark and there was no longer enough light to shoot, a hyena crossed the open on his way around the hill.

'That bastard crosses there every night,' the man said. 'Every night for two weeks.'

'He's the one makes the noise at night. I don't mind it. They're a filthy animal though.'

Drinking together, with no pain now except the discomfort of lying in the one position, the boys lighting a fire, its shadow jumping on the tents, he could feel the return of acquiescence in this life of pleasant surrender. She *was* very good to him. He had been cruel and unjust in the afternoon. She was a fine woman, marvellous really. And just then it occurred to him that he was going to die.

It came with a rush; not as a rush of water nor of wind; but of a sudden evil-smelling emptiness and the odd thing was that the hyena slipped lightly along the edge of it.

'What is it, Harry?' she asked him.

'Nothing,' he said. 'You had better move over to the other side. To windward.'

'Did Molo change the dressing?'

'Yes. I'm just using the boric now.'

'How do you feel?'

'A little wobbly.'

'I'm going in to bathe,' she said. 'I'll be right out. I'll eat with you and then we'll put the cot in.'

So, he said to himself, we did well to stop the quarrelling. He had never quarrelled much with this woman, while with the women that he loved he had quarrelled so much they had finally, always, with the corrosion of the quarrelling, killed what they had together. He had loved too much, demanded too much, and he wore it all out.

He thought about alone in Constantinople that time, having quarrelled in Paris before he had gone out. He had whored the whole time and then, when that was over, and he had failed to kill his loneliness, but only made it worse, he had written her, the first one, the one who left him, a letter telling her how he had never been able to kill it. . . . How when he thought he saw her outside the Regence one time it made him go all faint and sick inside, and that he would follow a woman who looked like her in some way, along the Boulevard, afraid to see it was not she, afraid to lose the feeling it gave him. How every one he had slept with had only made him miss her more. How what she had done could never matter since he knew he could not cure himself of loving her. He wrote this letter at the Club, cold sober, and mailed it to New York asking her to write him at the office in Paris. That seemed safe. And that night missing her so much it made him feel hollow sick inside, he wandered up past Maxim's, picked a girl up and took her out to supper. He had gone to a place to dance with her afterward, she danced badly, and left her for a hot Armenian slut, that swung her belly against him so it almost scalded. He took her away from a British gunner subaltern after a row. The gunner asked him outside and they fought in the street on the cobbles in the dark. He'd hit him twice, hard, on the side of the jaw and when he didn't go down he knew he was in for a fight. The gunner hit him in the body, then beside his eye. He swung with his left again and landed and the gunner fell on him and grabbed his coat and tore the sleeve off and he clubbed him twice behind the ear and then smashed him with his right as he pushed him away. When the gunner went down his head hit first and he ran with the girl because they heard the M.P.'s coming. They got into a taxi and drove out to Rimmily Hissa along the Bosphorus, and around, and back in the cool night and went to bed and she felt as over-ripe as she looked but smooth, rose-petal, syrupy, smooth-bellied, big-breasted and needed no pillow under her buttocks, and he left her before she was awake looking blousy enough in the first daylight and turned up at the Pera Palace with a black eye, carrying his coat because one sleeve was missing.

That same night he left for Anatolia and he remembered, later on that trip, riding all day through fields of the poppies that they raised for opium and how strange it made you feel, finally, and all the distances seemed wrong, to where they had made the attack with the newly arrived Constantine officers, that did not know a god-damned thing, and the artillery had fired into the troops and the British observer had cried like a child.

That was the day he'd first seen dead men wearing white ballet skirts and upturned shoes with pompons on them. The Turks had come steadily and lumpily and he had seen the skirted men running and the officers shooting into them and running then themselves and he and the British observer had run too until his lungs ached and his mouth was full of the taste of pennies and they stopped behind some rocks and there were the Turks coming as lumpily as ever. Later he had seen the things that he could never think of and later still he had seen much worse. So when he got back to Paris that time he could not talk about it or stand to have it mentioned. And there in the café as he passed was that American poet with a pile of saucers in front of him and a stupid look on his potato face talking about the Dada movement with a Roumanian who said his name was Tristan Tzara, who always wore a monocle and had a headache, and, back at the apartment with his wife that now he loved again, the quarrel all over, the madness all over, glad to be home, the office sent his mail up to the flat. So then the letter in answer to the one he'd written came in on a platter one morning and when he saw the handwriting he went cold all over and tried to slip the letter underneath another. But his wife said, 'Who is that letter from, dear?' and that was the end of the beginning of that.

He remembered the good times with them all, and the quarrels. They always picked the finest places to have the quarrels. And why had they always quarrelled when he was feeling best? He had never written any of that because, at first, he never wanted to hurt any one and then it seemed as though there was enough to write without it. But he had always thought that he would write it finally. There was so much to write. He had seen the world change; not just the events; although he had seen many of them and had watched the people, but he had seen the subtler change and he could remember how the people were at different times. He had been in it and he had watched it and it was his duty to write of it; but now he never would.

'How do you feel?' she said. She had come out from the tent now after her bath.

'All right.'

'Could you eat now?' He saw Molo behind her with the folding table and the other boy with the dishes.

'I want to write,' he said.

'You ought to take some broth to keep your strength up.'

'I'm going to die tonight,' he said. 'I don't need my strength up.'

'Don't be melodramatic, Harry, please,' she said.

'Why don't you use your nose? I'm rotted half way up my thigh now. What the hell should I fool with broth for? Molo bring whiskey-soda.'

'Please take the broth,' she said gently.

'All right.'

The broth was too hot. He had to hold it in the cup until it cooled enough to take it and then he just got it down without gagging.

'You're a fine woman,' he said. 'Don't pay any attention to me.'

She looked at him with her well-known, well-loved face from *Spur* and *Town & Country*, only a little the worse for drink, only a little the worse for bed, but *Town & Country* never showed those good breasts and those useful thighs and those lightly small-of-back-caressing hands, and as he looked and saw her well-known pleasant smile, he felt death come again.

This time there was no rush. It was a puff, as of a wind that makes a candle flicker and the flame go tall.

'They can bring my net out later and hang it from the tree and build the fire up. I'm not going in the tent tonight. It's not worth moving. It's a clear night. There won't be any rain.'

So this was how you died, in whispers that you did not hear. Well, there would be no more quarrelling. He could promise that. The one experience that he had never had he was not going to spoil now. He probably would. You spoiled everything. But perhaps he wouldn't.

'You can't take dictation, can you?'

'I never learned,' she told him.

'That's all right.'

There wasn't time, of course, although it seemed as though it telescoped so that you might put it all into one paragraph if you could get it right.

There was a log house, chinked white with mortar, on a hill above the lake. There was a bell on a pole by the door to call the people in to meals. Behind the house were fields and behind the fields was the timber. A line of lombardy poplars ran from the house to the dock. Other poplars ran along the point. A road went up to the hills along the edge of the timber and along that road he picked blackberries. Then that log house was burned down and all the guns that had been on deer foot racks above the open fire place were burned and afterwards their barrels, with the lead melted in the magazines, and the stocks burned away, lay out on the heap of ashes that were used to make lye for the big iron soap kettles, and you asked Grandfather if you could have them to play with, and he said, no. You see they were his guns still and he never bought any others. Nor did he hunt any more. The house was rebuilt in the same place out of lumber now and painted white and from its porch you saw the poplars and the lake beyond; but there were never any more guns. The barrels of the guns that had hung on the deer feet on the wall of the log house lay out there on the heap of ashes and no one ever touched them.

In the Black Forest, after the war, we rented a trout stream and there were two ways to walk to it. One was down the valley from Triberg and around the valley road in the shade of the trees that bordered the white road, and then up a side road that went up through the hills past many small farms, with the big Schwarzwald houses, until that road crossed the stream. That was where our fishing began.

The other way was to climb steeply up to the edge of the woods and then go across the top of the hills through the pine woods, and then out to the edge of a meadow and down across this meadow to the bridge. There were birches along the stream and it was not big, but narrow, clear and fast, with pools where it had cut under the roots of the birches. At the Hotel in Triberg the proprietor had a fine season. It was very pleasant and we were all great friends. The next year came the inflation and the money he had made the year before was not enough to buy supplies to open the hotel and he hanged himself.

You could dictate that, but you could not dictate the Place Contre-scarpe where the flower sellers dyed their flowers in the street and the dye ran over the paving where the autobus started and the old men and the women, always drunk on wine and bad marc; and the children with their noses running in the cold; the smell of dirty sweat and poverty and drunkenness at the Café des Amateurs and the whores at the Bal Musette they lived above. The concierge who entertained the trooper of the Garde Republicaine in her loge, his horse-hair-plumed helmet on a chair. The locataire across the hall whose husband was a bicycle racer and her joy that morning at the crémerie when she had opened L'Auto and seen where he placed third in Paris-Tours, his first big race. She had blushed and laughed and then gone upstairs crying with the yellow sporting paper in her hand. The husband of the woman who ran the Bal Musette drove a taxi and when he, Harry, had to take an early plane the husband knocked upon the door to wake him and they each drank a glass of white wine at the zinc of the bar before they started. He knew his neighbors in that quarter then because they all were poor.

Around that Place there were two kinds; the drunkards and the sportifs. The drunkards killed their poverty that way; the sportifs took it out in exercise. They were the descendants of the Communards and it was no struggle for them to know their politics. They knew who had shot their fathers, their relatives, their brothers, and their friends when the Versailles troops came in and took the town after the Commune and executed any one they could catch with calloused hands, or who wore a cap, or carried any other sign he was a working man. And in that poverty, and in that quarter across the street from a Boucherie Chevaline and a wine co-operative he had written the start of all he was to do. There never was another part of Paris that he loved like that, the sprawling trees, the old white plastered houses painted brown below, the long green of the autobus in that round square, the purple flower dye upon the paving, the sudden drop down the hill of the rue Cardinal Lemoine to the River, and the other way the narrow crowded world of the rue Mouffetard. The street that ran up toward the Pantheon and the other that he always took with the bicycle, the only asphalted street in all that quarter, smooth under the tires, with the high narrow houses and the cheap tall hotel where Paul Verlaine had died. There were only two rooms in the apartments where they lived and he had a room on the top floor of that hotel that cost him sixty francs a month where he did his writing, and from it he could see the roofs and chimney pots and all the hills of Paris.

From the apartment you could only see the wood and coal man's place. He sold wine too, bad wine. The golden horse's head outside the Boucherie Chevaline where the carcasses hung yellow gold and red in the open window, and the green painted co-operative where they bought their wine; good wine and cheap. The rest was plaster walls and the windows

*of the neighbors. The neighbors who, at night, when some one lay drunk
in the street, moaning and groaning in that typical French ivresse that
you were propaganded to believe did not exist, would open their windows and then the murmur of talk.*

*'Where is the policeman? When you don't want him the bugger is
always there. He's sleeping with some concierge. Get the Agent.' Till
some one threw a bucket of water from a window and the moaning
stopped. 'What's that? Water. Ah, that's intelligent.' And the windows
shutting. Marie, his femme de ménage, protesting against the eight-
hour day saying, 'If a husband works until six he gets only a little drunk
on the way home and does not waste too much. If he works only until
five he is drunk every night and one has no money. It is the wife of the
working man who suffers from this shortening of hours.'*

'Wouldn't you like some more broth?' the woman asked him
now.

'No, thank you very much. It is awfully good.'

'Try just a little.'

'I would like a whiskey-soda.'

'It's not good for you.'

'No. It's bad for me. Cole Porter wrote the words and the
music. This knowledge that you're going mad for me.'

'You know I like you to drink.'

'Oh yes. Only it's bad for me.'

When she goes, he thought, I'll have all I want. Not all I want
but all there is. Ayee he was tired. Too tired. He was going to
sleep a little while. He lay still and death was not there. It must
have gone around another street. It went in pairs, on bicycles,
and moved absolutely silently on the pavements.

*No, he had never written about Paris. Not the Paris that he cared
about. But what about the rest that he had never written?*

*What about the ranch and the silvered gray of the sage brush, the
quick, clear water in the irrigation ditches, and the heavy green of the
alfalfa. The trail went up into the hills and the cattle in the summer were
shy as deer. The bawling and the steady noise and slow moving mass
raising a dust as you brought them down in the fall. And behind the
mountains, the clear sharpness of the peak in the evening light and,
riding down along the trail in the moonlight, bright across the valley.
Now he remembered coming down through the timber in the dark holding the horse's tail when you could not see and all the stories that he
meant to write.*

About the half-wit chore boy who was left at the ranch that time and told not to let any one get any hay, and that old bastard from the Forks who had beaten the boy when he had worked for him stopping to get some feed. The boy refusing and the old man saying he would beat him again. The boy got the rifle from the kitchen and shot him when he tried to come into the barn and when they came back to the ranch he'd been dead a week, frozen in the corral, and the dogs had eaten part of him. But what was left you packed on a sled wrapped in a blanket and roped on and you got the boy to help you haul it, and the two of you took it out over the road on skis, and sixty miles down to town to turn the boy over. He having no idea that he would be arrested. Thinking he had done his duty and that you were his friend and he would be rewarded. He'd helped to haul the old man in so everybody could know how bad the old man had been and how he'd tried to steal some feed that didn't belong to him, and when the sheriff put the handcuffs on the boy he couldn't believe it. Then he'd started to cry. That was one story he had saved to write. He knew at least twenty good stories from out there and he had never written one. Why?

'You tell them why,' he said.
'Why what, dear?'
'Why nothing.'
She didn't drink so much, now, since she had him. But if he lived he would never write about her, he knew that now. Nor about any of them. The rich were dull and they drank too much, or they played too much backgammon. They were dull and they were repetitious. He remembered poor Julian and his romantic awe of them and how he had started a story once that began, 'The very rich are different from you and me.' And how some one had said to Julian, Yes, they have more money. But that was not humorous to Julian. He thought they were a special glamorous race and when he found they weren't it wrecked him just as much as any other thing that wrecked him.

He had been contemptuous of those who wrecked. You did not have to like it because you understood it. He could beat anything, he thought, because no thing could hurt him if he did not care.

All right. Now he would not care for death. One thing he had always dreaded was the pain. He could stand pain as well as any man, until it went on too long, and wore him out, but here he had something that had hurt frightfully and just when he had felt it breaking him, the pain had stopped.

He remembered long ago when Williamson, the bombing officer, had been hit by a stick bomb some one in a German patrol had thrown as he was coming in through the wire that night and, screaming, had begged every one to kill him. He was a fat man, very brave, and a good officer, although addicted to fantastic shows. But that night he was caught in the wire, with a flare lighting him up and his bowels spilled out into the wire, so when they brought him in, alive, they had to cut him loose. Shoot me, Harry. For Christ sake shoot me. They had had an argument one time about our Lord never sending you anything you could not bear and some one's theory had been that meant that at a certain time the pain passed you out automatically. But he had always remembered Williamson, that night. Nothing passed out Williamson until he gave him all his morphine tablets that he had always saved to use himself and then they did not work right away.

Still this now, that he had, was very easy; and if it was no worse as it went on there was nothing to worry about. Except that he would rather be in better company.

He thought a little about the company that he would like to have.

No, he thought, when everything you do, you do too long, and do too late, you can't expect to find the people still there. The people all are gone. The party's over and you are with your hostess now.

I'm getting as bored with dying as with everything else, he thought.

'It's a bore,' he said out loud.

'What is, my dear?'

'Anything you do too bloody long.'

He looked at her face between him and the fire. She was leaning back in the chair and the firelight shone on her pleasantly lined face and he could see that she was sleepy. He heard the hyena make a noise just outside the range of the fire.

'I've been writing,' he said. 'But I got tired.'

'Do you think you will be able to sleep?'

'Pretty sure. Why don't you turn in?'

'I like to sit here with you.'

'Do you feel anything strange?' he asked her.

'No. Just a little sleepy.'

'I do,' he said.

He had just felt death come by again.

'You know the only thing I've never lost is curiosity,' he said to her.

'You've never lost anything. You're the most complete man I've ever known.'

'Christ,' he said. 'How little a woman knows. What is that? Your intuition?'

Because, just then, death had come and rested its head on the foot of the cot and he could smell its breath.

'Never believe any of that about a scythe and a skull,' he told her. 'It can be two bicycle policemen as easily, or be a bird. Or it can have a wide snout like a hyena.'

It had moved up on him now, but it had no shape any more. It simply occupied space.

'Tell it to go away.'

It did not go away but moved a little closer.

'You've got a hell of a breath,' he told it. 'You stinking bastard.'

It moved up closer to him still and now he could not speak to it, and when it saw he could not speak it came a little closer, and now he tried to send it away without speaking, but it moved in on him so its weight was all upon his chest, and while it crouched there and he could not move, or speak, he heard the woman say, 'Bwana is asleep now. Take the cot up very gently and carry it into the tent.'

He could not speak to tell her to make it go away and it crouched now, heavier, so he could not breathe. And then, while they lifted the cot, suddenly it was all right and the weight went from his chest.

★ ★ ★

It was morning and had been morning for some time and he heard the plane. It showed very tiny and then made a wide circle and the boys ran out and lit the fires, using kerosene, and piled on grass so there were two big smudges at each end of the level place and the morning breeze blew them toward the camp and the plane circled twice more, low this time, and then glided down and levelled off and landed smoothly and, coming walking toward him, was old Compton in slacks, a tweed jacket and a brown felt hat.

'What's the matter, old cock?' Compton said.

'Bad leg,' he told him. 'Will you have some breakfast?'

'Thanks. I'll just have some tea. It's the Puss Moth you know. I won't be able to take the Memsahib. There's only room for one. Your lorry is on the way.'

Helen had taken Compton aside and was speaking to him. Compton came back more cheery than ever.

'We'll get you right in,' he said. 'I'll be back for the Mem. Now I'm afraid I'll have to stop at Arusha to refuel. We'd better get going.'

'What about the tea?'

'I don't really care about it, you know.'

The boys had picked up the cot and carried it around the green tents and down along the rock and out onto the plain and along past the smudges that were burning brightly now, the grass all consumed, and the wind fanning the fire, to the little plane. It was difficult getting him in, but once in he lay back in the leather seat, and the leg was stuck straight out to one side of the seat where Compton sat. Compton started the motor and got in. He waved to Helen and to the boys and, as the clatter moved into the old familiar roar, they swung around with Compie watching for warthog holes and roared, bumping, along the stretch between the fires and with the last bump rose and he saw them all standing below, waving, and the camp beside the hill, flattening now, and the plain spreading, clumps of trees, and the bush flattening, while the game trails ran now smoothly to the dry waterholes, and there was a new water that he had never known of. The zebra, small rounded backs now, and the wilde-beeste, big-headed dots seeming to climb as they moved in long fingers across the plain, now scattering as the shadow came to-ward them, they were tiny now, and the movement had no gal-lop, and the plain as far as you could see, gray-yellow now and ahead old Compie's tweed back and the brown felt hat. Then they were over the first hills and the wildebeeste were trailing up them, and then they were over mountains with sudden depths of green-rising forest and the solid bamboo slopes, and then the heavy forest again, sculptured into peaks and hollows until they crossed, and hills sloped down and then another plain, hot now, and purple brown, bumpy with heat and Compie looking back to see how he was riding. Then there were other mountains dark ahead.

And then instead of going on to Arusha they turned left, he evidently figured that they had the gas, and looking down he saw a pink sifting cloud, moving over the ground, and in the air, like the first snow in a blizzard, that comes from nowhere, and he knew the locusts were coming up from the South. Then they began to climb and they were going to the East it seemed, and then it darkened and they were in a storm, the rain so thick it seemed like flying through a waterfall, and then they were out and Compie turned his head and grinned and pointed and there, ahead, all he could see, as wide as all the world, great, high, and unbelievably white in the sun, was the square top of Kilimanjaro. And then he knew that there was where he was going.

Just then the hyena stopped whimpering in the night and started to make a strange, human, almost crying sound. The woman heard it and stirred uneasily. She did not wake. In her dream she was at the house on Long Island and it was the night before her daughter's début. Somehow her father was there and he had been very rude. Then the noise the hyena made was so loud she woke and for a moment she did not know where she was and she was very afraid. Then she took the flashlight and shone it on the other cot that they had carried in after Harry had gone to sleep. She could see his bulk under the mosquito bar but somehow he had gotten his leg out and it hung down alongside the cot. The dressings had all come down and she could not look at it.

'Molo,' she called, 'Molo! Molo!'

Then she said, 'Harry, Harry!' Then her voice rising, 'Harry! Please. Oh Harry!'

There was no answer and she could not hear him breathing.

Outside the tent the hyena made the same strange noise that had awakened her. But she did not hear him for the beating of her heart.

THE SHORT HAPPY LIFE OF
FRANCIS MACOMBER

It was now lunch time and they were all sitting under the double green fly of the dining tent pretending that nothing had happened.

'Will you have lime juice or lemon squash?' Macomber asked.

'I'll have a gimlet,' Robert Wilson told him.

'I'll have a gimlet too. I need something,' Macomber's wife said.

'I suppose it's the thing to do,' Macomber agreed. 'Tell him to make three gimlets.'

The mess boy had started them already, lifting the bottles out of the canvas cooling bags that sweated wet in the wind that blew through the trees that shaded the tents.

'What had I ought to give them?' Macomber asked.

'A quid would be plenty,' Wilson told him. 'You don't want to spoil them.'

'Will the headman distribute it?'

'Absolutely.'

Francis Macomber had, half an hour before, been carried to his tent from the edge of the camp in triumph on the arms and shoulders of the cook, the personal boys, the skinner and the porters. The gun-bearers had taken no part in the demonstration. When the native boys put him down at the door of his tent, he had shaken all their hands, received their congratulations, and then gone into the tent and sat on the bed until his wife came in. She did not speak to him when she came in and he left the tent at once to wash his face and hands in the portable wash basin outside and go over to the dining tent to sit in a comfortable canvas chair in the breeze and the shade.

'You've got your lion,' Robert Wilson said to him, 'and a damned fine one too.'

Mrs. Macomber looked at Wilson quickly. She was an extremely handsome and well-kept woman of the beauty and social position which had, five years before, commanded five thousand dollars as the price of endorsing, with photographs, a beauty product which she had never used. She had been married to Francis Macomber for eleven years.

'He is a good lion, isn't he?' Macomber said. His wife looked at him now. She looked at both these men as though she had never seen them before.

One, Wilson, the white hunter, she knew she had never truly seen before. He was about middle height with sandy hair, a stubby mustache, a very red face and extremely cold blue eyes with faint white wrinkles at the corners that grooved merrily when he smiled. He smiled at her now and she looked away from his face at the way his shoulders sloped in the loose tunic he wore with the four big cartridges held in loops where the left breast pocket should have been, at his big brown hands, his old slacks, his very dirty boots and back to his red face again. She noticed where the baked red of his face stopped in a white line that marked the circle left by his Stetson hat that hung now from one of the pegs of the tent pole.

'Well, here's to the lion,' Robert Wilson said. He smiled at her again and, not smiling, she looked curiously at her husband.

Francis Macomber was very tall, very well built if you did not mind that length of bone, dark, his hair cropped like an oarsman, rather thin-lipped, and was considered handsome. He was dressed in the same sort of safari clothes that Wilson wore except that his were new, he was thirty-five years old, kept himself very fit, was good at court games, had a number of big-game fishing records, and had just shown himself, very publicly, to be a coward.

'Here's to the lion,' he said. 'I can't ever thank you for what you did.'

Margaret, his wife, looked away from him and back to Wilson.

'Let's not talk about the lion,' she said.

Wilson looked over at her without smiling and now she smiled at him.

'It's been a very strange day,' she said. 'Hadn't you ought to put your hat on even under the canvas at noon? You told me that, you know.'

'Might put it on,' said Wilson.

'You know you have a very red face, Mr. Wilson,' she told him and smiled again.

'Drink,' said Wilson.

'I don't think so,' she said. 'Francis drinks a great deal, but his face is never red.'

'It's red today,' Macomber tried a joke.

'No,' said Margaret. 'It's mine that's red today. But Mr. Wilson's is always red.'

'Must be racial,' said Wilson. 'I say, you wouldn't like to drop my beauty as a topic, would you?'

'I've just started on it.'

'Let's chuck it,' said Wilson.

'Conversation is going to be so difficult,' Margaret said.

'Don't be silly, Margot,' her husband said.

'No difficulty,' Wilson said. 'Got a damn fine lion.'

Margot looked at them both and they both saw that she was going to cry. Wilson had seen it coming for a long time and he dreaded it. Macomber was past dreading it.

'I wish it hadn't happened. Oh, I wish it hadn't happened,' she said and started for her tent. She made no noise of crying but they could see that her shoulders were shaking under the rose-colored, sun-proofed shirt she wore.

'Women upset,' said Wilson to the tall man. 'Amounts to nothing. Strain on the nerves and one thing'n another.'

'No,' said Macomber. 'I suppose that I rate that for the rest of my life now.'

'Nonsense. Let's have a spot of the giant killer,' said Wilson. 'Forget the whole thing. Nothing to it anyway.'

'We might try,' said Macomber. 'I won't forget what you did for me though.'

'Nothing,' said Wilson. 'All nonsense.'

So they sat there in the shade where the camp was pitched under some wide-topped acacia trees with a boulder-strewn cliff behind them, and a stretch of grass that ran to the bank of a boulder-filled stream in front with forest beyond it, and drank their just-cool lime drinks and avoided one another's eyes while the boys set the table for lunch. Wilson could tell that the boys all knew about it now and when he saw Macomber's personal boy looking curiously at his master while he was putting dishes on the table he snapped at him in Swahili. The boy turned away with his face blank.

'What were you telling him?' Macomber asked.

'Nothing. Told him to look alive or I'd see he got about fifteen of the best.'

'What's that? Lashes?'

'It's quite illegal,' Wilson said. 'You're supposed to fine them.'

'Do you still have them whipped?'

'Oh, yes. They could raise a row if they chose to complain. But they don't. They prefer it to the fines.'

'How strange!' said Macomber.

'Not strange, really,' Wilson said. 'Which would you rather do? Take a good birching or lose your pay?'

Then he felt embarrassed at asking it and before Macomber could answer he went on, 'We all take a beating every day, you know, one way or another.'

This was no better. 'Good God,' he thought. 'I am a diplomat, aren't I?'

'Yes, we take a beating,' said Macomber, still not looking at him. 'I'm awfully sorry about that lion business. It doesn't have to go any further, does it? I mean no one will hear about it, will they?'

'You mean will I tell it at the Mathaiga Club?' Wilson looked at him now coldly. He had not expected this. So he's a bloody four-letter man as well as a bloody coward, he thought. I rather liked him too until today. But how is one to know about an American?

'No,' said Wilson. 'I'm a professional hunter. We never talk about our clients. You can be quite easy on that. It's supposed to be bad form to ask us not to talk though.'

He had decided now that to break would be much easier. He would eat, then, by himself and could read a book with his meals. They would eat by themselves. He would see them through the safari on a very formal basis – what was it the French called it? Distinguished consideration – and it would be a damn sight easier than having to go through this emotional trash. He'd insult him and make a good clean break. Then he could read a book with his meals and he'd still be drinking their whiskey. That was the phrase for it when a safari went bad. You ran into another white hunter and you asked, 'How is everything going?' and he answered, 'Oh, I'm still drinking their whiskey,' and you knew everything had gone to pot.

'I'm sorry,' Macomber said and looked at him with his American face that would stay adolescent until it became middle-aged, and Wilson noted his crew-cropped hair, fine eyes only faintly shifty, good nose, thin lips and handsome jaw. 'I'm sorry I didn't realize that. There are lots of things I don't know.'

So what could he do, Wilson thought. He was all ready to break it off quickly and neatly and here the beggar was apologizing after he had just insulted him. He made one more attempt. 'Don't worry about me talking,' he said. 'I have a living to make. You know in Africa no woman ever misses her lion and no white man ever bolts.'

'I bolted like a rabbit,' Macomber said.

Now what in hell were you going to do about a man who talked like that, Wilson wondered.

Wilson looked at Macomber with his flat, blue, machine-gunner's eyes and the other smiled back at him. He had a pleasant smile if you did not notice how his eyes showed when he was hurt.

'Maybe I can fix it up on buffalo,' he said. 'We're after them next, aren't we?'

'In the morning if you like,' Wilson told him. Perhaps he had been wrong. This was certainly the way to take it. You most certainly could not tell a damned thing about an American. He was all for Macomber again. If you could forget the morning. But, of course, you couldn't. The morning had been about as bad as they come.

'Here comes the Memsahib,' he said. She was walking over from her tent looking refreshed and cheerful and quite lovely. She had a very perfect oval face, so perfect that you expected her to be stupid. But she wasn't stupid, Wilson thought, no, not stupid.

'How is the beautiful red-faced Mr. Wilson? Are you feeling better, Francis, my pearl?'

'Oh, much,' said Macomber.

'I've dropped the whole thing,' she said, sitting down at the table. 'What importance is there to whether Francis is any good at killing lions? That's not his trade. That's Mr. Wilson's trade. Mr. Wilson is really very impressive killing anything. You do kill anything, don't you?'

'Oh, anything,' said Wilson. 'Simply anything.' They are, he thought, the hardest in the world; the hardest, the cruelest, the most predatory and the most attractive and their men have soft-ened or gone to pieces nervously as they have hardened. Or is it that they pick men they can handle? They can't know that much at the age they marry, he thought. He was grateful that he had gone through his education on American women before now because this was a very attractive one.

'We're going after buff in the morning,' he told her.

'I'm coming,' she said.

'No, you're not.'

'Oh, yes, I am. Mayn't I, Francis?'

'Why not stay in camp?'

'Not for anything,' she said. 'I wouldn't miss something like today for anything.'

When she left, Wilson was thinking, when she went off to cry, she seemed a hell of a fine woman. She seemed to understand, to realize, to be hurt for him and for herself and to know how things really stood. She is away for twenty minutes and now she is back, simply enamelled in that American female cruelty. They are the damnedest women. Really the damnedest.

'We'll put on another show for you tomorrow,' Francis Macomber said.

'You're not coming,' Wilson said.

'You're very mistaken,' she told him. 'And I want *so* to see you perform again. You were lovely this morning. That is if blowing things' heads off is lovely.'

'Here's the lunch,' said Wilson. 'You're very merry, aren't you?'

'Why not? I didn't come out here to be dull.'

'Well, it hasn't been dull,' Wilson said. He could see the boulders in the river and the high bank beyond with the trees and he remembered the morning.

'Oh, no,' she said. 'It's been charming. And tomorrow. You don't know how I look forward to tomorrow.'

'That's eland he's offering you,' Wilson said.

'They're the big cowy things that jump like hares, aren't they?'

'I suppose that describes them,' Wilson said.

'It's very good meat,' Macomber said.

'Did you shoot it, Francis?' she asked.

'Yes.'

'They're not dangerous, are they?'

'Only if they fall on you,' Wilson told her.

'I'm so glad.'

'Why not let up on the bitchery just a little, Margot,' Macomber said, cutting the eland steak and putting some mashed potato, gravy and carrot on the down-turned fork that tined through the piece of meat.

'I suppose I could,' she said, 'since you put it so prettily.'

'Tonight we'll have champagne for the lion,' Wilson said. 'It's a bit too hot at noon.'

'Oh, the lion,' Margot said. 'I'd forgotten the lion!'

So, Robert Wilson thought to himself, she *is* giving him a ride, isn't she? Or do you suppose that's her idea of putting up a good show? How should a woman act when she discovers her husband is a bloody coward? She's damn cruel but they're all cruel. They govern, of course, and to govern one has to be cruel sometimes. Still, I've seen enough of their damn terrorism.

'Have some more eland,' he said to her politely.

That afternoon, late, Wilson and Macomber went out in the motor car with the native driver and the two gun-bearers. Mrs. Macomber stayed in the camp. It was too hot to go out, she said, and she was going with them in the early morning. As they drove off Wilson saw her standing under the big tree, looking pretty rather than beautiful in her faintly rosy khaki, her dark hair drawn back off her forehead and gathered in a knot low on her neck, her face as fresh, he thought, as though she were in England. She waved to them as the car went off through the swale of high grass and curved around through the trees into the small hills of orchard bush.

In the orchard bush they found a herd of impala, and leaving the car they stalked one old ram with long, wide-spread horns and Macomber killed it with a very creditable shot that knocked the buck down at a good two hundred yards and sent the herd off bounding wildly and leaping over one another's backs in long, leg-drawn-up leaps as unbelievable and as floating as those one makes sometimes in dreams.

'That was a good shot,' Wilson said. 'They're a small target.'

'Is it a worth-while head?' Macomber asked.

'It's excellent,' Wilson told him. 'You shoot like that and you'll have no trouble.'

'Do you think we'll find buffalo tomorrow?'

'There's a good chance of it. They feed out early in the morning and with luck we may catch them in the open.'

'I'd like to clear away that lion business,' Macomber said. 'It's not very pleasant to have your wife see you do something like that.'

I should think it would be even more unpleasant to do it, Wilson thought, wife or no wife, or to talk about it having done it. But he said, 'I wouldn't think about that any more. Any one could be upset by his first lion. That's all over.'

But that night after dinner and a whiskey and soda by the fire before going to bed, as Francis Macomber lay on his cot with the mosquito bar over him and listened to the night noises it was not all over. It was neither all over nor was it beginning. It was there exactly as it happened with some parts of it indelibly emphasized and he was miserably ashamed at it. But more than shame he felt cold, hollow fear in him. The fear was still there like a cold slimy hollow in all the emptiness where once his confidence had been and it made him feel sick. It was still there with him now.

It had started the night before when he had wakened and heard the lion roaring somewhere up along the river. It was a deep sound and at the end there were sort of coughing grunts that made him seem just outside the tent, and when Francis Macomber woke in the night to hear it he was afraid. He could hear his wife breathing quietly, asleep. There was no one to tell he was afraid, nor to be afraid with him, and, lying alone, he did not know the Somali proverb that says a brave man is always frightened three times by a lion; when he first sees his track, when he first hears him roar and when he first confronts him. Then while they were eating breakfast by lantern light out in the dining tent, before the sun was up, the lion roared again and Francis thought he was just at the edge of camp.

'Sounds like an old-timer,' Robert Wilson said, looking up from his kippers and coffee. 'Listen to him cough.'

'Is he very close?'

'A mile or so up the stream.'

'Will we see him?'

'We'll have a look.'

'Does his roaring carry that far? It sounds as though he were right in camp.'

'Carries a hell of a long way,' said Robert Wilson. 'It's strange the way it carries. Hope he's a shootable cat. The boys said there was a very big one about here.'

'If I get a shot, where should I hit him,' Macomber asked, 'to stop him?'

'In the shoulders,' Wilson said. 'In the neck if you can make it. Shoot for bone. Break him down.'

'I hope I can place it properly,' Macomber said.

'You shoot very well,' Wilson told him. 'Take your time. Make sure of him. The first one in is the one that counts.'

'What range will it be?'

'Can't tell. Lion has something to say about that. Don't shoot unless it's close enough so you can make sure.'

'At under a hundred yards?' Macomber asked.

Wilson looked at him quickly.

'Hundred's about right. Might have to take him a bit under. Shouldn't chance a shot at much over that. A hundred's a decent range. You can hit him wherever you want at that. Here comes the Memsahib.'

'Good morning,' she said. 'Are we going after that lion?'

'As soon as you deal with your breakfast,' Wilson said. 'How are you feeling?'

'Marvellous,' she said. 'I'm very excited.'

'I'll just go and see that everything is ready.' Wilson went off. As he left the lion roared again.

'Noisy beggar,' Wilson said. 'We'll put a stop to that.'

'What's the matter, Francis?' his wife asked him.

'Nothing,' Macomber said.

'Yes, there is,' she said. 'What are you upset about?'

'Nothing,' he said.

'Tell me,' she looked at him. 'Don't you feel well?'

'It's that damned roaring,' he said. 'It's been going on all night, you know.'

'Why didn't you wake me,' she said. 'I'd love to have heard it.'

'I've got to kill the damned thing,' Macomber said, miserably.

'Well, that's what you're out here for, isn't it?'

'Yes. But I'm nervous. Hearing the thing roar gets on my nerves.'

'Well then, as Wilson said, kill him and stop his roaring.'

'Yes, darling,' said Francis Macomber. 'It sounds easy, doesn't it?'

'You're not afraid, are you?'

'Of course not. But I'm nervous from hearing him roar all night.'

'You'll kill him marvellously,' she said. 'I know you will. I'm awfully anxious to see it.'

'Finish your breakfast and we'll be starting.'

'It's not light yet,' she said. 'This is a ridiculous hour.'

Just then the lion roared in a deep-chested moaning, suddenly guttural, ascending vibration that seemed to shake the air and ended in a sigh and a heavy, deep-chested grunt.

'He sounds almost here,' Macomber's wife said.

'My God,' said Macomber. 'I hate that damned noise.'

'It's very impressive.'

'Impressive. It's frightful.'

Robert Wilson came up then carrying his short, ugly, shockingly big-bored .505 Gibbs and grinning.

'Come on,' he said. 'Your gun-bearer has your Springfield and the big gun. Everything's in the car. Have you solids?'

'Yes.'

'I'm ready,' Mrs. Macomber said.

'Must make him stop that racket,' Wilson said. 'You get in front. The Memsahib can sit back here with me.'

They climbed into the motor car and, in the gray first daylight, moved off up the river through the trees. Macomber opened the breech of his rifle and saw he had metal-cased bullets, shut the bolt and put the rifle on safety. He saw his hand was trembling. He felt in his pocket for more cartridges and moved his fingers over the cartridges in the loops of his tunic front. He turned back to where Wilson sat in the rear seat of the doorless, box-bodied motor car beside his wife, them both grinning with excitement, and Wilson leaned forward and whispered.

'See the birds dropping. Means the old boy has left his kill.'

On the far bank of the stream Macomber could see, above the trees, vultures circling and plummeting down.

'Chances are he'll come to drink along here,' Wilson whispered. 'Before he goes to lay up. Keep an eye out.'

They were driving slowly along the high bank of the stream which here cut deeply to its boulder-filled bed, and they wound in and out through big trees as they drove. Macomber was watching the opposite bank when he felt Wilson take hold of his arm. The car stopped.

'There he is,' he heard the whisper. 'Ahead and to the right. Get out and take him. He's a marvellous lion.'

Macomber saw the lion now. He was standing almost broadside, his great head up and turned toward them. The early morning breeze that blew toward them was just stirring his dark mane, and the lion looked huge, silhouetted on the rise of bank in the gray morning light, his shoulders heavy, his barrel of a body bulking smoothly.

'How far is he?' asked Macomber, raising his rifle.

'About seventy-five. Get out and take him.'

'Why not shoot from where I am?'

'You don't shoot them from cars,' he heard Wilson saying in his ear. 'Get out. He's not going to stay there all day.'

Macomber stepped out of the curved opening at the side of the front seat, onto the step and down onto the ground. The lion still stood looking majestically and coolly toward this object that his eyes only showed in silhouette, bulking like some super-rhino. There was no man smell carried toward him and he watched the object, moving his great head a little from side to side. Then watching the object, not afraid, but hesitating before going down the bank to drink with such a thing opposite him, he saw a man figure detach itself from it and he turned his heavy head and swung away toward the cover of the trees as he heard a cracking crash and felt the slam of a .30-06 220-grain solid bullet that bit his flank and ripped in sudden hot scalding nausea through his stomach. He trotted, heavy, big-footed, swinging wounded full-bellied, through the trees toward the tall grass and cover, and the crash came again to go past him ripping the air apart. Then it crashed again and he felt the blow as it hit his lower ribs and ripped on through, blood sudden hot and frothy in his mouth, and he galloped toward the high grass where he could crouch and not be seen and make them bring the crashing thing close enough so he could make a rush and get the man that held it.

Macomber had not thought how the lion felt as he got out of the car. He only knew his hands were shaking and as he walked away from the car it was almost impossible for him to make his legs move. They were stiff in the thighs, but he could feel the muscles fluttering. He raised the rifle, sighted on the junction of the lion's head and shoulders and pulled the trigger. Nothing happened though he pulled until he thought his finger would break. Then he knew he had the safety on and as he lowered the rifle to move the safety over he moved another frozen pace forward, and the lion seeing his silhouette flow clear of the silhouette of the car, turned and started off at a trot, and, as Macomber fired, he heard a whunk that meant that the bullet was home; but the lion kept on going. Macomber shot again and every one saw the bullet throw a spout of dirt beyond the trotting lion. He shot again, remembering to lower his aim, and they all heard the bullet hit, and the lion went into a gallop and was in the tall grass before he had the bolt pushed forward.

Macomber stood there feeling sick at his stomach, his hands that held the Springfield still cocked, shaking, and his wife and Robert Wilson were standing by him. Beside him too were the two gun-bearers chattering in Wakamba.

'I hit him,' Macomber said. 'I hit him twice.'

'You gut-shot him and you hit him somewhere forward,' Wilson said without enthusiasm. The gun-bearers looked very grave. They were silent now.

'You may have killed him,' Wilson went on. 'We'll have to wait a while before we go in to find out.'

'What do you mean?'

'Let him get sick before we follow him up.'

'Oh,' said Macomber.

'He's a hell of a fine lion,' Wilson said cheerfully. 'He's gotten into a bad place though.'

'Why is it bad?'

'Can't see him until you're on him.'

'Oh,' said Macomber.

'Come on,' said Wilson. 'The Memsahib can stay here in the car. We'll go to have a look at the blood spoor.'

'Stay here, Margot,' Macomber said to his wife. His mouth was very dry and it was hard for him to talk.

'Why?' she asked.

'Wilson says to.'

'We're going to have a look,' Wilson said. 'You stay here. You can see even better from here.'

'All right.'

Wilson spoke in Swahili to the driver. He nodded and said, 'Yes, Bwana.'

Then they went down the steep bank and across the stream, climbing over and around the boulders and up the other bank, pulling up by some projecting roots, and along it until they found where the lion had been trotting when Macomber first shot. There was dark blood on the short grass that the gun-bearers pointed out with grass stems, and that ran away behind the river bank trees.

'What do we do?' asked Macomber.

'Not much choice,' said Wilson. 'We can't bring the car over. Bank's too steep. We'll let him stiffen up a bit and then you and I'll go in and have a look for him.'

'Can't we set the grass on fire?' Macomber asked.

'Too green.'

'Can't we send beaters?'

Wilson looked at him appraisingly. 'Of course we can,' he said. 'But it's just a touch murderous. You see, we know the lion's wounded. You can drive an unwounded lion – he'll move on ahead of a noise – but a wounded lion's going to charge. You can't see him until you're right on him. He'll make himself perfectly flat in cover you wouldn't think would hide a hare. You can't very well send boys in there to that sort of a show. Somebody bound to get mauled.'

'What about the gun-bearers?'

'Oh, they'll go with us. It's their *shauri*. You see, they signed on for it. They don't look too happy though, do they?'

'I don't want to go in there,' said Macomber. It was out before he knew he'd said it.

'Neither do I,' said Wilson very cheerily. 'Really no choice though.' Then, as an afterthought, he glanced at Macomber and saw suddenly how he was trembling and the pitiful look on his face.

'You don't have to go in, of course,' he said. 'That's what I'm hired for, you know. That's why I'm so expensive.'

'You mean you'd go in by yourself? Why not leave him there?'

Robert Wilson, whose entire occupation had been with the lion and the problem he presented, and who had not been thinking about Macomber except to note that he was rather windy, suddenly felt as though he had opened the wrong door in a hotel and seen something shameful.

'What do you mean?'

'Why not just leave him?'

'You mean pretend to ourselves he hasn't been hit?'

'No. Just drop it.'

'It isn't done.'

'Why not?'

'For one thing, he's certain to be suffering. For another, some one else might run onto him.'

'I see.'

'But you don't have to have anything to do with it.'

'I'd like to,' Macomber said. 'I'm just scared, you know.'

'I'll go ahead when we go in,' Wilson said, 'with Kongoni tracking. You keep behind me and a little to one side. Chances are we'll hear him growl. If we see him we'll both shoot. Don't worry about anything. I'll keep you backed up. As a matter of fact, you know, perhaps you'd better not go. It might be much better. Why don't you go over and join the Memsahib while I just get it over with?'

'No, I want to go.'

'All right,' said Wilson. 'But don't go in if you don't want to. This is my *shauri* now, you know.'

'I want to go,' said Macomber.

They sat under a tree and smoked.

'Want to go back and speak to the Memsahib while we're waiting?' Wilson asked.

'No.'

'I'll just step back and tell her to be patient.'

'Good,' said Macomber. He sat there, sweating under his arms, his mouth dry, his stomach hollow feeling, wanting to find courage to tell Wilson to go on and finish off the lion without him. He could not know that Wilson was furious because he had not noticed the state he was in earlier and sent him back to his wife. While he sat there Wilson came up. 'I have your big gun,' he said. 'Take it. We've given him time, I think. Come on.'

Macomber took the big gun and Wilson said:

'Keep behind me and about five yards to the right and do exactly as I tell you.' Then he spoke in Swahili to the two gun-bearers who looked the picture of gloom.

'Let's go,' he said.

'Could I have a drink of water?' Macomber asked. Wilson spoke to the older gun-bearer, who wore a canteen on his belt, and the man unbuckled it, unscrewed the top and handed it to Macomber, who took it noticing how heavy it seemed and how hairy and shoddy the felt covering was in his hand. He raised it to drink and looked ahead at the high grass with the flat-topped trees behind it. A breeze was blowing toward them and the grass rippled gently in the wind. He looked at the gun-bearer and he could see the gun-bearer was suffering too with fear.

Thirty-five yards into the grass the big lion lay flattened out along the ground. His ears were back and his only movement was a slight twitching up and down of his long, black-tufted tail. He had turned at bay as soon as he had reached this cover and he was sick with the wound through his full belly, and weakening with the wound through his lungs that brought a thin foamy red to his mouth each time he breathed. His flanks were wet and hot and flies were on the little openings the solid bullets had made in his tawny hide, and his big yellow eyes, narrowed with hate, looked straight ahead, only blinking when the pain came as he breathed, and his claws dug in the soft baked earth. All of him, pain, sickness, hatred and all of his remaining strength, was tightening into an absolute concentration for a rush. He could hear the men talking and he waited, gathering all of himself into this preparation for a charge as soon as the men would come into the grass. As he heard their voices his tail stiffened to twitch up and down, and, as they came into the edge of the grass, he made a coughing grunt and charged.

Kongoni, the old gun-bearer, in the lead watching the blood spoor, Wilson watching the grass for any movement, his big gun ready, the second gun-bearer looking ahead and listening,

Macomber close to Wilson, his rifle cocked, they had just moved into the grass when Macomber heard the blood-choked coughing grunt, and saw the swishing rush in the grass. The next thing he knew he was running; running wildly, in panic in the open, running toward the stream.

He heard the *ca-ra-wong!* of Wilson's big rifle, and again in a second crashing *carawong!* and turning saw the lion, horrible-looking now, with half his head seeming to be gone, crawling toward Wilson in the edge of the tall grass while the red-faced man worked the bolt on the short ugly rifle and aimed carefully as another blasting *carawong!* came from the muzzle, and the crawling, heavy, yellow bulk of the lion stiffened and the huge, mutilated head slid forward and Macomber, standing by himself in the clearing where he had run, holding a loaded rifle, while two black men and a white man looked back at him in contempt, knew the lion was dead. He came toward Wilson, his tallness all seeming a naked reproach, and Wilson looked at him and said:

'Want to take pictures?'

'No,' he said.

That was all any one had said until they reached the motor car. Then Wilson had said:

'Hell of a fine lion. Boys will skin him out. We might as well stay here in the shade.'

Macomber's wife had not looked at him nor he at her and he had sat by her in the back seat with Wilson sitting in the front seat. Once he had reached over and taken his wife's hand without looking at her and she had removed her hand from his. Looking across the stream to where the gun-bearers were skinning out the lion he could see that she had been able to see the whole thing. While they sat there his wife had reached forward and put her hand on Wilson's shoulder. He turned and she had leaned forward over the low seat and kissed him on the mouth.

'Oh, I say,' said Wilson, going redder than his natural baked color.

'Mr. Robert Wilson,' she said. 'The beautiful red-faced Mr. Robert Wilson.'

Then she sat down beside Macomber again and looked away across the stream to where the lion lay, with uplifted, white-muscled, tendon-marked naked forearms, and white bloating belly, as the black men fleshed away the skin. Finally the gun-bearers brought the skin over, wet and heavy, and climbed in behind with it, rolling it up before they got in, and the motor car started. No one had said anything more until they were back in camp.

That was the story of the lion. Macomber did not know how the lion had felt before he started his rush, nor during it when the unbelievable smash of the .505 with a muzzle velocity of two tons had hit him in the mouth, nor what kept him coming after that, when the second ripping crash had smashed his hind quarters and he had come crawling on toward the crashing, blasting thing that had destroyed him. Wilson knew something about it and only expressed it by saying, 'Damned fine lion,' but Macomber did not know how Wilson felt about things either. He did not know how his wife felt except that she was through with him.

His wife had been through with him before but it never lasted. He was very wealthy, and would be much wealthier, and he knew she would not leave him ever now. That was one of the few things that he really knew. He knew about that, about motor cycles – that was earliest – about motor cars, about duck-shooting, about fishing, trout, salmon and big-sea, about sex in books, many books, too many books, about all court games, about dogs, not much about horses, about hanging on to his money, about most of the other things his world dealt in, and about his wife not leaving him. His wife had been a great beauty and she was still a great beauty in Africa, but she was not a great enough beauty any more at home to be able to leave him and better herself and she knew it and he knew it. She had missed the chance to leave him and he knew it. If he had been better with women she would probably have started to worry about him getting another new, beautiful wife; but she knew too much about him to worry about him either. Also, he had always had a great tolerance which seemed the nicest thing about him if it were not the most sinister.

All in all they were known as a comparatively happily married couple, one of those whose disruption is often rumored but never occurs, and as the society columnist put it, they were adding more than a spice of *adventure* to their much envied and ever-enduring *Romance* by a *Safari* in what was known as *Darkest Africa* until the Martin Johnsons lighted it on so many silver screens where they were pursuing *Old Simba* the lion, the buffalo, *Tembo* the elephant and as well collecting specimens for the Museum of Natural History. This same columnist had reported them *on the verge* at least three times in the past and they had been. But they always made it up. They had a sound basis of union. Margot was too beautiful for Macomber to divorce her and Macomber had too much money for Margot ever to leave him.

It was now about three o'clock in the morning and Francis Macomber, who had been asleep a little while after he had stopped thinking about the lion, wakened and then slept again, woke suddenly, frightened in a dream of the bloody-headed lion standing over him, and listening while his heart pounded, he realized that his wife was not in the other cot in the tent. He lay awake with that knowledge for two hours.

At the end of that time his wife came into the tent, lifted her mosquito bar and crawled cozily into bed.

'Where have you been?' Macomber asked in the darkness.

'Hello,' she said. 'Are you awake?'

'Where have you been?'

'I just went out to get a breath of air.'

'You did, like hell.'

'What do you want me to say, darling?'

'Where have you been?'

'Out to get a breath of air.'

'That's a new name for it. You *are* a bitch.'

'Well, you're a coward.'

'All right,' he said. 'What of it?'

'Nothing as far as I'm concerned. But please let's not talk, darling, because I'm very sleepy.'

'You think that I'll take anything.'

'I know you will, sweet.'

'Well, I won't.'

'Please, darling, let's not talk. I'm so very sleepy.'

'There wasn't going to be any of that. You promised there wouldn't be.'

'Well, there is now,' she said sweetly.

'You said if we made this trip that there would be none of that. You promised.'

'Yes, darling. That's the way I meant it to be. But the trip was spoiled yesterday. We don't have to talk about it, do we?'

'You don't wait long when you have an advantage, do you?'

'Please let's not talk. I'm so sleepy, darling.'

'I'm going to talk.'

'Don't mind me then, because I'm going to sleep.' And she did.

At breakfast they were all three at the table before daylight and Francis Macomber found that, of all the many men that he had hated, he hated Robert Wilson the most.

'Sleep well?' Wilson asked in his throaty voice, filling a pipe. 'Did you?'

'Topping,' the white hunter told him.

You bastard, thought Macomber, you insolent bastard.

So she woke him when she came in, Wilson thought, looking at them both with his flat, cold eyes. Well, why doesn't he keep his wife where she belongs? What does he think I am, a bloody plaster saint? Let him keep her where she belongs. It's his own fault.

'Do you think we'll find buffalo?' Margot asked, pushing away a dish of apricots.

'Chance of it,' Wilson said and smiled at her. 'Why don't you stay in camp?'

'Not for anything,' she told him.

'Why not order her to stay in camp?' Wilson said to Macomber.

'You order her,' said Macomber coldly.

'Let's not have any ordering, nor,' turning to Macomber, 'any silliness, Francis,' Margot said quite pleasantly.

'Are you ready to start?' Macomber asked.

'Any time,' Wilson told him. 'Do you want the Memsahib to go?'

'Does it make any difference whether I do or not?'

The hell with it, thought Robert Wilson. The utter complete hell with it. So this is what it's going to be like. Well, this is what it's going to be like, then.

'Makes no difference,' he said.

'You're sure you wouldn't like to stay in camp with her yourself and let me go out and hunt the buffalo?' Macomber asked.

'Can't do that,' said Wilson. 'Wouldn't talk rot if I were you.'

'I'm not talking rot. I'm disgusted.'

'Bad word, disgusted.'

'Francis, will you please try to speak sensibly,' his wife said.

'I speak too damned sensibly,' Macomber said. 'Did you ever eat such filthy food?'

'Something wrong with the food?' asked Wilson quietly.

'No more than with everything else.'

'I'd pull yourself together, laddybuck,' Wilson said very quietly. 'There's a boy waits at table that understands a little English.'

'The hell with him.'

Wilson stood up and puffing on his pipe strolled away, speaking a few words in Swahili to one of the gun-bearers who was standing waiting for him. Macomber and his wife sat on at the table. He was staring at his coffee cup.

'If you make a scene I'll leave you, darling,' Margot said quietly.

'No, you won't.'

'You can try it and see.'

'You won't leave me.'

'No,' she said. 'I won't leave you and you'll behave yourself.'

'Behave myself? That's a way to talk. Behave myself.'

'Yes. Behave yourself.'

'Why don't *you* try behaving?'

'I've tried it so long. So very long.'

'I hate that red-faced swine,' Macomber said. 'I loathe the sight of him.'

'He's really *very* nice.'

'Oh, *shut up*,' Macomber almost shouted. Just then the car came up and stopped in front of the dining tent and the driver and the two gun-bearers got out. Wilson walked over and looked at the husband and wife sitting there at the table.

'Going shooting?' he asked.

'Yes,' said Macomber, standing up. 'Yes.'

'Better bring a woolly. It will be cool in the car,' Wilson said.

'I'll get my leather jacket,' Margot said.

'The boy has it,' Wilson told her. He climbed into the front with the driver and Francis Macomber and his wife sat, not speaking, in the back seat.

Hope the silly beggar doesn't take a notion to blow the back of my head off, Wilson thought to himself. Women *are* a nuisance on safari.

The car was grinding down to cross the river at a pebbly ford in the gray daylight and then climbed, angling up the steep bank, where Wilson had ordered a way shovelled out the day before so they could reach the parklike wooded rolling country on the far side.

It was a good morning, Wilson thought. There was a heavy dew and as the wheels went through the grass and low bushes he could smell the odor of the crushed fronds. It was an odor like verbena and he liked this early morning smell of the dew, the crushed bracken and the look of the tree trunks showing black through the early morning mist, as the car made its way through the untracked, parklike country. He had put the two in the back seat out of his mind now and was thinking about buffalo. The buffalo that he was after stayed in the daytime in a thick swamp where it was impossible to get a shot, but in the night they fed out into an open stretch of country and if he could come between them and their swamp with the car, Macomber would have a good chance at them in the open. He did not want to hunt buff with Macomber in thick cover. He did not want to hunt buff or anything else with Macomber at all, but he was a professional hunter and he had hunted with some rare ones in his time. If they got buff today there would only be rhino to come and the poor man would have gone through his dangerous game and things might pick up. He'd have nothing more to do with the woman and Macomber would get over that too. He must have gone through plenty of that before by the look of things. Poor beggar. He must have a way of getting over it. Well, it was the poor sod's own bloody fault.

He, Robert Wilson, carried a double size cot on safari to accommodate any windfalls he might receive. He had hunted for a certain clientele, the international, fast, sporting set, where the women did not feel they were getting their money's worth unless they had shared that cot with the white hunter. He despised them when he was away from them although he liked some of them well enough at the time, but he made his living by them; and their standards were his standards as long as they were hiring him.

They were his standards in all except the shooting. He had his own standards about the killing and they could live up to them or get some one else to hunt them. He knew, too, that they all respected him for this. This Macomber was an odd one though. Damned if he wasn't. Now the wife. Well, the wife. Yes, the wife. Hm, the wife. Well he'd dropped all that. He looked around at them. Macomber sat grim and furious. Margot smiled at him. She looked younger today, more innocent and fresher and not so professionally beautiful. What's in her heart God knows, Wilson thought. She hadn't talked much last night. At that it was a pleasure to see her.

The motor car climbed up a slight rise and went on through the trees and then out into a grassy prairie-like opening and kept in the shelter of the trees along the edge, the driver going slowly and Wilson looking carefully out across the prairie and all along its far side. He stopped the car and studied the opening with his field glasses. Then he motioned to the driver to go on and the car moved slowly along, the driver avoiding warthog holes and driving around the mud castles ants had built. Then, looking across the opening, Wilson suddenly turned and said,

'By God, there they are!'

And looking where he pointed, while the car jumped forward and Wilson spoke in rapid Swahili to the driver, Macomber saw three huge, black animals looking almost cylindrical in their long heaviness, like big black tank cars, moving at a gallop across the far edge of the open prairie. They moved at a stiff-necked, stiff bodied gallop and he could see the upswept wide black horns on their heads as they galloped heads out; the heads not moving.

'They're three old bulls,' Wilson said. 'We'll cut them off before they get to the swamp.'

The car was going a wild forty-five miles an hour across the open and as Macomber watched, the buffalo got bigger and bigger until he could see the gray, hairless, scabby look of one huge bull and how his neck was a part of his shoulders and the shiny black of his horns as he galloped a little behind the others that were strung out in that steady plunging gait; and then, the car swaying as though it had just jumped a road, they drew up close and he could see the plunging hugeness of the bull, and the dust in his sparsely haired hide, the wide boss of horn and his outstretched, wide-nostrilled muzzle, and he was raising his rifle when Wilson shouted, 'Not from the car, you fool!' and he had no fear, only hatred of Wilson, while the brakes clamped on and the car skidded, plowing sideways to an almost stop and Wilson was out on one side and he on the other, stumbling as his feet hit the still speeding-by of the earth, and then he was shooting at the bull as he moved away, hearing the bullets whunk into him, emptying his rifle at him as he moved steadily away, finally remembering to get his shots forward into the shoulder, and as he fumbled to re-load, he saw the bull was down. Down on his knees, his big head tossing, and seeing the other two still galloping he shot at the leader and hit him. He shot again and missed and he heard the *carawonging* roar as Wilson shot and saw the leading bull slide forward onto his nose.

'Get that other,' Wilson said. 'Now you're shooting!'

But the other bull was moving steadily at the same gallop and he missed, throwing a spout of dirt, and Wilson missed and the dust rose in a cloud and Wilson shouted, 'Come on. He's too far!' and grabbed his arm and they were in the car again, Macomber and Wilson hanging on the sides and rocketing swayingly over the uneven ground, drawing up on the steady, plunging, heavy-necked, straight-moving gallop of the bull.

They were behind him and Macomber was filling his rifle, dropping shells onto the ground, jamming it, clearing the jam, then they were almost up with the bull when Wilson yelled 'Stop,' and the car skidded so that it almost swung over and Macomber fell forward onto his feet, slammed his bolt forward and fired as far forward as he could aim into the galloping, rounded black back, aimed and shot again, then again, then again, and the bullets, all of them hitting, had no effect on the buffalo that he could see. Then Wilson shot, the roar deafening him, and he could see the bull stagger. Macomber shot again, aiming carefully, and down he came, onto his knees.

'All right,' Wilson said. 'Nice work. That's the three.'

Macomber felt a drunken elation.

'How many times did you shoot?' he asked.

'Just three,' Wilson said. 'You killed the first bull. The biggest one. I helped you finish the other two. Afraid they might have got into cover. You had them killed. I was just mopping up a little. You shot damn well.'

'Let's go to the car,' said Macomber. 'I want a drink.'

'Got to finish off that buff first,' Wilson told him. The buffalo was on his knees and he jerked his head furiously and bellowed in pig-eyed, roaring rage as they came toward him.

'Watch he doesn't get up,' Wilson said. Then, 'Get a little broadside and take him in the neck just behind the ear.'

Macomber aimed carefully at the center of the huge, jerking, rage-driven neck and shot. At the shot the head dropped forward.

'That does it,' said Wilson. 'Got the spine. They're a hell of a looking thing, aren't they?'

'Let's get the drink,' said Macomber. In his life he had never felt so good.

In the car Macomber's wife sat very white-faced. 'You were marvellous, darling,' she said to Macomber. 'What a ride.'

'Was it rough?' Wilson asked.

'It was frightful. I've never been more frightened in my life.'

'Let's all have a drink,' Macomber said.

'By all means,' said Wilson. 'Give it to the Memsahib.' She drank the neat whiskey from the flask and shuddered a little when she swallowed. She handed the flask to Macomber who handed it to Wilson.

'It was frightfully exciting,' she said. 'It's given me a dreadful headache. I didn't know you were allowed to shoot them from cars though.

'No one shot from cars,' said Wilson coldly.

'I mean chase them from cars.'

'Wouldn't ordinarily,' Wilson said. 'Seemed sporting enough to me though while we were doing it. Taking more chance driving that way across the plain full of holes and one thing and another than hunting on foot. Buffalo could have charged us each time we shot if he liked. Gave him every chance. Wouldn't mention it to any one though. It's illegal if that's what you mean.'

'It seemed very unfair to me,' Margot said, 'chasing those big helpless things in a motor car.'

'Did it?' said Wilson.

'What would happen if they heard about it in Nairobi?'

'I'd lose my licence for one thing. Other unpleasantnesses,' Wilson said, taking a drink from the flask. 'I'd be out of business.'

'Really?'

'Yes, really.'

'Well,' said Macomber, and he smiled for the first time all day. 'Now she has something on you.'

'You have such a pretty way of putting things, Francis,' Margot Macomber said. Wilson looked at them both. If a four-letter man marries a five-letter woman, he was thinking, what number of letters would their children be? What he said was, 'We lost a gun-bearer. Did you notice it?'

'My God, no,' Macomber said.

'Here he comes,' Wilson said. 'He's all right. He must have fallen off when we left the first bull.'

Approaching them was the middle-aged gun-bearer, limping along in his knitted cap, khaki tunic, shorts and rubber sandals, gloomy-faced and disgusted looking. As he came up he called out to Wilson in Swahili and they all saw the change in the white hunter's face.

'What does he say?' asked Margot.

'He says the first bull got up and went into the bush,' Wilson said with no expression in his voice.

'Oh,' said Macomber blankly.

'Then it's going to be just like the lion,' said Margot, full of anticipation.

'It's not going to be a damned bit like the lion,' Wilson told her. 'Did you want another drink, Macomber?'

'Thanks, yes,' Macomber said. He expected the feeling he had had about the lion to come back but it did not. For the first time in his life he really felt wholly without fear. Instead of fear he had a feeling of definite elation.

'We'll go and have a look at the second bull,' Wilson said. 'I'll tell the driver to put the car in the shade.'

'What are you going to do?' asked Margaret Macomber.

'Take a look at the buff,' Wilson said.

'I'll come.'

'Come along.'

The three of them walked over to where the second buffalo bulked blackly in the open, head forward on the grass, the massive horns swung wide.

'He's a very good head,' Wilson said. 'That's close to a fifty-inch spread.'

Macomber was looking at him with delight.

'He's hateful looking,' said Margot. 'Can't we go into the shade?'

'Of course,' Wilson said. 'Look,' he said to Macomber, and pointed. 'See that patch of bush?'

'Yes.'

'That's where the first bull went in. The gun-bearer said when he fell off the bull was down. He was watching us helling along and the other two buff galloping. When he looked up there was the bull up and looking at him. Gun-bearer ran like hell and the bull went off slowly into that bush.'

'Can we go in after him now?' asked Macomber eagerly.

Wilson looked at him appraisingly. Damned if this isn't a strange one, he thought. Yesterday he's scared sick and today he's a ruddy fire eater.

'No, we'll give him a while.'

'Let's please go into the shade,' Margot said. Her face was white and she looked ill.

They made their way to the car where it stood under a single, wide-spreading tree and all climbed in.

'Chances are he's dead in there,' Wilson remarked. 'After a little we'll have a look.'

Macomber felt a wild unreasonable happiness that he had never known before.

'By God, that was a chase,' he said. 'I've never felt any such feeling. Wasn't it marvellous, Margot?'

'I hated it.'

'Why?'

'I hated it,' she said bitterly. 'I loathed it.'

'You know I don't think I'd ever be afraid of anything again,' Macomber said to Wilson. 'Something happened in me after we first saw the buff and started after him. Like a dam bursting. It was pure excitement.'

'Cleans out your liver,' said Wilson. 'Damn funny things happen to people.'

Macomber's face was shining. 'You know something did happen to me,' he said. 'I feel absolutely different.'

His wife said nothing and eyed him strangely. She was sitting far back in the seat and Macomber was sitting forward talking to Wilson who turned sideways talking over the back of the front seat.

'You know, I'd like to try another lion,' Macomber said. 'I'm really not afraid of them now. After all, what can they do to you?'

'That's it,' said Wilson. 'Worst one can do is kill you. How does it go? Shakespeare. Damned good. See if I can remember. Oh, damned good. Used to quote it to myself at one time. Let's see. "By my troth, I care not; a man can die but once; we owe God a death and let it go which way it will, he that dies this year is quit for the next." Damned fine, eh?'

He was very embarrassed, having brought out this thing he had lived by, but he had seen men come of age before and it always moved him. It was not a matter of their twenty-first birthday.

It had taken a strange chance of hunting, a sudden precipitation into action without opportunity for worrying beforehand, to bring this about with Macomber, but regardless of how it had happened it had most certainly happened. Look at the beggar now, Wilson thought. It's that some of them stay little boys so long, Wilson thought. Sometimes all their lives. Their figures stay boyish when they're fifty. The great American boy-men. Damned strange people. But he liked this Macomber now. Damned strange fellow. Probably meant the end of cuckoldry too. Well, that would be a damned good thing. Damned good thing. Beggar had probably been afraid all his life. Don't know what started it. But over now. Hadn't had time to be afraid with the buff. That and being angry too. Motor car too. Motor cars made it familiar. Be a damn fire eater now. He'd seen it in the war work the same way. More of a change than any loss of virginity. Fear gone like an operation. Something else grew in its place. Main thing a man had. Made him into a man. Women knew it too. No bloody fear.

From the far corner of the seat Margaret Macomber looked at the two of them. There was no change in Wilson. She saw Wilson as she had seen him the day before when she had first realized what his great talent was. But she saw the change in Francis Macomber now.

'Do you have that feeling of happiness about what's going to happen?' Macomber asked, still exploring his new wealth.

'You're not supposed to mention it,' Wilson said, looking in the other's face. 'Much more fashionable to say you're scared. Mind you, you'll be scared too, plenty of times.'

'But you *have* a feeling of happiness about action to come?'

'Yes,' said Wilson. 'There's that. Doesn't do to talk too much about all this. Talk the whole thing away. No pleasure in anything if you mouth it up too much.'

'You're both talking rot,' said Margot. 'Just because you've chased some helpless animals in a motor car you talk like heroes.'

'Sorry,' said Wilson. 'I have been gassing too much.' She's worried about it already, he thought.

'If you don't know what we're talking about why not keep out of it?' Macomber asked his wife.

'You've gotten awfully brave, awfully suddenly,' his wife said contemptuously, but her contempt was not secure. She was very afraid of something.

Macomber laughed, a very natural hearty laugh. 'You know I *have*,' he said. 'I really have.'

'Isn't it sort of late?' Margot said bitterly. Because she had done the best she could for many years back and the way they were together now was no one person's fault.

'Not for me,' said Macomber.

Margot said nothing but sat back in the corner of the seat.

'Do you think we've given him time enough?' Macomber asked Wilson cheerfully.

'We might have a look,' Wilson said. 'Have you any solids left?'

'The gun-bearer has some.'

Wilson called in Swahili and the older gun-bearer, who was

skinning out one of the heads, straightened up, pulled a box of
solids out of his pocket and brought them over to Macomber,
who filled his magazine and put the remaining shells in his
pocket.

'You might as well shoot the Springfield,' Wilson said.
'You're used to it. We'll leave the Mannlicher in the car with the
Memsahib. Your gun-bearer can carry your heavy gun. I've this
damned cannon. Now let me tell you about them.' He had saved
this until the last because he did not want to worry Macomber.
'When a buff comes he comes with his head high and thrust
straight out. The boss of the horns covers any sort of a brain shot.
The only shot is straight into the nose. The only other shot is
into his chest or, if you're to one side, into the neck or the
shoulders. After they've been hit once they take a hell of a lot of
killing. Don't try anything fancy. Take the easiest shot there is.
They've finished skinning out that head now. Should we get
started?'

He called to the gun-bearers, who came up wiping their
hands, and the older one got into the back.

'I'll only take Kongoni,' Wilson said. 'The other can watch to
keep the birds away.'

As the car moved slowly across the open space toward the
island of brushy trees that ran in a tongue of foliage along a dry
water course that cut the open swale, Macomber felt his heart
pounding and his mouth was dry again, but it was excitement,
not fear.

'Here's where he went in,' Wilson said. Then to the gun-
bearer in Swahili, 'Take the blood spoor.'

The car was parallel to the patch of bush. Macomber, Wilson
and the gun-bearer got down. Macomber, looking back, saw his
wife, with the rifle by her side, looking at him. He waved to her
and she did not wave back.

The brush was very thick ahead and the ground was dry. The
middle-aged gun-bearer was sweating heavily and Wilson had
his hat down over his eyes and his red neck showed just ahead
of Macomber. Suddenly the gun-bearer said something in Swahili to Wilson and ran forward.

'He's dead in there,' Wilson said. 'Good work,' and he turned
to grip Macomber's hand and as they shook hands, grinning at
each other, the gun-bearer shouted wildly and they saw him
coming out of the bush sideways, fast as a crab, and the bull
coming, nose out, mouth tight closed, blood dripping, massive

head straight out, coming in a charge, his little pig eyes blood-shot as he looked at them. Wilson, who was ahead, was kneeling shooting, and Macomber, as he fired, unhearing his shot in the roaring of Wilson's gun, saw fragments like slate burst from the huge boss of the horns, and the head jerked, he shot again at the wide nostrils and saw the horns jolt again and fragments fly, and he did not see Wilson now and, aiming carefully, shot again with the buffalo's huge bulk almost on him and his rifle almost level with the on-coming head, nose out, and he could see the little wicked eyes and the head started to lower and he felt a sudden white-hot, blinding flash explode inside his head and that was all he ever felt.

Wilson had ducked to one side to get in a shoulder shot. Macomber had stood solid and shot for the nose, shooting a touch high each time and hitting the heavy horns, splintering and chipping them like hitting a slate roof, and Mrs. Macomber, in the car, had shot at the buffalo with the 6.5 Mannlicher as it seemed about to gore Macomber and had hit her husband about two inches up and a little to one side of the base of his skull.

Francis Macomber lay now, face down, not two yards from where the buffalo lay on his side and his wife knelt over him with Wilson beside her.

'I wouldn't turn him over,' Wilson said.

The woman was crying hysterically.

'I'd get back in the car,' Wilson said. 'Where's the rifle?'

She shook her head, her face contorted. The gun-bearer picked up the rifle.

'Leave it as it is,' said Wilson. Then, 'Go get Abdulla so that he may witness the manner of the accident.'

He knelt down, took a handkerchief from his pocket, and spread it over Francis Macomber's crew-cropped head where it lay. The blood sank into the dry, loose earth.

Wilson stood up and saw the buffalo on his side, his legs out, his thinly-haired belly crawling with ticks. 'Hell of a good bull,' his brain registered automatically. 'A good fifty inches, or better. Better.' He called to the driver and told him to spread a blanket over the body and stay by it. Then he walked over to the motor car where the woman sat crying in the corner.

'That was a pretty thing to do,' he said in a toneless voice. 'He *would* have left you too.'

'Stop it,' she said.

'Of course it's an accident,' he said. 'I know that.'

'Stop it,' she said.

'Don't worry,' he said. 'There will be a certain amount of unpleasantness but I will have some photographs taken that will be very useful at the inquest. There's the testimony of the gun-bearers and the driver too. You're perfectly all right.'

'Stop it,' she said.

'There's a hell of a lot to be done,' he said. 'And I'll have to send a truck off to the lake to wireless for a plane to take the three of us into Nairobi. Why didn't you poison him? That's what they do in England.'

'Stop it. Stop it. Stop it,' the woman cried.

Wilson looked at her with his flat blue eyes.

'I'm through now,' he said. 'I was a little angry. I'd begun to like your husband.'

'Oh, please stop it,' she said. 'Please stop it.'

'That's better,' Wilson said. 'Please is much better. Now I'll stop.'

OLD MAN AT THE BRIDGE

An old man with steel rimmed spectacles and very dusty clothes sat by the side of the road. There was a pontoon bridge across the river and carts, trucks, and men, women and children were crossing it. The mule-drawn carts staggered up the steep bank from the bridge with soldiers helping push against the spokes of the wheels. The trucks ground up and away heading out of it all and the peasants plodded along in the ankle deep dust. But the old man sat there without moving. He was too tired to go any farther.

It was my business to cross the bridge, explore the bridgehead beyond and find out to what point the enemy had advanced. I did this and returned over the bridge. There were not so many carts now and very few people on foot, but the old man was still there.

'Where do you come from?' I asked him.

'From San Carlos,' he said, and smiled.

That was his native town and so it gave him pleasure to mention it and he smiled.

'I was taking care of animals,' he explained.

'Oh,' I said, not quite understanding.

'Yes,' he said, 'I stayed, you see, taking care of animals. I was the last one to leave the town of San Carlos.'

He did not look like a shepherd nor a herdsman and I looked at his black dusty clothes and his gray dusty face and his steel rimmed spectacles and said, 'What animals were they?'

'Various animals,' he said, and shook his head. 'I had to leave them.'

I was watching the bridge and the African looking country of the Ebro Delta and wondering how long now it would be before we would see the enemy, and listening all the while for the first noises that would signal that ever mysterious event called contact, and the old man still sat there.

'What animals were they?' I asked.

'There were three animals altogether,' he explained. 'There were two goats and a cat and then there were four pairs of pigeons.'

'And you had to leave them?' I asked.

'Yes. Because of the artillery. The captain told me to go because of the artillery.'

'And you have no family?' I asked, watching the far end of the bridge where a few last carts were hurrying down the slope of the bank.

'No,' he said, 'only the animals I stated. The cat, of course, will be all right. A cat can look out for itself, but I cannot think what will become of the others.'

'What politics have you?' I asked.

'I am without politics,' he said. 'I am seventy-six years old. I have come twelve kilometers now and I think now I can go no further.'

'This is not a good place to stop,' I said. 'If you can make it, there are trucks up the road where it forks for Tortosa.'

'I will wait a while,' he said, 'and then I will go. Where do the trucks go?'

'Towards Barcelona,' I told him.

'I know no one in that direction,' he said, 'but thank you very much. Thank you again very much.'

He looked at me very blankly and tiredly, then said, having to share his worry with some one, 'The cat will be all right, I am sure. There is no need to be unquiet about the cat. But the others. Now what do you think about the others?'

'Why they'll probably come through it all right.'

'You think so?'

'Why not,' I said, watching the far bank where now there were no carts.

'But what will they do under the artillery when I was told to leave because of the artillery?'

'Did you leave the dove cage unlocked?' I asked.

'Yes.'

'Then they'll fly.'

'Yes, certainly they'll fly. But the others. It's better not to think about the others,' he said.

'If you are rested I would go,' I urged. 'Get up and try to walk now.'

'Thank you,' he said and got to his feet, swayed from side to side and then sat down backwards in the dust.

'I was taking care of animals,' he said dully, but no longer to me. 'I was only taking care of animals.'

There was nothing to do about him. It was Easter Sunday and the Fascists were advancing toward the Ebro. It was a gray overcast day with a low ceiling so their planes were not up. That and the fact that cats know how to look after themselves was all the good luck that old man would ever have.

PART TWO

STORIES AND FRAGMENTS FROM POSTHUMOUS COLLECTIONS

UNCOLLECTED STORIES PUBLISHED IN HEMINGWAY'S LIFETIME

THE DENUNCIATION

Chicote's in the old days in Madrid was a place sort of like The Stork, without the music and the debutantes, or the Waldorf's men's bar if they let girls in. You know, they came in, but it was a man's place and they didn't have any status. Pedro Chicote was the proprietor and he had one of those personalities that make a place. He was a great bartender and he was always pleasant, always cheerful, and he had a lot of zest. Now zest is a rare enough thing and few people have it for long. It should not be confused with showmanship either. Chicote had it and it was not faked or put on. He was also modest, simple and friendly. He really was as nice and pleasant and still as marvelously efficient as George, the chasseur at the Ritz bar in Paris, which is about the strongest comparison you can make to anyone who has been around, and he ran a fine bar.

In those days the snobs among the rich young men of Madrid hung out at something called the Nuevo Club and the good guys went to Chicote's. A lot of people went there that I did not like, the same as at The Stork, say, but I was never in Chicote's that it wasn't pleasant. One reason was that you did not talk politics there. There were cafés where you went for politics and nothing else but you didn't talk politics at Chicote's. You talked plenty of the other five subjects though and in the evening the best looking girls in the town showed up there and it was the place to start an evening from, all right, and we had all started some fine ones from there.

Then it was the place where you dropped in to find out who was in town, or where they had gone to if they were out of town. And if it was summer, and there was no one in town, you could always sit and enjoy a drink because the waiters were all pleasant.

It was a club only you didn't have to pay any dues and you could pick a girl up there. It was the best bar in Spain, certainly, and I think one of the best bars in the world, and all of us that used to hang out there had a great affection for it.

Another thing was that the drinks were wonderful. If you ordered a martini it was made with the best gin that money could buy, and Chicote had a barrel whiskey that came from Scotland that was so much better than the advertised brands that it was

pitiful to compare it with ordinary Scotch. Well, when the revolt started, Chicote was up at San Sebastian running the summer place he had there. He is still running it and they say it is the
best bar in Franco's Spain. The waiters took over the Madrid
place and they are still running it, but the good liquor is all gone
now.

Most of Chicote's old customers are on Franco's side; but
some of them are on the Government side. Because it was a very
cheerful place, and because really cheerful people are usually the
bravest, and the bravest get killed quickest, a big part of Chicote's old customers are now dead. The barrel whiskey had all
been gone for many months now and we finished the last of the
yellow gin in May of 1938. There's not much there to go for
now so I suppose Luis Delgado, if he had come to Madrid a little
later, might have stayed away from there and not gotten into that
trouble. But when he came to Madrid in the month of November of 1937 they still had the yellow gin and they still had Indian
quinine water. They do not seem worth risking your life for, so
maybe he just wanted to have a drink in the old place. Knowing
him, and knowing the place in the old days, it would be perfectly understandable.

They had butchered a cow at the Embassy that day and the
porter had called up at the Hotel Florida to tell us that they had
saved us ten pounds of fresh meat. I walked over to get it
through the early dusk of a Madrid winter. Two assault guards
with rifles sat on chairs outside the Embassy gate and the meat
was waiting at the porter's lodge.

The porter said it was a very good cut but that the cow was
lean. I offered him some roasted sunflower seeds and some
acorns from the pocket of my mackinaw jacket and we joked a
little standing outside the lodge on the gravel of the Embassy
driveway.

I walked home across the town with the meat heavy under my
arm. They were shelling up the Gran Via and I went into Chicote's to wait it out. It was noisy and crowded and I sat at a little
table in one corner against the sandbagged window with the
meat on the bench beside me and drank a gin and tonic water.
It was that week that we discovered they still had tonic water.
No one had ordered any since the war started and it was still the
same price as before the revolt. The evening papers were not yet
out so I bought three party tracts from an old woman. They
were ten centavos apiece and I told her to keep the change from

a peseta. She said God would bless me. I doubted this but read the three leaflets and drank the gin and tonic.

A waiter I had known in the old days came over to the table and said something to me.

'No,' I said. 'I don't believe it.'

'Yes,' he insisted, slanting his tray and his head in the same direction. 'Don't look now. There he is.'

'It's not my business,' I told him.

'Nor mine either.'

He went away and I bought the evening papers which had just come in from another old woman and read them. There was no doubt about the man the waiter had pointed out. We both knew him very well. All I could think was: the fool. The utter bloody fool.

Just then a Greek comrade came over and sat down at the table. He was a company commander in the Fifteenth Brigade who had been buried by an airplane bomb which had killed four other men and he had been sent in to be under observation for a while and then sent to a rest home or something of the sort.

'How are you, John?' I asked him. 'Try one of these.'

'What you call that drink, Mr. Emmunds?'

'Gin and tonic.'

'What is that kind of tonic?'

'Quinine. Try one.'

'Listen, I don't drink very much but is a quinine very good for fever. I try little one.'

'What did the doctor say about you, John?'

'Is a no necessity see doctor. I am all right. Only I have like buzzing noises all the time in the head.'

'You have to go to see him, John.'

'I go all right. But he not understand. He says I have no papers to admit.'

'I'll call up about it,' I said. 'I know the people there. Is the doctor a German?'

'That's right,' said John. 'Is a German. No talk English very good.'

Just then the waiter came over. He was an old man with a bald head and very old-fashioned manners which the war had not changed. He was very worried.

'I have a son at the front,' he said. 'I have another son killed. Now about this.'

'It is thy problem.'

'And you? Already I have told you.'

'I came in here to have a drink before eating.'

'And I work here. But tell me.'

'It is thy problem,' I said. 'I am not a politician.'

'Do you understand Spanish, John?' I asked the Greek comrade.

'No, I understand few words but I speak Greek, English, Arabic. One time I speak good Arabic. Listen, you know how I get buried?'

'No. I knew you were buried. That's all.'

He had a dark good-looking face and very dark hands that he moved about when he talked. He came from one of the islands and he spoke with great intensity.

'Well, I tell you now. You see I have very much experience in war. Before I am captain in Greek army too. I am good soldier. So when I see plane come over there when we are in trenches there at Fuentes del Ebro I look at him close. I look at plane come over, bank, turn like this' (he turned and banked with his hands), 'look down on us and I say, "Ah ha. Is for the General Staff. Is made the observation. Pretty soon come others."

'So just like I say come others. So I am stand there and watch. I watch close. I look up and I point out to company what happens. Is come three and three. One first and two behind. Is pass one group of three and I say to company, "See? Now is pass one formation."

'Is pass the other three and I say to company, "Now is hokay. Now is all right. Now is nothing more to worry." That the last thing I remember for two weeks.'

'When did it happen?'

'About one month ago. You see is my helmet forced down over my face when am buried by bomb so I have the air in that helmet to breathe until they dig me out but I know nothing about that. But in that air I breathe is the smoke from the explosion and that make me sick for long time. Now am I hokay, only with the ringing in the head. What you call this drink?'

'Gin and tonic. Schweppes Indian tonic water. This was a very fancy café before the war and this used to cost five pesetas when there were only seven pesetas to the dollar. We just found out they still have the tonic water and they're charging the same price for it. There's only a case left.'

'Is a good drink all right. Tell me, how was this city before the war?'

'Fine. Like now only lots to eat.'

The waiter came over and leaned toward the table.

'And if I don't?' he said. 'It is my responsibility.'

'If you wish to, go to the telephone and call this number. Write it down.'

He wrote it down. 'Ask for Pepé,' I said.

'I have nothing against him,' the waiter said. 'But it is the *Causa*. Certainly such a man is dangerous to our cause.'

'Don't the other waiters recognize him?'

'I think so. But no one has said anything. He is an old client.'

'I am an old client, too.'

'Perhaps then he is on our side now, too.'

'No,' I said. 'I know he is not.'

'I have never denounced anyone.'

'It is your problem. Maybe one of the other waiters will denounce him.'

'No. Only the old waiters know him and the old waiters do not denounce.'

'Bring another of the yellow gins and some bitters,' I said. 'There is tonic water still in the bottle.'

'What's he talk about?' asked John. 'I only understand little bit.'

'There is a man here that we both knew in the old days. He used to be a marvelous pigeon shot and I used to see him at shoots. He is a fascist and for him to come here now, no matter what his reasons, is very foolish. But he was always very brave and very foolish.'

'Show him to me.'

'There at that table with the flyers.'

'Which one?'

'With the very brown face; the cap over one eye. Who is laughing now.'

'He is fascist?'

'Yes.'

'That's a closest I see fascist since Fuentes del Ebro. Is a many fascist here?'

'Quite a few from time to time.'

'Is drink the same drink as you,' said John. 'We drink that other people think we fascists, eh? Listen you ever been South America, West Coast, Magallanes?'

'No.'

'Is all right. Only too many oc-toe-pus.'

'Too many what?'

'Oc-toe-pus.' He pronounced it with the accent on the toe as oc-*toe*-pus. 'You know with the eight arms.'

'Oh,' I said. 'Octopus.'

'Oc-toe-pus,' said John. 'You see I am diver too. Is a good place to work all right make plenty money only too many oc-*toe*-pus.'

'Did they bother you?'

'I don't know about that. First time I go down in Magallanes harbor I see oc-*toe*-pus. He is stand on his feet like this.' John pointed his fingers on the table and brought his hands up, at the same time bringing up his shoulders and raising his eyebrows. 'He is stand up taller than I am and he is look me right in the eye. I jerk cord for them to bring me up.'

'How big was he, John?'

'I cannot say absolutely because the glass in the helmet make distort a little. But the head was big around more than four feet any*way*. And he was stand on his feet like on *tip*-toes and look at me like this.' (He peered in my face.) 'So when I get up out of water they take off the helmet and so I say I don't go down there any more. Then the man of the job says, "What a matter with you, John? The oc-toe-pus is more afraid of you than you afraid of oc-toe-pus." So I say to him "Impossible!" What you say we drink some more this fascist drink?'

'All right,' I said.

I was watching the man at the table. His name was Luis Delgado and the last time I had seen him had been in 1933 shooting pigeons at Saint Sebastian and I remembered standing with him up on top of the stand watching the final of the big shoot. We had a bet, more than I could afford to bet, and I believed a good deal more than he could afford to lose that year, and when he paid coming down the stairs, I remembered how pleasant he was and how he made it seem a great privilege to pay. Then I remembered our standing at the bar having a martini, and I had that wonderful feeling of relief that comes when you have bet yourself out of a bad hole and I was wondering how badly the bet had hit him. I had shot rottenly all week and he had shot beautifully but drawn almost impossible birds and he had bet on himself steadily.

'Should we match a *duro*?' he asked.

'You really want to?'

'Yes, if you like.'

'For how much?'

He took out a notecase and looked in it and laughed.

'I'd say for anything you like,' he said. 'But suppose we say for eight thousand pesetas. That's what seems to be there.'

That was close to a thousand dollars then.

'Good,' I said, all the fine inner quiet gone now and the hollow that gambling makes come back again. 'Who's matching who?'

'I'll match you.'

We shook the heavy five-peseta pieces in our cupped hands; then each man laid his coin on the back of his left hand, each coin covered with the right hand.

'What's yours?' he asked.

I uncovered the big silver piece with the profile of Alfonso XIII as a baby showing.

'Heads,' I said.

'Take these damned things and be a good man and buy me a drink.' He emptied out the notecase. 'You wouldn't like to buy a good Purdey gun would you?'

'No,' I said. 'But look, Luis, if you need some money – '

I was holding the stiffly folded, shiny-heavy-paper, green thousand-peseta notes toward him.

'Don't be silly, Enrique,' he said. 'We've been gambling, haven't we?'

'Yes. But we know each other quite well.'

'Not that well.'

'Right,' I said. 'You're the judge of that. Then what will you drink?'

'What about a gin and tonic? That's a marvelous drink you know.'

So we had a gin and tonic and I felt very badly to have broken him and I felt awfully good to have won the money, and a gin and tonic never tasted better to me in all my life. There is no use to lie about these things or pretend you do not enjoy winning; but this boy Luis Delgado was a very pretty gambler.

'I don't think if people gambled for what they could afford it would be very interesting. Do you, Enrique?'

'I don't know. I've never been able to afford it.'

'Don't be silly. You have lots of money.'

'No I haven't,' I said. 'Really.'

'Oh, everyone has money,' he said. 'It's just a question of selling something or other to get hold of it.'

'I don't have much. Really.'

'Oh, don't be silly. I've never known an American who wasn't rich.'

I guess that was the truth all right. He wouldn't have met them at the Ritz bar or at Chicote's either in those days. And now he was back in Chicote's and all the Americans he would meet there now were the kind he would never have met; except me, and I was a mistake. But I would have given plenty not to have seen him in there.

Still, if he wanted to do an absolutely damn fool thing like that it was his own business. But as I looked at the table and remembered the old days I felt badly about him and I felt very badly too that I had given the waiter the number of the counter-espionage bureau in Seguridad headquarters. He could have had Seguridad by simply asking on the telephone. But I had given him the shortest cut to having Delgado arrested in one of those excesses of impartiality, righteousness and Pontius Pilatry, and the always–dirty desire to see how people act under an emotional conflict, that makes writers such attractive friends.

The waiter came over.

'What do you think?' he asked.

'I would never denounce him myself,' I said, now trying to undo for myself what I had done with the number. 'But I am a foreigner and it is your war and your problem.'

'But you are with us.'

'Absolutely and always. But it does not include denouncing old friends.'

'But for me?'

'For you it is different.'

I knew this was true and there was nothing else to say, only I wished I had never heard of any of it.

My curiosity as to how people would act in this case had been long ago, and shamefully, satisfied. I turned to John and did not look at the table where Luis Delgado was sitting. I knew he had been flying with the fascists for over a year, and here he was, in a loyalist uniform, talking to three young loyalist flyers of the last crop that had been trained in France.

None of those new kids would know him and I wondered whether he had come to try to steal a plane or for what. Whatever he was there for, he was a fool to come to Chicote's now.

'How do you feel, John?' I asked.

'Feel good,' said John. 'Is a good drink hokay. Makes me feel little bit drunk maybe. Is a good for the buzzing in the head.'

The waiter came over. He was very excited.

'I have denounced him,' he said.

'Well then,' I said, 'now you haven't any problem.'

'No,' he said proudly. 'I have denounced him. They are on their way now to get him.'

'Let's go,' I said to John. 'There is going to be some trouble here.'

'Is best go then,' said John. 'Is a plenty trouble always come, even if you do best to avoid. How much we owe?'

'You aren't going to stay?' the waiter asked.

'No.'

'But you gave me the telephone number.'

'I know it. You get to know too many telephone numbers if you stay around in this town.'

'But it was my duty.'

'Yes. Why not? Duty is a very strong thing.'

'But now?'

'Well, you felt good about it just now, didn't you? Maybe you will feel good about it again. Maybe you will get to like it.'

'You have forgotten the package,' the waiter said. He handed me the meat which was wrapped in two envelopes which had brought copies of the *Spur* to the piles of magazines which accumulated in one of the office rooms of the Embassy.

'I understand,' I said to the waiter. 'Truly.'

'He was an old client and a good client. Also I have never denounced anyone before. I did not denounce for pleasure.'

'Also I should not speak cynically or brutally. Tell him that I denounced him. He hates me anyway by now for differences in politics. He'd feel badly if he knew it was you.'

'No. Each man must take his responsibility. But you understand?'

'Yes,' I said. Then lied. 'I understand and I approve.' You have to lie very often in a war and when you have to lie you should do it quickly and as well as you can.

We shook hands and I went out the door with John. I looked back at the table where Luis Delgado sat as I went out. He had another gin and tonic in front of him and everyone at the table was laughing at something he had said. He had a very gay, brown face, and shooter's eyes, and I wondered what he was passing himself off as.

He was a fool to go to Chicote's. But that was exactly the sort of thing that he would do in order to be able to boast of it when he was back with his own people.

As we went out of the door and turned to walk up the street, a big Seguridad car drew up in front of Chicote's and eight men got out of it. Six with submachine guns took up positions outside the door. Two in plain clothes went inside. A man asked us for our papers and when I said, 'Foreigners,' he said to go along; that it was all right.

In the dark going up the Gran Via there was much new broken glass on the sidewalk and much rubble under foot from the shelling. The air was still smoky and all up the street it smelled of high explosive and blasted granite.

'Where you go eat?' asked John.

'I have some meat for all of us, and we can cook it in the room.'

'I cook it,' said John. 'I cook good. I remember one time when I cook on ship – '

'It will be pretty tough,' I said. 'It's just been freshly butchered.'

'Oh no,' said John. 'Is a no such thing as a tough meat in a war.'

People were hurrying by in the dark on their way home from the cinemas where they had stayed until the shelling was over.

'What's a matter that fascist he come to that café where they know him?'

'He was crazy to do it.'

'Is a trouble with a war,' John said. 'Is a too many people crazy.'

'John,' I said, 'I think you've got something there.'

Back at the hotel we went in the door past the sandbags piled to protect the porter's desk and I asked for the key, but the porter said there were two comrades upstairs in the room taking a bath. He had given them the keys.

'Go on up, John,' I said. 'I want to telephone.'

I went over to the booth and called the same number I had given the waiter.

'Hello? Pepé?'

A thin-lipped voice came over the phone. '¿Qué tal Enrique?'

'Listen, Pepé, did you pick up a certain Luis Delgado at Chicote's?'

'Sí, hombre, sí. Sin novedad. Without trouble.'

'He doesn't know anything about the waiter?'

'No, *hombre*, no.'

'Then don't tell him. Tell him I denounced him then, will you? Nothing about the waiter.'

'Why when it will make no difference? He is a spy. He will be shot. There is no choice in the matter.'

'I know,' I said. 'But it makes a difference.'

'As you want, *hombre*. As you want. When shall I see thee?'

'Lunch tomorrow. We have some meat.'

'And whiskey before. Good, *hombre*, good.'

'*Salud*, Pepé, and thank you.'

'*Salud*, Enrique. It is nothing. *Salud*.'

It was a strange and very deadly voice and I never got used to hearing it, but as I walked up the stairs now, I felt much better.

All we old clients of Chicote's had a sort of feeling about the place. I knew that was why Luis Delgado had been such a fool as to go back there. He could have done his business some place else. But if he was in Madrid he had to go there. He had been a good client as the waiter had said and we had been friends. Certainly any small acts of kindness you can do in life are worth doing. So I was glad I had called my friend Pepé at Seguridad headquarters because Luis Delgado was an old client of Chicote's and I did not wish him to be disillusioned or bitter about the waiters there before he died.

THE BUTTERFLY AND THE TANK

On this evening I was walking home from the censorship office
to the Florida Hotel and it was raining. So about halfway home
I got sick of the rain and stopped into Chicote's for a quick one.
It was the second winter of shelling in the siege of Madrid and
everything was short including tobacco and people's tempers
and you were a little hungry all the time and would become
suddenly and unreasonably irritated at things you could do nothing about such as the weather. I should have gone on home. It
was only five blocks more, but when I saw Chicote's doorway I
thought I would get a quick one and then do those six blocks up
the Gran Via through the mud and rubble of the streets broken
by the bombardment.

The place was crowded. You couldn't get near the bar and all
the tables were full. It was full of smoke, singing, men in uniform, and the smell of wet leather coats, and they were handing
drinks over a crowd that was three deep at the bar.

A waiter I knew found a chair from another table and I sat
down with a thin, white-faced, Adam's-appled German I knew
who was working at the censorship and two other people I did
not know. The table was in the middle of the room a little on
your right as you go in.

You couldn't hear yourself talk for the singing and I ordered
a gin and Angostura and put it down against the rain. The place
was really packed and everybody was very jolly; maybe getting
just a little bit too jolly from the newly made Catalan liquor most
of them were drinking. A couple of people I did not know
slapped me on the back and when the girl at our table said something to me, I couldn't hear it and said, 'Sure.'

She was pretty terrible looking now I had stopped looking
around and was looking at our table; really pretty terrible. But
it turned out, when the waiter came, that what she had asked
me was to have a drink. The fellow with her was not very forceful looking but she was forceful enough for both of them. She
had one of those strong, semi-classical faces and was built like a
lion tamer; and the boy with her looked as though he ought to
be wearing an old school tie. He wasn't though. He was wearing
a leather coat just like all the rest of us. Only it wasn't wet because they had been there since before the rain started. She had

on a leather coat too and it was becoming to the sort of face she had.

By this time I was wishing I had not stopped into Chicote's but had gone straight on home where you could change your clothes and be dry and have a drink in comfort on the bed with your feet up, and I was tired of looking at both of these young people. Life is very short and ugly women are very long and sitting there at the table I decided that even though I was a writer and supposed to have an insatiable curiosity about all sorts of people, I did not really care to know whether these two were married, or what they saw in each other, or what their politics were, or whether he had a little money, or she had a little money, or anything about them. I decided they must be in the radio. Any time you saw really strange looking civilians in Madrid they were always in the radio. So to say something I raised my voice above the noise and asked, 'You in the radio?'

'We are,' the girl said. So that was that. They were in the radio.

'How are you comrade?' I said to the German.

'Fine. And you?'

'Wet,' I said, and he laughed with his head on one side.

'You haven't got a cigarette?' he asked. I handed him my next to the last pack of cigarettes and he took two. The forceful girl took two and the young man with the old school tie face took one.

'Take another,' I shouted.

'No thanks,' he answered and the German took it instead.

'Do you mind?' he smiled.

'Of course not,' I said. I really minded and he knew it. But he wanted the cigarettes so badly that it did not matter. The singing had died down momentarily, or there was a break in it as there is sometimes in a storm, and we could all hear what we said.

'You been here long?' the forceful girl asked me. She pronounced it bean as in bean soup.

'Off and on,' I said.

'We must have a serious talk,' the German said. 'I want to have a talk with you. When can we have it?'

'I'll call you up,' I said. This German was a very strange German indeed and none of the good Germans liked him. He lived under the delusion that he could play the piano, but if you kept him away from pianos he was all right unless he was exposed to liquor, or the opportunity to gossip, and nobody had even been able to keep him away from those two things yet.

Gossip was the best thing he did and he always knew something new and highly discreditable about anyone you could mention in Madrid, Valencia, Barcelona, and other political centers.

Just then the singing really started in again, and you cannot gossip very well shouting, so it looked like a dull afternoon at Chicote's and I decided to leave as soon as I should have bought a round myself.

Just then it started. A civilian in a brown suit, a white shirt, black tie, his hair brushed straight back from a rather high forehead, who had been clowning around from table to table, squirted one of the waiters with a flit gun. Everybody laughed except the waiter who was carrying a tray full of drinks at the time. He was indignant.

'*No hay derecho,*' the waiter said. This means, 'You have no right to do that,' and is the simplest and the strongest protest in Spain.

The flit gun man, delighted with his success, and not seeming to give any importance to the fact that it was well into the second year of the war, that he was in a city under siege where everyone was under a strain, and that he was one of only four men in civilian clothes in the place, now squirted another waiter.

I looked around for a place to duck to. This waiter, also, was indignant and the flit gun man squirted him twice more, lightheartedly. Some people still thought it was funny, including the forceful girl. But the waiter stood, shaking his head. His lips were trembling. He was an old man and he had worked in Chicote's for ten years that I knew of.

'*No hay derecho,*' he said with dignity.

People had laughed, however, and the flit gun man, not noticing how the singing had fallen off, squirted his flit gun at the back of a waiter's neck. The waiter turned, holding his tray.

'*No hay derecho,*' he said. This time it was no protest. It was an indictment and I saw three men in uniform start from a table for the flit gun man and the next thing all four of them were going out the revolving door in a rush and you heard a smack when someone hit the flit gun man on the mouth. Somebody else picked up the flit gun and threw it out the door after him.

The three men came back in looking serious, tough and very

righteous. Then the door revolved and in came the flit gun man. His hair was down in his eyes, there was blood on his face, his necktie was pulled to one side and his shirt was torn open. He had the flit gun again and as he pushed, wild-eyed and white-faced, into the room he made one general, unaimed, challenging squirt with it, holding it toward the whole company.

I saw one of the three men start for him and I saw this man's face. There were more men with him now and they forced the flit gun man back between two tables on the left of the room as you go in, the flit gun man struggling wildly now, and when the shot went off I grabbed the forceful girl by the arm and dove for the kitchen door.

The kitchen door was shut and when I put my shoulder against it it did not give.

'Get down here behind the angle of the bar,' I said. She knelt there.

'Flat,' I said and pushed her down. She was furious.

Every man in the room except the German, who lay behind a table, and the public-school-looking boy who stood in a corner drawn up against the wall, had a gun up. On a bench along the wall three over-blonde girls, their hair dark at the roots, were standing on tiptoe to see and screaming steadily.

'I'm not afraid,' the forceful one said. 'This is ridiculous.'

'You don't want to get shot in a café brawl,' I said. 'If that flit king has any friends here this can be very bad.'

But he had no friends, evidently, because people began putting their pistols away and somebody lifted down the blonde screamers and everyone who had started over there when the shot came drew back away from the flit man who lay, quietly, on his back on the floor.

'No one is to leave until the police come,' someone shouted from the door.

Two policemen with rifles, who had come in off the street patrol, were standing by the door and at this announcement I saw six men form up just like the line-up of a football team coming out of a huddle and head out through the door. Three of them were the men who had first thrown the flit king out. One of them was the man who shot him. They went right through the policemen with the rifles like good interference taking out an end and a tackle. And as they went out one of the policemen got his rifle across the door and shouted, 'No one can leave. Absolutely no one.'

'Why did those men go? Why hold us if anyone's gone?'

'They were mechanics who had to return to their air field,' someone said.

'But if anyone's gone it's silly to hold the others.'

'Everyone must wait for the Seguridad. Things must be done legally and in order.'

'But don't you see that if any person has gone it is silly to hold the others?'

'No one can leave. Everyone must wait.'

'It's comic,' I said to the forceful girl.

'No it's not. It's simply horrible.'

We were standing up now and she was staring indignantly at where the flit king was lying. His arms were spread wide and he had one leg drawn up.

'I'm going over to help that poor wounded man. Why has no one helped him or done anything for him?'

'I'd leave him alone,' I said. 'You want to keep out of this.'

'But it's simply inhuman. I've nurse's training and I'm going to give him first aid.'

'I wouldn't,' I said. 'Don't go near him.'

'Why not?' She was very upset and almost hysterical.

'Because he's dead,' I said.

When the police came they held everybody there for three hours. They commenced by smelling of all the pistols. In this manner they would detect one which had been fired recently. After about forty pistols they seemed to get bored with this and anyway all you could smell was wet leather coats. Then they sat at a table placed directly behind the late flit king, who lay on the floor looking like a gray wax caricature of himself, with gray wax hands and a gray wax face, and examined people's papers.

With his shirt ripped open you could see the flit king had no undershirt and the soles of his shoes were worn through. He looked very small and pitiful lying there on the floor. You had to step over him to get to the table where two plain clothes policemen sat and examined everyone's identification papers. The husband lost and found his papers several times with nervousness. He had a safe conduct pass somewhere but he had mislaid it in a pocket and he kept on searching and perspiring until he found it. Then he would put it in a different pocket and have to go searching again. He perspired heavily while doing this and it made his hair very curly and his face red. He now looked as though he should have not only an old school tie but one of those little caps boys in the lower forms wear. You have heard how events age people. Well, this shooting had made him look about ten years younger.

While we were waiting around I told the forceful girl I thought the whole thing was a pretty good story and that I would write it sometime. The way the six had lined up in single file and rushed that door was very impressive. She was shocked and said that I could not write it because it would be prejudicial to the cause of the Spanish Republic. I said that I had been in Spain for a long time and that they used to have a phenomenal number of shootings in the old days around Valencia under the monarchy, and that for hundreds of years before the Republic people had been cutting each other with large knives called *navajas* in Andalucia, and that if I saw a comic shooting in Chicote's during the war I could write about it just as though it had been in New York, Chicago, Key West or Marseilles. It did not have anything to do with politics. She said I shouldn't. Probably a lot of other people will say I shouldn't too. The German seemed to think it was a pretty good story, however, and I gave him the last of the Camels. Well, anyway, finally, after about three hours the police said we could go.

They were sort of worried about me at the Florida because in those days, with the shelling, if you started for home on foot and didn't get there after the bars were closed at seven-thirty, people worried. I was glad to get home and I told the story while we were cooking supper on an electric stove and it had quite a success.

Well, it stopped raining during the night, and the next morning it was a fine, bright, cold early winter day and at twelve forty-five I pushed open the revolving doors at Chicote's to try a little gin and tonic before lunch. There were very few people there at that hour and two waiters and the manager came over to the table. They were all smiling.

'Did they catch the murderer?' I asked.

'Don't make jokes so early in the day,' the manager said. 'Did *you* see him shot?'

'Yes,' I told him.

'Me too,' he said. 'I was just here when it happened.' He pointed to a corner table. 'He placed the pistol right against the man's chest when he fired.'

'How late did they hold people?'

'Oh, until past two this morning.'

'They only came for the *fiambre*,' using the Spanish slang word for corpse, the same used on menus for cold meat, 'at eleven o'clock this morning.'

'But you don't know about it yet,' the manager said.

'No. He doesn't know,' a waiter said.

'It is a very rare thing,' another waiter said. '*Muy raro.*'

'And sad too,' the manager said. He shook his head.

'Yes. Sad and curious,' the waiter said. 'Very sad.'

'Tell me.'

'It is a very rare thing,' the manager said.

'Tell me. Come on, tell me.'

The manager leaned over the table in great confidence.

'In the flit gun, you know,' he said. 'He had eau de cologne. Poor fellow.'

'It was not a joke in such bad taste, you see?' the waiter said.

'It was really just gaiety. No one should have taken offense,' the manager said. 'Poor fellow.'

'I see,' I said. 'He just wanted everyone to have a good time.'

'Yes,' said the manager. 'It was really just an unfortunate misunderstanding.'

'And what about the flit gun?'

'The police took it. They have sent it around to his family.'

'I imagine they will be glad to have it,' I said.

'Yes,' said the manager. 'Certainly. A flit gun is always useful.'

'Who was he?'

'A cabinet maker.'

'Married?'

'Yes, the wife was here with the police this morning.'

'What did she say?'

'She dropped down by him and said, "Pedro what have they done to thee, Pedro? Who has done this to thee? Oh, Pedro."'

'Then the police had to take her away because she could not control herself,' the waiter said.

'It seems he was feeble of the chest,' the manager said. 'He fought in the first days of the movement. They said he fought in the Sierra but he was too weak in the chest to continue.'

'And yesterday afternoon he just went out on the town to cheer things up,' I suggested.

'No,' said the manager. 'You see it is very rare. Everything is *muy raro*. This I learn from the police who are very efficient if given time. They have interrogated comrades from the shop where he worked. This they located from the card of his syndi-

cate which was in his pocket. Yesterday he bought the flit gun
and *agua de colonia* to use for a joke at a wedding. He had an-
nounced this intention. He bought them across the street. There
was a label on the cologne bottle with the address. The bottle
was in the washroom. It was there he filled the flit gun. After
buying them he must have come in here when the rain started.'

'I remember when he came in,' a waiter said.

'In the gaiety, with the singing, he became gay too.'

'He was gay all right,' I said. 'He was practically floating
around.'

The manager kept on with the relentless Spanish logic.

'That is the gaiety of drinking with a weakness of the chest,'
he said.

'I don't like this story very well,' I said.

'Listen,' said the manager. 'How rare it is. His gaiety comes in
contact with the seriousness of the war like a butterfly – '

'Oh, very like a butterfly,' I said. 'Too much like a butterfly.'

'I am not joking,' said the manager. 'You see it? Like a butterfly and a tank.'

This pleased him enormously. He was getting into the real
Spanish metaphysics.

'Have a drink on the house,' he said. 'You must write a story
about this.'

I remembered the flit gun man with his gray wax hands and
his gray wax face, his arms spread wide and his legs drawn up and
he did look a little like a butterfly; not too much, you know. But
he did not look very human either. He reminded me more of a
dead sparrow.

'I'll take gin and Schweppes quinine tonic water,' I said.

'You must write a story about it,' the manager said. 'Here.
Here's luck.'

'Luck,' I said. 'Look, an English girl last night told me I
shouldn't write about it. That it would be very bad for the
cause.'

'What nonsense,' the manager said. 'It is very interesting and
important, the misunderstood gaiety coming in contact with the
deadly seriousness that is here always. To me it is the rarest and
most interesting thing which I have seen for some time. You
must write it.'

'All right,' I said. 'Sure. Has he any children?'

'No,' he said. 'I asked the police. But you must write it and
you must call it "The Butterfly and the Tank."'

'The title is very elegant,' the manager said. 'It is pure lit-erature.'

'All right,' I said. 'Sure. That's what we'll call it. "The Butter-fly and the Tank." '

And I sat there on that bright cheerful morning, the place smelling clean and newly aired and swept, with the manager who was an old friend and who was now very pleased with the literature we were making together and I took a sip of the gin and tonic water and looked out the sandbagged window and thought of the wife kneeling there and saying, 'Pedro. *Pedro*, who has done this to thee, Pedro?' And I thought that the police would never be able to tell her that even if they had the name of the man who pulled the trigger.

NIGHT BEFORE BATTLE

At this time we were working in a shell-smashed house that overlooked the Casa del Campo in Madrid. Below us a battle was being fought. You could see it spread out below you and over the hills, could smell it, could taste the dust of it, and the noise of it was one great slithering sheet of rifle and automatic rifle fire rising and dropping, and in it came the crack of the guns and the bubbly rumbling of the outgoing shells fired from the batteries behind us, the thud of their bursts, and then the rolling yellow clouds of dust. But it was just too far to film well. We had tried working closer but they kept sniping at the camera and you could not work.

The big camera was the most expensive thing we had and if it was smashed we were through. We were making the film on almost nothing and all the money was in the cans of film and the cameras. We could not afford to waste film and you had to be awfully careful of the cameras.

The day before we had been sniped out of a good place to film from and I had to crawl back holding the small camera to my belly, trying to keep my head lower than my shoulders, hitching along on my elbows, the bullets whocking into the brick wall over my back and twice spurting dirt over me.

Our heaviest attacks were made in the afternoon, God knows why, as the fascists then had the sun at their backs, and it shone on the camera lenses and made them blink like a helio and the Moors would open up on the flash. They knew all about helios and officers' glasses from the Riff and if you wanted to be properly sniped, all you had to do was use a pair of glasses without shading them adequately. They could shoot too, and they had kept my mouth dry all day.

In the afternoon we moved up into the house. It was a fine place to work and we made a sort of a blind for the camera on a balcony with the broken latticed curtains; but, as I said, it was too far.

It was not too far to get the pine studded hillside, the lake and the outline of the stone farm buildings that disappeared in the sudden smashes of stone dust from the hits by high explosive shells, nor was it too far to get the clouds of smoke and dirt that thundered up on the hill crest as the bombers droned over. But at eight hundred to a thousand yards the tanks looked like small mud-colored beetles bustling in the trees and spitting tiny flashes and the men behind them were toy men who lay flat, then crouched and ran, and then dropped to run again, or to stay where they lay, spotting the hillside as the tanks moved on. Still we hoped to get the shape of the battle. We had many close shots and would get others with luck and if we could get the sudden fountainings of earth, the puffs of shrapnel, the rolling clouds of smoke and dust lit by the yellow flash and white blossoming of grenades that is the very shape of battle we would have something that we needed.

So when the light failed we carried the big camera down the stairs, took off the tripod, made three loads, and then, one at a time, sprinted across the fire-swept corner of the Paseo Rosales into the lee of the stone wall of the stables of the old Montana Barracks. We knew we had a good place to work and we felt cheerful. But we were kidding ourselves plenty that it was not too far.

'Come on, let's go to Chicote's,' I said when we had come up the hill to the Hotel Florida.

But they had to repair a camera, to change film and seal up what we had made so I went alone. You were never alone in Spain and it felt good for a change.

As I started to walk down the Gran Via to Chicote's in the April twilight I felt happy, cheerful and excited. We had worked hard, and I thought well. But walking down the street alone, all my elation died. Now that I was alone and there was no excitement, I knew we had been too far away and any fool could see the offensive was a failure. I had known it all day but you are often deceived by hope and optimism. But remembering how it looked now, I knew this was just another blood bath like the Somme. The people's army was on the offensive finally. But it was attacking in a way that could do only one thing: destroy itself. And as I put together now what I had seen all day and what I had heard, I felt plenty bad.

I knew in the smoke and din of Chicote's that the offensive was a failure and I knew it even stronger when I took my first drink at the crowded bar. When things are all right and it is you that is feeling low a drink can make you feel better. But when things are really bad and you are all right, a drink just makes it clearer. Now, in Chicote's it was so crowded that you had to make room with your elbows to get your drink to your mouth. I had one good long swallow and then someone jostled me so that I spilled part of the glass of whiskey and soda. I looked around angrily and the man who had jostled me laughed.

'Hello fish face,' he said.

'Hello you goat.'

'Let's get a table,' he said. 'You certainly looked sore when I bumped you.'

'Where did you come from?' I asked. His leather coat was dirty and greasy, his eyes were hollow and he needed a shave. He had the big Colt automatic that had belonged to three other men that I had known of, and that we were always trying to get shells for, strapped to his leg. He was very tall and his face was smoke-darkened and grease-smudged. He had a leather helmet with a heavy leather padded ridge longitudinally over the top and a heavily padded leather rim.

'Where'd you come from?'

'Casa del Campo,' he said, pronouncing it in a sing-song mocking way we had heard a page boy use in calling in the lobby of a hotel in New Orleans one time and still kept as a private joke.

'There's a table,' I said as two soldiers and two girls got up to go. 'Let's get it.'

We sat at this table in the middle of the room and I watched him raise his glass. His hands were greasy and the forks of both thumbs black as graphite from the back spit of the machine gun. The hand holding the drink was shaking.

'Look at them.' He put out the other hand. It was shaking too. 'Both the same,' he said in that same comic lilt. Then, seriously, 'You been down there?'

'We're making a picture of it.'

'Photograph well?'

'Not too.'

'See us?'

'Where?'

'Attack on the farm. Three twenty-five this afternoon.'

'Oh, yes.'

'Like it?'

'Nope.'

'Me either,' he said. 'Listen the whole thing is just as crazy as a bedbug. Why do they want to make a frontal attack against positions like those? Who in hell thought it up?'

'An S.O.B. named Largo Caballero,' said a short man with thick glasses who was sitting at the table when we came over to it. 'The first time they let him look through a pair of field glasses he became a general. This is his masterpiece.'

We both looked at the man who spoke. Al Wagner, the tank man, looked at me and raised what had been his eyebrows before they were burnt off. The little man smiled at us.

'If anyone around here speaks English you're liable to get shot, comrade,' Al said to him.

'No,' said the little short man. 'Largo Caballero is liable to be shot. He ought to be shot.'

'Listen, comrade,' said Al. 'Just speak a little quieter, will you? Somebody might overhear you and think we were with you.'

'I know what I'm talking about,' said the short man with the very thick glasses. I looked at him carefully. He gave you a certain feeling that he did.

'Just the same it isn't always a good thing to say what you know,' I said. 'Have a drink?'

'Certainly,' he said. 'It's all right to talk to you. I know you. You're all right.'

'I'm not *that* all right,' I said. 'And this is a public bar.'

'A public bar is the only private place there is. Nobody can hear what we say here. What is your unit, comrade?'

'I've got some tanks about eight minutes from here on foot,' Al told him. 'We are through for the day and I have the early part of this evening off.'

'Why don't you ever get washed?' I said.

'I plan to,' said Al. 'In your room. When we leave here. Have you got any mechanic's soap?'

'No.'

'That's all right,' he said. 'I've got a little here with me in my pocket that I've been saving.'

The little man with the thick-lensed glasses was looking at Al intently.

'Are you a party member, comrade?' he asked.

'Sure,' said Al.

'I know Comrade Henry here is not,' the little man said.

'I wouldn't trust him then,' Al said. 'I never do.'

'You bastid,' I said. 'Want to go?'

'No,' Al said. 'I need another drink very badly.'

'I know all about Comrade Henry,' the little man said. 'Now let me tell you something more about Largo Caballero.'

'Do we have to hear it?' Al asked. 'Remember I'm in the people's army. You don't think it will discourage me, do you?'

'You know his head is swelled so badly now he's getting sort of mad. He is Prime Minister and War Minister and nobody can even talk to him any more. You know he's just a good honest trade union leader somewhere between the late Sam Gompers and John L. Lewis but this man Araquistain who invented him?'

'Take it easy,' said Al. 'I don't follow.'

'Oh, Araquistain invented him! Araquistain who is Ambassador in Paris now. He made him up you know. He called him the Spanish Lenin and then the poor man tried to live up to it and somebody let him look through a pair of field glasses and he thought he was Clausewitz.'

'You said that before,' Al told him coldly. 'What do you base it on?'

'Why three days ago in the Cabinet meeting he was talking about military affairs. They were talking about this business we've got now and Jesus Hernandez, just ribbing him, you know, asked him what was the difference between tactics and strategy. Do you know what the old boy said?'

'No,' Al said. I could see this new comrade was getting a little on his nerves.

'He said, "In tactics you attack the enemy from in front. In strategy you take him from the sides." Now isn't that something?'

'You better run along, comrade,' Al said. 'You're getting so awfully discouraged.'

'But we'll get rid of Largo Caballero,' the short comrade said. 'We'll get rid of him right after his offensive. This last piece of stupidity will be the end of him.'

'O.K., comrade,' Al told him. 'But I've got to attack in the morning.'

'Oh, you are going to attack again?'

'Listen, comrade. You can tell me any sort of crap you want because it's interesting and I'm grown up enough to sort things out. But don't ask me any questions, see? Because you'll be in trouble.'

'I just meant it personally. Not as information.'

'We don't know each other well enough to ask personal questions, comrade,' Al said. 'Why don't you just go to another table and let Comrade Henry and me talk. I want to ask him some things.'

'*Salud*, comrade,' the little man said, standing up. 'We'll meet another time.'

'Good,' said Al. 'Another time.'

We watched him go over to another table. He excused himself, some soldiers made room for him, and as we watched we could see him starting to talk. They all looked interested.

'What do you make of that little guy?' Al asked.

'I don't know.'

'Me either,' Al said. 'He certainly had this offensive sized up.' He took a drink and showed his hand. 'See? It's all right now. I'm not any rummy either. I never take a drink before an attack.'

'How was it today?'

'You saw it. How did it look?'

'Terrible.'

'That's it. That's the word for it all right. It was terrible. I guess he's using strategy and tactics both now because we are attacking from straight in front and from both sides. How's the rest of it going?'

'Duran took the new race track. The *hipódromo*. We've narrowed down on the corridor that runs up into University City. Up above we crossed the Coruña road. And we're stopped at the Cerro de Aguilar since yesterday morning. We were up that way this morning. Duran lost over half his brigade, I heard. How is it with you?'

'Tomorrow we're going to try those farm houses and the church again. The church on the hill, the one they call the hermit, is the objective. The whole hillside is cut by those gullies and it's all enfiladed at least three ways by machine-gun posts. They're dug deep all through there and it's well done. We haven't got enough artillery to give any kind of real covering fire to keep them down and we haven't heavy artillery to blow them out. They've got anti-tanks in those three houses and an anti-tank battery by the church. It's going to be murder.'

'When's it for?'

'Don't ask me. I've got no right to tell you that.'

'If we have to film it, I meant,' I said. 'The money from the film all goes for ambulances. We've got the Twelfth Brigade in the counter-attack at the Argada Bridge. And we've got the Twelfth again in that attack last week by Pingarrón. We got some good tank shots there.'

'The tanks were no good there,' Al said.

'I know,' I said, 'but they photographed very well. What about tomorrow?'

'Just get out early and wait,' he said. 'Not too early.'

'How you feel now?'

'I'm awfully tired,' he said. 'And I've got a bad headache. But I feel a lot better. Let's have another one and then go up to your place and get a bath.'

'Maybe we ought to eat first.'

'I'm too dirty to eat. You can hold a place and I'll go get a bath and join you at the Gran Via.'

'I'll go up with you.'

'No. It's better to hold a place and I'll join you.' He leaned his head forward on the table. 'Boy I got a headache. It's the noise in those buckets. I never hear it any more but it does something to your ears just the same.'

'Why don't you go to bed?'

'No. I'd rather stay up with you for a while and then sleep when I got back down there. I don't want to wake up twice.'

'You haven't got the horrors, have you?'

'No,' he said. 'I'm fine. Listen, Hank. I don't want to talk a lot of crap but I think I'm going to get killed tomorrow.'

I touched the table three times with my fingertips.

'Everybody feels like that. I've felt like that plenty of times.'

'No,' he said. 'It's not natural with me. But where we've got to go tomorrow doesn't make sense. I don't even know that I can get them up there. You can't make them move if they won't go. You can shoot them afterwards. But at the time if they won't go they won't go. If you shoot them they still won't go.'

'Maybe it will be all right.'

'No. We've got good infantry tomorrow. They'll go anyway. Not like those yellow bastids we had the first day.'

'Maybe it will be all right.'

'No,' he said. 'It won't be all right. But it will be just exactly as good as I can make it. I can make them start all right and I can take them up to where they will have to quit one at a time. Maybe they can make it. I've got three I can rely on. If only one of the good ones doesn't get knocked out at the start.'

'Who are your good ones?'

'I've got a big Greek from Chicago that will go anywhere. He's just as good as they come. I've got a Frenchman from Marseille that's got his left shoulder in a cast with two wounds still draining that asked to come out of the hospital in the Palace

Hotel for this show and has to be strapped in and I don't know how he can do it. Just technically I mean. He'd break your bloody heart. He used to be a taxi driver.' He stopped. 'I'm talking too much. Stop me if I talk too much.'

'Who's the third one?' I asked.

'The third one? Did I say I had a third one?'

'Sure.'

'Oh, yes,' he said. 'That's me.'

'What about the others?'

'They're mechanics, but they couldn't learn to soldier. They can't size up what's happening. And they're all afraid to die. I tried to get them over it,' he said. 'But it comes back on them every attack. They look like tank men when you see them by the tanks with the helmets on. They look like tank men when they get in. But when they shut the traps down there's really nothing inside. They aren't tank men. And so far we haven't had time to make new ones.'

'Do you want to take the bath?'

'Let's sit here a little while longer,' he said. 'It's nice here.'

'It's funny all right, with a war right down the end of the street so you can walk to it, and then leave it and come here.'

'And then walk back to it,' Al said.

'What about a girl? There's two American girls at the Florida. Newspaper correspondents. Maybe you could make one.'

'I don't want to have to talk to them. I'm too tired.'

'There's the two Moor girls from Ceuta at that corner table.'

He looked over at them. They were both dark and bushy-headed. One was large and one was small and they certainly both looked strong and active.

'No,' said Al. 'I'm going to see plenty Moors tomorrow without having to fool with them tonight.'

'There's plenty of girls,' I said. 'Manolita's at the Florida. That Seguridad bird she lives with has gone to Valencia and she's being true to him with everybody.'

'Listen, Hank, what are you trying to promote me?'

'I just wanted to cheer you up.'

'Grow up,' he said. 'What's one more?'

'One more.'

'I don't mind dying a bit,' he said. 'Dying is just a lot of crap. Only it's wasteful. The attack is wrong and it's wasteful. I can handle tanks good now. If I had time I could make good tankists too. And if we had tanks that were a little bit faster the anti-tanks wouldn't bother them the way it does when you haven't got the mobility. Listen, Hank, they aren't what we thought they were though. Do you remember when everybody thought if we only had tanks?'

'They were good at Guadalajara.'

'Sure. But those were the old boys. They were soldiers. And it was against Italians.'

'But what's happened?'

'A lot of things. The mercenaries signed up for six months. Most of them were Frenchmen. They soldiered good for five but now all they want to do is live through the last month and go home. They aren't worth a damn now. The Russians that came out as demonstrators when the government bought the tanks were perfect. But they're pulling them back now for China they say. The new Spaniards are some of them good and some not. It takes six months to make a good tank man, I mean to know anything. And to be able to size up and work intelligently you have to have a talent. We've been having to make them in six weeks and there aren't so many with a talent.'

'They make fine flyers.'

'They'll make fine tank guys too. But you have to get the ones with a vocation for it. It's sort of like being a priest. You have to be cut out for it. Especially now they've got so much anti-tank.'

They had pulled down the shutters in Chicote's and now they were locking the door. No one would be allowed in now. But you had a half an hour more before they closed.

'I like it here,' said Al. 'It isn't so noisy now. Remember that time I met you in New Orleans when I was on a ship and we went in to have a drink in the Monteleone bar and that kid that looked just like Saint Sebastian was paging people with that funny voice like he was singing and I gave him a quarter to page Mr. B. F. Slob?'

'That's the same way you said "Casa del Campo." '

'Yeah,' he said. 'I laugh every time I think of that.' Then he went on, 'You see, now, they're not frightened of tanks any more. Nobody is. We aren't either. But they're still useful. Really useful. Only with the anti-tank now they're so damn vulnerable. Maybe I ought to be in something else. *Not really*. Because they're still useful. But the way they are now you've got to have a vocation for them. You got to have a lot of political development to be a good tank man now.'

'You're a good tank man.'

'I'd like to be something else tomorrow,' he said. 'I'm talking awfully wet but you have a right to talk wet if it isn't going to hurt anybody else. You know I like tanks too, only we don't use them right because the infantry don't know enough yet. They just want the old tank ahead to give them some cover while they go. That's no good. Then they get to depending on the tanks and they won't move without them. Sometimes they won't even deploy.'

'I know.'

'But you see if you had tankists that knew their stuff they'd go out ahead and develop the machine-gun fire and then drop back behind the infantry and fire on the gun and knock it out and give the infantry covering fire when they attacked. And other tanks could rush the machine-gun posts as though they were cavalry. And they could straddle a trench and enfilade and put flaking fire down it. And they could bring up infantry when it was right to or cover their advance when that was best.'

'But instead?'

'Instead it's like it will be tomorrow. We have so damned few guns that we're just used as slightly mobile armored artillery units. And as soon as you are standing still and being light artillery, you've lost your mobility and that's your safety and they start sniping at you with the anti-tanks. And if we're not that we're just sort of iron perambulators to push ahead of the infantry. And lately you don't know whether the perambulator will push or whether the guys inside will push them. And you never know if there's going to be anybody behind you when you get there.'

'How many are you now to a brigade?'

'Six to a battalion. Thirty to a brigade. That's in principle.'

'Why don't you come along now and get the bath and we'll go and eat?'

'All right. But don't you start taking care of me or thinking I'm worried or anything because I'm not. I'm just tired and I wanted to talk. And don't give me any pep talk either because we've got a political commissar and I know what I'm fighting for and I'm not worried. But I'd like things to be efficient and used as intelligently as possible.'

'What made you think I was going to give you any pep talk?'

'You started to look like it.'

'All I tried to do was see if you wanted a girl and not to talk too wet about getting killed.'

'Well, I don't want any girl tonight and I'll talk just as wet as I please unless it does damage to others. Does it damage you?'

'Come on and get the bath,' I said. 'You can talk just as bloody wet as you want.'

'Who do you suppose that little guy was that talked as though he knew so much?'

'I don't know,' I said. 'But I'm going to find out.'

'He made me gloomy,' said Al. 'Come on. Let's go.'

The old waiter with the bald head unlocked the outside door of Chicote's and let us out into the street.

'How is the offensive, comrades?' he said at the door.

'It's O.K., comrade,' said Al. 'It's all right.'

'I am happy,' said the waiter. 'My boy is in the One Hundred and Forty-fifth Brigade. Have you seen them?'

'I am of the tanks,' said Al. 'This comrade makes a cinema. Have you seen the Hundred and Forty-fifth?'

'No,' I said.

'They are up the Extremadura road,' the old waiter said. 'My boy is political commissar of the machine-gun company of his battalion. He is my youngest boy. He is twenty.'

'What party are you, comrade?' Al asked him.

'I am of no party,' the waiter said. 'But my boy is a Communist.'

'So am I,' said Al. 'The offensive, comrade, has not yet reached a decision. It is very difficult. The fascists hold very strong positions. You, in the rear-guard, must be as firm as we will be at the front. We may not take these positions now but we have proved we now have an army capable of going on the offensive and you will see what it will do.'

'And the Extremadura road?' asked the old waiter, still holding on to the door. 'Is it very dangerous there?'

'No,' said Al. 'It's fine up there. You don't need to worry about him up there.'

'God bless you,' said the waiter. 'God guard you and keep you.'

Outside in the dark street, Al said, 'Jees he's kind of confused politically, isn't he?'

'He is a good guy,' I said. 'I've known him for a long time.'

'He seems like a good guy,' Al said. 'But he ought to get wise to himself politically.'

The room at the Florida was crowded. They were playing the

gramophone and it was full of smoke and there was a crap game going on the floor. Comrades kept coming in to use the bathtub and the room smelt of smoke, soap, dirty uniforms, and steam from the bathroom.

The Spanish girl called Manolita, very neat, demurely dressed, with a sort of false French chic, with much joviality, much dignity and closely set cold eyes, was sitting on the bed talking with an English newspaper man. Except for the gramophone it wasn't very noisy.

'It *is* your room, isn't it?' the English newspaper man said.

'It's in my name at the desk,' I said. 'I sleep in it sometimes.'

'But whose is the whiskey?' he asked.

'Mine,' said Manolita. 'They drank that bottle so I got another.'

'You're a good girl, daughter,' I said. 'That's three I owe you.'

'Two,' she said. 'The other was a present.'

There was a huge cooked ham, rosy and white edged in a half-opened tin on the table beside my typewriter and a comrade would reach up, cut himself a slice of ham with his pocket knife, and go back to the crap game. I cut myself a slice of ham.

'You're next on the tub,' I said to Al. He had been looking around the room.

'It's nice here,' he said. 'Where did the ham come from?'

'We bought it from the *intendencia* of one of the brigades,' she said. 'Isn't it beautiful?'

'Who's we?'

'He and I,' she said, turning her head toward the English correspondent. 'Don't you think he's cute?'

'Manolita has been most kind,' said the Englishman. 'I hope we're not disturbing you.'

'Not at all,' I said. 'Later on I might want to use the bed but that won't be until much later.'

'We can have a party in my room,' Manolita said. 'You aren't cross are you, Henry?'

'Never,' I said. 'Who are the comrades shooting craps?'

'I don't know,' said Manolita. 'They came in for baths and then they stayed to shoot craps. Everyone has been very nice. You know my bad news?'

'No.'

'It's very bad. You knew my fiancé who was in the police and went to Barcelona?'

'Yes. Sure.'

Al went into the bathroom.

'Well, he was shot in an accident and I haven't any one I can depend on in police circles and he never got me the papers he had promised me and today I heard I was going to be arrested.'

'Why?'

'Because I have no papers and they say I hang around with you people and with people from the brigades all the time so I am probably a spy. If my fiancé had not gotten himself shot it would have been all right. Will you help me?'

'Sure,' I said. 'Nothing will happen to you if you're all right.'

'I think I'd better stay with you to be sure.'

'And if you're not all right that would be fine for me, wouldn't it?'

'Can't I stay with you?'

'No. If you get in trouble call me up. I never heard you ask anybody any military questions. I think you're all right.'

'I'm *really* all right,' she said then, leaning over, away from the Englishman. 'You think it's all right to stay with him? Is *he* all right?'

'How do I know?' I said. 'I never saw him before.'

'You're being cross,' she said. 'Let's not think about it now but everyone be happy and go out to dinner.'

I went over to the crap game.

'You want to go out to dinner?'

'No, comrade,' said the man handling the dice without looking up. 'You want to get in the game?'

'I want to eat.'

'We'll be here when you get back,' said another crap shooter. 'Come on, roll, I've got you covered.'

'If you run into any money bring it up here to the game.'

There was one in the room I knew besides Manolita. He was from the Twelfth Brigade and he was playing the gramophone. He was a Hungarian, a sad Hungarian, not one of the cheerful kind.

'*Salud camarade*,' he said. 'Thank you for your hospitality.'

'Don't you shoot craps?' I asked him.

'I haven't that sort of money,' he said. 'They are aviators with contracts. Mercenaries . . . They make a thousand dollars a month. They were on the Teruel front and now they have come here.'

'How did they come up here?'

'One of them knows you. But he had to go out to his field. They came for him in a car and the game had already started.'

'I'm glad you came up,' I said. 'Come up any time and make yourself at home.'

'I came to play the new discs,' he said. 'It does not disturb you?'

'No. It's fine. Have a drink.'

'A little ham,' he said.

One of the crap shooters reached up and cut a slice of ham.

'You haven't seen this guy Henry around that owns the place, have you?' he asked me.

'That's me.'

'Oh,' he said. 'Sorry. Want to get in the game?'

'Later on,' I said.

'O.K.,' he said. Then his mouth full of ham, 'Listen you tar heel bastid. Make your dice hit the wall and bounce.'

'Won't make no difference to you, comrade,' said the man handling the dice.

Al came out of the bathroom. He looked all clean except for some smudges around his eyes.

'You can take those off with a towel,' I said.

'What?'

'Look at yourself once more in the mirror.'

'It's too steamy,' he said. 'To hell with it, I feel clean.'

'Let's eat,' I said. 'Come on, Manolita. You know each other?'

I watched her eyes run over Al.

'How are you?' Manolita said.

'I say that is a sound idea,' the Englishman said. 'Do let's eat. But where?'

'Is that a crap game?' Al said.

'Didn't you see it when you came in?'

'No,' he said. 'All I saw was the ham.'

'It's a crap game.'

'You go and eat,' Al said. 'I'm staying here.'

As we went out there were six of them on the floor and Al Wagner was reaching up to cut a slice of ham.

'What do you do, comrade?' I heard one of the flyers say to Al.

'Tanks.'

'Tell me they aren't any good any more,' said the flyer.

'Tell you a lot of things,' Al said. 'What you got there? Some dice?'

'Want to look at them?'

'No,' said Al. 'I want to handle them.'

We went down the hall, Manolita, me and the tall English-man, and found the boys had left already for the Gran Via res-taurant. The Hungarian had stayed behind to replay the new discs. I was very hungry and the food at the Gran Via was lousy. The two who were making the film had already eaten and gone back to work on the bad camera.

This restaurant was in the basement and you had to pass a guard and go through the kitchen and down a stairs to get to it. It was a racket.

They had a millet and water soup, yellow rice with horse meat in it, and oranges for dessert. There had been another dish of chickpeas with sausage in it that everybody said was terrible but it had run out. The newspaper men all sat at one table and the other tables were filled with officers and girls from Chicote's, people from the censorship, which was then in the telephone building across the street, and various unknown citizens.

The restaurant was run by an anarchist syndicate and they sold you wine that was all stamped with the label of the royal cellars and the date it had been put in the bins. Most of it was so old that it was either corked or just plain faded out and gone to pieces. You can't drink labels and I sent three bottles back as bad before we got a drinkable one. There was a row about this.

The waiters didn't know the different wines. They just brought you a bottle of wine and you took your chances. They were as different from the Chicote's waiters as black from white. These waiters were all snotty, all over-tipped and they regularly had special dishes such as lobster or chicken that they sold extra for gigantic prices. But these had all been bought up before we got there so we just drew the soup, the rice and the oranges. The place always made me angry because the waiters were a crooked lot of profiteers and it was about as expensive to eat in, if you had one of the special dishes, as 21 or the Colony in New York.

We were sitting at the table with a bottle of wine that just wasn't bad, you know you could taste it starting to go, but it wouldn't justify making a row about, when Al Wagner came in. He looked around the room, saw us and came over.

'What's the matter?' I said.

'They broke me,' he said.

'It didn't take very long.'

'Not with those guys,' he said. 'That's a big game. What have they got to eat?'

I called a waiter over.

'It's too late,' he said. 'We can't serve anything now.'

'This comrade is in the tanks,' I said. 'He has fought all day and he will fight tomorrow and he hasn't eaten.'

'That's not my fault,' the waiter said. 'It's too late. There isn't anything more. Why doesn't the comrade eat with his unit? The army has plenty of food.'

'I asked him to eat with me.'

'You should have said something about it. It's too late now. We are not serving anything any more.'

'Get the head waiter.'

The head waiter said the cook had gone home and there was no fire in the kitchen. He went away. They were angry because we had sent the bad wine back.

'The hell with it,' said Al. 'Let's go somewhere else.'

'There's no place you can eat at this hour. They've got food. I'll just have to go over and suck up to the head waiter and give him some more money.'

I went over and did just that and the sullen waiter brought a plate of cold sliced meats, then half a spiny lobster with mayonnaise, and a salad of lettuce and lentils. The head waiter sold this out of his private stock which he was holding out either to take home, or sell to late comers.

'Cost you much?' Al asked.

'No,' I lied.

'I'll bet it did,' he said. 'I'll fix up with you when I get paid.'

'What do you get now?'

'I don't know yet. It was ten pesetas a day but they've raised it now I'm an officer. But we haven't got it yet and I haven't asked.'

'Comrade,' I called the waiter. He came over, still angry that the head waiter had gone over his head and served Al. 'Bring another bottle of wine, please.'

'What kind?'

'Any that is not too old so that the red is faded.'

'It's all the same.'

I said the equivalent of like hell it is in Spanish, and the waiter brought over a bottle of Château Mouton-Rothschild 1906 that was just as good as the last claret we had was rotten.

'Boy that's wine,' Al said. 'What did you tell him to get that?'

'Nothing. He just made a lucky draw out of the bin.'

'Most of that stuff from the palace stinks.'

'It's too old. This is a hell of a climate on wine.'

'There's that wise comrade,' Al nodded across at another table.

The little man with the thick glasses that had talked to us about Largo Caballero was talking with some people I knew were very big shots indeed.

'I guess he's a big shot,' I said.

'When they're high enough up they don't give a damn what they say. But I wish he would have waited until after tomorrow. It's kind of spoiled tomorrow for me.'

I filled his glass.

'What he said sounded pretty sensible,' Al went on. 'I've been thinking it over. But my duty is to do what I'm ordered to do.'

'Don't worry about it and get some sleep.'

'I'm going to get in that game again if you'll let me take a thousand pesetas,' Al said. 'I've got a lot more than that coming to me and I'll give you an order on my pay.'

'I don't want any order. You can pay me when you get it.'

'I don't think I'm going to draw it,' Al said. 'I certainly sound wet, don't I? And I know gambling's bohemianism too. But in a game like that is the only time I don't think about tomorrow.'

'Did you like that Manolita girl? She liked you.'

'She's got eyes like a snake.'

'She's not a bad girl. She's friendly and she's all right.'

'I don't want any girl. I want to get back in that crap game.'

Down the table Manolita was laughing at something the new Englishman had said in Spanish. Most of the people had left the table.

'Let's finish the wine and go,' Al said. 'Don't you want to get in that game?'

'I'll watch you for a while,' I said and called the waiter over to bring us the bill.

'Where you go?' Manolita called down the table.

'To the room.'

'We come by later on,' she said. 'This man is very funny.'

'She is making most awful sport of me,' the Englishman said. 'She picks up on my errors in Spanish. I say, doesn't *leche* mean milk?'

'That's one interpretation of it.'

'*Does* it mean something beastly too?'

'I'm afraid so,' I said.

'You know it *is* a beastly language,' he said. 'Now Manolita, stop pulling my leg. I say stop it.'

'I'm not pulling your leg,' Manolita laughed. 'I never touched your leg. I am just laughing about the *leche*.'

'But it *does* mean milk. Didn't you just hear Edwin Henry say so?'

Manolita started to laugh again and we got up to go.

'He's a silly piece of work,' Al said. 'I'd almost like to take her away because he's so silly.'

'You can never tell about an Englishman,' I said. It was such a profound remark that I knew we had ordered too many bottles. Outside, in the street, it was turning cold and in the moonlight the clouds were passing very big and white across the wide, building-sided canyon of the Gran Via and we walked up the sidewalk with the day's fresh shell holes neatly cut in the cement, their rubble still not swept away, on up the rise of the hill toward the Plaza Callao where the Florida Hotel faced down the other little hill where the wide street ran that ended at the front.

We went past the two guards in the dark outside the door of the hotel and listened a minute in the doorway as the shooting down the street strengthened into a roll of firing, then dropped off.

'If it keeps up I guess I ought to go down,' Al said listening.

'That wasn't anything,' I said. 'Anyway that was off to the left by Carabanchel.'

'It sounded straight down in the Campo.'

'That's the way the sound throws here at night. It always fools you.'

'They aren't going to counterattack us tonight,' Al said. 'When they've got those positions and we are up that creek they aren't going to leave their positions to try to kick us out of that creek.'

'What creek?'

'You know the name of that creek.'

'Oh. *That* creek.'

'Yeah. Up that creek without a paddle.'

'Come on inside. You didn't have to listen to that firing. That's the way it is every night.'

We went inside, crossed the lobby, passing the night watchman at the concierge's desk and the night watchman got up and went with us to the elevator. He pushed a button and the elevator came down. In it was a man with a white curly sheep's wool jacket, the wool worn inside, a pink bald head, and a pink, angry face. He had six bottles of champagne under his arms and in his hands and he said, 'What the hell's the idea of bringing the elevator down?'

'You've been riding in the elevator for an hour,' the night watchman said.

'I can't help it,' said the wooly jacket man. Then to me, 'Where's Frank?'

'Frank who?'

'You know Frank,' he said. 'Come on, help me with this elevator.'

'You're drunk,' I said to him. 'Come on, skip it and let us get upstairs.'

'So would you be drunk,' said the white wooly jacket man. 'So would you be drunk comrade old comrade. Listen, where's Frank?'

'Where do you think he is?'

'In this fellow Henry's room where the crap game is.'

'Come on with us,' I said. 'Don't fool with those buttons. That's why you stop it all the time.'

'I can fly anything,' said the wooly jacket man. 'And I can fly this old elevator. Want me to stunt it?'

'Skip it,' Al said to him. 'You're drunk. We want to get to the crap game.'

'Who are you? I'll hit you with a bottle full of champagne wine.'

'Try it,' said Al. 'I'd like to cool you, you rummy fake Santa Claus.'

'A rummy fake Santa Claus,' said the bald man. 'A rummy fake Santa Claus. And that's the thanks of the Republic.'

We had gotten the elevator stopped at my floor and were walking down the hall. 'Take some bottles,' said the bald man. Then, 'Do you know why I'm drunk?'

'No.'

'Well, I won't tell you. But you'd be surprised. A rummy Claus. Well well well. What are you in, comrade?'

'Tanks.'

'And you, comrade?'

'Making a picture.'

'And I'm a rummy fake Santa Claus. Well. Well. Well. I repeat. Well. Well. Well.'

'Go and drown in it,' said Al. 'You rummy fake Santa Claus.'

We were outside the room now. The man in the white wooly coat took hold of Al's arm with his thumb and forefinger.

'You amuse me, comrade,' he said. 'You truly amuse me.'

I opened the door. The room was full of smoke and the game looked just as when we had left it except the ham was all gone off the table and the whiskey all gone out of the bottle.

'It's Baldy,' said one of the crap shooters.

'How do you do, comrades,' said Baldy, bowing. 'How do you do? How do you do? How do you do?'

The game broke up and they all started to shoot questions at him.

'I have made my report, comrades,' Baldy said. 'And here is a little champagne wine. I am no longer interested in any but the picturesque aspects of the whole affair.'

'Where did your wingmen muck off to?'

'It wasn't their fault,' said Baldy. 'I was engaged in contemplating a terrific spectacle and I was ob-*livious* of the fact that I had any wingmen until all of those Fiats started coming down over, past and under me and I realized that my trusty little air-o-plane no longer had any tail.'

'Jees I wish you weren't drunk,' said one of the flyers.

'But I *am* drunk,' said Baldy. 'And I hope all you gentlemen and comrades will join me because I am very happy tonight even though I have been insulted by an ignorant tank man who has called me a rummy fake Santa Claus.'

'I wish you were sober,' the other flyer said. 'How'd you get back to the field?'

'Don't ask me any questions,' Baldy said with great dignity. 'I returned in a staff car of the Twelfth Brigade. When I alighted with my trusty par-a-chute there was a tendency to regard me as a criminal fascist due to my inability to master the Lanish Spanguage. But all difficulties were smoothed away when I convinced them of my identity and I was treated with rare consideration. Oh boy you ought to have seen that Junker when she started to burn. That's what I was watching when the Fiats dove on me. Oh boy I wish I could tell you.'

'He shot a tri-motor Junker down today over the Jarama and his wingmen mucked off on him and he got shot down and bailed out,' one of the flyers said. 'You know him. Baldy Jackson.'

'How far did you drop before you pulled your rip cord, Baldy?' asked another flyer.

'All of six thousand feet and I think my diaphragm is busted loose in front from when she came taut. I thought it would cut me in two. There must have been fifteen Fiats and I wanted to get completely clear. I had to fool with the chute plenty to get down on the right side of the river. I had to slip her plenty and hit pretty hard. The wind was good.'

'Frank had to go back to Alcalá,' another flyer said. 'We started a crap game. We got to get back there before daylight.'

'I am in no mood to toy with the dice,' said Baldy. 'I am in a mood to drink champagne wine out of glasses with cigarette butts in them.'

'I'll wash them,' said Al.

'For Comrade Fake Santa Claus,' said Baldy. 'For old Comrade Claus.'

'Skip it,' said Al. He picked up the glasses and took them to the bathroom.

'Is he in the tanks?' asked one of the flyers.

'Yes. He's been there since the start.'

'They tell me the tanks aren't any good any more,' a flyer said.

'You told him that once,' I said. 'Why don't you lay off? He's been working all day.'

'So have we. But I mean really they aren't any good, are they?'

'Not so good. But he's good.'

'I guess he's all right. He looks like a nice fellow. What kind of money do they make?'

'They got ten pesetas a day,' I said. 'Now he gets a lieutenant's pay.'

'Spanish lieutenant?'

'Yes.'

'I guess he's nuts all right. Or has he got politics?'

'He's got politics.'

'Oh, well,' he said. 'That explains it. Say Baldy, you must have had a hell of a time bailing out with that wind pressure with the tail gone.'

'Yes, comrade,' said Baldy.

'How did you feel?'

'I was thinking all the time, comrade.'

'Baldy, how many bailed out of the Junker?'

'Four,' said Baldy, 'out of a crew of six. I was sure I'd killed

the pilot. I noticed when he quit firing. There's a co-pilot that's
a gunner too and I'm pretty sure I got him too. I must have
because he quit firing too. But maybe it was the heat. Anyhow
four came out. Would you like me to describe the scene? I can
describe the scene very well.'

He was sitting on the bed now with a large water glass of
champagne in his hand and his pink head and pink face were
moist with sweat.

'Why doesn't anyone drink to me?' asked Baldy. 'I would like
all comrades to drink to me and then I will describe the scene in
all its horror and its beauty.'

We all drank.

'Where was I?' asked Baldy.

'Just coming out of the McAlester Hotel,' a flyer said. 'In all
your horror and your beauty – don't clown, Baldy. Oddly
enough we're interested.'

'I will describe it,' said Baldy. 'But first I must have more
champagne wine.' He had drained the glass when we drank to
him.

'If he drinks like that he'll go to sleep,' another flyer said.
'Only give him half a glass.'

Baldy drank it off.

'I will describe it,' he said. 'After another little drink.'

'Listen, Baldy, take it easy will you? This is something we
want to get straight. You got no ship now for a few days but
we're flying tomorrow and this is important as well as interesting.'

'I made my report,' said Baldy. 'You can read it out at the
field. They'll have a copy.'

'Come on, Baldy, snap out of it.'

'I will describe it eventually,' said Baldy. He shut and opened
his eyes several times, then said, 'Hello Comrade Santa Claus' to
Al. 'I will describe it eventually. All you comrades have to do is
listen.'

And he described it.

'It was very strange and very beautiful,' Baldy said and drank
off the glass of champagne.

'Cut it out, Baldy,' a flyer said.

'I have experienced profound emotions,' Baldy said. 'Highly
profound emotions. Emotions of the deepest dye.'

'Let's get back to Alcalá,' one flyer said. 'That pink head isn't
going to make sense. What about the game?'

'He's going to make sense,' another flyer said. 'He's just wind-ing up.'

'Are you criticizing me?' asked Baldy. 'Is *that* the thanks of the Republic?'

'Listen, Santa Claus,' Al said. 'What was it like?'

'Are you asking me?' Baldy stared at him. 'Are *you* putting questions to me? Have you ever been in action, comrade?'

'No,' said Al. 'I got these eyebrows burnt off when I was shav-ing.'

'Keep your drawers on, comrade,' said Baldy. 'I will describe the strange and beautiful scene. I'm a writer, you know, as well as a flyer.'

He nodded his head in confirmation of his own statement.

'He writes for the Meridian, Mississippi, *Argus*,' said a flyer. 'All the time. They can't stop him.'

'I have talent as a writer,' said Baldy. 'I have a fresh and original talent for description. I have a newspaper clipping which I have lost which says so. Now I will launch myself on the description.'

'O.K. What did it look like?'

'Comrades,' said Baldy. 'You can't describe it.' He held out his glass.

'What did I tell you?' said a flyer. 'He couldn't make sense in a month. He never could make sense.'

'You,' said Baldy, 'you unfortunate little fellow. All right. When I banked out of it I looked down and of course she had been pouring back smoke but she was holding right on her course to get over the mountains. She was losing altitude fast and I came up and over and dove on her again. There were still wingmen then and she'd lurched and started to smoke twice as much and then the door of the cockpit came open and it was just like looking into a blast furnace, and then they started to come out. I'd half rolled, dove, and then pulled up out of it and I was looking back and down and they were coming out of her, out through the blast furnace door, dropping out trying to get clear, and the chutes opened up and they looked like great big beauti-ful morning glories opening up and she was just one big thing of flame now like you never saw and going round and round and there were four chutes just as beautiful as anything you could see just pulling slow against the sky and then one started to burn at the edge and as it burned the man started to drop fast and I was watching him when the bullets started to come by and the Fiats right behind them and the bullets and the Fiats.'

'You're a writer all right,' said one flyer. 'You ought to write for *War Aces*. Do you mind telling me in plain language what happened?'

'No,' said Baldy. 'I'll tell you. But you know, no kidding, it was something to see. And I never shot down any big tri-motor Junkers before and I'm happy.'

'Everybody's happy, Baldy. Tell us what happened, really.'

'O.K.,' said Baldy. 'I'll just drink a little wine and then I'll tell you.'

'How were you when you sighted them?'

'We were in a left echelon of V's. Then we went into a left echelon of echelons and dove onto them with all four guns until you could have touched them before we rolled out of it. We crippled three others. The Fiats were hanging up in the sun. They didn't come down until I was sightseeing all by myself.'

'Did your wingmen muck off?'

'No. It was my fault. I started watching the spectacle and they were gone. There isn't any formation for watching spectacles. I guess they went on and picked up the echelon. I don't know. Don't ask me. And I'm tired. I was elated. But now I'm tired.'

'You're sleepy you mean. You're rum-dumb and sleepy.'

'I am simply tired,' said Baldy. 'A man in my position has the right to be tired. And if I become sleepy I have the right to be sleepy. Don't I Santa Claus?' he said to Al.

'Yeah,' said Al. 'I guess you have the right to be sleepy. I'm even sleepy myself. Isn't there going to be any crap game?'

'We got to get him out to Alcalá and we've got to get out there too,' a flyer said. 'Why? You lost money in the game?'

'A little,' said Al.

'You want to try to pass for it once?' the flyer asked him.

'I'll shoot a thousand,' Al said.

'I'll fade you,' the flyer said. 'You guys don't make much, do you?'

'No,' said Al. 'We don't make much.'

He laid the thousand-peseta note down on the floor, rolled the dice between his palms so they clicked over and over, and shot them out on the floor with a snap. Two ones showed.

'They're still your dice,' the flyer said, picking up the bill and looking at Al.

'I don't need them,' said Al. He stood up.

'Need any dough?' the flyer asked him. Looking at him curiously.

'Got no use for it,' Al said.

'We've got to get the hell out to Alcalá,' the flyer said. 'We'll have a game some night soon. We'll get hold of Frank and the rest of them. We could get up a pretty good game. Can we give you a lift?'

'Yes. Want a ride?'

'No,' Al said. 'I'm walking. It's just down the street.'

'Well, we're going out to Alcalá. Does anybody know the password for tonight?'

'Oh, the chauffeur will have it. He'll have gone by and picked it up before dark.'

'Come on, Baldy. You drunken sleepy bum.'

'Not me,' said Baldy. 'I am a potential ace of the people's army.'

'Takes ten to be an ace. Even if you count Italians. You've only got one, Baldy.'

'It wasn't Italians,' said Baldy. 'It was Germans. And you didn't see her when she was all hot like that inside. She was a raging inferno.'

'Carry him out,' said a flyer. 'He's writing for that Meridian, Mississippi, paper again. Well, so long. Thanks for having us up in the room.'

They all shook hands and they were gone. I went to the head of the stairs with them. The elevator was no longer running and I watched them go down the stairs. One was on each side of Baldy and he was nodding his head slowly. He was really sleepy now.

In their room the two I was working on the picture with were still working over the bad camera. It was delicate, eye-straining work and when I asked, 'Do you think you'll get her?' the tall one said, 'Yes. Sure. We have to. I make a piece now which was broken.'

'What was the party?' asked the other. 'We work always on this damn camera.'

'American flyers,' I said. 'And a fellow I used to know who's in tanks.'

'Goot fun? I am sorry not to be there.'

'All right,' I said. 'Kind of funny.'

'You must get sleep. We must all be up early. We must be fresh for tomorrow.'

'How much more have you got on that camera?'

'There it goes again. Damn such shape springs.'

'Leave him alone. We finish it. Then we all sleep. What time you call us?'

'Five?'

'All right. As soon as is light.'

'Good night.'

'*Salud*. Get some sleep.'

'*Salud*,' I said. 'We've got to be closer tomorrow.'

'Yes,' he said. 'I have thought so too. Much closer. I am glad you know.'

Al was asleep in the big chair in the room with the light on his face. I put a blanket over him but he woke.

'I'm going down.'

'Sleep here. I'll set the alarm and call you.'

'Something might happen with the alarm,' he said. 'I better go down. I don't want to get there late.'

'I'm sorry about the game.'

'They'd have broke me anyway,' he said. 'Those guys are poisonous with dice.'

'You had the dice there on that last play.'

'They're poisonous fading you too. They're strange guys too. I guess they don't get overpaid. I guess if you are doing it for dough there isn't enough dough to pay for doing it.'

'Want me to walk down with you?'

'No,' he said, standing up, and buckling on the big web-belted Colt he had taken off when he came back after dinner to the game. 'No, I feel fine now. I've got my perspective back again. All you need is a perspective.'

'I'd like to walk down.'

'No. Get some sleep. I'll go down and I'll get a good five hours' sleep before it starts.'

'That early?'

'Yeah. You won't have any light to film by. You might as well stay in bed.' He took an envelope out of his leather coat and laid it on the table. 'Take this stuff, will you, and send it to my brother in N.Y. His address is on the back of the envelope.'

'Sure. But I won't have to send it.'

'No,' he said. 'I don't think you will now. But there's some pictures and stuff they'll like to have. He's got a nice wife. Want to see her picture?'

He took it out of his pocket. It was inside his identity book.

It showed a pretty, dark girl standing by a rowboat on the shore of a lake.

'Up in the Catskills,' said Al. 'Yeah. He's got a nice wife. She's a Jewish girl. Yes,' he said. 'Don't let me get wet again. So long, kid. Take it easy. I tell you truly I feel O.K. now. And I didn't feel good when I came out this afternoon.'

'Let me walk down.'

'No. You might have trouble coming back through the Plaza de España. Some of those guys are nervous at night. Good night. See you tomorrow night.'

'That's the way to talk.'

Upstairs in the room above mine, Manolita and the Englishman were making quite a lot of noise. So she evidently hadn't been arrested.

'That's right. That's the way to talk,' Al said. 'Takes you sometimes three or four hours to get so you can do it though.'

He'd put the leather helmet on now with the raised padded ridge and his face looked dark and I noticed the dark hollows under his eyes.

'See you tomorrow night at Chicote's,' I said.

'That's right,' he said, and wouldn't look me in the eye. 'See you tomorrow night at Chicote's.'

'What time?'

'Listen, that's enough,' he said. 'Tomorrow night at Chicote's. We don't have to go into the time.' And he went out.

If you hadn't known him pretty well and if you hadn't seen the terrain where he was going to attack tomorrow, you would have thought he was very angry about something. I guess somewhere inside of himself he was angry, very angry. You get angry about a lot of things and you, yourself, dying uselessly is one of them. But then I guess angry is about the best way that you can be when you attack.

UNDER THE RIDGE

In the heat of the day with the dust blowing, we came back, dry-mouthed, nose-clogged and heavy-loaded, down out of the battle to the long ridge above the river where the Spanish troops lay in reserve.

I sat down with my back against the shallow trench, my shoulders and the back of my head against the earth, clear now from even stray bullets, and looked at what lay below us in the hollow. There was the tank reserve, the tanks covered with branches chopped from olive trees. To their left were the staff cars, mud-daubed and branch-covered, and between the two a long line of men carrying stretchers wound down through the gap to where, on the flat at the foot of the ridge, ambulances were loading. Commissary mules loaded with sacks of bread and kegs of wine, and a train of ammunition mules, led by their drivers, were coming up the gap in the ridge, and men with empty stretchers were walking slowly up the trail with the mules.

To the right, below the curve of the ridge, I could see the entrance to the cave where the brigade staff was working, and their signaling wires ran out of the top of the cave and curved on over the ridge in the shelter of which we lay.

Motorcyclists in leather suits and helmets came up and down the cut on their cycles or, where it was too steep, walking them, and leaving them beside the cut, walked over to the entrance to the cave and ducked inside. As I watched, a big Hungarian cyclist that I knew came out of the cave, tucked some papers in his leather wallet, walked over to his motorcycle and, pushing it up through the stream of mules and stretcher-bearers, threw a leg over the saddle and roared on over the ridge, his machine churning a storm of dust.

Below, across the flat where the ambulances were coming and going, was the green foliage that marked the line of the river. There was a large house with a red tile roof and there was a gray stone mill, and from the trees around the big house beyond the river came the flashes of our guns. They were firing straight at us and there were the twin flashes, then the throaty, short *bung-bung* of the three-inch pieces and then the rising cry of the shells coming toward us and going on over our heads. As always, we were short of artillery. There were only four batteries down there, when there should have been forty, and they were firing only two guns at a time. The attack had failed before we came down.

'Are you Russians?' a Spanish soldier asked me.

'No, Americans,' I said. 'Have you any water?'

'Yes, comrade.' He handed over a pigskin bag. These troops in reserve were soldiers only in name and from the fact that they were in uniform. They were not intended to be used in the attack, and they sprawled along this line under the crest of the ridge, huddled in groups, eating, drinking and talking, or simply sitting dumbly, waiting. The attack was being made by an International Brigade.

We both drank. The water tasted of asphalt and pig bristles.

'Wine is better,' the soldier said. 'I will get wine.'

'Yes. But for the thirst, water.'

'There is no thirst like the thirst of battle. Even here, in reserve, I have much thirst.'

'That is fear,' said another soldier. 'Thirst is fear.'

'No,' said another. 'With fear there is thirst, always. But in battle there is much thirst even when there is no fear.'

'There is always fear in battle,' said the first soldier.

'For you,' said the second soldier.

'It is normal,' the first soldier said.

'For you.'

'Shut your dirty mouth,' said the first soldier. 'I am simply a man who tells the truth.'

It was a bright April day and the wind was blowing wildly so that each mule that came up the gap raised a cloud of dust, and the two men at the ends of a stretcher each raised a cloud of dust that blew together and made one, and below, across the flat, long streams of dust moved out from the ambulances and blew away in the wind.

I felt quite sure I was not going to be killed on that day now, since we had done our work well in the morning, and twice during the early part of the attack we should have been killed and were not; and this had given me confidence. The first time had been when we had gone up with the tanks and picked a place from which to film the attack. Later I had a sudden distrust for the place and we had moved the cameras about two hundred yards to the left. Just before leaving, I had marked the place in quite the oldest way there is of marking a place, and within ten minutes a six-inch shell had lit on the exact place where I had been and there was no trace of any human being ever having been there. Instead, there was a large and clearly blasted hole in the earth.

Then, two hours later, a Polish officer, recently detached from the battalion and attached to the staff, had offered to show us the positions the Poles had just captured and, coming from under the lee of a fold of hill, we had walked into machine-gun fire that we had to crawl out from under with our chins tight to the ground and dust in our noses, and at the same time made the sad discovery that the Poles had captured no positions at all that day but were a little further back than the place they had started from. And now, lying in the shelter of the trench, I was wet with sweat, hungry and thirsty and hollow inside from the now-finished danger of the attack.

'You are sure you are not Russians?' asked a soldier. 'There are Russians here today.'

'Yes. But we are not Russians.'

'You have the face of a Russian.'

'No,' I said. 'You are wrong, comrade. I have quite a funny face but it is not the face of a Russian.'

'He has the face of a Russian,' pointing at the other one of us who was working on a camera.

'Perhaps. But still he is not Russian. Where you from?'

'Extremadura,' he said proudly.

'Are there any Russians in Extremadura?' I asked.

'No,' he told me, even more proudly. 'There are no Russians in Extremadura, and there are no Extremadurans in Russia.'

'What are your politics?'

'I hate all foreigners,' he said.

'That's a broad political program.'

'I hate the Moors, the English, the French, the Italians, the Germans, the North Americans and the Russians.'

'You hate them in that order?'

'Yes. But perhaps I hate the Russians the most.'

'Man, you have very interesting ideas,' I said. 'Are you a fascist?'

'No. I am an Extremaduran and I hate foreigners.'

'He has very rare ideas,' said another soldier. 'Do not give him too much importance. Me, I like foreigners. I am from Valencia. Take another cup of wine, please.'

I reached up and took the cup, the other wine still brassy in my mouth. I looked at the Extremaduran. He was tall and thin.

His face was haggard and unshaven, and his cheeks were sunken. He stood straight up in his rage, his blanket cape around his shoulders.

'Keep your head down,' I told him. 'There are many lost bullets coming over.'

'I have no fear of bullets and I hate all foreigners,' he said fiercely.

'You don't have to fear bullets,' I said, 'but you should avoid them when you are in reserve. It is not intelligent to be wounded when it can be avoided.'

'I am not afraid of anything,' the Extremaduran said.

'You are very lucky, comrade.'

'It's true,' the other, with the wine cup, said. 'He has no fear, not even of the *aviones*.'

'He is crazy,' another soldier said. 'Everyone fears planes. They kill little but make much fear.'

'I have no fear. Neither of planes nor of nothing,' the Extremaduran said. 'And I hate every foreigner alive.'

Down the gap, walking beside two stretcher-bearers and seeming to pay no attention at all to where he was, came a tall man in International Brigade uniform with a blanket rolled over his shoulder and tied at his waist. His head was held high and he looked like a man walking in his sleep. He was middle-aged. He was not carrying a rifle and, from where I lay, he did not look wounded.

I watched him walking alone down out of the war. Before he came to the staff cars he turned to the left and his head still held high in that strange way, he walked over the edge of the ridge and out of sight.

The one who was with me, busy changing film in the hand cameras, had not noticed him.

A single shell came in over the ridge and fountained in the dirt and black smoke just short of the tank reserve.

Someone put his head out of the cave where brigade headquarters was and then disappeared inside. I thought it looked like a good place to go, but knew they would all be furious in there because the attack was a failure, and I did not want to face them. If an operation was successful they were happy to have motion pictures of it. But if it was a failure everyone was in such a rage there was always a chance of being sent back under arrest.

'They may shell us now,' I said.

'That makes no difference to me,' said the Extremaduran. I was beginning to be a little tired of the Extremaduran.

'Have you any more wine to spare?' I asked. My mouth was still dry.

'Yes, man. There are gallons of it,' the friendly soldier said. He was short, big-fisted and very dirty, with a stubble of beard about the same length as the hair on his cropped head. 'Do you think they will shell us now?'

'They should,' I said. 'But in this war you can never tell.'

'What is the matter with this war?' asked the Extremaduran angrily. 'Don't you like this war?'

'Shut up!' said the friendly soldier. 'I command here, and these comrades are our guests.'

'Then let him not talk against our war,' said the Extremaduran. 'No foreigners shall come here and talk against our war.'

'What town are you from, comrade?' I asked the Extremaduran.

'Badajoz,' he said. 'I am from Badajoz. In Badajoz, we have been sacked and pillaged and our women violated by the English, the French and now the Moors. What the Moors have done now is no worse than what the English did under Wellington. You should read history. My great-grandmother was killed by the English. The house where my family lived was burned by the English.'

'I regret it,' I said. 'Why do you hate the North Americans?'

'My father was killed by the North Americans in Cuba while he was there as a conscript.'

'I am sorry for that, too. Truly sorry. Believe me. And why do you hate the Russians?'

'Because they are the representatives of tyranny and I hate their faces. You have the face of a Russian.'

'Maybe we better get out of here,' I said to the one who was with me and who did not speak Spanish. 'It seems I have the face of a Russian and it's getting me into trouble.'

'I'm going to sleep,' he said. 'This is a good place. Don't talk so much and you won't get into trouble.'

'There's a comrade here that doesn't like me. I think he's an anarchist.'

'Well, watch out he doesn't shoot you, then. I'm going to sleep.'

Just then two men in leather coats, one short and stocky, the other of medium height, both with civilian caps, flat, high-cheekboned faces, wooden-holstered Mauser pistols strapped to their legs, came out of the gap and headed toward us.

The taller of them spoke to me in French. 'Have you seen a French comrade pass through here?' he asked. 'A comrade with a blanket tied around his shoulders in the form of a bandoleer? A comrade of about forty-five or fifty years old? Have you seen such a comrade going in the direction away from the front?'

'No,' I said. 'I have not seen such a comrade.'

He looked at me a moment and I noticed his eyes were a grayish-yellow and that they did not blink at all.

'Thank you, comrade,' he said, in his odd French, and then spoke rapidly to the other man with him in a language I did not understand. They went off and climbed the highest part of the ridge, from where they could see down all the gullies.

'There is the true face of Russians,' the Extremaduran said.

'Shut up!' I said. I was watching the two men in the leather coats. They were standing there, under considerable fire, looking carefully over all the broken country below the ridge and toward the river.

Suddenly one of them saw what he was looking for, and pointed. Then the two started to run like hunting dogs, one straight down over the ridge, the other at an angle as though to cut someone off. Before the second one went over the crest I could see him drawing his pistol and holding it ahead of him as he ran.

'And how do you like that?' asked the Extremaduran.

'No better than you,' I said.

Over the crest of the parallel ridge I heard the Mausers' jerky barking. They kept it up for more than a dozen shots. They must have opened fire at too long a range. After all the burst of shooting there was a pause and then a single shot.

The Extremaduran looked at me sullenly and said nothing. I thought it would be simpler if the shelling started. But it did not start.

The two in the leather coats and civilian caps came back over the ridge, walking together, and then down to the gap, walking downhill with that odd bent-kneed way of the two-legged animal coming down a steep slope. They turned up the gap as a tank came whirring and clanking down and moved to one side to let it pass.

The tanks had failed again that day, and the drivers coming

down from the lines in their leather helmets, the tank turrets open now as they came into the shelter of the ridge, had the straight-ahead stare of football players who have been removed from a game for yellowness.

The two flat-faced men in the leather coats stood by us on the ridge to let the tank pass.

'Did you find the comrade you were looking for?' I asked the taller one of them in French.

'Yes, comrade. Thank you,' he said and looked me over very carefully.

'What does he say?' the Extremaduran asked.

'He says they found the comrade they were looking for,' I told him. The Extremaduran said nothing.

We had been all that morning in the place the middle-aged Frenchman had walked out of. We had been there in the dust, the smoke, the noise, the receiving of wounds, the death, the fear of death, the bravery, the cowardice, the insanity and failure of an unsuccessful attack. We had been there on that plowed field men could not cross and live. You dropped and lay flat; making a mound to shield your head; working your chin into the dirt; waiting for the order to go up that slope no man could go up and live.

We had been with those who lay there waiting for the tanks that did not come; waiting under the inrushing shriek and roaring crash of the shelling; the metal and the earth thrown like clods from a dirt fountain; and overhead the cracking, whispering fire like a curtain. We knew how those felt, waiting. They were as far forward as they could get. And men could not move further and live, when the order came to move ahead.

We had been there all morning in the place the middle-aged Frenchman had come walking away from. I understood how a man might suddenly, seeing clearly the stupidity of dying in an unsuccessful attack; or suddenly seeing it clearly, as you can see clearly and justly before you die; seeing its hopelessness, seeing its idiocy, seeing how it really was, simply get back and walk away from it as the Frenchman had done. He could walk out of it not from cowardice, but simply from seeing too clearly; knowing suddenly that he had to leave it; knowing there was no other thing to do.

The Frenchman had come walking out of the attack with great dignity and I understood him as a man. But, as a soldier, these other men who policed the battle had hunted him down, and the death he had walked away from had found him when he was just over the ridge, clear of the bullets and the shelling, and walking toward the river.

'And that,' the Extremaduran said to me, nodding toward the battle police.

'Is war,' I said. 'In war, it is necessary to have discipline.'

'And to live under that sort of discipline we should die?'

'Without discipline everyone will die anyway.'

'There is one kind of discipline and another kind of discipline,' the Extremaduran said. 'Listen to me. In February we were here where we are now and the fascists attacked. They drove us from the hills that you Internationals tried to take today and that you could not take. We fell back to here; to this ridge. Internationals came up and took the line ahead of us.'

'I know that,' I said.

'But you do not know this,' he went on angrily. 'There was a boy from my province who became frightened during the bombardment, and he shot himself in the hand so that he could leave the line because he was afraid.'

The other soldiers were all listening now. Several nodded.

'Such people have their wounds dressed and are returned at once to the line,' the Extremaduran went on. 'It is just.'

'Yes,' I said. 'That is as it should be.'

'That is as it should be,' said the Extremaduran. 'But this boy shot himself so badly that the bone was all smashed and there surged up an infection and his hand was amputated.'

Several soldiers nodded.

'Go on, tell him the rest,' said one.

'It might be better not to speak of it,' said the cropped-headed, bristly-faced man who said he was in command.

'It is my duty to speak,' the Extremaduran said.

The one in command shrugged his shoulders. 'I did not like it either,' he said. 'Go on, then. But I do not like to hear it spoken of either.'

'This boy remained in the hospital in the valley since February,' the Extremaduran said. 'Some of us have seen him in the hospital. All say he was well liked in the hospital and made himself as useful as a man with one hand can be useful. Never was he under arrest. Never was there anything to prepare him.'

The man in command handed me the cup of wine again without saying anything. They were all listening; as men who cannot read or write listen to a story.

'Yesterday, at the close of day, before we knew there was to be an attack. Yesterday, before the sun set, when we thought today was to be as any other day, they brought him up the trail in the gap there from the flat. We were cooking the evening meal and they brought him up. There were only four of them. Him, the boy Paco, those two you have just seen in the leather coats and the caps, and an officer from the brigade. We saw the four of them climbing together up the gap, and we saw Paco's hands were not tied, nor was he bound in any way.

'When we saw him we all crowded around and said, "Hello, Paco. How are you, Paco? How is everything, Paco, old boy, old Paco?"

'Then he said, "Everything's all right. Everything is good except this" – and showed us the stump.

'Paco said, "That was a cowardly and foolish thing. I am sorry that I did that thing. But I try to be useful with one hand. I will do what I can with one hand for the Cause." '

'Yes,' interrupted a soldier. 'He said that. I heard him say that.'

'We spoke with him,' the Extremaduran said. 'And he spoke with us. When such people with the leather coats and the pistols come it is always a bad omen in a war, as is the arrival of people with map cases and field glasses. Still we thought they had brought him for a visit, and all of us who had not been to the hospital were happy to see him, and as I say, it was the hour of the evening meal and the evening was clear and warm.'

'This wind only rose during the night,' a soldier said.

'Then,' the Extremaduran went on somberly, 'one of *them* said to the officer in Spanish, "Where is the place?"

' "Where is the place this Paco was wounded?" asked the officer.'

'I answered him,' said the man in command. 'I showed the place. It is a little further down than where you are.'

'Here is the place,' said a soldier. He pointed, and I could see it was the place. It showed clearly that it was the place.

'Then one of them led Paco by the arm to the place and held him there by the arm while the other spoke in Spanish. He spoke in Spanish, making many mistakes in the language. At first we wanted to laugh, and Paco started to smile. I could not understand all the speech, but it was that Paco must be punished as an example, in order that there would be no more self-inflicted wounds, and that all others would be punished in the same way.

'Then, while the one held Paco by the arm; Paco, looking very ashamed to be spoken of this way when he was already ashamed and sorry; the other took his pistol out and shot Paco in the back of the head without any word to Paco. Nor any word more.'

The soldiers all nodded.

'It was thus,' said one. 'You can see the place. He fell with his mouth there. You can see it.'

I had seen the place clearly enough from where I lay.

'He had no warning and no chance to prepare himself,' the one in command said. 'It was very brutal.'

'It is for this that I now hate Russians as well as all other foreigners,' said the Extremaduran. 'We can give ourselves no illusions about foreigners. If you are a foreigner, I am sorry. But for myself, now, I can make no exceptions. You have eaten bread and drunk wine with us. Now I think you should go.'

'Do not speak in that way,' the man in command said to the Extremaduran. 'It is necessary to be formal.'

'I think we had better go,' I said.

'You are not angry?' the man in command said. 'You can stay in this shelter as long as you wish. Are you thirsty? Do you wish more wine?'

'Thank you very much,' I said. 'I think we had better go.'

'You understand my hatred?' asked the Extremaduran.

'I understand your hatred,' I said.

'Good,' he said and put out his hand. 'I do not refuse to shake hands. And that you, personally, have much luck.'

'Equally to you,' I said. 'Personally, and as a Spaniard.'

I woke the one who took the pictures and we started down the ridge toward brigade headquarters. The tanks were all coming back now and you could hardly hear yourself talk for the noise.

'Were you talking all that time?'

'Listening.'

'Hear anything interesting?'

'Plenty.'

'What do you want to do now?'

'Get back to Madrid.'

'We should see the general.'

'Yes,' I said. 'We must.'

The general was coldly furious. He had been ordered to make the attack as a surprise with one brigade only, bringing everything up before daylight. It should have been made by at least a division. He had used three battalions and held one in reserve. The French tank commander had got drunk to be brave for the attack and finally was too drunk to function. He was to be shot when he sobered up.

The tanks had not come up in time and finally had refused to advance, and two of the battalions had failed to attain their objectives. The third had taken theirs, but it formed an untenable salient. The only real result had been a few prisoners, and these had been confided to the tank men to bring back and the tank men had killed them. The general had only failure to show, and they had killed his prisoners.

'What can I write on it?' I asked.

'Nothing that is not in the official communiqué. Have you any whiskey in that long flask?'

'Yes.'

He took a drink and licked his lips carefully. He had once been a captain of Hungarian Hussars, and he had once captured a gold train in Siberia when he was a leader of irregular cavalry with the Red Army and held it all one winter when the thermometer went down to forty below zero. We were good friends and he loved whiskey, and he is now dead.

'Get out of here now,' he said. 'Have you transport?'

'Yes.'

'Did you get any pictures?'

'Some. The tanks.'

'The tanks,' he said bitterly. 'The swine. The cowards. Watch out you don't get killed,' he said. 'You are supposed to be a writer.'

'I can't write now.'

'Write it afterwards. You can write it all afterwards. And don't get killed. Especially, don't get killed. Now, get out of here.'

He could not take his own advice because he was killed two months later. But the oddest thing about that day was how marvelously the pictures we took of the tanks came out. On the screen they advanced over the hill irresistibly, mounting the crests like great ships, to crawl clanking on toward the illusion of victory we screened.

The nearest any man was to victory that day was probably the Frenchman who came, with his head held high, walking out of the battle. But his victory only lasted until he had walked half-way down the ridge. We saw him lying stretched out there on the slope of the ridge, still wearing his blanket, as we came walking down the cut to get into the staff car that would take us to Madrid.

NOBODY EVER DIES

The house was built of rose-colored plaster that had peeled and faded with the dampness and from its porch you could see the sea, very blue, at the end of the street. There were laurel trees along the sidewalk that grew high enough to shade the upper porch and in the shade it was cool. A mockingbird hung in a wicker cage at a corner of the porch, and it was not singing now, nor even chirping, because a young man of about twenty-eight, thin, dark, with bluish circles under his eyes and a stubble of beard, had just taken off a sweater that he wore and spread it over the cage. The young man was standing now, his mouth slightly open, listening. Someone was trying the locked and bolted front door.

As he listened he heard the wind in the laurels close beside the porch, the horn of a taxi coming along the street and the voices of the children playing in a vacant lot. Then he heard a key turn again in the lock of the front door. He heard it unlock the door, heard the door pulled against the bolt, and then the lock being turned again. At the same time he heard the sound of a bat against a baseball and shrill shouting in Spanish from the vacant lot. He stood there, moistening his lips, and listened while some-one tried the back door.

The young man, who was named Enrique, took off his shoes and, putting them down carefully, moved softly along the tiling of the porch until he could look down at the back door. There was no one there. He slipped back to the front of the house and, keeping out of sight, looked down the street.

A Negro in a narrow-brimmed flat-topped straw hat and a gray alpaca coat and black trousers was walking along the side-walk under the laurel trees. Enrique watched, but there was no one else. He stood there for some time watching and listening, then he took his sweater off the bird cage and put it on.

He had been sweating heavily while he had been listening and now he was cold in the shade and the cool northeast wind. The sweater covered a leather shoulder holster, the leather ringed and salt-whitened with perspiration, that he wore with a forty-five-caliber Colt pistol which, by its constant pressure, had given him a boil a little below his armpit. He lay down on a canvas cot now close to the wall of the house. He was still listening.

The bird chirped and hopped about the cage and the young man looked up at it. Then he got up and unhooked the door of the cage and opened it. The bird cocked his head at the open door and drew it back, then jerked his head forward again, his bill pointing at an angle.

'Go on,' the young man said softly. 'It's not a trick.'

He put his hand into the cage and the bird flew against the back, fluttering against the withes.

'You're silly,' the young man said. He took his hand out of the cage. 'I'll leave it open.'

He lay face down on the cot, his chin on his folded arms, and he was still listening. He heard the bird fly out of the cage and then he heard him sing in one of the laurel trees.

'It was foolish to keep the bird if the house is supposed to be empty,' he thought. 'It is just such foolishness that makes all the trouble. How can I blame others when I am that stupid?'

In the vacant lot the boys were still playing baseball and it was quite cool now. The young man unbuckled the leather shoulder holster and laid the big pistol by his leg. Then he went to sleep.

When he woke it was dark and the street light on the corner shone through the leaves of the laurels. He stood up and walked to the front of the house and, keeping in the shadow and the shelter of the wall, looked up and down the street. A man in a narrow-brimmed, flat-topped straw hat stood under a tree on the corner. Enrique could not see the color of his coat or trousers, but he was a Negro.

Enrique went quickly to the back of the porch but there was no light there except that which shone on the weedy field from the back windows of the next two houses. There could be any number of people in the back. He knew that, since he could no longer really hear as he had in the afternoon, because a radio was going in the second house away.

Suddenly there came the mechanical crescendo of a siren and the young man felt a prickling wave go over his scalp. It came as suddenly as a person blushes, it felt like prickly heat, and it was gone as quickly as it came. The siren was on the radio; it was part of an advertisement, and the announcer's voice followed, 'Gavis tooth paste. Unaltering, insuperable, the best.'

Enrique smiled in the dark. It was time someone should be coming now.

After the siren on the recorded announcements came a crying baby which the announcer said would be satisfied with Malta-

Malta, and then there was a motor horn and a customer who demanded green gas. 'Don't tell me any stories. I asked for green gas. More economical, more mileage. The best.'

Enrique knew all the advertisements by heart. They had not changed in the fifteen months that he had been away at war; they must still be using the same discs in the broadcasting station, and still the siren had deceived him and given him that thin, quick prickle across the scalp that was as definite a reaction to danger as a bird dog stiffening to the warm scent of quail.

He had not had that prickle when he started. Danger and the fear of it had once made him feel empty in his stomach. They had made him feel weak as you are weak with a fever, and he had known the inability to move; when you must force movement forward by legs that feel as dead as though they were asleep. That was all gone now, and he did without difficulty whatever he should do. The prickling was all that remained of the vast capacity for fear some brave men start with. It was his only remaining reaction to danger except for the perspiring which, he knew, he would always have, and now it served as a warning and nothing more.

As he stood, looking out at the tree where the man with the straw hat sat now, on the curb, a stone fell on the tiled floor of the porch. Enrique looked for it against the wall but did not find it. He passed his hands under the cot but it was not there. As he knelt, another pebble fell on the tiled floor, bounced and rolled into the corner toward the side of the house and into the street. Enrique picked it up. It was a smooth-feeling ordinary pebble and he put it in his pocket and went inside the house and down the stairs to the back door.

He stood to one side of the door and took the Colt out of the holster and held it, heavy in his right hand.

'The victory,' he said very quietly in Spanish, his mouth disdaining the word, and shifted softly on his bare feet to the other side of the door.

'To those who earn it,' someone said outside the door. It was a woman's voice, giving the second half of the password, and it spoke quickly and unsteadily.

Enrique drew back the double bolt on the door and opened it with his left hand, the Colt still in his right.

There was a girl there in the dark, holding a basket. She wore a handkerchief over her head.

'Hello,' he said and shut the door and bolted it. He could hear her breathing in the dark. He took the basket from her and patted her shoulder.

'Enrique,' she said, and he could not see the way her eyes were shining nor the look on her face.

'Come upstairs,' he said. 'There is someone watching the front of the house. Did he see you?'

'No,' she said. 'I came across the vacant lot.'

'I will show him to you. Come up to the porch.'

They went up the stairs, Enrique carrying the basket. He put it down by the bed and walked to the edge of the porch and looked. The Negro who wore the narrow-brimmed flat-topped straw hat was gone.

'So,' Enrique said quietly.

'So what?' asked the girl, holding his arm now and looking out.

'So he is gone. What is there to eat?'

'I am sorry you were here alone all day,' she said. 'It was so stupid that I had to wait until it was dark to come. I have wanted to come all day.'

'It was stupid to be here at all. They brought me here from the boat before daylight and left me, with a password and nothing to eat, in a house that is watched. You cannot eat a password. I should not be put in a house that is being watched for other reasons. It is very Cuban. But at least, in the old days we ate. How are you, Maria?'

In the dark she kissed him, hard, on the mouth. He felt the tight-pressed fullness of her lips and the way her body shivered against his and then came the stab of white pain in the small of his back.

'Ayee! Be careful.'

'What is it?'

'The back.'

'What of the back? Is it a wound?'

'You should see it,' he said.

'Can I see it now?'

'Afterwards. We must eat and get out of here. What have they stored here?'

'Too many things. Things left over from the failure of April. Things kept for the future.'

'The long-distant future,' he said. 'Did they know it was watched?'

'I am sure not.'

'What is there?'

'There are some rifles in cases. There are boxes of ammunition.'

'Everything should be moved tonight.' His mouth was full. 'There will be years of work before we will need this again.'

'Do you like the *escabeche*?'

'It's very good; sit here close.'

'Enrique,' she said, sitting tight against him. She put a hand on his thigh and with the other she stroked the back of his neck. 'My Enrique.'

'Touch me carefully,' he said, eating. 'The back is bad.'

'Are you happy to be back from the war?'

'I have not thought about it,' he said.

'Enrique, how is Chucho?'

'Dead at Lérida.'

'Felipe?'

'Dead. Also at Lérida.'

'And Arturo?'

'Dead at Teruel.'

'And Vicente?' she asked in a flat voice, her two hands folded on his thigh now.

'Dead. At the attack across the road at Celadas.'

'Vicente is my brother.' She sat stiff and alone now, her hands away from him.

'I know,' said Enrique. He went on eating.

'He is my only brother.'

'I thought you knew,' said Enrique.

'I did not know and he is my brother.'

'I am sorry, Maria. I should have said it another way.'

'And he is dead? You know he is dead? It is not just a report?'

'Listen. Rogello, Basilio, Esteban, Felo and I are alive. The others are dead.'

'All?'

'All,' said Enrique.

'I cannot stand it,' said Maria. 'Please, I cannot stand it.'

'It does no good to discuss it. They are dead.'

'But it is not only that Vicente is my brother. I can give up my brother. It is the flower of our party.'

'Yes. The flower of the party.'

'It is not worth it. It has destroyed the best.'

'Yes. It is worth it.'

'How can you say that? That is criminal.'

'No. It is worth it.'

She was crying now and Enrique went on eating. 'Don't cry,' he said. 'The thing to do is to think how we can work to take their places.'

'But he is my brother. Don't you understand? *My brother.*'

'We are all brothers. Some are dead and others still live. They send us home now, so there will be some left. Otherwise there would be none. Now we must work.'

'But why were they all killed?'

'We were with an attack division. You are either killed or wounded. We others have been wounded.'

'How was Vicente killed?'

'He was crossing the road when he was struck by machine-gun fire from a farmhouse on the right. The road was enfiladed from that house.'

'Were you there?'

'Yes. I had the first company. We were on his right. We took the house but it took some time. They had three machine guns there. Two in the house, one in the stable. It was difficult to approach. We had to get a tank up to put fire on the window before we could rush the last gun. I lost eight men. It was too many.'

'And where was that?'

'Celadas.'

'I never heard of it.'

'No,' said Enrique. 'The operation was not a success. No one will ever hear of it. That was where Vicente and Ignacio were killed.'

'And you say such things are justified? That men like that should die in failures in a foreign country?'

'There are no foreign countries, Maria, where people speak Spanish. Where you die does not matter, if you die for liberty. Anyway, the thing to do is live and not to die.'

'But think of who have died – away from here – and in failures.'

'They did not go to die. They went to fight. The dying is an accident.'

'But the failures. My brother is dead in a failure. Chucho in a failure. Ignacio in a failure.'

'They are just a part. Some things we had to do were impossible. Many that looked impossible we did. But sometimes the people on your flank would not attack. Sometimes there was not enough artillery. Sometimes we were ordered to do things not in sufficient force – as at Celadas. Those make the failures. But in the end, it was not a failure.'

She did not answer and he finished eating.

The wind was fresh now in the trees and it was cold on the porch. He put the dishes back in the basket and wiped his mouth on the napkin. He wiped his hands carefully and then put his arm around the girl. She was crying.

'Don't cry, Maria,' he said. 'What has happened has happened. We must think of what there is to do. There is much to do.'

She said nothing and he could see her face in the light from the street lamp looking straight ahead.

'We must check all romanticism. This place is an example of that romanticism. We must stop terrorism. We must proceed so that we will never again fall into revolutionary adventurism.'

The girl still said nothing and he looked at her face that he had thought of all the months when he had thought of anything except his work.

'You talk like a book,' she said. 'Not like a human being.'

'I am sorry,' he said. 'It is only lessons I have learned. It is things I know must be done. To me it is more real than anything.'

'All that is real to me are the dead,' she said.

'We honor them. But they are not important.'

'You talk like a book again,' she said angrily. 'Your heart is a book.'

'I am sorry, Maria. I thought you would understand.'

'All I understand is the dead,' she said.

He knew this was not true because she had not seen them dead as he had in the rain in the olive groves of the Jarama, in the heat in the smashed houses of Quijorna, and in the snow at Teruel. But he knew that she blamed him for being alive when Vicente was dead and suddenly – in the small and unconditioned human part of him which was left, and which he did not realize was still there – he was hurt deeply.

'There was a bird,' he said. 'A mockingbird in a cage.'

'Yes.'

'I let it go.'

'Aren't you kind!' she said scornfully. 'Are soldiers all sentimental?'

'I am a good soldier.'

'I believe it. You talk like one. What kind of soldier was my brother?'

'Very good. Gayer than me. I was not gay. It is a lack.'

'But you practice self-criticism and you talk like a book.'

'It would be better if I were gayer,' he said. 'I could never learn it.'

'And the gay ones are all dead.'

'No,' he said. 'Basilio is gay.'

'Then he'll die,' she said.

'Maria? Do not talk like that. You talk like a defeatist.'

'You talk like a book,' she told him. 'Please do not touch me. You have a dry heart and I hate you.'

Now he was hurt again, he who had thought that his heart was dry, and that nothing could hurt ever again except the pain, and sitting on the bed he leaned forward.

'Pull up my sweater,' he said.

'I don't want to.'

He pulled up the back and leaned over. 'Maria, look there,' he said. 'That is not from a book.'

'I cannot see,' she said. 'I do not want to see.'

'Put your hand across the lower back.'

He felt her fingers touch that huge sunken place a baseball could have been pushed through, that grotesque scar from the wound the surgeon had pushed his rubber-gloved fist through in cleaning, which had run from one side of the small of his back through to the other. He felt her touch it and he shrank quickly inside. Then she was holding him tight and kissing him, her lips an island in the sudden white sea of pain that came in a shining, unbearable, rising, blinding wave and swept him clean. The lips there, still there; then over-whelmed, and the pain gone as he sat, alone, wet with sweat and Maria crying and saying, 'Oh, Enrique. Forgive me. Please forgive me.'

'It is all right,' Enrique said. 'There is nothing to forgive. But it was not out of any book.'

'But does it hurt always?'

'Only when I am touched or jarred.'

'And the spinal cord?'

'It was touched a very little. Also the kidneys, but they are all right. The shell fragment went in one side and out the other. There are other wounds lower down and on my legs.'

'Enrique, please forgive me.'

'There is nothing to forgive. But it is not nice that I cannot make love and I am sorry that I am not gay.'

'We can make love after it is well.'

'Yes.'

'And it will be well.'

'Yes.'

'And I will take care of you.'

'No. I will take care of you. I do not mind this thing at all. Only the pain of touching or jarring. It does not bother me. Now we must work. We must leave this place now. Everything that is here must be moved tonight. It must be stored in a new and unsuspected place and in one where it will not deteriorate. It will be a long time before we will need it. There is much to be done before we will ever reach that stage again. Many must be educated. These cartridges may no longer serve by then. This climate ruins the primers. And we must go now. I am a fool to have stayed here this long and the fool who put me here will answer to the committee.'

'I am to take you there tonight. They thought this house was safe for you to stay today.'

'This house is a folly.'

'We will go now.'

'We should have gone before.'

'Kiss me, Enrique.'

'We'll do it very carefully,' he said.

Then, in the dark on the bed, holding himself carefully, his eyes closed, their lips against each other, the happiness there with no pain, the being home suddenly there with no pain, the being alive returning and no pain, the comfort of being loved and still no pain; so there was a hollowness of loving, now no longer hollow, and the two sets of lips in the dark, pressing so that they were happily and kindly, darkly and warmly at home and without pain in the darkness, there came the siren cutting, suddenly, to rise like all the pain in the world. It was the real siren, not the one of the radio. It was not one siren. It was two. They were coming both ways up the street.

He turned his head and then stood up. He thought that coming home had not lasted very long.

'Go out the door and across the lot,' he said. 'Go. I can shoot from up here and make a diversion.'

'No, you go,' she said. 'Please, I will stay here to shoot and they will think you're inside.'

'Come on,' he said. 'We'll both go. There's nothing to defend here. This stuff is useless. It's better to get away.'

'I want to stay,' she said. 'I want to protect you.'

She reached for the pistol in the holster under his arm and he slapped her face. 'Come on. Don't be a silly girl. *Come on!*'

They were going down the stairs now and he felt her close beside him. He swung the door open and together they stepped out the door and were clear of the building. He turned and locked the door. 'Run, Maria,' he said. 'Across the lot in that direction. Go!'

'I want to go with you.'

He slapped her again quickly. 'Run. Then dive in the weeds and crawl. Forgive me, Maria. But go. I go the other way. Go,' he said. 'Damn you. *Go.*'

They started into the weeds at the same time. He ran twenty paces and then, as the police cars stopped in front of the house, the sirens dying, he dropped flat and started to crawl.

The weed pollen was dusty in his face and as he wriggled steadily along, the sand-burrs stabbing his hands and knees sharply and minutely, he heard them coming around the house. They had surrounded it.

He crawled steadily, thinking hard, giving no importance to the pain.

'But *why* the sirens?' he thought. '*Why* no third car from the rear? Why no spotlight or a searchlight on this field? Cubans,' he thought. 'Can they be this stupid and theatrical? They must have thought there was no one in the house. They must have come only to seize the stuff. But *why* the sirens?'

Behind him he heard them breaking in the door. They were all around the house. He heard two blasts on a whistle from close to the house and he wriggled steadily on.

'The fools,' he thought. 'But they must have found the basket and the dishes by now. What people! What a way to raid a house!'

He was almost to the edge of the lot now and he knew that he must rise and make a dash across the road for the far houses. He had found a way of crawling that hurt little. He could adjust himself to almost any movement. It was the brusque changes that hurt, and he dreaded rising to his feet.

In the weeds he rose on one knee, took the shock of the pain, held through it, and then brought it on again as he drew the other foot alongside his knee in order to rise.

He started to run toward the house across the street, at the back of the next lot, when the clicking on of the searchlight caught him so that he was full in the beam, looking toward it, the blackness a sharp line on either side.

The searchlight was from the police car that had come silently, without siren, and posted itself at one back corner of the lot.

As Enrique rose to his feet, thin, gaunt, sharply outlined in the beam, pulling at the big pistol in the holster under his armpit, the submachine guns opened on him from the darkened car.

The feeling is that of being clubbed across the chest and he only felt the first one. The other clubbing thuds that came were echoes.

He went forward onto his face in the weeds and as he fell, or perhaps it was between the time the searchlight went on and the first bullet reached him, he had one thought. 'They are not so stupid. Perhaps something can be done with them.'

If he had had time for another thought it would have been to hope there was no car at the other corner. But there was a car at the other corner and its searchlight was going over the field. Its wide beam was playing over the weeds, where the girl, Maria, lay hidden. In the dark car the machine gunners, their guns poised, followed the sweep of the beam with the fluted, efficient ugliness of the Thompson muzzles.

In the shadow of the tree, behind the darkened car from which the searchlight played, there was a Negro standing. He wore a flat-topped, narrow-brimmed straw hat and an alpaca coat. Under his shirt he wore a string of blue voodoo beads. He was standing quietly watching the lights working.

The searchlights played on over the weedfield where the girl lay flat against the ground, her chin in the earth. She had not moved since she heard the burst of firing. She could feel her heart beating against the ground.

'Do you see her?' asked one of the men in the car.

'Let them beat through the weeds for the other side,' the lieutenant in the front seat said. '*Hola*,' he called to the Negro under the tree. 'Go to the house and tell them to beat toward us through the weeds in extended order. Are there only the two?'

'Only two,' the Negro said in a quiet voice. 'We have the other one.'

'Go.'

'Yes sir, Lieutenant,' the Negro said.

Holding his straw hat in both hands he started to run along the edge of the field toward the house where, now, lights shone from all the windows.

In the field the girl lay, her hands clasped across the top of her head. 'Help me to bear this,' she said into the weeds, speaking to no one, for there was no one there. Then, suddenly, personally, sobbing, 'Help me, Vicente. Help me, Felipe. Help me, Chucho. Help me, Arturo. Help me now, Enrique. Help me.'

At one time she would have prayed, but she had lost that and now she needed something.

'Help me not to talk if they take me,' she said, her mouth against the weeds. 'Keep me from talking, Enrique. Keep me from ever talking, Vicente.'

Behind her she could hear them going through the weeds like beaters in a rabbit drive. They were spread wide and advancing like skirmishers, flashing their electric torches in the weeds.

'Oh, Enrique,' she said, 'help me.'

She brought her hands down from her head and clenched them by her sides. 'It is better so,' she thought. 'If I run they will shoot. It will be simpler.'

Slowly she got up and ran toward the car. The searchlight was full on her and she ran seeing only it, into its white, blinding eye. She thought this was the best way to do it.

Behind her they were shouting. But there was no shooting. Someone tackled her heavily and she went down. She heard him breathing as he held her.

Someone else took her under the arm and lifted her. Holding her by the two arms they walked her toward the car. They were not rough with her, but they walked her steadily toward the car.

'No,' she said. 'No. No.'

'It's the sister of Vicente Irtube,' said the lieutenant. 'She should be useful.'

'She's been questioned before,' said another.

'Never seriously.'

'No,' she said. 'No. No.' She cried aloud, 'Help me, Vicente! Help me, help me, Enrique!'

'They're dead,' said someone. 'They won't help you. Don't be silly.'

'Yes,' she said. 'They will help me. It is the dead that will help me. Oh, yes, yes, yes! It is our dead that will help me!'

'Take a look at Enrique then,' said the lieutenant. 'See if he will help you. He's in the back of that car.'

'He's helping me now,' the girl, Maria, said. 'Can't you see he's helping me now? Thank you, Enrique. Oh, thank you!'

'Come on,' said the lieutenant. 'She's crazy. Leave four men to guard the stuff and we will send a truck for it. We'll take this crazy up to headquarters. She can talk up there.'

'No,' said Maria, taking hold of his sleeve. 'Can't you see everyone is helping me now?'

'No,' said the lieutenant. 'You are crazy.'

'No one dies for nothing,' said Maria. 'Everyone is helping me now.'

'Get them to help you in about an hour,' said the lieutenant.

'They will,' said Maria. 'Please don't worry. Many, many people are helping me now.'

She sat there holding herself very still against the back of the seat. She seemed now to have a strange confidence. It was the same confidence another girl her age had felt a little more than five hundred years before in the market place of a town called Rouen.

Maria did not think of this. Nor did anyone in the car think of it. The two girls named Jeanne and Maria had nothing in common except this sudden strange confidence which came when they needed it. But all of the policemen in the car felt uncomfortable about Maria now as she sat very straight with her face shining in the arc light.

The cars started and in the back seat of the front car men were putting the machine guns back into the heavy canvas cases, slipping the stocks out and putting them in their diagonal pockets, the barrels with the handgrips in the big flapped pouch, the magazines in the narrow webbed pockets.

The Negro with the flat straw hat came out from the shadow of the house and hailed the first car. He got up into the front seat, making two who rode there beside the driver, and the four cars turned onto the main road that led toward the sea-drive into La Havana.

Sitting crowded on the front seat of the car, the Negro reached under his shirt and put his fingers on the string of blue voodoo beads. He sat without speaking, his fingers holding the beads. He had been a dock worker before he got a job as a stool pigeon for the Havana police and he would get fifty dollars for this night's work. Fifty dollars is a lot of money now in La Havana, but the Negro could no longer think about the money. He turned his head a little, very slowly, as they came onto the lighted driveway of the Malecon and, looking back, saw the girl's face, shining proudly, and her head held high.

The Negro was frightened and he put his fingers all the way around the string of blue voodoo beads and held them tight. But they could not help his fear because he was up against an older magic now.

THE GOOD LION

Once upon a time there was a lion that lived in Africa with all the other lions. The other lions were all bad lions and every day they ate zebras and wildebeests and every kind of antelope. Sometimes the bad lions ate people too. They ate Swahilis, Umbulus and Wandorobos and they especially liked to eat Hindu traders. All Hindu traders are very fat and delicious to a lion.

But this lion, that we love because he was so good, had wings on his back. Because he had wings on his back the other lions all made fun of him.

'Look at him with the wings on his back,' they would say and then they would all roar with laughter.

'Look at what he eats,' they would say because the good lion only ate pasta and scampi because he was so good.

The bad lions would roar with laughter and eat another Hindu trader and their wives would drink his blood, going lap, lap, lap with their tongues like big cats. They only stopped to growl with laughter or to roar with laughter at the good lion and to snarl at his wings. They were very bad and wicked lions indeed.

But the good lion would sit and fold his wings back and ask politely if he might have a Negroni or an Americano and he always drank that instead of the blood of the Hindu traders. One day he refused to eat eight Masai cattle and only ate some tagliatelli and drank a glass of pomodoro.

This made the wicked lions very angry and one of the lionesses, who was the wickedest of them all and could never get the blood of Hindu traders off her whiskers even when she rubbed her face in the grass, said, 'Who are you that you think you are so much better than we are? Where do you come from, you pasta-eating lion? What are you doing here anyway?' She growled at him and they all roared without laughter.

'My father lives in a city where he stands under the clock tower and looks down on a thousand pigeons, all of whom are his subjects. When they fly they make a noise like a rushing river. There are more palaces in my father's city than in all of Africa and there are four great bronze horses that face him and they all have one foot in the air because they fear him.

'In my father's city men go on foot or in boats and no real horse would enter the city for fear of my father.'

'Your father was a griffon,' the wicked lioness said, licking her whiskers.

'You are a liar,' one of the wicked lions said. 'There is no such city.'

'Pass me a piece of Hindu trader,' another very wicked lion said. 'This Masai cattle is too newly killed.'

'You are a worthless liar and the son of a griffon,' the wickedest of all the lionesses said. 'And now I think I shall kill you and eat you, wings and all.'

This frightened the good lion very much because he could see her yellow eyes and her tail going up and down and the blood caked on her whiskers and he smelled her breath which was very bad because she never brushed her teeth ever. Also she had old pieces of Hindu trader under her claws.

'Don't kill me,' the good lion said. 'My father is a noble lion and always has been respected and everything is true as I said.'

Just then the wicked lioness sprang at him. But he rose into the air on his wings and circled the group of wicked lions once, with them all roaring and looking at him. He looked down and thought, 'What savages these lions are.'

He circled them once more to make them roar more loudly. Then he swooped low so he could look at the eyes of the wicked lioness who rose on her hind legs to try and catch him. But she missed him with her claws.

'*Adios*,' he said, for he spoke beautiful Spanish, being a lion of culture.

'*Au revoir*,' he called to them in his exemplary French.

They all roared and growled in African lion dialect.

Then the good lion circled higher and higher and set his course for Venice. He alighted in the Piazza and everyone was delighted to see him. He flew up for a moment and kissed his father on both cheeks and saw the horses still had their feet up and the Basilica looked more beautiful than a soap bubble. The Campanile was in place and the pigeons were going to their nests for the evening.

'How was Africa?' his father said.

'Very savage, father,' the good lion replied.

'We have night lighting here now,' his father said.

'So I see,' the good lion answered like a dutiful son.

'It bothers my eyes a little,' his father confided to him. 'Where are you going now, my son?'

'To Harry's Bar,' the good lion said.

'Remember me to Cipriani and tell him I will be in some day soon to see about my bill,' said his father.

'Yes, father,' said the good lion and he flew down lightly and walked to Harry's Bar on his own four paws.

In Cipriani's nothing was changed. All of his friends were there. But he was a little changed himself from being in Africa.

'A Negroni, Signor Barone?' asked Mr. Cipriani.

But the good lion had flown all the way from Africa and Africa had changed him.

'Do you have any Hindu trader sandwiches?' he asked Cipriani.

'No, but I can get some.'

'While you are sending for them, make me a very dry martini.' He added, 'With Gordon's gin.'

'Very good,' said Cipriani. 'Very good indeed.'

Now the lion looked about him at the faces of all the nice people and he knew that he was at home but that he had also traveled. He was very happy.

THE FAITHFUL BULL

One time there was a bull and his name was not Ferdinand and he cared nothing for flowers. He loved to fight and he fought with all the other bulls of his own age, or any age, and he was a champion.

His horns were as solid as wood and they were as sharply pointed as the quill of a porcupine. They hurt him, at the base, when he fought and he did not care at all. His neck muscles lifted in a great lump that is called in Spanish the *morillo* and this *morillo* lifted like a hill when he was ready to fight. He was always ready to fight and his coat was black and shining and his eyes were clear.

Anything made him want to fight and he would fight with deadly seriousness exactly as some people eat or read or go to church. Each time he fought he fought to kill and the other bulls were not afraid of him because they came of good blood and were not afraid. But they had no wish to provoke him. Nor did they wish to fight him.

He was not a bully nor was he wicked, but he liked to fight as men might like to sing or to be the King or the President. He never thought at all. Fighting was his obligation and his duty and his joy.

He fought on the stony, high ground. He fought under the cork-oak trees and he fought in the good pasture by the river. He walked fifteen miles each day from the river to the high, stony ground and he would fight any bull that looked at him. Still he was never angry.

That is not really true, for he was angry inside himself. But he did not know why, because he could not think. He was very noble and he loved to fight.

So what happened to him? The man who owned him, if anyone can own such an animal, knew what a great bull he was and still he was worried because this bull cost him so much money by fighting with other bulls. Each bull was worth over one thousand dollars and after they had fought the great bull they were worth less than two hundred dollars and sometimes less than that.

So the man, who was a good man, decided that he would keep the blood of this bull in all of his stock rather than send him to the ring to be killed. So he selected him for breeding.

But this bull was a strange bull. When they first turned him into the pasture with the breeding cows, he saw one who was young and beautiful and slimmer and better muscled and shinier and more lovely than all the others. So, since he could not fight, he fell in love with her and he paid no attention to any of the others. He only wanted to be with her, and the others meant nothing to him at all.

The man who owned the bull ranch hoped that the bull would change, or learn, or be different than he was. But the bull was the same and he loved whom he loved and no one else. He only wanted to be with her, and the others meant nothing to him at all.

So the man sent him away with five others bulls to be killed in the ring, and at least the bull could fight, even though he was faithful. He fought wonderfully and everyone admired him and the man who killed him admired him the most. But the fighting jacket of the man who killed him and who is called the matador was wet through by the end, and his mouth was very dry.

'*Que toro más bravo*,' the matador said as he handed his sword to his sword handler. He handed it with the hilt up and the blade dripping with the blood from the heart of the brave bull who no longer had any problems of any kind and was being dragged out of the ring by four horses.

'Yes. He was the one the Marqués of Villamayor had to get rid of because he was faithful,' the sword handler, who knew everything, said.

'Perhaps we should all be faithful,' the matador said.

A MAN OF THE WORLD

The blind man knew the sounds of all the different machines in the Saloon. I don't know how long it took him to learn the sounds of the machines but it must have taken him quite a time because he only worked one saloon at a time. He worked two towns though and he would start out of The Flats along after it was good and dark on his way up to Jessup. He'd stop by the side of the road when he heard a car coming and their lights would pick him up and either they would stop and give him a ride or they wouldn't and would go on by on the icy road. It would depend on how they were loaded and whether there were women in the car because the blind man smelled plenty strong and especially in winter. But someone would always stop for him because he was a blind man.

Everybody knew him and they called him Blindy which is a good name for a blind man in that part of the country, and the name of the saloon that he threw his trade to was The Pilot. Right next to it was another saloon, also with gambling and a dining room, that was called The Index. Both of these were the names of mountains and they were both good saloons with old-days bars and the gambling was about the same in one as in the other except you ate better in The Pilot probably, although you got a better sizzling steak at The Index. Then The Index was open all night long and got the early morning trade and from daylight until ten o'clock in the morning the drinks were on the house. They were the only saloons in Jessup and they did not have to do that kind of thing. But that was the way they were.

Blindy probably preferred The Pilot because the machines were right along the left-hand wall as you came in and faced the bar. This gave him better control over them than he would have had at The Index where they were scattered on account it was a bigger place with more room. On this night it was really cold outside and he came in with icicles on his mustache and small pus icicles out of both eyes and he didn't look really very good. Even his smell was froze but that wasn't for very long and he started to put out almost as soon as the door was shut. It was always hard for me to look at him but I was looking at him carefully because I knew he always rode and I didn't see how he would be frozen up so bad. Finally I asked him.

'Where you walk from, Blindy?'

'Willie Sawyer put me out of his car down below the railway bridge. There weren't no more cars come and I walked in.'

'What did he put you afoot for?' somebody asked.

'Said I smelled too bad.'

Someone had pulled the handle on a machine and Blindy started listening to the whirr. It came up nothing. 'Any dudes playing?' he asked me.

'Can't you hear?'

'Not yet.'

'No dudes, Blindy, and it's a Wednesday.'

'I know what night it is. Don't start telling me what night it is.'

Blindy went down the line of machines feeling in all of them to see if anything had been left in the cups by mistake. Naturally there wasn't anything, but that was the first part of his pitch. He came back to the bar where we were and Al Chaney asked him to have a drink.

'No,' Blindy said. 'I got to be careful on those roads.'

'What you mean those roads?' somebody asked him. 'You only go on one road. Between here and The Flats.'

'I been on lots of roads,' Blindy said. 'And any time I may have to take off and go on more.'

Somebody hit on a machine but it wasn't any heavy hit. Blindy moved on it just the same. It was a quarter machine and the young fellow who was playing it gave him a quarter sort of reluctantly. Blindy felt it before he put it in his pocket.

'Thank you,' he said. 'You'll never miss it.'

The young fellow said, 'Nice to know that,' and put a quarter back in the machine and pulled down again.

He hit again but this time pretty good and he scooped in the quarters and gave a quarter to Blindy.

'Thanks,' Blindy said. 'You're doing fine.'

'Tonight's my night,' the young fellow who was playing said.

'Your night is my night,' Blindy said and the young fellow went on playing but he wasn't doing any good any more and Blindy was so strong standing by him and he looked so awful and finally the fellow quit playing and came over to the bar. Blindy had run him out but he had no way of noticing it because the fellow didn't say anything, so Blindy just checked the machines again with his hand and stood there waiting for someone else to come in and make a play.

There wasn't any play at the wheel nor at the crap table and at the poker game there were just gamblers sitting there and cutting each other up. It was a quiet evening on a week night in town and there wasn't any excitement. The place was not making a nickel except at the bar. But at the bar it was pleasant and the place had been nice until Blindy had come in. Now everybody was figuring they might as well go next door to The Index or else cut out and go home.

'What will yours be, Tom?' Frank the bartender asked me. 'This is on the house.'

'I was figuring on shoving.'

'Have one first then.'

'The same with ditch,' I said. Frank asked the young fellow, who was wearing heavy Oregon Cities and a black hat and was shaved clean and had a snow-burned face, what he would drink and the young fellow took the same. The whiskey was Old Forester.

I nodded to him and raised my drink and we both sipped at the drinks. Blindy was down at the far end of the machines. I think he figured maybe no one would come in if they saw him at the door. Not that he was self-conscious.

'How did that man lose his sight?' the young fellow asked me.

'I wouldn't know,' I told him.

'Him fight?' the stranger said. He shook his head.

'Yeah,' Frank said. 'He got that high voice out of the same fight. Tell him, Tom.'

'I never heard of it.'

'No. You wouldn't of,' Frank said. 'Of course not. You wasn't here, I suppose. Mister, it was a night about as cold as tonight. Maybe colder. It was a quick fight too. I didn't see the start of it. Then they come fighting out of the door of The Index. Blackie, him that's Blindy now, and this other boy Willie Sawyer, and they were slugging and kneeing and gouging and biting and I see one of Blackie's eyes hanging down on his cheek. They were fighting on the ice of the road with the snow all banked up and the light from this door and The Index door, and Hollis Sands was right behind Willie Sawyer who was gouging for the eye and Hollis kept hollering, 'Bite it off! Bite it off just like it was a grape!' Blackie was biting onto Willie Sawyer's face and he had a good holt and it give way with a jerk and then he had another good holt and they were down on the ice now and Willie Sawyer was gouging him to make him let go and then

Blackie gave a yell like you've never heard. Worse than when they cut a boar.'

Blindy had come up opposite us and we smelled him and turned around.

' "Bite it off just like it was a grape," ' he said in his high-pitched voice and looked at us, moving his head up and down. 'That was the left eye. He got the other one without no advice. Then he stomped me when I couldn't see. That was the bad part.' He patted himself.

'I could fight good then,' he said. 'But he got the eye before I knew even what was happening. He got it with a lucky gouge. Well,' Blindy said without any rancor, 'that put a stop to my fighting days.'

'Give Blackie a drink,' I said to Frank.

'Blindy's the name, Tom. I earned that name. You seen me earn it. That's the same fellow who put me adrift down the road tonight. Fellow bit the eye. We ain't never made friends.'

'What did you do to him?' the stranger asked.

'Oh, you'll see him around,' Blindy said. 'You'll recognize him any time you see him. I'll let it come as a surprise.'

'You don't want to see him,' I told the stranger.

'You know that's one of the reasons I'd like to see sometimes,' Blindy said. 'I'd like to just have one good look at him.'

'You know what he looks like,' Frank told him. 'You went up and put your hands on his face once.'

'Did it again tonight too,' Blindy said happily. 'That's why he put me out of the car. He ain't got no sense of humor at all. I told him on a cold night like this he'd ought to bundle up so the whole inside of his face wouldn't catch cold. He didn't even think that was funny. You know that Willie Sawyer he'll never be a man of the world.'

'Blackie, you have one on the house,' Frank said. 'I can't drive you home because I only live just down the road. But you can sleep in the back of the place.'

'That's mighty good of you, Frank. Only just don't call me Blackie. I'm not Blackie any more. Blindy's my name.'

'Have a drink, Blindy.'

'Yes, sir,' Blindy said. His hand reached out and found the glass and he raised it accurately to the three of us.

'That Willie Sawyer,' he said. 'Probably alone home by himself. That Willie Sawyer he don't know how to have any fun at all.'

GET A SEEING-EYED DOG

'And what did we do then?' he asked her. She told him.

'That part is very strange. I can't remember that at all.'

'Can you remember the safari leaving?'

'I should. But I don't. I remember the women going down the trail to the beach for the water with the pots on their heads and I remember the flock of geese the *toto* drove back and forth to the water. I remember how slowly they all went and they were always going down or coming up. There was a very big tide too and the flats were yellow and the channel ran by the far island. The wind blew all the time and there were no flies and no mosquitoes. There was a roof and a cement floor and the poles that held the roof up, and the wind blew through them all the time. It was cool all day and lovely and cool at night.'

'Do you remember when the big dhow came in and careened on the low tide?'

'Yes, I remember her and the crew coming ashore in her boats and coming up the path from the beach, and the geese were afraid of them and so were the women.'

'That was the day we caught so many fish but had to come in because it was rough.'

'I remember that.'

'You're remembering well today,' she said. 'Don't do it too much.'

'I'm sorry you didn't get to fly to Zanzibar,' he said. 'That upper beach from where we were was a fine place to land. You could have landed and taken off from there quite easily.'

'We can always go to Zanzibar. Don't try to remember too much today. Would you like me to read to you? There's always something in the old *New Yorker*s that we missed.'

'No, please don't read,' he said. 'Just talk. Talk about the good days.'

'Do you want to hear about what it's like outside?'

'It's raining,' he said. 'I know that.'

'It's raining a big rain,' she told him. 'There won't be any tourists out with this weather. The wind is very wild and we can go down and sit by the fire.'

'We could anyway. I don't care about them any more. I like to hear them talk.'

'Some of them are awful,' she said. 'But some of them are quite nice. I think it's really the nicest ones that go out to Torcello.'

'That's quite true,' he said. 'I hadn't thought of that. There's really nothing for them to see unless they are a bit too nice.'

'Can I make you a drink?' she asked. 'You know how worthless a nurse I am. I wasn't trained for it and I haven't any talent. But I can make drinks.'

'Let's have a drink.'

'What do you want?'

'Anything,' he said.

'I'll make a surprise. I'll make it downstairs.'

He heard the door open and close and her feet on the stairs and he thought, I must get her to go on a trip. I must figure out some way to do it. I have to think up something practical. I've got this now for the rest of my life and I must figure out ways not to destroy her life and ruin her with it. She has been so good and she was not built to be good. I mean this sort of good. I mean good every day and dull good.

He heard her coming up the stairs and noticed the difference in her tread when she was carrying two glasses and when she had walked down bare-handed. He heard the rain on the window-pane and he smelled the beech logs burning in the fireplace. As she came into the room he put his hand out for the drink and closed his hand on it and felt her touch the glass with her own.

'It's our old drink for out here,' she said. 'Campari and Gordon's with ice.'

'I'm certainly glad you're not a girl who would say "on the rocks." '

'No,' she said. 'I wouldn't ever say that. We've *been* on the rocks.'

'On our own two feet when the chips were down and for keeps,' he remembered. 'Do you remember when we barred those phrases?'

'That was in the time of my lion. Wasn't he a wonderful lion? I can't wait till we see him.'

'I can't either,' he said.

'I'm sorry.'

'Do you remember when we barred that phrase?'

'I nearly said it again.'

'You know,' he told her, 'we're awfully lucky to have come

here. I remember it so well that it is palpable. That's a new word
and we'll bar it soon. But it really is wonderful. When I hear the
rain I can see it on the stones and on the canal and on the lagoon,
and I know the way the trees bend in every wind and how the
church and the tower are in every sort of light. We couldn't have
come to a better place for me. It's really perfect. We've got the
good radio and a fine tape recorder and I'm going to write better
than I ever could. If you take your time with the tape recorder
you can get the words right. I can work slow and I can see the
words when I say them. If they're wrong I hear them wrong and
I can do them over and work on them until I get them right.
Honey, in lots of ways we couldn't have it better.'

'Oh, Philip –'

'Shit,' he said. 'The dark is just the dark. This isn't like the real
dark. I can see very well inside and now my head is better all the
time and I can remember and I can make up well. You wait and
see. Didn't I remember better today?'

'You remember better all the time. And you're getting
strong.'

'I am strong,' he said. 'Now if you –'

'If me what?'

'If you'd go away for a while and get a rest and a change from
this.'

'Don't you want me?'

'Of course I want you, darling.'

'Then why do we have to talk about me going away? I know
I'm not good at looking after you but I can do things other
people can't do and we do love each other. You love me and
you know it and we know things nobody else knows.'

'We do wonderful things in the dark,' he said.

'And we did wonderful things in the daytime too.'

'You know I rather like the dark. In some ways it is an im-
provement.'

'Don't lie too much,' she said. 'You don't have to be so
bloody noble.'

'Listen to it rain,' he said. 'How is the tide now?'

'It's way out and the wind has driven the water even further
out. You could almost walk to Burano.'

'All except one place,' he said. 'Are there many birds?'

'Mostly gulls and terns. They are down on the flats and when
they get up the wind catches them.'

'Aren't there any shore birds?'

'There are a few working on the part of the flats that only comes out when we have this wind and this tide.'

'Do you think it will ever be spring?'

'I don't know,' she said. 'It certainly doesn't act like it.'

'Have you drunk all your drink?'

'Just about. Why don't you drink yours?'

'I was saving it.'

'Drink it up,' she said. 'Wasn't it awful when you couldn't drink at all?'

'No, you see,' he said. 'What I was thinking about when you went downstairs was that you could go to Paris and then to London and you'd see people and could have some fun and then you'd come back and it would have to be spring by then and you could tell me all about everything.'

'No,' she said.

'I think it would be intelligent to do,' he said. 'You know this is a long sort of stupid business and we have to learn to pace ourselves. And I don't want to wear you out. You know –'

'I wish you wouldn't say "you know" so much.'

'You see? That's one of the things. I could learn to talk in a non-irritating way. You might be mad about me when you came back.'

'What would you do nights?'

'Nights are easy.'

'I'll bet they are. I suppose you've learned how to sleep too.'

'I'm going to,' he told her and drank half the drink. 'That's part of The Plan. You know this is how it works. If you go away and have some fun then I have a good conscience. Then for the first time in my life with a good conscience I sleep automatically. I take a pillow which represents my good conscience and I put my arms around it and off I go to sleep. If I wake up by any odd chance I just think beautiful happy dirty thoughts. Or I make wonderful fine good resolutions. Or I remember things. You know I want you to have fun –'

'Please don't say "you know." '

'I'll concentrate on not saying it. It's barred but I forget and let the bars down. Anyway I don't want you just to be a seeing-eyed dog.'

'I'm not and you know it. Anyway it's seeing-eye not seeing-eyed.'

'I knew that,' he told her. 'Come and sit here, would you mind very much?'

She came and sat by him on the bed and they both heard the rain hard against the pane of the window and he tried not to feel her head and her lovely face the way a blind man feels and there was no other way that he could touch her face except that way. He held her close and kissed the top of her head. I will have to try it another day, he thought. I must not be so stupid about it. She feels so lovely and I love her so much and have done her so much damage and I must learn to take good care of her in every way I can. If I think of her and of her only, everything will be all right.

'I won't say "you know" all the time any more,' he told her. 'We can start with that.'

She shook her head and he could feel her tremble.

'You say it all you want,' she said and kissed him.

'Please don't cry, my blessed,' he said.

'I don't want you to sleep with any lousy pillow,' she said.

'I won't. Not *any* lousy pillow.'

Stop it, he said to himself. Stop it right now.

'Look, *tu*,' he said. 'We'll go down now and have lunch in our old fine place by the fire and I'll tell you what a wonderful kitten you are and what lucky kittens we are.'

'We really are.'

'We'll work everything out fine.'

'I just don't want to be sent away.'

'Nobody is ever going to send you away.'

But walking down the stairs feeling each stair carefully and holding to the banister he thought, I must get her away and get her away as soon as I can without hurting her. Because I am not doing too well at this. That I can promise you. But what else can you do? Nothing, he thought. There's nothing you can do. But maybe, as you go along, you will get good at it.

Drafts and Fragments first published in
THE NICK ADAMS STORIES

THREE SHOTS

Nick was undressing in the tent. He saw the shadows of his father and Uncle George cast by the fire on the canvas wall. He felt very uncomfortable and ashamed and undressed as fast as he could, piling his clothes neatly. He was ashamed because undressing reminded him of the night before. He had kept it out of his mind all day.

His father and uncle had gone off across the lake after supper to fish with a jack light. Before they shoved the boat out his father told him that if any emergency came up while they were gone he was to fire three shots with the rifle and they would come right back. Nick went back from the edge of the lake through the woods to the camp. He could hear the oars of the boat in the dark. His father was rowing and his uncle was sitting in the stern trolling. He had taken his seat with his rod ready when his father shoved the boat out. Nick listened to them on the lake until he could no longer hear the oars.

Walking back through the woods Nick began to be frightened. He was always a little frightened of the woods at night. He opened the flap of the tent and undressed and lay very quietly between the blankets in the dark. The fire was burned down to a bed of coals outside. Nick lay still and tried to go to sleep. There was no noise anywhere. Nick felt if he could only hear a fox bark or an owl or anything he would be all right. He was not afraid of anything definite as yet. But he was getting very afraid. Then suddenly he was afraid of dying. Just a few weeks before at home, in church, they had sung a hymn, 'Some day the silver cord will break.' While they were singing the hymn Nick had realized that some day he must die. It made him feel quite sick. It was the first time he had ever realized that he himself would have to die sometime.

That night he sat out in the hall under the night light trying to read *Robinson Crusoe* to keep his mind off the fact that some day the silver cord must break. The nurse found him there and threatened to tell his father on him if he did not go to bed. He went in to bed and as soon as the nurse was in her room came out again and read under the hall light until morning.

Last night in the tent he had had the same fear. He never had it except at night. It was more a realization than a fear at first.

But it was always on the edge of fear and became fear very quickly when it started. As soon as he began to be really frightened he took the rifle and poked the muzzle out the front of the tent and shot three times. The rifle kicked badly. He heard the shots rip off through the trees. As soon as he had fired the shots it was all right.

He lay down to wait for his father's return and was asleep before his father and uncle had put out their jack light on the other side of the lake.

'Damn that kid,' Uncle George said as they rowed back. 'What did you tell him to call us in for? He's probably got the heebie-jeebies about something.'

Uncle George was an enthusiastic fisherman and his father's younger brother.

'Oh, well. He's pretty small,' his father said.

'That's no reason to bring him into the woods with us.'

'I know he's an awful coward,' his father said, 'but we're all yellow at that age.'

'I can't stand him,' George said. 'He's such an awful liar.'

'Oh, well, forget it. You'll get plenty of fishing anyway.'

They came into the tent and Uncle George shone his flashlight into Nick's eyes.

'What was it, Nickie?' said his father. Nick sat up in bed.

'It sounded like a cross between a fox and a wolf and it was fooling around the tent,' Nick said. 'It was a little like a fox but more like a wolf.' He had learned the phrase 'cross between' that same day from his uncle.

'He probably heard a screech owl,' Uncle George said.

In the morning his father found two big basswood trees that leaned across each other so that they rubbed together in the wind.

'Do you think that was what it was, Nick?' his father asked.

'Maybe,' Nick said. He didn't want to think about it.

'You don't want to ever be frightened in the woods, Nick. There is nothing that can hurt you.'

'Not even lightning?' Nick asked.

'No, not even lightning. If there is a thunder storm get out into the open. Or get under a beech tree. They're never struck.'

'Never?' Nick asked.

'I never heard of one,' said his father.

'Gee, I'm glad to know that about beech trees,' Nick said.

Now he was undressing again in the tent. He was conscious

of the two shadows on the wall although he was not watching them. Then he heard a boat being pulled up on the beach and the two shadows were gone. He heard his father talking with someone.

Then his father shouted, 'Get your clothes on, Nick.'

He dressed as fast as he could. His father came in and rummaged through the duffel bags.

'Put your coat on, Nick,' his father said, absentmindedly.

THE INDIANS MOVED AWAY

The Petoskey road ran straight uphill from Grandpa Bacon's farm. His farm was at the end of the road. It always seemed, though, that the road started at his farm and ran to Petoskey, going along the edge of the trees up the long hill, steep and sandy, to disappear into the woods where the long slope of fields stopped short against the hardwood timber.

After the road went into the woods it was cool and the sand firm underfoot from the moisture. It went up and down hills through the woods with berry bushes and beech saplings on either side that had to be periodically cut back to keep them from effacing the road altogether. In the summer the Indians picked the berries along the road and brought them down to the cottage to sell them, packed in the buckets, wild red raspberries crushing with their own weight, covered with basswood leaves to keep them cool; later blackberries, firm and fresh shining, pails of them. The Indians brought them, coming through the woods to the cottage by the lake. You never heard them come but there they were, standing by the kitchen door with the tin buckets full of berries. Sometimes Nick, lying reading in the hammock, smelt the Indians coming through the gate past the woodpile and around the house. Indians all smelled alike. It was a sweetish smell that all Indians had. He had smelled it first when Grandpa Bacon rented the shack by the point to Indians and after they had left he went inside the shack and it all smelled that way. Grandpa Bacon could never rent the shack to white people after that and no more Indians rented it because the Indian who had lived there had gone into Petoskey to get drunk on the Fourth of July and, coming back, had lain down to go to sleep on the Pere Marquette railway tracks and been run over by the midnight train. He was a very tall Indian and had made Nick an ash canoe paddle. He had lived alone in the shack and drank pain killer and walked through the woods alone at night. Many Indians were that way.

There were no successful Indians. Formerly there had been – old Indians who owned farms and worked them and grew old and fat with many children and grandchildren. Indians like Simon Green who lived on Hortons Creek and had a big farm. Simon Green was dead, though, and his children had sold the farm to divide the money and gone off somewhere.

THE INDIANS MOVED AWAY

Nick remembered Simon Green sitting in a chair in front of the blacksmith shop at Hortons Bay, perspiring in the sun while his horses were being shod inside. Nick spading up the cool moist dirt under the eaves of the shed for worms dug with his fingers in the dirt and heard the quick clang of the iron being hammered. He sifted dirt into his can of worms and filled back the earth he had spaded, patted it smooth with the spade. Outside in the sun Simon Green sat in the chair.

'Hello, Nick,' he said as Nick came out.

'Hello, Mr. Green.'

'Going fishing?'

'Yes.'

'Pretty hot day,' Simon smiled. 'Tell your dad we're going to have lots of birds this fall.'

Nick went on across the field back of the shop to the house to get his cane pole and creel. On his way down to the creek Simon Green passed along the road in his buggy. Nick was just going into the brush and Simon did not see him. That was the last he had seen of Simon Green. He died that winter and the next summer his farm was sold. He left nothing besides his farm. Everything had been put back into the farm. One of the boys wanted to go on farming but the others overruled him and the farm was sold. It did not bring one half as much as everyone expected.

The Green boy, Eddy, who had wanted to go on farming, bought a piece of land over back of Spring Brook. The other two boys bought a poolroom in Pellston. They lost money and were sold out. That was the way the Indians went.

THE LAST GOOD COUNTRY

'Nickie,' his sister said to him. 'Listen to me, Nickie.'

'I don't want to hear it.'

He was watching the bottom of the spring where the sand rose in small spurts with the bubbling water. There was a tin cup on a forked stick that was stuck in the gravel by the spring. Adams looked at it and at the water rising and then flowing clear in its gravel bed beside the sandy road. He could see both ways on the road and he looked up the hill and then down to the dock and the lake. Behind him was a thick cedar swamp and his back was against a big cedar tree. His sister was sitting on the moss beside him and she had her arm around his shoulders.

He took the cup and dipped it down into the spring and handed the cup to his sister. She drank some and handed the cup back and he dipped another cup and drank feeling the cold of the water and tasting the faint clean iron rusty taste of the cup.

'They're waiting for you to come home to supper,' his sister said. 'There's two of them. They came in a buggy and they asked where you were.'

'Did anybody tell them?'

'Nobody knew where you were but me. Did you get many, Nickie?'

'I got twenty-six.'

'Are they good ones?'

'Just the size they want for the dinners.'

'Oh Nickie I wish you wouldn't sell them.'

'She gives me a dollar a pound,' Nick Adams said.

His sister was tanned brown and she had dark brown eyes and dark brown hair with yellow streaks in it from the sun. She and Nick loved each other and they did not love the others. They always thought of everyone else in the family as the others.

'They know about everything, Nickie,' his sister said hopelessly. 'They said they were going to make an example of you and send you to the reform school.'

'They've only got proof on one thing,' Nick told her. 'But I guess I have to go away for a while.'

'Can I go?'

'No. I'm sorry, Littless. How much money have we got?'

'Fourteen dollars and sixty-five cents. I brought it.'

'Did they say anything else?'

'No. Only that they were going to stay till you came home.'

'Our mother will get tired of feeding them.'

'She gave them lunch already.'

'What were they doing?'

'Just sitting around on the screen porch. They asked our mother for your rifle but I'd hid it in the wood-shed when I saw them by the fence.'

'Were you expecting them?'

'Yes. Weren't you?'

'I guess so. God-damn them.'

'God-damn them for me too,' his sister said. 'Aren't I old enough to go now? I hid the rifle. I brought the money.'

'I'd worry about you,' Nick Adams told her. 'I don't even know where I'm going.'

'Sure you do.'

'If there's two of us they'd look harder. A boy and a girl show up.'

'I'd go like a boy,' she said. 'I always wanted to be a boy anyway. They couldn't tell anything about me if my hair was cut.'

'No,' Nick Adams said. 'That's true.'

'Let's think something out good,' she said. 'Please Nick please. I know I'm only your sister, Littless. But I could be lots of use and you'd be lonely without me. Wouldn't you be?'

'I'm lonely now thinking about going away from you.'

'See? And we may have to be away for years. Who can tell? Take me Nickie. Please take me.' She kissed him and held onto him with both her arms. Nick Adams looked at her and tried to think straight. It was difficult. But there was no choice.

'No, I can't take you.'

'Please. I'd be good and I'd help and I wouldn't be a nuisance.'

'I know it. You'd be wonderful. But I can't do it.'

'Would you if I were a boy?'

'No. I'm in trouble and it's my own fault and I mustn't get anybody else in trouble. Especially you.'

He looked up and down the road and up at the sky where the big high afternoon clouds were riding and at the white caps on the lake out beyond the point.

'Please,' his sister said.

'I told you,' he said. 'I made up my mind.'

'All right,' she said. 'But I think you're wrong. And I hate to think you're wrong.'

'I was wrong to get in the trouble and stupid too. How did I ever get so stupid?'

'I don't think it would be stupid to take me. It might be wrong. But it wouldn't be stupid and we've done wrong already.'

'You and I've never done anything wrong together.'

'I don't mean that kind of wrong like you and Trudy. I mean I've stolen for you and I keep your secrets and now I'm warning you about them.'

'Thanks,' he said. 'Now I have to figure out what to do.'

'Can't I come?'

'No, Littless,' he said. 'People wouldn't understand.'

'I don't care if they understand.'

'Listen,' he said. 'If I took you people would look twice as hard for us.'

'I guess so,' she admitted. 'And the family would help them.'

'That's the trouble,' Nick said. 'Let me plan now. I have to figure out what to do.'

Looking up the road he saw a buggy coming down the hill and he took his sister by the wrist and said, 'Come on back. Get out of sight.'

Behind the big cedars they lay flat against the springy moss with their faces down and heard the soft noise of the horses' hooves in the sand and the small noise of the wheels. Neither of the men in the buggy was talking but Nick Adams smelled them as they went past and he smelled the sweated horses. He sweated himself until they were well past on their way to the dock because he thought they might stop to water at the spring or to get a drink.

'Look at them, Littless,' he said.

'It's them.'

'Come on,' Nick told her. He crawled back into the swamp pulling his sack of fish. This part of the swamp was mossy still and not muddy and when they were well out of sight he stood up and put the sack behind the trunk of a cedar.

'Did you get to see them?' his sister asked.

'I know one of them,' Nick Adams said. 'He's a no good son of a bitch.'

'He said he'd been after you for four years.'

'I know.'

'The other one, the big one with the spit tobacco face and the blue suit, is the one from downstate.'

'Good,' Nick said. 'Now I know them both. But who told them I was down at the grist mill? That's where they're going.'

'Somebody must have told them. Maybe they just thought it out. Anybody could have told them you'd gone to fish the creek.'

'I guess so. But now I don't know whether it's safe to take her the trout.'

'I'll take them to her.'

'No. They're too heavy. I'll take them through the swamp and to the woods in back of the hotel. You go straight to the hotel and see if she's there and if everything's all right. And if it is you'll find me there by the big basswood tree.'

'It's a long way there through the swamp, Nickie.'

'It's a long way back from reform school too.'

'Can't I come with you through the swamp? I'll go in then and see her while you stay out and come back out with you and take them in.'

'All right,' Nick said. 'But I wish you'd do it the other way.'

'Why, Nickie?'

'Because you'll see them maybe on the road and you can tell me where they've gone.'

'All right. I just wanted to stay with you as long as I could.'

'I'll see you in the second growth wood lot in back of the hotel where the big basswood is.'

Nick waited more than an hour in the second growth timber and his sister had not come. When she came she was excited and he knew she was tired.

'They're at our house,' she said. 'They're sitting out on the screen porch and drinking whiskey and ginger ale and they've unhitched and put their horses up. They say they're going to wait till you come back. It was our mother told them you'd gone fishing at the creek. I don't think she meant to. Anyway I hope not.'

'What about Mrs. Packard?'

'I saw her in the kitchen of the hotel and she asked me if I'd seen you and I said no. She said she was waiting for you to bring her some fish for tonight. She was worried. You might as well take them in.'

'Good,' he said. 'They're nice and fresh. I repacked them in ferns.'

'Can I come in with you?'

'Sure,' Nick said.

The hotel was a long wooden building with a porch that fronted on the lake. There were wide wooden steps that led down to the pier that ran far out into the water and there were natural cedar railings alongside the steps and natural cedar railings around the porch. There were chairs made of natural cedar on the porch and in them sat middle-aged people wearing white clothes. There were pipes with spring water bubbling out of them set on the lawn and little paths led to them. The water tasted like rotten eggs because these were mineral springs and Nick and his sister used to drink from them as a matter of discipline. Now coming toward the rear of the hotel where the kitchen was they crossed a plank bridge over a small brook that ran into the lake beside the hotel, and slipped into the back door of the kitchen.

'Wash them and put them in the ice box Nickie,' Mrs. Packard said. 'I'll weigh them later.'

'Mrs. Packard,' Nick said. 'Could I speak to you a minute?'

'Speak up,' she said. 'Can't you see I'm busy?'

'If I could have the money now.'

Mrs. Packard was a handsome woman in a gingham apron. She had a beautiful complexion and she was very busy and her kitchen help was there as well.

'You don't mean you want to sell trout. Don't you know that's against the law?'

'I know,' Nick said. 'I brought you the fish for a present. I mean my time for the wood I split and corded.'

'I'll get it,' she said. 'I have to go to the Annex.'

Nick and his sister followed her outside and on the board sidewalk that led to the ice-house from the kitchen she stopped and put her hands in her apron pocket and took out a pocket book.

'You get out of here,' she said quickly and kindly. 'And get out of here fast. How much do you need?'

'I've got sixteen dollars,' Nick said.

'Take twenty,' she told him. 'And keep that tyke out of trouble. Let her go home and keep an eye on them until you're clear.'

'When did you hear about them?'

She shook her head at him.

'Buying is as bad or worse than selling,' she said. 'You stay away until things quiet down. Nickie you're a good boy no matter what anybody says. You see Packard if things get bad. Come here nights if you need anything. I sleep light. Just knock on the window.'

'You aren't going to serve them tonight are you Mrs. Packard? You're not going to serve them for the dinners?'

'No,' she said. 'But I'm not going to waste them. Packard can eat half a dozen and I know other people that can. Be careful Nickie and let it blow over. Keep out of sight.'

'Littless wants to go with me.'

'Don't you dare take her,' Mrs. Packard said. 'You come by tonight and I'll have some stuff made up for you.'

'Could you let me take a skillet?'

'I'll have what you need. Packard knows what you need. I don't give you any more money so you'll keep out of trouble.'

'Do you want me to find some one who can get the fish for you?'

'No. There won't be trout dinners for a while,' Mrs. Packard said.

'I'd like to see Mr. Packard about getting a few things.'

'He'll get you anything you need. But don't you go near the store Nick.'

'I'll get Littless to take him a note. What time can I come by and get the things? I'd like to get started.'

'You just tap on the window. Packard will have everything fixed up. He knows what you'll need. Don't you worry Nickie and don't do anything bad.'

'Can't I go and see him at the store?'

'No. You keep away from the store.'

The brother and sister went back toward the woods and looked back at the brown wood hotel.

'I wish Mrs. Packard was our mother,' the girl said.

'We might as well not talk against her,' Nick said. 'She's our mother. Why do you suppose I said I had sixteen dollars?'

'It sounds better,' his sister told him. 'Thirteen dollars and sixty-five cents isn't dignified to tell other people.'

'I ought to go and see Mr. Packard,' Nick said. 'It isn't practical for him to make up an antfill [?illegible] for me when he doesn't know what I've got or where I'm going. It doesn't make sense even.'

'I didn't think so either,' his sister said. 'But she was being so nice about it. She was in a hurry too because she had the dinners as well as feeding the resorters.'

'Look Littless,' Nick said. 'You go to the store and buy a pencil and a pad of paper and buy yourself a nickel's worth of any kind of candy you want. I'll write Mr. Packard a note.'

He gave his sister a quarter and she said, 'What kind of candy do you want?'

'I don't feel like any kind of candy.'

'I'll be right back,' his sister said. 'Don't you worry Nickie.'

Nick sat against the basswood tree and waited for her and thought. Thinking about the thing itself made him feel bad and did no good. It had happened now. It was really no worse than when he had first known they had the proof. It had to go along like this and he was lucky he was not at home when they came.

They were in the big hemlocks on the hill behind the house now. It was evening and the sun was down beyond the hills on the other side of the lake.

'I've found everything,' his sister said. 'It's going to make a pretty big pack Nickie.'

'I know it.'

'If I was going you wouldn't need anything more, hardly.'

'What are they doing?'

'They ate a big supper and now they're sitting out on the porch and drinking. They're telling each other stories about how smart they are.'

'They aren't very smart so far.'

'They're going to starve you out,' his sister said. 'A couple of nights in the woods and you'll be back. You hear a loon holler a couple of times when you got an empty stomach and you'll be back.'

'What did our mother give them for supper?'

'Awful,' his sister said.

'Good.'

'I've located everything on the list. Our mother's gone to bed with a sick headache. She wrote your father.'

'Did you see the letter?'

'No. It's in her room with the list of stuff to get from the store tomorrow. She's going to have to make a new list when she finds everything is gone in the morning.'

'How much are they drinking?'

'They've drunk about a bottle I guess.'

'I wish we could put knock-out drops in it.'

'I could put them in if you'll tell me how. Do you put them in the bottle?'

'No. In the glass. But we haven't got any.'

'Would there be any in the medicine cabinet?'

'No.'

'I could put paragoric in the bottle. They have another bottle. Or calomel. I know we've got those.'

'No,' said Nick. 'You try to get me about half the other bottle. When they're asleep. Put it in any old medicine bottle.'

'I better go and watch them,' his sister said. 'My I wish we had knock-out drops. I never even heard of them.'

'They aren't really drops,' Nick told her. 'It's chloral hydrage. Whores give it to lumberjacks in their drinks when they're going to jack roll them.'

'It sounds pretty bad,' his sister said. 'But we probably ought to have some for in emergencies.'

'Let me kiss you,' her brother said. 'Just for in an emergency.'

'Who will you kiss when you go away?'

'Nobody,' he said. 'Trudy maybe if I can find her.'

'I thought you were through with her.'

'I was. But I'm not sure now.'

'You wouldn't go and make her another baby would you?'

'I don't know.'

'They'll put you in the reform school for that if you keep doing it.'

'I heard that.'

'Well let's not talk about it,' his sister said. 'I promised myself I'd never even think about it. I don't want to think about that while you're gone and have the family talk about it and me know it's true. Where's she now?'

'I'm going to find her.'

'Really? Nickie you shouldn't. Please don't.'

'I think I have to, Littless.'

'I know where she is if you have to find her.'

'Where is she?'

'At the Indian Play.'

'Really?'

'Why would I tell except to keep you from having trouble finding her? Why wouldn't I tell you the truth when I love you?'

'Why didn't you tell me before?'

'Nickie you ought to learn not to ask too much. I thought we'd go away together and I'd take care of you and you'd take care of me and you know where I thought we'd go. I thought we'd hunt and fish and eat and read and sleep together and not worry and love each other and be kind and good.'

'When did you find out?'

'This afternoon. I saw Joubert on the bridge fishing when I went home. He asked about you and said Trudy was at the play and Billy had a job there too. He tried to get a job but they wouldn't take him. He can't swim well enough to play water base-ball.'

'Was that all he said?'

'He said for me to ask you if you had forgotten what sweet grass smells like.'

'I'm sorry Littless,' Nick said. 'I'm not a good brother, and I'm not a good man and I'm not a good friend even.'

'But you would have taken me truly if you thought it wouldn't make trouble wouldn't you?'

'Of course.'

'And this is your second best hope isn't it?'

'It isn't even that.'

'I don't mind as long as it's second best.'

'Let's go down and watch them drinking,' Nick said. 'I'd like to hear them talk sitting in our own house.'

'Will you promise not to get angry and do anything bad?'

'Sure.'

'Nor to the horses. It's not the horses' fault.'

'Not the horses either.'

'I wish we had knock-out drops,' his sister said loyal.

'Well we haven't,' Nick told her. 'I guess there aren't any this side of Boyne City.'

They sat in the woodshed and they watched the two men sitting at the table on the screened porch. The moon had not risen and it was dark but the outlines of the men showed against the lightness that the lake made behind them. They were not talking now but were both leaning forward on the table. Then Nick heard the clink of ice against a bucket.

'The ginger-ale's gone,' one of the men said.

'I said it wouldn't last,' the other said. 'But you were the one said we had plenty.'

'Get some water. There's a pail and a dipper in the kitchen.'

'I've drunk enough. I'm going to turn in.'

'Aren't you going to stay up for if that kid comes in?'

'No. I'm going to get some sleep. You stay up.'

'Do you think he'll come in tonight?'

'I don't know. I'm going to get some sleep. You wake me when you get sleepy.'

'I can stay up all night,' the local warden said. 'Many's the night I've stayed up all night for jack-lighters and never shut an eye.'

'Me too,' the downstate man said. 'But now I'm going to get a little sleep.'

Nick and his sister watched him go in the door. Their mother had told the two men they could sleep in the bedroom next to the living room. They saw when he struck a match. Then the window was dark again. They watched the other warden sitting at the table until he put his head on his arms. Then they heard him snoring.

'We'll give him a little while to make sure he's solid asleep. Then we'll get the stuff,' Nick said.

'You get over outside the fence,' his sister said. 'It doesn't matter if I'm moving around. But he might wake up and see you.'

'All right,' Nick agreed. 'I'll get everything out of here. Most of it's here.'

'Can you find everything without a light?'

'Sure. Where's the rifle?'

'Flat on the back upper rafter. Don't slip or make the wood fall down, Nickie.'

'Don't you worry.'

She came out to the fence at the far corner where Nick was making up his pack beyond the big hemlock that had been struck by lightning the summer before and had fallen in a storm that autumn. The moon was just rising now behind the far hills and enough moonlight came through the trees for Nick to see clearly what he was packing. His sister put down the sack she was carrying and said, 'They're sleeping like pigs Nickie.'

'Good.'

'The downstate one was snoring just like the one outside. I think I got everything.'

'You good old Littless.'

'I'm going to walk with you for a way. I can be back before anybody's up.'

'Fine.'

'You don't mind do you Nickie?'

'No.'

'Nickie.'

'What?'

'I have to tell you something.'

'Tell it.'

'I wrote a note to our mother and told her I was going with you to keep you out of trouble and not to tell anybody and that you'd take good care of me. I put it under her door. It's locked.'

'Oh shit,' Nick said. Then he said, 'I'm sorry, Littless.'

'Now it's not your fault and I can't make it worse for you.'

'You're awful.'

'You said she was your second choice.'

'Not even that.'

'Can't we be happy now?'

'Sure.'

'I brought the whiskey,' she said hopefully. 'I left some in the bottle. One of them can't be sure the other didn't drink it. Anyway they have another bottle.'

'Did you bring a blanket for you?'

'Of course.'

'We better get going.'

'We're all right if we're going where I think. The only thing makes the pack bigger is my blanket. I'll carry the rifle.'

'All right. What kind of shoes have you?'

'I've got my work-moccassins.'

'What did you bring to read?'

'Lorna Doone and Kidnapped and Wuthering Heights.'

'They're all too old for you but Kidnapped.'

'Lorna Doone isn't.'

'We'll read it out loud,' Nick said. 'That way it lasts longer. But Littless you've made things sort of hard now and we better go. Those bastards can't be as stupid as they act. Maybe it was just because they were drinking.'

'I'm all ready to go,' his sister said. 'Let me help you strap the pack.'

'You know you haven't had any sleep at all and that we have to travel?'

'I know. I'm really like the snoring one at the table says he was.'

'Maybe he was that way once too,' Nick said. 'But what you have to do is keep your feet in good shape. Do the moccassins chafe?'

'No. And my feet are tough from barefoot all summer.'

'Mine are good too,' said Nick. 'Come on. Let's go.'

They started off walking on the soft hemlock needles and the trees were high and there was no brush between the tree trunks.

They walked up-hill and the moon came through the trees and showed Nick with the very big pack and his sister carrying the .22 rifle. When they were at the top of the hill they looked back and saw the lake in the moonlight. It was clear enough so they could see the dark point and beyond were the high hills of the far shore.

'We might as well say goodbye to it,' Nick Adams said.

'Goodbye lake,' Littless said. 'I love you too.'

They went down from the hill and across the long field and through the orchard and then through a rail fence and into a field of stubble. Going through the stubble field they looked to the right and saw the slaughter house and the big barn in the hollow and the old log farm house on the other high land that overlooked the lake. The long road of Lombardy poplars that ran to the lake was in the moonlight.

'Does it hurt your feet, Littless?' Nick asked.

'No,' his sister said.

'I came this way on account of the dogs,' Nick said. 'They'd shut up as soon as they knew it was us. But somebody might hear them bark.'

'I know,' she said. 'And as soon as they shut up afterwards they'd know it was us.'

Ahead they could see the dark of the rising line of hills beyond the road. They came to the end of one cut field of grain and crossed the little sunken creek that ran down to the spring house. Then they climbed across the rise of another stubble field and there was another rail fence and the sandy road with the second growth timber solid beyond it.

'Wait till I climb over and I'll help you,' Nick said. 'I want to look at the road.'

From the top of the fence he saw the roll of the country and the dark timber by their own house and the bright of the lake in the moonlight. Then he was looking at the road.

'They can't track us the way we've come and I don't [. . .] they would notice tracks in this deep sand,' he said to his sister. 'We can keep to the two sides of the road if it isn't too scratchy.'

'Nickie, honestly I don't think they're intelligent enough to track anybody. Look how they just waited for you to come back and then practically got drunk before supper and afterwards.'

'They came down to the dock,' Nick said. 'That was where I was. If you hadn't have told me they would have picked me up.'

'They didn't have to be so intelligent to figure you would be on the big creek when our mother let them know you might have gone fishing. After I left they must have found all the boats were there and that would make them think you were fishing the creek. Everybody knows you usually fish below the grist mill and the cider mill. They were just slow thinking it out.'

'All right,' Nick said. 'But they were awfully close then.'

His sister handed him the rifle through the fence, butt toward him, and then crawled between the rails. She stood beside him on the road and he put his hand on her head and stroked it.

'Are you awfully tired Littless?'

'No. I'm fine. I'm too happy to be tired.'

'Until you're too tired you walk in the sandy part of the road where their horses made holes in the sand. It's so soft and dry tracks won't show and I'll walk on the side where it's hard.'

'I can walk on the side too.'

'No. I don't want you to get scratched.'

They climbed, but with constant small descents, toward the height of land that separated the two lakes. There was close, heavy, second-growth timber on both sides of the road and blackberry and raspberry bushes grew from the edge of the road to the timber. Ahead they could see the top of each hill as a notch in the timber. The moon was well on its way down now.

'How do you feel Littless?' Nick asked his sister.

'I feel wonderful. Nickie is it always this nice when you run away from home?'

'No. Usually it's lonesome.'

'How lonesome have you ever been?'

'Bad black lonesome. Awful.'

'Do you think you'll get lonesome with me?'

'No.'

'You don't mind you're with me instead of going to Trudy?'

'What do you talk about her for all the time?'

'I haven't been. Maybe you were thinking about her and you thought I was.'

'You're too smart,' Nick said. 'I thought about her because you told me where she was and when I knew where she was I wondered what she would be doing and all that.'

'I guess I shouldn't have come.'

'I told you that you shouldn't come.'

'Oh hell,' his sister said. 'Are we going to be like the others and have fights? I'll go back now. You don't have to have me.'

'Shut up,' Nick said.

'Please don't say that, Nickie. I'll go back or I'll stay just as you want. I'll go back whenever you tell me to. But I won't have fights. Haven't we seen enough fights in families?'

'Yes,' said Nick.

'I know I forced you to take me. But I fixed it so you wouldn't get in trouble about it. And I did keep them from catching you.'

They had reached the height of land from where they could see the lake again although from here it looked narrow now and almost like a big river.

'We cut across country here,' Nick said. 'Then we'll hit that old logging road. Here's where you go back from if you want to go back.'

He took off his pack and put it back into the timber and his sister leaned the rifle on it.

'Sit down Littless and take a rest,' he said. 'We're both tired.'

Nick lay with his head on the pack and his sister lay by him with her head on his shoulder.

'I'm not going back Nickie unless you tell me to,' she said. 'I just don't want fights. Promise me we won't have fights?'

'Promise.'

'I won't talk about Trudy.'

'The hell with Trudy.'

'I want to be useful and a good partner.'

'You are. You won't mind if I get restless and mix it up with being lonesome?'

'No. We'll take good care of each other and have fun. We can have a lovely time.'

'All right. We'll start to have it now.'

'I've been having it all the time.'

'We just have one pretty hard stretch and then a really hard stretch and then we'll be there. We might as well wait until it gets light to start. You go to sleep Littless. Are you warm enough?'

'Oh yes Nickie. I've got my sweater.'

She curled up beside him and was asleep. In a little while Nick was sleeping too. He slept for two hours until the morning light woke him.

Nick had circled around through the second-growth timber until they had come onto the old logging road.

'We couldn't leave tracks going into it from the main road,' he told his sister.

The old road was so over-grown that he had to stoop many times to avoid hitting branches.

'It's like a tunnel,' his sister said.

'It opens up after a while.'

'Have I ever been here before?'

'No. This goes up way beyond where I ever took you hunting.'

'Does it come out on the secret place?'

'No, Littless. We have to go through some long bad slashings. Nobody gets in where we're going.'

They kept on along the road and then took another road that was even more over-grown. Then they came out into a clearing. There was fire-weed and brush in the clearing and the old cabins of the logging camp. They were very old and some of the roofs had fallen in. But there was a spring by the road and they both drank at it. The sun wasn't up yet and they both felt hollow and empty in the early morning after the night of walking.

'All this beyond was hemlock forest,' Nick said. 'They only cut it for the bark and they never used the logs.'

'But what happens to the road?'

'They must have cut up at the far end first and hauled and piled the bark by the road to snake it out. Then finally they cut everything right to the road and piled the bark here and then pulled out.'

'Is the secret place beyond all this slashing?'

'Yes. We go through the slashing and then some more road and then another slashing and then we come to virgin timber.'

'How did they leave it when they cut all this?'

'I don't know. It belonged to somebody that wouldn't sell I guess. They stole a lot from the edges and paid stumpage on it. But the good part's still there and there isn't any passable road into it.'

'But why can't people go down the creek? The creek has to come from somewhere.'

They were resting before they started the bad travelling through the slashing and Nick wanted to explain.

'Look Littless. The creek crosses the main road we were on and it goes through a farmer's land. The farmer has it fenced for a pasture and he runs people off that want to fish. So they stop at the bridge on his land. Then below where they would hit if they cut across his pasture on the other side from his house, on that section of the creek he runs a bull. The bull is mean and he really runs everybody off. He's the meanest bull I ever saw and he just stays there mean all the time and hunts for people. Then after him the farmer's land ends and there's a section of cedar swamp with sink holes and you'd have to know it to get through. And then, even if you know it, it's bad. Below that is the secret place. We're going in over the hills and sort of in the back way. Then below the secret place there's real swamp. Bad swamp that you can't get through. Now we better start the bad part.'

The bad part and the part that was worse were behind them now. Nick had climbed over many logs that were higher than his head and others that were up to his waist. He would take the rifle and lay it down on the top of the log and pull his sister up and then she would slide down on the far side or he would lower himself down and take the rifle and help the girl down. They went over and around piles of brush and it was hot in the slashing and the pollen from the ragweed and the fireweed dusted the girl's hair and made her sneeze.

'Damn slashings,' she said to Nick. They were resting on top of a big log ringed where they sat by the cutting of the bark peelers. The ring was grey in the rotting grey log and all around were other long grey trunks with the brilliant and worthless weeds growing.

'This is the last one,' Nick said.

'I hate them,' his sister said. 'And the damn weeds are like flowers in a tree cemetery if nobody took care of it.'

'You see why I didn't want to try to make it in the dark.'

'We couldn't.'

'No. And nobody's going to chase us through here. Now we come into the good part.'

They came from the hot sun of the slashings into the shade of the great trees. The slashings had run up to the top of a ridge and over and then the forest began. They were walking on the brown forest floor now and it was springy and cool under their feet. There was no underbrush and the trunks of the trees rose sixty feet high before there were any branches. It was cool in the shade of the trees and high up in them Nick could hear the breeze that was rising. No sun came through as they walked and Nick knew there would be no sun through the high top branches until nearly noon. His sister put her hand in his and walked close to him.

'I'm not scared Nickie. But it makes me feel very strange.'

'Me too,' Nick said. 'Always.'

'I never was in woods like these.'

'This is all the virgin timber left around here.'

'Do we go through it very long?'

'Quite a way.'

'I'd be afraid if I were alone.'

'It makes me feel strange. But I'm not afraid.'

'I said that first.'

'I know. Maybe we say it because we are afraid.'

'No. I'm not afraid because I'm with you. But I know I'd be afraid alone. Did you ever come here with anyone else?'

'No. Only by myself.'

'And you weren't afraid?'

'No. But I always feel strange. Like the way I ought to feel in church.'

'Nickie where we're going to live isn't as solemn as this is it?'

'No. Don't you worry. There it's cheerful. You just enjoy this Littless. This is good for you. This is the way forests were in the olden days.'

'I love the olden days. But I wouldn't want it all this solemn.'

'It wasn't all solemn. But the hemlock forests were.'

'It's wonderful walking. I thought behind our house was wonderful. But this is better. Nickie do you believe in God? You don't have to answer if you don't want to.'

'I don't know.'

'All right. You don't have to say it. But you don't mind if I say my prayers at night?'

'No. I'll remind you if you forget.'

'Thank you. Because this kind of woods makes me feel awfully religious.'

'That's why they build cathedrals to be like this.'

'You've never seen a cathedral have you?'

'No. But I've read about them and I can imagine them. This is the best one we have around here.'

'Do you think we can go to Europe some time and see cathedrals?'

'Sure we will. But first I have to get out of this trouble and learn how to make some money.'

'Do you think you'll ever make money writing?'

'If I get good enough.'

'Couldn't you maybe make it if you wrote cheerfuller things? That isn't my opinion. Our mother said everything you write is morbid.'

'It's too morbid for the St. Nicholas,' Nick said. 'They didn't say it. But they didn't like it.'

'But the St. Nicholas is our favourite magazine.'

'I know,' said Nick. 'But I'm too morbid for it already. And I'm not even grown up.'

'When is a man grown up? When he's married?'

'No. Until you're grown up they sent you to reform school. After you're grown up they send you to the Penitentiary.'

'I'm glad you're not grown up there.'

'They're not going to send me anywhere,' Nick said. 'And let's not talk morbid even if I write morbid.'

'I didn't say it was morbid.'

'I know. Everybody else does though.'

'Let's be cheerful Nickie,' his sister said. 'These woods make us too solemn.'

'We'll be out of them pretty soon,' Nick told her. 'Then you'll see where we're going to live. Are you hungry, Littless?'

'A little.'

'I'll bet,' Nick said. 'We'll eat a couple of apples.'

They were coming down a long hill when they saw sunlight ahead through the tree trunks. Now, at the edge of the timber there was wintergreen growing and some partridge berries and the forest floor began to be alive with growing things. Through the tree trunks they saw an open meadow that sloped to where white birches grew along the stream. Below the meadow and the line of the birches there was the dark green of a cedar swamp and far beyond the swamp there were dark blue hills. There was an arm of the lake between the swamp and the hills. But from here they could not see. They only felt from the distances that it was there.

'Here's the spring,' Nick said to his sister. 'And here's the stones where I camped before.'

'It's a beautiful, beautiful place, Nickie,' his sister said. 'Can we see the lake too?'

'There's a place where we can see it. But it's better to camp here. I'll get some wood and we'll make breakfast.'

'The fire stones are very old.'

'It's a very old place,' Nick said. 'The fire stones are Indian.'

'How did you come to it straight through the woods with no trail and no blazes?'

'Didn't you see the direction sticks on the three ridges?'

'No.'

'I'll show them to you sometime.'

'Are they yours?'

'No. They're from the old days.'

'Why didn't you show them to me?'

'I don't know,' Nick said. 'I was showing off I guess.'

'Nickie they'll never find us here.'

'I hope not,' Nick said.

At about the time that Nick and his sister were entering the first of the slashings the warden who was sleeping on the screen porch of the house that stood in the shade of the trees above the lake was wakened by the sun that, rising above the slope of open land behind the house, shone full on his face. During the night the warden had gotten up for a drink of water and when he had come back from the kitchen he had lain down on the floor with a cushion from one of the chairs for a pillow. Now he waked, realized where he was, and got to his feet. He had slept on his right side because he had a thirty-eight Smith and Wesson revolver in a shoulder holster under his left armpit. Now, awake, he felt for the gun, looked away from the sun, which hurt his eyes, and went into the kitchen where he dipped up a drink of water from the pail beside the kitchen table. The hired girl was building a fire in the stove and the warden said to her, 'What about some breakfast?'

'No breakfast,' she said. She slept in a cabin out behind the house and had come into the kitchen a half an hour before. The sight of the warden lying on the floor of the screen porch and the nearly empty bottle of whiskey on the table had frightened and disgusted her. Then it had made her angry.

'What do you mean no breakfast?' the warden said still holding the dipper.

'Just that.'

'Why?'

'Nothing to eat.'

'What about coffee?'

'No coffee.'

'Tea?'

'No tea. No bacon. No corn-meal. No salt. No pepper. No coffee. No Borden's canned cream. No Aunt Jemima buckwheat flour. No nothing.'

'What are you talking about? There was plenty to eat last night.'

'There isn't now. Chipmunks must have carried it away.'

The warden from downstate had gotten up when he heard them talking and come into the kitchen.

'How *you* feel this morning?' the hired girl asked him.

The warden ignored the hired girl and said, 'What is it Evans?'

'That son of a bitch came in here last night and got himself a pack load of grub.'

'Don't you swear in my kitchen,' the hired girl said.

'Come out here,' the downstate warden said. They both went out on the screen porch and shut the kitchen door.

'What does that mean Evans?' the downstate man pointed at the quart of old Green River which had less than a quarter in it. 'How skunk drunk were you?'

'I drank the same as you. I sat up by the table –'

'Doing what?'

'Waiting for the goddamn Adams boy if he showed.'

'And drinking.'

'Not drinking. Then I got up and went in the kitchen and got a drink of water about half past four and I lay down here in front of the door to take it easier.'

'Why didn't you lie down in front of the kitchen door?'

'I could see him better from here if he came.'

'So what happened?'

'He must have come in the kitchen through a window maybe, and loaded that stuff.'

'Bullshit.'

'What were you doing?' the local warden asked.

'I was sleeping the same as you.'

'Okay. Let's quit fighting about it. That doesn't do any good.'

'Tell that hired girl to come out here.'

The hired girl came out and the downstate man said to her, 'You tell Mrs. Adams we want to speak to her.'

The hired girl did not say anything but went into the main part of the house shutting the door after her.

'You better pick up the full and the empty bottles,' the downstate man said. 'There isn't enough of this to do any good. You want a drink of it?'

'No thanks. I've got to work today.'

'I'll take one,' the downstate man said. 'It hasn't been shared right.'

'I didn't drink any of it after you left,' the local warden said doggedly.

'Why do you keep on with that bullshit?'

'It isn't bullshit.'

The downstate man put the bottle down. 'All right,' he said to the hired girl who had opened and shut the door behind her. 'What did she say?'

'She has a sick headache and she can't see you. She says you have a warrant. She says for you to search the place if you want to and then go.'

'What did she say about the boy?'

'She hasn't seen the boy and she doesn't know anything about him.'

'Where are the other kids?'

'They're visiting at Charlevoix.'

'Who are they visiting?'

'I don't know. She doesn't know. They went to the dance and they were going to stay over Sunday with friends.'

'Who was that kid that was around here yesterday?'

'I didn't see any kid around here yesterday.'

'There was.'

'Maybe some friend of the children asking for them. Maybe some resorter's kid. Was it a boy or a girl?'

'A girl about eleven or twelve. Brown hair and brown eyes. Freckles. Very tanned. Wearing over-hauls and a boy's shirt. Barefooted.'

'Sounds like anybody,' the hired girl said. 'Did you say eleven or twelve years old?'

'Oh shit,' said the man from downstate. 'You can't get anything out of these moss-backs.'

'If I'm a moss-back what's he?' The hired girl looked at the local warden. 'What's Mr. Evans? His kids and me went to the same school house.'

'Who was the girl?' Evans asked her. 'Come on Suzy. I can find out anyway.'

'I wouldn't know,' Suzy, the hired girl, said. 'It seems like all kinds of people come by here now. I feel just like I'm in a big city.'

'You don't want to get in any trouble do you Suzy?' Evans said.

'No Sir.'

'I mean it.'

'You don't want to get in any trouble either do you?' Suzy asked him.

Out at the barn after they were hitched up the downstate man said, 'We didn't do so good did we?'

'He's loose now,' Evans said. 'He's got grub and he must have his rifle. But he's still in the area. I can get him. Can you track?'

'No. Not really. Can you?'

'In snow.' The warden laughed. 'But we don't have to track. We have to think out where he'll be.'

'He didn't load up with all that stuff to go South. He'd just take a little something and head for the railway.'

'I couldn't tell what was missing from the wood shed except that pack with the shelter halves [?illegible]. But he had a big pack load from the kitchen. He's heading in somewhere. I got to check on all his habits and his friends and where he used to go. You block him off at Charlevoix and Petoskey and St. Ignace and Sheboygan. Where would you go if you were him?'

'I'd go to the Upper Peninsula.'

'Me too. He's been up there too. The ferry is the easiest place to pick him up. But there's Sheboygan and he knows that country too.'

'We better go down and see Packard. We were going to check that today.'

'What's to prevent him going down by East Jordan and Grand Traverse?'

'Nothing. But that isn't his country. He'll go someplace that he knows.'

Suzy came out when they were opening the gate in the fence.

'Can I ride down to the store with you? I've got to get some groceries.'

'What makes you think we're going to the store?'

'Yesterday you were talking about going to see Mr. Packard.'

'How are you going to get your groceries back?'

'I guess I can get a lift with somebody on the road or coming up the lake. This is Saturday.'

'All right. Climb up,' the local warden said.

'Thank you Mr. Evans,' Suzy said.

At the General Store and Post-office Evans hitched the team at the rack and he and the downstate man stood and talked before they went in.

'I couldn't say anything with that damned Suzy.'

'Sure.'

'Packard's a fine man. There isn't anybody better liked in this country. You'd never get a conviction on that trout business against him. Nobody's going to scare him and we don't want to antagonize him.'

'Do you think he'll co-operate?'

'Not if you act rough.'

'We'll go see him.'

Inside the store Suzy had gone straight through past the glass show cases, the opened barrels, the boxes, the shelves of canned goods seeing nothing nor anyone until she came to the post office with its lock boxes and its general delivery and stamp window. The window was down and she went straight on to the back of the store. Mr. Packard was opening a packing box with a crowbar. He looked at her and smiled.

'Mr. John,' the hired girl said speaking very fast. 'There's two wardens coming in that's after Nickie. He cleared out last night and his kid sister's gone with him. Don't let on about that. His mother knows it and it's all right. Anyhow she isn't going to say anything.'

'Did he take all your groceries?'

'Most of them.'

'You pick out what you need and make a list and I'll check it over with you.'

'They're coming in now.'

'You go out the back and come in the front again. I'll go and talk to them.'

Suzy walked around the long frame building and climbed the front steps again. This time she noticed everything as she came in. She knew the Indians who had brought in the baskets and she knew the two Indian boys who were looking at the fishing tackle in the first show cases on the left. She knew all the patent medicines in the next case and who usually bought them. She had clerked one summer in the store and she knew what the penciled code letters and numbers mean that were on the card board boxes that held shoes, winter over-shoes, wool socks, mittens, caps, and sweaters. She knew what the baskets were worth that the Indians had brought in and that it was too late in the season for them to bring a good price.

'Why did you bring them in so late Mrs. Tabeshaw?' she asked.

'Too much fun fourth of July,' the Indian woman laughed.

'How's Billy?' Suzy asked.

'I don't know Suzy I no see him four weeks now.'

'Why don't you take them down to the hotel and try and sell them to the resorters?' Suzy said.

'Maybe,' Mrs. Tabeshaw said. 'I took once.'

'You ought to take them every day.'

'Long walk,' Mrs. Tabeshaw said.

While Suzy was talking to the people she knew and making a list of what she needed for the house the two wardens were in the back of the store with Mr. John Packard.

Mr. John had gray blue eyes and dark hair and a dark mustache and he always looked as though he had wandered into a general store by accident. He had been away from Northern Michigan once for eighteen years when he was a young man and he looked more like a peace officer or an honest gambler than a store keeper. He had owned good saloons in his time and run them well. But when the country had been lumbered off he had stayed and bought farming land. Finally when the county had gone local option he had bought this store. He already owned the hotel. But he said he didn't like a hotel without a bar and so he almost never went near it. Mrs. Packard ran the hotel. She was more ambitious than Mr. John and Mr. John said he didn't want to waste time with people who had enough money to take a vacation anywhere in the country. They wanted and then came to a hotel without a bar and spent their time sitting on the porch in rocking chairs. He called the resorters change of lifers and he made fun of them to Mrs. Packard but she loved him and never minded when he teased her.

'I don't mind if you call them change of lifers,' she told him one night in bed. 'I had the damn thing but I'm still all the woman you can handle aren't I?'

She liked the resorters because some of them brought culture and Mr. John said they loved culture like a lumberjack loved Peerless the great chewing tobacco. He really respected her love of culture because she said she loved it just like he loved good bonded whiskey and she said, 'Packard you don't have to care about culture. I won't bother you with it. But it makes me feel wonderful.'

Mr. John said she could have culture until hell wouldn't hold it just so long as he never had to go to a Chautauqua or a Self Betterment course. He had been to camp meetings and a Revival but he had never been to a Chautauqua. He said a camp meeting or a revival was bad enough but at least there was some sexual intercourse afterwards by those who got really aroused although he never knew anyone to pay their bills after a camp meeting or a revival. Mrs. Packard, he told Nick Adams, would get worried about the salvation of his immortal soul after she had been to a big revival by somebody like Gypsy Smith that great Evangelist, but finally it would turn out that he, Packard, looked like Gypsy Smith and everything would be fine finally. But a Chautauqua was something strange. Culture maybe was better than religion Mr. John thought. But it was a cold proposition. But still they were crazy for it. He could see it was more than a fad though.

'Compared to religion it's sort of a dry fuck, Nickie,' he had told Nick Adams. 'But it's sure got a hold on them. It must be sort of like the Holy Rollers only in the brain. You ever see the extent they go in for it over at Wequetousing [?] and Roaring Brook?'

'No,' Nick said.

'You study it sometime and tell me what you think. You going to be a writer you ought to get in on it early. Don't let them get too far ahead of you.'

Mr. John liked Nick Adams because he said he had original sin. Nick did not understand this but he was proud.

'You're going to have things to repent, boy,' Mr. John had told Nick. 'That's one of the best things there is. You can always decide whether to repent them or not. But the thing is to have them.'

'I don't want to do anything bad,' Nick had said.

'I don't want you to,' Mr. John had said. 'But you're alive and you're going to do things. Don't you lie and don't you steal. Everybody has to lie. But you pick out somebody you never lie to.'

'I'll pick out you.'

'That's right. Don't you ever lie to me no matter what and I won't lie to you.'

'I'll try,' Nick had said.

'That isn't it,' Mr. John said. 'It has to be absolute.'

'All right,' Nick said. 'I'll never lie to you.'

'I don't mean I want you telling me everything,' Mr. John said. 'Like if you jerk off.'

'I don't jerk off,' Nick told him. 'I fuck.'

'I guess as simple a word for it as any,' Mr. John said. 'But don't you do it anymore than you have to.'

'I know. I started it too early I guess.'

'So did I,' Mr. John said. 'But don't do it when you're drunk and always make water afterwards and wash yourself good with soap and water.'

'Yes Sir,' Nick had said. 'I don't have much trouble with it lately.'

'What became of your girl?'

'Somebody said she was working up at the Soo.'

'She was a beautiful girl and I always liked her,' Mr. John had said.

'So did I,' Nick said.

'Try and not feel too bad about it.'

'I can't help it,' Nick said. 'None of it was her fault. She's just built that way. If I ran into her again I guess I'd get mixed up with her again.'

'Maybe not.'

'Maybe too. I'd try not to.'

Mr. John was thinking about Nick when he went out to the back counter where the two men were waiting for him. He looked them over as he stood there and he didn't like either of them. He had always disliked the local man Evans and had no respect for him but he sensed that the downstate man was dangerous. He had not analysed it yet but he saw the man had very flat eyes and a mouth that was tighter than just a tobacco chewer's mouth needed to be. He had a real elk's tooth too on his watch-chain. It was really a fine tusk from about a five-year-old bull. It was a beautiful tusk and Mr. John looked at it again and at the over-large bulge the man's shoulder holster made under his coat.

'Did you kill that bull with that cannon you're carrying around under your arm?' Mr. John asked the downstate man.

The downstate man looked at Mr. John un-appreciatively.

'No,' he said. 'I killed that bull out in the thoroughfare country in Wyoming with a Winchester 45–70.'

'You're a big-gun man eh?' Mr. John said. He looked under the counter. 'Have big feet too. Do you need that big a cannon when you go out hunting kids?'

'What do you mean, kids,' the downstate man said. He was one ahead.

'I mean the kid you're looking for.'

'You said kids,' the downstate man said.

Mr. John moved in. It was necessary. 'What's Evans carry when he goes after a boy who's licked his own boy twice? You must be heavily armed Evans. That boy could lick you too.'

'Why don't you produce him and we could try it,' Evans said.

'You said kids, Mr. Packard,' the downstate man said. 'What made you say that?'

'Looking at you, you cock-sucker,' Mr. John said. 'You splay-footed bastard.'

'Why don't you come out from behind that counter if you want to talk like that?' the downstate man said.

'You're talking to the United States Postmaster,' Mr. John said. 'You're talking without witnesses except for Turd-face Evans. I suppose you know why they call him Turd-face. You can figure it out. You're a detective.'

He was happy now. He had drawn the attack and he felt now as he used to feel in the old days before he made a living from feeding and bedding resorters who rocked in rustic chairs on the front porch of his hotel while they looked out over the lake.

'Listen, Splay-foot, I remember you very well now. Don't you remember me Splayzey?'

The downstate man looked at him. But he did not remember him.

'I remember you in Cheyenne the day Tom Horn was hanged,' Mr. John told him. 'You were one of the ones that framed him with promises from the association. Do you remember now? Who owned the Saloon in Medicine Bow when you worked for the people that gave it to Tom? Is that why you ended up doing what you're doing? Haven't you got any memory?'

'When did you come back here?'

'Two years after they dropped Tom.'

'I'll be god-damned.'

'Do you remember when I gave you that bull tusk when we were packing out from Greybull?'

'Sure. Listen, Jim, I got to get this kid.'

'My name's John,' Mr. John said. 'John Packard. Come on in back and have a drink. You want to get to know this other character. His name is Crut-Face Evans. We used to call him Turd-Face. I just changed it now out of kindness.'

'Mr. John,' said Mr. Evans. 'Why don't you be friendly and co-operative?'

'I just changed your name didn't I?' said Mr. John. 'What kind of co-operation do you boys want?'

In the back of the store Mr. John took a bottle off a low shelf in the corner and handed it to the downstate man.

'Drink up Splayzey,' he said. 'You look like you need it.'

They each took a drink and then Mr. John asked, 'What are you after this kid for?'

'Violation of the game laws,' the downstate man said.

'What particular violation?'

'He killed a great blue heron the twelfth of last month.'*

'Two men with guns out after a boy because he killed a great blue heron the twelfth of last month,' Mr. John said. 'How many trout fingerlings do you suppose a bird like that eats in a day?'

'They're a protected bird,' Evans said. 'There've been other violations.'

'But this is the one you've got proof of.'

'That's about it.'

'What were the other violations?'

'Plenty.'

'But you haven't got proof.'

'I didn't say that,' Evans said. 'But we've got proof on this.'

'And the date was the twelfth?'

'That's right,' said Evans.

'Why don't you ask some questions instead of answering them?' the downstate man said to his partner. Mr. John laughed. 'Let him alone Splayzey,' he said. 'I like to see that great brain work.'

'How well do you know the boy?' the downstate man asked. 'Pretty well.'

'Ever do any business with him?'

'He buys a little stuff here once in a while. Pays cash.'

'Do you have any idea where he'd head for?'

'He's got folks in Oklahoma.'

'When did you see him last?' Evans asked.

*Hemingway intended to change blue heron to buck deer.

'Come on, Evans,' the downstate man said. 'You're wasting our time. Thanks for the drink, Jim.'

'John,' Mr. John said. 'What's your name Splayzey?'

'Porter. Henry J. Porter.'

'Splayzey you're not going to do any shooting at that boy.'

'I'm going to bring him in.'

'You always were a murderous bastard.'

'Come on Evans,' the downstate man said. 'We're wasting time in here.'

'You remember what I said about the shooting,' Mr. John said very quietly.

'I heard you,' the downstate man said.

The two men went out through the store and unhitched their light wagon and drove off. Mr. John watched them go up the road. Evans was driving and the downstate man was talking to him.

Henry J. Porter, Mr. John thought. The only name I can remember for him is Splayzey. He had such big feet he had to have made to order boats. Splayfoot they called him. Then Splayzey. It was his tracks by the spring where that Nester's boy was shot that they hung Tom for. Splayzey. Splayzey what? Maybe I never did know. Splay-foot Splayzey. Splayfoot Porter? No it wasn't Porter.

'I'm sorry about those baskets, Mrs. Tabeshaw,' he said. 'It's too late in the season now and they don't carry over. But if you'd be patient with them down at the hotel you'd get rid of them.'

'You buy them sell at the hotel,' Mrs. Tabeshaw suggested.

'No. They'd buy them better from you,' Mr. John told her. 'You're a fine looking woman.'

'Long time ago,' Mrs. Tabeshaw said.

'Suzy I'd like to see you,' Mr. John said.

In the back of the store he said, 'Tell me about it.'

'I told you already. They came for Nickie and I was waiting for him. When they were sleeping drunk Nickie got his stuff and pulled out. He's got grub for two weeks easy and he's got his rifle and young Littless went with him.'

'Why did she go?'

'I don't know, Mr. John. I guess she wanted to look after him and keep him from doing anything bad. You know him.'

'You live up by Evanses. How much do you think he knows about where Nick uses?'

'All he can. But I don't know how much.'

'Where do you think they went?'

'I wouldn't know Mr. John. Nickie knows a lot of country.'

'That man with Evans is no good. He's really bad.'

'He isn't very smart.'

'He's smarter than he acts. The booze has him down. But he's smart and he's bad. I used to know him.'

'What do you want me to do?'

'Nothing, Suzy. Let me know about anything.'

'I'll add up my stuff Mr. John and you can check it.'

'How are you going home?'

'I can get the boat up to Henry's Dock and then get a row boat from the cottage and row down and get the stuff. Mr. John what will they do with Nickie?'

'That's what I'm worried about.'

'They were talking about getting him put in the reform school.'

'I wish he hadn't killed that buck.'

'So does he. He told me he was reading in a book about how you could crease something with a bullet and it wouldn't do it any harm. It would just stun it and Nickie wanted to try it. He said it was a damn fool thing to do. But he wanted to try it. Then he hit the buck and broke his neck. He felt awful about it. He felt awful about trying to crease it in the first place.'

'I know.'

'Then it must have been Evans found the meat where he had it hung up in the old Spring House. Anyway somebody took it.'

'Who could have told Evans?'

'I think it was just that boy of his found it. He trails around after Nick all the time. You never see him. He could have seen Nickie kill the buck. That boy's no good Mr. John. But he sure can trail around after anybody. He's liable to be in this room right now.'

'No,' said Mr. John. 'But he could be listening outside.'

'I think he's after Nick by now,' the girl said.

'Did you hear them say anything about him at the house?'

'They never mentioned him,' Suzy said.

'Evans must have left him home to do the chores. I don't think we have to worry about him till they get home to Evans's.'

'I can row up to the lake to home this afternoon and get one of our kids to let me know if Evans hires anyone to do the chores. That will mean he's turned that boy loose.'

'Both the men are too old to trail anybody.'

'But that boy's terrible, Mr. John, and he knows too much about Nickie and where he would go. He'd find them and then bring the men up to them.'

'Come in back of the Post Office,' Mr. John said.

Back of the filing slits and the lock-boxes and the registry book and the flat stamp books in place along with the cancellation stamps and their pads, with the General Delivery window down, so that Suzy felt again the glory of office that had been hers when she had helped out in the store Mr. John said, 'Where do you think they went Suzy?'

'I wouldn't know, true. Somewhere not too far or he wouldn't take Littless. Somewhere that's really good or he wouldn't take her. They know about the trout for trout dinners too Mr. John.'

'That boy?'

'Sure.'

'Maybe we better do something about the boy.'

'I'd kill him. I'm pretty sure that's why Littless went along. So Nickie wouldn't kill him.'

'You fix it up so we keep track of them.'

'I will. But you have to think out something Mr. John. Mrs. Adams she's just broke down. She just gets a sick headache like always. Here. You better take this letter.'

'You drop it in the box,' Mr. John said. 'That's United States Mail.'

'I wanted to kill them both last night when they were asleep.'

'No,' Mr. John told her. 'Don't talk that way and don't think that way.'

'Didn't you ever want to kill anybody Mr. John?'

'Yes. But it's wrong and it doesn't work out.'

'My father killed a man.'

'It didn't do him any good.'

'He couldn't help it.'

'You have to learn to help it,' Mr. John said. 'You get along now Suzy.'

'I'll see you tonight or in the morning,' Suzy said. 'I wish I still worked here Mr. John.'

'So do I, Suzy. But Mrs. Packard doesn't see it that way.'

'I know,' said Suzy. 'That's the way everything is.'

Nick and his sister were lying on a browse bed under a lean-to that they had built together in the edge of the hemlock forest looking out over the slope of the hill to the cedar swamp and the blue hills beyond.

'If it isn't comfortable, Littless, we can feather in some more balsam on that hemlock. We'll be tired tonight and this will do. But we can fix it up really good tomorrow.'

'It feels lovely,' his sister said. 'Lie loose and really feel it Nickie.'

'It's a pretty good camp,' Nick said. 'And it doesn't show. We'll only use little fires.'

'Would a fire show across to the hills?'

'It might,' Nick said. 'A fire shows a long way at night. But I'll stake out a blanket behind it. That way it won't show.'

'Nickie wouldn't it be nice if there wasn't anyone after us and we were just here for fun?'

'Don't start thinking that way so soon,' Nick said. 'We just started. Anyway if we were just here for fun we wouldn't be here.'

'I'm sorry Nickie.'

'You don't need to be,' Nick told her. 'Look, Littless, I'm going down to get a few trout for supper.'

'Can I come?'

'No. You stay here and take a rest. You had a tough day. You read a while or just lie quiet.'

'It was tough in the slashings wasn't it? I thought it was really hard. Did I do all right?'

'You did wonderfully and you were wonderful making camp. But you take it easy now.'

'I'll try to invent something for camp. Have we got a name for this camp?'

'Let's call it camp number one,' Nick said.

He went down the hill toward the creek and when he had come almost to the bank he stopped and cut himself a willow stick about four feet long and trimmed it, leaving the bark on. He could see the clear fast water of the stream. It was narrow and deep and the banks were mossy here before the stream entered the swamp. The dark clear water flowed fast and its rushing made bulges on the surface. Nick did not go close to it as he knew it flowed under the banks and he did not want to frighten a fish by walking on the bank. There must be quite a few up here in the open now, he thought. It's pretty late in the summer.

He took a coil of silk line out of a tobacco pouch he carried in the left breast pocket of his shirt and cut a length that was not quite as long as the willow stick and fastened it to the tip where he had notched it lightly. Then he fastened on a hook that he took from the pouch; put the pouch away, buttoned his pocket and then holding the shank of the hook he tested the pull of the line and the bend of the willow. He laid his rod down now and went back to where the trunk of a small birch tree dead for several years lay on its side in the grove of birches that bordered the cedars by the stream. He rolled the log over and found several earth worms under it. They were not big. But they were red and lively and he put them in a flat round tin with holes punched in the top that had once held Copenhagen snuff. He put some dirt over them and rolled the log back. This was the third year he had found bait at this same place and he had always replaced this log so that it was as he had found it.

Nobody knows how big this creek is, he thought. It picks up an awful volume of water in that bad swamp up above. Now he looked up the creek and down it and up the hill to the hemlock forest where the camp was. Then he walked to where he had left the pole with the line and the hook and baited the hook carefully and spat on it for good luck. Holding the pole and the line with the baited hook in his right hand he walked very carefully and gently toward the back of the narrow, heavy flowing stream.

It was so narrow here that his willow pole would have spanned it and as he came close to the bank he heard the turbulent rush of the water. He stopped by the bank, out of sight of anything in the stream, and took two lead shot, split down one side, out of the tobacco pouch and bent them on the line about a foot above the hook, clinching them with his teeth.

He swung the hook on which the two worms curled out over the water and dropped it gently in so that it sunk, swirling in the fast water, and he lowered the tip of the willow pole to let the current take the line and the baited hook under the bank. He felt the line straighten and a sudden heavy firmness. He swung up on the pole and it bent almost double in his hand. He felt the throbbing, jerking pull that did not yield as he pulled. Then it yielded rising in the water with the line, heavy wildness of movement in the narrow deep current and the trout was torn out of the water and flapping in the air sailed over Nick's shoulder and onto the bank behind him. Nick saw him shine in the sun and then he found him where he was tumbling in the ferns. He was strong and heavy in Nick's hands and he had a pleasant smell and Nick saw how dark his back was and how brilliant his spots were colored and how bright the edges of his fins were. They were white on the edge with a black line behind and then there was the lovely golden sunset colour of his belly. Nick held him in his right hand and he could just reach around him.

He's pretty big for the skillet, he thought. But I've hurt him and I have to kill him.

He knocked the trout's head sharply against the handle of his hunting knife and laid him against the trunk of a birch tree.

'Damn,' he said. 'He's a perfect size for Mrs. Packard and her trout dinners. But he's pretty big for Littless and me.'

I better go up stream and find a shallow and try to get a couple of small ones, he thought. Damn didn't he feel like something when I horsed him out though? They can talk all they want about playing them but people that have never horsed them out don't know what they can make you feel. What if it only lasts that long? It's the time when there's no give at all and then they start to come and what they do to you on the way up and into the air.

This is a strange creek, he thought. It's funny when you have to hunt for small ones.

He found his pole where he had thrown it. The hook was bent and he straightened it. Then he picked up the heavy fish and started up the stream.

There's one shallow, pebbly part just after she comes out of the upper swamp, he thought. I can get a couple of small ones there. Littless might not like this big one. If she gets homesick I'll have to take her back. I wonder what those old boys are doing now? I don't think that god-damn Evans kid knows about this place. That son of a bitch. I don't think anybody fished in here but Indians. You should have been an Indian, he thought. It would have saved you a lot of trouble.

He made his way up the creek keeping back from the stream but once stepping onto a piece of bank where the stream flowed under ground. A big trout broke out in a violence that made a slashing wake in the water. He was a trout so big that it hardly seemed he could turn in the stream.

'When did you come up?' Nick said when the fish had gone under the bank again further up-stream. 'Boy what a trout.'

At the pebbly shallow stretch he caught two small trout. They were beautiful fish too, firm and hard and he gutted the three fish and tossed the guts into the stream then washed the trout carefully in the cold water and then wrapped them in a small faded sugar sack from his pocket.

It's a good thing that girl likes fish, he thought. I wish we would have picked some berries. I know where I can always get some though. He started back up the hill slope toward their camp. The sun was down behind the hill and the weather was good. He looked out across the swamp and up in the sky above where the arm of the lake would be he saw a fish hawk flying.

He came up to the lean-to very quietly and his sister did not hear him. She was lying on her side reading. Seeing her he spoke softly not to startle her.

'What did you do, you monkey?'

She turned and looked at him and smiled and shook her head.

'I cut it off,' she said.

'How?'

'With a scissors. How did you think?'

'How did you see to do it?'

'I just held it out and cut it. It's easy. Do I look like a boy?'

'Like a wild boy of Borneo.'

'I couldn't cut it like a Sunday school boy. Does it look too wild?'

'No.'

'It's very exciting,' she said. 'Now I'm your sister but I'm a boy too. Do you think it will change me into a boy?'

'No.'

'I wish it would.'

'You're crazy, Littless.'

'Maybe I am. Do I look like an idiot boy?'

'A little.'

'You can make it neater. You can see to cut it with a comb.'

'I'll have to make it a little better but not much. Are you hungry, idiot brother?'

'Can't I just be an unidiot brother?'

'I don't want to trade you for a brother.'

'You have to now, Nickie don't you see? It was something we had to do. I should have asked you but I knew it was something we had to do so I said it for a surprise.'

'I like it,' Nick said. 'The hell with everything. I like it very much.'

'Thank you Nickie so much. I was laying trying to rest like you said. But all I could do was imagine things to do for you. I was going to get you a chewing tobacco can full of knock-out drops from some big saloon in some place like Sheboygan.'

'Who did you get them from?'

Nick was sitting down now and his sister sat on his lap and held her arms around his neck and rubbed her cropped head against his cheek.

'I got them from the Queen of the Whores,' she said. 'And you know the name of the saloon?'

'No.'

'The Royal Ten Dollar Gold Piece Inn and Emporium.'

'What did you do there?'

'I was a whore's assistant.'

'What's a whore's assistant do?'

'Oh she carries the whore's train when she walks and opens her carriage door and shows her to the right room. It's like a Lady in Waiting I guess.'

'What's she say to the whore?'

'She'll say anything that comes into her mind as long as it's polite.'

'Like what, brother?'

'Like, "Well ma'am it must be pretty tiring on a hot day like today to be just a bird in a gilded cage." Things like that.'

'What's the whore say?'

'She says, "Yes indeedy. It sure is sweetness." Because this whore I was the whore's assistant to is of humble origin.'

'What kind of origin are you?'

'I'm the sister or the brother of a morbid writer and I'm delicately brought up. This makes me intensely desirable to the main whore and to all of her circle.'

'Did you get the knock-out drops?'

'Of course. She said, "Hon take these little old Drops." Thank you I said. "Give my regards to your morbid brother and ask him to stop by the Emporium anytime he is at Sheboygan." '

'Get off my lap,' Nick said.

'That's just the way they talk in the Emporium,' Littless said. 'I have to get supper. Aren't you hungry?'

'I'll get supper.'

'No,' Nick said. 'You keep on talking.'

'Don't you think we're going to have fun Nickie?'

'We're having fun now.'

'Do you want me to tell you about the other thing I did for you?'

'You mean before you decided to do something practical and cut off your hair?'

'This was practical enough. Wait till you hear it. Can I kiss you while you're making supper?'

'Wait a while and I'll tell you. What was it you were going to do?'

'Well I guess I was ruined morally last night when I stole the whiskey. Do you think you can be ruined morally by just one thing like that?'

'No. Anyway the bottle was open.'

'Yes. But I took the empty pint bottle and the quart bottle with the whiskey in it out to the kitchen and I poured the pint bottle full and some spilled on my hand and I licked it off and I thought that probably ruined me morally.'

'How'd it taste?'

'Awfully strong and funny and a little sick making.'

'That wouldn't ruin you morally.'

'Well I'm glad because if I was ruined morally how could I exercise a good influence on you?'

'I don't know,' Nick said. 'What was it you were going to do?'

He had his fire made and the skillet resting on it and he was laying strips of bacon in the skillet. His sister was watching and she had her hands folded across her knees and he watched her unclasp her hands and put one arm down and lean on it and put her legs out straight. She was practicing being a boy.

'I've got to learn to put my hands right.'

'Keep them away from your head.'

'I know. It would be easy if there was some boy my own age to copy.'

'Copy me.'

'That would be natural, wouldn't it? You won't laugh though?'

'Maybe.'

'Gee I hope I won't start to be a girl while we're on the trip.'

'Don't worry.'

'We have the same shoulders and the same kind of legs.'

'What was the other thing you were going to do?'

Nick was cooking the trout now. The bacon was curled brown on a fresh cut chip of wood from the piece of fallen timber they were using for the fire fat. Nick basted them and then turned them and basted them again. It was getting dark and he had rigged a piece of canvas behind the little fire so that it would not be seen.

'What were you going to do?' he asked again. Littless leaned forward and spat toward the fire.

'How was that?'

'You missed the skillet anyway.'

'Oh it's pretty bad. I got it out of the Bible. I was going to take three spikes, one for each of them, and drive them into the temples of those two and that boy while they slept.'

'What were you going to drive them in with?'

'A muffled hammer.'

'How do you muffle a hammer?'

'I'd muffle it all right.'

'That nail thing's pretty rough to try.'

'Well that girl did it in the Bible and since I've seen armed men drunk and asleep and circulated among them at night and stolen their whiskey why shouldn't I go the whole way especially if I learned it in the Bible?'

'They didn't have a muffled hammer in the Bible.'

'I guess I mixed it up with muffled oars.'

'Maybe. And we don't want to kill anybody. That's why you came along.'

'I know. But crime comes easy for you and me Nickie. We're different from the others. Then I thought if I was ruined morally I might as well be useful.'

'You're crazy, Littless,' he said. 'Listen, does tea keep you awake?'

'I don't know. I never had it at night. Only peppermint tea.'

'I'll make it very weak and put canned cream in it.'

'I don't need it, Nickie, if we're short.'

'It will just give the milk a little taste.'

They were eating now. Nick had cut them each two slices of rye bread and he soaked one slice for each in the bacon fat in the skillet. They ate that and the trout that were crisp outside and cooked well and very tender inside. Then they put the trout skeletons in the fire and ate the bacon made in a sandwich with the other piece of bread and then Littless drank the weak tea with the condensed milk in it and Nick tapped two slivers of wood into the holes he had punched in the can.

'Did you have enough?'

'Plenty. The trout was wonderful and the bacon too. Weren't we lucky they had rye bread?'

'Eat an apple,' he said. 'Maybe we'll have something good tomorrow. Maybe I should have made a bigger supper Littless.'

'No. I had plenty.'

'You're sure you're not hungry?'

'No. I'm full. I've got some chocolate if you'd like some.'

'Where'd you get it?'

'From my saviour.'

'Where?'

'My saviour where I save everything.'

'Oh.'

'This is fresh. Some is the hard kind from the kitchen. We can start on that and save the other for special. Look my saviour's got a draw string like a tobacco pouch. We can use it for nuggets and things like that. Do you think we'll get out west Nickie on this trip?'

'I haven't got it figured yet.'

'I'd like to get my saviour packed full of nuggets worth sixteen dollars an ounce.'

Nick cleaned up the skillet and put the pack in at the head of the lean-to. The blanket was spread over the browse bed and he put the other one on it and tucked it under on Littless's side. He cleaned out the two quart tin pail he'd made tea in and filled it with cold water from the spring. When he came back from the spring his sister was in the bed asleep, her head on the pillow she had made by rolling her blue jeans around her moccasins. He kissed her but she did not wake and he put on his old mackinaw coat and felt in the pack sack until he found the pint bottle of whiskey.

He opened it and smelled it and it smelled very good. He dipped a half a cup of water out of the small pail he had brought from the spring and poured a little of the whiskey in it. Then he sat and sipped this very slowly letting it stay under his tongue before he brought it slowly back over his tongue and swallowed it.

He watched the small coals of the fire brighten with the light evening breeze and he tasted the whiskey and cold water and looked at the coals and thought. Then he finished the cup, dipped up some cold water and drank it and went to bed. The rifle was under his left leg and his head was on the good hard pillow his moccasins and the rolled trousers made and he pulled his side of the blanket tight around him and said his prayers and went to sleep.

In the night he was cold and he spread his mackinaw coat over his sister and rolled back over closer to her so that there was more of his side of the blanket under him. He felt for the gun and tucked it under his leg again. The air was cold and sharp to breathe and he smelled the cut hemlock and balsam boughs. He had not realized how tired he was until the cold had waked him. Now he lay comfortable again feeling the warmth of his sister's body against his back and he thought I must take good care of her and keep her happy and get her back safely. He listened to her breathing and to the quiet of the night and then he was asleep again.

It was just light enough to see the far hills beyond the swamp when he woke. He lay quietly and stretched the stiffness from his body then he sat up and pulled on his khaki trousers and put on his moccasins. He watched his sister sleeping with the collar of the warm mackinaw coat under her chin, and her high cheekbones and brown freckled skin light rose under the brown, her chopped off hair showing the beautiful line of her head and emphasizing her straight nose and her close set ears. He wished he could draw her face and he watched the way her long lashes lay on her cheeks.

She looks like a small wild animal, he thought, and she sleeps like one. How would you say her head looks? he thought. I guess the nearest is that it looks as though some one had cut her hair off on a wooden block with an ax. It has a sort of a carved look.

He loved his sister very much and she loved him too much. But, he thought, I guess those things straighten out. At least I hope so.

There's no sense waking anyone up, he thought. She must have been really tired if I'm as tired as I am. If we are all right here we are doing just what we should do; staying out of sight until things quiet down and that downstate man pulls out. I've got to feed her better though. It's a shame I couldn't have outfitted really good.

We've got a lot of things though. The pack was heavy enough. But what we want to get today is berries. I better get a partridge or a couple if I can. We can get good mushrooms too. We'll have to be careful about the bacon but we won't need it with the shortening. Maybe I fed her too light last night. She's used to lots of milk too and sweet things. Don't worry about it. We'll feed good. It's a good thing she likes trout. They were really good. Don't worry about her. She'll eat wonderfully. But Nick boy you certainly didn't feed her too much yesterday. Better to let her sleep than to wake her up now. There's plenty for you to do.

He started to get some things out of the pack very carefully and his sister smiled in her sleep. The brown skin came taut over her cheek bones when she smiled and the under colour showed. She did not wake and he started to prepare to make breakfast and get the fire ready. There was plenty of wood cut and he built a very small fire and made tea while he waited to start breakfast. He drank his tea straight and ate three dried apricots and he tried to read in Lorna Doone. But he had read it and it did not have magic any more and he knew it was a loss on this trip.

Late in the afternoon, when they had made camp, he had put some prunes in a tin pail to soak and he put them on the fire now to stew. In the pack he found the prepared buckwheat flour and he put it out with an enameled sauce pan and a tin cup to mix the flour with water to make a batter. He had the tin of vegetable shortening and he cut a piece off the top of an empty flour sack and wrapped it around a cut stick and tied it tight with a piece of fish line. Littless had brought four old flour sacks and he was proud of her.

He mixed the batter and put the skillet on the fire greasing it with the shortening which he spread with the cloth on the stick. First it made the skillet shine darkly then it sizzled and spat and he greased again and poured the batter smoothly and watched it bubble and then start to firm around the edges. He watched the rising and the forming of the texture and the gray colour of the cake. He loosened it from the pan with a fresh clean chip and flipped it and caught it, the beautiful browned side up; the other sizzling. He could feel its weight but see it growing in buoyancy in the skillet.

'Good morning,' his sister said. 'Did I sleep awfully late?'

'No, devil.'

She stood up with her shirt hanging down her brown legs.

'You've done everything.'

'No. I just started the cakes.'

'Doesn't that one smell wonderful? I'll go to the spring and wash and come and help.'

'Don't wash in the spring.'

'I'm not white man,' she said. She was gone behind the lean-to.

'Where did you leave the soap?' she asked.

'It's by the spring. There's an empty lard basket. Bring the butter will you. It's in the spring.'

'I'll be right back.'

There was a half a pound of butter and she brought it wrapped in the oiled paper in the empty lard bucket.

They ate the buckwheat cakes with butter and Log Cabin syrup out of a tin Log Cabin can. The top of the chimney unscrewed and the syrup poured from the chimney. They were both very hungry and the cakes were delicious with the butter melting on them and running down into the cut places with the syrup. They ate the prunes out of the tin cups and drank the juice. Then they drank tea from the same cups.

'Prunes taste like a celebration,' Littless said. 'Think of that. How did you sleep Nickie?'

'Good.'

'Thank you for putting the mackinaw on me. Wasn't it a lovely night though?'

'Yes. Did you sleep all night?'

'I'm still asleep. Nickie can we stay here always?'

'I don't think so. You'd grow up and have to get married.'

'I'm going to get married to you anyway. I want to be your common law wife. I read about it in the paper.'

'That's where you read about the Unwritten Law.'

'Sure. I'm going to be your common law wife under the Unwritten Law. Can't I Nickie?'

'No.'

'I will. I'll surprise you. All you have to do is live a certain time as man and wife. I'll get them to count this time now. It's just like Homesteading.'

'I won't let you file.'

'You can't help yourself. That's the Unwritten Law. I've thought it out lots of times. I'll get cards printed Mrs. Nick Adams, Cross Village, Michigan – Common Law Wife. I'll hand these out to a few people openly each year until the time's up.'

'I don't think it would work.'

'I've got another scheme. We'll have a couple of children while I'm a minor. Then you have to marry me under the Unwritten Law.'

'That's not the Unwritten Law.'

'I get mixed up on it.'

'Anyway nobody knows yet if it works.'

'It must,' she said. 'Mr. Thaw is counting on it.'

'Mr. Thaw might make a mistake.'

'Why Nickie Mr. Thaw practically invented the Unwritten Law.'

'I thought it was his lawyer.'

'Well Mr. Thaw put it in action anyway.'

'I don't like Mr. Thaw,' Nick Adams said.

'That's good. There's things about him I don't like either. But he certainly made the paper more interesting reading didn't he?'

'He gives the others something new to hate.'

'They hate Mr. Stanford White too.'

'I think they're jealous of both of them.'

'I believe that's true Nickie. Just like they're jealous of us.'

'Think anybody is jealous of us now?'

'Not right now maybe. Our mother will think we're fugitives from justice steeped in sin and iniquity. It's a good thing she doesn't know I got you that whiskey.'

'I tried it last night. It's very good.'

'Oh I'm glad. That's the first whiskey I ever stole anywhere. Isn't it wonderful that it's good? I didn't think anything about those people could be good.'

'I've got to think about them too much. Let's not talk about them,' Nick said.

'All right. What are we going to do today?'

'What would you like to do?'

'I'd like to go to Mr. John's store and get everything we need.'

'We can't do that.'

'I know it. What do you plan to really do?'

'We ought to get a partridge or some partridges. We've always got trout. But I don't want you to get tired of trout.'

'Were you ever tired of trout?'

'No. But they say people get tired of them.'

'I wouldn't get tired of them,' Littless said. 'You get tired of pike right away. But you never get tired of trout nor of perch. I know, Nickie. True.'

'You don't get tired of wall-eyed pike either,' Nick said. 'Only of shovel nose. Boy you sure get tired of them.'

'I don't like the pitch-fork bones,' his sister said. 'It's a fish that surfeits you.'

'We'll clean up here and I'll find a place to cache the shells and we'll make a trip for berries and try to get some birds.'

'I'll bring two lard pails and a couple of the sacks,' his sister said.

'Littless,' Nick said. 'You remember about going to the bath-room will you please?'

'Of course.'

'That's important.'

'I know it. You remember too.'

'I will.'

Nick went back into the timber and buried the carton of .22 Long Rifles and the loose boxes of .22 Shorts under the brown needled floor at the base of a big hemlock. He put back the packed needles he had cut with his knife and made a small cut as far up as he could reach on the heavy bark of the tree. He took a bearing on the tree and then came out onto the hillside and walked down to the lean-to.

It was a lovely morning now. The day was high and clear blue and no clouds had come yet. Nick was happy with his sister and he thought, No matter how this thing comes out we might as well have a good happy time. He had already learned there was only one day at a time and that it was always the day you were in. It would be today until it was tonight and tomorrow would be today again. This was the main thing he had learned so far.

Today was a good day and coming down to the camp with his rifle he was happy although their trouble was like a fish hook caught in his pocket that pricked him occasionally as he walked. They left the pack inside the lean-to. There were great odds against a bear bothering it in the daytime because any bear would be down below feeding on berries around the swamp. But Nick buried the bottle of whiskey up behind the spring. Littless was not back yet and Nick sat down on the log of the fallen tree they were using for firewood and checked his rifle. They were going after partridges so he pulled out the tube of the magazine and poured the long-rifle cartridges into his hand and then put them into a chamois pouch and filled the magazine with .22 shorts. They made less noise and would not tear the meat up if he could not get head shots.

He was all ready now and wanted to start. Where's that girl anyway? he thought. Then he thought, Don't get excited. You told her to take her time. Don't get nervous. But he was nervous and it made him angry at himself.

'Here I am,' his sister said. 'I'm sorry that I took so long. I went too far away I guess.'

'You're fine,' Nick said. 'Let's go. You have the pails?'

'Uh-huh and covers too.'

They started down across the hill to the creek. Nick looked carefully up the stream and along the hillside. His sister watched him. She had the pails in one of the sacks and carried it along over her shoulder by the other sack.

'Aren't you taking a pole Nickie?' she asked him.

'No. I'll cut one if we fish.'

He moved ahead of his sister holding the rifle in one hand keeping a little way away from the stream. He was hunting now.

'It's a strange creek,' his sister said.

'It's the biggest small stream I've ever known,' Nick told her.

'It's deep and scary for a little stream.'

'It keeps having new springs,' Nick said. 'And it digs under the bank and it digs down. It's awful cold water Littless. Feel it.'

'Gee,' she said. It was numbing cold.

'The sun warms it a little,' Nick said. 'But not much. We'll hunt along easy. There's a berry patch down below.'

They went along down the creek. Nick was studying the banks. He had seen a mink's track and shown it to his sister and they had seen tiny ruby crowned kinglets that were hunting insects and let the boy and girl come close as they moved sharply and delicately in the cedars. They had seen cedar wax wings so calm and gentle and distinguished moving in their lovely elegance with the magic wax touches on their wing coverts and their tails, and Littless had said, 'They're the most beautiful Nickie. There couldn't be more simple beautiful birds.'

'They're built like your face,' he said.

'No Nickie. Don't make fun. Cedar wax wings make me so proud and happy that I cry.'

'When they wheel and light and then move so proud and friendly and gently,' Nick said.

They had gone on and suddenly Nick had raised the rifle and shot before his sister could see what he was looking at. Then she heard the sound of a big bird tossing and beating its wings on the ground. She saw Nick pumping the gun and shoot twice more and each time she heard another pounding of wings in the willow brush. Then there was the whirring noise of wings as large brown birds burst out of the willows and one bird flew only a little way and lit in the willows and with its crested head on one side looked down bending the collar of feathers on his neck where the other birds were still thumping. The bird looking down from the red willow brush was beautiful, plump, heavy and looked so stupid with his head turned down and as Nick raised his rifle slowly his sister whispered, 'No, Nickie. Please no. We've got plenty.'

'All right,' Nick said. 'You want to take him?'

'No, Nickie. No.'

Nick went forward into the willows and picked up the three grouse and batted their heads against the butt of the rifle stock and laid them out on the moss.

His sister felt them, warm and full breasted and beautifully feathered.

'Wait till we eat them,' Nick said. He was very happy.

'I'm sorry for them now,' his sister said. 'They were enjoying the morning just like we were.'

She looked up at the grouse still in the tree.

'It does look a little silly still staring down,' she said.

'It's enjoying the morning just like we were,' Nick said. 'This time of year the Indians call them fool hens. After they've been hunted they get smart. They're not the real fool hens. These never get smart. They're willow grouse. These are ruffed grouse.'

'I hope we'll get smart,' his sister said. 'Tell him to go away Nickie.'

'You tell him.'

'Go away Partridge.'

The grouse did not move.

Nick raised the rifle and the grouse looked at him. Nick knew he could not shoot the bird without making his sister sad and he made a noise blowing out so his tongue rattled and lips shook like a grouse bursting from cover and the bird looked at him fascinated.

'We better not annoy him,' Nick said.

'I'm sorry, Nickie,' his sister said. 'He *is* stupid.'

'Wait till we eat them,' Nick told her. 'You'll see why we hunt them.'

'Are they out of season too?'

'Sure. But they are full grown and nobody but us would ever hunt them. I kill plenty of great horned owls and a great horned owl will kill a partridge every day if he can. They hunt all the time and they kill all the good birds.'

'He certainly could kill that one easy,' his sister said. 'I don't feel bad anymore. Do you want a bag to carry them in?'

'I'll draw them and then pack them in the bag with some ferns. It isn't so far to the berries now.'

They sat against one of the cedars and Nick opened the birds and took out their warm entrails and feeling the inside of the birds hot on his right hand he found the edible parts of the giblets and cleaned them and then washed them in the stream. When the birds were cleaned he smoothed their feathers and wrapped them in ferns and put them in the flour sack. He tied the mouth of the flour sack and two corners with a piece of fish line and slung it over his shoulder and then went back to the stream and dropped the entrails in and tossed some bright pieces of lung in to see the trout rise in the rapid heavy flow of the water.

'They'd make good bait but we don't need bait now,' he said. 'Our trout are all in the stream and we'll take them when we need them.'

'This stream would make us rich if it was near home,' his sister said.

'It would be fished out then. This is the last really wild stream there is except in another awful country to get to beyond the foot of the lake. I never brought anybody here to fish.'

'Who ever fishes it?'

'Nobody I know.'

'Is it a virgin stream?'

'No. Indians fish it. But they're gone now since they quit cutting hemlock bark and the camps closed down.'

'Does the Evans boy know?'

'Not him,' Nick said. But then he thought about it and it made him feel sick. He could see the Evans boy.

'What're you thinking Nickie?'

'I wasn't thinking.'

'You were thinking. You tell me. We're partners.'

'He might know,' Nick said. 'God damn it. He might know.'

'But you don't know that he knows.'

'No. That's the trouble. If I did I'd get out.'

'Maybe he's back at camp now,' his sister said.

'Don't talk that way. Do you want to bring him?'

'No,' she said. 'Please Nickie. I'm sorry I brought it up.'

'I'm not,' Nick said. 'I'm grateful. I knew it anyway. Only I'd stopped thinking about it. I have to think about things now the rest of my life.'

'You always thought about things.'

'Not like this.'

'Let's go down and get the berries anyway,' Littless said. 'There isn't anything we can do now to help is there?'

'No,' Nick said. 'We'll pick the berries and get back to camp.'

But Nick was trying to accept it now and think his way all the way through it. He must not get in a panic about it. Nothing had changed. Things were just as they were when he had decided to come here and let things blow over. The Evans boy could have followed him here before. But it was very unlikely. He could have followed him one time when he had gone in from the road through the Hodges place, but it was doubtful. Nobody had been fishing the stream. He could be sure of that. But the Evans boy did not care about fishing.

'All that bastard cares about is trailing me,' he said.

'I know it Nickie.'

'This is three times he's made us trouble.'

'I know it, Nickie. But don't you kill him.'

That's why she came along, Nick thought. That's why she's here. I can't do it while she's along.

'I know I mustn't kill him,' he said. 'There's nothing we can do now. Let's not talk about it.'

'As long as you don't kill him,' his sister said. 'There's nothing we can't get out of and nothing that won't blow over.'

'Let's get back to camp,' Nick said.

'Without the berries?'

'We'll get the berries another day.'

'Are you nervous Nickie?'

'Yes. I'm sorry.'

'But what good will we be back at camp?'

'We'll know quicker.'

'Can't we just go along the way we were going?'

'Not now. I'm not scared, Littless. And don't you be scared. But something's made me nervous.'

Nick had cut up away from the stream into the edge of the timber and they were walking in the shade of the trees. They would come onto the camp now from above.

From the timber they approached the camp carefully. Nick went ahead with the rifle. The camp had not been visited.

'You stay here,' Nick told his sister. 'I'm going to have a look beyond.' He left the sack with the birds and the berry pails with Littless and went well upstream. As soon as he was out of sight of his sister he changed the .22 shorts in the rifle for the long rifles. I won't kill him, he thought, but anyway it's the right thing to do. He made a careful search of the country. He saw no sign of anyone and he went down to the stream and then down stream and back up to the camp.

'I'm sorry I was nervous, Littless,' he said. 'We might as well have a good lunch and then we won't have to worry about a fire showing at night.'

'I'm worried now too,' she said.

'Don't you be worried. It's just like it was before.'

'But he drove us back from getting the berries without him even being here.'

'I know. But he's not been here. Maybe he's never even been to this creek ever. Maybe we'll never see him again.'

'He makes me scared Nickie worse when he's not here than when he's here.'

'I know. But there isn't any use being scared.'

'What are we going to do?'

'Well we better wait to cook until night.'

'Why did you change?'

'He won't be around here at night. He can't come through the swamp in the dark. We don't have to worry about him early in the morning and late in the evening nor in the dark. We'll have to be like the deer and only be out then. We'll lay up in the daytime.'

'Maybe he'll never come.'

'Sure. Maybe.'

'But I can stay though can't I?'

'I ought to get you home.'

'No. Please Nickie. Who's going to keep you from killing him then?'

'Listen, Littless, don't ever talk about killing and remember I never talked about killing. There isn't any killing nor ever going to be any.'

'True?'

'True.'

'I'm so glad.'

'Don't even be that. Nobody ever talked about it.'

'All right. I never thought about it nor spoke about it.'

'Me either.'

'Of course you didn't.'

'I never even thought about it.'

No, he thought. You never even thought about it. Only all day and all night. But you mustn't think about it in front of her because she can feel it because she is your sister and you love each other.

'Are you hungry Littless?'

'Not really.'

'Eat some of the hard chocolate and I'll get some fresh water from the spring.'

'I don't have to have anything.'

They looked across to where the big white clouds of the eleven o'clock breeze were coming up over the blue hills beyond the swamp. The sky was a high clear blue and the clouds came up white and detached themselves from behind the hills and moved high in the sky as the breeze freshened and the shadows of the clouds moved over the swamp and across the hillside. The wind blew in the trees now and was cool as they lay in the shade. The water from the spring was cold and fresh in the tin pail and the chocolate was not quite bitter but was hard and crunched as they chewed it.

'It's as good as the water in the spring where we were when we first saw them,' his sister said. 'It tastes even better after the chocolate.'

'We can cook if you're hungry.'

'I'm not if you're not.'

'I'm always hungry. I was a fool not to go on and get the berries.'

'No. You came back to find out.'

'Look, Littless. I know a place back by the slashing we came through where we can get berries. I'll cache everything and we can go in there through the timber all the way and pick a couple of pails full and then we'll have them ahead for tomorrow. It isn't a bad walk.'

'All right. But I'm fine.'

'Aren't you hungry?'

'No. Not at all now after the chocolate. I'd love to just stay and read. We had a nice walk when we were hunting.'

'All right,' Nick said. 'Are you tired from yesterday?'

'Maybe a little.'

'We'll take it easy. I'll read Wuthering Heights.'

'Is it too old to read out loud to me?'

'No.'

'Will you read it?'

'Sure.'

CROSSING THE MISSISSIPPI

The Kansas City train stopped at a siding just east of the Mississippi River and Nick looked out at the road that was half a foot deep with dust. There was nothing in sight but the road and a few dust-grayed trees. A wagon lurched along through the ruts, the driver slouching with the jolts of his spring seat and letting the reins hang slack on the horses' backs.

Nick looked at the wagon and wondered where it was going, whether the driver lived near the Mississippi and whether he ever went fishing. The wagon lurched out of sight up the road and Nick thought of the World Series game going on in New York. He thought of Happy Felsch's home run in the first game he had watched at the White Sox Park, Slim Solee swinging far forward, his knee nearly touching the ground and the white dot of the ball on its far trajectory toward the green fence at center field, Felsch, his head down, tearing for the stuffed white square at first base and then the exulting roar from the spectators as the ball landed in a knot of scrambling fans in the open bleachers.

As the train started and the dusty trees and brown road commenced to move past, the magazine vendor came swaying down the aisle.

'Got any dope on the Series?' Nick asked him.

'White Sox won the final game,' the news butcher answered, making his way down the aisle of the chair car with the sea-legs roll of a sailor. His answer gave Nick a comfortable glow. The White Sox had licked them. It was a fine feeling. Nick opened his Saturday Evening Post and commenced reading, occasionally looking out of the window to watch for any glimpse of the Mississippi. Crossing the Mississippi would be a big event he thought, and he wanted to enjoy every minute of it.

The scenery seemed to flow past in a stream of road, telegraph poles, occasional houses and flat brown fields. Nick had expected bluffs for the Mississippi shore but finally, after an endless seeming bayou had poured past the window, he could see out of the window the engine of the train curving out onto a long bridge above a broad, muddy brown stretch of water. Desolate hills were on the far side that Nick could now see and on the near side a flat mud bank. The river seemed to move solidly downstream, not to flow but to move like a solid, shifting lake, swirling a little where the abutments of the bridge jutted out. Mark Twain, Huck Finn, Tom Sawyer, and LaSalle crowded each other in Nick's mind as he looked up the flat, brown plain of slow-moving water. Anyhow I've seen the Mississippi, he thought happily to himself.

NIGHT BEFORE LANDING

Walking around the deck in the dark Nick passed the Polish officers sitting in a row of deck chairs. Someone was playing the mandolin. Leon Chocianowicz put out his foot in the dark.

'Hey, Nick,' he said, 'where you going?'

'Nowhere. Just walking.'

'Sit here. There's a chair.'

Nick sat in the empty chair and looked out at the men passing against the light from the sea. It was a warm night in June. Nick leaned back in the chair.

'Tomorrow we get in,' Leon said. 'I heard it from the wireless man.'

'I heard it from the barber,' Nick said.

Leon laughed and spoke in Polish to the man in the next deck chair. He leaned forward and smiled at Nick.

'He doesn't speak English,' Leon said. 'He says he heard it from Gaby.'

'Where's Gaby?'

'Up in a lifeboat with somebody.'

'Where's Galinski?'

'Maybe with Gaby.'

'No,' said Nick. 'She told me she couldn't stand him.'

Gaby was the only girl on the boat. She had blonde hair which was always coming down, a loud laugh, a good body, and a bad odor of some sort. An aunt, who had not left her cabin since the boat sailed, was taking her back to her family in Paris. Her father had something to do with the French Line and she dined at the captain's table.

'Why doesn't she like Galinski?' Leon asked.

'She said he looked like a porpoise.'

Leon laughed again. 'Come on,' he said, 'let's go find him and tell him.'

They stood up and walked over to the rail. Overhead the lifeboats were swung out ready to be lowered. The ship was listed, the decks slanted and the lifeboats hung slanted and widely swinging. The water slipped softly, great patches of phosphorescent kelp churned out and sucked and bubbled under.

'She makes good time,' Nick said, looking down at the water.

'We're in the Bay of Biscay,' Leon said. 'Tomorrow we ought to see the land.'

They walked around the deck and down a ladder back to the stern to watch the wake phosphorescent and turning like plowed land in perspective. Above them was the gun platform with two sailors walking up and down beside the gun black against the faint glow from the water.

'They're zigzagging,' Leon watched the wake.

'All day.'

'They say these boats carry the German mails and that's why they're never sunk.'

'Maybe,' said Nick. 'I don't believe it.'

'I don't either. But it's a nice idea. Let's go find Galinski.'

They found Galinski in his cabin with a bottle of cognac. He was drinking out of a tooth mug.

'Hello, Anton.'

'Hello, Nick. Hello, Leon. Haff a drink.'

'You tell him, Nick.'

'Listen, Anton. We've got a message for you from a beautiful lady.'

'I know your beautiful lady. You take that beautiful lady and stick her up a funnel.'

Lying on his back he put his feet against the springs and mattress of the upper berth and pushed.

'Carper!' he shouted. 'Hey, Carper! Wake up and drink.'

Over the edge of the upper bunk looked a face. It was a round face with steel-rimmed spectacles.

'Don't ask me to drink when I'm drunk.'

'Come on down and drink,' Galinski bellowed.

'No,' from the upper berth. 'Give me the liquor up here.'

He had rolled over against the wall again.

'He's been drunk for two weeks,' Galinski said.

'I'm sorry,' came the voice from the upper berth. 'That can't be an accurate statement because I only met you ten days ago.'

'Haven't you been drunk for two weeks, Carper,' Nick said.

'Of course,' the Carper said, talking to the wall. 'But Galinski has no right to say so.'

Galinski jogged him up and down by pushing with his feet.

'I take it back, Carper,' he said. 'I don't think you're drunk.'

'Don't make ridiculous statements,' the Carper said faintly.

'What are you doing, Anton,' Leon asked.

'Thinking about my girl in Niagara Falls.'

'Come on, Nick,' said Leon. 'We'll leave this porpoise.'

'Did she tell you I was a porpoise?' Galinski asked. 'She told me I was a porpoise. You know what I said to her in French. "Mademoiselle Gaby, you have got nothing that has any interest for me." Take a drink, Nick.'

He reached out the bottle and Nick swallowed some of the brandy.

'Leon?'

'No. Come on, Nick. We'll leave him.'

'I go on duty with the men at midnight,' Galinski said.

'Don't get drunk,' Nick said.

'I have never been drunk.'

In the upper bunk the Carper muttered something.

'What you say, Carper?'

'I was calling on God to strike him.'

'I have neffer been drunk,' Galinski repeated and poured the tooth mug half full of cognac.

'Go on, God,' the Carper said. 'Strike him.'

'I have neffer been drunk. I have neffer slept with a woman.'

'Come on. Do your stuff, God. Strike him.'

'Come on, Nick. Let's get out.'

Galinski handed the bottle to Nick. He took a swallow and followed the tall Pole out.

Outside the door they heard Galinski's voice shouting, 'I have neffer been drunk. I have neffer slept with a woman. I have neffer told a lie.'

'Strike him,' came the Carper's thin voice. 'Don't take that stuff from him, God. Strike him.'

'They're a fine pair,' Nick said.

'What about this Carper? Where does he come from?'

'He was two years in the ambulance before. They sent him home. He got fired out of college and now he's going back.'

'He drinks too much.'

'He isn't happy.'

'Let's get a bottle of wine and sleep out in a lifeboat.'

'Come on.'

They stopped at the smoking room bar and Nick bought a bottle of red wine. Leon stood at the bar, tall in his French uniform. Inside the smoking room two big poker games were going on. Nick would have liked to play but not on the last night. Everybody was playing. It was smoky and hot with all the port-holes closed and shuttered. Nick looked at Leon. 'Want to play?'

'No. Let's drink the wine and talk.'

'Let's get two bottles then.'

They went out of the hot room onto the deck carrying the bottles. It was not hard to climb out onto one of the lifeboats although it scared Nick to look down at the water as he climbed out on the davits. Inside the boat they made themselves comfortable with life belts to lie back against the thwarts. There was a feeling of being between the sea and the sky. It was not like being on the throbbing of the big boat.

'This is good,' said Nick.

'I sleep in one of these every night.'

'I'd be afraid I'd walk in my sleep,' Nick said. He was uncorking the wine. 'I sleep on the deck.'

He handed the bottle to Leon. 'Keep this and open the other bottle for me,' the Pole said.

'You take it,' Nick said. He drew the cork from the second bottle and clinked it across the dark with Leon. They drank.

'You'll get better wine than this in France,' Leon said.

'I won't be in France.'

'I forgot. I wish we were going to soldier together.'

'I wouldn't be any good,' Nick said. He looked over the gunwale of the boat at the dark water below. He had been frightened coming out on the davits.

'I wonder if I'll be scared,' he said.

'No,' Leon said. 'I don't think so.'

'It will be fun to see all the planes and that stuff.'

'Yes,' said Leon. 'I am going to fly as soon as I can transfer.'

'I couldn't do that.'

'Why not?'

'I don't know.'

'You mustn't think about being scared.'

'I don't. Really I don't. I never worry about it. I just thought because it made me feel funny coming out onto the boat just now.'

Leon lay on his side, the bottle straight up beside his head.

'We don't have to think about being scared,' he said. 'We're not that kind.'

'The Carper's scared,' Nick said.

'Yes. Galinski told me.'

'That's what he was sent back for. That's why he's drunk all the time.'

'He's not like us,' Leon said. 'Listen, Nick. You and me, we've got something in us.'

'I know. I feel that way. Other people can get killed but not me. I feel that absolutely.'

'That's it. That's what we've got.'

'I wanted to get into the Canadian army but they wouldn't take me.'

'I know. You told me.'

They both drank. Nick lay back and looked at the cloud of smoke from the funnel against the sky. The sky was beginning to lighten. Maybe the moon was going to come up.

'Have you got a girl, Leon?'

'No.'

'None at all?'

'No.'

'I got one,' Nick said.

'You live with her?'

'We're engaged.'

'I never slept with a girl.'

'I've been with them in houses.'

Leon took a drink. The bottle angled blackly from his mouth against the sky.

'That isn't what I mean. I done that. I don't like it. I mean sleep all night with one you love.'

'My girl would have slept with me.'

'Sure. If she loved you she'd sleep with you.'

'We're going to get married.'

SUMMER PEOPLE

Halfway down the gravel road from Hortons Bay, the town, to the lake there was a spring. The water came up in a tile sunk beside the road, lipping over the cracked edge of the tile and flowing away through the close-growing mint into the swamp. In the dark Nick put his arm down into the spring but could not hold it there because of the cold. He felt the featherings of the sand spouting up from the spring cones at the bottom against his fingers. Nick thought, I wish I could put all of myself in there. I bet that would fix me. He pulled his arm out and sat down at the edge of the road. It was a hot night.

Down the road through the trees he could see the white of the Bean house on its piles over the water. He did not want to go down to the dock. Everybody was down there swimming. He did not want Kate with Odgar around. He could see the car on the road beside the warehouse. Odgar and Kate were down there. Odgar with that fried-fish look in his eye every time he looked at Kate. Didn't Odgar know anything? Kate wouldn't ever marry him. She wouldn't ever marry anybody that didn't make her. And if they tried to make her she would curl up inside of herself and be hard and slip away. He could make her do it all right. Instead of curling up hard and slipping away she would open out smoothly, relaxing, untightening, easy to hold. Odgar thought it was love that did it. His eyes got walleyed and red at the edges of the lids. She couldn't bear to have him touch her. It was all in his eyes. Then Odgar would want them to be just the same friends as ever. Play in the sand. Make mud images. Take all-day trips in the boat together. Kate always in her bathing suit. Odgar looking at her.

Odgar was thirty-two and had been twice operated on for varicocele. He was ugly to look at and everybody liked his face. Odgar could never get it and it meant everything in the world to him. Every summer he was worse about it. It was pitiful. Odgar was awfully nice. He had been nicer to Nick than anybody ever had. Now Nick could get it if he wanted it. Odgar would kill himself, Nick thought, if he knew it. I wonder how he'd kill himself. He couldn't think of Odgar dead. He probably wouldn't do it. Still people did. It wasn't just love. Odgar thought just love would do it. Odgar loved her

enough, Godnose. It was liking, and liking the body, and intro-
ducing the body, and persuading, and taking chances, and never
frightening, and assuming about the other person, and always
taking never asking, and gentleness and liking, and making liking and happiness, and joking and making people not afraid. And
making it all right afterwards. It wasn't loving. Loving was
frightening. He, Nicholas Adans, could have what he wanted
because of something in him. Maybe it did not last. Maybe he
would lose it. He wished he could give it to Odgar, or tell Odgar
about it. You couldn't ever tell anybody about anything.
Especially Odgar. No, not especially Odgar. Anybody, anywhere. That had always been his first mistake, talking. He had
talked himself out of too many things. There ought to be something you could do for the Princeton, Yale and Harvard virgins,
though. Why weren't there any virgins in state universities?
Coeducation maybe. They met girls who were out to marry and
the girls helped them along and married them. What would
become of fellows like Odgar and Harvey and Mike and all the
rest? He didn't know. He hadn't lived long enough. They were
the best people in the world. What became of them? How the
hell could he know. How could he write like Hardy and
Hamsun when he only knew ten years of life. He couldn't. Wait
till he was fifty.

In the dark he kneeled down and took a drink from the spring.
He felt all right. He knew he was going to be a great writer. He
knew things and they couldn't touch him. Nobody could. Only
he did not know enough things. That would come all right. He
knew. The water was cold and made his eyes ache. He had swallowed too big a gulp. Like ice cream. That's the way with drinking with your nose underwater. He'd better go swimming.
Thinking was no good. It started and went on so. He walked
down the road, past the car and the big warehouse on the left
where apples and potatoes were loaded onto the boats in the fall,
past the white-painted Bean house where they danced by lantern light sometimes on the hardwood floor, out on the dock to
where they were swimming.

They were all swimming off the end of the dock. As Nick
walked along the rough boards high above the water he heard
the double protest of the long springboard and a splash. The
water lapped below in the piles. That must be the Ghee, he
thought. Kate came up out of the water like a seal and pulled
herself up the ladder.

'It's Wemedge,' she shouted to the others. 'Come on in, Wemedge. It's wonderful.'

'Hi, Wemedge,' said Odgar. 'Boy it's great.'

'Where's Wemedge?' It was the Ghee, swimming far out.

'Is this man Wemedge a nonswimmer?' Bill's voice very deep and bass over the water.

Nick felt good. It was fun to have people yell at you like that. He scuffed off his canvas shoes, pulled his shirt over his head and stepped out of his trousers. His bare feet felt the sandy planks of the dock. He ran very quickly out the yielding plank of the springboard, his toes shoved against the end of the board, he tightened and he was in the water, smoothly and deeply, with no consciousness of the dive. He had breathed in deeply as he took off and now went on and on through the water, holding his back arched, feet straight and trailing. Then he was on the surface, floating face down. He rolled over and opened his eyes. He did not care anything about swimming, only to dive and be under-water.

'How is it, Wemedge?' The Ghee was just behind him.

'Warm as piss,' Nick said.

He took a deep breath, took hold of his ankles with his hands, his knees under his chin, and sank slowly down into the water. It was warm at the top but he dropped quickly into cool, then cold. As he neared the bottom it was quite cold. Nick floated down gently against the bottom. It was marly and his toes hated it as he uncurled and shoved hard against it to come up to the air. It was strange coming up from underwater into the dark. Nick rested in the water, barely paddling and comfortable. Odgar and Kate were talking together up on the dock.

'Have you ever swum in a sea where it was phosphorescent, Carl?'

'No.' Odgar's voice was unnatural talking to Kate.

We might rub ourselves all over with matches, Nick thought. He took a deep breath, drew his knees up, clasped tight and sank, this time with his eyes open. He sank gently, first going off to one side, then sinking head first. It was no good. He could not see underwater in the dark. He was right to keep his eyes shut when he first dove in. It was funny about reactions like that. They weren't always right, though. He did not go all the way down but straightened out and swam along and up through the cool, keeping just below the warm surface water. It was funny how much fun it was to swim underwater and how little fun there was in plain swimming. It was fun to swim on the surface in the ocean. That was the buoyancy. But the taste of the brine and the way it made you thirsty. Fresh water was better. Just like this on a hot night. He came up for air just under the projecting edge of the dock and climbed up the ladder.

'Oh, dive, Wemedge, will you?' Kate said. 'Do a good dive.' They were sitting together on the dock leaning back against one of the big piles.

'Do a noiseless one, Wemedge,' Odgar said.

'All right.'

Nick, dripping, walked out on the springboard, remembering how to do the dive. Odgar and Kate watched him, black in the dark, standing at the end of the board, poise and dive as he had learned from watching a sea otter. In the water as he turned to come up to the air Nick thought, Gosh, if I could only have Kate down here. He came up in a rush to the surface, feeling water in his eyes and ears. He must have started to take a breath.

'It was perfect. Absolutely perfect,' Kate shouted from the dock.

Nick came up the ladder.

'Where are the men?' he asked.

'They're swimming way out in the bay,' Odgar said.

Nick lay down on the dock beside Kate and Odgar. He could hear the Ghee and Bill swimming way out in the dark.

'You're the most wonderful diver, Wemedge,' Kate said, touching his back with her foot. Nick tightened under the contact.

'No,' he said.

'You're a wonder, Wemedge,' Odgar said.

'Nope,' Nick said. He was thinking, thinking if it was possible to be with somebody underwater, he could hold his breath three minutes, against the sand on the bottom, they could float up together, take a breath and go down, it was easy to sink if you knew how. He had once drunk a bottle of milk and peeled and eaten a banana underwater to show off, had to have weights, though, to hold him down, if there was a ring at the bottom, something he could get his arm through, he could do it all right. Gee, how it would be, you couldn't ever get a girl though, a girl couldn't go through with it, she'd swallow water, it would drown Kate, Kate wasn't really any good underwater, he wished there was a girl like that, maybe he'd get a girl like that, probably never, there wasn't anybody but him that was that way underwater. Swimmers, hell, swimmers were slobs, nobody knew about the water but him, there was a fellow up at Evanston that could hold his breath six minutes but he was crazy. He wished he was a fish, no he didn't. He laughed.

'What's the joke, Wemedge?' Odgar said in his husky, near-to-Kate voice.

'I wished I was a fish,' Nick said.

'That's a good joke,' said Odgar.

'Sure,' said Nick.

'Don't be an ass, Wemedge,' said Kate.

'Would you like to be a fish, Butstein?' he said, lying with his head on the planks, facing away from them.

'No,' said Kate. 'Not tonight.'

Nick pressed his back hard against her foot.

'What animal would you like to be, Odgar?' Nick said.

'J. P. Morgan,' Odgar said.

'You're nice, Odgar,' Kate said. Nick felt Odgar glow.

'I'd like to be Wemedge,' Kate said.

'You could always be Mrs. Wemedge,' Odgar said.

'There isn't going to be any Mrs. Wemedge,' Nick said. He tightened his back muscles. Kate had both her legs stretched out against his back as though she were resting them on a log in front of a fire.

'Don't be too sure,' Odgar said.

'I'm awful sure,' Nick said. 'I'm going to marry a mermaid.'

'She'd be Mrs. Wemedge,' Kate said.

'No she wouldn't,' Nick said. 'I wouldn't let her.'

'How would you stop her?'

'I'd stop her all right. Just let her try it.'

'Mermaids don't marry,' Kate said.

'That'd be all right with me,' Nick said.

'The Mann Act would get you,' said Odgar.

'We'd stay outside the four-mile limit,' Nick said. 'We'd get food from the rumrunners. You could get a diving suit and come and visit us, Odgar. Bring Butstein if she wants to come. We'll be at home every Thursday afternoon.'

'What are we going to do tomorrow?' Odgar said, his voice becoming husky, near to Kate again.

'Oh, hell, let's not talk about tomorrow,' Nick said. 'Let's talk about my mermaid.'

'We're through with your mermaid.'

ERNEST HEMINGWAY

'All right,' Nick said. 'You and Odgar go and talk. I'm going to think about her.'

'You're immoral, Wemedge. You're disgustingly immoral.'

'No, I'm not. I'm honest.' Then, lying with his eyes shut, he said, 'Don't bother me. I'm thinking about her.'

He lay there thinking of his mermaid while Kate's insteps pressed against his back and she and Odgar talked.

Odgar and Kate talked but he did not hear them. He lay, no longer thinking, quite happy.

Bill and the Ghee had come out of the water farther down the shore, walked down the beach up to the car and then backed it out onto the dock. Nick stood up and put on his clothes. Bill and the Ghee were in the front seat, tired from the long swim. Nick got in behind with Kate and Odgar. They leaned back. Bill drove roaring up the hill and turned onto the main road. On the main highway Nick could see the lights of other cars up ahead, going out of sight, then blinding as they mounted a hill, blinking as they came near, then dimmed as Bill passed. The road was high along the shore of the lake. Big cars out from Charlevoix, rich Jews riding behind their chauffeurs, came up and passed, hogging the road and not dimming their lights. They passed like railway trains. Bill flashed the spotlights on cars alongside the road in the trees, making the occupants change their positions. Nobody passed Bill from behind, although a spotlight played on the back of their heads for some time until Bill drew away. Bill slowed, then turned abruptly onto the sandy road that ran up through the orchard to the farmhouse. The car, in low gear, moved steadily up through the orchard. Kate put her lips to Nick's ear.

'In about an hour, Wemedge,' she said. Nick pressed his thigh hard against hers. The car circled at the top of the hill above the orchard and stopped in front of the house.

'Aunty's asleep. We've got to be quiet,' Kate said.

'Good night, men,' Bill whispered. 'We'll stop by in the morning.'

'Good night, Smith,' whispered the Ghee. 'Good night, Butstein.'

'Good night, Ghee,' Kate said.

Odgar was staying at the house.

'Good night, men,' Nick said. 'See you, Morgen.'

'Night, Wemedge,' Odgar said from the porch.

Nick and the Ghee walked down the road into the orchard.

Nick reached up and took an apple from one of the Duchess trees. It was still green but he sucked the acid juice from the bite and spat out the pulp.

'You and the Bird took a long swim, Ghee,' he said.

'Not so long, Wemedge,' the Ghee answered.

They came out from the orchard past the mailbox onto the hard state highway. There was a cold mist in the hollow where the road crossed the creek. Nick stopped on the bridge.

'Come on, Wemedge,' the Ghee said.

'All right,' Nick agreed.

They went on up the hill to where the road turned into the grove of trees around the church. There were no lights in any of the houses they passed. Hortons Bay was asleep. No motor cars had passed them.

'I don't feel like turning in yet,' Nick said.

'Want me to walk with you?'

'No, Ghee. Don't bother.'

'All right.'

'I'll walk up as far as the cottage with you,' Nick said. They unhooked the screen door and went into the kitchen. Nick opened the meat safe and looked around.

'Want some of this, Ghee?' he said.

'I want a piece of pie,' the Ghee said.

'So do I,' Nick said. He wrapped up some fried chicken and two pieces of cherry pie in oiled paper from the top of the icebox.

'I'll take this with me,' he said. The Ghee washed down his pie with a dipper full of water from the bucket.

'If you want anything to read, Ghee, get it out of my room,' Nick said. The Ghee had been looking at the lunch Nick had wrapped up.

'Don't be a damn fool, Wemedge,' he said.

'That's all right, Ghee.'

'All right. Only don't be a damn fool,' the Ghee said. He opened the screen door and went out across the grass to the cottage. Nick turned off the light and went out, hooking the screen door shut. He had the lunch wrapped up in a newspaper and crossed the wet grass, climbed the fence and went up the road through the town under the big elm trees, past the last cluster of R.F.D. mailboxes at the crossroads and out onto the Charlevoix highway. After crossing the creek he cut across a field, skirted the edge of the orchard, keeping to the edge of the

clearing, and climbed the rail fence into the wood lot. In the
center of the wood lot four hemlock trees grew close together.
The ground was soft with pine needles and there was no dew.
The wood lot had never been cut over and the forest floor was
dry and warm without underbrush. Nick put the package of
lunch by the base of one of the hemlocks and lay down to wait.
He saw Kate coming through the trees in the dark but did not
move. She did not see him and stood a moment, holding the
two blankets in her arms. In the dark it looked like some enormous pregnancy. Nick was shocked. Then it was funny.

'Hello, Butstein,' he said. She dropped the blankets.

'Oh, Wemedge. You shouldn't have frightened me like that.
I was afraid you hadn't come.'

'Dear Butstein,' Nick said. He held her close against him, feeling her body against his, all the sweet body against his body. She
pressed close against him.

'I love you so, Wemedge.'

'Dear, dear old Butstein,' Nick said.

They spread the blankets, Kate smoothing them flat.

'It was awfully dangerous to bring the blankets,' Kate said.

'I know,' Nick said. 'Let's undress.'

'Oh, Wemedge.'

'It's more fun.' They undressed sitting on the blankets. Nick
was a little embarrassed to sit there like that.

'Do you like me with my clothes off, Wemedge?'

'Gee, let's get under,' Nick said. They lay between the rough
blankets.* He was hot against her cool body, hunting for it, then
it was all right.

'Is it all right?'

Kate pressed all the way up for answer.

'Is it fun?'

'Oh, Wemedge. I've wanted it so. I've needed it so.'

They lay together in the blankets. Wemedge slid his head
down, his nose touching along the line of the neck, down between her breasts. It was like piano keys.

'You smell so cool,' he said.

He touched one of her small breasts with his lips gently. It
came alive between his lips, his tongue pressing against it. He felt
the whole feeling coming back again and, sliding his hands
down, moved Kate over. He slid down and she fitted close in

*The following passage appears to have been deleted by Hemingway

against him. She pressed tight in against the curve of his abdomen. She felt wonderful there. He searched, a little awkwardly, then found it. He put both hands over her breasts and held her to him. Nick kissed hard against her back. Kate's head dropped forward.

'Is it good this way?' he said.

'I love it. I love it. I love it. Oh, come, Wemedge. Please come. Come, come. Please, Wemedge. Please, please, Wemedge.'†

'There it is,' Nick said.

He was suddenly conscious of the blanket rough against his bare body.

'Was I bad, Wemedge?' Kate said.

'No, you were good,' Nick said. His mind was working very hard and clear. He saw everything very sharp and clear. 'I'm hungry,' he said.

'I wish we could sleep here all night.' Kate cuddled against him.

'It would be swell,' Nick said. 'But we can't. You've got to get back to the house.'

'I don't want to go,' Kate said.

Nick stood up, a little wind blowing on his body. He pulled on his shirt and was glad to have it on. He put on his trousers and shoes.

'You've got to get dressed, Stut,' he said. She lay there, the blankets pulled over her head.

'Just a minute,' she said. Nick got the lunch from over the hemlock. He opened it up.

'Come on, get dressed, Stut,' he said.

'I don't want to,' Kate said. 'I'm going to sleep here all night.' She sat up in the blankets. 'Hand me those things, Wemedge.'

Nick gave her the clothes.

'I've just thought of it,' Kate said. 'If I sleep out here they'll just think that I'm an idiot and came out here with the blankets and it will be all right.'

'You won't be comfortable,' Nick said.

'If I'm uncomfortable I'll go in.'

'Let's eat before I have to go,' Nick said.

'I'll put something on,' Kate said.

They sat together and ate the fried chicken and each ate a piece of cherry pie.

† deletion ends

Nick stood up, then kneeled down and kissed Kate.

'Good night, Stut,' he said.

'Good night, Wemedge,' she said and kissed him. 'Didn't we have fun?' Her eyes shone in the dark.

'Gee,' said Wemedge. Then, 'I wish I didn't have to go.'

'Go on,' said Kate. 'Before anything more happens.'

'Oh Stut,' Wemedge said. 'You're the only one.'

Kate crept down into the blankets. 'I'm all right,' she said.

Nick went off through the woods, avoiding the clearing and the orchard, down to the road. He was glowing, but coming through the mist by the creek bottom it died down. He was very sleepy coming up the hill. It was an effort getting up the last part.

He came through the wet grass to the cottage and upstairs to his room, walking carefully not to creak. It was good to be in bed, sheets, stretching out full length, digging his head in the pillow. Good in bed, comfortable, happy, fishing tomorrow, he prayed as he always prayed when he remembered it, for the family, himself, to be a great writer, Kate, the men, Odgar, for good fishing, poor old Odgar, poor old Odgar, sleeping up there at the cottage, maybe not fishing, maybe not sleeping all night. Still there wasn't anything you could do, not a thing.

WEDDING DAY

He had been in swimming and was washing his feet in the wash bowl after having walked up the hill. The room was hot and Dutch and Luman were both standing around looking nervous. Nick got a clean suit of underwear, clean silk socks, new garters, a white shirt and collar out from the drawer of the bureau and put them on. He stood in front of the mirror and tied his tie. Dutch and Luman reminded him of dressing rooms before fights and football games. He enjoyed their nervousness. He wondered if it would be this way if he were going to be hanged. Probably. He could never realize anything until it happened. Dutch went out for a corkscrew and came in and opened the bottle.

'Take a good shot, Dutch.'

'After you, Stein.'

'No. What the hell. Go on and drink.'

Dutch took a good long pull. Nick resented the length of it. After all, that was the only bottle of whiskey there was. Dutch passed the bottle to him. He handed it to Luman. Luman took a shot not quite as long as Dutch's.

'All right, Stein, old kid.' He handed the bottle to Nick.

Nick took a couple of swallows. He loved whiskey. Nick pulled on his trousers. He wasn't thinking at all. Horny Bill, Art Meyer and the Ghee were dressing upstairs. They ought to have liquor. Christ, why wasn't there any more than one bottle.

After the wedding was over they got into John Kotesky's Ford and drove over the hill road to the lake. Nick paid John Kotesky five dollars and Kotesky helped him carry the bags down to the rowboat. They both shook hands with Kotesky and then his Ford went back up along the road. They could hear it for a long time. Nick could not find the oars where his father had hidden them for him in the plum trees back of the ice house and Helen waited for him down at the boat. Finally he found them and carried them down to the shore.

It was a long row across the lake in the dark. The night was hot and depressing. Neither of them talked much. A few people had spoiled the wedding. Nick rowed hard when they were near shore and shot the boat up on the sandy beach. He pulled it up and Helen stepped out. Nick kissed her. She kissed him back hard the way he had taught her with her mouth a little open so their tongues could play with each other. They held tight to each other and then walked up to the cottage. It was dark and long. Nick unlocked the door and then went back to the boat to get the bags. He lit the lamps and they looked through the cottage together.

ON WRITING

It was getting hot, the sun hot on the back of his neck.

Nick had one good trout. He did not care about getting many trout. Now the stream was shallow and wide. There were trees along both banks. The trees of the left bank made short shadows on the current in the forenoon sun. Nick knew there were trout in each shadow. He and Bill Smith had discovered that on the Black River one hot day. In the afternoon, after the sun had crossed toward the hills, the trout would be in the cool shadows on the other side of the stream.

The very biggest ones would lie up close to the bank. You could always pick them up there on the Black. Bill and he had discovered it. When the sun was down they all moved out into the current. Just when the sun made the water blinding in the glare before it went down you were liable to strike a big trout anywhere in the current. It was almost impossible to fish then, the surface of the water was blinding as a mirror in the sun. Of course you could fish upstream, but in a stream like the Black or this you had to wallow against the current and in a deep place the water piled up on you. It was no fun to fish upstream although all the books said it was the only way.

All the books. He and Bill had fun with the books in the old days. They all started with a fake premise. Like fox hunting. Bill Bird's dentist in Paris said, in fly fishing you pit your intelligence against that of the fish. That's the way I'd always thought of it, Ezra said. That was good for a laugh. There were so many things good for a laugh. In the States they thought bullfighting was a joke. Ezra thought fishing was a joke. Lots of people think poetry is a joke. Englishmen are a joke.

Remember when they pushed us over the *barrera* in front of the bull at Pamplona because they thought we were Frenchmen? Bill's dentist is as bad the other way about fishing. Bill Bird, that is. Once Bill meant Bill Smith. Now it means Bill Bird. Bill Bird was in Paris now.

When he married he lost Bill Smith, Odgar, the Ghee, all the old gang. Was it because they were virgins? The Ghee certainly was not. No, he lost them because he admitted by marrying that something was more important than the fishing.

He had built it all up. Bill had never fished before they met.

Everyplace they had been together. The Black, the Sturgeon, the Pine Barrens, the Upper Minnie, all the little streams. Most about fishing he and Bill had discovered together. They worked on the farm and fished and took long trips in the woods from June to October. Bill always quit his job every spring. So did he. Ezra thought fishing was a joke.

Bill forgave him the fishing he had done before they met. He forgave him all the rivers. He was really proud of them. It was like a girl about other girls. If they were before they did not matter. But after was different.

That was why he lost them, he guessed.

They were all married to fishing. Ezra thought fishing was a joke. So did most everybody. He'd been married to it before he married Helen. Really married to it. It wasn't any joke.

So he lost them all. Helen thought it was because they didn't like her.

Nick sat down on a boulder in the shade and hung his sack down into the river. The water swirled around both sides of the boulder. (It was cool in the shade. The bank of the river was sandy under the edge of the trees. There were mink tracks in the sand.)

He might as well be out of the heat. The rock was dry and cool. He sat letting the water run out of his boots down the side of the rock.

Helen thought it was because they did not like her. She really did. Gosh, he remembered the horror he used to have of people getting married. It was funny. Probably it was because he had always been with older people, nonmarrying people.

Odgar always wanted to marry Kate. Kate wouldn't ever marry anybody. She and Odgar always quarreled about it but Odgar did not want anybody else and Kate wouldn't have anybody. She wanted them to be just as good friends and Odgar wanted to be friends and they were always miserable and quarreling trying to be.

It was the Madame planted all that asceticism. The Ghee went with girls in houses in Chicago but he had it, too. Nick had had it, too. It was all a fake. You had this fake ideal planted in you and then you lived your life to it.

All the love went into fishing and the summer.

He had loved it more than anything. He had loved digging potatoes with Bill in the fall, the long trips in the car, fishing in the bay, reading in the hammock on the front porch, swimming off the dock, playing baseball at Charlevoix and Petoskey, living at the Bay, the Madame's cooking, the way she had servants serve the food, eating in the dining room looking down across the long fields and the point to the lake, talking with her, drinking with Bill's old man, the fishing trips away from the farm, just lying around.

He loved the long summer. It used to be that he felt sick when the first of August came and he realized that there were only four more weeks before the trout season closed. Now sometimes he had it that way in dreams. He would dream that the summer was nearly gone and he hadn't been fishing. It made him feel sick in the dream, as though he had been in jail.

The hills at the foot of Walloon Lake, storms on the lake coming up in the motorboat, holding an umbrella over the engine to keep the waves that came in off the spark plug, pumping out, running the boat in big storms delivering vegetables around the lake, climbing up, sliding down, the wave following behind, coming up from the foot of the lake with the groceries, the mail and the Chicago paper under a tarpaulin, sitting on them to keep them dry, too rough to land, drying out in front of the fire, the wind in the hemlocks and the wet pine needles underfoot when he was barefoot going for the milk. Getting up at daylight to row across the lake and hike over the hills after a rain to fish in Hortons Creek.

Hortons always needed a rain. Shultz's was no good if it rained, running muddy and overflowing, running through the grass. Where were the trout when a stream was like that?

That was where a bull chased him over the fence and he lost his pocketbook with all the hooks in it.

If he knew then what he knew about bulls now. Where were Maera and Algabeno now? August the Feria at Valencia, Santander, bad fights at St. Sebastien. Sanchez Mejias killing six bulls. The way phrases from bullfight papers kept coming into his head all the time until he had to quit reading them. The *corrida* of the Miuras. In spite of his notorious defects in the execution of the *pase natural*. The flower of Andalucia. *Chiquelín el camelista*. Juan Terremoto. Belmonte Vuelve?

Maera's kid brother was a bullfighter now. That was the way it went.

His whole inner life had been bullfights all one year. Chink pale and miserable about the horses. Don never minded them, he said. 'And then suddenly I knew I was going to love bullfighting.' That must have been Maera. Maera was the greatest man he'd ever known. Chink knew it, too. He followed him around in the *encierro*.

He, Nick, was the friend of Maera and Maera waved at them from Box 87 above their *sobrepuerta* and waited for Helen to see him and waved again and Helen worshipped him and there were three picadors in the box and all the other picadors did their stuff right down in front of the box and looked up and waved before and after and he said to Helen that picadors only worked for each other, and of course it was true. And it was the best pic-ing he ever saw and the three pics in the box with their Cordoba hats nodded at each good *vara* and the other pics waved up at them and then did their stuff. Like the time the Portuguese were in and the old pic threw his hat into the ring hanging on over the *barrera* watching young Da Veiga. That was the saddest thing he'd ever seen. That was what that fat pic wanted to be, a *caballero en plaza*.

God, how that Da Veiga kid could ride. That was riding. It didn't show well in the movies.

The movies ruined everything. Like talking about something good. That was what had made the war unreal. Too much talking.

Talking about anything was bad. Writing about anything actual was bad. It always killed it.

The only writing that was any good was what you made up, what you imagined. That made everything come true. Like when he wrote 'My Old Man' he'd never seen a jockey killed and the next week Georges Parfrement was killed at that very jump and that was the way it looked. Everything good he'd ever written he'd made up. None of it had ever happened. Other things had happened. Better things, maybe. That was what the family couldn't understand. They thought it all was experience.

That was the weakness of Joyce. Daedalus in *Ulysses* was Joyce himself, so he was terrible. Joyce was so damn romantic and intellectual about him. He'd made Bloom up, Bloom was wonderful. He'd made Mrs. Bloom up. She was the greatest in the world.

That was the way with Mac. Mac worked too close to life. You had to digest life and then create your own people. Mac had stuff, though.

Nick in the stories was never himself. He made him up. Of course he'd never seen an Indian woman having a baby. That was what made it good. Nobody knew that. He'd seen a woman have a baby on the road to Karagatch and tried to help her. That was the way it was.

He wished he could always write like that. He would sometime. He wanted to be a great writer. He was pretty sure he would be. He knew it in lots of ways. He would in spite of everything. It was hard, though.

It was hard to be a great writer if you loved the world and living in it and special people. It was hard when you loved so many places. Then you were healthy and felt good and were having a good time and what the hell.

He always worked best when Helen was unwell. Just that much discontent and friction. Then there were times when you had to write. Not conscience. Just peristaltic action. Then you felt sometimes like you could never write but after a while you knew sooner or later you would write another good story.

It was really more fun than anything. That was really why you did it. He had never realized that before. It wasn't conscience. It was simply that it was the greatest pleasure. It had more bite to it than anything else. It was so damn hard to write well, too.

There were so many tricks.

It was easy to write if you used the tricks. Everybody used them. Joyce had invented hundreds of new ones. Just because they were new didn't make them any better. They would all turn into clichés.

He wanted to write like Cezanne painted.

Cezanne started with all the tricks. Then he broke the whole thing down and built the real thing. It was hell to do. He was the greatest. The greatest for always. It wasn't a cult. He, Nick, wanted to write about country so it would be there like Cezanne had done it in painting. You had to do it from inside yourself. There wasn't any trick. Nobody had ever written about country like that. He felt almost holy about it. It was deadly serious. You could do it if you would fight it out. If you'd lived right with your eyes.

It was a thing you couldn't talk about. He was going to work on it until he got it. Maybe never, but he would know as he got near it. It was a job. Maybe for all his life.

People were easy to do. All this smart stuff was easy. Against this age, skyscraper primitives, Cummings when he was smart, it was automatic writing, not *The Enormous Room*, that was a book, it was one of the great books. Cummings worked hard to get it.

Was there anybody else? Young Asch had something but you couldn't tell. Jews go bad quickly. They all start with something. Mac had something. Don Stewart had the most next to Cummings. Sometimes in the Haddocks. Ring Lardner, maybe. Very maybe. Old guys like Sherwood. Older guys like Dreiser. Was there anybody else? Young guys, maybe. Great unknowns. There are never any unknowns, though.

They weren't after what he was after.

He could see the Cezannes. The portrait at Gertrude Stein's. She'd know it if he ever got things right. The two good ones at the Luxembourg, the ones he'd seen every day at the loan exhibit at Bernheim's. The soldiers undressing to swim, the house through the trees, one of the trees with a house beyond, not the lake one, the other lake one. The portrait of the boy. Cezanne could do people, too. But that was easier, he used what he got from the country to do people with. Nick could do that, too. People were easy. Nobody knew anything about them. If it sounded good they took your word for it. They took Joyce's word for it.

He knew just how Cezanne would paint this stretch of river. God, if he were only here to do it. They died and that was the hell of it. They worked all their lives and then got old and died.

Nick, seeing how Cezanne would do the stretch of river and the swamp, stood up and stepped down into the stream. The water was cold and actual. He waded across the stream, moving in the picture. He kneeled down in the gravel on the bank and reached down into the trout sack. It lay in the stream where he had dragged it across the shallows. The old boy was alive. Nick opened the mouth of the sack and slid the trout into the shallow water and watched him move off through the shallows, his back out of water, threading between rocks toward the deep current.

'He was too big to eat,' Nick said. 'I'll get a couple of little ones in front of camp for supper.'

He climbed the bank of the stream, reeling up his line and started through the brush. He ate a sandwich. He was in a hurry and the rod bothered him. He was not thinking. He was holding something in his head. He wanted to get back to camp and get to work.

He moved through the brush, holding the rod close to him. The line caught on a branch. Nick stopped and cut the leader and reeled the line up. He went through the brush now easily, holding the rod out before him.

Ahead of him he saw a rabbit, flat out on the trail. He stopped, grudging. The rabbit was barely breathing. There were two ticks on the rabbit's head, one behind each ear. They were gray, tight with blood, as big as grapes. Nick pulled them off, their heads tiny and hard, with moving feet. He stepped on them on the trail.

Nick picked up the rabbit, limp, with dull button eyes, and put it under a sweet fern bush beside the trail. He felt its heart beating as he laid it down. The rabbit lay quiet under the bush. It might come to, Nick thought. Probably the ticks had attached themselves to it as it crouched in the grass. Maybe after it had been dancing in the open. He did not know.

He went on up the trail to the camp. He was holding something in his head.

First published in

THE COMPLETE SHORT STORIES

(1987)

A TRAIN TRIP

My father touched me and I was awake. He stood by the bed in the dark. I felt his hand on me and I was wide awake in my head and saw and felt things but all the rest of me was asleep.

'Jimmy,' he said, 'are you awake?'

'Yes.'

'Get dressed then.'

'All right.'

He stood there and I wanted to move but I was really still asleep.

'Get dressed, Jimmy.'

'All right,' I said but I lay there. Then the sleep was gone and I moved out of bed.

'Good boy,' my father said. I stood on the rug and felt for my clothes at the foot of the bed.

'They're on the chair,' my father said. 'Put on your shoes and stockings too.' He went out of the room. It was cold and complicated getting dressed; I had not worn shoes and stockings all summer and it was not pleasant putting them on. My father came back in the room and sat on the bed.

'Do the shoes hurt?'

'They pinch.'

'If the shoe pinches put it on.'

'I'm putting it on.'

'We'll get some other shoes,' he said. 'It's not even a principle, Jimmy. It's a proverb.'

'I see.'

'Like two against one is nigger fun. That's a proverb too.'

'I like that one better than about the shoe,' I said.

'It's not so true,' he said. 'That's why you like it. The pleasanter proverbs aren't so true.' It was cold and I tied my other shoe and was finished dressing.

'Would you like button shoes?' my father asked.

'I don't care.'

'You can have them if you like,' he said. 'Everybody ought to have button shoes if they like.'

'I'm all ready.'

'Where are we going?'

'We're going a long way.'

'Where to?'

'Canada.'

'We'll go there too,' he said. We went out to the kitchen. All the shutters were closed and there was a lamp on the table. In the middle of the room was a suitcase, a duffel bag, and two rucksacks. 'Sit down at the table,' my father said. He brought the frying pan and the coffee pot from the stove and sat down beside me and we ate ham and eggs and drank coffee with condensed cream in it.

'Eat all you can.'

'I'm full.'

'Eat that other egg.' He lifted the egg that was left in the pan with the pancake turner and put it on my plate. The edges were crisped from the bacon fat. I ate it and looked around the kitchen. If I was going away I wanted to remember it and say goodbye. In the corner the stove was rusty and half the lid was broken off the hot water reservoir. Above the stove there was a wooden-handled dish mop stuck in the edge of one of the rafters. My father threw it at a bat one evening. He left it there to remind him to get a new one and afterwards I think to remind him of the bat. I caught the bat in the landing net and kept him in a box with screen over it for a while. He had tiny eyes and tiny teeth and he kept himself folded in the box. We let him loose down on the shore of the lake in the dark and he flew out over the lake, flying very lightly and with flutters and flew down close over the water and then high and turned and flew over us and back into the trees in the dark. There were two kitchen tables, one that we ate on and one we did dishes on. They were both covered with oilcloth. There was a tin bucket for carrying lake water to fill the reservoir and a granite bucket for well water. There was a roller towel on the pantry door and dish towels on a rack over the stove. The broom was in the corner. The wood box was half full and all the pans were hanging against the wall.

I looked all around the kitchen to remember it and I was awfully fond of it.

'Well,' said my father. 'Do you think you'll remember it?'

'I think so.'

'And what will you remember?'

'All the fun we've had.'

'Not just filling the wood box and hauling water?'

'That's not hard.'

'No,' he said. 'That's not hard. Aren't you sorry to go away?'

'Not if we're going to Canada.'

'We won't stay there.'

'Won't we stay there a while?'

'Not very long.'

'Where do we go then?'

'We'll see.'

'I don't care where we go,' I said.

'Try and keep that way,' my father said. He lit a cigarette and offered me the package. 'You don't smoke?'

'No.'

'That's good,' he said. 'Now you go outdoors and climb up on the ladder and put the bucket on the chimney and I'll lock up.'

I went outside. It was still dark but along the edge of the hills it was lightening. The ladder was leaning against the roof and I found the old berry pail beside the woodshed and climbed the ladder. The leather soles of my shoes felt insecure and slippery on the rungs. I put the bucket over the top of the stove pipe to keep out the rain and to keep squirrels and chipmunks from climbing in. From the roof I looked down through the trees to the lake. Looking down on the other side was the woodshed roof, the fence and the hills. It was lighter than when I started to climb the ladder and it was cold and very early in the morning. I looked at the trees and the lake again to remember them and all around; at the hills in back and the woods off on the other side of the house and down again at the woodshed roof and I loved them all very much, the woodshed and the fence and the hills and the woods and I wished we were just going on a fishing trip and not going away. I heard the door shut and my father put all the bags out on the ground. Then he locked the door. I started down the ladder.

'Jimmy,' my father said.

'Yes.'

'How is it up there on the roof?'

'I'm coming down.'

'Go on up. I'm coming up a minute,' he said and climbed up very slowly and carefully. He looked all around the way I had done. 'I don't want to go either,' he said.

'Why do we have to go?'

'I don't know,' he said. 'But we do.'

We climbed down the ladder and my father put it in the

woodshed. We carried the things down to the dock. The motor boat was tied beside the dock. There was dew on the oilcloth cover, the engine, and the seats were wet with dew. I took off the cover and wiped the seats dry with a piece of waste. My father lifted down the bags from the dock and put them in the stern of the boat. Then I untied the bow line and the stern line and got back in the boat and held onto the dock. My father primed the engine through a petcock, rocking the wheel twice to suck the gasoline into the cylinder, then he cranked the flywheel over and the engine started. I held the boat to the dock with a twist of the line around a spile. The propeller churned up the water and the boat pulled against the dock making the water swirl through the spiles.

'Let her go, Jimmy,' my father said and I cast off the line and we started away from the dock. I saw the cottage through the trees with the windows shuttered. We were going straight out from the dock and the dock became shorter and the shoreline opened out.

'You take her,' my father said and I took the wheel and turned her out toward the point. I looked back and saw the beach and the dock and the boat house and the clump of balm of Gilead trees and then we were past the clearing and there was the cove with the mouth of the little stream coming into the lake and the bank high with hemlock trees and then the wooded shoreline of the point and then I had to watch for the sand bar that came way out beyond the point. There was deep water right up to the edge of the bar and I went along the edge of the channel and then out around the end seeing the channel bank slope off underwater and the pickerel weed growing underwater and sucked toward us by the propeller and then we were past the point and when I looked back the dock and the boat house were out of sight and there was only the point with three crows walking on the sand and an old log half covered in the sand and ahead the open lake.

I heard the train and then saw it coming, first in a long curve looking very small and hurried and cut into little connected sections; moving with the hills and the hills moving with the trees behind it. I saw a puff of white from the engine and heard the whistle then another puff and heard the whistle again. It was still early in the morning and the train was on the other side of a tamarack swamp. There was running water on each side of the tracks, clear spring water with a brown swamp bottom and there was a mist over the center of the swamp. The trees that had been killed in the forest fires were gray and thin and dead in the mist but the mist was not foggy. It was cold and white and early morning. The train was coming straight down the tracks now getting closer and closer and bigger and bigger. I stepped back from the tracks and looked back at the lake with the two grocery stores and the boat houses, the long docks going out into the water and close by the station the gravelled patch around the artesian well where the water came straight up in the sunlight out of a brown water-film covered pipe. The water was splashing in the fountain basin, in back was the lake with a breeze coming up, there were woods along the shore and the boat we had come in was tied to the dock.

The train stopped, the conductor and the brakeman got down and my father said good-bye to Fred Cuthbert who was going to take care of the boat in his boat house.

'When will you be back?'

'I don't know, Fred,' my father said. 'Give her a coat of paint in the spring.'

'Good-bye, Jimmy,' Fred said. 'Take good care of yourself.'

'Good-bye, Fred.'

We shook hands with Fred and got on the train. The conductor got on in the car ahead and the brakeman picked up the little box we had stepped up on and swung aboard the train as it started. Fred stood there on the station platform and I watched the station, Fred standing there, then walking away, the water splashing up out of the pipe in the sun and then ties and the swamp and the station very small and the lake looking different and from a new angle and then we were out of sight and crossed the Bear River and went through a cut and there were only the ties and the rails running back and fireweed growing beside the track and nothing more to look at to remember. It was all new now looking out from the platform and the woods had that new look of woods you do not know and if you passed a lake it was the same way. It was just a lake and new and not like a lake you had lived on.

'You'll get all cinders out here,' my father said.

'I guess we'd better go in,' I said. I felt funny with so much new country. I suppose it really looked just the same as the country where we lived but it did not feel the same. I suppose every patch of hardwood with the leaves turning looks alike but when you see a beech woods from the train it does not make you happy; it only makes you want the woods where you live. But I did not know that then. I thought it would all be like where we lived only more of it and that it would be just the same and give you the same feeling, but it didn't. We did not have anything to do with it. The hills were worse than the woods. Perhaps all the hills in Michigan look the same but up in the car I looked out of the window and I would see woods and swamps and we would cross a stream and it was very interesting and then we would pass hills with a farmhouse and the woods behind them and they were the same hills but they were different and everything was a little different. I suppose, of course, that hills that a railroad runs by can *not* be the same. But it was not the way I had thought it was going to be. But it was a fine day early in the fall. The air was fine with the window open and in a little while I was hungry. We had been up since before it was light and now it was almost half past eight. My father came back down the car to our seat.

'How do you feel, Jimmy?'

'Hungry.'

He gave me a bar of chocolate and an apple out of his pocket.

'Come on up to the smoker,' he said and I followed him through the car and into the next one ahead. We sat down in a seat, my father inside next to the window. It was dirty in the smoker and the black leather on the seats had been burned by cinders.

'Look at the seats opposite us,' my father said to me without looking toward them. Opposite us two men sat side by side. The man on the inside was looking out the window and his right wrist was handcuffed to the left wrist of the man who sat beside him. In the seat ahead of them were two other men. I could only see their backs but they sat the same way. The two men who sat on the aisle were talking.

'In a day coach,' the man opposite us said. The man who sat in front of him spoke without turning around.

'Well why didn't we take the night train?'

'Did you want to sleep with these?'

'Sure. Why not?'

'It's more comfortable this way.'

'The hell it's comfortable.'

The man who was looking out of the window looked at us and winked. He was a little man and he wore a cap. There was a bandage around his head under the cap. The man he was handcuffed to wore a cap also but his neck was thick, he was dressed in a blue suit and he wore a cap as though it was only for travelling.

The two men on the next seat were about the same size and build but the one on the aisle had the thicker neck.

'How about something to smoke, Jack?' the man who had winked said to my father over the shoulder of the man he was handcuffed to. The thick-necked man turned and looked at my father and me. The man who had winked smiled. My father took out a package of cigarettes.

'You want to give him a cigarette?' asked the guard. My father reached the package across the aisle.

'I'll give it to him,' said the guard. He took the package in his free hand, squeezed it, put it in his handcuffed hand and holding it there took out a cigarette with his free hand and gave it to the man beside him. The man next to the window smiled at us and the guard lit the cigarette for him.

'You're awfully sweet to me,' he said to the guard.

The guard reached the package of cigarettes back across the aisle.

'Have one,' my father said.

'No thanks. I'm chewing.'

'Making a long trip?'

'Chicago.'

'So are we.'

'It's a fine town,' the little man next to the window said. 'I was there once.'

'I'll say you were,' the guard said. 'I'll say you were.'

We moved up and sat in the seat directly opposite them. The guard in front looked around. The man with him looked down at the floor.

'What's the trouble,' asked my father.

'These gentlemen are wanted for murder.'

The man next to the window winked at me.

'Keep it clean,' he said. 'We're all gentlemen here.'

'Who was killed?' asked my father.

'An Italian,' said the guard.

'Who?' asked the little man very brightly.

'An Italian,' the guard repeated to my father.

'Who killed him?' asked the little man looking at the sergeant and opening his eyes wide.

'You're pretty funny,' the guard said.

'No sir,' the little man said. 'I just asked you, Sergeant, *who* killed this Italian.'

'*He* killed this Italian,' the prisoner on the front seat said looking toward the detective. '*He* killed this Italian with his bow and arrow.'

'Cut it out,' said the detective.

'Sergeant,' the little man said. '*I* did not kill this Italian. *I* would not kill an Italian. *I* do not *know* an Italian.'

'Write it down and use it against him,' the prisoner on the front seat said. 'Everything he says will be used against him. *He* did not kill this Italian.'

'Sergeant,' asked the little man, 'who did kill this Italian?'

'You did,' said the detective.

'Sergeant,' said the little man. 'That is a falsehood. I did not kill this Italian. I refuse to repeat it. I did not kill this Italian.'

'Everything he says must be used against him,' said the other prisoner. 'Sergeant, why did you kill this Italian?'

'It was an error, Sergeant,' the little prisoner said. 'It was a grave error. You should never have killed this Italian.'

'Or that Italian,' the other prisoner said.

'Shut to hell up the both of you,' said the sergeant. 'They're dope heads,' he said to my father. 'They're crazy as bed bugs.'

'Bed bugs?' said the little man, his voice rising. 'There are no bed bugs on me, Sergeant.'

'He comes from a long line of English earls,' said the other prisoner. 'Ask the senator there,' he nodded at my father.

'Ask the little man there,' said the first prisoner. 'He's just George Washington's age. He cannot tell a lie.'

'Speak up, boy,' the big prisoner stared at me.

'Cut it out,' the guard said.

'Yes, Sergeant,' said the little prisoner. 'Make him cut it out. He's got no right to bring in the little lad.'

'I was a boy myself once,' the big prisoner said.

'Shut your goddam mouth,' the guard said.

'That's right, Sergeant,' began the little prisoner.

'Shut *your* goddam mouth.' The little prisoner winked at me.

'Maybe we better go back to the other car,' my father said to me. 'See you later,' he said to the two detectives.

'Sure. See you at lunch.' The other detective nodded. The little prisoner winked at us. He watched us go down the aisle. The other prisoner was looking out of the window. We walked back through the smoker to our seats in the other car.

'Well, Jimmy, what do you make of that?'
'I don't know.'
'Neither do I,' said my father.

At lunch at Cadillac we were sitting at the counter before they came in and they sat apart at a table. It was a good lunch. We ate chicken pot pie and I drank a glass of milk and ate a piece of blueberry pie with ice cream. The lunch room was crowded. Looking out the open door you could see the train. I sat on my stool at the lunch counter and watched the four of them eating together. The two prisoners ate with their left hands and the detectives with their right hands. When the detectives wanted to cut up their meat they used the fork in their left hand and that pulled the prisoner's right hand toward them. Both the hands that were fastened together were on the table. I watched the little prisoner eating and he, without seeming to do it purposefully, made it very uncomfortable for the sergeant. He would jerk without seeming to know it and he held his hand so the sergeant's left hand was always being pulled. The other two ate as comfortably as they could. They were not as interesting to watch anyway.

'Why don't you take them off while we eat?' the little man said to the sergeant. The sergeant did not say anything. He was reaching for his coffee and as he picked it up the little man jerked and he spilled it. Without looking toward the little man the sergeant jerked out with his arm and the steel cuffs yanked the little man's wrist and the sergeant's wrist hit the little man in the face.

'Son of a bitch,' the little man said. His lip was cut and he sucked it.

'Who?' asked the sergeant.

'Not you,' said the little man. 'Not you with me chained to you. Certainly not.'

The sergeant moved his wrist under the table and looked at the little man's face.

'What do you say?'

'Not a thing,' said the little man. The sergeant looked at his face and then reached for his coffee again with his handcuffed hand. The little man's right hand was pulled out across the table as the sergeant reached. The sergeant lifted the coffee cup and as he raised it to drink it it jerked out of his hand and the coffee spilled all over everything. The sergeant brought the handcuffs up into the little man's face twice without looking at him. The little man's face was bloody and he sucked his lip and looked at the table.

'You got enough?'

'Yes,' said the little man. 'I've got plenty.'

'You feel quieter now?'

'Very quiet,' said the little man. 'How do you feel?'

'Wipe your face off,' said the sergeant. 'Your mouth is bloody.'

We saw them get on the train two at a time and we got on too and went to our seats. The other detective, not the one they called Sergeant but the one handcuffed to the big prisoner, had not taken any notice of what happened at the table. He had watched it but he had not seemed to notice it. The big prisoner had not said anything but had watched everything.

There were cinders in the plush of our seat in the train and my father brushed the seat with a newspaper. The train started and I looked out the open window and tried to see Cadillac but you could not see much, only the lake, and factories and a fine smooth road along near the tracks. There were a lot of sawdust piles along the lake shore.

'Don't put your head out, Jimmy,' my father said. I sat down. There was nothing much to see anyway.

'That is the town Al Moegast came from,' my father said.

'Oh,' I said.

'Did you see what happened at the table?' my father asked.

'Yes.'

'Did you see everything?'

'I don't know.'

'What do you think the little one made that trouble for?'

'I guess he wanted to make it uncomfortable so they would take the handcuffs off.'

'Did you see anything else?'

'I saw him get hit three times in the face.'

'Where did you watch when he hit him?'

'I watched his face. I watched the sergeant hit him.'

'Well,' my father said. 'While the sergeant hit him in the face with the handcuff on his right hand he picked up a steel-bladed knife off the table with his left hand and put it in his pocket.'

'I didn't see.'

'No,' my father said. 'Every man has two hands, Jimmy. At least to start with. You ought to watch both of them if you're going to see things.'

'What did the other two do?' I asked. My father laughed.

'I didn't watch them,' he said.

We sat there in the train after lunch and I looked out of the window and watched the country. It did not mean so much now because there was so much else going on and I had seen a lot of country but I did not want to suggest that we go up into the smoker until my father said to. He was reading and I guess my restlessness disturbed him.

'Don't you ever read, Jimmy?' he asked me.

'Not much,' I said. 'I don't have time.'

'What are you doing now?'

'Waiting.'

'Do you want to go up there?'

'Yes.'

'Do you think we ought to tell the sergeant?'

'No,' I said.

'It's an ethical problem,' he said and shut the book.

'Do you want to tell him?' I asked.

'No,' my father said. 'Besides a man is held to be innocent until the law has proved him guilty. He may not have killed that Italian.'

'Are they dope fiends?'

'I don't know whether they use dope or not,' my father said. 'Many people use it. But using cocaine or morphine or heroin doesn't make people talk the way they talked.'

'What does?'

'I don't know,' said my father. 'What makes anyone talk the way they do?'

'Let's go up there,' I said. My father got the suitcase down, opened it up and put the book in it and something out of his pocket. He locked the suitcase and we went up to the smoker. Walking along the aisle of the smoker I saw the two detectives and the two prisoners sitting quietly. We sat down opposite them.

The little man's cap was down over the bandage around his head and his lips were swollen. He was awake and looking out of the window. The sergeant was sleepy, his eyes would shut and then open, stay open a while and then shut. His face looked very heavy and sleepy. Ahead on the next seat the other two were both sleepy. The prisoner leaned toward the window side of the seat and the detective toward the aisle. They were not comfortable that way and as they got sleepier, they both leaned toward each other.

The little man looked at the sergeant and then across at us. He did not seem to recognize us and looked all down the car. He seemed to be looking at all the men in the smoker. There were not very many passengers. Then he looked at the sergeant again. My father had taken another book out of his pocket and was reading.

'Sergeant,' the little man said. The sergeant held his eyes open and looked at the prisoner.

'I got to go to the can,' the little man said.

'Not now,' the sergeant shut his eyes.

'Listen, Sergeant,' the little man said. 'Didn't you ever have to go to the can?'

'Not now,' the sergeant said. He did not want to leave the half asleep half awake state he was in. He was breathing slowly and heavily but when he would open his eyes his breathing would stop. The little man looked across at us but did not seem to recognize us.

'Sergeant,' he said. The sergeant did not answer. The little man ran his tongue over his lips. 'Listen Sergeant, I got to go to the can.'

'All right,' the sergeant said. He stood up and the little man stood up and they walked down the aisle. I looked at my father. 'Go on,' he said, 'if you want to.' I walked after them down the aisle.

They were standing at the door.

'I want to go in alone,' the prisoner said.

'No you don't.'

'Go on. Let me go in alone.'

'No.'

'Why not? You can keep the door locked.'

'I won't take them off.'

'Go on, Sergeant. Let me go in alone.'

'We'll take a look,' the sergeant said. They went inside and the sergeant shut the door. I was sitting on the seat opposite the door to the toilet. I looked down the aisle at my father. Inside I could hear them talking but not what they were saying. Someone turned the handle inside the door to open it and then I heard something fall against it and hit twice against the door. Then it fell on the floor. Then there was a noise as when you pick a rabbit up by the hind legs and slap its head against a stump to kill it. I was looking at my father and motioning. There was that noise three times and then I saw something come out from under the door. It was blood and it came out very slowly and smoothly. I ran down the aisle to my father. 'There's blood coming out under the door.'

'Sit down there,' my father said. He stood up, went across the aisle and touched the detective on the shoulder. The detective looked up.

'Your partner went up to the washroom,' my father said.

'Sure,' said the detective. 'Why not?'

'My boy went up there and said he saw blood coming out from under the door.'

The detective jumped up and jerked the other prisoner over on the seat. The other prisoner looked at my father.

'Come on,' the detective said. The prisoner sat there. 'Come on,' the detective said and the prisoner did not move. 'Come on or I'll blow your can off.'

'What's it all about, your excellency?' the prisoner asked.

'Come on, you bastard,' the detective said.

'Aw, keep it clean,' the prisoner said.

They were going down the aisle, the detective ahead holding a gun in his right hand and the prisoner handcuffed to him hanging back. The passengers were standing up to see. 'Stay where you are,' my father said. He took hold of me by the arm.

The detective saw the blood under the door. He looked around at the prisoner. The prisoner saw him looking and stood still. 'No,' he said. The detective holding his gun in his right hand jerked down hard with his left hand and the prisoner slipped forward on his knees. 'No,' he said. The detective watching the door and the prisoner shifted the revolver so he held it by the muzzle and hit the prisoner suddenly at the side of the head. The prisoner slipped down with his head and hands on the floor. 'No,' he said shaking his head on the floor. 'No. No. No.'

The detective hit him again and then again and he was quiet. He lay on the floor on his face with his head bent down on his chest. Watching the door, the detective laid the revolver down on the floor and leaning over unlocked the handcuff from the wrist of the prisoner. Then he picked up the revolver and stood up. Holding the revolver in his right hand he pulled the cord with his left to stop the train. Then he reached for the handle of the door.

The train was starting to slow.

'Get away from that door,' we heard someone say inside the door.

'Open it up,' said the detective and stepped back.

'Al,' the voice said. 'Al, are you all right?'

The detective stood just to one side of the door. The train was slowing down.

'Al,' said the voice again. 'Answer me if you're all right.'

There was no answer. The train stopped. The brakeman opened the door. 'What the hell?' he said. He looked at the man on the floor, the blood and the detective holding the revolver. The conductor was coming down from the other end of the car.

'There's a fellow in there that's killed a man,' the detective said.

'The hell there is. He's gone out the window,' said the brakeman.

'Watch that man,' said the detective. He opened the door to the platform. I went across the aisle and looked out the window. Along the tracks there was a fence. Beyond the fence was the woods. I looked up and down the tracks. The detective came running by; then ran back. There was no one in sight. The detective came back in the car and they opened the door of the washroom. The door would not swing open because the sergeant was lying across it on the floor. The window was open about halfway. The sergeant was still breathing. They picked him up and carried him out into the car and they picked up the prisoner and put him in a seat. The detective put the handcuff through the handle of a big suitcase. Nobody seemed to know what to do or whether to look after the sergeant or try and find the little man or what. Everybody had gotten out of the train and looked down the tracks and in the edge of the woods. The brakeman had seen the little man run across the tracks and into the woods. The detective went into the woods a couple of times and then came out. The prisoner had taken the sergeant's gun and nobody seemed to want to go very far into the woods after him. Finally they started the train to get to a station where they could send for the state constabulary and send out a description of the little man. My father helped them with the sergeant. He washed off the wound, it was between the collarbone and the neck, and sent me to get paper and towels from the washroom and folded them over and made a plug for it and tied it tight in with a sleeve from the sergeant's shirt. They laid him out as comfortably as they could and my father washed off his face. His head had been banged against the floor of the washroom and he was still unconscious but my father said the wound was not serious. At the station they took him off and the detective took the other prisoner off too. The other prisoner's face was white and he had a bruised bump on the side of his head. He looked silly when they took him off and seemed anxious to move very fast to do whatever they told him. My father came back in the car from helping them with the sergeant. They had put him in a motor truck that was at the station and were going to drive him to a hospital. The detective was sending wires. We were standing on the platform and the train started and I saw the prisoner standing there, leaning the back of his head against the wall of the station. He was crying.

I felt pretty bad about everything and we went in the smoker. The brakeman had a bucket and a bunch of waste and was mopping up and washing where the blood had been.

'How was he, Doc?' he said to my father.

'I'm not a doctor,' my father said. 'But I think he'll be all right.'

'Two big dicks,' said the brakeman. 'And they couldn't handle that one little shrimp.'

'Did you see him get out the window?'

'Sure,' said the brakeman. 'Or I saw him just after he lit on the tracks.'

'Did you recognize him?'

'No. Not when I first saw him. How do you think he stabbed him, Doc?'

'He must have jumped up on him from behind,' my father said.

'Wonder where he got the knife?'

'I don't know,' said my father.

'That other poor boob,' said the brakeman. 'He never even tried to make a break.'

'No.'

'That detective gave him his though. Did you see it, Doc?'

'Yes.'

'That poor boob,' the brakeman said. It was damp and clean where he had washed. We went back to our seats in the other car. My father sat and did not say anything and I wondered what he was thinking.

'Well, Jimmy,' he said, after a while.

'Yes.'

'What do you think of it all now?'

'I don't know.'

'Neither do I,' said my father. 'Do you feel bad?'

'Yes.'

'So do I. Were you scared?'

'When I saw the blood,' I said. 'And when he hit the prisoner.'

'That's healthy.'

'Were you scared?'

'No,' my father said. 'What was the blood like?' I thought a minute.

'It was thick and smooth.'

'Blood is thicker than water,' my father said. 'That's the first proverb you run up against when you lead an active life.'

'It doesn't mean that,' I said. 'It means about family.'

'No,' said my father. 'It means just that, but it always surprises you. I remember the first time I found it out.'

'When was that?'

'I felt my shoes full of it. It was very warm and thick. It was just like water in your rubber boots when we go duck hunting except it was warm and thicker and smoother.'

'When was that?'

'Oh, a long time ago,' said my father.

THE PORTER

When we went to bed my father said I might as well sleep in the lower berth because I would want to look out the window early in the morning. He said an upper berth did not make any difference to him and he would come to bed after a while. I undressed and put my clothes in the hammock and put on pajamas and got into bed. I turned off the light and pulled up the window curtain but it was cold if I sat up to look out and lying down in bed I could not see anything. My father took a suitcase out from under my berth, opened it on the bed, took out his pajamas and tossed them up to the upper berth, then he took a book out and the bottle and filled his flask.

'Turn on the light,' I said.

'No,' he said. 'I don't need it. Are you sleepy, Jim?'

'I guess so.'

'Get a good sleep,' he said and closed the suitcase and put it back under the berth.

'Did you put your shoes out?'

'No,' I said. They were in the hammock and I got up to get them but he found them and put them out in the aisle. He shut the curtain.

'Aren't you going to bed, sir?' the porter asked him.

'No,' my father said. 'I'm going to read a while up in the washroom.'

'Yes, sir,' the porter said. It was fine lying between the sheets with the thick blanket pulled up and it all dark and the country dark outside. There was a screen across the lower part of the window that was open and the air came in cold. The green curtain was buttoned tight and the car swayed but felt very solid and was going fast and once in a while you would hear the whistle. I went to sleep and when I woke up I looked out and we were going very slowly and crossing a big river. There were lights shining on the water and the iron framework of a bridge going by the window and my father was getting into the upper berth.

'Are you awake, Jimmy?'

'Yes. Where are we?'

'We're crossing into Canada now,' he said. 'But in the morning we'll be out of it.'

I looked out of the window to see Canada but all I could see were railway yards and freight cars. We stopped and two men came by with torches and stopped and hit on the wheels with hammers. I could not see anything but the men crouching over by the wheels and opposite us freight cars and I crawled down in bed again.

'Where are we in Canada?' I asked.

'Windsor,' my father said. 'Good night, Jim.'

When I woke up in the morning and looked out we were going through fine country that looked like Michigan only with higher hills and the trees were all turning. I got dressed in all but my shoes and reached under the curtain for them. They were shined and I put them on and unbuttoned the curtain and went out in the aisle. The curtains were buttoned all down the aisle and everybody seemed to be still asleep. I went down to the washroom and looked in. The nigger porter was asleep in one corner of the leather cushioned seat. His cap was down over his eyes and his feet were up on one of the chairs. His mouth was open, his head was tipped back and his hands were together in his lap. I went on to the end of the car and looked out but it was drafty and cindery and there was no place to sit down. I went back to the washroom and went in very carefully so as not to wake the porter and sat down by the window. The washroom smelt like brass spittoons in the early morning. I was hungry and I looked out of the window at the fall country and watched the porter asleep. It looked like good shooting country. There was lots of brush on the hills and patches of woods and fine looking farms and good roads. It was a different kind of looking country than Michigan. Going through it it all seemed to be connected and in Michigan one part of the country hasn't any connection with another. There weren't any swamps either and none of it looked burnt over. It all looked as though it belonged to somebody but it was nice looking country and the beeches and the maples were turned and there were lots of scrub oaks that had fine colored leaves too and when there was brush there was lots of sumac that was bright red. It looked like good country for rabbits and I tried to see some game but it went by too fast to concentrate looking and the only birds you could see were birds flying. I saw a hawk hunting over a field and his mate too. I saw flickers flying in the edge of the woods and I figured they were going south. I saw bluejays twice but the train was no good for seeing birds. It slid the country all sideways if you looked straight at anything and you had to just let it go by, looking ahead a little

all the time. We passed a farm with a long meadow and I saw a
flock of killdeer plover feeding. Three of them flew up when the
train went by and circled off over the woods but the rest kept on
feeding. We made a big curve so I could see the other cars
curved ahead and the engine with the drive wheels going very
fast away up ahead and a river valley down below us and then I
looked around and the porter was awake and looking at me.

'What do you see?' he said.

'Not much.'

'You certainly do look at it.'

I did not say anything but I was glad he was awake. He kept
his feet up on the chair but reached up and put his cap straight.

'That your father that stayed up here reading?'

'Yes.'

'He certainly can drink liquor.'

'He's a great drinker.'

'He certainly is a great drinker. That's it, a great drinker.'

I did not say anything.

'I had a couple with him,' the porter said. 'And I got plenty
of effect but he sat there half the night and never showed a
thing.'

'He never shows anything,' I said.

'No sir. But if he keeps up that way he's going to kill his
whole insides.'

I did not say anything.

'You hungry, boy?'

'Yes,' I said. 'I'm very hungry.'

'We got a diner on now. Come on back and we'll get a little
something.'

We went back through two other cars, all with the curtains
closed all along the aisles, to the diner and through the tables
back to the kitchen.

'Hail fellow well met,' the porter said to the chef.

'Uncle George,' the chef said. There were four other niggers
sitting at a table playing cards.

'How about some food for the young gentleman and myself?'

'No sir,' said the chef. 'Not until I can get it ready.'

'Could you drink?' said George.

'No sir,' said the chef.

'Here it is,' said George. He took a pint bottle out of his side
pocket. 'Courtesy of the young gentleman's father.'

'He's courteous,' said the chef. He wiped his lips.

ERNEST HEMINGWAY

'The young gentleman's father is the world's champion.'

'At what?'

'At drinking.'

'He's mighty courteous,' said the chef. 'How did you eat last night?'

'With that collection of yellow boys.'

'They all together still?'

'Between Chicago and Detroit. We call 'em the White Eskimos now.'

'Well,' said the chef. 'Everything's got its place.' He broke two eggs on the side of a frying pan. 'Ham and eggs for the son of the champion?'

'Thanks,' I said.

'How about some of that courtesy?'

'Yes sir.'

'May your father remain undefeated,' the chef said to me. He licked his lips. 'Does the young gentleman drink too?'

'No sir,' said George. 'He's in my charge.'

The chef put the ham and eggs on two plates.

'Seat yourselves, gentlemen.'

George and I sat down and he brought us two cups of coffee and sat down opposite us.

'You willing to part with another example of that courtesy?'

'For the best,' said George. 'We got to get back to the car. How is the railroad business?'

'Rails are firm,' said the chef. 'How's Wall Street?'

'The bears are bulling again,' said George. 'A lady bear ain't safe today.'

'Bet on the Cubs,' said the chef. 'The Giants are too big for the league.'

George laughed and the chef laughed.

'You're a very courteous fellow,' George said. 'Fancy meeting you here.'

'Run along,' said the chef. 'Lackawannius is calling you.'

'I love that girl,' said George. 'Who touches a hair –'

'Run along,' said the chef. 'Or those yellow boys will get you.'

'It's a pleasure, sir,' said George. 'It's a very real pleasure.'

'Run along.'

'Just one more courteous action.'

The chef wiped his lips. 'God speed the parting guest,' he said.

'I'll be in for breakfast,' George said.

'Take your unearned increment,' the chef said. George put the bottle in his pocket.

'Good-bye to a noble soul,' he said.

'Get the hell out of here,' said one of the niggers who was playing cards.

'Good-bye, gentlemen all,' George said.

'Good night, sir,' said the chef. We went out.

We went back up to our car and George looked at the number board. There was a number twelve and a number five showing. George pulled a little thing down and the numbers disappeared.

'You better sit here and be comfortable,' he said.

I sat down in the washroom and waited and he went down the aisle. In a little while he came back.

'They're all happy now,' he said. 'How do you like the rail-road business, Jimmy?'

'How did you know my name?'

'That's what your father calls you, ain't it?'

'Sure.'

'Well,' he said.

'I like it fine,' I said. 'Do you and the chef always talk that way?'

'No, James,' he said. 'We only talk that way when we're en-thused.'

'Just when you have a drink,' I said.

'Not that alone. When we're enthused from any cause. The chef and I are kindred spirits.'

'What are kindred spirits?'

'Gentlemen with the same outlook on life.'

I did not say anything and the bell buzzed. George went out, pulled the little thing in the box and came back in the room.

'Did you ever see a man cut with a razor?'

'No.'

'Would you like to have it explained?'

'Yes.'

The bell buzzed again. 'I'd better go see,' George went out.

He came back and sat down by me. 'The use of the razor,' he said, 'is an art not alone known to the barbering profession.' He looked at me. 'Don't you make them big eyes,' he said. 'I'm only lecturing.'

'I'm not scared.'

'I should say you're not,' said George. 'You're here with your greatest friend.'

'Sure,' I said. I figured he was pretty drunk.

'Your father got a lot of this?' He took out the bottle.

'I don't know.'

'Your father is a type of noble Christian gentleman.' He took a drink.

I didn't say anything.

'Returning to the razor,' George said. He reached in the inside pocket of his coat and brought out a razor. He laid it closed on the palm of his left hand.

The palm was pink.

'Consider the razor,' George said. 'It toils not, neither does it spin.'

He held it out on the palm of his hand. It had a black bone handle. He opened it up and held it in his right hand with the blade out straight.

'You got a hair from your head?'

'How do you mean?'

'Pull one out. My own are very tenacious.'

I pulled out a hair and George reached for it. He held it in his left hand looking at it carefully then flicked the razor and cut it in two. 'Keenness of edge,' he said. Still looking at the little end of hair that was left he turned the razor in his hand and flicked the blade back the other direction. The blade cut the hair off close to his finger and thumb. 'Simplicity of action,' George said. 'Two admirable qualities.'

The buzzer rang and he folded the razor and handed it to me.

'Guard the razor,' he said and went out. I looked at it and opened it and shut it. It was just an ordinary razor. George came back and sat down beside me. He took a drink. There was no more in the bottle. He looked at it and put it back in his pocket.

'The razor, please,' he said. I handed it to him. He put it on the palm of his left hand.

'You have observed,' he said, 'keenness of edge and simplicity of action. Now a greater than these two. Security of manipulation.'

He picked up the razor in his right hand, gave it a little flip and the blade came open and lay back, edge out across his knuckles. He showed me his hand; the handle of the razor was in his fist, the blade was open across the knuckles, held in place by his forefinger and his thumb. The blade was solidly in place all across his fist, the edge out.

'You observe it?' George said. 'Now for that great requisite skill in the use of.'

He stood up and patted out with his right hand, his fist closed, the blade open across the knuckles. The razor blade shone in the sun coming through the window. George ducked and jabbed three times with the blade. He stepped back and flicked it twice in the air. Then holding his head down and his left arm around his neck he whipped his fist and the blade back and forth, back and forth, ducking and dodging. He slashed one, two, three, four, five, six. He straightened up. His face was sweaty and he folded the razor and put it in his pocket.

'Skill in the use of,' he said. 'And in the left hand preferably a pillow.'

He sat down and wiped his face. He took off his cap and wiped the leather band inside. He went over and took a drink of water.

'The razor's a delusion,' he said. 'The razor's no defense. Anybody can cut you with a razor. If you're close enough to cut them they're bound to cut you. If you could have a pillow in your left hand you'd be all right. But where you going to get a pillow when you need a razor? Who you going to cut in bed? The razor's a delusion, Jimmy. It's a nigger weapon. A regular nigger weapon. But now you know how they use it. Bending a razor back over the hand is the only progress the nigger ever made. Only nigger ever knew how to defend himself was Jack Johnson and they put him in Leavenworth. And what would I do to Jack Johnson with a razor. It none of it makes any difference, Jimmy. All you get in this life is a point of view. Fellows like me and the chef got a point of view. Even if he's got a wrong point of view he's better off. A nigger gets delusions like old Jack or Marcus Garvey and they put him in the pen. Look where my delusion about the razor would take me. Nothing's got any value, Jimmy. Liquor makes you feel like I'll feel in an hour. You and me aren't even friends.'

'Yes we are.'

'Good old Jimmy,' he said. 'Look at the deal they gave this poor old Tiger Flowers. If he was white he'd have made a million dollars.'

'Who was he?'

'He was a fighter. A damn good fighter.'

'What did they do to him?'

'They just took him down the road in one way or another all the time.'

'It's a shame,' I said.

'Jimmy, there's nothing to the whole business. You get syphed up from women or if you're married your wife'll run around. In the railroad business you're away from home nights. The kind of a girl you want is the kind of a girl that'll jig you because she can't help it. You want her because she can't help it and you lose her because she can't help it and a man's only got so many orgasms to his whole life and what difference does it make when you feel worse after liquor.'

'Don't you feel all right?'

'No I don't. I feel bad. If I didn't feel bad I wouldn't talk that way.'

'My father feels bad sometimes too in the morning.'

'He does?'

'Sure.'

'What does he do for it?'

'He exercises.'

'Well, I got twenty-four berths to make up. Maybe that's the solution.'

It was a long day on the train after the rain started. The rain made the windows of the train wet so you could not see outside clearly and then it made everything outside look the same anyway. We went through many towns and cities but it was raining in all of them and when we crossed the Hudson River at Albany it was raining hard. I stood out in the vestibule and George opened the door so I could see out but there was only the wet iron of the bridge and the rain coming down into the river and the train with water dripping. It smelled good outside though. It was a fall rain and the air coming in through the open door smelled fresh and like wet wood and iron and it felt like fall up at the lake. There were plenty of other people in the car but none of them looked very interesting. A nice looking woman asked me to sit down next to her and I did but she turned out to have a boy of her own just my age and was going to a place in New York to be superintendent of schools. I wished I could have gone back with George to the kitchen of the dining car and heard him talk with the chef. But during the regular daytime George talked just like anyone else, except even less, and very polite, but I noticed him drinking lots of ice water.

It had stopped raining outside but there were big clouds over the mountains. We were going along the river and the country was very beautiful and I had never seen anything like it before except in the illustrations of a book at Mrs. Kenwood's where we used to go for Sunday dinner up at the lake. It was a big book and it was always on the parlor table and I would look at it while waiting for dinner. The engravings were like this country now after the rain with the river and the mountains going up from it and the gray stone. Sometimes there would be a train across on the other side of the river. The leaves on the trees were turned by the fall and sometimes you saw the river through the branches of the trees and it did not seem old and like the illustrations but instead it seemed like a place to live in and where you could fish and eat your lunch and watch the train go by. But mostly it was dark and unreal and sad and strange and classical like the engravings. That may have been because it was just after a rain and the sun had not come out. When the wind blows the leaves off the trees they are cheerful and good to walk through and the trees are the same, only they are without leaves. But when the leaves fall from the rain they are dead and wet and flat to the ground and the trees are changed and wet and unfriendly. It was very beautiful coming along the Hudson but it was the sort of thing I did not know about and it made me wish we were back at the lake. It gave me the same feeling that the engravings in the book did and the feeling was confused with the room where I always looked at the book and it being someone else's house and before dinner and wet trees after the rain and the time in the north when the fall is over and it is wet and cold and the birds are gone and the woods are no more fun to walk in and it rains and you want to stay inside with a fire. I do not suppose I thought of all those things because I have never thought much and never in words but it was the feeling of all those things that the country along the Hudson River gave me. The rain can make all places strange, even places where you live.

BLACK ASS AT THE CROSS ROADS

We had reached the cross roads before noon and had shot a French civilian by mistake. He had run across the field on our right beyond the farmhouse when he saw the first jeep come up. Claude had ordered him to halt and when he had kept on running across the field Red shot him. It was the first man he had killed that day and he was very pleased.

We had all thought he was a German who had stolen civilian clothes, but he turned out to be French. Anyway his papers were French and they said he was from Soissons.

'*Sans doute c'était un Collabo*,' Claude said.

'He ran, didn't he?' Red asked. 'Claude told him to halt in good French.'

'Put him in the game book as a Collabo,' I said. 'Put his papers back on him.'

'What was he doing up here if he comes from Soissons?' Red asked. 'Soissons's way the hell back.'

'He fled ahead of our troops because he was a collaborator,' Claude explained.

'He's got a mean face.' Red looked down at him.

'You spoiled it a little,' I said. 'Listen, Claude. Put the papers back and leave the money.'

'Someone else will take it.'

'*You* won't take it,' I said. 'There will be plenty of money coming through on Krauts.'

Then I told them where to put the two vehicles and where to set up shop and sent Onésime across the field to cross the two roads and get into the shuttered *estaminet* and find out what had gone through on the escape-route road.

Quite a little had gone through, always on the road to the right. I knew plenty more had to come through and I paced the distances back from the road to the two traps we had set up. We were using Kraut weapons so the noise would not alarm them if anyone heard the noise coming up on the cross roads. We set the traps well beyond the cross roads so that we would not louse up the cross roads and make it look like a shambles. We wanted them to hit the cross roads fast and keep coming.

'It is a beautiful *guet-apens*,' Claude said and Red asked me what was that. I told him it was only a trap as always. Red said he must remember the word. He now spoke his idea of French about half the time and if given an order perhaps half the time he would answer in what he thought was French. It was comic and I liked it.

It was a beautiful late summer day and there were very few more to come that summer. We lay where we had set up and the two vehicles covered us from behind the manure pile. It was a big rich manure pile and very solid and we lay in the grass behind the ditch and the grass smelled as all summers smell and the two trees made a shade over each trap. Perhaps I had set up too close but you cannot ever be too close if you have fire power and the stuff is going to come through fast. One hundred yards is all right. Fifty yards is ideal. We were closer than that. Of course in that kind of thing it always seems closer.

Some people would disagree with this setup. But we had to figure to get out and back and keep the road as clean looking as possible. There was nothing much you could do about vehicles, but other vehicles coming would normally assume they had been destroyed by aircraft. On this day, though, there was no aircraft. But nobody coming would know there had not been aircraft through here. Anybody making their run on an escape route sees things differently too.

'*Mon Capitaine*,' Red said to me. 'If the point comes up they will not shoot the shit out of us when they hear these Kraut weapons?'

'We have observation on the road where the point will come from the two vehicles. They'll flag them off. Don't sweat.'

'I am not sweating,' Red said. 'I have shot a proved collaborator. The only thing we have killed today and we will kill many Krauts in this setup. *Pas vrai*, Onie?'

Onésime said, '*Merde*' and just then we heard a car coming very fast. I saw it come down the beech-tree bordered road. It was an overloaded gray-green camouflaged Volkswagen and it was filled with steel-helmeted people looking as though they were racing to catch a train. There were two aiming stones by the side of the road that I had taken from a wall by the farm, and as the Volkswagen crossed the notch of the cross roads and came toward us on the good straight escape road that crossed in front of us and led up a hill, I said to Red, 'Kill the driver at the first stone.' To Onésime I said, 'Traverse at body height.'

The Volkswagen driver had no control of his vehicle after

Red shot. I could not see the expression on his face because of
the helmet. His hands relaxed. They did not crisp tight nor hold
on the wheel. The machine gun started firing before the driver's
hands relaxed and the car went into the ditch spilling the occupants in slow motion. Some were on the road and the second
outfit gave them a small carefully hoarded burst. One man rolled
over and another started to crawl and while I watched Claude
shot them both.

'I think I got that driver in the head,' Red said.

'Don't be too fancy.'

'She throws a little high at this range,' Red said. 'I shot for the
lowest part of him I could see.'

'Bertrand,' I called over to the second outfit. 'You and your
people get them off the road, please. Bring me all the *Feldbuchen*
and you hold the money for splitting. Get them off fast. Go on
and help, Red. Get them into the ditch.'

I watched the road to the west beyond the *estaminet* while the
cleaning up was going on. I never watched the cleaning up unless I had to take part in it myself. Watching the cleaning up is
bad for you. It is no worse for me than for anyone else. But I was
in command.

'How many did you get, Onie?'

'All eight, I think. Hit, I mean.'

'At this range –'

'It's not very sporting. But after all it's their machine gun.'

'We have to get set now fast again.'

'I don't think the vehicle is shot up badly.'

'We'll check her afterwards.'

'Listen,' Red said. I listened, then blew the whistle twice and
everybody faded back, Red hauling the last Kraut by one leg
with his head shuddering and the trap was set again. But nothing
came and I was worried.

We were set up for a simple job of assassination astride an
escape route. We were not astride, technically, because we did
not have enough people to set up on both sides of the road and
we were not technically prepared to cope with armored vehicles. But each trap had two German *Panzerfausten*. They were
much more powerful and simpler than the general-issue American bazooka, having a bigger warhead and you could throw
away the launching tube; but lately, many that we had found in
the German retreat had been booby-trapped and others had
been sabotaged. We used only those as fresh as anything in that

market could be fresh and we always asked a German prisoner to fire off samples taken at random from the lot.

German prisoners who had been taken by irregulars were often as co-operative as head waiters or minor diplomats. In general we regarded the Germans as perverted Boy Scouts. This is another way of saying they were splendid soldiers. We were not splendid soldiers. We were specialists in a dirty trade. In French we said, '*un métier très sale.*'

We knew, from repeated questionings, that all Germans coming through on this escape route were making for Aachen and I knew that all we killed now we would not have to fight in Aachen nor behind the West Wall. This was simple. I was pleased when anything was that simple.

The Germans we saw coming now were on bicycles. There were four of them and they were in a hurry too but they were very tired. They were not cyclist troops. They were just Germans on stolen bicycles. The leading rider saw the fresh blood on the road and then he turned his head and saw the vehicle and he put his weight hard down on his right pedal with his right boot and we opened on him and on the others. A man shot off a bicycle is always a sad thing to see, although not as sad as a horse shot with a man riding him nor a milk cow gut-shot when she walks into a fire fight. But there is something about a man shot off a bicycle at close range that is too intimate. These were four men and four bicycles. It was very intimate and you could hear the thin tragic noise the bicycles made when they went over onto the road and the heavy sound of men falling and the clatter of equipment.

'Get them off the road quick,' I said. 'And hide the four *vélos.*'

As I turned to watch the road one of the doors of the *estaminet* opened and two civilians wearing caps and working clothes came out each carrying two bottles. They sauntered across the cross roads and turned to come up in the field behind the ambush. They wore sweaters and old coats, corduroy trousers and country boots.

'Keep them covered, Red,' I said. They advanced steadily and then raised the bottles high above their heads, one bottle in each hand as they came in.

'For Christ sake, get down,' I called, and they got down and came crawling through the grass with the bottles tucked under their arms.

'*Nous sommes des copains,*' one called in a deep voice, rich with alcohol.

'Advance, rum–dumb *copains*, and be recognized,' Claude answered.

'We are advancing.'

'What do you want out here in the rain?' Onésime called.

'We bring the little presents.'

'Why didn't you give the little presents when I was over there?' Claude asked.

'Ah, things have changed, *camarade*.'

'For the better?'

'*Rudement,*' the first rummy *camarade* said. The other, lying flat and handing us one of the bottles, asked in a hurt tone, '*On dit pas bonjour aux nouveaux camarades?*'

'*Bonjour,*' I said. '*Tu veux battre?*'

'If it's necessary. But we came to ask if we might have the *vélos*.'

'After the fight,' I said. 'You've made your military service?'

'Naturally.'

'Okay. You take a German rifle each and two packs of ammo and go up the road two hundred yards on our right and kill any Germans that get by us.'

'Can't we stay with you?'

'We're specialists,' Claude said. 'Do what the captain says.'

'Get up there and pick out a good place and don't shoot back this way.'

'Put on these arm bands,' Claude said. He had a pocket full of arm bands. 'You're *Franc-tireurs*.' He did not add the rest of it.

'Afterwards we can have the *vélos*?'

'One apiece if you don't have to fight. Two apiece if you fight.'

'What about the money?' Claude asked. 'They're using our guns.'

'Let them keep the money.'

'They don't deserve it.'

'Bring any money back and you'll get your share. *Allez vite. Débine-toi.*'

'*Ceux sont des poivrots pourris,*' Claude said.

'They had rummies in Napoleon's time too.'

'It's probable.'

'It's certain,' I said. 'You can take it easy on that.'

We lay in the grass and it smelled of true summer and the flies, the ordinary flies and the big blue flies started to come to the dead that were in the ditch and there were butterflies around the edges of the blood on the black-surfaced road. There were yellow butterflies and white butterflies around the blood and the streaks where the bodies had been hauled.

'I didn't know butterflies ate blood,' Red said.

'I didn't either.'

'Of course when we hunt it's too cold for butterflies.'

'When we hunt in Wyoming the picket pin gophers and the prairie dogs are holed up already. That's the fifteenth of September.'

'I'm going to watch and see if they really eat it,' Red said.

'Want to take my glasses?'

He watched and after a while he said, 'I'll be damned if I can tell. But it sure interests them.' Then he turned to Onésime and said, 'Piss *pauvre* Krauts, Onie. *Pas de* pistol, *pas de binoculaire*. Fuck-all *rien*.'

'*Assez de sous*,' Onésime said. 'We're doing all right on the money.'

'No fucking place to spend it.'

'Some day.'

'*Je veux* spend *maintenant*,' Red said.

Claude opened one of the two bottles with the cork screw on his Boy Scout German knife. He smelled it and handed it to me.

'*C'est du gnôle.*'

The other outfit had been working on their share. They were our best friends but as soon as we were split they seemed like the others and the vehicles seemed like the rear echelon. You split too easy, I thought. You want to watch that. That's one more thing you can watch.

I took a drink from the bottle. It was very strong raw spirits and all it had was fire. I handed it back to Claude who gave it to Red. Tears came into his eyes when he swallowed it.

'What do they make it out of up here, Onie?'

'Potatoes, I think, and parings from horses' hooves they get at the blacksmith shop.'

I translated to Red. 'I taste everything but the potatoes,' he said.

'They age it in rusty nail kegs with a few old nails to give it zest.'

'I better take another to take the taste out of my mouth,' Red said. '*Mon Capitaine*, should we die together?'

'*Bonjour, toute le monde,*' I said. This was an old joke we had about an Algerian who was about to be guillotined on the pavement outside the Santé who replied with that phrase when asked if he had any last words to say.

'To the butterflies,' Onésime drank.

'To the nail kegs,' Claude raised the bottle.

'Listen,' Red said and handed the bottle to me. We all heard the noise of a tracked vehicle.

'The fucking jackpot,' Red said. 'Along ongfong de la patree, le fucking jackpot ou le more.' He sang softly, the nail keg juice no good to him now. I took another good drink of the juice as we lay and checked everything and looked up the road to our left. Then it came in sight. It was a Kraut half-track and it was crowded to standing room only.

When you set a trap on an escape route you have four or, if you can afford them, five Teller mines, armed, on the far side of the road. They lie like round checker counters wider than the biggest soup plates and toad squatted in their thick deadliness. They are in a semi-circle, covered with cut grass and connected by a heavy tarred line which may be procured at any ship chandler's. One end of this line is made fast to a kilometer marking, called a *borne*, or to a tenth of a kilometer stone, or any other completely solid object, and the line runs loosely across the road and is coiled in the first or second section of the trap.

The approaching overloaded vehicle was of the type where the driver looks out through slits and its heavy machine guns now showed high in anti-aircraft position. We were all watching it closely as it came nearer, so very overcrowded. It was full of combat S.S. and we could see the collars now and faces were clear then clearer.

'Pull the cord,' I called to the second outfit and as the cord took up its slack and commenced to tighten the mines moved out of their semi-circle and across the road looking, I thought, like nothing but green grass-covered Teller mines.

Now the driver would see them and stop or he would go on and hit them. You should not attack an armored vehicle while it was moving, but if he braked I could hit him with the big-headed German bazooka.

The half-track came on very fast and now we could see the faces quite clearly. They were all looking down the road where the point would come from. Claude and Onie were white and Red had a twitch in the muscle of his cheek. I felt hollow as always. Then someone in the half-track saw the blood and the Volkswagen in the ditch and the bodies. They were shouting in German and the driver and the officer with him must have seen the mines across the road and they came to a tearing swerving halt and had started to back when the bazooka hit. It hit while both outfits were firing from the two traps. The people in the half-track had mines themselves and were hurrying to set up their own road block to cover what had gone through because when the Kraut bazooka hit and the vehicle went up we all dropped our heads and everything rained down as from a fountain. It rained metal and other things. I checked on Claude and Onie and Red and they were all firing. I was firing too with a Smeizer on the slits and my back was wet and I had stuff all over my neck, but I had seen what fountained up. I could not understand why the vehicle had not been blown wide open or overturned. But it just blew straight up. The fifties from the vehicle were firing and there was so much noise you could not hear. No one showed from the half-track and I thought it was over and was going to wave the fifties off, when someone inside threw a stick grenade that exploded just beyond the edge of the road.

'They're killing their dead,' Claude said. 'Can I go up and put a couple into her?'

'I can hit her again.'

'No. Once was enough. My whole back's tattooed.'

'Okay. Go on.'

He crawled forward, snaking in the grass under the fire of the fifties and pulled the pin from a grenade and let the lever snap loose and held the grenade smoking gray and then lobbed it underhand up over the side of the half-track. It exploded with a jumping roar and you could hear the fragments whang against the armor.

'Come on out,' Claude said in German. A German machine-gun pistol started shooting from the right-hand slit. Red hit the slit twice. The pistol fired again. It was obvious it was not being aimed.

'Come on out,' Claude called. The pistol shot again, making a noise like children rattling a stick along a picket fence. I shot back making the same silly noise.

'Come on back, Claude,' I said. 'You fire on one slit, Red. Onie, you fire on the other.'

When Claude came back fast I said, 'Fuck that Kraut. We'll

use up another one. We can get more. The point will be up anyway.'

'This is their rear guard,' Onie said. 'This vehicle.'

'Go ahead and shoot it,' I said to Claude. He shot it and there was no front compartment and then they went in after what would be left of the money and the paybooks. I had a drink and waved to the vehicles. The men on the fifties were shaking their hands over their heads like fighters. Then I sat with my back against the tree to think and to look down the road.

They brought what paybooks there were and I put them in a canvas bag with the others. Not one of them was dry. There was a great deal of money, also wet, and Onie and Claude and the other outfit cut off a lot of S.S. patches and they had what pistols were serviceable and some that weren't and put it all in the canvas sack with the red stripes around it.

I never touched the money. That was their business and I thought it was bad luck to touch it anyway. But there was plenty of prize money. Bertrand gave me an Iron Cross, first class, and I put it in the pocket of my shirt. We kept some for a while and then we gave them all away. I never liked to keep anything. It's bad luck in the end. I had stuff for a while that I wished I could have sent back afterwards or to their families.

The outfit looked as though they had been showered by chunks and particles from an explosion in an abattoir and the other people did not look too clean when they came out from the body of the half-track. I did not know how badly I must have looked myself until I noticed how many flies there were around my back and neck and shoulders.

The half-track lay across the road and any vehicle passing would have to slow down. Everyone was rich now and we had lost no one and the place was ruined. We would have to fight on another day and I was sure this was the rear guard and all we would get now would be strays and unfortunates.

'Disarm the mines and pick up everything and we will go back to the farmhouse and clean up. We can interdict the road from there like in the book.'

They came in heavily loaded and everyone was very cheerful. We left the vehicles where they were and washed up at the pump in the farmyard and Red put iodine on the metal cuts and scratches and sifted Sulfa on Onie and Claude and me and then Claude took care of Red.

'Haven't they got anything to drink in that farmhouse?' I asked René.

'I don't know. We've been too busy.'

'Get in and see.'

He found some bottles of red wine that was drinkable and I sat around and checked the weapons and made jokes. We had very severe discipline but no formality except when we were back at Division or when we wanted to show off.

'*Encore un coup manqué*,' I said. That was a very old joke and it was a phrase that a crook we had with us for a while always uttered when I would let something worthless go by to wait for something good.

'It's terrible,' said Claude.

'It's intolerable,' said Michel.

'Me, I can go no further,' Onésime said.

'*Moi, je suis la France*,' Red said.

'You fight?' Claude asked him.

'*Pas moi*,' Red answered. 'I command.'

'You fight?' Claude asked me.

'*Jamais*.'

'Why is your shirt covered with blood?'

'I was attending the birth of a calf.'

'Are you a midwife or a veterinary?'

'I give only the name, rank and serial number.'

We drank some more wine and watched the road and waited for the point to come up.

'*Où est la* fucking point?' Red asked.

'I am not in their confidence.'

'I'm glad it didn't come up while we had the little *accrochage*,' Onie said. 'Tell me, *mon Capitaine*, how did you feel when you let the thing go?'

'Very hollow.'

'What did you think about?'

'I hoped to Christ it would not trickle out.'

'We were certainly lucky they were loaded with stuff.'

'Or that they didn't back up and deploy.'

'Don't ruin my afternoon,' Marcel said.

'Two Krauts on bicycles,' Red said. 'Approaching from the west.'

'Plucky chaps,' I said.

'*Encore un coup manqué*,' said Onie.

'Anybody want them?'

Nobody wanted them. They were pedaling steadily, slumped forward and their boots were too big for the pedals.

'I'll try one with the M-1,' I said. Auguste handed it to me and I waited until the first German on the bicycle was past the half-track and clear of the trees and then had the sight on him, swung with him and missed.

'*Pas bon*,' said Red and I tried it again swinging further ahead. The German fell in the same disconcerting heartbreaking way and lay in the road with the *vélo* upside down and a wheel still spinning. The other cyclist sprinted on and soon the *copains* were firing. We heard the hard *ta-bung* of their shots which had no effect on the cyclist who kept on pedaling until he was out of sight.

'*Copains* no bloody *bon*,' Red said.

Then we saw the *copains* falling back to retire onto the main body. The French of the outfit were ashamed and sore.

'*On peut les fusiller?*' Claude asked.

'No. We don't shoot rummies.'

'*Encore un coup manqué*,' said Onie and everybody felt better but not too good.

The first *copain* who had a bottle in his shirt which showed when he stopped and presented arms said, '*Mon Capitaine, on a fait un véritable massacre.*'

'Shut up,' said Onie. 'And hand me your pieces.'

'But we were the right flank,' the *copain* said in his rich voice.

'You're shit,' Claude said. 'You venerable alcoholic. Shut up and fuck off.'

'*Mais on a battu.*'

'Fought, shit,' Marcel said. '*Foute moi le camp.*'

'*On peut fusiller les copains?*' Red asked. He had remembered it like a parrot.

'You shut up too,' I said. 'Claude, I promised them two *vélos*.'

'It's true,' Claude said.

'You and I will go down and give them the worst two and remove the Kraut and the *vélo*. You others keep the road cut.'

'It was not like this in the old days,' one of the *copains* said.

'Nothing's ever going to be like it was in the old days. You were probably drunk in the old days anyway.'

We went first to the German in the road. He was not dead but was shot through both lungs. We took him as gently as we could and laid him down as comfortable as we could and I took off his tunic and shirt and we sifted the wounds with Sulfa and Claude put a field dressing on him. He had a nice face and he did not look more than seventeen. He tried to talk but he couldn't. He was trying to take it the way he'd always heard you should.

Claude got a couple of tunics from the dead and made a pillow for him. Then he stroked his head and held his hand and felt his pulse. The boy was watching him all the time but he could not talk. The boy never looked away from him and Claude bent over and kissed him on the forehead.

'Carry that bicycle off the road,' I said to the *copains*.

'*Cette putain guerre*,' Claude said. 'This dirty whore of a war.'

The boy did not know that it was me who had done it to him and so he had no special fear of me and I felt his pulse too and I knew why Claude had done what he had done. I should have kissed him myself if I was any good. It was just one of those things that you omit to do and that stay with you.

'I'd like to stay with him for a little while,' Claude said.

'Thank you very much,' I said. I went over to where we had the four bicycles behind the trees and the *copains* were standing there like crows.

'Take this one and that one and *foute moi le camp*.' I took off their brassards and put them in my pocket.

'But we fought. That's worth two.'

'Fuck off,' I said. 'Did you hear me? Fuck off.'

They went away disappointed.

A boy about fourteen came out from the *estaminet* and asked for the new bicycle.

'They took mine early this morning.'

'All right. Take it.'

'What about the other two?'

'Run along and keep off the road until the column gets up here.'

'But you are the column.'

'No,' I said. 'Unfortunately we are not the column.'

The boy mounted the bicycle which was undamaged and rode down to the *estaminet*. I walked back under the hot summer sky to the farmyard to wait for the point. I didn't know how I could feel any worse. But you can all right. I can promise you that.

'Will we go into the big town tonight?' Red asked me.

'Sure. They're taking it now, coming in from the west. Can't you hear it?'

'Sure. You could hear it since noon. Is it a good town?'

'You'll see it as soon as the column gets up and we fit in and

go down that road past the *estaminet*.' I showed him on the map.
'You can see it in about a mile. See the curve before you drop
down?'

'Are we going to fight any more?'

'Not today.'

'You got another shirt?'

'It's worse than this.'

'It can't be worse than this one. I'll wash this one out. If you
have to put it on wet it won't hurt on a hot day like this. You
feeling bad?'

'Yeah. Very.'

'What's holding Claude up?'

'He's staying with the kid I shot until he dies.'

'Was it a kid?'

'Yeah.'

'Oh shit,' Red said.

After a while Claude came back wheeling the two *vélos*. He
handed me the boy's *Feldbuch*.

'Let me wash your shirt good too, Claude. I got Onie's and
mine washed and they're nearly dry.'

'Thanks very much, Red,' Claude said. 'Is there any of the
wine left?'

'We found some more and some sausage.'

'Good,' Claude said. He had the black ass bad too.

'We're going in the big town after the column overruns us.
You can see it only a little more than a mile from here,' Red told
him.

'I've seen it before,' Claude said. 'It's a good town.'

'We aren't going to fight any more today.'

'We'll fight tomorrow.'

'Maybe we won't have to.'

'Maybe.'

'Cheer up.'

'Shut up. I'm cheered up.'

'Good,' Red said. 'Take this bottle and the sausage and I'll
wash the shirt in no time.'

'Thank you very much,' Claude said. We were splitting it
even between us and neither of us liked our share.

LANDSCAPE WITH FIGURES

It was very strange in that house. The elevator, of course, no longer ran. The steel column it slid up and down on was bent and there were several marble stairs in the six flights which were broken so that you had to walk carefully on the edges as you climbed so that you would not fall through. There were doors which opened onto rooms where there were no longer any rooms and you could swing a perfectly sound-looking door open and step across the door sill into space: that floor and the next three floors below having been blasted out of the front of the apartment house by direct hits by high explosive shells. Yet the two top floors had four rooms on the front of the house which were intact and there was still running water in the back rooms on all of the floors. We called this house the Old Homestead.

The front line had, at the very worst moment, been directly below this apartment house along the upper edge of the little plateau that the boulevard circled and the trench and the weather-rotted sandbags were still there. They were so close you could throw a broken tile or a piece of mortar from the smashed apartment house down into them as you stood on one of the balconies. But now the line had been pushed down from the lip of the plateau, across the river and up into the pine-studded slope of the hill that rose behind the old royal hunting lodge that was called the Casa del Campo. It was there that the fighting was going on, now, and we used the Old Homestead both as an observation post and as an advantage point to film from.

In those days it was very dangerous and always cold and we were always hungry and we joked a great deal.

Each time a shell bursts in a building it makes a great cloud of brick and plaster dust and when this settles it coats the surface of a mirror so that it is as powdered as the windows which have been calcimined over in a new building. There was a tall unbroken mirror in one of the rooms of that house giving off the stairs as you climbed and on its dusty surface I printed, with my finger, in large letters DEATH TO JOHNNY and we then sent Johnny, the cameraman, into that room on some pretext. When he opened the door, during a shelling, and saw that ghostly announcement staring at him from the glass he went into a white, deadly, Dutch rage and it was quite a time before we were friends again.

Then the next day when we were loading the equipment into a car in front of the hotel I got into the car and cranked up the glass of the side window as it was bitterly cold. As the glass rose I saw, printed on it with large red letters in what must have been a borrowed lipstick, ED IS A LICE. We used the car for several days with that mysterious, to the Spaniards, slogan. They must have taken it for the initials or slogan of some Holland-American revolutionary organization perhaps resembling the F.A.I. or the C.N.T.

Then there was the day when the great British authority on let us forget just what came to town. He had a huge, German-type steel helmet which he wore on all expeditions in the direction of the front. This was an item of clothing which none of the rest of us affected. It was the general theory that since there were not many steel helmets these should be reserved for the shock troops and his wearing of this helmet formed in us an instant prejudice against the Great Authority.

We had met in the room of an American woman journalist who had a splendid electric heater. The Authority took an instant fancy to this very pleasant room and named it the Club. His proposal was that everyone should bring their own liquor there and be able to enjoy it in the warmth and pleasant atmosphere. As the American girl was exceedingly hard-working and had been trying, perhaps not too successfully, to keep her room from becoming in any sense the Club, this definite baptism and classification came as rather a blow to her.

We were working there in the Old Homestead the next day, shielding the camera lens as carefully as possible against the glare of the afternoon sun with a screen of broken matting, when the Authority arrived accompanied by the American girl. He had heard us discussing the location at the Club and had come to pay a visit. I was using a pair of field glasses, eight power, small Zeisses that you could cover with your two hands so that they gave no reflection, and was observing from the shadow in the angle of the broken balcony. The attack was about to start and we were waiting for the planes to come over and commence the bombardment which substituted for adequate artillery preparation due to the Government's then shortage of heavy artillery.

We had worked in the house, concealing ourselves as carefully as rats do because the success of our work and the possibility of continued observation depended altogether on not drawing any fire on the seemingly deserted building. Now into the room came the Great Authority, and drawing up one of the empty chairs, seated himself in the exact center of the open balcony, steel helmet, over-sized binoculars and all. The camera was at an angle on one side of the balcony window as carefully camouflaged as a machine gun. I was in the angle of shadow on the other, invisible to anyone on the hillside, and always careful never to move across the sunny open space. The Authority was seated in plain sight in the middle of the sunny patch looking, in his steel hat, like the head of all the general staffs in the world, his glasses blinking in the sun like a helio.

'Look,' I said to him. 'We have to work here. From where you're sitting your glasses make a blink that everybody on that hill can see.'

'Ay dount think theys aneh dainjah een a house,' the Authority said with calm and condescending dignity.

'If you ever hunted mountain sheep,' I said, 'you know they can see you as far as you can see them. Do you see how clearly you see the men with your glasses? They have glasses too.'

'Ay dount think theys aneh dainjah een a house,' the Authority repeated. 'Wheah are the tanks?'

'There,' I said. 'Under the trees.'

The two cameramen were making grimaces and shaking their clenched fists over their heads in fury.

'I go to take the big camera into the back,' Johnny said.

'Keep well back, daughter,' I said to the American girl. Then, to the Authority, 'They take you for somebody's staff, you know. They see that tin hat and those glasses and they think we're running the battle. You're asking for it, you know.'

He repeated his refrain.

It was at that minute that the first one hit us. It came with a noise like a bursted steam pipe combined with a ripping of canvas and with the burst and the roar and rattle of broken plaster and the dust smoke over us I had the girl out of the room and into the back of the apartment. As I dove through the door something with a steel hat on passed me going for the stairs. You may think a rabbit moves fast when it first jumps and starts zig-zagging away, but the Authority moved through that smoke-filled hall, down those tricky stairs, out the door, and down the street faster than any rabbit. One of the cameramen said he had no speed on the lens of his Leica which would stop him in motion. This of course is inaccurate but it gives the effect.

Anyway they shelled the house fast for about a minute. They came on such a flat trajectory you hardly had time to hold a breath between the rush and the jolt and roar of the burst. Then after the last one we waited a couple of minutes to see if it had stopped, had a drink of water from the tap in the kitchen sink, and found a new room to set up the camera. The attack was just starting.

The American girl was very bitter against the Authority. '*He* brought me here,' she said. '*He* said it was quite safe. And *he* went away and did not even say good-bye.'

'He *cahnt* be a gentleman,' I said. 'Look, daughter. Watch. Now. There it goes.'

Below us some men stood up, half crouching, and ran forward toward a stone house in a patch of trees. The house was disappearing in the sudden fountainings of dust clouds from the shells that were registering on it. The wind blew the dust clear after each shell so that the house kept showing plainly through the dust as a ship comes out of a fog and ahead of the men a tank lurched fast like a round-topped, gun-snouted beetle and went out of sight in the trees. As you watched, the men who were running forward threw themselves flat. Then another tank went forward on the left and into the trees and you could see the flash of its firing and in the smoke that blew from the house one of the men who was on the ground stood up and ran wildly back toward the trench that they had left when they attacked. Another got up and ran back, holding his rifle in one hand, his other hand on his head. Then they were running back from all along the line. Some fell as they ran. Others lay on the ground without ever having got up. They were scattered all over the hillside.

'What's happened?' the girl asked.

'The attack has failed,' I said.

'Why?'

'It wasn't pushed home.'

'Why? Wasn't it just as dangerous for them to run back as to go forward?'

'Not quite.'

The girl held the field glasses to her eyes. Then she put them down.

'I can't see any more,' she said. The tears were running down her cheeks and her face was working. I had never seen her cry before and we had seen many things you could cry about if you were going to cry. In a war everybody of all ranks including generals cries at some time or another. This is true, no matter what people tell you, but it is to be avoided, and is avoided, and I had not seen this girl doing it before.

'And that's an attack?'

'That's an attack,' I said. 'Now you've seen one.'

'And what will happen?'

'They may send them again if there's enough people left to lead them. I doubt if they will. You can count the losses out there if you like.'

'Are those men all dead?'

'No. Some are too badly wounded to move. They will bring them in in the dark.'

'What will the tanks do now?'

'They'll go home if they're lucky.'

But one of them was already unlucky. In the pine woods a black dirty column of smoke began to rise and was then blown sideways by the wind. Soon it was a rolling black cloud and in the greasy black smoke you could see the red flames. There was an explosion and a billowing of white smoke and then the black smoke rolled higher; but from a wider base.

'That's a tank,' I said. 'Burning.'

We stood and watched. Through the glasses you could see two men get out of an angle of the trench and start up a slant of the hill carrying a stretcher. They seemed to move slowly and ploddingly. As you watched the man in front sank onto his knees and then sat down. The man behind had dropped to the ground. He crawled forward. Then with his arm under the first man's shoulder he started to crawl, dragging him toward the trench. Then he stopped moving and you saw that he was lying flat on his face. They both lay there not moving now.

They had stopped shelling the house and it was quiet now. The big farmhouse and walled court showed clear and yellow against the green hillside that was scarred white with the dirt where the strong points had been fortified and the communication trenches dug. There was smoke from small fires rising now over the hillside where men were cooking. And up the slope toward the big farmhouse lay the casualties of the attack like many scattered bundles on the green slope. The tank was burning black and greasy in the trees.

'It's horrible,' the girl said. 'It's the first time I've ever seen it. It's really horrible.'

'It always has been.'

'Don't you hate it?'

'I hate it and I always have hated it. But when you have to do it you ought to know how. That was a frontal attack. They are just murder.'

'Are there other ways to attack?'

'Oh sure. Lots of them. But you have to have knowledge and discipline and trained squad and section leaders. And most of all you ought to have surprise.'

'It makes now too dark to work,' Johnny said putting the cap over his telephoto lens. 'Hello you old lice. Now we go home to the hotel. Today we work pretty good.'

'Yes,' said the other one. 'Today we have got something very good. It is too dom bad the attack is no good. Is better not to think about it. Sometime we film a successful attack. Only always with a successful attack it rains or snows.'

'I don't want to see any more ever,' the girl said. 'I've seen it now. Nothing would ever make me see it for curiosity or to make money writing about it. Those are *men* as we are. Look at them there on that hillside.'

'You are not men,' said Johnny. 'You are a womans. Don't make a confusion.'

'Comes now the steel hat man,' said the other looking out of the window. 'Comes now with much dignity. I wish I had bomb to throw to make suddenly a surprise.'

We were packing up the cameras and equipment when the steel-hatted Authority came in.

'Hullo,' he said. 'Did you make some good pictures? I have a car in one of the back streets to take you home, Elizabeth.'

'I'm going home with Edwin Henry,' the girl said.

'Did the wind die down?' I asked him conversationally.

He let that go by and said to the girl, 'You won't come?'

'No,' she said. 'We are all going home together.'

'I'll see you at the Club tonight,' he said to me very pleasantly.

'You don't belong to the Club any more,' I told him, speaking as nearly English as I could.

We all started down the stairs together, being very careful about the holes in the marble, and walking over and around the new damage. It seemed a very long stairway. I picked up a brass nose-cap flattened and plaster marked at the end and handed it to the girl called Elizabeth.

'I don't want it,' she said and at the doorway we all stopped and let the steel-hatted man go on ahead alone. He walked with great dignity across the part of the street where you were sometimes fired on and continued on, with dignity, in the shelter of the wall opposite. Then, one at a time, we sprinted across to the lee of the wall. It is the third or fourth man to cross an open space who draws the fire, you learn after you have been around a while, and we were always pleased to be across that particular place.

So we walked up the street now, protected by the wall, four abreast, carrying the cameras and stepping over the new iron fragments, the freshly broken bricks, and the blocks of stone, and watching the dignity of the walk of the steel-hatted man ahead who no longer belonged to the Club.

'I hate to write a dispatch,' I said. 'It's not going to be an easy one to write. This offensive is gone.'

'What's the matter with you, boy?' asked Johnny.

'You must write what can be said,' the other one said gently. 'Certainly something can be said about a day so full of events.'

'When will they get the wounded back?' the girl asked. She wore no hat and walked with a long loose stride and her hair, which was a dusty yellow in the fading light, hung over the collar of her short, fur-collared jacket. It swung as she turned her head. Her face was white and she looked ill.

'I told you as soon as it gets dark.'

'God make it get dark quick,' she said. 'So that's war. That's what I've come here to see and write about. Were those two men killed who went out with the stretcher?'

'Yes,' I said. 'Positively.'

'They moved so *slowly*,' the girl said pitifully.

'Sometimes it's very hard to make the legs move,' I said. 'It's like walking in deep sand or in a dream.'

Ahead of us the man in the steel hat was still walking up the street. There was a line of shattered houses on his left and the brick wall of the barracks on his right. His car was parked at the end of the street where ours was also standing in the lee of a house.

'Let's take him back to the Club,' the girl said. 'I don't want anyone to be hurt tonight. Not their feelings nor anything. Heh!' she called. 'Wait for us. We're coming.'

He stopped and looked back, the great heavy helmet looking ridiculous as he turned his head, like the huge horns on some harmless beast. He waited and we came up.

'Can I help you with any of that?' he asked.

'No. The car's just there ahead.'

'We're all going to the Club,' the girl said. She smiled at him. 'Would you come and bring a bottle of something?'

'That would be so nice,' he said. 'What should I bring?'

'Anything,' the girl said. 'Bring anything you like. I have to do some work first. Make it seven thirtyish.'

'Will you ride home with me?' he asked her. 'I'm afraid the other car is crowded with all that bit.'

'Yes,' she said. 'I'd like to. Thank you.'

They got in one car and we loaded all the stuff into the other.

'What's the matter, boy?' Johnny said. 'Your girl go home with somebody else?'

'The attack upset her. She feels very badly.'

'A woman who doesn't upset by an attack is no woman,' said Johnny.

'It was a very unsuccessful attack,' said the other. 'Fortunately she did not see it from too close. We must never let her see one from close regardless of the danger. It is too strong a thing. From where she saw it is only a picture. Like old-fashioned battle scene.'

'She has a kind heart,' said Johnny. 'Different than you, you old lice.'

'I have a kind heart,' I said. 'And it's louse. Not lice. Lice is the plural.'

'I like lice better,' said Johnny. 'It sounds more determined.'

But he put up his hand and rubbed out the words written in lipstick on the window.

'We make a new joke tomorrow,' he said. 'It's all right now about the writing on the mirror.'

'Good,' I said. 'I'm glad.'

'You old lice,' said Johnny and slapped me on the back.

'Louse is the word.'

'No. Lice. I like much better. Is many times more determined.'

'Go to hell.'

'Good,' said Johnny, smiling happily. 'Now we are all good friends again. In a war we must all be careful not to hurt each other's feelings.'

I GUESS EVERYTHING REMINDS
YOU OF SOMETHING

'It's a very good story,' the boy's father said. 'Do you know how good it is?'

'I didn't want her to send it to you, Papa.'

'What else have you written?'

'That's the only story. Truly I didn't want her to send it to you. But when it won the prize –'

'She wants me to help you. But if you can write that well you don't need anyone to help you. All you need is to write. How long did it take you to write that story?'

'Not very long.'

'Where did you learn about that type of gull?'

'In the Bahamas I guess.'

'You never went to the Dog Rocks nor to Elbow Key. There weren't any gulls nor terns nested at Cat Key nor Bimini. At Key West you would only have seen least terns nesting.'

'Killem Peters. Sure. They nest on the coral rocks.'

'Right on the flats,' his father said. 'Where would you have known gulls like the one in the story?'

'Maybe you told me about them, Papa.'

'It's a very fine story. It reminds me of a story I read a long time ago.'

'I guess everything reminds you of something,' the boy said.

That summer the boy read books that his father found for him in the library and when he would come over to the main house for lunch, if he had not been playing baseball or had not been down at the club shooting, he would often say he had been writing.

'Show it to me when you want to or ask me about any trouble,' his father said. 'Write about something that you know.'

'I am,' the boy said.

'I don't want to look over your shoulder or breathe down your neck,' his father said. 'If you want, though, I can set you some simple problems about things we both know. It would be good training.'

'I think I'm going all right.'

'Don't show it to me until you want to then. How did you like "Far Away and Long Ago"?'

'I liked it very much.'

'The sort of problems I meant were: we could go into the market together or to the cockfight and then each of us write down what we saw. What it really was that you saw that stayed with you. Things like the handler opening the rooster's bill and blowing in his throat when the referee would let them pick up and handle them before pitting again. The small things. To see what we each saw.'

The boy nodded and then looked down at his plate.

'Or we can go into the café and shake a few rounds of poker dice and you write what it was in the conversation that you heard. Not try to write everything. Only what you heard that meant anything.'

'I'm afraid that I'm not ready for that yet, Papa. I think I'd better go on the way I did in the story.'

'Do that then. I don't want to interfere or influence you. Those were just exercises. I'd have been glad to do them with you. They're like five-finger exercises. Those weren't especially good. We can make better ones.'

'Probably it's better for me to go on the way it was in the story.'

'Sure,' his father said.

I could not write that well when I was his age, his father thought. I never knew anyone else that could either. But I never knew anyone else that could shoot better at ten than this boy could; not just show-off shooting, but shooting in competition with grown men and professionals. He shot the same way in the field when he was twelve. He shot as though he had built-in radar. He never took a shot out of range nor let a driven bird come too close and he shot with beautiful style and an absolute timing and precision on high pheasants and in pass shooting at ducks.

At live pigeons, in competition, when he walked out on the cement, spun the wheel and walked to the metal plaque that marked the black stripe of his yardage, the pros were silent and watching. He was the only shooter that the crowd became dead silent for. Some of the pros smiled as though at a secret when he put his gun to his shoulder and looked back to see where the heel of the stock rested against his shoulder. Then his cheek went down against the comb, his left hand was far forward, his weight was forward on his left foot. The muzzle of the gun rose and lowered, then swept to left, to right, and back to center. The heel of his right foot lifted gently as all of him leaned behind the two loads in the chambers.

'Ready,' he said in that low, hoarse voice that did not belong to a small boy.

'Ready,' answered the trapper.

'Pull,' said the hoarse voice and from whichever of the five traps the gray racing pigeon came out, and at whatever angle his wings drove him in full, low flight above the green grass toward the white, low fence, the load of the first barrel swung into him and the load from the second barrel drove through the first. As the bird collapsed in flight, his head falling forward, only the great shots saw the impact of the second load driving through onto the bird already dead in the air.

The boy would break his gun and walk back in off the cement toward the pavilion, no expression on his face, his eyes down, never giving any recognition to applause and saying, 'Thanks,' in the strange hoarse voice if some pro said, 'Good bird, Stevie.'

He would put his gun in the rack and wait to watch his father shoot and then the two of them would walk off together to the outdoor bar.

'Can I drink a Coca-Cola, Papa?'

'Better not drink more than half a one.'

'All right. I'm sorry I was so slow. I shouldn't have let the bird get hard.'

'He was a strong, low driver, Stevie.'

'Nobody'd ever have known it if I hadn't been slow.'

'You're doing all right.'

'I'll get my speed back. Don't worry, Papa. Just this little bit of Coke won't slow me.'

His next bird died in the air as the spring arm of the sunken trap swung him up from the opening in the hidden trench into driving flight. Everyone could see the second barrel hit him in the air before he hit the ground. He had not gone a yard from the trap.

As the boy came in one of the local shooters said, 'Well, you got an easy one, Stevie.'

The boy nodded and put up his gun. He looked at the score-board. There were four other shooters before his father. He went to find him.

'You've got your speed back,' his father said.

'I heard the trap,' the boy said. 'I don't want to throw you off, Papa. You can hear all of them I know. But now the number

two trap is about twice as loud as any of the others. They ought
to grease it. Nobody's noticed it I don't think.'

'I always swing on the noise of the trap.'

'Sure. But if it's extra loud it's to your left. Left is loud.'

His father did not draw a bird from the number two trap for
the next three rounds. When he did he did not hear the trap and
killed the bird with his second barrel far out so that it just hit the
fence to fall inside.

'Geez, Papa, I'm sorry,' the boy said. 'They greased it. I should
have kept my damned mouth shut.'

It was the night after the last big international shoot that they
had ever shot in together that they had been talking and the boy
had said, 'I don't understand how anyone ever misses a pigeon.'

'Don't ever say that to anybody else,' his father said.

'No. I mean it really. There's no reason ever to miss one. The
one I lost on I hit twice but it fell dead outside.'

'That's how you lose.'

'I understand that. That's how I lost. But I don't see how any
real shooter can miss one.'

'Maybe you will in twenty years,' his father said.

'I didn't mean to be rude, Papa.'

'That's all right,' his father said. 'Only don't say it to other
people.'

He was thinking of that when he wondered about the story
and about the boy's writing. With all his unbelievable talent the
boy had not become the shooter he was on live birds by himself
nor without being taught and disciplined. He had forgotten now
all about the training. He had forgotten how when he started to
miss live birds his father would take his shirt off him and show
him the bruise on his arm where he had placed the gun incor-
rectly. He had cured him of that by having him always look back
at his shoulder to be sure he had mounted the gun before he
called for a bird.

He had forgotten the discipline of weight on your forward
foot, keep your head down and swing. How do you know your
weight is on your forward foot? By raising your right heel. Head
down, swing and speed. Now it doesn't matter what your score
is. I want you to take them as soon as they leave the trap. Never
look at any part of the bird but the bill. Swing with their bills. If
you can't see the bill swing where it would be. What I want
from you now is speed.

The boy was a wonderful natural shot but he had worked with

him to make him a perfect shot and each year when he would take him and start on his speed he would start killing a six or eight out of ten. Then move to nine out of ten; hang there, and then move up to a twenty out of twenty only to be beaten by the luck that separated perfect shooters in the end.

He never showed his father the second story. It was not finished to his satisfaction at the end of vacation. He said he wanted to get it absolutely right before he showed it. As soon as he got it right he was going to send it to his father. He had had a very good vacation, he said, one of the best and he was glad he had such good reading too and he thanked his father for not pushing him too hard on the writing because after all a vacation is a vacation and this had been a fine one, maybe one of the very best, and they certainly had had some wonderful times they certainly had.

It was seven years later that his father read the prize-winning story again. It was in a book that he found in checking through some books in the boy's old room. As soon as he saw it he knew where the story had come from. He remembered the long-ago feeling of familiarity. He turned through the pages and there it was, unchanged and with the same title, in a book of very good short stories by an Irish writer. The boy had copied it exactly from the book and used the original title.

In the last five of the seven years between the summer of the prize-winning story and the day his father ran onto the book the boy had done everything hateful and stupid that he could, his father thought. But it was because he was sick his father had told himself. His vileness came on from a sickness. He was all right until then. But that had all started a year or more after that last summer.

Now he knew that boy had never been any good. He had thought so often looking back on things. And it was sad to know that shooting did not mean a thing.

GREAT NEWS FROM THE MAINLAND

For three days it blew out of the south bending the fronds of the royal palms until they were parted in a line forward and away from the gray trunks that bent with the heavy wind. As the wind increased the dark green stems of the fronds blew wildly as the wind killed them. The branches of the mango trees shook and snapped in the wind and its heat burned the mango flowers until they were brown and dusty and their stems dried. The grass dried and there was no more moisture in the soil and it was dust in the wind.

The wind blew day and night for five days and when it stopped half the palm fronds hung dead against the trunks, the green mangos lay on the ground and on the trees and the blossoms were dead and the stems dry. The mango crop was gone along with all the other things that went that year.

The call he had put in on the telephone came through from the mainland and the man said, 'Yes, Dr. Simpson,' and then heard the cracker voice say, 'Mr. Wheeler? Well sir that boy of yours certainly surprised us all today. He really did. We were giving him the usual sodium pentothal before the shock treatment and I've always noticed that boy has an unusual resistance to sodium pentothal. Never took drugs did he?'

'Not as far as I know.'

'No? Well naturally one never knows. But he certainly put on a performance today. Threw five of us around just as though we were children. Five grown men I tell you. Had to postpone the treatment. Of course he has a morbid fear of electric shock that's completely unjustified and that's why I use the sodium pentothal but there was no question of administering it today. Now I regard it as an excellent sign. He hasn't revolted against anything Mr. Wheeler. This is the most favorable sign I've seen. That boy's really making progress Mr. Wheeler. I was proud of him. Why I said to him, "Stephen I didn't know you had it in you." You can be proud and satisfied at the way he's getting along. He wrote me one of the most interesting and significant letters right after the incident. I'm sending it over to you. You didn't get the other letters? That's right. That's right there was a little delay in getting them off. My secretary has been literally swamped, you know how it is Mr. Wheeler and I'm a busy man. Well he used the vilest language of course when he was resisting the treatment but he apologized to me in the most gentlemanly way. You should see that boy now Mr. Wheeler. He's taking care of his appearance now. He's just the typical fashion plate of a young college gentleman.'

'What about the treatment?'

'Oh he'll get the treatment. I'll just have to double up on the quantity of the sodium pentothal first. His resistance to that is simply amazing. You understand these are extra treatments that he requested himself of course. There might be something masochistic in that. He even suggested that himself in his letter. But I don't think so. I think that boy's beginning to get a grasp of reality. I'm sending you the letter. You can be very encouraged about that boy Mr. Wheeler.'

'How's the weather over there?'

'What's that? Oh the weather. Well it's just a bit off from what I'd describe as typical for this time of year. No it's not entirely typical. There has been some unreasonable weather to be frank. You call up anytime Mr. Wheeler. I wouldn't be upset or worried about the progress that boy's making for a moment. I'll send you his letter. You could almost describe it as a brilliant letter. Yes Mr. Wheeler. No Mr. Wheeler I'd say everything's going finely Mr. Wheeler. There's nothing to worry about. You'd like to talk to him? I'll see that your call goes through at the hospital. Tomorrow is better perhaps. He's naturally a little exhausted after the treatment. Tomorrow would be better. You say he didn't have the treatment? That's quite correct Mr. Wheeler. I had no idea that boy was capable of anything like that strength. That's correct. The treatment is for tomorrow. I'll just increase the sodium pentothal. These additional treatments he requested himself, remember. Give him a call day after tomorrow. That's a free day for him and he will have had a rest. That's right Mr. Wheeler that's right. You have no cause for anxiety. I would say his progress could not be more satisfactory. Today's Tuesday. You call him on Thursday. Any time Thursday.'

The wind was back in the south on Thursday. There was not much it could do now to trees except blow the dead brown palm branches and burn the few mango blossoms whose stems had not died. But it yellowed the leaves of the alamo trees and blew dust and stripped leaves over the swimming pool. It blew dust through the screens into the house and sifted it into the books and over the pictures. The milk cows lay with their rumps against the wind and the cuds they chewed were gritty. The winds always come in Lent, Mr. Wheeler remembered. That was the local name for them. All bad winds had local names and bad writers always became literary about them. He had resisted this as he had resisted writing that the palm branches blew forward making a line against the trunk as the hair of young women parts and blows forward when they stand with their backs to a storm. He had resisted writing of the scent of the mango blooms when they had walked together on the night before the wind started and the noise of the bees in them outside his window. There were no bees now and he refused to use the foreign word for this wind. There had been too much bad literature made about the foreign names for winds and he knew too many of those names. Mr. Wheeler was writing in longhand because he did not wish to uncover the typewriter in the Lenten wind.

The houseboy who had been a contemporary and a friend of his son when they were both growing up came in and said, 'The call to Stevie is ready.'

'Hi Papa,' Stephen said in a hoarse voice. 'I'm fine Papa really fine. This is the time. I've really got this thing beat now. You have no idea. I've really got a grasp of reality now. Dr. Simpson? Oh he's fine. I really have confidence in him. He's a good man Papa. I really have faith in him. He's more down to earth than the majority of those people. He's giving me a few extra treatments. How's everybody? Good. How's the weather? Good that's fine. No difficulty about treatments. No. Not at all. Everything's fine really. Glad everything's so good with you. This time I've really got the answer. Well we mustn't waste money on the telephone. Give my love to everyone. Good-bye Papa. See you soon.'

'Stevie sent you his best,' I said to the houseboy.

He smiled happily, remembering the old days.

'That's nice of him. How is he?'

'Fine,' I said. 'He says everything is fine.'

THE STRANGE COUNTRY

Miami was hot and muggy and the land wind that blew from the Everglades brought mosquitoes even in the morning.

'We'll get out as soon as we can,' Roger said. 'I'll have to get some money. Do you know anything about cars?'

'Not very much.'

'You might look and see what there is advertised in the classified in the paper and I'll get some money here to Western Union.'

'Can you get it just like that?'

'If I get the call through in time so my lawyer can get it off.'

They were up on the thirteenth floor of a hotel on Biscayne Boulevard and the bellboy had just gone down for the papers and some other purchases. There were two rooms and they overlooked the bay, the park and the traffic passing on the Boulevard. They were registered under their own names.

'You take the corner one,' Roger had said. 'It will have a little breeze in it maybe. I'll get on the telephone in the other room.'

'What can I do to help?'

'You run through the classifieds on motorcars for sale in one paper and I'll take the other.'

'What sort of a car?'

'A convertible with good rubber. The best one we can get.'

'How much money do you think we'll have?'

'I'm going to try for five thousand.'

'That's wonderful. Do you think you can get it?'

'I don't know. I'll get going on him now,' Roger said and went into the other room. He shut the door and then opened it. 'Do you still love me?'

'I though that was all settled,' she said. 'Please kiss me now before the boy comes back.'

'Good.'

He held her solidly against him and kissed her hard.

'That's better,' she said. 'Why did we have to have separate rooms?'

'I thought I might have to be identified to get the money.'

'Oh.'

'If we have any luck we won't have to stay in these.'

'Can we really do it all that fast?'

'If we have any luck.'

'Then can we be Mr. and Mrs. Gilch?'

'Mr. and Mrs. Stephen Gilch.'

'Mr. and Mrs. Stephen Brat-Gilch.'

'I'd better make the call.'

'Don't stay away an awfully long time though.'

They had lunch at a seafood restaurant owned by Greeks. It was an air-conditioned oasis against the heavy heat of the town and the food had certainly originally come out of the ocean but it was to Eddy's cooking of the same things as old re-used grease is to fresh browned butter. But there was a good bottle of really cold, dry, resiny tasting Greek white wine and for dessert they had cherry pie.

'Let's go to Greece and the islands,' she said.

'Haven't you ever been there?'

'One summer. I loved it.'

'We'll go there.'

By two o'clock the money was at the Western Union. It was thirty-five hundred instead of five thousand and by three-thirty they had bought a used Buick convertible with only six thousand miles on it. It had two good spares, set-in well fenders, a radio, a big spotlight, plenty of luggage space in the rear and it was sand colored.

By five-thirty they had made various other purchases, checked out of the hotel and the doorman was stowing their bags into the back of the car. It was still deadly hot.

Roger, who was sweating heavily in his heavy uniform, as suitable to the subtropics in summer as shorts would be to Labrador in winter, tipped the doorman and got into the car and they drove along Biscayne Boulevard and turned west to get onto the road to Coral Gables and the Tamiami Trail.

'How do you feel?' he asked the girl.

'Wonderful. Do you think it's true?'

'I know it's true because it's so damned hot and we didn't get the five thousand.'

'Do you think we paid too much for the car?'

'No. Just right.'

'Did you get the insurance?'

'Yes. And joined the A.A.A.'

'Aren't we fast?'

'We're terrific.'

'Have you got the rest of the money?'

'Sure. Pinned in my shirt.'

'That's our bank.'

'It's all we've got.'

'How do you think it will last?'

'It won't have to last. I'll make some more.'

'It will have to last for a while.'

'It will.'

'Roger.'

'Yes, daughter.'

'Do you love me?'

'I don't know.'

'Say it.'

'I don't know. But I'm going to damn well find out.'

'I love you. Hard. Hard. Hard.'

'You keep that up. That will be a big help to me.'

'Why don't you say you love me?'

'Let's wait.'

She had been holding her hand on his thigh while he drove and now she took it away.

'All right,' she said. 'We'll wait.'

They were driving west now on the broad Coral Gables road through the flat heat-stricken outskirts of Miami, past stores, filling stations and markets with cars with people going home from the city passing them steadily. Now they passed Coral Gables to their left with the buildings that looked out of the Basso Veneto rising from the Florida prairie and ahead the road stretched straight and heat-welted across what had once been the Everglades. Roger drove faster now and the movement of the car through the heavy air made the air cool as it came in through the scoop in the dash and the slanted glass of the ventilators.

'She's a lovely car,' the girl said. 'Weren't we lucky to get her?'

'Very.'

'We're pretty lucky don't you think?'

'So far.'

'You've gotten awfully cautious on me.'

'Not really.'

'But we can be jolly can't we?'

'I'm jolly.'

'You don't sound awfully jolly.'

'Well maybe then I'm not.'

'Couldn't you be though? You see I really am.'

'I will be,' Roger said. 'I promise.'

Looking ahead at the road he had driven so many times in his life, seeing it stretch ahead, knowing it was the same road with the ditches on either side and the forest and the swamps, knowing that only the car was different, that only who was with him was different, Roger felt the old hollowness coming inside of him and knew he must stop it.

'I love you, daughter,' he said. He did not think it was true. But it sounded all right as he said it. 'I love you very much and I'm going to try to be very good to you.'

'And you're going to be jolly.'

'And I'm going to be jolly.'

'That's wonderful,' she said. 'Have we started already?'

'We're on the road.'

'When will we see the birds?'

'They're much further in this time of year.'

'Roger.'

'Yes, Bratchen.'

'You don't have to be jolly if you don't feel like it. We'll be jolly enough. You feel however you feel and I'll be jolly for us both. I can't help it today.'

He saw on ahead where the road turned to the right and ran northwest through the forest swamp instead of west. That was good. That was really much better. Pretty soon they would come to the big osprey's nest in the dead cypress tree. They had just passed the place where he had killed the rattlesnake that winter driving through here with David's mother before Andrew was born. That was the year they both bought Seminole shirts at the trading post at Everglades and wore them in the car. He had given the big rattlesnake to some Indians that had come in to trade and they were pleased with the snake because he had a fine hide and twelve rattles and Roger remembered how heavy and thick he was when he lifted him with his huge, flattened head hanging and how the Indian smiled when he took him. That was the year they shot the wild turkey as he crossed the road that early morning coming out of the mist that was just thinning with the first sun, the cypresses showing black in the silver mist and the turkey brown-bronze and lovely as he stepped onto the road, stepping high-headed, then crouching to run, then flopping on the road.

'I'm fine,' he told the girl. 'We get into some nice country now.'

'Where do you think we'll get to tonight?'

'We'll find some place. Once we get to the gulf side this breeze will be a sea breeze instead of a land breeze and it will be cool.'

'That will be lovely,' the girl said. 'I hated to think of staying the first night in that hotel.'

'We were awfully lucky to get away. I didn't think we could do it that quickly.'

'I wonder how Tom is.'

'Lonely,' Roger said.

'Isn't he a wonderful guy?'

'He's my best friend and my conscience and my father and my brother and my banker. He's like a saint. Only jolly.'

'I never knew anybody as fine,' she said. 'It breaks your heart the way he loves you and the boys.'

'I wish he could have them all summer.'

'Won't you miss them terribly?'

'I miss them all the time.'

They had put the wild turkey in the back of the seat and he had been so heavy, warm and beautiful with the shining bronze plumage, so different from the blues and blacks of a domestic turkey, and David's mother was so excited she could hardly speak. And then she had said, 'No. Let me hold him. I want to see him again. We can put him away later.' And he had put a newspaper on her lap and she had tucked the bird's bloodied head under his wing, folding the wing carefully over it, and sat there stroking and smoothing his breast feathers while he, Roger, drove. Finally she said, 'He's cold now' and had wrapped him in the paper and put him in the back of the seat again and said, 'Thank you for letting me keep him when I wanted him so much.' Roger had kissed her while he drove and she had said, 'Oh Roger we're so happy and we always will be won't we?' That was just around this next slanting turn the road makes up ahead. The sun was down to the top of the treetops now. But they had not seen the birds.

'You won't miss them so much you won't be able to love me will you?'

'No. Truly.'

'I understand it making you sad. But you were going to be away from them anyway weren't you?'

'Sure. Please don't worry, daughter.'

'I like it when you say daughter. Say it again.'

'It comes at the end of a sentence,' he said. 'Daughter.'

'Maybe it's because I'm younger,' she said. 'I love the kids. I love them all three, hard, and I think they're wonderful. I didn't know there were kids like that. But Andy's too young for me to marry and I love you. So I forget about them and just am as happy as I can be to be with you.'

'You're good.'

'I'm not really. I'm awfully difficult. But I do know when I love someone and I've loved you ever since I can remember. So I'm going to try to be good.'

'You're being wonderful.'

'Oh I can be much better than this.'

'Don't try.'

'I'm not going to for a while. Roger I'm so happy. We'll be happy won't we?'

'Yes, daughter.'

'And we can be happy for always can't we? I know it sounds silly me being Mother's daughter and you with everyone. But I believe in it and it's possible. I know it's possible. I've loved you all my life and if that's possible it's possible to be happy isn't it? Say it is anyway.'

'I think it is.'

He'd always said it was. Not in this car though. In other cars in other countries. But he had said it enough in this country too and he had believed it. It would have been possible too. Everything was possible once. It was possible on this road on that stretch that now lay ahead where the canal ran clear and flowing by the right-hand side of the road where the Indian poled his dugout. There was no Indian there now. That was before. When it was possible. Before the birds were gone. That was the other year before the turkey. That year before the big rattlesnake was the year they saw the Indian poling the dugout and the buck in the bow of the dugout with his white throat and chest, his slender legs with the delicate shaped hoofs, shaped like a broken heart, drawn up and his head with the beautiful miniature horns looking toward the Indian. They had stopped the car and spoken to the Indian but he did not understand English and grinned and the small buck lay there dead with his eyes open looking straight at the Indian. It was possible then and for five years after. But what was possible now? Nothing was possible now unless he himself was and he must say the things if there was ever to be a chance of them being true. Even if it were wrong to say them he must say them. They never could be true unless he said them.

He had to say them and then perhaps he could feel them and then perhaps he could believe them. And then perhaps they would be true. Perhaps is an ugly word, he thought, but it is even worse on the end of your cigar.

'Have you got cigarettes?' he asked the girl. 'I don't know whether that lighter works.'

'I haven't tried it. I haven't smoked. I've felt so unnervous.'

'You don't just smoke when you're nervous do you?'

'I think so. Mostly.'

'Try the lighter.'

'All right.'

'Who was the guy you married?'

'Oh let's not talk about him.'

'No. I just meant who was he?'

'No one you know.'

'Don't you really want to tell me about him?'

'No, Roger. No.'

'All right.'

'I'm sorry,' she said. 'He was English.'

'Was?'

'Is. But I like *was* better. Besides you said was.'

'Was is a good word,' he said. 'It's a hell of a lot better word than perhaps.'

'All right. I don't understand it at all but I believe you. Roger?'

'Yes, daughter.'

'Do you feel any better?'

'Much. I'm fine.'

'All right. I'll tell you about him. He turned out to be gay. That was it. He hadn't said anything about it and he didn't act that way at all. Not at all. Truly. You probably think I'm stupid. But he didn't in any way. He was absolutely beautiful. You know how they can be. And then I found out about it. Right away of course. The same night actually. Now is it all right not to talk about it?'

'Poor Helena.'

'Don't call me Helena. Call me daughter.'

'My poor daughter. My darling.'

'That's a nice word too. You mustn't mix it with daughter though. It's no good that way. Mummy knew him. I thought she might have said something. She just said she'd never noticed and when I said, "You might have noticed," she said, "I thought

you knew what you were doing and I had no call to interfere."
I said, "Couldn't you just have said something or couldn't
somebody just have said something?" and she said, "Darling,
everyone thought you knew what you were doing. Everyone.
Everyone knows you don't care anything about it yourself and I
had every right to think you knew the facts of life in this right
little tight little island." '

She was sitting stiff and straight beside him now and she had
no tone in her voice at all. She didn't mimic. She simply used
the exact words or as exactly as she remembered them. Roger
thought they sounded quite exact.

'Mummy was a great comfort,' she said. 'She said a lot of
things to me that day.'

'Look,' Roger said. 'We'll throw it all away. All of it. We'll
throw it all away now right here beside the road. Any of it you
want to get rid of you can always tell me. But we've thrown it
all away now and we've really thrown it away.'

'I want it to be like that,' she said. 'That's how I started out.
And you know I said at the start we'd give it a miss.'

'I know. I'm sorry. But I'm glad really because now we have
thrown it away.'

'It's nice of you. But you don't have to make incantations or
exorcisions or any of that. I can swim without water wings. And
he *was* damned beautiful.'

'Spit it out. If that's the way you want it.'

'Don't be like that. You're so damned superior you don't have
to be superior. Roger?'

'Yes, Bratchen.'

'I love you very much and we don't have to do this any more
do we?'

'No. Truly.'

'I'm so glad. Now will we be jolly?'

'Sure we will. Look,' he said. 'There are the birds. The first of
them.'

They showed white in the cypress hammock that rose like an
island of trees out of the swamp on their left the sun shining on
them in the dark foliage and as the sun lowered more came
flying across the sky, flying white and slow, their long legs
stretched behind them.

'They're coming in for the night. They've been feeding out
in the marsh. Watch the way they brake with their wings and the
long legs slant forward to land.'

'Will we see the ibises too?'

'There they are.'

He had stopped the car and across the darkening swamp they could see the wood ibis crossing the sky with their pulsing flight to wheel and light in another island of trees.

'They used to roost much closer.'

'Maybe we will see them in the morning,' she said. 'Do you want me to make a drink while we've stopped?'

'We can make it while we drive. The mosquitoes will get to us here.'

As he started the car there were a few mosquitoes in it, the big black Everglades type, but the rush of the wind took them out when he opened the door and slapped them out with his hand and the girl found two enameled cups in the packages they had brought and the carton that held a bottle of White Horse. She wiped the cups out with a paper napkin, poured in Scotch, the bottle still in the carton, put in lumps of ice from the thermos jug and poured soda into them.

'Here's to us,' she said and gave him the cold enameled cup and he held it drinking slowly and driving on, holding the wheel with his left hand, driving along into the road that was dusky now. He put on the lights a little later and soon they cut far ahead into the dark and the two of them drank the whiskey and it was what they needed and made them feel much better. There is always a chance, Roger thought, when a drink can still do what it is supposed to do. This drink had done exactly what it should do.

'It tastes sort of slimy and slippery in a cup.'

'Enameled,' Roger said.

'That was pretty easy,' she said. 'Doesn't it taste wonderfully?'

'It's the first drink we've had all day. Except that resin wine at lunch. It's our good friend,' he said. 'The old giant killer.'

'That's a nice name for it. Did you always call it that?'

'Since the war. That's when we first used it for that.'

'This forest would be a bad place for giants.'

'I think they've been killed off a long time,' he said. 'They probably hunted them out with those big swamp buggies with the huge tires.'

'That must be very elaborate. It's easier with an enameled cup.'

'Tin cups make it taste even better,' he said. 'Not for giant killing. Just for how good it can be. But you ought to have ice cold spring water and the cup chilled in the spring and you look down in the spring and there are little plumes of sand that rise on the bottom where it's bubbling.'

'Will we have that?'

'Sure. We'll have everything. You can make a wonderful one with wild strawberries. If you have a lemon you cut half of it and squeeze it into the cup and leave the rind in the cup. Then you crush the wild strawberries into the cup and wash the sawdust off a piece of ice from the icehouse and put it in and then fill the cup with Scotch and then stir it till it's all mixed and cold.'

'Don't you put in any water?'

'No. The ice melts enough and there's enough juice in the strawberries and from the lemon.'

'Do you think there will still be wild strawberries?'

'I'm sure there will be.'

'Do you think there will be enough to make a shortcake?'

'I'm pretty sure there will be.'

'We better not talk about it. I'm getting awfully hungry.'

'We'll drive about another drink more,' he said. 'And then we ought to be there.'

They drove on in the night now with the swamp dark and high on both sides of the road and the good headlights lighting far ahead. The drinks drove the past away the way the headlights cut through the dark and Roger said,

'Daughter, I'll take another if you want to make it.'

When she had made it she said, 'Why don't you let me hold it and give it to you when you want it?'

'It doesn't bother me driving.'

'It doesn't bother me to hold it either. Doesn't it make you feel good?'

'Better than anything.'

'Not than anything. But awfully good.'

Ahead now were the lights of a village where the trees were cleared away and Roger turned onto a road that ran to the left and drove past a drugstore, a general store, a restaurant and along a deserted paved street that ran to the sea. He turned right and drove on another paved street past vacant lots and scattered houses until they saw the lights of a filling station and a neon sign advertising cabins. The main highway ran past there joining the sea road and the cabins were toward the sea. They stopped the car at the filling station and Roger asked the middle-aged man who came out looking blue-skinned in the light of the sign to check the oil and water and fill the tank.

'How are the cabins?' Roger asked.

'O.K., Cap,' the man said. 'Nice cabins. Clean cabins.'

'Got clean sheets?' Roger asked.

'Just as clean as you want them. You folks fixing to stay all night?'

'If we stay.'

'All night's three dollars.'

'How's for the lady to have a look at one?'

'Fine and dandy. She won't ever see no finer mattresses. Sheets plumb clean. Shower. Perfect cross ventilation. Modern plumbing.'

'I'll go in,' the girl said.

'Here take a key. You folks from Miami?'

'That's right.'

'Prefer the West Coast myself,' the man said. 'Your oil's O.K. and so's your water.'

The girl came back to the car.

'The one I saw is a splendid cabin. It's cool too.'

'Breeze right off the Gulf of Mexico,' the man said. 'Going to blow all night. All tomorrow. Probably part of Thursday. Did you try that mattress?'

'Everything looked marvelous.'

'My old woman keeps them so goddam clean it's a crime. She wears herself to death on them. I sent her up to the show to-night. Laundry's the biggest item. But she does it. There it is. I just got nine into her.' He went to hang up the hose.

'He's a little confusing,' Helena whispered. 'But it's quite nice and clean.'

'Well you going to take her?' the man asked.

'Sure,' Roger said. 'We'll take her.'

'Write in the book then.'

Roger wrote Mr. and Mrs. Robert Hutchins 9072 Surfside Drive Miami Beach and handed the book back.

'Any kin to the educator?' the man asked, making a note of the license number in the book.

'No. I'm sorry.'

'Nothing to be sorry about,' the man said. 'I never thought much of him. Just read about him in the papers. Like me to help you with anything?'

'No. I'll just run her in and we'll put our things in.'

'That's three and nine gallons makes five-fifty with the state tax.'

'Where can we get something to eat?' Roger asked.

'Two different places in town. Just about the same.'

'You prefer either one?'

'People speak pretty highly of the Green Lantern.'

'I think I've heard of it,' the girl said. 'Somewhere.'

'You might. Widow woman runs it.'

'I believe that's the place,' the girl said.

'Sure you don't want me to help you?'

'No. We're fine,' Roger said.

'Just one thing I'd like to say,' the man said. 'Mrs. Hutchins certainly is a fine looking woman.'

'Thank you,' Helena said. 'I think that's lovely of you. But I'm afraid it's just that beautiful light.'

'No,' he said. 'I mean it true. From the heart.'

'I think we'd better go in,' Helena said to Roger. 'I don't want you to lose me so early in the trip.'

Inside the cabin there was a double bed, a table covered with oilcloth, two chairs and a light bulb that hung down from the ceiling. There was a shower, a toilet and a washbowl with a mirror. Clean towels hung on a rack by the washbowl and there was a pole at one end of the room with some hangers.

Roger brought in the bags and Helena put the ice jug, the two cups, and the cardboard carton with the Scotch in it on the table with the paper bag full of White Rock bottles.

'Don't look gloomy,' she said. 'The bed is clean. The sheets anyway.'

Roger put his arm around her and kissed her.

'Put the light out please.'

Roger reached up to the light bulb and turned the switch. In the dark he kissed her, brushing his lips against hers, feeling them both fill without opening, feeling her trembling as he held her. Holding her tight against him, her head back now, he heard the sea on the beach and felt the wind cool through the window. He felt the silk of her hair over his arm and their bodies hard and taut and he dropped his hand on her breasts to feel them rise, quick-budding under his fingers.

'Oh Roger,' she said. 'Please. Oh please.'

'Don't talk.'

'Is that him? Oh he's lovely.'

'Don't talk.'

'He'll be good to me. Won't he. And I'll try to be good to him. But isn't he awfully big?'

'No.'

'Oh I love you so and I love him so. Do you think we should try now so we'll know? I can't stand it very much longer. Not knowing. I haven't been able to stand it all afternoon.'

'We can try.'

'Oh let's. Let's try. Let's try now.'

'Kiss me once more.'

In the dark he went into the strange country and it was very strange indeed, hard to enter, suddenly perilously difficult, then blindingly, happily, safely, encompassed; free of all doubts, all perils and all dreads, held unholdingly, to hold, to hold increasingly, unholdingly still to hold, taking away all things before, and all to come, bringing the beginning of bright happiness in darkness, closer, closer, closer now closer and ever closer, to go on past all belief, longer, finer, further, finer higher and higher to drive toward happiness suddenly, scaldingly achieved.

'Oh darling,' he said. 'Oh darling.'

'Yes.'

'Thank you my dear blessed.'

'I'm dead,' she said. 'Don't thank me. I'm dead.'

'Do you want —'

'No please. I'm dead.'

'Let's —'

'No. Please believe me. I don't know how to say it another way.'

Then later she said, 'Roger.'

'Yes, daughter.'

'Are you sure?'

'Yes, daughter.'

'And you're not disappointed because of anything?'

'No, daughter.'

'Do you think you'll get to love me?'

'I love you,' he lied. I love what we did he meant.

'Say it again.'

'I love you,' he lied again.

'Say it once more.'

'I love you,' he lied.

'That's three times,' she said, in the dark. 'I'll try to make it come true.'

The wind blew cool on them and the noise the palm leaves made was almost like rain and after a while the girl said, 'It will be lovely tonight but do you know what I am now?'

'Hungry.'

'Aren't you a wonderful guesser?'

'I'm hungry too.'

They ate at the Green Lantern and the widow woman squirted Flit under the table and brought them fresh mullet roe browned crisp and fried with good bacon. They drank cold Regal beer and ate a steak each with mashed potatoes. The steak was thin from grass-fed beef and not very good but they were hungry and the girl kicked her shoes off under the table and put both her bare feet on Roger's. She was beautiful and he loved to look at her and her feet felt very good on his.

'Does it do it to you?' she asked.

'Of course.'

'Can I feel?'

'If the widow woman isn't looking.'

'It does it to me too,' she said. 'Aren't our bodies nice to each other?'

They ate pineapple pie for dessert and each had another cold bottle of Regal fresh from deep in the melting ice water of the cooler.

'I have Flit on my feet,' she said. 'They'll be nicer when they don't have Flit on them.'

'They're lovely with Flit. Push really hard with them.'

'I don't want to push you out of the widow woman's chair.'

'All right. That's enough.'

'You never felt any better did you?'

'No,' Roger said truly.

'We don't have to go to the movies do we?'

'Not unless you want to very much.'

'Let's go back to our house and then start out terribly early in the morning.'

'That's fine.'

They paid the widow woman and took a couple of bottles of the cold Regal in a paper sack and drove back to the cabins and put the car in the space between cabins.

'The car knows about us already,' she said as they came in the cabin.

'It's nice that way.'

'I was sort of shy with him at the start but now I feel like he's our partner.'

'He's a good car.'

'Do you think the man was shocked?'

'No. Jealous.'

'Isn't he awfully old to be jealous?'

'Maybe. Maybe he's just pleased.'

'Let's not think about him.'

'I haven't thought about him.'

'The car will protect us. He's our good friend already. Did you see how friendly he was coming back from the widow woman's?'

'I saw the difference.'

'Let's not even put the light on.'

'Good,' Roger said. 'I'll take a shower or do you want one first?'

'No. You.'

Then waiting in the bed he heard her in the bath splashing and then drying herself and then she came into the bed very fast and long and cool and wonderful feeling.

'My lovely,' he said. 'My true lovely.'

'Are you glad to have me?'

'Yes, my darling.'

'And it's really all right?'

'It's wonderful.'

'We can do it all over the country and all over the world.'

'We're here now.'

'All right. We're here. Here. Where we are. Here. Oh the good, fine, lovely here in the dark. What a fine lovely wonderful here. So lovely in the dark. In the lovely dark. Please hear me here. Oh very gently here very gently please carefully Please Please very carefully Thank you carefully oh in the lovely dark.'

It was a strange country again but at the end he was not lonely and later, waking, it was still strange and no one spoke at all but it was their country now, not his nor hers, but theirs, truly, and they both knew it.

In the dark with the wind blowing cool through the cabin she said, 'Now you're happy and you love me.'

'Now I'm happy and I love you.'

'You don't have to repeat it. It's true now.'

'I know it. I was awfully slow wasn't I.'

'You were a little slow.'

'I'm awfully glad that I love you.'

'See?' she said. 'It isn't hard.'

'I really love you.'

'I thought maybe you would. I mean I hoped you would.'

'I do.' He held her very close and tight. 'I really love you. Do you hear me?'

It was true, too, a thing which surprised him greatly, especially when he found that it was still true in the morning.

They didn't leave the next morning. Helena was still sleeping when Roger woke and he watched her sleeping, her hair spread over the pillow, swept up from her neck and swung to one side, her lovely brown face, the eyes and the lips closed looking even more beautiful than when she was awake. He noticed her eyelids were pale in the tanned face and how the long lashes lay, the sweetness of her lips, quiet now like a child's asleep, and how her breasts showed under the sheet she had pulled up over her in the night. He thought he shouldn't wake her and he was afraid if he kissed her it might, so he dressed and walked down into the village, feeling hollow and hungry and happy, smelling the early morning smells and hearing and seeing the birds and feeling and smelling the breeze that still blew in from the Gulf of Mexico, down to the other restaurant a block beyond the Green Lantern. It was really a lunch counter and he sat on a stool and ordered coffee with milk and a fried ham and egg sandwich on rye bread. There was a midnight edition of the *Miami Herald* on the counter that some trucker had left and he read about the military rebellion in Spain while he ate the sandwich and drank the coffee. He felt the egg spurt in the rye bread as his teeth went through the bread, the slice of dill pickle, the egg and the ham, and he smelled them all and the good early morning coffee smell as he lifted the cup.

'They're having plenty of trouble over there aren't they,' the man behind the counter said to him. He was an elderly man with his face tanned to the line of the sweatband of his hat and freckled dead white above that. Roger saw he had a thin, mean cracker mouth and he wore steel-rimmed glasses.

'Plenty,' Roger agreed.

'All those European countries are the same,' the man said. 'Trouble after trouble.'

'I'll take another cup of coffee,' Roger said. He would let this one cool while he read the paper.

'When they get to the bottom of it they'll find the Pope there.' The man drew the coffee and put the pot of milk by it.

Roger looked up interestedly as he poured the milk into the cup.

'Three men at the bottom of everything,' the man told him. 'The Pope, Herbert Hoover, and Franklin Delano Roosevelt.'

Roger relaxed. The man went on to explain the interlocking interests of these three and Roger listened happily. America was a wonderful place he thought. Imagine buying a copy of *Bouvard et Pécuchet* when you could get this free with your breakfast. You are getting something else with the newspaper, he thought. But in the meantime there is this.

'What about the Jews?' he asked finally. 'Where do they come in?'

'The Jews are a thing of the past,' the man behind the counter told him. 'Henry Ford put them out of business when he published *The Protocols of the Elders of Zion.*'

'Do you think they're through?'

'Not a doubt of it, fella,' the man said. 'You've seen the last of them.'

'That surprises me,' Roger said.

'Let me tell you something else,' the man leaned forward. 'Some day old Henry will get the Pope the same way. He'll get him just like he got Wall Street.'

'Did he get Wall Street?'

'Oh boy,' the man said. 'They're through.'

'Henry must be going good.'

'Henry? You really said something then. Henry's the man of the ages.'

'What about Hitler?'

'Hitler's a man of his word.'

'What about the Russians?'

'You've asked the right man that question. Let the Russian bear stay in his own backyard.'

'Well that pretty well fixes things up,' Roger got up.

'Things look good,' the man behind the counter said. 'I'm an optimist. Once old Henry tackles the Pope you'll see all three of them crumble.'

'What papers do you read?'

'Any of them,' the man said. 'But I don't get my political views there. I think things out for myself.'

'What do I owe you?'

'Forty-five cents.'

'It was a first class breakfast.'

'Come again,' the man said and picked up the paper from where Roger had laid it on the counter. He's going to figure some more things out for himself, Roger thought.

Roger walked back to the tourist camp, buying a later edition of the *Miami Herald* at the drugstore. He also bought some razor blades, a tube of mentholated shaving cream, some Dentyne chewing gum, a bottle of Listerine and an alarm clock.

When he arrived at the cabin and opened the door quietly and put his package on the table beside the thermos jug, the enameled cups, the brown paper bag full of White Rock bottles, and the two bottles of Regal beer they had forgotten to drink, Helena was still asleep. He sat in the chair and read the paper and watched her sleep. The sun was high enough so that it did not shine on her face and the breeze came in the other window, blowing across her as she slept without stirring.

Roger read the paper trying to figure out from the various bulletins what had happened, really, and how it was going. She might as well sleep, he thought. We better get whatever there is each day now and as much and as well as we can because it's started now. It came quicker than I thought it would. I do not have to go yet and we can have a while. Either it will be over right away and the Government will put it down or there will be plenty of time. If I had not had these two months with the kids I would have been over there for it. I'd rather have been with the kids, he thought. It's too late to go now. It would probably be over before I would get there. Anyway there is going to be plenty of it from now on. There is going to be plenty of it for us all the rest of our lives. Plenty of it. Too damned much of it. I've had a wonderful time this summer with Tom and the kids and now I've got this girl and I'll see how long my conscience holds out and when I have to go I'll go to it and not worry about it until then. This is the start all right. Once it starts there isn't going to be any end to it. I don't see any end until we destroy them, there and here and everywhere. I don't see any end to it ever, he thought. Not for us anyway. But maybe they will win this first one in a hurry, he thought, and I won't have to go to this one.

The thing had come that he had expected and known would come and that he had waited all one fall for in Madrid and he was already making excuses not to go to it. Spending the time he had with the children had been a valid excuse and he knew nothing had been planned in Spain until later. But now it had come and what was he doing? He was convincing himself there was no need for him to go. It is liable all to be over before I can get there, he thought. There is going to be plenty of time.

There were other things that held him back too that he did not understand yet. They were the weaknesses that developed alongside his strengths like the crevices in a glacier under its covering of snow, or, if that is too pompous a comparison, like streaks of fat between muscles. These weaknesses were a part of the strengths unless they grew to dominate them; but they were mostly hidden and he did not understand them, nor know their uses. He did know, though, that this thing had come that he must go to and aid in every way he could, and yet he found varied reasons why he did not have to go.

They were all varyingly honest and they were all weak except one; he would have to make some money to support his children and their mothers and he would have to do some decent writing to make that money or he would not be able to live with himself. I know six good stories, he thought, and I'm going to write them. That will get them done and I have to do them to make up for that whoring on the Coast. If I can really do four out of the six that will pretty well balance me with myself and make up for that job of whoring; whoring hell, it wasn't even whoring it was like being asked to produce a sample of semen in a test tube that could be used for artificial insemination. You had an office to produce it in and a secretary to help you. Don't forget. The hell with these sexual symbols. What he meant was that he had taken money for writing something that was not the absolute best he could write. Absolute best hell. It was crap. Goosecrap. Now he had to atone for that and recover his respect by writing as well as he could and better than he ever had. That sounded simple, he thought. Try and do it some time.

But anyway if I do four as good as I can do and as straight as God could do them on one of his good days (Hi there Deity. Wish me luck Boy. Glad to hear you're doing so good yourself.) then I'll be straight with myself and if that six-play bastard Nicholson can sell two out of the four that will stake the kids while we are gone. We? Sure. We. Don't you remember about we? Like the little pig we we we all the way home. Only away from home. Home. That's a laugh. There isn't any home. Sure there is. This is home. All this. This cabin. This car. Those once fresh sheets. The Green Lantern and the widow woman and Regal beer. The drugstore and the breeze off the gulf. That crazy at the lunch counter and a ham and egg sandwich on rye. Make it two to go. One with a slice of raw onion. Fill her up and check the water and the oil please. Would you mind checking the tires please? The hiss of compressed air, administered courteously and free was home which was all oil-stained cement everywhere, all rubber worn on pavements, comfort facilities, and Cokes in red vending machines. The center line of highways was the boundary line of home.

You get to think like one of those Vast-Spaces-of-America writers, he said to himself. Better watch it. Better get a load of this. Look at your girl sleeping and know this: Home is going to be where people do not have enough to eat. Home is going to be wherever men are oppressed. Home is going to be wherever evil is strongest and can be fought. Home is going to be where you will go from now on.

But I don't have to go yet, he thought. He had some reasons to delay it. No you don't have to go yet, his conscience said. And I can write the stories, he said. Yes, you must write the stories and they must be as good as you can write and better. All right, Conscience, he thought. We have that all straightened out. I guess the way things are shaping up I had better let her sleep. You let her sleep, his conscience said. And you try very hard to take good care of her and not only that. You *take* good care of her. As good as I can, he told his conscience, and I'll write at least four good ones. They better be good, his conscience said. They will be, he said. They'll be the very best.

So having promised and decided that did he then take a pencil and an old exercise book and, sharpening the pencil, start one of the stories there on the table while the girl slept? He did not. He poured an inch and a half of White Horse into one of the enameled cups, unscrewed the top of the ice jug and putting his hand in the cool depth pulled out a chunk of ice and put it in the cup. He opened a bottle of White Rock and poured some alongside of the ice and then swirled the lump of ice around with his finger before he drank.

They've got Spanish Morocco, Sevilla, Pamplona, Burgos, Saragossa, he thought. We've got Barcelona, Madrid, Valencia and the Basque country. Both frontiers are still open. It doesn't look so bad. It looks good. I must get a good map though. I ought to be able to get a good map in New Orleans. Mobile maybe.

He figured it as well as he could without a map. Saragossa is bad, he thought. That cuts the railway to Barcelona. Saragossa was a good Anarchist town. Not like Barcelona or Lérida. But still plenty there. They can't have put up much of a fight. Maybe they haven't made their fight yet. They'd have to take Saragossa right away if they could. They would have to come up from Catalonia and take it.

If they could keep the Madrid-Valencia-Barcelona railway and open up Madrid-Saragossa-Barcelona and hold Irún it ought to be all right. With stuff coming in from France they ought to be able to build up in the Basque country and beat Mola in the north. That would be the toughest fight. That son of a bitch. He could not see the situation in the south except that the revolters would have to come up the valley of the Tagus to attack Madrid and they would probably try it from the north too. Would have to try it right away to try to force the passes of the Quadarramas the way Napoleon had done it.

I wish I had not been with the kids, he thought. I wish the hell I was there. No you don't wish you hadn't been with the kids. You can't go to everyone. Or you can't be at them the minute they start. You're not a firehorse and you have as much obligation to the kids as to anything in the world. Until the time comes when you have to fight to keep the world so it will be O.K. for them to live in, he corrected. But that sounded pompous so he corrected it to when it is more necessary to fight than to be with them. That was flat enough. That would come soon enough.

Figure this one out and what you have to do and then stick with that, he told himself. Figure it as well as you can and then really do what you have to do. All right, he said. And he went on figuring.

Helena slept until eleven-thirty and he had finished his second drink.

'Why didn't you wake me, darling?' she said when she opened her eyes and rolled toward him and smiled.

'You looked so lovely sleeping.'

'But we've missed our early start and the early morning on the road.'

'We'll have it tomorrow morning.'

'Give kiss.'

'Kiss.'

'Give hug a lug.'

'Big hugalug.'

'Feels better,' she said. 'Oh. Feels good.'

When she came out from the shower with her hair tucked under a rubber cap she said, 'Darling, you didn't have to drink because you were lonesome did you?'

'No. Just because I felt like it.'

'Did you feel badly though?'

'No. I felt wonderful.'

'I'm so glad. I'm ashamed. I just slept and slept.'

'We can swim before lunch.'

'I don't know,' she said. 'I'm so hungry. Do you think we could have lunch and then take a nap or read or something and then swim?'

'*Wunderbar.*'

'We shouldn't start and drive this afternoon?'

'See how you feel, daughter.'

'Come here,' she said.

He did. She put her arms around him and he felt her standing, fresh and cool from the shower, not dried yet, and he kissed her slowly and happily feeling the happy ache come in him where she had pressed firm against him.

'How's that?'

'That's fine.'

'Good,' she said. 'Let's drive tomorrow.'

The beach was white sand, almost as fine as flour, and it ran for miles. They took a long walk along it in the late afternoon, swimming out, lying in the clear water, floating and playing, and then swimming in to walk further along the beach.

'It's a lovelier beach than Bimini even,' the girl said.

'But the water's not as fine. It doesn't have that quality the Gulf Stream water has.'

'No I guess not. But after European beaches it's unbelievable.'

The clean softness of the sand made walking a sensual pleasure that could be varied from the dry, soft, powdery to the just moist and yielding to the firm cool sand of the line of the receding tide.

'I wish the boys were here to point out things and show me things and tell me about things.'

'I'll point out things.'

'You don't have to. You just walk ahead a little way and let me look at your back and your can.'

'You walk ahead.'

'No you.'

Then she came up to him and said, 'Come on. Let's run side by side.'

They jogged easily along the pleasant firm footing above the breaking waves. She ran well, almost too well for a girl, and when Roger forced the pace just a little she kept up easily. He kept the same pace and then lengthened it a little again. She kept even with him but said, 'Hi. Don't kill me,' and he stopped and kissed her. She was hot from the running and she said, 'No. Don't.'

'It's nice.'

'Must go in the water first,' she said. They dove into the surf that was sandy where it broke and swam out to the clean green water. She stood up with just her head and shoulders out.

'Kiss now.'

Her lips were salty and her face was wet with the seawater and as he kissed her she turned her head so that her sea wet hair swung against his shoulder.

'Awfully salty but awfully good,' she said. 'Hold very hard.'

He did.

'Here comes a big one,' she said. 'A really big one. Now lift high up and we'll go over together in the wave.'

The wave rolled them over and over holding tight onto each other his legs tight around hers.

'Better than drowning,' she said. 'So much better. Let's do it once more.'

They picked a huge wave this time and when it hung and curled to break Roger threw them across the line of its breaking and when it crashed down it rolled them over and over like a piece of driftwood onto the sand.

'Let's get clean and lie on the sand,' she said and they swam and dove in the clean water and then lay side by side on the cool, firm beach where the last inrush of the waves just touched their toes and ankles.

'Roger, do you still love me?'

'Yes, daughter. Very much.'

'I love you. You were nice to play.'

'I had fun.'

'We do have fun don't we.'

'It's been lovely all day.'

'We only had a half a day because I was a bad girl and slept so late.'

'That was a good sound thing to do.'

'I didn't do it to be good and sound. I did it because I couldn't help it.'

He lay alongside of her, his right foot touching her left, his leg touching hers and he put his hand on her head and neck.

'Old head's awfully wet. You won't catch a cold in the wind?'

'I don't think so. If we lived by the ocean all the time I'd have to get my hair cut.'

'No.'

'It looks nice. You'd be surprised.'

'I love it the way it is.'

'It's wonderful short for swimming.'

'Not for bed though.'

'I don't know,' she said. 'You'd still be able to tell I was a girl.'

'Do you think so?'

'I'm almost sure. I could always remind you.'

'Daughter?'

'What, darling?'

'Did you always like making love?'

'No.'

'Do you now?'

'What do you think?'

'I think that if I had a good look both ways down the beach and there was no one in sight we'd be all right.'

'It's an awfully lonely beach,' she said.

They walked back along the sea and the wind was still blowing and the rollers were breaking far out on the low tide.

'It seems so awfully simple and as though there were no problems at all,' the girl said. 'I found you and then all we ever had to do was eat and sleep and make love. Of course it's not like that at all.'

'Let's keep it like that for a while.'

'I think we have a right to for a little while. Maybe not a right to. But I think we can. But won't you be awfully bored with me?'

'No,' he said. He was not lonely after this last time as he had nearly always been no matter with whom or where. He had not had the old death loneliness since the first time the night before. 'You do something awfully good to me.'

'I'm glad if I really do. Wouldn't it be awful if we were the kind of people who grated on each other's nerves and had to have fights to love each other?'

'We're not like that.'

'I'll try not to be. But won't you be bored just with me?'

'No.'

'But you're thinking about something else now.'

'Yes. I was wondering if we could get a *Miami Daily News*.'

'That's the afternoon paper?'

'I just wanted to read about the Spanish business.'

'The military revolt?'

'Yes.'

'Will you tell me about it?'

'Sure.'

He told her about it as well as he could within the limitations of his knowledge and his information.

'Are you worried about it?'

'Yes. But I haven't thought about it all afternoon.'

'We'll see what there is in the paper,' she said. 'And tomorrow you can follow it on the radio in the car. Tomorrow we'll really get an early start.'

'I bought an alarm clock.'

'Weren't you intelligent? It's wonderful to have such an intelligent husband. Roger?'

'Yes, daughter.'

'What do you think they will have to eat at the Green Lantern?'

The next day they started early in the morning before sunrise and by breakfast they had done a hundred miles and were away from the sea and the bays with their wooden docks and fish packing houses and up in the monotonous pine and scrub palmetto of the cattle country. They ate at a lunch counter in a town in the middle of the Florida prairie. The lunch counter was on the shady side of the square and looked out on a red bricked court house with its green lawn.

'I don't know how I ever held out for that second fifty,' the girl said, looking at the menu.

'We should have stopped at Punta Gorda,' Roger said. 'That would have been sensible.'

'We said we'd do a hundred though,' the girl said. 'And we did it. What are you going to have, darling?'

'I'm going to have ham and eggs and coffee and a big slice of raw onion,' Roger told the waitress.

'How do you want the eggs?'

'Straight up.'

'The lady?'

'I'll have corned beef hash, browned, with two poached eggs,' Helena said.

'Tea, coffee, or milk?'

'Milk please.'

'What kind of juice?'

'Grapefruit please.'

'Two grapefruits. Do you mind the onion?' Roger asked.

'I love onions,' she said. 'Not as much as I love you though. And I never tried them for breakfast.'

'They're good,' Roger said. 'They get in there with the coffee and keep you from being lonely when you drive.'

'You're not lonely are you?'

'No, daughter.'

'We made quite good time didn't we?'

'Not really good. That's not much of a stretch for time with the bridges and the towns.'

'Look at the cowpunchers,' she said. Two men on cow ponies, wearing western work clothes, got down from their stock saddles and hitched their horses to the rail in front of the lunch room and walked down the sidewalk on their high-heeled boots.

'They run a lot of cattle around here,' Roger said. 'You have to watch for stock on all these roads.'

'I didn't know they raised many cattle in Florida.'

'An awful lot. Good cattle now too.'

'Don't you want to get a paper?'

'I'd like to,' he said. 'I'll see if the cashier has one.'

'At the drugstore,' the cashier said. 'St. Petersburg and Tampa papers at the drugstore.'

'Where is it?'

'At the corner. I doubt if you could miss it.'

'You want anything from the drugstore?' Roger asked the girl.

'Camels,' she said. 'Remember we have to fill the ice jug.'

'I'll ask them.'

Roger came back with the morning papers and a carton of cigarettes.

'It's not going so good.' He handed her one of the papers.

'Is there anything we didn't get on the radio?'

'Not much. But it doesn't look so good.'

'Can they fill the ice jug?'

'I forgot to ask.'

The waitress came with the two breakfasts and they both drank their cold grapefruit juice and started to eat. Roger kept on reading his paper so Helena propped hers against a water glass and read too.

'Have you any chili sauce?' Roger asked the waitress. She was a thin juke-joint looking blonde.

'You bet,' she said. 'You people from Hollywood?'

'I've been there.'

'Ain't she from there?'

'She's going there.'

'Oh Jesus me,' the waitress said. 'Would you write in my book?'

'I'd love to,' Helena said. 'But I'm not in pictures.'

'You will be, honey,' the waitress said. 'Wait a minute,' she said. 'I got a pen.'

She handed Helena the book. It was quite new and had a gray imitation leather cover.

'I only just got it,' she said. 'I only had this job a week.'

Helena wrote Helena Hancock on the first page in the rather flamboyant untypical hand that had emerged from the mixed ways of writing she had been taught at various schools.

'Jesus beat me what a name,' the waitress said. 'Wouldn't you write something with it?'

'What's your name?' Helena asked.

'Marie.'

To Marie from her friend Helena wrote above the florid name in the slightly suspect script.

'Gee thanks,' Marie said. Then to Roger, 'You don't mind writing do you?'

'No,' Roger said. 'I'd like to. What's your last name, Marie?'

'Oh that don't matter.'

He wrote Best always to Marie from Roger Hancock.

'You her father?' the waitress asked.

'Yes,' said Roger.

'Gee I'm glad she's going out there with her father,' the waitress said. 'Well I certainly wish you people luck.'

'We need it,' Roger said.

'No,' the waitress said. 'You don't need it. But I wish it to you anyway. Say you must have got married awfully young.'

'I was,' Roger said. I sure as hell was, he thought.

'I'll bet her mother was beautiful.'

'She was the most beautiful girl you ever saw.'

'Where's she now?'

'In London,' Helena said.

'You people certainly lead lives,' the waitress said. 'Do you want another glass of milk?'

'No thanks,' Helena said. 'Where are you from, Marie?'

'Fort Meade,' the waitress said. 'It's right up the road.'

'Do you like it here?'

'This is a bigger town. It's a step up I guess.'

'Do you have any fun?'

'I always have fun when there's any time. Do you want anything more?' she asked Roger.

'No. We have to roll.'

They paid the check and shook hands.

'Thanks very much for the quarter,' the waitress said. 'And for writing in my book. I guess I'll be reading about you in the papers. Good luck, Miss Hancock.'

'Good luck,' Helena said. 'I hope you have a good summer.'

'It'll be all right,' the waitress said. 'You be careful won't you.'

'You be careful too,' Helena said.

'O.K.,' Marie said. 'Only it's kind of late for me.'

She bit her lip and turned and went into the kitchen.

'She was a nice girl,' Helena said to Roger as they got into the car. 'I should have told her it was sort of late for me too. But I guess that only would have worried her.'

'We must fill the ice jug,' Roger said.

'I'll take it in,' Helena offered. 'I haven't done anything for us all day.'

'Let me get it.'

'No. You read the paper and I'll get it. Have we enough Scotch?'

'There's that whole other bottle in the carton that isn't opened.'

'That's splendid.'

Roger read the paper. I might as well, he thought. I'm going to drive all day.

'It only cost a quarter,' the girl said when she came back with the jug. 'But it's chipped awfully fine. Too fine I'm afraid.'

'We can get some more this evening.'

When they were out of the town and had settled down to the long black highway north through the prairie and the pines, into the hills of the lake country, the road striped black over the long,

varied peninsula, heavy with the mounting summer heat now
that they were away from the sea breeze; but with them making
their own breeze driving at a steady seventy on the straight long
stretches and feeling the country being put behind them, the girl
said, 'It's fun to drive fast isn't it? It's like making your own
youth.'

'How do you mean?'

'I don't know,' she said. 'Sort of foreshortening and telescop-
ing the world the way youth does.'

'I never thought much about youth.'

'I know it,' she said. 'But I did. You didn't think about it
because you never lost it. If you never thought about it you
couldn't lose it.'

'Go on,' he said. 'That doesn't follow.'

'It doesn't make good sense,' she said. 'I'll get it straightened
out though and then it will. You don't mind me talking when it
doesn't make completely good sense do you?'

'No, daughter.'

'You see if I made really completely good sense I wouldn't be
here.' She stopped. 'Yes I would. It's super good sense. Not
common sense.'

'Like surrealism?'

'Nothing like surrealism. I hate surrealism.'

'I don't,' he said. 'I liked it when it started. It kept on such a
long time after it was over was the trouble.'

'But things are never really successful until they are over.'

'Say that again.'

'I mean they aren't successful in America until they are over.
And they have to have been over for years and years before they
are successful in London.'

'Where did you learn all this, daughter?'

'I thought it out,' she said. 'I've had a lot of time to think
while I was waiting around for you.'

'You didn't wait so very much.'

'Oh yes I did. You'll never know.'

There was a choice to be made soon of two main highways
with very little difference in their mileage and he did not know
whether to take the one that he knew was a good road through
pleasant country but that he had driven many times with Andy
and David's mother or the newly finished highway that might
go through duller country.

That's no choice, he thought. We'll take the new one. The

hell with maybe starting something again like I had the other
night coming across the Tamiami Trail.

They caught the news broadcast on the radio, switching it off
through the soap operas of the forenoon and on at each hour.

'It isn't like fiddling while Rome burns,' Roger said. 'It's driving west northwest at seventy miles an hour away from a fire
that's burning up what you care about to the east and hearing
about it while you drive away from it.'

'If we keep on driving long enough we'll get to it.'

'We hit a lot of water first.'

'Roger. Do you have to go? If you have to go you should.'

'No dammit. I don't have to go. Not yet. I figured that
through yesterday morning while you were asleep.'

'Didn't I sleep though? It was shameful.'

'I'm awfully glad you did. Do you think you got enough last
night? It was awfully early when I woke you.'

'I had a wonderful sleep. Roger?'

'What, daughter?'

'We were mean to lie to that waitress.'

'She asked questions,' Roger said. 'It was simpler that way.'

'Could you have been my father?'

'If I'd begot you at fourteen.'

'I'm glad you're not,' she said. 'God it would be complicated.
It's complicated enough I suppose until I simplify it. Do you
think I'll bore you because I'm twenty-two and sleep all night
long and am hungry all the time?'

'And are the most beautiful girl I've ever seen and wonderful
and strange as hell in bed and always fun to talk to.'

'All right. Stop. Why am I strange in bed?'

'You are.'

'I said why?'

'I'm not an anatomist,' he said. 'I'm just the guy that loves
you.'

'Don't you like to talk about it?'

'No. Do you?'

'No. I'm shy about it and very frightened. Always frightened.'

'My old Bratchen. We were lucky weren't we?'

'Let's not even talk about how lucky. Do you think Andy and
Dave and Tom would mind?'

'No.'

'We ought to write to Tom.'

'We will.'

'What do you suppose he's doing now?'

Roger looked through the wheel at the clock on the dashboard.

'He will have finished painting and be having a drink.'

'Why don't we have one?'

'Fine.'

She made the drinks in the cups putting in handfuls of the finely chipped ice, the whiskey and White Rock. The new highway was wide now and ran far and clear ahead through the forest of pines that were tapped and scored for turpentine.

'It doesn't look like the Landes does it,' Roger said and lifting the cup felt the drink icy in his mouth. It was very good but the chipped ice melted fast.

'No. In the Landes there is yellow gorse in between the pines.'

'And they don't work the trees for turpentine with chain gangs either,' Roger said. 'This is all convict labor country through here.'

'Tell me how they work it.'

'It's pretty damned awful,' he said. 'The state contracts them out to the turpentine and lumber camps. They used to catch everyone off the trains during the worst of the Depression. All the people riding the trains looking for work. Going east or west or south. They'd stop the trains right outside of Tallahassee and round up the men and march them off to jail and then sentence them to chain gangs and contract them out to the turpentine and lumber outfits. This is a wicked stretch of country. It's old and wicked with lots of law and no justice.'

'Pine country can be so friendly too.'

'This isn't friendly. This is a bastard. There are lots of lawless people in it but the work is done by the prisoners. It's a slave country. The law's only for outsiders.'

'I'm glad we're going through it fast.'

'Yes. But we really ought to know it. How it's run. How it works. Who are the crooks and the tyrants and how to get rid of them.'

'I'd love to do that.'

'You ought to buck Florida politics some time and see what happens.'

'Is it really bad?'

'You couldn't believe it.'

'Do you know much about it?'

'A little,' he said. 'I bucked it for a while with some good people but we didn't get anywhere. We got the Bejesus beat out of us. On conversation.'

'Wouldn't you like to be in politics?'

'No. I want to be a writer.'

'That's what I want you to be.'

The road was unrolling now through some scattered hardwood and then across cypress swamps and hammock country and then ahead there was an iron bridge across a clear, dark-watered stream, beautiful and clear moving, with live oaks along its bank and a sign at the bridge that said it was the Senwannee (*sic*) River.

They were on it and over it and up the bank beyond and the road had turned north.

'It was like a river in a dream,' Helena said. 'Wasn't it wonderful so clear and so dark? Couldn't we go down it in a canoe some time?'

'I've crossed it up above and it's beautiful wherever you cross it.'

'Can't we make a trip on it sometime?'

'Sure. There's a place way up above where I've seen it as clear as a trout stream.'

'Wouldn't there be snakes?'

'I'm pretty sure there'd be a lot.'

'I'm afraid of them. Really afraid of them. But we could be careful couldn't we?'

'Sure. We ought to do it in the winter time.'

'There are such wonderful places for us to go,' she said. 'I'll always remember this river now and we saw it only like the lens clicking in a camera. We should have stopped.'

'Do you want to go back?'

'Not until we come to it going the other way. I want to go on and on and on.'

'We're either going to have to stop to get something to eat or else get sandwiches and eat them while we drive.'

'Let's have another drink,' she said. 'And then get some sandwiches. What kind do you think they'll have?'

'They ought to have hamburgers and maybe barbecue.'

The second drink was like the first, icy cold but quick melting in the wind and Helena held the cup out of the rush of the air and handed it to him when he drank.

'Daughter, are you drinking more than you usually do?'

'Of course. You didn't think I drank a couple of cups of whiskey and water every noon by myself before lunch did you?'

'I don't want you to drink more than you should.'

'I won't. But it's fun. If I don't want one I won't take one. I never knew about driving across the country and having our drinks on the way.'

'We could have fun stopping and poking around. Going down to the coast and seeing the old places. But I want us to get out west.'

'So do I. I've never seen it. We can always come back.'

'It's such a long way. But this is so much more fun than flying.'

'This is flying. Roger, will it be wonderful out west?'

'It always is to me.'

'Isn't it lucky I've never been out so we'll have it together?'

'We've got a lot of country to get through first.'

'It's going to be fun though. Do you think we'll come to the sandwich town pretty soon?'

'We'll take the next town.'

The next town was a lumbering town with one long street of frame and brick buildings along the highway. The mills were by the railroad and lumber was piled high along the tracks and there was the smell of cypress and pine sawdust in the heat. While Roger filled the gas and had the water, oil and air checked Helena ordered hamburger sandwiches and barbecued pork sandwiches with hot sauce on them in a lunch counter and brought them to the car in a brown paper bag. She had beer in another paper sack.

Back on the highway again, and out of the heat of the town, they ate the sandwiches and drank cold beer that the girl opened.

'I couldn't get any of our marriage beer,' she said. 'This was the only kind there was.'

'It's good and cold. Wonderful after the barbecue.'

'The man said it was about like Regal. He said I'd never be able to tell it from Regal.'

'It's better than Regal.'

'It had a funny name. It wasn't a German name either. But the labels soaked off.'

'It'll be on the caps.'

'I threw the caps away.'

'Wait till we get out west. They have better beer the further out you get.'

'I don't think they could have any better sandwich buns or any better barbecue. Aren't these good?'

'They're awfully good. This isn't a part of the country where you eat very good either.'

'Roger, will you mind terribly if I go to sleep for a little while after lunch? I won't if you're sleepy.'

'I'd love it if you went to sleep. I'm not sleepy at all really. I'd tell you if I was.'

'There's another bottle of beer for you. Dammit I forgot to look at the cap.'

'That's good. I like to drink it unknown.'

'But we could have remembered it for another time.'

'We'll get another new one.'

'Roger, would you really not mind if I went to sleep?'

'No, beauty.'

'I can stay awake if you want.'

'Please sleep and you'll wake up lonely and we can talk.'

'Good night, my dear Roger. Thank you very much for the trip and the two drinks and the sandwiches and the unknown beer and the way down upon the Swanee River and for where we are going.'

'You go to sleep, my baby.'

'I will. You wake me up if you want me.'

She slept curled up in the deep seat and Roger drove, watching the wide road ahead for stock, making fast time through the pine country, trying to keep around seventy to try to see how much he could get over sixty miles onto the speedometer in each hour. He had never been on this stretch of highway but he knew this part of the state and he was driving it now only to put it behind him. You shouldn't have to waste country but on a long trip you have to.

The monotony tires you, he thought. That and the fact there are no vistas. This would be a fine country on foot in cool weather but it is monotonous to drive through now.

I have not been driving long enough to settle into it yet. But I should have more resiliency than I have. I'm not sleepy. My eyes are bored I guess as well as tired. I am not bored, he thought. It is just my eyes and the fact that it is a long time since I have been sitting still so long. It is another game and I'll have to relearn it. About day after tomorrow we will start to make real distance and not be tired by it. I haven't sat still this long for a long time.

He reached forward and turned on the radio and tuned it. Helena did not wake so he left it on and let it blur in with his thinking and his driving.

It is awfully nice having her in the car asleep, he thought. She is good company even when she is asleep. You are a strange and lucky bastard, he thought. You are having much better luck than you deserve. You just thought you had learned something about being alone and you really worked at it and you did learn something. You got right to the edge of something. Then you backslid and ran with those worthless people, not quite as worthless as the other batch, but worthless enough and to spare. Probably they were even more worthless. You certainly were worthless with them. Then you got through that and got in fine shape with Tom and the kids and you knew you couldn't be happier and that there was nothing coming up except to be lonely again and then along comes this girl and you go right into happiness as though it were a country you were the biggest landowner in. Happiness is pre-war Hungary and you are Count Károlyi. Maybe not the biggest landowner but raised the most pheasant anyway. I wonder if she will like to shoot pheasant. Maybe she will. I can still shoot them. They don't bother me. I never asked her if she could shoot. Her mother shot quite well in that wonderful dope-head trance she had. She wasn't a wicked woman at the start. She was a very nice woman, pleasant and kind and successful in bed and I think she meant all the things she said to all the people. I really think she meant them. That is probably what made it so dangerous. It always sounded as though she meant them anyway. I suppose, though, it finally becomes a social defect to be unable to believe any marriage has not really been consummated until the husband has committed suicide. Things all ended so violently that started so pleasantly. But I suppose that is always the way with drugs. Though I suppose among those spiders who eat their mates some of the mate eaters are remarkably attractive. My dear she has never, really never, looked better. Dear Henry was just a *bonne bouche*. Henry was nice too. You know how much we all liked him.

None of those spiders take drugs either, he thought. Of course that's what I should remember about this child, exactly as you should remember the stalling speed of a plane, that her mother was her mother.

That's all very simple, he thought. But you know your own mother was a bitch. But you also know you are a bastard in quite different ways from her ways. So why should her stalling speed be the same as her mother's? Yours isn't.

No one had ever said it was. Hers I mean. What you said was that you should remember her mother as you would remember and so forth.

That's dirty too, he thought. For nothing, for no reason, when you need it most you have this girl, freely and of her own will, lovely, loving and full of illusions about you, and with her asleep beside you on the seat you start destroying her and denying her without any formalities of cocks crowing, twice nor thrice nor even on the radio.

You are a bastard, he thought and looked down at the girl asleep on the seat by him.

I suppose you start to destroy it for fear you will lose it, or that it will take too great a hold on you, or in case it shouldn't be true, but it is not very good to do. I would like to see you have something besides your kids you did not destroy sometime. This girl's mother was and is a bitch and your mother was a bitch. That ought to bring you closer to her and make you understand her. That doesn't mean she has to be a bitch any more than you have to be a heel. She thinks you are a much better guy than you are and maybe that will make you a better guy than you are. You've been good for a long time now and maybe you can be good. As far as I know you haven't done anything cruel since that night on the dock with that citizen with the wife and the dog. You haven't been drunk. You haven't been wicked. It's a shame you're not still in the church because you could make such a good confession.

She sees you the way you are now and you are a good guy as of the last few weeks and she probably thinks that is the way you have been all the time and that people just maligned you.

You really can start it all over now. You really can. *Please don't be silly*, another part of him said. You really can, he said to himself. You can be just as good a guy as she thinks you are and as you are at this moment. There is such a thing as starting it all over and you've been given a chance to and you can do it and you will do it. *Will you make all the promises again?* Yes. If necessary I will make all the promises and I will keep them. *Not all the promises? Knowing you have broken them?* He could not say anything to that. *You mustn't be a crook before you start.* No. I mustn't. *Say what you can truly do each day and then do it. Each day. Do it a day at a time and keep each day's promises to her and to yourself.* That way I can start it all new, he thought, and still be straight.

You're getting to be an awful moralist, he thought. If you don't watch out you will bore her. *When weren't you always a moralist?* At different times. *Don't fool yourself.* Well, at different places then. *Don't fool yourself.*

All right, Conscience, he said. Only don't be so solemn and didactic. Get a load of this, Conscience old friend, I know how useful and important you are and how you could have kept me out of all the trouble I have been in but couldn't you have a little lighter touch about it? I know that conscience speaks in italics but sometimes you seem to speak in very boldfaced Gothic script. I would take it just as well from you, Conscience, if you did not try to scare me; just as I would consider the Ten Commandments just as seriously if they were not presented as graven on stone tablets. You know, Conscience, it has been a long time since we were frightened by the thunder. Now with the lightning: There you have something. But the thunder doesn't impress us so much any more. *I'm trying to help you, you son of a bitch*, his conscience said.

The girl was still sleeping and they were coming up the hill into Tallahassee. She will probably wake when we stop at the first light, he thought. But she did not and he drove through the old town and turned off to the left on U.S. 319 straight south and into the beautiful wooded country that ran down toward the Gulf Coast.

There's one thing about you, daughter, he thought. Not only can you outsleep anybody I've ever known and have the best appetite I've ever seen linked with a build like yours but you have an absolutely heaven-given ability to not have to go to the bathroom.

Their room was on the fourteenth floor and it was not very cool. But with the fans on and the windows open it was better and when the bellboy had gone out Helena said, 'Don't be disappointed, darling. Please. It's lovely.'

'I thought I could get you an air-conditioned one.'

'They're awful to sleep in really. Like being in a vault. This will be fine.'

'We could have tried the other two. But they know me there.'

'They'll know us both here now. What's our name?'

'Mr. and Mrs. Robert Harris.'

'That's a splendid name. We must try to live up to it. Do you want to bathe first?'

'No. You.'

'All right. I'm going to really bathe though.'

'Go ahead. Go to sleep in the tub if you want.'

'I may. I didn't sleep all day did I?'

'You were wonderful. There was some pretty dull going too.'

'It wasn't bad. Lots of it was lovely. But New Orleans isn't really the way I thought it would be. Did you always know it was so flat and dull? I don't know what I expected. Marseilles I suppose. And to see the river.'

'It's only to eat and drink in. The part right around here doesn't look so bad at night. It's really sort of nice.'

'Let's not go out until it's dark. It's all right around here. Some of it is lovely.'

'We'll have that and then, in the morning, we'll be on our way.'

'That only leaves time for one meal.'

'That's all right. We'll come back in cold weather when we can really eat. Darling,' she said. 'This is the first sort of letdown we've had. So let's not let it let us down. We'll have long baths and some drinks and a meal twice as expensive as we can afford and we'll go to bed and make wonderful love.'

'The hell with New Orleans in the movies,' Roger said. 'We'll have New Orleans in bed.'

'Eat first. Didn't you order some White Rock and ice?'

'Yes. Do you want a drink?'

'No. I was just worried about you.'

'It will be along,' Roger said. There was a knock at the door. 'Here it is. You get started on the tub.'

'It's going to be wonderful,' she said. 'There will just be my nose out of water and the tips of my breasts maybe and my toes and I'm going to have it just as cold as it will run.'

The bellboy brought the pitcher of ice, the bottled water and the papers, took his tip and went out.

Roger made a drink and settled down to read. He was tired and it felt good to lie back on the bed with two pillows folded under his neck and read the evening and the morning papers. Things were not so good in Spain but it had not really taken shape yet. He read all the Spanish news carefully in the three papers and then read the other cable news and then the local news.

'Are you all right, darling?' Helena called from the bathroom.

'I'm wonderful.'

'Have you undressed?'

'Yes.'

'Do you have anything on?'

'No.'

'Are you very brown?'

'Still.'

'Do you know where we swam this morning was the loveliest beach I've ever seen.'

'I wonder how it can get so white and so floury.'

'Darling are you very, very brown?'

'Why?'

'I was just thinking about you.'

'Being in cold water's supposed to be good for that.'

'I'm brown under the water. You'd like it.'

'I like it.'

'You keep on reading,' she said. 'You are reading aren't you?'

'Yes.'

'Is Spain all right?'

'No.'

'I'm so sorry. Is it very bad?'

'No. Not yet. Really.'

'Roger?'

'Yes.'

'Do you love me?'

'Yes, daughter.'

'You go back and read now. I'll think about that here under-water.'

Roger lay back and listened to the noises that came up from the street below and read the papers and drank his drink. This was almost the best hour of the day. It was the hour he had always gone to the café alone when he had lived in Paris, to read the evening papers and have his aperitif. This town was nothing like Paris nor was it like Orleans either. Orleans wasn't much of a town either. It was pleasant enough though. Probably a better town to live in than this one. He didn't know the environs of this town though and he knew he was stupid about it.

He had always liked New Orleans, the little that he knew of

it, but it was a letdown to anyone who expected very much. And this certainly was not the month to hit it in.

The best time he had ever hit it was with Andy one time in the winter and another time driving through with David. The time going north with Andy they had not come through New Orleans. They had bypassed it to the north to save time and driven north of Lake Pontchartrain and across through Hammond to Baton Rouge on a new road that was being built so they made many detours and then they had gone north through Mississippi in the southern edge of the blizzard that was coming down from the north. When they had hit New Orleans was coming south again. But it was still cold and they had a wonderful time eating and drinking and the city had seemed gay and sharp with cold, instead of moist and damp and Andy had roamed all the antique shops and bought a sword with his Christmas money. He kept the sword in the luggage compartment behind the seat in the car and slept with it in his bed at night.

When he and David had come through it had been in the winter and they had made their headquarters in that restaurant he would have to try to find, the non-tourist one. He remembered it as in a cellar and having teakwood tables and chairs or else they sat on benches. It was probably not like that and was like a dream and he did not remember its name nor where it was located except he thought it was in the opposite direction from Antoine's, on an east and west, not a north and south street, and he and David had stayed in there two days. He probably had it mixed up with some other place. There was a place in Lyons and another near the Parc Monceau that always were merged in his dreams. That was one of the things about being drunk when you were young. You made places in your mind that afterwards you could never find and they were better than any places could ever be. He knew he hadn't been to this place with Andy though.

'I'm coming out,' she said.

'Feel how cool,' she said on the bed. 'Feel how cool all the way down. No don't go away. I like you.'

'No. Let me take a shower.'

'If you want. But I'd rather not. You don't wash the pickled onions do you before you put them in the cocktail? You don't wash the vermouth do you?'

'I wash the glass and the ice.'

'It's different. You're not the glass and the ice. Roger, please do that again. Isn't again a nice word?'

'Again and again,' he said.

Softly he felt the lovely curve from her hip bone up under her ribs and the apple slope of her breasts.

'Is it a good curve?'

He kissed her breasts and she said, 'Be awfully careful when they're so cold. Be very careful and kind. Do you know about them aching?'

'Yes,' he said. 'I know about aching.'

Then she said, 'The other one is jealous.'

Later she said, 'They didn't plan things right for me to have two breasts and you only one way to kiss. They made everything so far apart.'

His hand covered the other, the pressure between the fingers barely touching and then his lips wandered up over all the lovely coolness and met hers. They met and brushed very lightly, sweeping from side to side, losing nothing of the lovely outer screen and then he kissed her.

'Oh darling,' she said. 'Oh please darling. My dearest kind lovely love. Oh please, please, please my dear love.'

After quite a long time she said, 'I'm so sorry if I was selfish about your bath. But when I came out of mine I was selfish.'

'You weren't selfish.'

'Roger, do you still love me?'

'Yes, daughter.'

'Do you change how you feel afterwards?'

'No,' he lied.

'I don't at all. I just feel better afterwards. I mustn't tell you.'

'You tell me.'

'No. I won't tell you too much. But we do have a lovely time don't we?'

'Yes,' he said very truthfully.

'After we bathe we can go out.'

'I'll go now.'

'You know maybe we ought to stay tomorrow. I ought to have my nails done and my hair washed. I can do it all myself but you might like it better done properly. That way we could sleep late and then have part of one day in town and then leave the next morning.'

'That would be good.'

'I like New Orleans now. Don't you?'

'New Orleans is wonderful. It's changed a lot since we came here.'

'I'll go in. I'll only be a minute. Then you can bathe.'

'I only want a shower.'

Afterwards they went down in the elevator. There were Negro girls who ran the elevators and they were pretty. The elevator was full with a party from the floor above so they went down fast. Going down in the elevator made him feel hollower than ever inside. He felt Helena against him where they were crowded.

'If you ever get so that you don't feel anything when you see flying fish go out of water or when an elevator drops you better turn in your suit,' he said to her.

'I feel it still,' she said. 'Are those the only things you have to turn in your suit for?'

The door had opened and they were crossing the old-fashioned marble lobby crowded at this hour with people waiting for other people, people waiting to go to dinner, people just waiting, and Roger said, 'Walk ahead and let me see you.'

'Where do I walk to?'

'Straight toward the door of the air-conditioned bar.'

He caught her at the door.

'You're beautiful. You walk wonderfully and if I were here and saw you now for the first time I'd be in love with you.'

'If I saw you across the room I'd be in love with you.'

'If I saw you for the first time everything would turn over inside of me and I'd ache right through my chest.'

'That's the way I feel all of the time.'

'You can't feel that way all of the time.'

'Maybe not. But I can feel that way an awfully big part of the time.'

'Daughter, isn't New Orleans a fine place?'

'Weren't we lucky to come here?'

It felt very cold in the big high-ceilinged, pleasant, dark-wood panelled bar room and Helena, sitting beside Roger at a table, said, 'Look,' and showed him the tiny prickles of goose-flesh on her brown arm. 'You can do that to me too,' she said. 'But this time it's air conditioning.'

'It's really cold. It feels wonderful.'

'What should we drink?'

'Should we get tight?'

'Let's get a little tight.'

'I'll drink absinthe then.'

'Do you think I should?'

'Why don't you try it. Didn't you ever?'

'No. I was saving it to drink with you.'

'Don't make up things.'

'It's not made up. I truly did.'

'Daughter, don't make up a lot of things.'

'It's not made up. I didn't save my maidenly state because I thought it would bore you and besides I gave you up for a while. But I did save absinthe. Truly.'

'Do you have any real absinthe?' Roger asked the bar waiter.

'It's not supposed to be,' the waiter said. 'But I have some.'

'The real Couvet Pontarlier sixty-eighth-degree? Not the Tarragova?'

'Yes, sir,' the waiter said. 'I can't bring you the bottle. It will be in an ordinary Pernod bottle.'

'I can tell it,' Roger said.

'I believe you, sir,' the waiter said. 'Do you want a frappé or drip?'

'Straight drip. You have the dripping saucers?'

'Naturally, sir.'

'Without sugar.'

'Won't the lady want sugar, sir?'

'No. We'll let her try it without.'

'Very good, sir.'

After the waiter was gone Roger took Helena's hand under the table. 'Hello my beauty.'

'This is wonderful. Us here and this good old poison coming and we'll eat in some fine place.'

'And then go to bed.'

'Do you like bed as much as all that?'

'I never did. But I do now.'

'Why did you never?'

'Let's not talk about it.'

'We won't.'

'I don't ask you about everyone you've been in love with. We don't have to talk about London do we?'

'No. We can talk about you and how beautiful you are. You know you still move like a colt?'

'Roger, tell me, did I really walk so it pleased you?'

'You walk so that it breaks my heart.'

'All I do is keep my shoulders back and my head straight up and walk. I know there are tricks I ought to know.'

'When you look the way you do, daughter, there aren't any tricks. You're so beautiful that I'd be happy just to look at you.'

'Not permanently I hope.'

'Daytimes,' he said. 'Look, daughter. The one thing about absinthe is that you have to drink it awfully slowly. It won't taste strong mixed with the water but you have to believe it is.'

'I believe. Credo Roger.'

'I hope you'll never change it the way Lady Caroline did.'

'I'll never change it except for cause. But you're not like him at all.'

'I wouldn't want to be.'

'You're not. Someone tried to tell me you were at college. They meant it as a compliment I think but I was terribly angry and made an awful row with the English professor. They made us read you you know. I mean they made the others read it. I'd read it all. There isn't very much, Roger. Don't you think you ought to work more?'

'I'm going to work now as soon as we get out west.'

'Maybe we shouldn't stay tomorrow then. I'll be so happy when you work.'

'Happier than now?'

'Yes,' she said. 'Happier than now.'

'I'll work hard. You'll see.'

'Roger, do you think I'm bad for you? Do I make you drink or make love more than you should?'

'No, daughter.'

'I'm awfully glad if it's true because I want to be good for you. I know it's a weakness and silliness but I make up stories to myself in the daytime and in one of them I save your life. Sometimes it's from drowning and sometimes from in front of a train and sometimes in a plane and sometimes in the mountains. You can laugh if you want. And then there is one where I come into your life when you are disgusted and disappointed with all women and you love me so much and I take such good care of you that you get an epoch of writing wonderfully. That's a wonderful one. I was making it up again today in the car.'

'That's one I'm pretty sure I've seen in the movies or read somewhere.'

'Oh I know. I've seen it there too. And I'm sure I've read it too. But don't you think it happens? Don't you think I could be good for you? Not in a wishy-washy way or by giving you a little *baby* but really good for you so you'd write better than you ever wrote and be happy at the same time?'

'They do it in pictures. Why shouldn't we do it?'

The absinthe had come and from the saucers of cracked ice placed over the top of the glasses water, that Roger added from a small pitcher, was dripping down into the clear yellowish liquor turning it to an opalescent milkiness.

'Try that,' Roger said when it was the right cloudy color.

'It's very strange,' the girl said. 'And warming in the stomach. It tastes like medicine.'

'It is medicine. Pretty strong medicine.'

'I don't really need medicine yet,' the girl said. 'But this is awfully good. When will we be tight?'

'Almost any time. I'm going to have three. You take what you want. But take them slow.'

'I'll see how I do. I don't know anything about it yet except that it's like medicine. Roger?'

'Yes, daughter.'

He was feeling the warmth of the alchemist's furnace starting at the pit of his stomach.

'Roger, don't you think I really could be good for you the way I was in the story I made up?'

'I think we could be good to each other and for each other. But I don't like it to be on a basis of stories. I think the story business is bad.'

'But you see that's the way I am. I'm a story-maker-upper and I'm romantic I know. But that's how I am. If I was practical I'd never have come to Bimini.'

I don't know, Roger thought to himself. If that was what you wanted to do that was quite practical. You didn't just make up a story about it. And the other part of him thought: You must be slipping you bastard if the absinthe can bring the heel in you out that quickly. But what he said was, 'I don't know, daughter. I think the story business is dangerous. First you could make up stories about something innocuous, like me, and then there could be all sorts of other stories. There might be bad ones.'

'You're not so innocuous.'

'Oh yes I am. Or the stories are anyway. Saving me is fairly innocuous. But first you might be saving me and then next you might be saving the world. Then you might start saving yourself.'

'I'd like to save the world. I always wished I could. That's awfully big to make a story about. But I want to save you first.'

'I'm getting scared,' Roger said.

He drank some more of the absinthe and he felt better but he was worried.

'Have you always made up the stories?'

'Since I can remember. I've made them up about you for twelve years. I didn't tell you all the ones. There are hundreds of them.'

'Why don't you write instead of making up the stories?'

'I do write. But it's not as much fun as making up the stories and it's much harder. Then they're not nearly as good. The ones I make up are wonderful.'

'But you're always the heroine in the stories you write?'

'No. It's not that simple.'

'Well let's not worry about it now.' He took another sip of the absinthe and rolled it under his tongue.

'I never worried about it at all,' the girl said. 'What I wanted, always, was you and now I'm with you. Now I want you to be a great writer.'

'Maybe we'd better not even stop for dinner,' he said. He was still very worried and the absinthe warmth had moved up to his head now and he did not trust it there. He said to himself, What did you think could happen that would not have consequences? What woman in the world did you think could be as sound as a good secondhand Buick car? You've only known two sound women in your life and you lost them both. What will she want after that? And the other part of his brain said, Hail heel. The absinthe certainly brought you out early tonight.

So he said, 'Daughter, for now, let's just try to be good to each other and love each other' (he got the word out though the absinthe made it a difficult word for him to articulate) 'and as soon as we get out where we are going I will work just as hard and as well as I can.'

'That's lovely,' she said. 'And you don't mind my telling you I made up stories?'

'No,' he lied. 'They were very nice stories.' Which was true.

'Can I have another?' she asked.

'Sure.' He wished now they had never taken it although it was the drink he loved best of almost any in the world. But almost everything bad that had ever happened to him had happened when he was drinking absinthe; those bad things which were his own fault. He could tell that she knew something was wrong and he pulled hard against himself so that there would be nothing wrong.

'I didn't say something I shouldn't did I?'

'No, daughter. Here's to you.'

'Here's to us.'

The second one always tastes better than the first because certain taste buds are numbed against the bitterness of the wormwood so that without becoming sweet, or even sweeter, it becomes less bitter and there are parts of the tongue that enjoy it more.

'It is strange and wonderful. But all it does so far is just bring us to the edge of misunderstanding,' the girl said.

'I know,' he said. 'Let's stick together through it.'

'Was it that you thought I was ambitious?'

'It's all right about the stories.'

'No. It's not all right with you. I couldn't love you as much as I do and not know when you're upset.'

'I'm not upset,' he lied. 'And I'm not going to be upset,' he resolved. 'Let's talk about something else.'

'It will be wonderful when we're out there and you can work.'

She is a little obtuse, he thought. Or maybe does it affect her that way? But he said, 'It will be. But you won't be bored?'

'Of course not.'

'I work awfully hard when I work.'

'I'll work too.'

'That will be fun,' he said. 'Like Mr. and Mrs. Browning. I never saw the play.'

'Roger, do you have to make fun of it?'

'I don't know.' Now pull yourself together, he said to himself. Now is the time to pull yourself together. Be good now. 'I make fun of everything,' he said. 'I think it will be fine. And it's much better for you to be working when I'm writing.'

'Will you mind reading mine sometimes?'

'No. I'll love to.'

'Really?'

'No. Of course. I'll be really happy to. Really.'

'When you drink this it makes you feel as though you could do anything,' the girl said. 'I'm awfully glad I never drank it before. Do you mind if we talk about writing, Roger?'

'Hell no.'

'Why did you say "Hell no"?'

'I don't know,' he said. 'Let's talk about writing. Really. I mean it. What about writing?'

'Now you've made me feel like a fool. You don't have to take me in as an equal or a partner. I only meant I'd like to talk about it if you'd like to.'

'Let's talk about it. What about it?'

The girl began to cry, sitting straight up and looking at him. She did not sob nor turn her head away. She just looked at him and tears came down her cheeks and her mouth grew fuller but it did not twist nor break.

'Please, daughter,' he said. 'Please. Let's talk about it or anything else and I'll be friendly.'

She bit her lip and then said, 'I suppose I wanted to be partners even though I said I didn't.'

I guess that was part of the dream and why the hell shouldn't it be? Roger thought. What do you have to hurt her for you bastard? Be good now fast before you hurt her.

'You see I'd like to have you not just like me in bed but like me in the head and like to talk about things that interest us both.'

'We will,' he said. 'We will now. Bratchen daughter, what about writing, my dear beauty?'

'What I wanted to tell you was that drinking this made me feel the way I feel when I am going to write. That I could do anything and that I can write wonderfully. Then I write and it's just dull. The truer I try to make it the duller it is. And when it isn't true it's silly.'

'Give me a kiss.'

'Here?'

'Yes.'

He leaned over the table and kissed her. 'You're awfully beautiful when you cry.'

'I'm awfully sorry I cried,' she said. 'You don't really mind if we talk about it do you?'

'Of course not.'

'You see that was one of the parts of it I'd looked forward to.'

Yes, I guess it was, he thought. Well why shouldn't it be? And we'll do it. Maybe I will get to like it.

'What was it about writing?' he said. 'Besides how it seems it's going to be wonderful and then it turns out dull?'

'Wasn't it that way with you when you started?'

'No. When I started I'd feel as though I could do anything and while I was doing it I would feel like I was making the whole world and when I would read it I would think this is so good I couldn't have written it. I must have read it somewhere. Probably in the *Saturday Evening Post*.'

'Weren't you ever discouraged?'

'Not when I started. I thought I was writing the greatest stories ever written and that people just didn't have sense enough to know it.'

'Were you really that conceited?'

'Worse probably. Only I didn't think I was conceited. I was just confident.'

'If those were your first stories, the ones I read, you had a right to be confident.'

'They weren't,' he said. 'All those first confident stories were lost. The ones you read were when I wasn't confident at all.'

'How were they lost, Roger?'

'It's an awful story. I'll tell it to you sometime.'

'Wouldn't you tell it to me now?'

'I hate to because it's happened to other people and to better writers than I am and that makes it sound as though it were made up. There's no reason for it ever happening and yet it's happened many times and it still hurts like a bastard. No it doesn't really. It has a scar over it now. A good thick scar.'

'Please tell me about it. If it's a scar and not a scab it won't hurt to will it?'

'No, daughter. Well I was very methodical in those days and I kept original manuscripts in one cardboard folder and typed originals in another and carbons in another. I guess it wasn't so cockeyed methodical. I don't know how else you'd do it. Oh the hell with this story.'

'No tell me.'

'Well I was working at the Lausanne Conference and it was the holidays coming up and Andrew's mother who was a lovely girl and very beautiful and kind –'

'I was never jealous of her,' the girl said. 'I was jealous of David's and Tom's mother.'

'You shouldn't be jealous of either of them. They were both wonderful.'

'I was jealous of Dave's and Tom's mother,' Helena said. 'I'm not now.'

'That's awfully white of you,' Roger said. 'Maybe we ought to send her a cable.'

'Go on with the story, please, and don't be bad.'

'All right. The aforesaid Andy's mother thought she would bring down my stuff so I could have it with me and be able to do some work while we had the holiday together. She was going to bring it to me as a surprise. She hadn't written anything about it and when I met her at Lausanne I didn't know anything about it. She was a day late and had wired about it. The only thing I knew was that she was crying when I met her and she cried and cried and when I would ask her what was the matter she told me it was too awful to tell me and then she would cry again. She cried as though her heart was broken. Do I have to tell this story?'

'Please tell me.'

'All that morning she would not tell me and I thought of all the worst possible things that could have happened and asked her if they had happened. But she just shook her head. The worst thing I could think of was that she had *tromper*-ed me or fallen in love with someone else and when I asked her that she said, "Oh how can you say that?" and cried some more. I felt relieved then and then, finally, she told me.

'She had packed all the manuscript folders in a suitcase and left the suitcase with her other bags in her first class compartment in the Paris–Lausanne–Milan Express in the Gare de Lyon while she went out on the quai to buy a London paper and a bottle of Evian water. You remember the Gare de Lyon and how they would have sort of push tables with papers and magazines and mineral water and small flasks of cognac and sandwiches with ham between sliced long pointed-end bread wrapped in paper and other push carts with pillows and blankets that you rented? Well when she got back into the compartment with her paper and her Evian water the suitcase was gone.

'She did everything there was to be done. You know the French police. The first thing she had to do was show her *carte d'identité* and try to prove she was not an international crook herself and that she did not suffer from hallucinations and that she was sure she actually had such a suitcase and were the papers of political importance and besides, madame, surely there exist copies. She had that all night and the next day when a detective came and searched the flat for the suitcase and found a shotgun of mine and demanded to know if I had a *permis de chasse* I think there was some doubt in the minds of the police whether she should be allowed to proceed to Lausanne and she said the detective had followed her to the train and appeared in the compartment just before the train pulled out and said, "You are quite sure madame that all your baggage is intact now? That you have not lost anything else? No other important papers?"

'So I said, "But it's all right really. You *can't* have brought the originals and the typed originals and the carbons."

' "But I did," she said. "Roger, I know I did." It was true too. I found out it was true when I went up to Paris to see. I remember walking up the stairs and opening the door to the flat, unlocking it and pulling back on the brass handle of the sliding lock and the odor of Eau de Tavel in the kitchen and the dust that had sifted in through the windows on the table in the dining room and going to the cupboard where I kept the stuff in the dining room and it was all gone. I was sure it would be there; that some of the manila folders would be there because I could see them there so clearly in my mind. But there was nothing there at all, not even my paper clips in a cardboard box nor my pencils and erasers nor my pencil sharpener that was shaped like a fish, nor my envelopes with the return address typed in the upper left-hand corner, nor my international postage coupons that you enclosed for them to send the manuscripts back with and that were kept in a small Persian lacquered box that had a pornographic painting inside of it. They were all gone. They had all been packed in the suitcase. Even the red stick of wax was gone that I had used to seal letters and packages. I stood there and looked at the painting inside the Persian box and noticed the curious over-proportion of the parts represented that always characterizes pornography and I remember thinking how much I disliked pornographic pictures and painting and writing and how after this box had been given to me by a friend on his return from Persia I had only looked at the painted interior once to please the friend and that after that I had only used the box as a convenience to keep coupons and stamps in and had never seen the pictures. I felt almost as though I could not breathe when I saw that there really were no folders with originals, nor folders with typed copies, nor folders with carbons and then I locked the door of the cupboard and went into the next room, which was the bedroom, and lay down on the bed and put a pillow between my legs and my arms around another pillow and lay there very quietly. I had never put a pillow between my legs before and I had never lain with my arms around a pillow but now I needed them very badly. I knew everything I had ever written and everything that I had great confidence in was gone. I had rewritten them so many times and gotten them just how I wanted them and I knew I could not write them again because once I had them right I forgot them completely and each time I ever read them I wondered at them and at how I had ever done them.

'So I lay there without moving with the pillows for friends and I was in despair. I had never had despair before, true despair, nor have I ever had it since. My forehead lay against the Persian shawl that covered the bed, which was only a mattress and springs set on the floor and the bed cover was dusty too and I smelt the dust and lay there with my despair and the pillows were my only comfort.'

'What were they that were gone,' the girl asked.

'Eleven stories, a novel, and poems.'

'Poor poor Roger.'

'No. I wasn't so poor because there were more inside. Not them. But to come. But I was in bad shape. You see I hadn't believed they could be gone. Not everything.'

'What did you do?'

'Nothing very practical. I lay there for a while.'

'Did you cry?'

'No. I was all dried up inside like the dust in the house. Weren't you ever in despair?'

'Of course. In London. But I could cry.'

'I'm sorry, daughter. I got to thinking about this thing and I forgot. I'm awfully sorry.'

'What did you do?'

'Let's see. I got up and went down the stairs and spoke to the concierge and she asked me about madame. She was worried because the police had been to the flat and had asked her questions but she was still cordial. She asked me if we had found the valise that had been stolen and I said no and she said it was dirty luck and a great misfortune and was it true that all my works were in it. I said yes and she said but how was it there were no copies? I said the copies were there too. Then she said *Mais ça alors*. Why were copies made to lose them with the originals? I said madame had packed them by mistake. It was a great mistake, she said. A fatal mistake. But monsieur can remember them surely. No, I said. But, she said, monsieur will have to remember them. *Il faut le souvienne rappeler. Oui*, I said, *mais ce n'est pas possible. Je ne m'en souviens plus. Mais il faut faire un effort*, she said. *Je le ferais*, I said. But it's useless. *Mais qu'est-ce que monsieur va faire*? she asked. Monsieur has worked here for three years. I have seen monsieur work at the café on the corner. I've seen monsieur at work at the table in the dining room when I've brought things up. *Je sais que monsieur travaille comme un sourd. Qu'est-ce que il faut faire maintenant? Il faut recommencer*, I said. Then the concierge started to cry. I put my arm around her and she smelled of armpit sweat and dust and old black clothes and her hair smelled rancid and she cried with her head on my chest. Were there poems too? she asked. Yes, I said. What unhappiness, she said. But you can recall those surely. *Je tâcherai de la faire*, I said. Do it, she said. Do it tonight.

'I will, I told her. Oh monsieur, she said, madame is beautiful and amiable and *tous le qu'il y a de gentil* but what a grave error it was. Will you drink a glass of marc with me? Of course, I told her, and, sniffing, she left my chest to find the bottle and the two small glasses. To the new works, she said. To them, I said. Monsieur will be a member of the Académie Française. No, I said. The Académie Americaine, she said. Would you prefer rum? I have some rum. No, I said. Marc is very good. Good, she said. Another glass. Now, she said, go out and get yourself drunk and, since Marcelle is not coming to do the flat, as soon as my husband comes in to hold down this dirty loge I will go upstairs and clean the place up for you to sleep tonight. Do you want me to buy anything for you? Do you want me to make breakfast? I asked her. Certainly, she said. Give me ten francs and I'll bring you the change. I'd make you dinner but you ought to eat out tonight. Even though it is more expensive. *Allez voir des amis et manger quelque part*. If it wasn't for my husband I'd come with you.

'Come on and have a drink at the Café des Amateurs now, I said. We'll have a hot grog. No I can't leave this cage until my husband comes, she said. *Débine-toi maintenant*. Leave me the key. It will all be in order when you get back.

'She was a fine woman and I felt better already because I knew there was only one thing to do; to start over. But I did not know if I could do it. Some of the stories had been about boxing, and some about baseball and others about horse racing. They were the things I had known best and had been closest to and several were about the first war. Writing them I had felt all the emotion

I had to feel about those things and I had put it all in and all the knowledge of them that I could express and I had rewritten and rewritten until it was all in them and all gone out of me. Because I had worked on newspapers since I was very young I could never remember anything once I had written it down; as each day you wiped your memory clear with writing as you might wipe a blackboard clear with a sponge or a wet rag; and I still had that evil habit and now it had caught up with me.

'But the concierge, and the smell of the concierge, and her practicality and determination hit my despair as a nail might hit it if it were driven in cleanly and soundly and I thought I must do something about this; something practical; something that will be good for me even if it cannot help about the stories. Already I was half glad the novel was gone because I could see already, as you begin to see clearly over the water when a rain-storm lifts on the ocean as the wind carries it out to sea, that I could write a better novel. But I missed the stories as though they were a combination of my house, and my job, my only gun, my small savings and my wife; also my poems. But the despair was going and there was only missing now as after a great loss. Missing is very bad too.'

'I know about missing,' the girl said.

'Poor daughter,' he said. 'Missing is bad. But it doesn't kill you. But despair would kill you in just a little time.'

'Really kill you?'

'I think so,' he said.

'Can we have another?' she asked. 'Will you tell me the rest? This is the sort of thing I always wondered about.'

'We can have another,' Roger said. 'And I'll tell you the rest if it doesn't bore you.'

'Roger, you mustn't say that about boring me.'

'I bore the hell out of myself sometimes,' he said. 'So it seemed normal I might bore you.'

'Please make the drink and then tell me what happened.'

JUVENILIA AND PRE-PARIS STORIES

JUDGMENT OF MANITOU

Dick Haywood buttoned the collar of his mackinaw up about his ears, took down his rifle from the deer horns above the fireplace of the cabin and pulled on his heavy fur mittens. 'I'll go and run that line toward Loon River, Pierre,' he said. 'Holy quill pigs, but it's cold.' He glanced at the thermometer. 'Forty-two below! Well, so long, Pierre.' Pierre merely grunted, as, twisting on his snowshoes, Dick started out over the crust with the swinging snowshoe stride of the traveler of the barren grounds.

In the doorway of the cabin Pierre stood looking after Dick as he swung along. He grinned evilly to himself, 'De tief will tink it a blame sight cooler when he swingin' by one leg in the air like Wah-boy, the rabbit; he would steal my money, would he!' Pierre slammed the heavy door shut, threw some wood on the fire and crawled into his bunk.

As Dick Haywood strode along he talked to himself as to the travelers of the 'silent places.' 'Wonder why Pierre is so grouchy just because he lost that money? Bet he just misplaced it somewhere. All he does now is to grunt like a surly pig and every once in a while I catch him leering at me behind my back. If he thinks I stole his money why don't he say so and have it out with me! Why, he used to be so cheerful and jolly; when we agreed at Missainabal to be pardners and trap up here in the Ungava district, I thought he'd be a jolly good companion, but now he hasn't spoken to me for the last week, except to grunt or swear in that Cree lingo.'

It was a cold day, but it was the dry, invigorating cold of the northland and Dick enjoyed the crisp air. He was a good traveller on snowshoes and rapidly covered the first five miles of the trap line, but somehow he felt that something was following him and he glanced around several times only to be disappointed each time. 'I guess it's only the Kootzie-ootzie,' he muttered to himself, for in the North whenever men do not understand a thing they blame it on the 'little bad god of the Crees.' Suddenly, as Dick entered a growth of spruce, he was jerked off his feet, high into the air. When his head had cleared from the bang it had received by striking the icy crust, he saw that he was suspended in the air by a rope which was attached to a spruce tree, which had been bent over to form the spring for a snare, such as is used to capture rabbits. His fingers barely touched the crust, and as he struggled and the cord grew tighter on his leg he saw what he had sensed to be following him. Slowly out of the woods trotted a band of gaunt, white, hungry timber wolves, and squatted on their haunches in a circle round him.

Back in the cabin Pierre as he lay in his bunk was awakened by a gnawing sound overhead, and idly looking up at the rafter he saw a red squirrel busily gnawing away at the leather of his lost wallet. He thought of the trap he had set for Dick, and springing from his bunk he seized his rifle, and coatless and gloveless ran madly out along the trail. After a gasping, breathless, choking run he came upon the spruce grove. Two ravens left off picking at the shapeless something that had once been Dick Haywood, and flapped lazily into a neighboring spruce. All over the bloody snow were the tracks of My-in-gau, the timber wolf.

As he took a step forward Pierre felt the clanking grip of the toother bear trap, that Dick had come to tend, close on his feet. He fell forward, and as he lay on the snow he said, 'It is the judgment of Manitou; I will save My-in-gau, the wolf, the trouble.'

And he reached for the rifle.

A MATTER OF COLOUR

'What, you never heard the story about Joe Gans' first fight?' said old Bob Armstrong, as he tugged at one of his gloves.

'Well, son, that kid I was just giving the lesson to reminded me of the Big Swede that gummed the best frame-up we ever almost pulled off.

'The yarn's a classic now; but I'll give it to you just as it happened.

'Along back in 1902 I was managing a sort of a new lightweight by the name of Montana Dan Morgan. Well, this Dan person was one of those rough and ready lads, game and all that, but with no footwork, but with a kick like a mule in his right fin, but with a weak left that wouldn't dent melted butter. I'd gotten along pretty well with the bird, and we'd collected sundry shekels fighting dockwallopers and stevedores and preliminary boys out at the old Olympic club.

'Dan was getting to be quite a sizable scrapper, and by using his strong right mitt and stalling along, he managed to achieve quite a reputation. So I matched the lad with Jim O'Rourke, the old trial horse, and the boy managed to hang one on Jim's jaw that was good for the ten-second anesthetic.

'So when Pete McCarthy came around one day and said he had an amateur that wanted to break in, and would I sign Dan up with him for twenty rounds out at Vernon, I fell for it strong. Joe Gans, Pete said, was the amateur's name, and I'd never heard of him at that time.

'I thought that it was kind of strange when Pete came around with a contract that had a $500 forfeit clause in it for non-appearance, but we intended to appear all right, so I signed up.

'Well, we didn't train much for the scrap, and two days before it was to come off, Dan comes up to me and says: "Bob, take a look at this hand."

'He stuck out his right mauler, and there, just above the wrist, was a lump like a pigeon egg.

' "Holy smokes! Danny, where did you get that?"

' "The bag busted loose while I was punchin' it," says Danny, "and me right banged into the framework."

' "Well, you've done it now," I yelped. "There's that 500 iron men in the forfeit, and I've put down everything I've got on you to win by K. O."

' "It can't be helped," says Dan. "That bag wasn't fastened proper; I'll fight anyway."

' "Yes, you will, with that left hand of yours, that couldn't punch a ripple in a bowl of soup."

' "Bob," says Danny, "I've got a scheme. You know the way the ring is out there at the Olympic? Up on the stage with that old cloth drop curtain in back? Well, in the first round, before they find out about this bad flipper of mine, I'll rush the smoke up against the curtain (you know Joe Gans was a 'pusson of color') and you have somebody back there with a baseball bat, and swat him on the head from behind the curtain."

'Say! I could have thrown a fit. It was so blame simple. We just couldn't lose, you see. It comes off so quick nobody gets wise. Then we collects and beats it!

'So I goes out and pawns my watch to put another twenty down on Dan to win by a knockout. Then we went out to Vernon and I hired a big husky Swede to do the slapstick act.

'The day of the fight dawned bright and clear, as the sporting writers say, only it was foggy. I installed the husky Swede back of the old drop curtain just behind the ropes. You see, I had every cent we had down on Dan, about 600 round ones and the 500 in the forfeit. A couple of ham and egg fighters mauled each other in the prelims, and then the bell rings for our show.

'I tied Dan's gloves on, gives him a chew of gum and my blessing, and he climbs over the ropes into the squared circle. This Joe Gans, he's champion now, had quite a big following among the Oakland gang, and so we had no very great trouble getting our money covered. Joe's black, you know, and the Swede behind the scenes had his instructions: "Just as soon as the white man backs the black man up against the ropes, you swing on the black man's head with the bat from behind the curtain."

'Well, the gong clangs and Dan rushes the smoke up against the ropes, according to instructions.

'Nothing doing from behind the curtain! I motioned wildly at the Swede looking out through the peephole.

'Then Joe Gans rushes Dan up against the ropes. Whunk! comes a crack and Dan drops like a poled over ox.

'Holy smoke! The Swede had hit the wrong man! All our kale was gone! I climbed into the ring, grabbed Dan and dragged him into the dressing room by the feet. There wasn't any need for the referee to count ten; he might have counted 300.

'There was the Swede.

'I lit into him: "You miserable apology for a low-grade im-becile! You evidence of God's carelessness! Why in the name of the Prophet did you hit the white man instead of the black man?"

' "Mister Armstrong," he says, "you no should talk at me like that – I bane color blind!" '

SEPI JINGAN

' "Velvet's" like red hot pepper; "P. A." like cornsilk. Give me a package of "Peerless".'

Billy Tabeshaw, long, lean, copper-colored, hamfaced and Ojibway, spun a Canadian quarter onto the counter of the little northwoods country store and stood waiting for the clerk to get his change from the till under the notion counter.

'Hey, you robber!' yelled the clerk. 'Come back here!'

We all had a glimpse of a big, wolfish-looking, husky dog vanishing through the door with a string of frankfurter sausages bobbing, snake-like, behind him.

'Darn that blasted cur! Them sausages are on you, Bill.'

'Don't cuss the dog. I'll stand for the meat. What's it set me back?'

'Just twenty-nine cents, Bill. There was three pounds of 'em at ten cents, but I et one of 'em myself.'

'Here's thirty cents. Go buy yourself a picture post-card.'

Bill's dusky face cracked across in a white-toothed grin. He put his package of tobacco under his arm and slouched out of the store. At the door he crooked a finger at me and I followed him out into the cool twilight of the summer evening.

At the far end of the wide porch three pipes glowed in the dusk.

'Ish,' said Bill, 'they're smoking "Stag!" It smells like dried apricots. Me for "Peerless." '

Bill is not the redskin of the popular magazine. He never says 'ugh.' I have yet to hear him grunt or speak of the Great White Father at Washington. His chief interests are the various brands of tobacco and his big dog, 'Sepi Jingan.'

We strolled off down the road. A little way ahead, through the gathering darkness, we could see a blurred figure. A whiff of smoke reached Bill's nostrils. 'Gol, that guy is smoking "Giant"! No, it's "Honest Scrap"! Just like burnt rubber hose. Me for "Peerless." '

The edge of the full moon showed above the hill to the east. To our right was a grassy bank. 'Let's sit down,' Bill said. 'Did I ever tell you about Sepi Jingan?'

'Like to hear it,' I replied.

'You remember Paul Black Bird?'

'The new fellow who got drunk last fourth of July and went to sleep on the Pere Marquette tracks?'

'Yes. He was a bad Indian. Up on the upper peninsula he couldn't get drunk. He used to drink all day – everything. But he couldn't get drunk. Then he would go crazy; but he wasn't drunk. He was crazy because he couldn't get drunk.

'Paul was Jack-fishing [spearing fish illegally] over on Witch Lake up on the upper, and John Brandar, who was game warden, went over to pinch him. John always did a job like that alone; so next day, when he didn't show up, his wife sent me over to look for him. I found him, all right. He was lying at the end of the portage, all spread out, face down and a pike-pole stuck through his back.

'They raised a big fuss and the sheriff hunted all over for Paul; but there never was a white man yet could catch an Indian in the Indian's own country.

'But with me, it was quite different. You see, John Brandar was my cousin.

'I took Sepi, who was just a pup then, and we trailed him (that was two years ago). We trailed him to the Soo, lost the trail, picked it up at Garden River, in Ontario; followed him along the north shore to Michipicoten; and then he went up to Missainabie and 'way up to Moose Factory. We were always just behind him, but we never could catch up. He doubled back by the Abittibi and finally thought he'd ditched us. He came down to this country from Mackinaw.

'We trailed him, though, but lost the scent and just happened to hit this place. We didn't know he was here, but he had us spotted.

'Last fourth of July I was walking by the P. M. tracks with Sepi when something hit me alongside the head and everything went black.

'When I came to, there was Paul Black Bird standing over me with a pike-pole and grinning at me!

' "Well," he smiled, "you have caught up with me; ain't you glad to see me?"

'There was where he made a mistake. He should have killed me then and everything would have been all right for him. He would have, if he had been either drunk or sober, but he had been drinking and was crazy. That was what saved me.

'He kept prodding me with the pike-pole and kidding me. "Where's your dog, dog man? You and he have followed me. I will kill you both and then slide you onto the rails."

'All the time I kept wondering where Sepi was. Finally I saw him. He was crawling with his belly on the earth, toward Black Bird. Nearer and nearer he crawled and I prayed that Paul wouldn't see him.

'Paul sat there, cussing and pricking me with the long pike-pole. Sepi crawled closer and closer. I watched him out of the tail of my eye while I looked at Paul.

'Suddenly Sepi sprang like a shaggy thunderbolt. With a side snap of his head, his long, wolf jaws caught the throat.

'It was really a very neat job, considering. The Pere Marquette Resort Limited removed all the traces. So, you see, when you said that Paul Black Bird was drunk and lay down on the Pere Marquette tracks you weren't quite right. That Indian couldn't get drunk. He only got crazy on drink.

'That's why you and me are sittin' here, lookin' at the moon, and my debts are paid and I let Sepi steal sausages at Hauley's store.

'Funny, ain't it?

'You take my advice and stay off that "Tuxedo" – "Peerless" is the only tobacco.

'Come on, Sepi.'

THE MERCENARIES

If you are honestly curious about pearl fishing conditions in the Marquesas, the possibility of employment on the projected Trans Gobi Desert Railway, or the potentialities of any of the hot tamale republics, go to the Cafe Cambrinus on Wabash Avenue, Chicago. There at the rear of the dining room where the neo-bohemians struggle nightly with their spaghetti and ravioli is a small smoke-filled room that is a clearinghouse for the camp followers of fortune. When you enter the room, and you will have no more chance than the zoological entrant in the famous camel-needle's eye gymkhana of entering the room unless you are approved by Cambrinus, there will be a sudden silence. Then a varying number of eyes will look you over with that detached intensity that comes of a periodic contemplation of death. This inspection is not mere boorishness. If you're recognized favourably, all right; if you are unknown, all right; Cambrinus has passed on you. After a time the talk picks up again. But one time the door was pushed open, men looked up, glances of recognition shot across the room, a man half rose from one of the card tables, his hand behind him, two men ducked to the floor, there was a roar from the doorway, and what had had its genesis in the Malay Archipelago terminated in the back room of the Cambrinus. But that's not this.

I came out of the wind scoured nakedness of Wabash Avenue in January into the cosy bar of the Cambrinus and, armed with a smile from Cambrinus himself, passed through the dining room where the waiters were clearing away the debris of the table d'hotes and sweeping out into the little back room. The two men I had seen in the café before were seated at one of the three tables with half empty bottles of an unlabeled beverage known to the initiates as 'Kentucky Brew' before them. They nodded and I joined them.

'Smoke?' asked the taller of the two, a gaunt man with a face the color of half-tanned leather, shoving a package of cheap cigarettes across the table.

'It is possible the gentleman would prefer one of these,' smiled the other with a flash of white teeth under a carefully pointed mustache, and pushed a monogrammed cigarette box across to me with a small, well-manicured hand.

'Shouldn't wonder,' grunted the big man, his adam's apple

rising and falling above his flannel shirt collar. 'Can't taste em myself.' He took one of his own cigarettes and rolled the end between thumb and forefinger until a tiny mound of tobacco piled up on the table before him, then carefully picked up the stringy wad and tucked it under his tongue, lighting the half-cigarette that remained.

'It is droll, that manner of smoking a cigarette, is it not?' smiled the dark little man as he held a match for me. I noted a crossed-cannon monogram on his box as I handed it back to him.

'Artigliere français?' I questioned.

'Mais oui, Monsieur; le soixante-quinze!' he smiled again, his whole face lighting up.

'Say,' broke in the gaunt man, eyeing me thoughtfully; 'Artill'ry ain't your trade, is it?'

'No, takes too much brains,' I said.

'That's too darn bad. It don't,' the leather-faced man replied to my answer and observation.

'Why?' said I.

'There's a good job now.' He rolled the tobacco under his tongue and drew a deep inhalation on his cigarette butt. 'For gunners. Peru verstus and against Chile. Two hundred dollars a month – '

'In gold,' smiled the Frenchman, twisting his mustache.

'In gold,' continued the leather-face. 'We got the dope from Cambrinus. Artillery officers they want. We saw the consul. He's fat and important and oily. "War with Chile? Reediculous!" he says. I talked spiggotty to him for awhile and we come to terms. Napoleon here –'

The Frenchman bowed, 'Lieutenant Denis Ricaud.'

'Napoleon here –,' continued leather-face unmoved, 'and me are officers in the Royal Republican Peruvian Army with tickets to New York.' He tapped his coat pocket. 'There we see the Peruvian consul and present papers,' he tapped his pocket again, 'and are shipped to Peru via way of the Isthmus. Let's have a drink.'

He pushed the button under the table and Antonino the squat Sardinian waiter poked his head in the door.

'If you haven't had one, perhaps you'd try a Cognac-Benedictine?' asked the leather-faced man. I nodded, thinking. 'Tre Martell-Benedictine, Nino. It's all right with Cambrinus.'

Antonino nodded and vanished. Ricaud flashed his smile at me, 'And you will hear people denounce the absinthe as an evil beverage!'

I was puzzling over the drink leather-face had ordered, for there is only one place in the world where people drink that smooth, insidious, brainrotting mixture. And I was still puzzling when Antonino returned with the drinks, not in liqueur glasses, but in big full cock-tail containers.

'These are mine altogether in toto,' said the leather-face, pulling out a roll of bills. 'Me and Napoleon are now being emolumated at the rate of two hundred dollars per month –'

'Gold!' smiled Ricaud.

'Gold!' calmly finished leather-face. 'Say, my name is Graves, Perry Graves.' He looked across the table at me.

'Mine's Rinaldi. Rinaldi Renaldo,' I said.

'Wop?' asked Graves, lifting his eyebrows and his adam's apple simultaneously.

'Grandfather was Italian,' I replied.

'Wop, eh,' said Graves unhearingly, then lifted his glass. 'Napoleon, and you, Signor Resolvo, I'd like to propose a toast. You say "A bas Chile!" Napoleon. You say "Delenda Chile!" Risotto. I drink "To Hell with Chile!" ' We all sipped our glasses.

'Down with Chile,' said Graves meditatively, then in an argumentative tone, 'They're not a bad lot, those Chillies!'

'Ever been there?' I asked.

'Nope,' said Graves, 'a rotten bad lot those dirty Chillies.'

'Capitaine Graves is a propagandiste to himself,' smiled Ricaud, and lit a cigarette.

'We'll rally round the doughnut. The Peruvian doughnut,' mused Graves, disembowelling another cigarette. 'Follow the doughnut, my boys, my brave boys. Vive la doughnut. Up with the Peruvian doughnut and down with the chile concarne. A dirty rotten lot those Chillies!'

'What is the doughnut, mon cher Graves?' asked Ricaud, puzzled.

'Make the world safe for the doughnut, the grand old Peruvian doughnut. Don't give up the doughnut. Remember the doughnut. Peru expects every doughnut to do his duty,' Graves was chanting in a monotone. 'Wrap me in the doughnut, my brave boys. No, it doesn't sound right. It ain't got something a slogum ought to have. But those Chillies are a rotten lot!'

'The Capitaine is très patriotic, n'est-ce pas? The doughnut is the national symbol of Peru, I take it?' asked Ricaud.

'Never been there. But we'll show those dirty Chillies they can't trample on the grand old Peruvian doughnut though, Napoleon!' said Graves, fiercely banging his fist on the table.

'Really, we should know more of the country at whose disposal we have placed our swords,' murmured Ricaud, apologetically. 'What I wonder is the flag of Peru?'

'Can't use the sword myself,' said Graves dourly, raising his glass. 'That reminds me of something. Say, you ever been to Italy?'

'Three years,' I replied.

'During the war?' Graves shot a look at me.

'Durante la guerra,' I said.

'Good boy! Ever hear of Il Lupo?'

Who in Italy has not heard of Il Lupo, the Wolf? The Italian ace of aces and second only to the dead Baracca. Any school boy can tell the number of his victories and the story of his combat with Baron Von Hauser, the great Austrian pilot. How he brought Von Hauser back alive to the Italian lines, his gun jammed, his observer dead in the cockpit.

'Is he a brave man?' asked Graves, his face tightening up.

'Of course!' I said.

'Certainment!' said Ricaud, who knew the story as well as I did.

'He is not,' said Graves quietly, the leather mask of his face crinkled into a smile. 'I'll leave it to you Napoleon, and to you, Signor Riposso, if he is a brave man. The war is over –'

'I seem to have heard as much somewheres,' murmured Ricaud.

'The war is over,' calmly proceeded Graves. 'Before it, I was a top kicker of field artillery. At the end I was a captain of field artillery, acting pro tempor for the time being. After awhile, they demoted us all to our pre-war rank and I took a discharge. It's a long tumble from captain to sergeant. You see, I was an officer, but not a gentleman. I could command a battery, but I've got a rotten taste in cigarettes. But I wasn't no worse off than lots of other old non-coms. Some were majors even and lieutenant colonels. Now they're all non-coms again or out. Napoleon here is a gentleman. You can tell it to look at him. But I ain't. That ain't the point of this, and I ain't kicking if that's the way they want to run their army.' He raised his glass.

'Down with the Chillies!'

'After the Armistice I rated some leave and got an order of movement good for Italy, and went down through Genoa and Pisa and hit Rome, and a fella said it was good weather in Sicily. That's where I learned to drink this.' He noted his glass was empty and pushed the button under the table. 'Too much of this ain't good for a man.'

I nodded.

'You go across from a place called Villa San Giovanni on a ferry to Messina, where you can get a train. One way it goes to Palermo. The other way to Catania. It was just which and together with me which way to go. There was quite a crowd of us standing there where the two trains were waiting, and a woman came up to me and smiled and said, "You are the American captain, Forbes, going to Taormina?"

'I wasn't, of course, and a gentleman like Napoleon here would have said how sorry he was but that he was not Captain Forbes, but I don't know. I saluted and when I looked at her I admitted that I was that captain enroute on the way to nowheres by Taormina, wherever it should be. She was so pleased, but said that she had not expected me for three or four days, and how was dear Dyonisia?

'I'd been out at the Corso Cavalli in Rome and had won money on a dog named Dyonisia that came from behind in the stretch and won the prettiest race you ever saw, so I said without lying any that Dyonisia was never better in her life. And Bianca, how was she, dear girl? Bianca, so far as I knew, was enjoying the best of health. So all this time we were getting into a first class compartment and the Signora, whose name I hadn't caught, was exclaiming what a funny and lucky thing it was that we had met up. She had known me instantly from Dyonisia's description. And wasn't it fine that the war was over and we could all get a little pleasure again, and what a fine part we Americans had played. That was while some of the Europeans still admitted that the United States had been in the war.

'It's all lemon orchards and orange groves along the right-hand side of the railway, and so pretty that it hurts to look at it. Hills terraced and yellow fruit shining through the green leaves and darker green of olive trees on the hills, and streams with wide dry pebbly beds cutting down to the sea and old stone houses, and everything all color. And over on the left-hand side you've got the sea, lots bluer than the Bay of Naples, and the coast of Calabria over across is purple like no other place there is. Well, the Signora was just as good to look at as the scenery. Only she was different. Blue-black hair and a face colored like old ivory and eyes like inkwells and full red lips and one of those smiles, you know what they're like, Signor Riscossa.'

'But what has this most pleasant adventure to do with the valor of the Wolf, Capitain?' asked Ricaud, who had his own ideas about the points of women.

'A whole lot, Napoleon,' continued Graves. 'She had those red lips, you know –'

'To the loup! Curse her red lips!' exclaimed Ricaud, impatiently.

'God bless her red lips, Napoleon. And after awhile the little train stopped at a station called Jardini, and she said that this was our getting off place, and that Taormina was the town up on the hill. There was a carriage waiting, and we got in and drove up the pipe elbow road to the little town way up above. I was very gallant and dignified. I'd like to have had you see me, Napoleon.

'That evening we had dinner together, and I'm telling you it wasn't no short order chow. First a Martell-Benedictine and then an antipasto di magro of all kind of funny things you couldn't figure out but that ate great. Then a soup, clear, and after, these little flat fish like baby flounders cooked like those soft-shelled crabs you get at Rousseau's in New Orleans. Roast young turkey with a funny dressing and the Bronte wine that's like melted up rubies. They grow the grapes on Aetna and they're not allowed to ship it out of the country, off the island, you know. For dessert we had these funny crumpily things they call *pasticceria* and black turkish coffee, with a liqueur called Cointreau.

'After the meal, we sat out in the garden under the orange trees, jasmine matted on the walls, and the moon making all the shadows blue-black and her hair dusky and her lips red. Away off you could see the moon on the sea and the snow up on the shoulder of Aetna mountain. Everything white as plaster in the moonlight or purple like the Calabria coast, and away down below the lights of Jardini blinking yellow. It seemed she and her husband didn't get along so well. He was a flyer up in Istery of Hystery or somewheres, I didn't care much, with the Wop army of preoccupation, and she was pleased and happy that I had come to cheer her up for a few days. And I was too.

'Well, the next morning we were eating breakfast, or what they call breakfast, rolls, coffee, and oranges, with the sun shining in through the big swinging-door windows, when the door opens, and in rushed – an Eyetalian can't come into a room without rushing, excuse me, Signor Disolvo – a good-looking fellow with a scar across his cheek and a beautiful blue theatrical looking cape and shining black boots and a sword, crying "Carissima!"

'Then he saw me sitting at the breakfast table, and his "Carissi-ma!" ended in a sort of gurgle. His face got white, all except that scar that stood out like a bright red welt.

' "What is this?" he said in Eyetalian, and whipped out his sword. Then I placed him. I seen that good-looking, scarred face on the covers of lots of the illustrated magazines. It was the Lupo. The Signora was crying among the breakfast dishes, and she was scared. But the Lupo was magnificent. He was doing the dramatic, and he was doing it great. He had anything I ever seen beat.

' "Who are you, you son of a dog?" he said to me. Funny how that expression is international, ain't it, among all countries?

' "Captain Perry Graves, at your service," I said. It was a funny situation, the dashing, handsome, knock em dead Wolf full of righteous wrath, and opposite him old Perry Graves, as homely as you see him now. I didn't look like the side of a triangle, but there was something about me she liked, I guess.

' "Will you give me the satisfaction of a gentleman?" he snapped out.

' "Certainly," I said, bowing.

' "Here and now?" he said.

' "Surely," I said, and bowed again.

' "You have a sword?" he asked, in a sweet tone.

' "Excuse me a minute," I said, and went and got my bag and my belt and gun.

' "You have a sword?" he asked, when I came back.

' "No," said I.

' "I will get you one," says he, in his best Lupo manner.

' "I don't wish a sword," I said.

' "You won't fight me? You dirty dog, I'll cut you down!" '
Graves's face was as hard as his voice was soft.

' "I will fight you here and now," I said to him. "You have a pistol, so have I. We will stand facing each other across the table with our left hands touching." The table wasn't four feet across. "The Signora will count one, two, three. We will start firing at the count of three. Firing across the table." '

Then the control of the situation shifted from the handsome Lupo to Perry Graves. ''Cause just as sure as it was that he would kill me with a sword was the fact that if he killed me at that three foot range with his gun I would take him with me. He knew it too, and he started to sweat. That was the only sign. Big drops of sweat on his forehead. He unbuckled his cape and took out his gun. It was one of those little 7.65 mm. pretty ugly, short little gats.

'We faced across the table and rested our hands on the board, I remember my fingers were in a coffee cup, our right hands with the pistols were below the edge. My big forty-five made a big handful. The Signora was still crying. The Lupo said to her, "Count, you slut!" She was sobbing hysterically.

' "Emeglio!" called the Lupo. A servant came to the door, his face scared and white. "Stand at the end of the table," commanded the Wolf, "and count slowly and clearly, Una-Dua-Tre!"

'The servant stood at the end of the table. I didn't watch the Wolf's eyes like he did mine. I looked at his wrist where his hand disappeared under the table.

' "Una!" said the waiter. I watched the Lupo's hand.

' "Dua!" and his hand shot up. He'd broken under the strain and was going to fire and try and get me before the signal. My old gat belched out and a big forty-five bullet tore his out of his hand as it went off. You see, he hadn't never heard of shooting from the hip.

'The Signora jumped up, screaming, and threw her arms around him. His face was burning red with shame, and his hand was quivering from the sting of the smash. I shoved my gun into the holster and got my musette bag and started for the door, but stopped at the table and drank my coffee standing. It was cold, but I like my coffee in the morning. There wasn't another word said. She was clinging to his neck and crying, and he was standing there, red and ashamed. I walked to the door and opened it, and looked back, and her eye flickered at me over his shoulder. Maybe it was a wink, maybe not. I shut the door and walked out of the courtyard down the road to Jardini. Wolf, hell no, he was a coyote. A coyote, Napoleon, is a wolf that is not a wolf. Now do you think he was a brave man, Signor Disporto?'

I said nothing. I was thinking of how this leather-faced old adventurer had matched his courage against admittedly one of the most fearless men in Europe.

'It is a question of standards,' said Ricaud, as the fresh glasses arrived. 'Lupo is brave, of course. The adventure of Von Hauser is proof. Also, mon capitain, he is Latin. That you cannot understand, for you have courage without imagination. It is a gift from God, monsieur.' Ricaud smiled, shaking his head sadly. 'I wish I have it. I have died a thousand times, and I am not a coward. I will die many more before I am buried, but it is, what you call it, Graves, my trade. We go now to a little war. Perhaps a joke war, eh? But one dies as dead in Chile as on Montfaucon. I envy you, Graves, you are American.

'Signor Rinaldi, I like you to drink with me to Captain Perry Graves, who is so brave he makes the bravest flyer in your country look like a coward!' He laughed, and raised his glass.

'Aw, say, Napoleon!' broke in Graves, embarrassedly, 'Let's change that to "Vive la doughnut!" '

PAULINE SNOW

Pauline Snow was the only beautiful girl we ever had out at the Bay. She was like an Easter Lily coming up straight and lithe and beautiful out of a dung heap. When her father and mother died she came to live with the Blodgetts. Then Art Simons started coming around to the Blodgetts' in the evenings.

Art couldn't come to most places at the Bay, but old Blodgett liked to have him around. Blodgett said he brightened up the place. Art would go out to the stable with Blodgett when he was doing the chores and tell him stories, looking around first to see that no one would overhear. Old Blodgett would come in, his face as red as a turkey's wattles, and laugh, and slap Art on the back. And then laugh and laugh, his face getting redder all the time.

Art began to take Pauline for walks after supper. She was frightened at first of Art, with his thick blunt fingers, and his manner of always touching her when he talked, and didn't want to go. But old Blodgett made fun of her.

'Art's the only regular fellow around the Bay!' he'd say, and clap Art across the shoulders. 'Be a sport, Pauline!'

Pauline's big eyes would look frightened – but she went off with him in the dusk along the road. There was a red line of afterglow along the hills toward Charlevoix, and Pauline said to Art, 'Don't you think that's awfully pretty, Art?'

'We didn't come down here to talk about sunsets, kiddo!' said Art, and put his arm around her.

After a while some of the neighbors made a complaint, and they sent Pauline away to the correction school down at Coldwater. Art was away for awhile, and then came back and married one of the Jenkins girls.

ED PAIGE

Stanley Ketchell came to Boyne City once, barn storming with a burlesque show. He had a forfeit posted that he'd knock anybody out inside of six rounds. Everybody was lumbering then, and Ed Paige came in with a bunch of the boys from White's camp number two to see the show. When the big scene came where Ketchell's manager made the offer, Ed went up on the stage.

It was a wonderful slashing, tearing-in battle, and there were lots of people claimed Ed shaded Ketchell. Anyway Ed received the hundred dollars for staying the limit, and he hasn't done anything much since. He just thinks about the time he fought Stanley Ketchell. For awhile people used to point Ed out. But now most everyone has forgotten all about it, and quite a few say they'll never believe Ed really did it.

BOB WHITE

Bob White was drafted and went over with a base hospital unit. About three days before the armistice he got to France. Bob told the Odd Fellows a lot of things about the war the first lodge night he was home.

Bob had an iron cross he said he got off'n a dead German officer. And the noise forty miles back of the front was wors'n right up in the trenches. Bob didn't like the French people. Some of them used cattle to plow with and all the French girls have black teeth. And they ain't like our girls. Bob was with the best French families, too, and he ought to know. According to Bob, the French soldiers never did any fighting in the war either. They were all old men and were always working on the roads. The Marines didn't really do any fighting either, Bob says. He saw a lot of Marines, and they were all M.P.s around the docks and in Paris.

The people out at the Bay don't think much of France or the Marines either, for that matter, now that Bob's back with news right direct.

OLD MAN HURD – AND MRS. HURD

Old Man Hurd has a face that looks indecent. He hasn't any whiskers, and his chin kind of slinks in and his eyes are red rimmed and watery, and the edges of his nostrils are always red and raw. Hurd's shanty is in a hollow on the forty down back of our place and you can hear him cursing his horses when he's dragging. He's just a little man and he comes up to get our swill that we always leave for his pigs in a big carbide can out back. When he finds something in the swill that he thinks the pigs won't like, you can hear him cursing us and the swill under his breath.

He's an Evan and goes to church and prayer meeting regular. Nobody has ever seen him smile, but sometimes we can hear him singing a song that goes:

> Reeligiun makes me happy,
> Reeligiun makes me happy,
> Reeligiun makes me happy,
> I'm-on-my-way!

Mrs. Hurd is a large woman with a big, comely, simple face, and she's about twenty years younger than the Old Man. She's about forty now, and when she was eighteen her father died and left her the old Amacker place. She tried to run the place, but she couldn't do it. She didn't have enough money to get to Grand Rapids, and in those days there weren't summer people to work for as there is now. And she told my mother once – 'I was a right likely-looking girl then, too.'

Hurd used to come up to the old Amacker place every night and not say anything, but just look at what a mess she was making of trying to run the place. He wouldn't offer to help her split wood or anything. He'd just stand and look at her and the hopeless way she was muddling. After standing there a while, he'd say, 'Sarah, you'd better marry me.'

So after a while she married him, and she told my mother, 'the awful part about it was that he looked then just like he looks now.'

BILLY GILBERT

Billy Gilbert was an Ojibway that lived up near Susan Lake. Mrs. Billy was the nicest looking Indian woman in upper Michigan, and they had two fat, brown little kids named Beulah and Prudence. Billy and Mrs. Billy both had gone to Mount Pleasant to school, and Billy was a good farmer. Along in 1915, nobody at the Bay knew why, Billy went up to the Soo and enlisted in the Black Watch.

This summer Billy came home. He had two scraps of ribbon sewed on his tunic over his heart and three gold pencil stripes on his left sleeve. Nobody around the Bay knew that the ribbons stood for the M.M. and the D.C.M., all the boys that came back had ribbons on, some had three and four, you could buy them at the camps where you were discharged; but everybody made a lot of fun of his kilts.

'Look at the Injun with skirts on!' loafers would holler. And when he rested his pack and lit a cigarette, someone was sure to say, 'Oh look at her! She smokes!' That was always good for a laugh. It wasn't the kind of homecoming Billy had pictured.

He hiked up the road to Susan Lake and found his shack empty. The door was padlocked and his garden was sod and there was quack grass in his young orchard, choking the young trees that the rabbits hadn't girdled. Billy turned down the road to a neighbor's.

'Mrs. Gilbert?' said the man in the doorway, looking amusedly at Billy's kilts. 'She went off with Simon Green's boy. Sold the place to G—— at Charlevoix. It ain't been farmed this year. You're Billy, eh? Well, they're living down the State somewheres.' The neighbor stood in the doorway holding a lamp.

Billy turned away, struggled into his pack and swung into his Highlander's stride down the road in the dusk, his bonnet cocked on one side, his bare knees swinging under his kilts as they had swung down the Bapaume-Cambrai Road. His face was as stolid as ever, but his eyes looked a long way through the dark. Then he commenced whistling. And the tune he whistled was:

> It's a long way to Tipperary,
> It's a long way to go.

PORTRAIT OF THE IDEALIST IN LOVE

The elevated tracks were just below the open windows of the office. Across the tracks was another office building. Trains passed along the tracks and stopping at the station shut off the view of the other building. Sometimes pigeons lit on the ledge of the office windows and flew down to light on the tracks. Moving trains did not cut off the view of the buildings opposite but showed them through open windows and the quick segments of the platform. It was lunch hour and there was no one in the office except Ralph Williams who was finishing a letter to the sister of the girl he was engaged to. He took the last sheet out of the typewriter and read over the letter.

My Dear Isabelle,

I am taking this means of talking to you because your ideas and mine are so greatly different on various subjects that it would be extremely difficult to come to any conclusion through talking.

I have seen that something growing between us, something that I do not wish to see. If I am wrong I want to remedy my errors. Those feelings have been hurting me more than you can imagine. More than the slights which you told me you noticed when I first came down to see Irma. Those days to me were wonderful for I was awakening from a sleep which I thought was everlasting and was perhaps my reason for seemingly neglecting small attentions toward you – because I was finding the love that I had looked for and, after finding it, did not wish to lose it. I tried to make amends after you told me about them sitting in the North Shore Hotel quite a few long months ago. I regretted them and was sincerely sorry for my negligence. My efforts in that direction, however, seem to have been in vain and are apparently a failure. It is hurting me to think that a member of the family that I have learned to love reflecting through Irma has found a place in her mind for ill feelings and ill will toward the man who hopes sometime to be her Brother in Law. It is not that my feelings toward you have lessened. You are simply permitting yourself to think so.

The nature of my living, my experiences, my feelings, and my ideals have caused me to think a little more than the average man of my age. And I know why you are allowing these feelings to enter your mind.

Through 23 years of my life I have, through some unknown reason, reverenced an ideal peculiar to mankind, an ideal which has grown in magnitude to such a high estate of thought that even the slightest reference to it causes a feeling of resentment to show in me from within, and I cannot help it showing. So I am going to continue feeling as I do but with the determination to try and keep it within my heart whether it may wound or not.

The difference between a person with an ideal and one who lacks an ideal is the difference between the person who guides his life by what he thinks and sees materially and the person who has enough of the visionary in him to adopt as his guide a dream which has not yet come true or perhaps never come true. I am adhering to mine. It is all in giving a little more than what I would ask or take. I have always thought, and thought, and thought perhaps too much so, but always placing myself in the other person's position and thinking what I would do under the circumstances in their position, then continuing in the path of what I think is just. When one continues to do what is right he can never go very far wrong. You have read of men, men of wealth, who have won place and power and happiness by means and methods which have stirred up the ill will of their fellow beings causing an indifference to their standing with their fellow men because of an ideal.

Like mercy, thoughtfulness, consideration, and good will bless both those who give and those who receive it. They are virtues worth cultivating and practicing, not merely at Christmas, but from January to December. That is and has been my policy. You perhaps will not agree with me on this subject. You may say, I do not practice these things. If you still think that way, I am sorry, I can do nothing more than I have been for when one shows a kindness for others, when one thinks less of making themselves happy than making others happy, they feel unselfish, they are thoughtful and they come nearer obeying the commandment, 'Thou shalt love thy neighbor as thyself.'

Unselfishness, consideration and good will are built primarily on honest, unstinted, and unselfish good will on our own parts. It is the deliberate cultivation of good will by playing up to people's prejudices, their natural likes and dislikes. That is what I have tried to do many times. It is why Irma and I love each other; it is why I love all of you folks. To you these feelings of mine may be prejudiced, but they're only that in your mind – to us they are reasonable likes and dislikes. You do not understand why I should have it. That Ideal to me is You, a woman. Then what do you suppose the nature of that Ideal is in the woman I love? You do not like it because I do not enter into the things you like with as much zeal as you wish, and I know that you are not the only one that feels that way. You did not like it because I did not smile or laugh at the object of your humor the other night. With the amount of modesty which my ideal of a woman possesses, you among them and also Clara, I could not see the humour or amusement in the nature of form of a woman's limbs that you could, making comparisons with others.

My idea is a woman, the works of a Greater Being than Ourselves, of nature, no matter what forms they may take, and, when that ideal is marred by casting un-called-for reflections upon them, my reasons for resentment are apparent.

I know that I do not enter into a lot of jests and humorous pastimes, bringing forth amusement, and I have seen that it has been noticed at different times before this. I have regretted it always. Years ago when I was much younger, when attending picnics or parties when I did not enter into the amusements and mirthful pranks with the enthusiasm that perhaps I should have, it was noticed and I was often told about it. I have often tried to overcome these feelings so that they might not show on the surface, but I see I have not been successful and that they are still noticed.

I do not like to see things which do not add charm or grace to a woman because of the nature of my living and the formation of my ideal, because I think deeper and have a higher standard for such things than the average man has. Ideals are the most powerful forces known to man, but they entered my mind, I think, before they should have, and I made them entirely centered on that one object. We all must have them, why I chose that one, I have never understood, but I am glad I did. I do know that the man with ideals, the man who refuses to tarnish, lower, or barter his ideals or ideal, no matter how high the price or what the cost, can never feel abjectly poor, can never feel alone in the mind and spirit and soul.

These likes and dislikes so you make yourself think they are something uncalled for and to you, you think I am prejudiced against some act, some word or statement. However, they may be very reasonable after all, since people have them and since you want the thoughtfulness, good will and love, it is necessary that you overlook some of them or that thoughtfulness and good will cannot be obtained. Sometimes other people like very bad things, and our way may be a better way of doing the same thing. It is then the natural course for us to fight for our way to the death that sometimes people will see the reasonableness of our method and think of it in the same way.

Now I am willing to go more than halfway to accomplish and overcome my feelings, to do my part to try to please everyone and if you are willing to come a little way we will forget what has passed.

I have always had a policy of when I wanted to make a friend the only way I found it can be done is to watch for opportunities to do them a service. To do this or that person a favor, and with persistent actions it seldom fails. For good friends appreciate those things; whether they show it or not, you know they are your friends. If I find that I may lose them, I look for some repulsive habit and then try to remedy it or rid myself of it entirely. Isabelle have I in a way succeeded in doing it entirely? Isabelle have I in a way succeeded in doing that with you even in part, by writing this letter to you?

I haven't the slightest idea what you will think or how you will accept this letter, but I am hoping that I have to some extent been able to tell you why I have felt as I have.

If I have caused you to feel indifferently towards me, if it is my fault that a growing dislike for me has entered your mind, all that I can say is that I am sorry. I have simply been myself, my natural self, and regret that I have made you feel in such a way.

Sincerely your humble brother to be,
Ralph Spencer Williams

He had been eating his lunch while he read the letter. He corrected an awkward sentence in the fifth from the last paragraph, addressed an envelope on the typewriter, folded the letter, sealed it, and placed it in the basket for out-going mail. Then he put the paper his lunch had been wrapped in into the wastebasket, blew the crumbs off his desk, and walked over to the window. He looked across at the drugstore under the elevated on the other side of the street. What he wanted was a good, cool, double lemon coca-cola. It was a good, cool, stimulating drink. A man was better off without stimulants but sometimes they were a good thing. They had their place like everything else and the thing to do was not to abuse them. He put on his hat.

THE ASH HEEL'S TENDON

In a former unenlightened time there was a saying, 'In vino veritas,' which meant roughly that under the influence of the cup that queers a man sloughed off his dross of reserve and conventionality and showed the true metal of his self. The true self might be happy, might be poetic, might be morbid, or might be extremely pugnacious. In the rude nomenclature of our forefathers these revealed conditions were denominated in order – laughing, sloppy crying and fighting jags.

A man with his shell removed by the corrosive action of alcohol might present as unattractive an appearance as the shrunken, misshapen nudity of an unprotected hermit crab. Another with a rock-like exterior might prove to be genial, generous and companionable under the influence. But there were men in those days on whose inner personality alcohol had no more effect than a sluicing of the pyramids with vinegar would have on the caskets within.

Such men were spoken of as having wonderful heads; the head being popularly misconceived as the spot of greatest resistance in the body's fight against alcohol. As a matter of physiological fact, they were the possessors of non-absorbent stomachs. But you couldn't build a barroom saga around a non-absorbent stomach. That would be almost as difficult as persuading a badly shot up doughboy that he had made war on the German government and in no sense had opposed the German people.

This yarn deals with non-absorbent stomachs, shooting, and the Hand of God and the true seat of the emotions. It does not handle them in that order, however, as it begins with the Hand of God.

Back in the days before cocktails were drunk out of teacups Hand Evans was a gun. Now a gun is a widely divergent character from a gunman. A gunman, and present styles seem to tend toward the two-gun man, is an individual with chaps, a broad-brimmed hat, a southern drawl, a habit of working his jaws so his cheek muscles will bulge in the close-ups (the same effect can be acquired by chewing gum consistently) and two immense pistols in open holsters tied low on his hairy pants. He may look hard but he is really very kind-hearted and will come out all right in the last reel. Usually he is someone else in disguise anyway.

A gun has not a single one of the gunman's predominant characteristics. Instead he is a quiet, unattractive, rather colorless, professional death producer. His form as a killer may vary, but as a class, he likes to work in pairs and to work close. The gun's preference for close work may be accounted for by the fact that he is often an execrable shot. There is small opportunity for practice with the automatic pistol in a city, but at ten feet no great skill is required. Also every gun has his weak point, what Jack Farrell (who, while he was on the force, had seen the rise and assisted at the fall of most of the killing brethren from Killer King to Kansas City Blackie) called his ash heel's tendon. The first two members of the trilogy of W.W. and the Song claimed many. All had their vulnerable spots.

Hand Evans was the exception. Hand was short for Hand of God. That irreverent specimen of the nomenclature of the underworld had followed him east from Seattle. After he had done his first job in the middle west Rocky Heifitz, who ran the saloon at Ninth and Grand, held forth to a brace of initiates who leaned on the bar while he punctuated his harangue with stabs of a pudgy forefinger.

'If that bird is the Hand of God, I'll say the Lord has some straight left. That's what that bird is – Gawd's Straight Left. And I hope to tell ya it's a left like Peter Jackson's, too. One of these that shoots faster than you can lamp it and won't take no for an answer. You gaudy dancers that are sacking around here and making a play to be bump-off artists better not run in with The Hand.'

Thus spoke Rocky as he sliced off the surplus collar with a wooden spatula.

There were elements of style about Hand's execution of his first commission. Certain requests required the erasure of one Scotty Duncan, who was possessed of more than a desirable degree of knowledge and was suspected of being in communication with those representatives of the law known as 'The Flatties.' Hand's terms were 'two hundred down, getaway money, and two hundred mailed General Delivery, Chicago.' This of course was an exorbitant price for a single bump-off job, but as he explained, 'You take or you leave it. I ain't no working stiff. Get some cheap hyjack if you want a sloppy job.' They took it. For the demise of Scotty Duncan, because of his police protection, must have none of the earmarks of a local accomplishment.

So, shortly after noon, as Scotty Duncan emerged from Wolf's, where he habitually lunched, Hand Evans, a cool, short, swarthy-faced little figure, stood in Heifitz's corridor, the outer swinging door ajar. With the unhurried accuracy of a champion billiard player making a shot requiring some little skill, he took a squat, ugly automatic pistol from his pocket and as Duncan appeared across the street in front of Wolf's he shot once, watched Duncan slump face down to the pavement, and then, replacing the gun in his pocket, walked to the bar.

Rocky set a bottle of whiskey in front of him and Hand poured a half-tumbler full.

'The head,' he remarked conversationally to Rocky, the bar-room being clear by arrangement, 'is cleaner, neater; and using soft-nosed stuff, you know a job is finished.'

He drained the whiskey, refused a chaser, and taking a soft hat and ulster from a peg on the wall, picked up a traveling bag and started for the rear entrance. 'Say Hand!' boomed Rocky, coming out from behind the bar, 'I'd like to shake hands with you.' He wiped his big hands on his apron and smiled admiringly at the dark little man.

'Don't call me Hand,' said Evans, very calmly, and opened the door that led into the alley. 'And I don't shake hands with nobody.'

And that was all the city saw of Hand Evans for some time.

Occasionally reports filtered back to the city about him. He was in New York. He'd done a croak there. He'd left New York. No one knew where he was. He was believed to be in the West again. Then he killed a man in New Orleans and was not heard of for a month or two until he appeared in Chicago again and there was another killing. The sequence was always the same. Hand Evans appeared in town. There was a killing with no witnesses or only favorable witnesses. Hand Evans disappeared. He worked for the highest bidder and he worked alone. He gave allegiance to no one and he split with no one.

The members of the oldest profession could get no hold on him and his only possible weakness was drink. He drank a great deal too much. But it had no visible effect on him. While his companions at the bar grew maudlin or quarrelsome, he was always Hand Evans, with all the rattlesnake's deadliness and without the serpent's warning signal.

So when he was seen at Rocky Heifitz's place after an absence of two years, his coming bred conjecture, consternation and in two cases, cold, deadly fear in those citizens of the city who would be aware of his coming. There was conjecture on the part of the entire district who were in the know; the coming of Hand Evans was a far surer presage of death than the most reliable banshee wail in Ireland. The district wondered who was going to die. There was paralyzing, gnawing, sinking fear at the pits of the stomachs of Pinky Miller and Ike Lantz. And there was joy in the heart of Jack Farrell.

Scotty Duncan's well-conducted exit had not stopped the leak that threatened to enlarge in the dike of security that protected the interests, and with a sudden pouring rush to carry them all on the flood into that dreader bayou of the discovered, the penitentiary. Pinky Miller and Ike Lantz knew of adequate reason why they should be called upon to shuffle off in the interest of protection. Fear that Hand Evans was in the city as an agent of that protection, that their loose-lippedness threatened, nauseated them, and they pictured Scotty Duncan lying on the pavement in front of Wolf's with a neat round puncture in his forehead and a hole big enough to put an egg in at the back. So they went to Jack Farrell.

'Hand Evans is in town,' said Pinky, looking across the desk at the square-jawed, ruddy complacency of Jack Farrell, the czar of the Fifteenth Street police station.

'I know it,' Jack spat accurately at the cuspidor in the corner and reinserted his cigar.

'What are you going to do about it?' demanded Ike.

'Nothing,' returned Farrell, looking at them amusedly from under his bushy white eyebrows.

'Nothing,' almost shouted Pinky in his phobia. 'Nothing. He's going to croak us. That's what he's going to do. And "nothing" you say.'

He pounded on the desk, and his face was pink with emotion. 'Don't you know he's out for me and Ike?'

'Sure,' said Jack Farrell, and again scored on the cuspidor.

'Don't kid us, Jack,' said Ike, who had himself better in hand, 'we know we're stools. But I seen Scotty Duncan. Don't kid us, Jack.'

Farrell removed his cigar, tipped back his chair and looked the two stool pigeons in the eye.

'I'm not kidding you birds. We ain't got nothing on Hand Evans. We know he bumped Scotty, but there ain't any proof.'

'How about Heifitz,' cut in Pinky whiningly.

'Heifitz. Heifitz, he'd swear he'd never seen Hand. There's

nothing of him anywhere's. All we can do is vag him or hold him for investigation and neither of them will hold him for more than twenty-four hours. He ain't no vag and there's nothing to investigate that we ain't went into already. Somebody's due for a one way trip to the land out of which's bourne no travelers return. You ain't afraid to die, are you, Pinky?'

'Don't kid, Jack,' said Ike, his racial fortitude giving him dignity beside the whining Pinky. 'Ain't there nothing that we can do?'

'Bump him yourselves and make a getaway or get something on him and I'll jug him.' Farrell puffed complacently on the cigar.

'You know we can't bump him. We ain't guns,' pleaded Ike.

'He drinks, don't he? And he'll drink with anybody. Maybe he ain't after you boys after all. Get him full and maybe he'll spill something. Get him full tonight at Heifitz's. I'll look out for you all I can, boys.'

'The hell of it is,' whined Pinky, 'it ain't as though he was just an ordinary gun. We might have some chance to get him, or we might get someone to croak him. But this guy's death. There ain't anybody could get him and he ain't got any weak points. And he'll kill anyone that tries to even pinch him.'

'Everybody's got weak points,' said Farrell. 'Now you birds get along out of here.'

The two stool pigeons opened the door and slipped out.

Farrell reached for a desk phone and called a number.

'Hello, Rocky? This is Jack. Anybody in the place? All right. Yes. I know he's after me. The two stools were just up. Scared to death. But we haven't anything on him. Yes. I understand why you can't testify on the other. The stools are going to try and get him oiled tonight. He's to get me tomorrow? I'd do the same thing in their place. Why bother with the stools when they can get the man higher up. All right. Yes. Get this Rocky. I'm sending a record over for the phonygraft. Tonight at about eleven thirty I'll call you from Wolf's across the street. Start the record. The one I sent over. He'll be drinking with some sacks the two stools will have there. Be ready to duck after you start the record. Yes. All right. So long Rocky.'

He hung up the receiver and clapping on his derby found a fresh cigar in the top drawer of his desk and started out of the door whistling.

That night Hand Evans stood, short, olive-faced and stony-eyed, his right foot elevated upon the brass rail of Rocky Heifitz's bar, his left hand encircling a bottle of whiskey from which he regularly filled the little glass that was before him. After filling the glass he drank it with his left hand. His right hand always hung by his side where there was a bulge in his coat pocket or rested on the bar where it could reach the other gun that he carried in the holster under his armpit. His eyes were on the mirror that paralleled the bar back of Rocky's head and that showed the panorama of the room and the swinging doors.

During the evening several men had approached Hand and offered to buy him drinks. To all he made the same reply. 'I'm buying my own liquor.' After that conversation was rather difficult. There was small likelihood of Hand spilling anything. If there is any truth in 'In vino veritas,' Hand's shell, peeled off, revealed only another and much harder shell beneath.

At a half hour before midnight the phone back of the bar jingled. Rocky answered. 'Hello? Wrong number,' and slammed down the receiver.

'Say, maybe there's one you ain't heard,' he said, and reached for the top disk of a pile of phonograph records.

'None of that damn jazz,' said the swarthy little man in front of the bar.

'This ain't jazz,' replied Rocky, adjusting a new needle. 'This is the genuwine high-brow stuff. This is soup and fish music. It's called Vesty the Gubby.'

He started the machine and the great tenor's voice poured out of the sounding box in Leoncavallo's soul-searing music. 'Laugh, Pagliacco, though your heart be breaking,' sang Caruso. Hand's face brightened, then clouded, and his eyes dropped to the floor. All through the singing of the heart-broken protest of the fool against the fate that forces him on to jest while all his life has tumbled about his ears, Hand looked at the floor. The shell was broken.

Hand didn't see the swinging door open, and Jack Farrell standing in the doorway. He only heard Caruso's mighty voice ringing out in Canio's soul-tortured lament. At the last note he raised both hands impulsively to applaud.

'Keep 'em up!' Jack Farrell's voice cracked like a shot and Hand turned to look into the muzzle of a forty-five in the Irishman's big freckled hand. 'Keep 'em up, Wop!'

He ran practiced fingers over Hand's coat, extracted the two pistols from the pocket and the shoulder holster, and then laughed into the swarthy face.

'Didn't have a weakness, eh? Couldn't be pinched? Kill

anyone that tried to pinch you, eh?' He slipped a pair of steel bracelets on Hand's wrists. 'You can put 'em down now. We got enough on them now so that Rocky here can tell what he knows of Scotty Duncan without any risk.'

Hand Evans stood immobile, looking at Farrell with all the poisonous hate of a back-broken rattlesnake in his eyes.

'You didn't have a weakness,' Farrell went on, gloatingly. 'Liquor didn't bother you. You didn't care any more about a woman than a slot machine. You were going to kill me tomorrow. But you had a weakness all right. Your real name is Guardalabene, ain't it?' Hand had not said a word since his arrest, but all his concentrated hate was in his eyes. His face was as immobile as ever.

'Guardalabene is his name, Rocky,' said Farrell, turning to the bar-tender. 'And what brought his hand away from his pocket was the wop voice. Your ash heel's tendon, Mr. Guardalabene, was Music. Call the station, will ya, Rocky?'

THE CURRENT

Stuyvesant Byng grinned at the maid who opened the door, and, as was customary when Stuyvesant Byng grinned, he received an answering smile.

'Miss Dorothy will be down, Mr. Stuyvesant. May I take your things?' She looked after him with more than approbation in her eyes. Women usually looked that way at Stuyvesant. On his way to Dorothy Hadley's that night he had stopped in at a telephone booth and two girls as they came out of the next booth nudged each other as he passed.

'That bird sure does an eye good,' remarked the first, following him with her eyes as she drew a lipstick from her vanity bag.

'Yeh, he's too good to be true. I'm weary of them too darn handsome guys. No collar ads in mine. Give me Henry the foundry hand who pays for what he gets, and gets what he pays for.' She laughed mirthlessly at her joke.

'Come on Evelyn, don't look at the door where he's went out all night. Handsome Harry has passed out of the picture.'

'I guess,' said the first, finishing her lipstick operation and considering herself in the mirror of her bag appraisingly, 'I guess he was too darn good looking. But I'd like to have a date with him for tonight.'

'I'd like to be Lady Astor – but we ain't. We got to blow down to Peccarraro's and maybe we rate a supper. Come on old war horse. We got to shimmy along.'

Stuyvesant Byng was unconscious of this of course. He didn't know that women usually looked after him and often commented on him, and tonight he was particularly unconscious of everything, because he was going to Dorothy Hadley's for a very definite purpose. He was going to propose to Dorothy, and he wasn't at all sure what her answer would be.

Stuy had proposed to girls before. Once in a canoe up at the lake, with the moon aiding and abetting, and once in his car going well over fifty miles an hour with one hand on the wheel. But he'd always come out of them all right, and his elder brother had pulled him out of the last one. Let's see. The last one was still quite vivid. He'd proposed aboard Harry's yacht. But he'd had the moon with him then, too; and there had never been any doubt as to the answer. Tonight was different. He was going to propose to Dorothy Hadley, and he had a hunch that she was going to turn him down. He lit a cigarette and substituted smoking for thinking for a moment. Stuyvesant Byng could never be really accused of thinking, but when he smoked he used his brain less than normally.

Then Dorothy came into the room, her hand outstretched. 'Hello, Stuy,' she smiled at him.

'Howdy, Do,' he grinned back and flicked his cigarette into the open fire.

Her hair was the first thing about Dorothy that everyone noticed. It was the raw gold color of old country burnished copper kettles, and it held all of the firelight and occasionally flashed a little of it back. Her hair was wonderful! The rest of her was altogether adorable and Stuy looked at her appreciatively.

'You always look wonderful, Do,' he said as she sank into one of the deep leather chairs before the fire. He sat on the arm of her chair and looked down at her glorious hair!

'What have you been doing since you got back Stuy? You haven't been around for ages?' she asked looking up at him. Stuy considered.

'Oh a bunch of us were up on the Nipigon last August. Sam Horne and Martin and Duntley and I. And then I went way up back up of beyond in Quebec with Sam Horne and we got a moose. Sam got it, to tell the truth. And I've been down at Pinehurst just lately dubbing around. Nobody much there.'

Stuy took out his cigarette case and offered it to Dorothy. She shook her head. Dorothy was the only girl Stuy knew that didn't smoke, and it always gave him a pleasant feeling to have her refuse. She thought he was merely thoughtless.

'What are you doing in town now Stuy, you old wild man?' Dorothy smiled and stroked his arm. It was peculiar with Dorothy. When she stroked your arm she did just that, she stroked your arm. Other girls – but not Dorothy. It meant nothing to her.

'Came up for the opera,' grinned Stuy.

Dorothy laughed tinklingly, like the chiming of one of those Chinese wind bells. 'You never went to the opera in your life that you weren't dragged. What are you up for, Stuy?'

'All right, Do. Now's as good a time as any.' His voice took on a different tone, his hand rested on her shoulder. She didn't shrink away, but looked steadily up into his eyes. 'I love you, Do. I want you to marry me.'

His hand still resting on her shoulder, she laughed again but this time not so merrily, and her eyes still looked up at his. 'Oh Stuy! You're so funny. I can't marry you. And you don't really love me you know.' Stuy's hand had fallen when she said 'funny.'

'Funny peculiar, not funny ha! ha! I mean,' she said gently and put her hand over his. 'I think the world of you Stuy. We've always been pals. But you've been in love with twenty girls while we've been palling around. You could never be really in love with any one. And besides, you're too good looking. I've got a snub nose, Stuy. Oh yes I have. I could never marry a man as good looking as you are. I'd never go out and have people say "Who is that red-haired girl with that wonderful handsome man over there?"'

'You're the most beautiful girl in the world!' said Stuy fervently.

Dorothy smiled quietly at him and pressed his hand. 'I wonder how many times you've said that, Stuy? You're fickle, boy. You're inconstant.' Her voice was very gentle. 'Oh I know I'm hurting you. I guess I mean to. You've never stuck to anything. You play a good game of polo. But you never would stick to it. One year you were runner-up in the National Open. The next year you didn't enter. You play lots better polo than at least two internationalists that I know, and you know the game of golf you can put up. But you're not a sticker, Stuy. And you'd be the same way in anything else. You're a philanderer, Stuy. I know that's an awfully old-fashioned word – but that's what you are old dear.' She stroked his arm again.

'Let me say something, Do.' Stuy's face was carmine and he was so good looking that Dorothy longed to be in his – well, Stuy was handsome. 'I've always loved you Do, ever since we were kids. I loved you from the time you were a little red-haired kid till now. It's been the big thing in my life. It's been the big strong current. It's like a river. The current always flows along, but the wind on the surface makes white caps, and it may look as though the river is flowing the other way. But the white caps are only on the surface. Underneath, the current flows strong, always the same way. My love for you has been the current, and any other girls have only been little waves on the surface. Don't you see, dear?'

'I see, Stuy dear. But seeing isn't believing,' said Dorothy very tenderly, and if Stuy had taken her in his arms then the story wouldn't have amounted to much for the reader. 'But I'll give you a chance, old boy. You've never stuck to anything. You've always philandered. Pick something out and make an absolute, unqualified success of it. Show you're a champion, not a runner-up. Don't always be an also-ran, Stuy. And then you can come and ask me again.'

'Do you mean business?' said Stuy, dolefully.

'Not necessarily. It's no harder than anything else and you've plenty of money anyway. It wouldn't be right to get any more. Anything hard, Stuy. And make a success of it. Be a champion, old boy.'

'By Gad, Do, I'll do it.' Stuy was on his feet and had Dorothy's hand in his great paw. 'I'll do it, Do. And then I'll –.'

'Come back here,' finished Dorothy for him, and he went out of the room with his mind alight with her smile.

At his room he called up Sam Horne, his best pal. Sam was out. 'Ask him to come over as soon as he comes in. It's very important.' Stuy hung up the receiver and began to pace up and down. After a while he went over to the cellaret and poured himself a drink. Just then Sam Horne burst in.

'What do you want with me at this time of night, you crazy Bingo? Solitary drinking, eh? Well, we'll soon remedy that. Where's another glass? What's up? Spill it out to Uncle Sam. Some girl going to marry you?' He circled the glass with his hand and put his feet up on the table.

'I've got to be a champion, Sam,' began Stuy earnestly.

'Easy!' said Sam. 'You cast the best fly on the Nipigon.'

'She wouldn't accept that,' returned Stuy.

'She, eh?' said Sam. 'Oh yes, of course She! Well, who is She? And why have you got to be a champion all of a sudden for She?'

Stuy explained at length. Sam, his feet still on the table, his top hat pushed far back on his head, poured himself out another drink, and as Stuy reached for the bottle Sam's fingers closed around it. 'Not for you boy. This isn't the stuff to make champions at anything but elbow crooking. Let's see. You couldn't ever make it at tennis. Not against Johnstone and Johnson and that crew. You might have once at golf, but not anymore. There won't be any polo to speak of for a year. You're out of luck Bingo.'

'You've forgotten something, old wiseness,' said Stuy.

'No, I hadn't forgotten it. I just didn't know whether to mention it or not. You know what Dawson said about you the last time you were down sparring at the club. "If Mr. Byng would go into the game there isn't a man in the ring today that could touch him at 154 pounds." I know that. And I know how much love you have for it.'

'She said – something hard,' mused Stuy.

'That's hard all right, all right. It's the hardest, dirtiest, worst game in the world Stuy old Bingo,' returned Sam.

Stuy got up and assumed a fighting pose. 'How does Slam Bing sound as a nom de guerre, Samivel? You see before you, old son, Slam Bing (the late Stuyvesant Byng), the future middleweight box fighter champion of the world,' said Stuy impressively.

'Gentlemen, Mr. Slam Bing, the Hoboken Horror,' nodded Sam and filled his glass.

The first eight months were awful. Stuy had always hated the thought of fighting, he hated punishment and was always in a cold sweat before he climbed through the ropes. He didn't have to take much punishment, though, for he possessed a left hand that was a shade faster than anything that had ever been seen in the middle-weight division before, and a right that wouldn't have been any more effective if it had been ballasted with the concrete-filled glove. He utterly outclassed the first few men he fought in preliminary bouts and soon possessed a more than local reputation. But he hated the whole thing. The smelly dressing room, the crowd, the smoke-filled close halls he fought in, the smell of everything, and all the faces that shone white and red from the ringside seats he loathed.

Sam Horne and old Dawson, who had been sparring partner to FitzSimmons, were always with him. Dawson made his matches for him, trained him and counseled him. Sam swung a towel to drive the air into his lungs between rounds, while Dawson sponged off his face and chest and chafed his legs and kneaded his arms and thighs, and poured advice into his ears. Stuy won all his first fights quickly. After the first few set-ups he ran up against some better opposition. He learned what it was to take punishment, to be hit hard and often. He had his first black eye, and he learned the thrill of the knockout. That feeling comparable to none when the perfectly timed punch crashes home, and the man who has been battering you slips down to the resined canvas floor unconscious.

And one night when, after eight rounds of fast and bitter fighting, Stuy's right swung to a spot a little to one side of the point of the jaw of a certain Hebrew Gentleman with an Irish name, and Stuy stooped and putting his gloves under the unconscious Celtic Semite's arms carried him to his corner while the crowded auditorium shouted and yelled for Slam Bing, he realized that he was very near the top of his profession.

'You got him, Bingo! You sure knocked him for a goal, old boy! Oh you've got the old wallop, kid!' Sam exulted as they forced their way through the crowd to Stuy's dressing room. Dawson was following with the bucket, sponge, towels and other paraphernalia. Stuy lay on his back on the couch in his dressing room, breathing heavily while Sam raved.

'Oh boy, when you were lugging toe to toe there in the sixth, I thought little Sammy would go clean off. And when you got him in the eighth, I hit old Dawson so hard I nearly knocked him up into the ring. I fight as hard as you do, Stuy.'

'It was a fight,' said Stuy in a tired tone. 'He was better than I thought. He jolted me a couple of times.'

'Yeah, and you jolted him, old Grampas. Eh, Dawson?' to the trainer who was coming in the door.

'Jolted him! You couldn't have hit him any harder if you'd had a fist full of lead. You hit him with everything but the water bucket. You're a heavyweight above the waist, Mr. Byng. That's where you have it on all these other middles. Well, there's only one better than that one you rocked to sleep tonight.' He uncorked a bottle of liniment. 'We get him next, Mr. Byng. How do you feel?'

'I'm all right, Dawson. But I wish to hell it was over with. All of it. Twice tonight I thought I'd give anything if I wasn't fighting. What do I fight for anyway? I don't have to fight?' he said testily.

'Oh yes you do, Stuy,' said Sam quietly.

'Yes I do,' said Stuy resignedly. 'But how I wish it was all over. When do we take on McGibbons, Dawson?'

'In about a month, Mr. Byng. At New Orleans. It's for twenty rounds.'

'You know I never fought twenty rounds, Dawson.' Stuy's voice was grouchy.

'You won't have to Mr. Byng neither,' grinned Dawson.

In McGibbons Stuy was meeting the champion of his class and one of the greatest, although one of the freakiest fighters that ever entered the squared circle. He was actually Irish, a rare thing in a pugilist nowadays, and was squat-built, with a simian face and the long arms of a gorilla. No one had ever knocked him down, much less knocked him out, and either of his hands carried the deadly knockout potion. He was a past master of every trick of the ring craft and saw no reason why he should not hold the championship for years to come. When his manager spoke to him about a match with Stuy, his ugly ape face was distorted by an evil, fang-revealing grin.

'Society Willie, boy, ain't he a pretty looker? All right, make it for twenty rounds if you can and he'll not be so pretty. Offer him an eighty-twenty split.'

After a lengthy session with Dawson, Seidman, Ape McGibbons' manager, returned to his principal. 'Did you make it eighty-twenty?' asked the sour Ape.

'I got something better than that, Mac. A winner-take-all. You got it all over this Byng thing. He's a set-up for you. You'll butcher him. Old Alec Dawson that used to spar with the Cornishman is handling him, and I took him for it. That gives you twenty-percent more. Ain't it a good move now, Mac?'

'I said eighty-twenty, you Jew swine. Now what if accidents happen? Why don't you do what I tell you?'

'There won't be no accidents, Mac. Believe you me. There can't be no accidents. There gotta be no accidents! You just knock him for a goal. Won't you now, Mac?'

'I gotta now, you hooker. But eighty-twenty listened a lot better to me. This winner-take-all stuff was all right in the old days when you hadda have it. But eighty-twenty means you get the eighty no matter what happens. And there's always accidents.'

'But Mac, listen! There's gotta be absolutely no accidents. You mustn't let there be none. You just rock him off.' Seidman combined apology, praise, confidence, and encouragement in his tone.

'All right, I see that. Shut up, will ye?' The Ape's temper was frayed.

During the preliminaries, Dawson, Sam and Stuy were up in Stuy's dressing room. Sam was as cheerful as ever. 'In less than two hours you'll be champion of this old world thing, Bingo. And I've got everything that belongs or ever will belong to the Horne family on you to win by a knockout.'

'He'll save your money for you, Mr. Horne. And don't try and knock me loose when he puts it over, either. How do you feel, Mr. Byng?'

'I'm all right, Alec. I just feel as though I'd like to call it all off and I'm scared to death and my knees may knock together. Otherwise I'm all right. I'll never fight again, Alec.' Stuy was in his fighting trunks and shoes, and wrapped in an old football blanket and a bathrobe.

'You're all right, Mr. Byng. But watch him all the time. Both his left and his right is bad. Keep him away with that left of yours, and don't be sure you've got him till you hear the ref counting. Don't let him fool you that he's in bad shape. And stay away from him! Don't infight him. Knock his can off. We stand to win twenty thousand dollars, Mr. Byng.' Dawson illustrated each word of his instructions as he talked. He was by far the most nervous of the three.

'You stand to win twenty thou, you mean, Al. Though I don't think the fighter's percentage will be that much.'

'You're too good to me, Mr. Byng. But just remember. Keep away from him. Don't let him fool you, and when you get the chance knock his can off!'

Sam, who had disappeared, poked his head in at the door. 'Come on. Our number's up. We're at the post. The wheel is going to spin. Come on, you box fighter. I've got a surprise for you, Stuy. Look over where the women are, you mitt slinger, as you go in. See if you can't notice a spot of color.'

'You crazy fool. She isn't here, is she?' snapped Stuy angrily.

'She's nowhere else, Bingo.' Sam was joyful.

'Who told you to bring her, you fool?'

'Nobody, it was all my own idea. I have them occasionally. Who are you fighting for, anyway?'

'Oh, you crazy damned fool,' moaned Stuy impotently. 'I didn't want her to even know about it until it was all over. What if I get crowned?' He was so angry, hopelessly angry, that he didn't notice where he was going and jostled into the outside spectators at the edge of the big indoor arena.

'That's all right. She knows all about it. She's here with her father. I explained all about it and you and the "hard thing" and all. And Stuy, you aren't going to get knocked for a loop or anything because she is here.'

They came down a long sloping aisle to the ring amid a roar of applause from all over the house, punctured by shouts of 'Oh, you Slammer!' 'You'll get him, Byng!' 'Kill the Ape!' Sam reached his stool up through the ropes, and Stuy, after bowing, seated himself on it and leaned back, his eyes searching the crowd.

'Over there,' pointed Sam. 'Are you blind? Wave to her!' Stuy waved where he could see the sheen of Dorothy's hair and a white splash that must be her face.

There was the usual tiresome wait for the champion to appear, and when he came shuffling down the aisle there was another roar. Then the introductions, the referee called the fighters together in the center of the ring for instructions, then the automatic gong clanged and the fight was on. It was so ghastly white in the ring from the light of the banked arcs that shone down on the canvas.

The Ape's chin was sunk on his chest, his shoulders hunched and his hairy long arms out, the left extended, the right curved. He moved with a queer, flat-footed shuffle, and his little blue eyes always avoided Stuy's.

Stuy, as Dawson said, was a heavyweight above his waist. He had terrific shoulders and long arms and thick wrists. His legs were well shaped but not in proportion with his upper body, and his deep chest had the breathing power of a racehorse. His hair was carefully brushed and his face was, as Dorothy had once said, 'too handsome.'

As they stepped back from shaking hands Stuy's left hand shot out, like the darting of a spear, into the Ape's face. But the Ape's head twisted sideways and his own right whanged against Stuy's ribs over the heart. 'Pretty boy!' said the Ape. 'You won't be so pretty, pretty soon.' He came tearing in with both hands, and Stuy met him with a straight left that brought him up like a poke in the face with a two-by-four. The Ape rushed again, and Stuy sidestepped, stepped in and brought his right up from the hip to the Ape's jaw. It was the old FitzSimmons shift. The Ape swayed groggily and seemed about to fall. His hands dropped low. Stuy shot a left to his head and stepped forward and crossed the right for the knockout, when he felt a terrific jar and heard dimly the ringing of the gong.

On his stool in the corner where Sam and Dawson had dragged him, he was revived with the smell of aromatic spirits of ammonia in his nostrils, Sam dousing him with water, while a handler he had not seen before shot great sweeps of air into his laboring lungs with flaps of a big towel. 'Keep away from him until you know you've got him! Keep away from him! Stall and cover up now! Just hang on. He got you with his left last round as you started to right cross him.'

Then came the clang of the gong. His stool was jerked out from under him and he was alone in the ring. But he was not alone, for there was the Ape coming toward him where he stood so unsteadily. He must stall and cover up until his head cleared and this hazy feeling left. He protected his jaw as well as he could while the Ape rushed him and showered punches on him. He dimly thought that he'd never seen so many gloves before. His nose felt huge, he knew that it was bleeding badly down onto his chest. How easy it would be to quit! How long was a round anyway? Only three minutes? It had been three hours already. They were in a clinch now, and the Ape was hooking kidney punches into the small of his back. Each one felt like a kick in the pit of the stomach. The referee broke them apart. There was blood on his silk shirt. Stuy covered up again and went into his shell. The Ape slugged away. How easy it would be to quit! Then he'd have peace and this would all be over. No, there was a current somewhere. He must go with the current. That was all that mattered, the steady current. The current that made things move. Dorothy was here, too. Why, he wondered? Then his head began to clear and a plan formed. The gong sounded and he staggered in a drunken zig-zag to his corner.

Dawson bent over him with the ammonia. Stuy muttered between his swollen lips as Dawson worked on the split nose, and sponged the blood out of his eyes. 'I'm all right now, Alec. Two can play that foxing game. I'm going to get him this round!'

When the gong boomed, he went out as groggily as before and retreated under the Ape's smashing attack. He could only see out of one eye now, but he did not attempt a counter blow. Just kept in his shell as much as possible and guarded the jaw. The crowd were yelling for the knockout. After a vicious rush by the Ape he slipped to his knees and heard the referee count. He rose at the count of seven, his hands by his side swaying. The Ape stepped close in a rush to finish the job, an evil look on his face. His punch started and Stuy's right hand came up like a flash from below his waist and crashed on the Ape's jaw with the force of a pile driver. The Ape's face convulsed, he swayed and, as he toppled, Stuy caught him again with a bone smashing swing. The referee counted ten, he might have counted a hundred, and then raised Stuy's gloved right hand above his head. Stuy grinned for the first time in a long time.

The auditorium was a bedlam. Sam had his arm around him and was yelling in his ear. Dawson was pounding him madly on the back. And towards the ring were working their way through the milling crowd a red-haired girl and a gentleman in evening dress.

Stuy slipped through the ropes to the floor and Dorothy was in his arms. 'Oh Stuy!' she sobbed. 'You're so homely and beautiful with your smashed bloody face. And I love you so. Oh why did you take to fighting? Oh I love you so! You're not a philanderer. You're much nicer than the dying gladiator. Oh I'm talking nonsense! But I love you, Stuy. And oh Stuy, you won't ever fight again, will you?' He pressed her close to him and grinned through his gory mush of a face. 'Don't worry, dearest. Don't worry.'

MODERN CLASSICS IN EVERYMAN'S LIBRARY

CHINUA ACHEBE
The African Trilogy
Things Fall Apart

ISABEL ALLENDE
The House of the Spirits

ISAAC ASIMOV
Foundation
Foundation and Empire
Second Foundation
(in 1 vol.)

MARGARET ATWOOD
The Handmaid's Tale

GIORGIO BASSANI
The Garden of the Finzi-Continis

SIMONE DE BEAUVOIR
The Second Sex

SAMUEL BECKETT
Molloy, Malone Dies,
The Unnamable
(US only)

SAUL BELLOW
The Adventures of Augie March

JORGE LUIS BORGES
Ficciones

RAY BRADBURY
The Stories of Ray Bradbury

MIKHAIL BULGAKOV
The Master and Margarita

JAMES M. CAIN
The Postman Always Rings Twice
Double Indemnity
Mildred Pierce
Selected Stories
(1 vol. US only)

ITALO CALVINO
If on a winter's night a traveler

ALBERT CAMUS
The Outsider (UK)
The Stranger (US)
The Plague, The Fall,
Exile and the Kingdom,
and Selected Essays
(in 1 vol.)

WILLA CATHER
Death Comes for the Archbishop
(US only)
My Ántonia
O Pioneers!

RAYMOND CHANDLER
The novels (2 vols)
Collected Stories

G. K. CHESTERTON
The Everyman Chesterton

KATE CHOPIN
The Awakening

JOSEPH CONRAD
Heart of Darkness
Lord Jim
Nostromo
The Secret Agent
Typhoon and Other Stories
Under Western Eyes
Victory

ROALD DAHL
Collected Stories

JOAN DIDION
We Tell Ourselves Stories in
Order to Live (US only)

UMBERTO ECO
The Name of the Rose

J. G. FARRELL
The Siege of Krishnapur
and Troubles

WILLIAM FAULKNER
The Sound and the Fury
(UK only)

F. SCOTT FITZGERALD
The Great Gatsby
This Side of Paradise
(UK only)

PENELOPE FITZGERALD
The Bookshop
The Gate of Angels
The Blue Flower
(in 1 vol.)
Offshore
Human Voices
The Beginning of Spring
(in 1 vol.)

FORD MADOX FORD
The Good Soldier
Parade's End

RICHARD FORD
The Bascombe Novels

E. M. FORSTER
Howards End
A Passage to India
A Room with a View,
Where Angels Fear to Tread
(in 1 vol., US only)

ANNE FRANK
The Diary of a Young Girl
(US only)

GEORGE MACDONALD
FRASER
Flashman
Flash for Freedom!
Flashman in the Great Game

KAHLIL GIBRAN
The Collected Works

GÜNTER GRASS
The Tin Drum

GRAHAM GREENE
Brighton Rock
The Human Factor

DASHIELL HAMMETT
The Maltese Falcon
The Thin Man
Red Harvest
(in 1 vol.)
The Dain Curse
The Glass Key
and Selected Stories
(in 1 vol.)

JAROSLAV HAŠEK
The Good Soldier Švejk

JOSEPH HELLER
Catch-22

ERNEST HEMINGWAY
A Farewell to Arms
The Collected Stories
(UK only)

MICHAEL HERR
Dispatches (US only)

PATRICIA HIGHSMITH
The Talented Mr. Ripley
Ripley Under Ground
Ripley's Game
(in 1 vol.)

JAMES JOYCE
Dubliners
A Portrait of the Artist as
a Young Man
Ulysses

FRANZ KAFKA
Collected Stories
The Castle
The Trial

MAXINE HONG KINGSTON
The Woman Warrior and
China Men
(US only)

RUDYARD KIPLING
Collected Stories
Kim

GIUSEPPE TOMASI DI
LAMPEDUSA
The Leopard

D. H. LAWRENCE
Collected Stories
The Rainbow
Sons and Lovers
Women in Love

DORIS LESSING
Stories

PRIMO LEVI
If This is a Man and The Truce
(UK only)
The Periodic Table

NAGUIB MAHFOUZ
The Cairo Trilogy
Three Novels of Ancient Egypt

THOMAS MANN
Buddenbrooks
Collected Stories (UK only)
Death in Venice and Other Stories
(US only)
Doctor Faustus
Joseph and His Brothers
The Magic Mountain

KATHERINE MANSFIELD
The Garden Party and Other
Stories

GABRIEL GARCÍA MÁRQUEZ
The General in His Labyrinth
Love in the Time of Cholera
One Hundred Years of Solitude

W. SOMERSET MAUGHAM
Collected Stories

CORMAC McCARTHY
The Border Trilogy

YUKIO MISHIMA
The Temple of the
Golden Pavilion

TONI MORRISON
Beloved
Song of Solomon

ALICE MUNRO
Carried Away: A Selection
of Stories

VLADIMIR NABOKOV
Lolita
Pale Fire
Pnin
Speak, Memory

V. S. NAIPAUL
Collected Short Fiction (US only)
A House for Mr Biswas

R. K. NARAYAN
Swami and Friends, The Bachelor
of Arts, The Dark Room,
The English Teacher
(in 1 vol.)
Mr Sampath – The Printer of
Malgudi, The Financial Expert,
Waiting for the Mahatma
(in 1 vol.)

IRÈNE NÉMIROVSKY
David Golder
The Ball
Snow in Autumn
The Courilof Affair
(in 1 vol.)

FLANN O'BRIEN
The Complete Novels

FRANK O'CONNOR
The Best of Frank O'Connor

MICHAEL ONDAATJE
The English Patient

GEORGE ORWELL
Animal Farm
Nineteen Eighty-Four
Essays
Burmese Days, Keep the Aspidistra
Flying, Coming Up for Air
(in 1 vol.)

ORHAN PAMUK
My Name is Red
Snow

BORIS PASTERNAK
Doctor Zhivago

SYLVIA PLATH
The Bell Jar (US only)

MARCEL PROUST
In Search of Lost Time
(4 vols, UK only)

PHILIP PULLMAN
His Dark Materials

JOSEPH ROTH
The Radetzky March

SALMAN RUSHDIE
Midnight's Children

PAUL SCOTT
The Raj Quartet (2 vols)

ALEXANDER SOLZHENITSYN
One Day in the Life of
Ivan Denisovich

MURIEL SPARK
The Prime of Miss Jean Brodie
The Girls of Slender Means
The Driver's Seat
The Only Problem
(in 1 vol.)

CHRISTINA STEAD
The Man Who Loved Children

JOHN STEINBECK
The Grapes of Wrath

ITALO SVEVO
Zeno's Conscience

JUNICHIRŌ TANIZAKI
The Makioka Sisters

JOHN UPDIKE
The Complete Henry Bech
Rabbit Angstrom

This book is set in BEMBO which was cut
by the punch-cutter Francesco Griffo
for the Venetian printer-publisher
Aldus Manutius in early 1495
and first used in a pamphlet
by a young scholar
named Pietro
Bembo.